Modern Short Stories

THE USES OF IMAGINATION

Revised Edition

Modern

Edited by ARTHUR MIZENER, CORNELL UNIVERSITY

Short Stories

THE USES OF IMAGINATION

Revised Edition

W · W · NORTON & COMPANY · INC · *New York*

Contents

Foreword

In any reasonably definable sense, the short story has existed as a literary form for less than a hundred years, and the significant differences among short stories are not historical differences but differences in mode, in the attitudes toward life which govern an author's sense of reality and the techniques of expression these attitudes dictate. For this reason above all, the best way to arrange a volume of short stories is by types or kinds rather than in a chronological pattern intended to indicate some not very significant historical development.

Arranging stories by types has critical and even practical advantages. Like the lyric poem, the short story is a concentrated and often elliptical form, dependent for its success on feeling and suggestion. But which elements in a given story are charged with feeling, and therefore highly suggestive, and which are merely literal or conventional depends on what kind of story it is. If we have been reading Henry James and have learned to focus our attention on those elements that are most suggestive in his kind of story, we may, if not warned, carry over to our reading of D. H. Lawrence the same focus of attention, and thus find ourselves scrutinizing with every care elements that are insignificant in Lawrence's kind of story, and failing to notice—or finding irrelevant—the elements that for Lawrence are the significant ones in the story. It is difficult not to believe that the familiar complaints against James—that his people are snobbish and that in his stories nothing happens—like the familiar complaints against Lawrence—that he is obsessed with sex and strident—are not so much stupid as a consequence of misdirected attention such as I have been trying to describe.

For the purpose of avoiding this kind of misdirected attention, it is useful to have stories that work in the same way grouped together and separated from stories that work in other ways, and an arrangement of this kind ought to be particularly useful for undergraduates who are in the early stages of learning how to read imaginative literature. Comparatively inexperienced readers almost instinctively try first to grasp the "moral" or "lesson" of a story. In their way, they are trying to find the governing attitudes of the story, and they are quite right to do so. But if they are to succeed, they must discover which elements of the story to focus their attention on, which ones will really reveal the story's implications. The kind of teaching that is going to make the most sense to students at this stage of development is the kind that begins with a group of stories that require the reader's attention to be focused on the same elements; what he learns to look for by studying the first story in a group will be the right thing for him to look for in all the other stories in the group. Then, when it is time for him to move on to a different kind of story, he ought to be duly warned that he is doing so by having examples of this second kind of story separately grouped.

I hope that the arrangement of the stories in this book will assist the learning process I have been describing. These stories were all chosen because they seem to me good ones, not because they fitted any preconceived scheme of presentation, and I believe they can be profitably read in almost any order the reader chooses. But after I had selected them, I found they fell into the groups into which this book divides them. The stories in each group require essentially the same kind of reading, and in the introductory essay for each group I have tried to suggest the kind of reading the stories require and why they do so.

The order in which the four groups of stories are arranged may be open to argument. In a purely critical sense, the "realistic" stories of the second group ought perhaps to be placed first. But because these stories are "realistic," because they are primarily concerned to show—in Hemingway's famous phrase—"the way it was," they seldom provide the reader with any comment on what is happening. What these stories mean is almost wholly implied by the action, almost never openly stated. Therefore, though the events of these stories are usually easy to recognize, their meaning is hard to determine. In the stories of the group I have placed first, the authors can—and do—direct the reader's attention to the meaning of the events. It is my experience as a teacher that students find such stories a good deal easier to understand than the stories of the second group.

I believe that the arrangement of these stories and the introductions to the four groups may be some help to teachers, but I very much hope no one will allow them to hinder his teaching the stories in any order that seems to him good. The important thing is that these are all wonderful stories.

Cornell University   A. M.
September, 1961

Foreword to the Revised Edition

This revised edition of *Modern Short Stories* has two main purposes. The first is to add to the original selection stories by writers who have either attracted the editor's interest since the first edition was published or have been recommended by teachers who have used the book. Altogether eight new stories have been added, slightly more than a fourth of the stories in the book. These are the stories by Doris Lessing, Flannery O'Connor, Mary McCarthy, F. J. Powers, Dan Jacobson, James Agee, Bernard Malamud, and Reynolds Price.

The second purpose is to increase the usefulness of the book for various kinds of courses. The general arrangement of the stories in the first edition has satisfied the majority of its users and has been kept, but a number of teachers have asked for more information about the stories than is given in the first edition. The amount of critical discussion needed to satisfy this request would clutter the book badly, and we have therefore put it in a separate teachers' handbook, to be used with this text. This handbook contains a discussion of every story in *Modern Short Stories*. Two or three stories from each of the book's four parts, chosen for their variety, have been discussed at some length; the rest of the stories are discussed more briefly.

In order to make this handbook as useful as possible to the teacher, we have added a set of questions for each story at the end of *Modern Short Stories*. These questions have been correlated with the discussions in the handbook: each set constitutes a structured analysis of the story based on the handbook's discussion of it. By using these questions to guide their study of the story, students will be helped to discover the most significant passages and to see for themselves some of the relations among them that are analyzed in the handbook. In the classroom, these questions will then serve the teacher as a starting point for the development of a conception of the story the students will already have begun to think about and be prepared to discuss, and one that the teacher can, with the help of the handbook, make fully meaningful and coherent for them.

In addition, the handbook also provides some suggestions for the teachers who want to use this book of stories in other ways than the one suggested by its plan of organization. Some teachers, for example, prefer to study the short story by examining its technical resources and then using particular stories to illustrate them. For such teachers the handbook provides a brief discussion of these technical resources and some suggestions for using the short stories in this book to illustrate them.

Finally, brief biographies of all the authors represented in *Modern Short Stories* have been added to this edition.

Cornell University   A. M.
January 1967

Part One

INTRODUCTION

All the stories in this first group show an attitude toward experience that is characteristic of our time. This attitude might be described as twentieth-century romanticism, in order to distinguish it from the several different kinds of romanticism that flourished at various times in the nineteenth century. What makes these twentieth-century writers romantic is that, like all other kinds of romantics, they are deeply disturbed by what seems to them the ambiguous relation between subject and object, by the tendency for what is outside us to exist independent of the subjective reality of emotions, convictions, and beliefs that exists inside us. The early nineteenth-century romantics temporarily solved this problem by accepting a special conception of the relation between the subjective observer and the objective reality he observed. This conception was worked out by Coleridge and simplified into a slogan by Wordsworth in his "Lines Composed a Few Miles Above Tintern Abbey," when he proclaimed himself a lover

>   of all the mighty world
> Of eye and ear,—both what they half create,
> And what perceive; well pleased to recognize
> In nature and the language of the sense
> The anchor of my purest thoughts, the nurse,
> The guide, the guardian of my heart, and soul
> Of all my moral being.

But this solution of the problem has not stood up. Men have continued to feel that there is a disturbing gap between "nature" and their "moral being." The scientific conception of external reality seems to be constantly reducing the possibilities that our perceptions create nature in any way, or that we can anchor our thoughts in nature. Some writers, like those in the third group of stories in this book, escape this difficulty by making the subjective sense of life the essential reality; for them, the objective world is either a kind of stage set or backdrop for the working out of man's inner life of feelings, or a symbolic demonstration of it.

But for the writers of the stories in the present group, the objective world is too convincingly real to be treated in these ways. No more than the writers in the third group are they prepared to surrender their subjective and emotionally charged conception of the nature of things. But neither will they surrender their sense of the alien autonomy of the objective world. Therefore they write stories in which the events and the characters are exactly as we believe them to be in the actual world, and people and places in these stories are described so accurately that they often approach being social history. Miss McCarthy is not quite sure *Artists in Uniform* ought even to be called a story. "I myself," she has written, "would not know quite what to call it: it was a fragment of autobiography. . . ." Dylan Thomas begins *A Story* with the sentence, "If you can call it a story." The journey up the Congo taken by Marlow in Conrad's *Heart of Darkness* was actually taken by Conrad in 1890, so that Conrad is able to represent the Belgian Congo as it was under the rule of the infamous Leopold II with a brilliance and precision that few historians have equaled. Fitzgerald's *Babylon Revisited* takes us to Paris in the 1920's—or, to be exact, into a bittersweet recollection of Paris in the 1920's—and it gives us an acute sense of the "feel" of that time and place: ". . . the snow of twenty-nine wasn't real snow. If you didn't want it to be snow, you just paid some money." Frank O'Connor, Katherine Anne Porter, and John Updike show us crucial stages in the process of growing up that most of us recognize at once from our own experience.

But if what happens in these stories is very lifelike and even historically accurate, the stories are at the same time strongly marked by the authors' feelings about what happens, by their conviction that the essential reality of things is created by what people feel about them. However accurately they represent what happens, this conviction that the significant reality is in the hearts of men requires them to put the main emphasis of their stories on how they feel about what happens.

The most obvious way to do that is to tell the story in the first person, as Conrad does in *Heart of Darkness*. In *Heart of Darkness*, all Conrad's wonderful eloquence is exercised to make us share Marlow's feelings about the events of the story. But substantially the same effect can be achieved when the story is told in the third person, as Fitzgerald's *Babylon Revisited* is. In *Babylon Revisited*, Fitzgerald makes Charlie Wales' thoughts and feelings so dominate the story that in the end we are on his side. Therefore, in reading one of these romantic stories, whether it is told in the first person or the third person, we must be particularly alert to detect the feelings about the events, though we must at the same time do full justice to the objective reality of the events. If we read this kind of story properly, we will come away with a strong sense of the personal, subjective experience of the protagonist and, at the same time, a belief that the events of the story have been shown us exactly as they must have happened, neither distorted nor censored to make us feel about them as the author wants us to feel.

Thus Conrad's *Heart of Darkness* shows us an unforgettably vivid picture of the African jungle and of the Europeans' exploitation of the African natives. It does not do so because Conrad wishes to persuade us to accept some "objective," historical view of these events, or to make us feel that nature is beneficent or savages noble. As a matter of fact, Conrad's jungle is ominous and terrifying and his savages are frankly, if innocently, savage. The darkness Conrad is really concerned with is not in the heart of Africa at all; it is in the hearts of men, and for all its magnificent actuality, the jungle Conrad describes is ultimately metaphorical, a means of making us see the full horror that Kurtz felt in his heart. "Yes," Marlow says of the jungle's leaping and howling savages, "it was ugly enough; but if you were man enough you would admit to yourself that there was in you just the faintest trace of a response to the terrible frankness of that noise. . . ." Everywhere in *Heart of Darkness* Marlow, who is a better man than most of us, is saying something like that.

There is no voice like Marlow's to guide us in *Babylon Revisited*. By writing it in the third person, Fitzgerald could represent with almost historical accuracy the Paris Charlie and Helen had lived in two years before and the Paris Peter and Marion live in now. But if you watch closely, you will see that this third person who is speaking in the story becomes almost identical with Charlie at the crucial points of the story. As a result we are led to judge the events as he does and thus, despite his unforgivable conduct of two years ago, to forgive him.

In theory, a story in the first person, with all its opportunities for the expression of the character's feelings, ought to emphasize subjective reality at the expense of objective reality much more than a story in the third person. But in fact, though *Babylon Revisited* is written in the third person, we share Charlie Wales' feelings at least as much as we do Marlow's in *Heart of Darkness*. Both stories achieve the kind of effect that is the peculiar triumph of the contemporary romantic story, the effect that results from representing events in an overwhelmingly lifelike way and at the same time convincing us that what ultimately counts is not these events themselves but what men feel in their hearts about them.

JOSEPH CONRAD

Heart of Darkness

The *Nellie*, a cruising yawl, swung to her anchor without a flutter of the sails, and was at rest. The flood had made, the wind was nearly calm, and being bound down the river, the only thing for it was to come to and wait for the turn of the tide.

The sea-reach of the Thames stretched before us like the beginning of an interminable waterway. In the offing the sea and the sky were welded together without a joint, and in the luminous space the tanned sails of the barges drifting up with the tide seemed to stand still in red clusters of canvas sharply peaked, with gleams of varnished sprits. A haze rested on the low shores that ran out to sea in vanishing flatness. The air was dark above Gravesend, and farther back still seemed condensed into a mournful gloom, brooding motionless over the biggest, and the greatest, town on earth.

The Director of Companies was our captain and our host. We four affectionately watched his back as he stood in the bows looking to seaward. On the whole river there was nothing that looked half so nautical. He resembled a pilot, which to a seaman is trustworthiness personified. It was difficult to realize his work was not out there in the luminous estuary, but behind him, within the brooding gloom.

Between us there was, as I have already said somewhere, the bond of the sea. Besides holding our hearts together through long periods of separation, it had the effect of making us tolerant of each other's yarns—and even convictions. The Lawyer—the best of old fellows had, because of his many years and many virtues, the only cushion on deck, and was lying on the only rug. The Ac-

5

countant had brought out already a box of dominoes, and was toying architecturally with the bones. Marlow sat cross-legged right aft, leaning against the mizzen-mast. He had sunken cheeks, a yellow complexion, a straight back, an ascetic aspect, and, with his arms dropped, the palms of hands outwards, resembled an idol. The director, satisfied the anchor had good hold, made his way aft and sat down amongst us. We exchanged a few words lazily. Afterwards there was silence on board the yacht. For some reason or other we did not begin that game of dominoes. We felt meditative, and fit for nothing but placid staring. The day was ending in a serenity of still and exquisite brilliance. The water shone pacifically; the sky, without a speck, was a benign immensity of unstained light; the very mist on the Essex marshes was like a gauzy and radiant fabric, hung from the wooded rises inland, and draping the low shores in diaphanous folds. Only the gloom to the west, brooding over the upper reaches, became more somber every minute, as if angered by the approach of the sun.

And at last, in its curved and imperceptible fall, the sun sank low, and from glowing white changed to a dull red without rays and without heat, as if about to go out suddenly, stricken to death by the touch of that gloom brooding over a crowd of men.

Forthwith a change came over the waters, and the serenity became less brilliant but more profound. The old river in its broad reach rested unruffled at the decline of day, after ages of good service done to the race that peopled its banks, spread out in the tranquil dignity of a waterway leading to the uttermost ends of the earth. We looked at the venerable stream not in the vivid flush of a short day that comes and departs forever, but in the august light of abiding memories. And indeed nothing is easier for a man who has, as the phrase goes, "followed the sea" with reverence and affection, than to evoke the great spirit of the past upon the lower reaches of the Thames. The tidal current runs to and fro in its unceasing service, crowded with memories of men and ships it had borne to the rest of home or to the battles of the sea. It had known and served all the men of whom the nation is proud, from Sir Francis Drake to Sir John Franklin, knights all, titled and untitled—the knights-errant of the sea. It had borne all the ships whose names are like jewels flashing in the

night of time, from the *Golden Hind* returning with her round
flanks full of treasure, to be visited by the Queen's Highness and
thus pass out of the gigantic tale, to the *Erebus* and *Terror*,
bound on other conquests—and that never returned. It had
known the ships and the men. They had sailed from Deptford,
from Greenwich, from Erith—the adventurers and the settlers;
kings' ships and the ships of men on 'Change; captains, admirals,
the dark "interlopers" of the Eastern trade, and the commissioned
"generals" of East India fleets. Hunters for gold or pursuers of
fame, they all had gone out on that stream, bearing the sword,
and often the torch, messengers of the might within the land,
bearers of a spark from the sacred fire. What greatness had not
floated on the ebb of that river into the mystery of an unknown
earth! . . . The dreams of men, the seed of commonwealths, the
germs of empires.

The sun set; the dusk fell on the stream, and lights began to
appear along the shore. The Chapman lighthouse, a three-legged
thing erect on a mud-flat, shone strongly. Lights of ships moved
in the fairway—a great stir of lights going up and going down.
And farther west on the upper reaches the place of the monstrous
town was still marked ominously on the sky, a brooding gloom
in sunshine, a lurid glare under the stars.

"And this also," said Marlow suddenly, "has been one of the
dark places on the earth."

He was the only man of us who still "followed the sea." The
worst that could be said of him was that he did not represent
his class. He was a seaman, but he was a wanderer, too, while
most seamen lead, if one may so express it, a sedentary life. Their
minds are of the stay-at-home order, and their home is always
with them—the ship; and so is their country—the sea. One ship
is very much like another, and the sea is always the same. In the
immutability of their surroundings the foreign shores, the foreign faces, the changing immensity of life, glide past, veiled not
by a sense of mystery but by a slightly disdainful ignorance; for
there is nothing mysterious to a seaman unless it be the sea itself,
which is the mistress of his existence and as inscrutable as Destiny.
For the rest, after his hours of work, a casual stroll or a casual spree
on shore suffices to unfold for him the secret of a whole continent, and generally he finds the secret not worth knowing. The

yarns of seamen have a direct simplicity, the whole meaning of which lies within the shell of a cracked nut. But Marlow was not typical (if his propensity to spin yarns be excepted), and to him the meaning of an episode was not inside like a kernel but outside, enveloping the tale which brought it out only as a glow brings out a haze, in the likeness of one of these misty halos that sometimes are made visible by the spectral illumination of moonshine.

His remark did not seem at all surprising. It was just like Marlow. It was accepted in silence. No one took the trouble to grunt even; and presently he said, very slow—

"I was thinking of very old times, when the Romans first came here, nineteen hundred years ago—the other day. . . . Light came out of this river since—you say Knights? Yes; but it is like a running blaze on a plain, like a flash of lightning in the clouds. We live in the flicker—may it last as long as the old earth keeps rolling! But darkness was here yesterday. Imagine the feelings of a commander of a fine—what d'ye call 'em?—trireme in the Mediterranean, ordered suddenly to the north; run overland across the Gauls in a hurry; put in charge of one of these craft the legionaries—a wonderful lot of handy men they must have been, too —used to build, apparently by the hundred, in a month or two, if we may believe what we read. Imagine him here—the very end of the world, a sea the color of lead, a sky the color of smoke, a kind of ship about as rigid as a concertina—and going up this river with stores, or orders, or what you like. Sand-banks, marshes, forests, savages,—precious little to eat fit for a civilized man, nothing but Thames water to drink. No Falernian wine here, no going ashore. Here and there a military camp lost in a wilderness, like a needle in a bundle of hay—cold, fog, tempests, disease, exile, and death,—death skulking in the air, in the water, in the bush. They must have been dying like flies here. Oh, yes—he did it. Did it very well, too, no doubt, and without thinking much about it either, except afterwards to brag of what he had gone through in his time, perhaps. They were men enough to face the darkness. And perhaps he was cheered by keeping his eye on a chance of promotion to the fleet at Ravenna by and by, if he had good friends in Rome and survived the awful climate. Or think of a decent young citizen in a toga—perhaps too much dice, you know—coming out here in the train of some prefect, or tax-gatherer, or trader even, to mend his fortunes. Land in a swamp, march through the woods, and in some inland post feel the savagery, the utter savagery, had closed round him,—all that mysterious life of the wilderness that stirs in the forest, in the jungles, in the hearts of wild men. There's no initiation either into such mysteries. He has to live in the midst of the incomprehensible, which is also detestable. And it has a fascination, too, that goes to work upon him. The fascination of the abomination—you know, imagine the growing regrets, the longing to escape, the powerless disgust, the surrender, the hate."

He paused.

"Mind," he began again, lifting one arm from the elbow, the palm of the hand outwards, so that, with his legs folded before him, he had the pose of a Buddha preaching in European clothes and without a lotus-flower—"Mind, none of us would feel exactly like this. What saves us is efficiency—the devotion to efficiency. But these chaps were not much account, really. They were no colonists; their administration was merely a squeeze, and nothing more, I suspect. They were conquerors, and for that you want only brute force—nothing to boast of, when you have it, since your strength is just an accident arising from the weakness of others. They grabbed what they could get for the sake of what was to be got. It was just robbery with violence, aggravated murder on a great scale, and men going at it blind—as is very proper for those who tackle a darkness. The conquest of the earth, which mostly means the taking it away from those who have a different complexion or slightly flatter noses than ourselves, is not a pretty thing when you look into it too much. What redeems it is the idea only. An idea at the back of it; not a sentimental pretense but an idea; and an unselfish belief in the idea—something you can set up, and bow down before, and offer a sacrifice to. . . ."

He broke off. Flames glided in the river, small green flames, red flames, white flames, pursuing, overtaking, joining, crossing each other—then separating slowly or hastily. The traffic of the great city went on in the deepening night upon the sleepless river. We looked on, waiting patiently—there was nothing else to do till the end of the flood, but it was only after a long silence, when he said, in a hesitating voice, "I suppose you fellows remember I did once turn fresh-water sailor for a bit," that we knew we were fated, before the ebb began to run, to hear one of Marlow's inconclusive experiences.

"I don't want to bother you much with what happened to me personally," he began, showing in this remark the weakness of many tellers of tales who seem so often unaware of what their audience would best like to hear; "yet to understand the effect of it on me you ought to know how I got out there, what I saw, how I went up that river to the place where I first met the poor chap. It was the farthest point of navigation and the culminating point of my experience. It seemed somehow to throw a kind of light on everything about me—and into my thoughts. It was somber enough, too—and pitiful—not extraordinary in any way —not very clear either. No, not very clear. And yet it seemed to throw a kind of light.

"I had then, as you remember, just returned to London after a lot of Indian Ocean, Pacific, China Seas—a regular dose of the East—six years or so, and I was loafing about, hindering you fellows in your work and invading your homes, just as though I had got a heavenly mission to civilize you. It was very fine for a time, but after a bit I did get tired of resting. Then I began to look for a ship—I should think the hardest work on earth. But the ships wouldn't even look at me. And I got tired of that game, too.

"Now when I was a little chap I had a passion for maps. I would look for hours at South America, or Africa, or Australia, and lose myself in all the glories of exploration. At that time there were many blank spaces on the earth, and when I saw one that looked particularly inviting on a map (but they all look that) I would put my finger on it and say, When I grow up I will go there. The North Pole was one of these places, I remember. Well, I haven't been there yet, and shall not try now. The glamour's off. Other places were scattered about the Equator, and in every sort of latitude all over the two hemispheres. I have been in some of them, and . . . well, we won't talk about that. But there was one yet—the biggest, the most blank, so to speak—that I had a hankering after.

"True, by this time it was not a blank space any more. It had got filled since my childhood with rivers and lakes and names.

It had ceased to be a blank space of delightful mystery—a white patch for a boy to dream gloriously over. It had become a place of darkness. But there was in it one river especially, a mighty big river, that you could see on the map, resembling an immense snake uncoiled, with its head in the sea, its body at rest curving afar over a vast country, and its tail lost in the depths of the land. And as I looked at the map of it in a shop-window, it fascinated me as a snake would a bird—a silly little bird. Then I remembered there was a big concern, a Company for trade on that river. Dash it all! I thought to myself, they can't trade without using some kind of craft on that lot of fresh water—steamboats! Why shouldn't I try to get charge of one? I went on along Fleet Street, but could not shake off the idea. The snake had charmed me.

"You understand it was a Continental concern, that Trading society; but I have a lot of relations living on the Continent, because it's cheap and not so nasty as it looks, they say.

"I am sorry to own I began to worry them. This was already a fresh departure for me. I was not used to getting things that way, you know. I always went my own road and on my own legs where I had a mind to go. I wouldn't have believed it of myself; but, then—you see—I felt somehow I must get there by hook or by crook. So I worried them. The men said 'My dear fellow,' and did nothing. Then—would you believe it?—I tried the women. I, Charlie Marlow, set the women to work—to get a job. Heavens! Well, you see, the notion drove me. I had an aunt, a dear enthusiastic soul. She wrote: 'It will be delightful. I am ready to do anything, anything for you. It is a glorious idea. I know the wife of a very high personage in the Administration, and also a man who has lots of influence with,' etc., etc. She was determined to make no end of fuss to get me appointed skipper of a river steamboat, if such was my fancy.

"I got my appointment—of course; and I got it very quick. It appears the Company had received news that one of their captains had been killed in a scuffle with the natives. This was my chance, and it made me the more anxious to go. It was only months and months afterwards, when I made the attempt to recover what was left of the body, that I heard the original quarrel arose from a misunderstanding about some hens. Yes, two black hens. Fresleven —that was the fellow's name, a Dane—thought himself wronged somehow in the bargain, so he went ashore and started to hammer the chief of the village with a stick. Oh, it didn't surprise me in the least to hear this, and at the same time to be told that Fresleven was the gentlest, quietest creature that ever walked on two legs. No doubt he was; but he had been a couple of years already out there engaged in the noble cause, you know, and he probably felt the need at last of asserting his self-respect in some way. Therefore he whacked the old nigger mercilessly, while a big crowd of his people watched him, thunderstruck, till some man—I was told the chief's son—in desperation at hearing the old chap yell, made a tentative jab with a spear at the white man—and of course it went quite easy between the shoulder blades. Then the whole population cleared into the forest, expecting all kinds of calamities to happen, while, on the other hand, the steamer Fresleven commanded left also in a bad panic, in charge of the engineer, I believe. Afterwards nobody seemed to trouble much about Fresleven's remains, till I got out and stepped into his shoes. I couldn't let it rest, though; but when an opportunity offered at last to meet my predecessor, the grass growing through his ribs was tall enough to hide his bones. They were all there. The supernatural being had not been touched after he fell. And the village was deserted, the huts gaped black, rotting, all askew within the fallen enclosures. A calamity had come to it, sure enough. The people had vanished. Mad terror had scattered them, men, women, and children, through the bush, and they had never returned. What became of the hens I don't know either. I should think the cause of progress got them, anyhow. However, through this glorious affair I got my appointment, before I had fairly begun to hope for it.

"I flew around like mad to get ready, and before forty-eight hours I was crossing the Channel to show myself to my employers, and sign the contract. In a very few hours I arrived in a city that always makes me think of a whited sepulcher. Prejudice no doubt. I had no difficulty in finding the Company's offices. It was the biggest thing in the town, and everybody I met was full of it. They were going to run an over-sea empire, and make no end of coin by trade.

"A narrow and deserted street in deep shadow, high houses, innumerable windows with venetian blinds, a dead silence, grass sprouting between the stones, imposing carriage archways right and left, immense double doors standing ponderously ajar. I slipped through one of these cracks, went up a swept and ungarnished staircase, as arid as a desert, and opened the first door I came to. Two women, one fat and the other slim, sat on straw-bottomed chairs, knitting black wool. The slim one got up and walked straight at me—still knitting with downcast eyes—and only just as I began to think of getting out of her way, as you would for a somnambulist, stood still, and looked up. Her dress was as plain as an umbrella-cover, and she turned round without a word and preceded me into a waiting-room. I gave my name, and looked about. Deal table in the middle, plain chairs all around the walls, on one end a large shining map, marked with all the colors of a rainbow. There was a vast amount of red—good to see at any time, because one knows that some real work is done in there, a deuce of a lot of blue, a little green, smears of orange, and, on the East Coast, a purple patch, to show where the jolly pioneers of progress drink the jolly lager-beer. However, I wasn't going into any of these. I was going into the yellow. Dead in the center. And the river was there—fascinating—deadly—like a snake. Ough! A door opened, a white-haired secretarial head, but wearing a compassionate expression, appeared, and a skinny forefinger beckoned me into the sanctuary. Its light was dim, and a heavy writing-desk squatted in the middle. From behind that structure came out an impression of pale plumpness in a frock coat. The great man himself. He was five feet six, I should judge, and had his grip on the handle-end of ever so many millions. He shook hands, I fancy, murmured vaguely, was satisfied with my French. *Bon voyage*.

"In about forty-five seconds I found myself again in the waiting-room with the compassionate secretary, who, full of desolation and sympathy, made me sign some document. I believe I undertook amongst other things not to disclose any trade secrets. Well, I am not going to.

"I began to feel slightly uneasy. You know I am not used to such ceremonies, and there was something ominous in the atmosphere. It was just as though I had been let into some conspiracy—I don't know—something not quite right; and I was glad to get out. In the outer room the two women knitted black wool feverishly. People were arriving, and the younger one was walking back and forth introducing them. The old one sat on her chair. Her flat cloth slippers were propped up on a footwarmer, and a cat reposed on her lap. She wore a starched white affair on her head, had a wart on one cheek, and silver-rimmed spectacles hung on the tip of her nose. She glanced at me above the glasses. The swift and indifferent placidity of that look troubled me. Two youths with foolish and cheery countenances were being piloted over, and she threw at them the same quick glance of unconcerned wisdom. She seemed to know all about them and about me, too. An eerie feeling came over me. She seemed uncanny and fateful. Often far away there I thought of these two, guarding the door of Darkness, knitting black wool as for a warm pall, one introducing, introducing continuously to the unknown, the other scrutinizing the cheery and foolish faces with unconcerned old eyes. *Ave!* Old knitter of black wool. *Morituri te salutant.*[1] Not many of those she looked at ever saw her again—not half, by a long way.

"There was yet a visit to the doctor. 'A simple formality,' assured me the secretary, with an air of taking an immense part in all my sorrows. Accordingly a young chap wearing his hat over the left eyebrow, some clerk I suppose,—there must have been clerks in the business, though the house was as still as a house in a city of the dead—came from somewhere upstairs, and led me forth. He was shabby and careless, with inkstains on the sleeves of his jacket, and his cravat was large and billowy, under a chin shaped like the toe of an old boot. It was a little too early for the doctor, so I proposed a drink, and thereupon he developed a vein of joviality. As we sat over our vermouths he glorified the Company's business, and by and by I expressed casually my surprise at him not going out there. He became very cool and collected all at once. 'I am not such a fool as I look, quoth Plato to his disciples,' he said sententiously, emptied his glass with great resolution, and we rose.

"The old doctor felt my pulse, evidently thinking of something else the while. 'Good, good for there,' he mumbled, and then with a certain eagerness asked me whether I would let him measure my head. Rather surprised, I said Yes, when he produced a thing like

[1] *Ave! Morituri te salutant.* Hail! They who are about to die salute you.

calipers and got the dimensions back and front and every way, taking notes carefully. He was an unshaven little man in a threadbare coat like a gaberdine, with his feet in slippers, and I thought him a harmless fool. 'I always ask leave, in the interests of science, to measure the crania of those going out there,' he said. 'And when they come back, too?' I asked. 'Oh, I never see them,' he remarked; 'and, moreover, the changes take place inside, you know.' He smiled, as if at some quiet joke. 'So you are going out there. Famous. Interesting, too.' He gave me a searching glance, and made another note. 'Ever any madness in your family?' he asked, in a matter-of-fact tone. I felt very annoyed. 'Is that question in the interests of science, too?' 'It would be,' he said, without taking notice of my irritation, 'interesting for science to watch the mental changes of individuals, on the spot, but . . .' 'Are you an alienist?' I interrupted. 'Every doctor should be—a little,' answered that original, imperturbably. 'I have a little theory which you Messieurs who go out there must help me to prove. This is my share in the advantages my country shall reap from the possession of such a magnificent dependency. The mere wealth I leave to others. Pardon my questions, but you are the first Englishman coming under my observation . . .' I hastened to assure him I was not in the least typical. 'If I were,' said I, 'I wouldn't be talking like this with you.' 'What you say is rather profound, and probably erroneous,' he said, with a laugh. 'Avoid irritation more than exposure to the sun. Adieu. How do you English say, eh? Good-by. Ah! Good-by. Adieu. In the tropics one must before everything keep calm.' . . . He lifted a warning forefinger. . . . '*Du calme, du calme. Adieu.*'

"One thing more remained to do—say good-by to my excellent aunt. I found her triumphant. I had a cup of tea—the last decent cup of tea for many days—and in a room that most soothingly looked just as you would expect a lady's drawing-room to look, we had a long quiet chat by the fireside. In the course of these confidences it became quite plain to me I had been represented to the wife of the high dignitary, and goodness knows to how many more people besides, as an exceptional and gifted creature—a piece of good fortune for the Company—a man you don't get hold of every day. Good heavens! and I was going to take charge of a two-penny-half-penny river-steamboat with a penny whistle attached! It appeared, however, I was also one of the Workers, with a capital—you know. Something like an emissary of light, something like a lower sort of apostle. There had been a lot of such rot let loose in print and talk just about that time, and the excellent woman, living right in the rush of all that humbug, got carried off her feet. She talked about 'weaning those ignorant millions from their horrid ways,' till, upon my word, she made me quite uncomfortable. I ventured to hint that the Company was run for profit.

" 'You forget, dear Charlie, that the laborer is worthy of his hire,' she said, brightly. It's queer how out of touch with truth women are. They live in a world of their own, and there has never been anything like it, and never can be. It is too beautiful altogether, and if they were to set it up it would go to pieces before the first sunset. Some confounded fact we men have been living contentedly with ever since the day of creation would start up and knock the whole thing over.

"After this I got embraced, told to wear flannel, be sure to write often, and so on—and I left. In the street—I don't know why—a queer feeling came to me that I was an impostor. Odd thing that I, who used to clear out for any part of the world at twenty-four hours' notice, with less thought than most men give to the crossing of a street, had a moment—I won't say of hesitation, but of startled pause, before this commonplace affair. The best way I can explain it to you is by saying that, for a second or two, I felt as though, instead of going to the center of a continent, I were about to set off for the center of the earth.

"I left in a French steamer, and she called in every blamed port they have out there, for, as far as I could see, the sole purpose of landing soldiers and custom-house officers. I watched the coast. Watching a coast as it slips by the ship is like thinking about an enigma. There it is before you—smiling, frowning, inviting, grand, mean, insipid, or savage, and always mute with an air of whispering, Come and find out. This one was almost featureless, as if still in the making, with an aspect of monotonous grimness. The edge of a colossal jungle, so dark-green as to be almost black, fringed with white surf, ran straight, like a ruled line, far, far away along a blue sea whose glitter was blurred by a creeping mist. The sun was fierce, the land seemed to glisten and drip with steam.

Here and there grayish-whitish specks showed up clustered inside the white surf, with a flag flying above them perhaps. Settlements some centuries old, and still no bigger than pinheads on the untouched expanse of their background. We pounded along, stopped, landed soldiers; went on, landed custom-house clerks to levy toll in what looked like a God-forsaken wilderness, with a tin shed and a flag-pole lost in it; landed more soldiers—to take care of the custom-house clerks, presumably. Some, I heard, got drowned in the surf; but whether they did or not, nobody seemed particularly to care. They were just flung out there, and on we went. Every day the coast looked the same, as though we had not moved; but we passed various places—trading places—with names like Gran' Bassam, Little Popo; names that seemed to belong to some sordid farce acted in front of a sinister backcloth. The idleness of a passenger, my isolation amongst all these men with whom I had no point of contact, the oily and languid sea, the uniform somberness of the coast, seemed to keep me away from the truth of things, within the toil of a mournful and senseless delusion. The voice of the surf heard now and then was a positive pleasure, like the speech of a brother. It was something natural, that had its reason, that had a meaning. Now and then a boat from the shore gave one a momentary contact with reality. It was paddled by black fellows. You could see from afar the white of their eyeballs glistening. They shouted, sang; their bodies streamed with perspiration; they had faces like grotesque masks—these chaps; but they had bone, muscle, a wild vitality, an intense energy of movement, that was as natural and true as the surf along their coast. They wanted no excuse for being there. They were a great comfort to look at. For a time I would feel I belonged still to a world of straightforward facts; but the feeling would not last long. Something would turn up to scare it away. Once, I remember, we came upon a man-of-war anchored off the coast. There wasn't even a shed there, and she was shelling the bush. It appears the French had one of their wars going on thereabouts. Her ensign dropped limp like a rag; the muzzles of the long six-inch guns stuck out all over the low hull; the greasy, slimy swell swung her up lazily and let her down, swaying her thin masts. In the empty immensity of earth, sky, and water, there she was, incomprehensible, firing into a continent. Pop, would go one of the six-inch guns; a small flame would dart and vanish, a little white smoke would disappear, a tiny projectile would give a feeble screech—and nothing happened. Nothing could happen. There was a touch of insanity in the proceeding, a sense of lugubrious drollery in the sight; and it was not dissipated by somebody on board assuring me earnestly there was a camp of natives—he called them enemies!—hidden out of sight somewhere.

"We gave her her letters (I heard the men in that lonely ship were dying of fever at the rate of three a day) and went on. We called at some more places with farcical names, where the merry dance of death and trade goes on in a still and earthy atmosphere as of an overheated catacomb; all along the formless coast bordered by dangerous surf, as if Nature herself had tried to ward off intruders; in and out of rivers, streams of death in life, whose banks were rotting into mud, whose waters, thickened into slime, invaded the contorted mangroves, that seemed to writhe at us in the extremity of an impotent despair. Nowhere did we stop long enough to get a particularized impression, but the general sense of vague and oppressive wonder grew upon me. It was like a weary pilgrimage amongst hints for nightmares.

"It was upward of thirty days before I saw the mouth of the big river. We anchored off the seat of the government. But my work would not begin till some two hundred miles farther on. So as soon as I could I made a start for a place thirty miles higher up.

"I had my passage on a little sea-going steamer. Her captain was a Swede, and knowing me for a seaman, invited me on the bridge. He was a young man, lean, fair, and morose, with lanky hair and a shuffling gait. As we left the miserable little wharf, he tossed his head contemptuously at the shore. 'Been living there?' he asked. I said, 'Yes,' 'Fine lot these government chaps—are they not?' he went on, speaking English with great precision and considerable bitterness. 'It is funny what some people will do for a few francs a month. I wonder what becomes of that kind when it goes up-country?' I said to him I expected to see that soon. 'So-o-o!' he exclaimed. He shuffled athwart, keeping one eye ahead vigilantly. 'Don't be too sure,' he continued. 'The other day I took up a man who hanged himself on the road. He was a Swede, too.' 'Hanged himself! Why, in God's name?' I cried. He kept on looking out watchfully. 'Who knows? The sun was too much for him, or the country perhaps.'

"At last we opened a reach. A rocky cliff appeared, mounds of turned-up earth by the shore, houses on a hill, others with iron roofs, amongst a waste of excavations, or hanging to the declivity. A continuous noise of the rapids above hovered over this scene of inhabited devastation. A lot of people, mostly black and naked, moved about like ants. A jetty projected into the river. A blinding sunlight drowned all this at times in a sudden recrudescence of glare. 'There's your Company's station,' said the Swede, pointing to three wooden barrack-like structures on the rocky slope. 'I will send your things up. Four boxes did you say? So. Farewell.'

"I came upon a boiler wallowing in the grass, then found a path leading up the hill. It turned aside for the boulders, and also for an undersized railway-truck lying there on its back with its wheels in the air. One was off. The thing looked as dead as the carcass of some animal. I came upon more pieces of decaying machinery, a stack of rusty rails. To the left a clump of trees made a shady spot, where dark things seemed to stir feebly. I blinked, the path was steep. A horn tooted to the right, and I saw the black people run. A heavy and dull detonation shook the ground, a puff of smoke came out of the cliff, and that was all. No change appeared on the face of the rock. They were building a railway. The cliff was not in the way or anything; but this objectless blasting was all the work going on.

"A slight clinking behind me made me turn my head. Six black men advanced in a file, toiling up the path. They walked erect and slow, balancing small baskets full of earth on their heads, and the clink kept time with their footsteps. Black rags were wound round their loins, and the short ends behind waggled to and fro like tails. I could see every rib, the joints of their limbs were like knots in a rope; each had an iron collar on his neck, and all were connected together with a chain whose bights swung between them, rhythmically clinking. Another report from the cliff made me think suddenly of that ship of war I had seen firing into a continent. It was the same kind of ominous voice; but these men could by no stretch of imagination be called enemies. They were called criminals, and the outraged law, like the bursting shells, had come to them, an insoluble mystery from the sea. All their meager breasts panted together, the violently dilated nostrils quivered, the eyes stared stonily up-hill. They passed me within six inches, without a glance, with that complete, deathlike indifference of unhappy savages. Behind this raw matter one of the reclaimed, the product of the new forces at work, strolled despondently, carrying a rifle by its middle. He had a uniform jacket with one button off, and seeing a white man on the path, hoisted his weapon to his shoulder with alacrity. This was simple prudence, white men being so much alike at a distance that he could not tell who I might be. He was speedily reassured, and with a large, white, rascally grin, and a glance at his charge, seemed to take me into partnership in his exalted trust. After all, I also was a part of the great cause of these high and just proceedings.

"Instead of going up, I turned and descended to the left. My idea was to let that chain-gang get out of sight before I climbed the hill. You know I am not particularly tender; I've had to strike and to fend off. I've had to resist and to attack sometimes—that's only one way of resisting—without counting the exact cost, according to the demands of such sort of life as I had blundered into. I've seen the devil of violence, and the devil of greed, and the devil of hot desire; but, by all the stars! these were strong, lusty, red-eyed devils, that swayed and drove men—men, I tell you. But as I stood on this hillside, I foresaw that in the blinding sunshine of that land I would become acquainted with a flabby, pretending, weak-eyed devil of a rapacious and pitiless folly. How insidious he could be, too, I was only to find out several months later and a thousand miles farther. For a moment I stood appalled, as though by a warning. Finally I descended the hill, obliquely, towards the trees I had seen.

"I avoided a vast artificial hole somebody had been digging on the slope, the purpose of which I found it impossible to divine. It wasn't a quarry or a sandpit, anyhow. It was just a hole. It might have been connected with the philanthropic desire of giving the criminals something to do. I don't know. Then I nearly fell into a very narrow ravine, almost no more than a scar in the hillside. I discovered that a lot of imported drainage-pipes for the settlement had been tumbled in there. There wasn't one that was not broken. It was a wanton smashup. At last I got under the trees. My purpose was to stroll into the shade for a moment; but no sooner within than it seemed to me I had stepped into the gloomy circle of some Inferno. The rapids were near, and an uninterrupted, uniform, headlong, rushing noise filled the mournful stillness of the grove, where not a breath stirred, not a leaf moved, with a mysterious sound—as though the tearing pace of the launched earth had suddenly become audible.

"Black shapes crouched, lay, sat between the trees leaning against the trunks, clinging to the earth, half coming out, half effaced within the dim light, in all the attitudes of pain, abandonment, and despair. Another mine on the cliff went off, followed by a slight shudder of the soil under my feet. The work was going on. The work! And this was the place where some of the helpers had withdrawn to die.

"They were dying slowly—it was very clear. They were not enemies, they were not criminals, they were nothing earthly now, —nothing but black shadows of disease and starvation, lying confusedly in the greenish gloom. Brought from all the recesses of the coast in all the legality of time contracts, lost in uncongenial surroundings, fed on unfamiliar food, they sickened, became inefficient, and were then allowed to crawl away and rest. These moribund shapes were free as air—and nearly as thin. I began to distinguish the gleam of the eyes under the trees. Then, glancing down, I saw a face near my hand. The black bones reclined at full length with one shoulder against the tree, and slowly the eyelids rose and the sunken eyes looked up at me, enormous and vacant, a kind of blind, white flicker in the depths of the orbs, which died out slowly. The man seemed young—almost a boy— but you know with them it's hard to tell. I found nothing else to do but to offer him one of my good Swede's ship's biscuits I had in my pocket. The fingers closed slowly on it and held—there was no other movement and no other glance. He had tied a bit of white worsted round his neck— Why? Where did he get it? Was it a badge—an ornament—a charm—a propitiatory act? Was there any idea at all connected with it? It looked startling round his black neck, this bit of white thread from beyond the seas.

"Near the same tree two more bundles of acute angles sat with their legs drawn up. One, with his chin propped on his knees, stared at nothing, in an intolerable and appalling manner: his brother phantom rested its forehead, as if overcome with a great weariness; and all about others were scattered in every pose of contorted collapse, as in some picture of a massacre or a pestilence. While I stood horror-struck, one of these creatures rose to his hands and knees, and went off on all-fours towards the river to drink. He lapped out of his hand, then sat up in the sunlight, crossing his shins in front of him, and after a time let his woolly head fall on his breastbone.

"I didn't want any more loitering in the shade, and I made haste towards the station. When near the buildings I met a white man, in such an unexpected elegance of get-up that in the first moment I took him for a sort of vision. I saw a high starched collar, white cuffs, a light alpaca jacket, snowy trousers, a clean necktie, and varnished boots. No hat. Hair parted, brushed, oiled, under a green-lined parasol held in a big white hand. He was amazing, and had a penholder behind his ear.

"I shook hands with this miracle, and I learned he was the Company's chief accountant, and that all the bookkeeping was done at this station. He had come out for a moment, he said, 'to get a breath of fresh air.' The expression sounded wonderfully odd, with its suggestion of sedentary desk-life. I wouldn't have mentioned the fellow to you at all, only it was from his lips that I first heard the name of the man who is so indissolubly connected with the memories of that time. Moreover, I respected the fellow. Yes; I respected his collars, his vast cuffs, his brushed hair. His appearance was certainly that of a hairdresser's dummy; but in the great demoralization of the land he kept up his appearance. That's backbone. His starched collars and got-up shirt-fronts were achievements of character. He had been out nearly three years; and, later, I could not help asking him how he managed to sport such linen. He had just the faintest blush, and said modestly, 'I've been teaching one of the native women about the station. It was difficult. She had a distaste for the work.' Thus this man had verily accomplished something. And he was devoted to his books, which were in apple-pie order.

"Everything else in the station was in a muddle,—heads, things, buildings. Strings of dusty niggers with splay feet arrived and departed; a stream of manufactured goods, rubbishy cottons, beads, and brass-wire set into the depths of darkness, and in return came a precious trickle of ivory.

"I had to wait in the station for ten days—an eternity. I lived in a hut in the yard, but to be out of the chaos I would sometimes get into the accountant's office. It was built of horizontal planks, and so badly put together that, as he bent over his high desk, he was barred from neck to heels with narrow strips of sunlight. There was no need to open the big shutter to see. It was hot there, too; big flies buzzed fiendishly, and did not sting, but stabbed. I sat generally on the floor, while, of faultless appearance (and even slightly scented), perching on a high stool, he wrote, he wrote. Sometimes he stood up for exercise. When a truckle-bed with a sick man (some invalid agent from up-country) was put in there, he exhibited a gentle annoyance. 'The groans of this sick person,' he said, 'distract my attention. And without that it is extremely difficult to guard against clerical errors in this climate.'

"One day he remarked, without lifting his head, 'In the interior you will no doubt meet Mr. Kurtz.' On my asking who Mr. Kurtz was, he said he was a first-class agent; and seeing my disappointment at this information, he added slowly, laying down his pen, 'He is a very remarkable person.' Further questions elicited from him that Mr. Kurtz was at present in charge of a trading post, a very important one, in the true ivory-country, at 'the very bottom of there. Sends in as much ivory as all the others put together. . . .' He began to write again. The sick man was too ill to groan. The flies buzzed in a great peace.

"Suddenly there was a growing murmur of voices and a great tramping of feet. A caravan had come in. A violent babble of uncouth sounds burst out on the other side of the planks. All the carriers were speaking together, and in the midst of the uproar the lamentable voice of the chief agent was heard 'giving it up' tearfully for the twentieth time that day. . . . He rose slowly. 'What a frightful row,' he said. He crossed the room gently to look at the sick man, and returning, said to me, 'He does not hear.' 'What! Dead?' I asked, startled. 'No, not yet,' he answered, with great composure. Then, alluding with a toss of the head to the tumult in the station-yard, 'When one has got to make correct entries, one comes to hate those savages—hate them to the death.' He remained thoughtful for a moment. 'When you see Mr. Kurtz,' he went on, 'tell him for me that everything here'—he glanced

at the desk—'is very satisfactory. I don't like to write to him—
with those messengers of ours you never know who may get hold
of your letter—at that Central Station.' He stared at me for a moment with his mild, bulging eyes. 'Oh, he will go far, very far,' he
began again. 'He will be a somebody in the Administration before long. They, above—the Council in Europe, you know—
mean him to be.'

"He turned to his work. The noise outside had ceased, and
presently in going out I stopped at the door. In the steady buzz
of flies the homeward-bound agent was lying flushed and insensible; the other, bent over his books, was making correct entries
of perfectly correct transactions; and fifty feet below the doorstep I could see the still tree-tops of the grove of death.

"Next day I left that station at last, with a caravan of sixty men,
for a two-hundred-mile tramp.

"No use telling you much about that. Paths, paths, everywhere;
a stamped-in network of paths spreading over the empty land,
through long grass, through burnt grass, through thickets, down
and up chilly ravines, up and down stony hills ablaze with heat;
and a solitude, a solitude, nobody, not a hut. The population had
cleared out a long time ago. Well, if a lot of mysterious niggers
armed with all kinds of fearful weapons suddenly took to traveling on the road between Deal and Gravesend, catching the yokels
right and left to carry heavy loads for them, I fancy every farm
and cottage thereabouts would get empty very soon. Only here
the dwellings were gone, too. Still I passed through several abandoned villages. There's something pathetically childish in the
ruins of grass walls. Day after day, with the stamp and shuffle of
sixty pair of bare feet behind me, each pair under a sixty-pound
load. Camp, cook, sleep, strike camp, march. Now and then a carrier dead in harness, at rest in the long grass near the path, with
an empty water-gourd and his long staff lying by his side. A great
silence around and above. Perhaps on some quiet night the tremor
of far-off drums, sinking, swelling, a tremor vast, faint; a sound
weird, appealing, suggestive, and wild—and perhaps with as profound a meaning as the sound of bells in a Christian country. Once
a white man in an unbuttoned uniform, camping on the path with
an armed escort of lank Zanzibaris, very hospitable and festive—
not to say drunk. Was looking after the upkeep of the road, he

declared. Can't say I saw any road or any upkeep, unless the body of a middle-aged Negro, with a bullet-hole in the forehead, upon which I absolutely stumbled three miles farther on, may be considered as a permanent improvement. I had a white companion, too, not a bad chap, but rather too fleshy and with the exasperating habit of fainting on the hot hillsides, miles away from the least bit of shade and water. Annoying, you know, to hold your own coat like a parasol over a man's head while he is coming-to. I couldn't help asking him once what he meant by coming there at all. 'To make money, of course. What do you think?' he said, scornfully. Then he got fever, and had to be carried in a hammock slung under a pole. As he weighed sixteen stone I had no end of rows with the carriers. They jibbed, ran away, sneaked off with their loads in the night—quite a mutiny. So, one evening, I made a speech in English with gestures, not one of which was lost to the sixty pairs of eyes before me, and the next morning I started the hammock off in front all right. An hour afterwards I came upon the whole concern wrecked in a bush—man, hammock, groans, blankets, horrors. The heavy pole had skinned his poor nose. He was very anxious for me to kill somebody, but there wasn't the shadow of a carrier near. I remembered the old doctor— 'It would be interesting for science to watch the mental changes of individuals, on the spot.' I felt I was becoming scientifically interesting. However, all that is to no purpose. On the fifteenth day I came in sight of the big river again, and hobbled into the Central Station. It was on a backwater surrounded by scrub and forest, with a pretty border of smelly mud on one side, and on the three others enclosed by a crazy fence of rushes. A neglected gap was all the gate it had, and the first glance at the place was enough to let you see the flabby devil was running that show. White men with long staves in their hands appeared languidly from amongst the buildings, strolling up to take a look at me, and then retired out of sight somewhere. One of them, a stout, excitable chap with black mustaches, informed me with great volubility and many digressions, as soon as I told him who I was, that my steamer was at the bottom of the river. I was thunderstruck. What, how, why? Oh, it was 'all right.' The 'manager himself' was there. All quite correct. 'Everybody had behaved splendidly! splendidly!' 'you must,' he said in agitation, 'go and see the general manager at once. He is waiting!'

"I did not see the real significance of that wreck at once. I fancy I see it now, but I am not sure—not at all. Certainly the affair was too stupid—when I think of it—to be altogether natural. Still. . . . But at the moment it presented itself simply as a confounded nuisance. The steamer was sunk. They had started two days before in a sudden hurry up the river with the manager on board, in charge of some volunteer skipper, and before they had been out three hours they tore the bottom out of her on stones, and she sank near the south bank. I asked myself what I was to do there, now my boat was lost. As a matter of fact, I had plenty to do in fishing my command out of the river. I had to set about it the very next day. That, and the repairs when I brought the pieces to the station, took some months.

"My first interview with the manager was curious. He did not ask me to sit down after my twenty-mile walk that morning. He was commonplace in complexion, in feature, in manners, and in voice. He was of middle size and of ordinary build. His eyes, of the usual blue, were perhaps remarkably cold, and he certainly could make his glance fall on one as trenchant and heavy as an ax. But even at these times the rest of his person seemed to disclaim the intention. Otherwise there was only an indefinable, faint expression of his lips, something stealthy—a smile—not a smile—I remember it, but I can't explain. It was unconscious, this smile was, though just after he had said something it got intensified for an instant. It came at the end of his speeches like a seal applied on the words to make the meaning of the commonest phrase appear absolutely inscrutable. He was a common trader, from his youth up employed in these parts—nothing more. He was obeyed, yet he inspired neither love nor fear, nor even respect. He inspired uneasiness. That was it! Uneasiness. Not a definite mistrust—just uneasiness—nothing more. You have no idea how effective such a . . . a . . . faculty can be. He had no genius for organizing, for initiative, or for order even. That was evident in such things as the deplorable state of the station. He had no learning, and no intelligence. His position had come to him—why? Perhaps because he was never ill. . . . He had served three terms of three years out there. . . . Because triumphant health in the general rout of constitutions is a kind of power in itself. When he went home on leave he rioted on a large scale—pompously. Jack ashore—with a difference—in externals only. This one could gather from his casual talk. He originated nothing, he could keep the routine going—that's all. But he was great. He was great by this little thing that it was impossible to tell what could control such a man. He never gave the secret away. Perhaps there was nothing within him. Such a suspicion made one pause—for out there there were no external checks. Once when various tropical diseases had laid low almost every 'agent' in the station, he was heard to say, 'Men who come out here should have no entrails.' He sealed the utterance with that smile of his, as though it had been a door opening into a darkness he had in his keeping. You fancied you had seen things—but the seal was on. When annoyed at meal-times by the constant quarrels of the white men about precedence, he ordered an immense round table to be made, for which a special house had to be built. This was the station's mess-room. Where he sat was the first place—the rest were nowhere. One felt this to be his unalterable conviction. He was neither civil nor uncivil. He was quiet. He allowed his 'boy'—an overfed young Negro from the coast—to treat the white men, under his very eyes, with provoking insolence.

"He began to speak as soon as he saw me. I had been very long on the road. He could not wait. Had to start without me. The up-river stations had to be relieved. There had been so many delays already that he did not know who was dead and who was alive, and how they got on—and so on, and so on. He paid no attention to my explanations, and, playing with a stick of sealing-wax, repeated several times that the situation was 'very grave, very grave.' There were rumors that a very important station was in jeopardy, and its chief, Mr. Kurtz, was ill. Hoped it was not true. Mr. Kurtz was . . . I felt weary and irritable. Hang Kurtz, I thought. I interrupted him by saying I had heard of Mr. Kurtz on the coast. 'Ah! So they talk of him down there,' he murmured to himself. Then he began again, assuring me Mr. Kurtz was the best agent he had, an exceptional man, of the greatest importance to the Company; therefore I could understand his anxiety. He was, he said, 'very, very uneasy.' Certainly he fidgeted on his chair a good deal, exclaimed, 'Ah, Mr. Kurtz!' broke the stick of sealing-wax and seemed dumfounded by the accident. Next thing he wanted

to know 'how long it would take to . . .' I interrupted him
again. Being hungry, you know, and kept on my feet too, I was
getting savage. 'How can I tell?' I said. 'I haven't even seen the
wreck yet—some months, no doubt.' All this talk seemed to me so
futile. 'Some months,' he said. 'Well, let us say three months before
we can make a start. Yes. That ought to do the affair.' I flung out
of his hut (he lived all alone in a clay hut with a sort of veranda)
muttering to myself my opinion of him. He was a chattering idiot.
Afterwards I took it back when it was borne in upon me startlingly
with what extreme nicety he had estimated the time requisite for
the 'affair.'

"I went to work the next day, turning, so to speak, my back on
that station. In that way only it seemed to me I could keep my
hold on the redeeming facts of life. Still, one must look about
sometimes; and then I saw this station, these men strolling aimlessly about in the sunshine of the yard. I asked myself sometimes
what it all meant. They wandered here and there with their absurd long staves in their hands, like a lot of faithless pilgrims
bewitched inside a rotten fence. The word 'ivory' rang in the
air, was whispered, was sighed. You would think they were praying to it. A taint of imbecile rapacity blew through it all, like a
whiff from some corpse. By Jove! I've never seen anything so
unreal in my life. And outside, the silent wilderness surrounding
this cleared speck on the earth struck me as something great and
invincible, like evil or truth, waiting patiently for the passing
away of this fantastic invasion.

"Oh, these months! Well, never mind. Various things happened.
One evening a grass shed full of calico, cotton prints, beads, and
I don't know what else, burst into a blaze so suddenly that you
would have thought the earth had opened to let an avenging fire
consume all that trash. I was smoking my pipe quietly by my dismantled steamer, and saw them all cutting capers in the light, with
their arms lifted high, when the stout man with mustaches came
tearing down to the river, a tin pail in his hand, assured me that
everybody was 'behaving splendidly, splendidly,' dipped about
a quart of water and tore back again. I noticed there was a hole
in the bottom of his pail.

"I strolled up. There was no hurry. You see the thing had gone
off like a box of matches. It had been hopeless from the very first.

The flame had leaped high, driven everybody back, lighted up everything—and collapsed. The shed was already a heap of embers glowing fiercely. A nigger was being beaten near by. They said he had caused the fire in some way; be that as it may, he was screeching most horribly. I saw him, later, for several days, sitting in a bit of shade looking very sick and trying to recover himself: afterwards he arose and went out—and the wilderness without a sound took him into its bosom again. As I approached the glow from the dark I found myself at the back of two men, talking. I heard the name of Kurtz pronounced, then the words, 'take advantage of this unfortunate accident.' One of the men was the manager. I wished him a good evening. 'Did you ever see anything like it—eh? it is incredible,' he said, and walked off. The other man remained. He was a first-class agent, young, gentlemanly, a bit reserved, with a forked little beard and a hooked nose. He was standoffish with the other agents, and they on their side said he was the manager's spy among them. As to me, I had hardly ever spoken to him before. We got into talk, and by and by we strolled away from the hissing ruins. Then he asked me to his room, which was in the main building of the station. He struck a match, and I perceived that this young aristocrat had not only a silver-mounted dressing-case but also a whole candle all to himself. Just at that time the manager was the only man supposed to have any right to candles. Native mats covered the clay walls; a collection of spears, assegais, shields, knives was hung up in trophies. The business intrusted to this fellow was the making of bricks—so I had been informed; but there wasn't a fragment of a brick anywhere in the station, and he had been there more than a year—waiting. It seems he could not make bricks without something, I don't know what—straw, maybe. Anyways, it could not be found there, and as it was not likely to be sent from Europe, it did not appear clear to me what he was waiting for. An act of special creation perhaps. However, they were all waiting—all the sixteen or twenty pilgrims of them—for something; and upon my word it did not seem an uncongenial occupation, from the way they took it, though the only thing that ever came to them was disease—as far as I could see. They beguiled the time by backbiting and intriguing against each other in a foolish kind of way. There was an air of plotting about that station, but nothing came of it, of course. It was as unreal as everything else—as the philanthropic pretense of the whole concern, as their talk, as their government, as their show of work. The only real feeling was a desire to get appointed to a trading-post where ivory was to be had, so that they could earn percentages. They intrigued and slandered and hated each other only on that account,—but as to effectually lifting a little finger—oh, no. By heavens! there is something after all in the world allowing one man to steal a horse while another must not look at the halter. Steal a horse straight out. Very well. He has done it. Perhaps he can ride. But there is a way of looking at a halter that would provoke the most charitable of saints into a kick.

"I had no idea why he wanted to be sociable, but as we chatted in there it suddenly occurred to me the fellow was trying to get at something—in fact, pumping me. He alluded constantly to Europe, to the people I was supposed to know there—putting leading questions as to my acquaintances in the sepulchral city, and so on. His little eyes glittered like mica discs—with curiosity—though he tried to keep up a bit of superciliousness. At first I was astonished, but very soon I became awfully curious to see what he would find out from me. I couldn't possibly imagine what I had in me to make it worth his while. It was very pretty to see how he baffled himself, for in truth my body was full only of chills, and my head had nothing in it but that wretched steamboat business. It was evident he took me for a perfectly shameless prevaricator. At last he got angry, and, to conceal a movement of furious annoyance, he yawned. I rose. Then I noticed a small sketch in oils, on a panel, representing a woman, draped and blindfolded, carrying a lighted torch. The background was somber—almost black. The movement of the woman was stately, and the effect of the torchlight on the face was sinister.

"It arrested me, and he stood by civilly, holding an empty half-pint champagne bottle (medical comforts) with the candle stuck in it. To my question he said Mr. Kurtz had painted this—in this very station more than a year ago—while waiting for means to go to his trading-post. 'Tell me, pray,' said I, 'who is this Mr. Kurtz?'

" 'The chief of the Inner Station,' he answered in a short tone, looking away. 'Much obliged,' I said, laughing. 'And you are the brickmaker of the Central Station. Everyone knows that.' He was silent for a while. 'He is a prodigy,' he said at last. 'He is an emissary of pity, and science, and progress, and devil knows what else. We want,' he began to declaim suddenly, 'for the guidance of the cause intrusted to us by Europe, so to speak, higher intelligence, wide sympathies, a singleness of purpose.' 'Who says that?' I asked. 'Lots of them,' he replied. 'Some even write that; and so *he* comes here, a special being, as you ought to know.' 'Why ought I to know?' I interrupted, really surprised. He paid no attention. 'Yes. Today he is chief of the best station, next year he will be assistant-manager, two years more and . . . but I daresay you know what he will be in two years' time. You are of the new gang—the gang of virtue. The same people who sent him specially also recommended you. Oh, don't say no. I've my own eyes to trust.' Light dawned upon me. My dear aunt's influential acquaintances were producing an unexpected effect upon that young man. I nearly burst into a laugh. 'Do you read the Company's confidential correspondence?' I asked. He hadn't a word to say. It was great fun. 'When Mr. Kurtz,' I continued, severely, 'is General Manager, you won't have the opportunity.'

"He blew the candle out suddenly, and we went outside. The moon had risen. Black figures strolled about listlessly, pouring water on the glow, whence proceeded a sound of hissing; steam ascended in the moonlight, the beaten nigger groaned somewhere. 'What a row the brute makes!' said the indefatigable man with the mustaches, appearing near us. 'Serves him right. Transgression —punishment—bang! Pitiless, pitiless. That's the only way. This will prevent all conflagrations for the future. I was just telling the manager. . . .' He noticed my companion, and became crestfallen all at once. 'Not in bed yet,' he said, with a kind of servile heartiness; 'it's so natural. Ha! Danger—agitation.' He vanished. I went on to the river-side, and the other followed me. I heard a scathing murmur at my ear, 'Heap of muffs—go to.' The pilgrims could be seen in knots gesticulating, discussing. Several had still their staves in their hands. I verily believe they took these sticks to bed with them. Beyond the fence the forest stood up spectrally in the moonlight, and through the dim stir, through the faint sounds of that lamentable courtyard, the silence of the land went home to one's very heart—its mystery, its greatness, the amazing reality of its concealed life. The hurt nigger moaned feebly somewhere near by, and then fetched a deep sigh that made me mend my pace away from there. I felt a hand introducing itself under my arm. 'My dear sir,' said the fellow, 'I don't want to be misunderstood, and especially by you, who will see Mr. Kurtz long before I can have that pleasure. I wouldn't like him to get a false idea of my disposition. . . .'

"I let him run on, this papier-mâché Mephistopheles, and it seemed to me that if I tried I could poke my forefinger through him, and would find nothing inside but a little loose dirt, maybe. He, don't you see, had been planning to be assistant-manager by and by under the present man, and I could see that the coming of that Kurtz had upset them both not a little. He talked precipitately, and I did not try to stop him. I had my shoulders against the wreck of my steamer, hauled up on the slope like a carcass of some big river animal. The smell of mud, of primeval mud, by Jove! was in my nostrils, the high stillness of primeval forest was before my eyes; there were shiny patches on the black creek. The moon had spread over everything a thin layer of silver—over the rank grass, over the mud, upon the wall of matted vegetation standing higher than the wall of a temple, over the great river I could see through a somber gap glittering, glittering, as it flowed broadly by without a murmur. All this was great, expectant, mute, while the man jabbered about himself. I wondered whether the stillness on the face of the immensity looking at us two were meant as an appeal or as a menace. What were we who had strayed in here? Could we handle that dumb thing, or would it handle us? I felt how big, how confoundedly big, was that thing that couldn't talk, and perhaps was deaf as well. What was in there? I could see a little ivory coming out from there, and I had heard Mr. Kurtz was in there. I had heard enough about it, too—God knows! Yet somehow it didn't bring any image with it—no more than if I had been told an angel or a fiend was in there. I believed it in the same way one of you might believe there are inhabitants in the planet Mars. I knew once a Scotch sailmaker who was certain, dead sure, there were people in Mars. If you asked him for some idea how they looked and behaved, he would get shy and mutter something about 'walking on all-fours.' If you as much as smiled, he would—though a man of sixty—offer to fight you. I would not have gone so far as to fight for Kurtz, but I went for him near enough to a lie. You know I hate, detest, and can't bear a lie, not because I am straighter than the rest of us, but simply because it appalls me. There is a taint of death, a flavor of mortality in lies—which is exactly what I hate and detest in the world—what I want to forget. It makes me miserable and sick, like biting something rotten would do. Temperament, I suppose. Well, I went near enough to it by letting the young fool there believe anything he liked to imagine as to my influence in Europe. I became in an instant as much of a pretense as the rest of the bewitched pilgrims. This simply because I had a notion it somehow would be of help to that Kurtz whom at the time I did not see—you understand. He was just a word for me. I did not see the man in the name any more than you do. Do you see him? Do you see the story? Do you see anything? It seems to me I am trying to tell you a dream—making a vain attempt, because no relation of a dream can convey the dream-sensation, that commingling of absurdity, surprise, and bewilderment in a tremor of struggling revolt, that notion of being captured by the incredible which is of the very essence of dreams. . . ."

He was silent for a while.

". . . No, it is impossible; it is impossible to convey the life-sensation of any given epoch of one's existence—that which makes its truth, its meaning—its subtle and penetrating essence. It is impossible. We live, as we dream—alone. . . ."

He paused again as if reflecting, then added—

"Of course in this you fellows see more than I could then. You · see me, whom you know. . . ."

It had become so pitch dark that we listeners could hardly see one another. For a long time already he, sitting apart, had been no more to us than a voice. There was not a word from anybody. The others might have been asleep, but I was awake. I listened, I listened on the watch for the sentence, for the word, that would give me the clew to the faint uneasiness inspired by this narrative that seemed to shape itself without human lips in the heavy night-air of the river.

". . . Yes—I let him run on," Marlow began again, "and think what he pleased about the powers that were behind me. I did! And there was nothing behind me! There was nothing but that wretched, old, mangled steamboat I was leaning against, while he talked fluently about 'the necessity for every man to get on.' 'And when one comes out here, you conceive, it is not to gaze at the moon.' Mr. Kurtz was a 'universal genius,' but even a genius would find it easier to work with 'adequate tools—intelligent men.' He did not make bricks—why, there was a physical impossibility in the way—as I was well aware; and if he did secretarial work for the manager, it was because 'no sensible man rejects wantonly the confidence of his superiors.' Did I see it? I saw it. What more did I want? What I really wanted was rivets, by heaven! Rivets. To get on with the work—to stop the hole. Rivets I wanted. There were cases of them down at the coast—cases—piled up—burst—split! You kicked a loose rivet at every second step in that station yard on the hillside. Rivets had rolled into the grove of death. You could fill your pockets with rivets for the trouble of stooping down—and there wasn't one rivet to be found where it was wanted. We had plates that would do, but nothing to fasten them with. And every week the messenger, a lone Negro, letter-bag on shoulder and staff in hand, left our station for the coast. And several times a week a coast caravan came in with trade goods—ghastly glazed calico that made you shudder only to look at it; glass beads, valued about a penny a quart, confounded spotted cotton handkerchiefs. And no rivets. Three carriers could have brought all that was wanted to set that steamboat afloat.

"He was becoming confidential now, but I fancy my unresponsive attitude must have exasperated him at last, for he judged it necessary to inform me he feared neither God nor devil, let alone any mere man. I said I could see that very well, but what I wanted was a certain quantity of rivets—and rivets were what really Mr. Kurtz wanted, if he had only known it. Now letters went to the coast every week. . . . 'My dear sir,' he cried, 'I write from dictation.' I demanded rivets. There was a way—for an intelligent man. He changed his manner; became very cold, and suddenly began to talk about a hippopotamus; wondered whether sleeping on board the steamer (I stuck to my salvage night and day) I wasn't disturbed. There was an old hippo that had the bad habit of getting out on the bank and roaming at night over the station grounds. The pilgrims used to turn out in a body and empty every rifle they could lay hands on at him. Some even had sat up o' nights for him. All this energy was wasted, though. 'That animal has a charmed life,' he said; 'but you can say this only of brutes in this country. No man—you apprehend me?—no man here bears a charmed life.' He stood there for a moment in the moonlight with his delicate hooked nose set a little askew, and his mica eyes glittering without a wink, then, with a curt good night, he strode off. I could see he was disturbed and considerably puzzled, which made me feel more hopeful than I had been for days. It was a great comfort to turn from that chap to my influential friend, the battered, twisted, ruined, tin-pot steamboat. I clambered on board. She rang under my feet like an empty Huntley & Palmer biscuit-tin kicked along a gutter; she was nothing so solid in make, and rather less pretty in shape, but I had expended enough hard work on her to make me love her. No influential friend would have served me better. She had given me a chance to come out a bit—to find out what I could do. No, I don't like work. I had rather laze about and think of all the fine things that can be done. I don't like work—no man does—but I like what is in the work,—the chance to find yourself. Your own reality—for yourself, not for others—what no other man can ever know. They can only see the mere show, and never can tell what it really means.

"I was not surprised to see somebody sitting aft, on the deck, with his legs dangling over the mud. You see I rather chummed with the few mechanics there were in that station, whom the other pilgrims naturally despised—on account of their imperfect manners, I suppose. This was the foreman—a boiler-maker by trade—a good worker. He was a lank, bony, yellow-faced man, with big intense eyes. His aspect was worried, and his head was as bald as the palm of my hand; but his hair in falling seemed to have stuck to his chin, and had prospered in the new locality, for his beard hung down to his waist. He was a widower with six young children (he had left them in charge of a sister of his to come out there), and the passion of his life was pigeon-flying. He was an enthusiast and a connoisseur. He would rave about pigeons. After work hours he used sometimes to come over from his hut for a talk about his children and his pigeons; at work, when he had to crawl in the mud under the bottom of the steamboat, he would tie up that beard of his in a kind of white serviette he brought for the purpose. It had loops to go over his ears. In the evening he could be seen squatted on the bank rinsing that wrapper in the creek with great care, then spreading it solemnly on a bush to dry.

"I slapped him on the back and shouted, 'We shall have rivets!' He scrambled to his feet exclaiming, 'No! Rivets!' as though he couldn't believe his ears. Then in a low voice, 'You . . . eh?' I don't know why we behaved like lunatics. I put my finger to the side of my nose and nodded mysteriously. 'Good for you!' he cried, snapped his fingers above his head, lifting one foot. I tried a jig. We capered on the iron deck. A frightful clatter came out of that hulk, and the virgin forest on the other bank of the creek sent it back in a thundering roll upon the sleeping station. It must have made some of the pilgrims sit up in their hovels. A dark figure obscured the lighted doorway of the manager's hut, vanished, then, a second or so after, the doorway itself vanished, too. We stopped, and the silence driven away by the stamping of our feet flowed back again from the recesses of the land. The great wall of vegetation, an exuberant and entangled mass of trunks, branches, leaves, boughs, festoons, motionless in the moonlight, was like a rioting invasion of soundless life, a rolling wave of plants, piled up, crested, ready to topple over the creek, to sweep every little man of us out of his little existence. And it moved not. A deadened burst of mighty splashes and snorts reached us from afar, as though an ichthyosaurus had been taking a bath of glitter in the great river. 'After all,' said the boiler-maker in a reasonable tone, 'why shouldn't we get the rivets?' Why not, indeed! I did not know of any reason why we shouldn't. 'They'll come in three weeks,' I said, confidently.

"But they didn't. Instead of rivets there came an invasion, an infliction, a visitation. It came in sections during the next three weeks, each section headed by a donkey carrying a white man in new clothes and tan shoes, bowing from that elevation right and left to the impressed pilgrims. A quarrelsome band of foot-sore sulky niggers trod on the heels of the donkeys; a lot of tents, campstools, tin boxes, white cases, brown bales would be shot down in the courtyard, and the air of mystery would deepen a little over the muddle of the station. Five such installments came, with their absurd air of disorderly flight with the loot of

Heart of Darkness · 37

innumerable outfit shops and provision stores, that, one would think, they were lugging, after a raid, into the wilderness for equitable division. It was an extricable mess of things decent in themselves but that human folly made look like the spoils of thieving.

"This devoted band called itself the Eldorado Exploring Expedition, and I believe they were sworn to secrecy. Their talk, however, was the talk of sordid buccaneers: it was reckless without hardihood, greedy without audacity, and cruel without courage; there was not an atom of foresight or of serious intention in the whole batch of them, and they did not seem aware these things are wanted for the work of the world. To tear treasure out of the bowels of the land was their desire, with no more moral purpose at the back of it than there is in burglars breaking into a safe. Who paid the expenses of the noble enterprise I don't know; but the uncle of our manager was leader of that lot.

"In exterior he resembled a butcher in a poor neighborhood, and his eyes had a look of sleepy cunning. He carried his fat paunch with ostentation on his short legs, and during the time his gang infested the station spoke to no one but his nephew. You could see these two roaming about all day long with their heads close together in an everlasting confab.

"I had given up worrying myself about the rivets. One's capacity for that kind of folly is more limited than you would suppose. I said Hang!—and let things slide. I had plenty of time for meditation, and now and then I would give some thought to Kurtz. I wasn't very interested in him. No. Still, I was curious to see whether this man, who had come out equipped with moral ideas of some sort, would climb to the top after all and how he would set about his work when there."

II

"One evening as I was lying flat on the deck of my steamboat, I heard voices approaching—and there were the nephew and the uncle strolling along the bank. I laid my head on my arm again, and had nearly lost myself in a doze, when somebody said in my ear, as it were: 'I am as harmless as a little child, but I don't like to be dictated to. Am I the manager—or am I not? I was ordered to send him there. It's incredible.' . . . I became aware that the two were standing on the shore alongside the forepart of the steamboat, just below my head. I did not move; it did not occur to me to move: I was sleepy. 'It *is* unpleasant,' grunted the uncle. 'He has asked the Administration to be sent there,' said the other, 'with the idea of showing what he could do; and I was instructed accordingly. Look at the influence that man must have. Is it not frightful?' They both agreed it was frightful, then made several bizarre remarks: 'Make rain and fine weather—one man—the Council—by the nose'—bits of absurd sentences that got the better of my drowsiness, so that I had pretty near the whole of my wits about me when the uncle said, 'The climate may do away with this difficulty for you. Is he alone there?' 'Yes,' answered the manager; 'he sent his assistant down the river with a note to me in these terms: "Clear this poor devil out of the country, and don't bother sending more of that sort. I had rather be alone than have the kind of men you can dispose of with me." It was more than a year ago. Can you imagine such impudence!' 'Anything since then?' asked the other, hoarsely. 'Ivory,' jerked the nephew; 'lots of it—prime sort—lots—most annoying, from him.' 'And with that?' questioned the heavy rumble. 'Invoice,' was the reply fired out, so to speak. Then silence. They had been talking about Kurtz.

"I was broad awake by this time, but, lying perfectly at ease, remained still, having no inducement to change my position. 'How did that ivory come all this way?' growled the elder man, who seemed very vexed. The other explained that it had come with a fleet of canoes in charge of an English half-caste clerk Kurtz had with him; that Kurtz had apparently intended to return himself, the station being by that time bare of goods and stores, but after coming three hundred miles, had suddenly decided to go back, which he started to do alone in a small dugout with four paddlers, leaving the half-caste to continue down the river with the ivory. The two fellows there seemed astounded at anybody attempting such a thing. They were at a loss for an adequate motive. As to me, I seemed to see Kurtz for the first time. It was a distinct glimpse: the dugout, four paddling savages, and the lone white man turning his back suddenly on the headquarters, on relief, on thoughts of home—perhaps; setting his face towards the depths of the wilderness, towards his empty and desolate station. I did not know the motive. Perhaps he was just simply a fine fellow who stuck to his work for its own sake. His name, you understand, had not been pronounced once. He was 'that man.' The half-caste, who, as far as I could see, had conducted a difficult trip with great prudence and pluck, was invariably alluded to as 'that scoundrel.' The 'scoun-drel' had reported that the 'man' had been very ill—had recovered imperfectly. . . . The two below me moved away then a few paces, and strolled back and forth at some little distance. I heard: 'Military post—doctor—two hundred miles—quite alone now—unavoidable delays—nine months—no news—strange rumors.' They approached again, just as the manager was saying, 'No one, as far as I know, unless a species of wandering trader—a pestilential fellow, snapping ivory from the natives.' Who was it they were talking about now? I gathered in snatches that this was some man supposed to be in Kurtz's district, and of whom the manager did not approve. 'We will not be free from unfair competition till one of these fellows is hanged for an example,' he said. 'Certainly,' grunted the other; 'get him hanged! Why not? Anything—anything can be done in this country. That's what I say; nobody here, you understand, *here*, can endanger your position. And why? You stand the climate—you outlast them all. The danger is in Europe; but there before I left I took care to—' They moved off and whispered, then their voices rose again. 'The extraordinary series of delays is not my fault. I did my best.' The fat man sighed. 'Very sad.' 'And the pestif-erous absurdity of his talk,' continued the other; 'he bothered me enough when he was here. "Each station should be like a beacon on the road towards better things, a center for trade, of course, but also for humanizing, improving, instructing." Conceive you—that ass! And he wants to be manager! No, it's—' Here he got choked by excessive indignation, and I lifted my head the least bit. I was surprised to see how near they were—right under me. I could have spat upon their hats. They were looking on the ground, absorbed in thought. The manager was switching his leg with a slender twig: his sagacious relative lifted his head. 'You have been well since you came out this time?' he asked. The other gave a start. 'Who? I? Oh! Like a charm—like a charm. But the rest—oh, my goodness! All sick.

They die so quick, too, that I haven't the time to send them out of the country—it's incredible!' 'H'm. Just so,' grunted the uncle. 'Ah! my boy, trust to this—I say, trust to this.' I saw him extend his short flipper of an arm for a gesture that took in the forest, the creek, the mud, the river,—seemed to beckon with a dishonoring flourish before the sunlit face of the land a treacherous appeal to the lurking death, to the hidden evil, to the profound darkness of its heart. It was so startling that I leaped to my feet and looked back at the edge of the forest, as though I had expected an answer of some sort to that black display of confidence. You know the foolish notions that come to one sometimes. The high stillness confronted these two figures with its ominous patience, waiting for the passing away of a fantastic invasion.

"They swore aloud together—out of sheer fright, I believe—then pretending not to know anything of my existence, turned back to the station. The sun was low; and leaning forward side by side, they seemed to be tugging painfully uphill their two ridiculous shadows of unequal length, that trailed behind them slowly over the tall grass without bending a single blade.

"In a few days the Eldorado Expedition went into the patient wilderness, that closed upon it as the sea closes over a diver. Long afterwards the news came that all the donkeys were dead. I know nothing as to the fate of the less valuable animals. They, no doubt, like the rest of us, found what they deserved. I did not inquire. I was then rather excited at the prospect of meeting Kurtz very soon. When I say very soon I mean it comparatively. It was just two months from the day we left the creek when we came to the bank below Kurtz's station.

"Going up that river was like traveling back to the earliest beginnings of the world, when vegetation rioted on the earth and the big trees were kings. An empty stream, a great silence, an impenetrable forest. The air was warm, thick, heavy, sluggish. There was no joy in the brilliance of sunshine. The long stretches of the waterway ran on, deserted, into the gloom of overshadowed distances. On silvery sandbanks hippos and alligators sunned themselves side by side. The broadening waters flowed through a mob of wooded islands; you lost your way on that river as you would in a desert, and butted all day long against shoals, trying to find the channel, till you thought yourself bewitched and cut off forever from everything you had known once—somewhere—far away—in another existence perhaps. There were moments when one's past came back to one, as it will sometimes when you have not a moment to spare to yourself; but it came in the shape of an unrestful and noisy dream, remembered with wonder amongst the overwhelming realities of this strange world of plants, and water, and silence. And this stillness of life did not in the least resemble a peace. It was the stillness of an implacable force brooding over an inscrutable intention. It looked at you with a vengeful aspect. I got used to it afterwards; I did not see it any more; I had no time. I had to keep guessing at the channel; I had to discern, mostly by inspiration, the signs of hidden banks; I watched for sunken stones; I was learning to clap my teeth smartly before my heart flew out, when I shaved by a fluke some infernal sly old snag that would have ripped the life out of the tin-pot steamboat and drowned all the pilgrims; I had to keep a look-out for the signs of dead wood we could cut up in the night for next day's steaming. When you have to attend to things of that sort, to the mere incidents of the surface, the reality—the reality, I tell you—fades. The inner truth is hidden—luckily, luckily. But I felt it all the same; I felt often its mysterious stillness watching me at my monkey tricks, just as it watches you fellows performing on your respective tight-ropes for—what is it? half-a-crown a tumble—"

"Try to be civil, Marlow," growled a voice, and I knew there was at least one listener awake besides myself.

"I beg your pardon. I forgot the heartache which makes up the rest of the price. And indeed what does the price matter, if the trick be well done? You do your tricks very well. And I didn't do badly either, since I managed not to sink that steamboat on my first trip. It's a wonder to me yet. Imagine a blindfolded man set to drive a van over a bad road. I sweated and shivered over that business considerably, I can tell you. After all, for a seaman, to scrape the bottom of the thing that's supposed to float all the time under his care is the unpardonable sin. No one may know of it, but you never forget the thump—eh? A blow on the very heart. You remember it, you dream of it, you wake up at night and think of it—years after—and go hot and cold all over. I don't pretend to say that steamboat floated all the time. More than once she had to wade for a bit, with twenty cannibals splashing around and pushing. We had enlisted some of these chaps on the way for a crew. Fine fellows—cannibals—in their place. They were men one could work with, and I am grateful to them. And, after all, they did not eat each other before my face: they had brought along a provision of hippo-meat which went rotten, and made the mystery of the wilderness stink in my nostrils. Phoo! I can sniff it now. I had the manager on board and three or four pilgrims with their staves—all complete. Sometimes we came upon a station close by the bank, clinging to the skirts of the unknown, and the white men rushing out of a tumble-down hovel, with great gestures of joy and surprise and welcome, seemed very strange—had the appearance of being held there captive by a spell. The word ivory would ring in the air for a while—and on we went again into the silence, along empty reaches, round the still bends, between the high walls of our winding way, reverberating in hollow claps the ponderous beat of the stern-wheel. Trees, trees, millions of trees, massive, immense, running up high; and at their foot, hugging the bank against the stream, crept the little begrimed steamboat, like a sluggish beetle crawling on the floor of a lofty portico. It made you feel very small, very lost, and yet it was not altogether depressing, that feeling. After all, if you were small, the grimy beetle crawled on—which was just what you wanted it to do. Where the pilgrims imagined it crawled to I don't know. To some place where they expected to get something, I bet! For me it crawled towards Kurtz—exclusively; but when the steam-pipes started leaking we crawled very slow. The reaches opened before us and closed behind, as if the forest had stepped leisurely across the water to bar the way for our return. We penetrated deeper and deeper into the heart of darkness. It was very quiet there. At night sometimes the roll of drums behind the curtain of trees would run up the river and remain sustained faintly, as if hovering in the air high over our heads, till the first break of day. Whether it meant war, peace, or prayer we could not tell. The dawns were heralded by the descent of a chill stillness; the wood-cutters slept, their fires burned low; the snapping of a twig would make you start. We were wanderers on a prehistoric earth, on an earth that wore the aspect of an unknown planet. We could have fancied ourselves the first of men taking possession of an accursed inheritance, to be subdued at the cost of profound anguish and of excessive toil. But suddenly, as we struggled round a bend, there would be a glimpse of rush walls, of peaked grass-roofs, a burst of yells, a whirl of black limbs, a mass of hands clapping, of feet stamping, of bodies swaying, of eyes rolling, under the droop of heavy and motionless foliage. The steamer toiled along slowly on the edge of a black and incomprehensible frenzy. The prehistoric man was cursing us, praying to us, welcoming us— who could tell? We were cut off from the comprehension of our surroundings; we glided past like phantoms, wondering and secretly appalled, as sane men would be before an enthusiastic outbreak in a madhouse. We could not understand because we were too far and could not remember, because we were traveling in the night of first ages, of those ages that are gone, leaving hardly a sign—and no memories.

"The earth seemed unearthly. We are accustomed to look upon the shackled form of a conquered monster, but there— there you could look at a thing monstrous and free. It was unearthly, and the men were— No, they were not inhuman. Well, you know, that was the worst of it—this suspicion of their not being inhuman. It would come slowly to one. They howled and leaped, and spun, and made horrid faces; but what thrilled you was just the thought of their humanity—like yours—the thought of your remote kinship with this wild and passionate uproar. Ugly. Yes, it was ugly enough; but if you were man enough you would admit to yourself that there was in you just the faintest trace of a response to the terrible frankness of that noise, a dim suspicion of there being a meaning in it which you —you so remote from the night of first ages—could comprehend. And why not? The mind of man is capable of anything —because everything is in it, all the past as well as all the future. What was there after all? Joy, fear, sorrow, devotion, valor, rage—who can tell?—but truth—truth stripped of its cloak of time. Let the fool gape and shudder—the man knows, and can look on without a wink. But he must at least be as much of a man as these on the shore. He must meet that truth with his own true stuff—with his own inborn strength. Principles won't do. Acquisitions, clothes, pretty rags—rags that would fly off at the first good shake. No; you want a deliberate belief. An appeal to me in this fiendish row—is there? Very well; I hear; I admit, but I have a voice, too, and for good or evil mine is the speech that cannot be silenced. Of course, a fool, what with sheer fright and fine sentiments, is always safe. Who's that grunting? You wonder I didn't go ashore for a howl and a dance? Well, no—I didn't. Fine sentiments, you say? Fine sentiments, be hanged! I had no time. I had to mess about with white-lead and strips of woolen blanket helping to put bandages on those leaky steam-pipes—I tell you. I had to watch the steering, and circumvent those snags, and get the tin-pot along by hook or by crook. There was surface-truth enough in these things to save a wiser man. And between whiles I had to look after the savage who was fireman. He was an improved specimen; he could fire up a vertical boiler. He was there below me, and, upon my word, to look at him was as edifying as seeing a dog in a parody of breeches and a feather hat, walking on his hind-legs. A few months of training had done for that really fine chap. He squinted at the steam-gauge and at the water-gauge with an evident effort of intrepidity—and he had filed teeth, too, the poor devil, and the wool of his pate shaved into queer patterns, and three ornamental scars on each of his cheeks. He ought to have been clapping his hands and stamping his feet on the bank, instead of which he was hard at work, a thrall to strange witchcraft, full of improving knowledge. He was useful because he had been instructed; and what he knew was this—that should the water in that transparent thing disappear, the evil spirit inside the boiler would get angry through the greatness of his thirst, and take a terrible vengeance. So he sweated and fired up and watched the glass fearfully (with an impromptu charm, made of rags, tied to his arm, and a piece of polished bone, as big as a watch, stuck flatways through his lower lip), while the wooden banks slipped past us slowly, the short noise was left behind, the interminable miles of silence—and we crept on, towards Kurtz. But the snags were thick, the water was treacherous and shallow, the boiler seemed indeed to have a sulky devil in it, and thus neither that fireman nor I had any time to peer into our creepy thoughts.

"Some fifty miles below the Inner Station we came upon a hut of reeds, an inclined and melancholy pole, with the unrecognizable tatters of what had been a flag of some sort flying from it, and a neatly stacked woodpile. This was unexpected. We came to the bank, and on the stack of firewood found a flat piece of board with some faded pencil-writing on it. When deciphered it said: 'Wood for you. Hurry up. Approach cautiously.' There was a signature, but it was illegible—not Kurtz —a much longer word. 'Hurry up.' Where? Up the river? 'Approach cautiously.' We had not done so. But the warning could not have been meant for the place where it could be only found after approach. Something was wrong above. But what —and how much? That was the question. We commented adversely upon the imbecility of that telegraphic style. The bush around said nothing, and would not let us look very far, either. A torn curtain of red twill hung in the doorway of the hut, and flapped sadly in our faces. The dwelling was dismantled; but we could see a white man had lived there not very long ago. There remained a rude table—a plank on two posts; a heap of rubbish reposed in a dark corner, and by the door I picked up a book. It had lost its covers, and the pages had been thumbed into a state of extremely dirty softness; but the back had been lovingly stitched afresh with white cotton thread, which looked clean yet. It was an extraordinary find. Its title was, *An Inquiry into some Points of Seamanship*, by a man Towser, Towson —some such name—Master in his Majesty's Navy. The matter looked dreary reading enough, with illustrative diagrams and repulsive tables of figures, and the copy was sixty years old. I handled this amazing antiquity with the greatest possible tenderness, lest it should dissolve in my hands. Within, Towson or Towser was inquiring earnestly into the breaking strain of ships' chains and tackle, and other such matters. Not a very enthralling book; but at the first glance you could see there a singleness of intention, an honest concern for the right way of going to work, which made these humble pages, thought out so many years ago, luminous with another than a professional light. The simple old sailor, with his talk of chains and purchases, made me forget the jungle and the pilgrims in a delicious sensation of having come upon something unmistakably real. Such a book being there was wonderful enough; but still more astounding were the notes penciled in the margin, and plainly referring to the text. I couldn't believe my eyes! They were in cipher! Yes, it looked like cipher. Fancy a man lugging with him a book of that description into this nowhere and studying it—and making notes—in cipher at that! It was an extravagant mystery.

"I had been dimly aware for some time of a worrying noise, and when I lifted my eyes I saw the woodpile was gone, and the manager, aided by all the pilgrims, was shouting at me from the river-side. I slipped the book into my pocket. I assure you to leave off reading was like tearing myself away from the shelter of an old and solid friendship.

"I started the lame engine ahead. 'It must be this miserable trader—this intruder,' exclaimed the manager, looking back malevolently at the place we had left. 'He must be English,' I said. 'It will not save him from getting into trouble if he is not careful,' muttered the manager darkly. I observed with assumed innocence that no man was safe from trouble in this world.

"The current was more rapid now, the steamer seemed at her last gasp, the stern-wheel flopped languidly, and I caught myself listening on tiptoe for the next beat of the boat, for in sober truth I expected the wretched thing to give up every moment. It was like watching the last flickers of a life. But still we crawled. Sometimes I would pick out a tree a little way ahead to measure our progress towards Kurtz by, but I lost it invariably before we got abreast. To keep the eyes so long on one thing was too much for human patience. The manager displayed a beautiful resignation. I fretted and fumed and took to arguing with myself whether or no I would talk openly with Kurtz; but before I could come to any conclusion it occurred to me that my speech or my silence, indeed any action of mine, would be a mere futility. What did it matter what anyone knew or ignored? What did it matter who was manager? One gets sometimes such a flash of insight. The essentials of this affair lay deep under the surface, beyond my reach, and beyond my power of meddling.

"Towards the evening of the second day we judged ourselves

about eight miles from Kurtz's station. I wanted to push on; but the manager looked grave, and told me the navigation up there was so dangerous that it would be advisable, the sun being very low already, to wait where we were till next morning. Moreover, he pointed out that if the warning to approach cautiously were to be followed, we must approach in daylight— not at dusk, or in the dark. This was sensible enough. Eight miles meant nearly three hours' steaming for us, and I could also see suspicious ripples at the upper end of the reach. Nevertheless, I was annoyed beyond expression at the delay, and most unreasonably, too, since one night more could not matter much after so many months. As we had plenty of wood, and caution was the word, I brought up in the middle of the stream. The reach was narrow, straight, with high sides like a railway cutting. The dusk came gliding into it long before the sun had set. The current ran smooth and swift, but a dumb immobility sat on the banks. The living trees, lashed together by the creepers and every living bush of the undergrowth, might have been changed into stone, even to the slenderest twig, to the lightest leaf. It was not sleep—it seemed unnatural, like a state of trance. Not the faintest sound of any kind could be heard. You looked on amazed, and began to suspect yourself of being deaf—then the night came suddenly, and struck you blind as well. About three in the morning some large fish leaped, and the loud splash made me jump as though a gun had been fired. When the sun rose there was a white fog, very warm and clammy, and more blinding than the night. It did not shift or drive; it was just there, standing all around you like something solid. At eight or nine, perhaps, it lifted as a shutter lifts. We had a glimpse of the towering multitude of trees, of the immense matted jungle, with the blazing little ball of the sun hanging over it—all perfectly still— and then the white shutter came down again, smoothly, as if sliding in greased grooves. I ordered the chain, which we had begun to heave in, to be paid out again. Before it stopped running with a muffled rattle, a cry, a very loud cry, as of infinite desolation, soared slowly in the opaque air. It ceased. A complaining clamor, modulated in savage discords, filled our ears. The sheer unexpectedness of it made my hair stir under my cap. I don't know how it struck the others: to me it seemed as though the mist itself had screamed, so suddenly, and apparently from all sides at once, did this tumultuous and mournful uproar arise. It culminated in a hurried outbreak of almost intolerably excessive shrieking, which stopped short, leaving us stiffened in a variety of silly attitudes, and obstinately listening to the nearly as appalling and excessive silence. 'Good God! What is the meaning—' stammered at my elbow one of the pilgrims,—a little fat man, with sandy hair and red whiskers, who wore side-spring boots, and pink pajamas tucked into his socks. Two others remained open-mouthed a whole minute, then dashed into the little cabin, to rush out incontinently and stand darting scared glances, with Winchesters at 'ready' in their hands. What we could see was just the steamer we were on, her outlines blurred as though she had been on the point of dissolving, and a misty strip of water, perhaps two feet broad, around her—and that was all. The rest of the world was nowhere, as far as our eyes and ears were concerned. Just nowhere. Gone, disappeared; swept off without leaving a whisper or a shadow behind.

"I went forward, and ordered the chain to be hauled in short, so as to be ready to trip the anchor and move the steamboat at once if necessary. 'Will they attack?' whispered an awed voice. 'We will be all butchered in this fog,' murmured another. The faces twitched with the strain, the hands trembled slightly, the eyes forgot to wink. It was very curious to see the contrast of expressions of the white men and of the black fellows of our crew, who were as much strangers to that part of the river as we, though their homes were only eight hundred miles away. The whites, of course, greatly discomposed, had besides a curious look of being painfully shocked by such an outrageous row. The others had an alert, naturally interested expression; but their faces were essentially quiet, even those of the one or two who grinned as they hauled at the chain. Several exchanged short, grunting phrases, which seemed to settle the matter to their satisfaction. Their headman, a young, broad-chested black, severely draped in dark-blue fringed cloths, with fierce nostrils and his hair all done up artfully in oily ringlets, stood near me. 'Aha!' I said, just for good fellowship's sake. 'Catch 'im,' he snapped, with a bloodshot widening of his eyes and a flash of sharp teeth—'catch 'im. Give 'im to us.' 'To you, eh?' I asked;

'what would you do with them?' 'Eat 'im!' he said, curtly, and, leaning his elbow on the rail, looked out into the fog in a dignified and profoundly pensive attitude. I would no doubt have been properly horrified, had it not occurred to me that he and his chaps must be very hungry: that they must have been growing increasingly hungry for at least this month past. They had been engaged for six months (I don't think a single one of them had any clear idea of time, as we at the end of countless ages have. They still belonged to the beginnings of time—had no inherited experience to teach them as it were), and of course, as long as there was a piece of paper written over in accordance with some farcical law or other made down the river, it didn't enter anybody's head to trouble how they would live. Certainly they had brought with them some rotten hippo-meat, which couldn't have lasted very long, anyway, even if the pilgrims hadn't, in the midst of a shocking hullabaloo, thrown a considerable quantity of it overboard. It looked like a high-handed proceeding; but it was really a case of legitimate self-defense. You can't breathe dead hippo waking, sleeping, and eating, and at the same time keep your precarious grip on existence. Besides that, they had given them every week three pieces of brass wire, each about nine inches long; and the theory was they were to buy their provisions with that currency in riverside villages. You can see how *that* worked. There were either no villages, or the people were hostile, or the director, who like the rest of us fed out of tins, with an occasional old he-goat thrown in, didn't want to stop the steamer for some more or less recondite reason. So, unless they swallowed the wire itself, or made loops of it to snare the fishes with, I don't see what good their extravagant salary could be to them. I must say it was paid with a regularity worthy of a large and honorable trading company. For the rest, the only thing to eat—though it didn't look eatable in the least—I saw in their possession was a few lumps of some stuff like half-cooked dough, of a dirty lavender color, they kept wrapped in leaves, and now and then swallowed a piece of, but so small that it seemed done more for the looks of the thing than for any serious purpose of sustenance. Why in the name of all the gnawing devils of hunger they didn't go for us—they were thirty to five—and have a good tuck-in for once, amazes me now when I think of it. They were big powerful men, with not much capacity to weigh the consequences, with courage, with strength, even yet, though their skins were no longer glossy and their muscles no longer hard. And I saw that something restraining, one of those human secrets that baffle probability, had come into play there. I looked at them with a swift quickening of interest—not because it occurred to me I might be eaten by them before very long, though I own to you that just then I perceived—in a new light, as it were—how unwholesome the pilgrims looked, and I hoped, yes, I positively hoped, that my aspect was not so—what shall I say?—so—unappetizing: a touch of fantastic vanity which fitted well with the dream-sensation that pervaded all my days at that time. Perhaps I had a little fever, too. One can't live with one's finger everlastingly on one's pulse. I had often 'a little fever,' or a little touch of other things—the playful paw-strokes of the wilderness, the preliminary trifling before the more serious on-slaught which came in due course. Yes; I looked at them as you would on any human being, with a curiosity of their im-pulses, motives, capacities, weaknesses, when brought to the test of an inexorable physical necessity. Restraint! What possible restraint? Was it superstition, disgust, patience, fear—or some kind of primitive honor? No fear can stand up to hunger, no patience can wear it out, disgust simply does not exist where hunger is; and as to superstition, beliefs, and what you may call principles, they are less than chaff in a breeze. Don't you know the devilry of lingering starvation, its exasperating torment, its black thoughts, its somber and brooding ferocity? Well, I do. It takes a man all his inborn strength to fight hunger properly. It's really easier to face bereavement, dishonor, and the perdition of one's soul—than this kind of prolonged hunger. Sad, but true. And these chaps, too, had no earthly reason for any kind of scruple. Restraint! I would just as soon have expected re-straint from a hyena prowling amongst the corpses of a battle-field. But there was the fact facing me—the fact dazzling, to be seen, like the foam on the depths of the sea, like a ripple on an unfathomable enigma, a mystery greater—when I thought of it—than the curious, inexplicable note of desperate grief in this savage clamor that had swept by us on the river-bank, behind the blind whiteness of the fog.

"Two pilgrims were quarreling in hurried whispers as to which bank. 'Left.' 'No, no; how can you? Right, right, of course.' 'It is very serious,' said the manager's voice behind me; 'I would be desolated if anything should happen to Mr. Kurtz before we came up.' I looked at him, and had not the slightest doubt he was sincere. He was just the kind of man who would wish to preserve appearances. That was his restraint. But when he muttered something about going on at once, I did not even take the trouble to answer him. I knew, and he knew, that it was impossible. Were we to let go our hold of the bottom, we would be absolutely in the air—in space. We wouldn't be able to tell where we were going to—whether up or down stream, or across—till we fetched against one bank or the other,—and then we wouldn't know at first which it was. Of course I made no move. I had no mind for a smash-up. You couldn't imagine a more deadly place for a shipwreck. Whether drowned at once or not, we were sure to perish speedily in one way or another. 'I authorize you to take all the risks,' he said, after a short silence. 'I refuse to take any,' I said, shortly; which was just the answer he expected, though its tone might have surprised him. 'Well, I must defer to your judgment. You are captain,' he said, with marked civility. I turned my shoulder to him in sign of my appreciation, and looked into the fog. How long would it last? It was the most hopeless lookout. The approach to this Kurtz grubbing for ivory in the wretched bush was beset by as many dangers as though he had been an enchanted princess sleeping in a fabulous castle. 'Will they attack, do you think?' asked the manager, in a confidential tone.

"I did not think they would attack, for several obvious reasons. The thick fog was one. If they left the bank in their canoes they would get lost in it, as we would be if we attempted to move. Still, I had also judged the jungle of both banks quite impenetrable—and yet eyes were in it, eyes that had seen us. The river-side bushes were certainly very thick; but the under-growth behind was evidently penetrable. However, during the short lift I had seen no canoes anywhere in the reach—certainly not abreast of the steamer. But what made the idea of attack inconceivable to me was the nature of the noise—of the cries we had heard. They had not the fierce character boding immediate hostile intention. Unexpected, wild, and violent as they had been, they had given me an irresistible impression of sorrow. The glimpse of the steamboat had for some reason filled those savages with unrestrained grief. The danger, if any, I expounded, was from our proximity to a great human passion let loose. Even extreme grief may ultimately vent itself in violence —but more generally takes the form of apathy. . . .

"You should have seen the pilgrims stare! They had no heart to grin, or even to revile me: but I believe they thought me gone mad—with fright, maybe. I delivered a regular lecture. My dear boys, it was no good bothering. Keep a look-out? Well, you may guess I watched the fog for the signs of lifting as a cat watches a mouse; but for anything else our eyes were of no more use to us than if we had been buried miles deep in a heap of cotton-wool. It felt like it, too—choking, warm, stifling. Besides, all I said, though it sounded extravagant, was absolutely true to fact. What we afterwards alluded to as an attack was really an attempt at repulse. The action was very far from being aggressive—it was not even defensive, in the usual sense: it was undertaken under the stress of desperation, and in its essence was purely protective.

"It developed itself, I should say, two hours after the fog lifted, and its commencement was at a spot, roughly speaking, about a mile and a half below Kurtz's station. We had just floundered and flopped round a bend, when I saw an islet, a mere grassy hummock of bright green, in the middle of the stream. It was the only thing of the kind; but as we opened the reach more, I perceived it was the head of a long sandbank, or rather of a chain of shallow patches stretching down the middle of the river. They were discolored, just awash, and the whole lot was seen just under the water, exactly as a man's backbone is seen running down the middle of his back under the skin. Now, as far as I did see, I could go to the right or to the left of this. I didn't know either channel, of course. The banks looked pretty well alike, the depth appeared the same; but as I had been informed the station was on the west side, I naturally headed for the western passage.

"No sooner had we fairly entered it than I became aware it

was much narrower than I had supposed. To the left of us there was the long uninterrupted shoal, and to the right a high, steep bank heavily overgrown with bushes. Above the bush the trees stood in serried ranks. The twigs overhung the current thickly, and from distance to distance a large limb of some tree projected rigidly over the stream. It was then well on in the afternoon, the face of the forest was gloomy, and a broad strip of shadow had already fallen on the water. In this shadow we steamed up—very slowly, as you may imagine. I sheered her well inshore—the water being deepest near the bank, as the sounding-pole informed me.

"One of my hungry and forbearing friends was sounding in the bows just below me. This steamboat was exactly like a decked scow. On the deck, there were two little teak-wood houses, with doors and windows. The boiler was in the fore-end, and the machinery right astern. Over the whole there was a light roof, supported on stanchions. The funnel projected through that roof, and in front of the funnel a small cabin built of light planks served for a pilot-house. It contained a couch, two campstools, a loaded Martini-Henry leaning in one corner, a tiny table, and the steering-wheel. It had a wide door in front and a broad shutter at each side. All these were always thrown open, of course. I spent my days perched up there on the extreme fore-end of that roof, before the door. At night I slept, or tried to, on the couch. An athletic black belonging to some coast tribe, and educated by my poor predecessor, was the helmsman. He sported a pair of brass earrings, wore a blue cloth wrapper from the waist to the ankles, and thought all the world of himself. He was the most unstable kind of fool I had ever seen. He steered with no end of a swagger while you were by; but if he lost sight of you, he became instantly the prey of an abject funk, and would let that cripple of a steamboat get the upper hand of him in a minute.

"I was looking down at the sounding-pole, and feeling much annoyed to see at each try a little more of it stick out of that river, when I saw my poleman give up the business suddenly, and stretch himself flat on the deck, without even taking the trouble to haul his pole in. He kept hold on it though, and it trailed in the water. At the same time the fireman, whom I could also see below me, sat down abruptly before his furnace and ducked his head. I was amazed. Then I had to look at the river mighty quick, because there was a snag in the fairway. Sticks, little sticks, were flying about—thick: they were whizzing before my nose, dropping below me, striking behind me against my pilot-house. All this time the river, the shore, the woods, were very quiet—perfectly quiet. I could only hear the heavy splashing thump of the stern-wheel and the patter of these things. We cleared the snag clumsily. Arrows, by Jove! We were being shot at! I stepped in quickly to close the shutter on the land-side. That fool-helmsman, his hands on the spokes, was lifting his knees high, stamping his feet, champing his mouth, like a reined-in horse. Confound him! And we were staggering within ten feet of the bank. I had to lean right out to swing the heavy shutter, and I saw a face amongst the leaves on the level with my own, looking at me very fierce and steady; and then suddenly, as though a veil had been removed from my eyes, I made out, deep in the tangled gloom, naked breasts, arms, legs, glaring eyes,—the bush was swarming with human limbs in movement, glistening, of bronze color. The twigs shook, swayed, and rustled, the arrows flew out of them, and then the shutter came to. 'Steer her straight,' I said to the helmsman. He held his head rigid, face forward; but his eyes rolled, he kept on lifting and setting down his feet gently, his mouth foamed a little. 'Keep quiet!' I said in a fury. I might just as well have ordered a tree not to sway in the wind. I darted out. Below me there was a great scuffle of feet on the iron deck; confused exclamations; a voice screamed, 'Can you turn back?' I caught sight of a V-shaped ripple on the water ahead. What? Another snag! A fusillade burst out under my feet. The pilgrims had opened with their Winchesters, and were simply squirting lead into that bush. A deuce of a lot of smoke came up and drove slowly forward. I swore at it. Now I couldn't see the ripple or the snag either. I stood in the doorway, peering, and the arrows came in swarms. They might have been poisoned, but they looked as though they wouldn't kill a cat. The bush began to howl. Our wood-cutters raised a warlike whoop; the report of a rifle just at my back deafened me. I glanced over my shoulder, and the pilot-house was yet full of noise and smoke when I made a dash at the wheel. The fool-nigger had dropped everything to throw the shutter open and let off that Martini-Henry. He stood before the wide opening, glaring, and I yelled at him to come back, while I straightened the sudden twist out of that steamboat. There was no room to turn even if I had wanted to, the snag was somewhere very near ahead in that confounded smoke, there was no time to lose, so I just crowded her into the bank—right into the bank, where I knew the water was deep.

"We tore slowly along the overhanging bushes in a whirl of broken twigs and flying leaves. The fusillade below stopped short, as I had foreseen it would when the squirts got empty. I threw my head back to a glinting whizz that traversed the pilot-house, in at one shutter-hole and out at the other. Looking past that mad helmsman, who was shaking the empty rifle and yelling at the shore, I saw vague forms of men running bent double, leaping, gliding, distinct, incomplete, evanescent. Something big appeared in the air before the shutter, the rifle went overboard, and the man stepped back swiftly, looked at me over his shoulder in an extraordinary, profound, familiar manner, and fell upon my feet. The side of his head hit the wheel twice, and the end of what appeared a long cane clattered round and knocked over a little campstool. It looked as though after wrenching that thing from somebody ashore he had lost his balance in the effort. The thin smoke had blown away, we were clear of the snag, and looking ahead I could see that in another hundred yards or so I would be free to sheer off, away from the bank; but my feet felt so very warm and wet that I had to look down. The man had rolled on his back and stared straight up at me; both his hands clutched that cane. It was the shaft of a spear that, either thrown or lunged through the opening, had caught him in the side just below the ribs; the blade had gone in out of sight, after making a frightful gash; my shoes were full; a pool of blood lay very still, gleaming dark-red under the wheel; his eyes shone with an amazing luster. The fusillade burst out again. He looked at me anxiously, gripping the spear like something precious, with an air of being afraid I would try to take it away from him. I had to make an effort to free my eyes from his gaze and attend to steering.

With one hand I felt above my head for the line of the steam-whistle, and jerked out screech after screech hurriedly. The tumult of angry and warlike yells was checked instantly, and then from the depths of the woods went out such a tremulous and prolonged wail of mournful fear and utter despair as may be imagined to follow the flight of the last hope from the earth. There was a great commotion in the bush; the shower of arrows stopped, a few dropping shots rang out sharply—then silence, in which the languid beat of the stern-wheel came plainly to my ears. I put the helm hard a-starboard at the moment when the pilgrim in pink pajamas, very hot and agitated, appeared in the doorway. 'The manager sends me—' he began in an official tone, and stopped short. 'Good God!' he said, glaring at the wounded man.

"We two whites stood over him, and his lustrous and inquiring glance enveloped us both. I declare it looked as though he would presently put to us some question in an understandable language; but he died without uttering a sound, without moving a limb, without twitching a muscle. Only in the very last moment, as though in response to some sign we could not see, to some whisper we could not hear, he frowned heavily, and that frown gave to his black death-mask an inconceivably somber, brooding, and menacing expression. The luster of inquiring glance faded swiftly into vacant glassiness. 'Can you steer?' I asked the agent eagerly. He looked very dubious; but I made a grab at his arm, and he understood at once I meant him to steer whether or no. To tell you the truth, I was morbidly anxious to change my shoes and socks. 'He is dead,' murmured the fellow, immensely impressed. 'No doubt about it,' said I tugging like mad at the shoe-laces. 'And by the way, I suppose Mr. Kurtz is dead as well by this time.'

"For the moment that was the dominant thought. There was a sense of extreme disappointment, as though I had found out I had been striving after something altogether without a substance. I couldn't have been more disgusted if I had traveled all this way for the sole purpose of talking with Mr. Kurtz. Talking with . . . I flung one shoe overboard, and became aware that that was exactly what I had been looking forward to—a talk with Kurtz. I made the strange discovery that I had never imagined him as doing, you know, but as discoursing. I didn't say to myself, 'Now I will never see him,' or 'Now I will never shake him by the hand,' but, 'Now I will never hear him.' The man presented himself as a voice. Not of course that I did not connect him with some sort of action. Hadn't I been told in all the tones of jealousy and admiration that he had collected, bartered, swindled, or stolen more ivory than all the other agents together? That was not the point. The point was in his being a gifted creature, and that of all his gifts the one that stood out pre-eminently, that carried with it a sense of real presence, was his ability to talk, his words—the gift of expression, the bewildering, the illuminating, the most exalted and the most contemptible, the pulsating stream of light, or the deceitful flow from the heart of an impenetrable darkness.

"The other shoe went flying unto the devil-god of that river. I thought, by Jove! it's all over. We are too late; he has vanished —the gift has vanished, by means of some spear, arrow, or club. I will never hear that chap speak after all,—and my sorrow had a startling extravagance of emotion, even such as I had noticed in the howling sorrow of these savages in the bush. I couldn't have felt more lonely desolation somehow, had I been robbed of a belief or had missed my destiny in life. . . . Why do you sigh in this beastly way, somebody? Absurd? Well, absurd. Good Lord! mustn't a man ever— Here, give me some tobacco." . . .

There was a pause of profound stillness, then a match flared, and Marlow's lean face appeared, worn, hollow, with downward folds and drooped eyelids, with an aspect of concentrated attention; and as he took vigorous draws at his pipe, it seemed to retreat and advance out of the night in the regular flicker of the tiny flame. The match went out.

"Absurd!" he cried. "This is the worst of trying to tell. . . . Here you all are, each moored with two good addresses, like a hulk with two anchors, a butcher round one corner, a policeman round another, excellent appetites, and temperature normal —you hear—normal from year's end to year's end. And you say, Absurd! Absurd be—exploded! Absurd! My dear boys, what can you expect from a man who out of sheer nervousness had just flung overboard a pair of new shoes! Now I think of it, it is amazing I did not shed tears. I am, upon the whole, proud of my fortitude. I was cut to the quick at the idea of having lost the inestimable privilege of listening to the gifted Kurtz. Of course I was wrong. The privilege was waiting for me. Oh, yes, I heard more than enough. And I was right, too. A voice. He was very little more than a voice. And I heard—him—it—this voice—other voices—all of them were so little more than voices—and the memory of that time itself lingers around me, impalpable, like a dying vibration of one immense jabber, silly, atrocious, sordid, savage, or simply mean, without any kind of sense. Voices, voices—even the girl herself—now—"

He was silent for a long time.

"I laid the ghost of his gifts at last with a lie," he began, suddenly. "Girl! What? Did I mention a girl? Oh, she is out of it—completely. They—the women I mean—are out of it —should be out of it. We must help them to stay in that beautiful world of their own, lest ours gets worse. Oh, she had to be out of it. You should have heard the disinterred body of Mr. Kurtz saying, 'My Intended.' You would have perceived directly then how completely she was out of it. And the lofty frontal bone of Mr. Kurtz! They say the hair goes on growing sometimes, but this—ah—specimen, was impressively bald. The wilderness had patted him on the head, and, behold, it was like a ball—an ivory ball; it had caressed him, and—lo!—he had withered; it had taken him, loved him, embraced him, got into his veins, consumed his flesh, and sealed his soul to its own by the inconceivable ceremonies of some devilish initiation. He was its spoiled and pampered favorite. Ivory? I should think so. Heaps of it, stacks of it. The old mud shanty was bursting with it. You would think there was not a single tusk left either above or below the ground in the whole country. 'Mostly fossil,' the manager had remarked, disparagingly. It was no more fossil than I am; but they call it fossil when it is dug up. It appears these niggers do bury the tusks sometimes—but evidently they couldn't bury this parcel deep enough to save the gifted Mr. Kurtz from his fate. We filled the steamboat with it, and had to pile a lot on the deck. Thus he could see and enjoy as long as he could see, because the appreciation of this favor had remained with him to the last. You should have heard him say, 'My ivory.' Oh, yes, I heard him. 'My Intended, my ivory, my station, my river, my—' everything belonged to him. It made me hold my breath in expectation of hearing the wilderness burst into a prodigious peal of laughter that would shake the fixed stars in their places. Everything belonged to him—but that was a trifle. The thing was to know what he belonged to, how many powers of darkness claimed him for their own. That was the reflection that made you creepy all over. It was impossible—it was not good for one either—trying to imagine. He had taken a high seat amongst the devils of the land—I mean literally. You can't understand. How could you? —with solid pavement under your feet, surrounded by kind neighbors ready to cheer you or to fall on you, stepping delicately between the butcher and the policeman, in the holy terror of scandal and gallows and lunatic asylums—how can you imagine what particular region of the first ages a man's untrammeled feet may take him into by the way of solitude—utter solitude without a policeman—by the way of silence—utter silence, where no warning voice of a kind neighbor can be heard whispering of public opinion? These little things make all the great difference. When they are gone you must fall back upon your own innate strength, upon your own capacity for faithfulness. Of course you may be too much of a fool to go wrong— too dull even to know you are being assaulted by the powers of darkness. I take it, no fool ever made a bargain for his soul with the devil: the fool is too much of a fool, or the devil too much of a devil—I don't know which. Or you may be such a thunderingly exalted creature as to be altogether deaf and blind to anything but heavenly sights and sounds. Then the earth for you is only a standing place—and whether to be like this is your loss or your gain I won't pretend to say. But most of us are neither one nor the other. The earth for us is a place to live in, where we must put up with sights, with sounds, with smells, too, by Jove!—breathe dead hippo, so to speak, and not be contaminated. And there, don't you see? your strength comes in, the faith in your ability for the digging of unostentatious holes to bury the stuff in—your power of devotion, not to yourself, but to an obscure, back-breaking business. And that's difficult enough. Mind, I am not trying to excuse or even explain—I

am trying to account to myself for—for—Mr. Kurtz—for the
shade of Mr. Kurtz. This initiated wraith from the back of
Nowhere honored me with its amazing confidence before it
vanished altogether. This was because it could speak English
to me. The original Kurtz had been educated partly in England,
and—as he was good enough to say himself—his sympathies were
in the right place. His mother was half-English, his father was
half-French. All Europe contributed to the making of Kurtz;
and by and by I learned that, most appropriately, the International
Society for the Suppression of Savage Customs had intrusted
him with the making of a report, for its future guidance. And
he had written it, too. I've seen it. I've read it. It was eloquent,
vibrating with eloquence, but too high-strung, I think. Seventeen
pages of close writing he had found time for! But this must have
been before his—let us say—nerves, went wrong, and caused
him to preside at certain midnight dances ending with unspeakable
rites, which—as far as I reluctantly gathered from what I heard
at various times—were offered up to him—do you understand?
—to Mr. Kurtz himself. But it was a beautiful piece of writing.
The opening paragraph, however, in the light of later information,
strikes me now as ominous. He began with the argument that we
whites, from the point of development we had arrived at, 'must
necessarily appear to them [savages] in the nature of supernatural
beings—we approach them with the might as of a deity,' and so on,
and so on. 'By the simple exercise of our will we can exert a power
for good practically unbounded,' etc., etc. From that point he
soared and took me with him. The peroration was magnificent,
though difficult to remember, you know. It gave me the notion of
an exotic Immensity ruled by an august Benevolence. It made me
tingle with enthusiasm. This was the unbounded power of eloquence—of words—of burning noble words. There were no
practical hints to interrupt the magic current of phrases, unless
a kind of note at the foot of the last page, scrawled evidently
much later, in an unsteady hand, may be regarded as the expo-
sition of a method. It was very simple, and at the end of that
moving appeal to every altruistic sentiment it blazed at you,
luminous and terrifying, like a flash of lightning in a serene sky:
'Exterminate all the brutes!' The curious part was that he had
apparently forgotten all about that valuable postscriptum, be-

cause, later on, when he in a sense came to himself, he repeatedly entreated me to take good care of 'my pamphlet' (he called it), as it was sure to have in the future a good influence upon his career. I had full information about all these things, and, besides, as it turned out, I was to have the care of his memory. I've done enough for it to give me the indisputable right to lay it, if I choose, for an everlasting rest in the dust-bin of progress, amongst all the sweepings and, figuratively speaking, all the dead cats of civilization. But then, you see, I can't choose. He won't be forgotten. Whatever he was, he was not common. He had the power to charm or frighten rudimentary souls into an aggravated witch-dance in his honor; he could also fill the small souls of the pilgrims with bitter misgivings: he had one devoted friend at least, and he had conquered one soul in the world that was neither rudimentary nor tainted with self-seeking. No; I can't forget him, though I am not prepared to affirm the fellow was exactly worth the life we lost in getting to him. I missed my late helmsman awfully,—I missed him even while his body was still lying in the pilot-house. Perhaps you will think it passing strange this regret for a savage who was no more account than a grain of sand in a black Sahara. Well, don't you see, he had done something, he had steered; for months I had him at my back—a help—an instrument. It was a kind of partnership. He steered for me—I had to look after him, I worried about his deficiencies, and thus a subtle bond had been created, of which I only became aware when it was suddenly broken. And the intimate profundity of that look he gave me when he received his hurt remains to this day in my memory—like a claim of distant kinship affirmed in a supreme moment.

"Poor fool! If he had only left that shutter alone. He had no restraint, no restraint—just like Kurtz—a tree swayed by the wind. As soon as I had put on a dry pair of slippers, I dragged him out, after first jerking the spear out of his side, which operation I confess I performed with my eyes shut tight. His heels leaped together over the little door-step; his shoulders were pressed to my breast; I hugged him from behind desperately. Oh! he was heavy, heavy; heavier than any man on earth, I should imagine. Then without more ado I tipped him overboard. The current snatched him as though he had been a wisp of grass, and I saw the body roll over twice before I lost sight of it forever. All the pilgrims and the manager were then congregated on the awning-deck about the pilot-house, chattering at each other like a flock of excited magpies, and there was a scandalized murmur at my heartless promptitude. What they wanted to keep that body hanging about for I can't guess. Embalm it, maybe. But I had also heard another, and a very ominous, murmur on the deck below. My friends the wood-cutters were likewise scandalized, and with a better show of reason—though I admit that the reason itself was quite inadmissible. Oh, quite! I had made up my mind that if my late helmsman was to be eaten, the fishes alone should have him. He had been a very second-rate helmsman while alive, but now he was dead he might have become a first-class temptation, and possibly cause some startling trouble. Besides, I was anxious to take the wheel, the man in pink pajamas showing himself a hopeless duffer at the business.

"This I did directly the simple funeral was over. We were going half-speed, keeping right in the middle of the stream, and I listened to the talk about me. They had given up Kurtz, they had given up the station; Kurtz was dead, and the station had been burnt—and so on—and so on. The red-haired pilgrim was beside himself with the thought that at least this poor Kurtz had been properly avenged. 'Say! We must have made a glorious slaughter of them in the bush. Eh? What do you think? Say?' He positively danced, the bloodthirsty little gingery beggar. And he had nearly fainted when he saw the wounded man! I could not help saying, 'You made a glorious lot of smoke, anyhow.' I had seen, from the way the tops of the bushes rustled and flew, that almost all the shots had gone too high. You can't hit any-thing unless you take aim and fire from the shoulder; but these chaps fired from the hip with their eyes shut. The retreat, I maintained—and I was right—was caused by the screeching of the steam-whistle. Upon this they forgot Kurtz, and began to howl at me with indignant protests.

"The manager stood by the wheel murmuring confidentially about the necessity of getting well away down the river before dark at all events, when I saw in the distance a clearing on the river-side and the outlines of some sort of building. 'What's this?' I asked. He clapped his hands in wonder. 'The station!'

he cried. I edged in at once, still going half-speed.

"Through my glasses I saw the slope of a hill interspersed with rare trees and perfectly free from undergrowth. A long decaying building on the summit was half buried in the high grass; the large holes in the peaked roof gaped black from afar; the jungle and the woods made a background. There was no enclosure or fence of any kind; but there had been one apparently, for near the house half-a-dozen slim posts remained in a row, roughly trimmed, and with their upper ends ornamented with round carved balls. The rails, or whatever there had been between, had disappeared. Of course the forest surrounded all that. The river-bank was clear, and on the water-side I saw a white man under a hat like a cart-wheel beckoning persistently with his whole arm. Examining the edge of the forest above and below, I was almost certain I could see movements—human forms gliding here and there. I steamed past prudently, then stopped the engines and let her drift down. The man on the shore began to shout, urging us to land. 'We have been attacked,' screamed the manager. 'I know—I know. It's all right,' yelled back the other, as cheerful as you please. 'Come along. It's all right. I am glad.'

"His aspect reminded me of something I had seen—something funny I had seen somewhere. As I maneuvered to get alongside, I was asking myself, 'What does this fellow look like?' Suddenly I got it. He looked like a harlequin. His clothes had been made of some stuff that was brown holland probably, but it was covered with patches all over, with bright patches, blue, red, and yellow, —patches on the back, patches on the front, patches on elbows, on knees; colored binding around his jacket, scarlet edging at the bottom of his trousers; and the sunshine made him look extremely gay and wonderfully neat withal, because you could see how beautifully all this patching had been done. A beardless, boyish face, very fair, no features to speak of, nose peeling, little blue eyes, smiles and frowns chasing each other over that open countenance like sunshine and shadow on a wind-swept plain. 'Look out, captain!' he cried; 'there's a snag lodged in here last night.' What! Another snag? I confess I swore shamefully. I had nearly holed my cripple, to finish off that charming trip. The harlequin on the bank turned his little pug-nose up to me. 'You English?' he asked, all smiles. 'Are you?' I shouted from the wheel. The smiles vanished, and he shook his head as if sorry for my disappointment. Then he brightened up. 'Never mind!' he cried, encouragingly. 'Are we in time?' I asked. 'He is up there,' he replied with a toss of the head up the hill, and becoming gloomy all of a sudden. His face was like the autumn sky, overcast one moment and bright the next.

"When the manager, escorted by the pilgrims, all of them armed to the teeth, had gone to the house this chap came on board. 'I say, I don't like this. These natives are in the bush,' I said. He assured me earnestly it was all right. 'They are simple people,' he added; 'well, I am glad you came. It took me all my time to keep them off.' 'But you said it was all right,' I cried. 'Oh, they meant no harm,' he said; and as I stared he corrected himself, 'Not exactly.' Then vivaciously, 'My faith, your pilot-house wants a clean-up!' In the next breath he advised me to keep enough steam on the boiler to blow the whistle in case of any trouble. 'One good screech will do more for you than all your rifles. They are simple people,' he repeated. He rattled away at such a rate he quite overwhelmed me. He seemed to be trying to make up for lots of silence, and actually hinted, laughing, that such was the case. 'Don't you talk with Mr. Kurtz?' I said. 'You don't talk with that man—you listen to him,' he exclaimed with severe exaltation. 'But now—' He waved his arm, and in the twinkling of an eye was in the uttermost depths of despondency. In a moment he came up again with a jump, possessed himself of both my hands, and shook them continuously, while he gabbled: 'Brother sailor . . . honor . . . pleasure . . . delight . . . introduce myself . . . Russian . . . son of an arch-priest . . . Government of Tambov. . . . What? Tobacco! English tobacco; the excellent English tobacco! Now, that's brotherly. Smoke? Where's a sailor that does not smoke?'

"The pipe soothed him, and gradually I made out he had run away from school, had gone to sea in a Russian ship; ran away again; served some time in English ships; was now reconciled with the arch-priest. He made a point of that. 'But when one is young one must see things, gather experience, ideas; enlarge the mind.' 'Here!' I interrupted. 'You can never tell! Here I met Mr. Kurtz,' he said, youthfully solemn and reproachful. I held my tongue after that. It appears he had persuaded a Dutch trading-house on the coast to fit him out with stores and goods, and had started for the interior with a light heart, and no more idea of what would happen to him than a baby. He had been wandering about that river for nearly two years alone, cut off from everybody and everything. 'I am not so young as I look. I am twenty-five,' he said. 'At first old Van Shuyten would tell me to go to the devil,' he narrated with keen enjoyment; 'but I stuck to him, and talked and talked, till at last he got afraid I would talk the hind-leg off his favorite dog, so he gave me some cheap things and a few guns, and told me he hoped he would never see my face again. Good old Dutchman, Van Shuyten. I've sent him one small lot of ivory a year ago, so that he can't call me a little thief when I get back. I hope he got it. And for the rest I don't care. I had some wood stacked for you. That was my old house. Did you see?'

"I gave him Towson's book. He made as though he would kiss me, but restrained himself. 'The only book I had left, and I thought I had lost it,' he said, looking at it ecstatically. 'So many accidents happen to a man going about alone, you know. Canoes get upset sometimes—and sometimes you've got to clear out so quick when the people get angry.' He thumbed the pages. 'You made notes in Russian?' I asked. He nodded. 'I thought they were written in cipher,' I said. He laughed, then became serious. 'I had lots of trouble to keep these people off,' he said. 'Did they want to kill you?' I asked. 'Oh, no!' he cried, and checked himself. 'Why did they attack us?' I pursued. He hesitated, then said shamefacedly, 'They don't want him to go.' 'Don't they?' I said, curiously. He nodded a nod full of mystery and wisdom. 'I tell you,' he cried, 'this man has enlarged my mind.' He opened his arms wide, staring at me with his little blue eyes that were perfectly round."

III

"I looked at him, lost in astonishment. There he was before me, in motley, as though he had absconded from a troupe of mimes, enthusiastic, fabulous. His very existence was improbable, inexplicable, and altogether bewildering. He was an insoluble problem. It was inconceivable how he had existed, how he had succeeded in getting so far, how he had managed to remain—why he did not instantly disappear. 'I went a little farther,' he said, 'then still a little farther—till I had gone so far that I don't know how I'll ever get back. Never mind. Plenty time. I can manage. You take Kurtz away quick—quick—I tell you.' The glamour of youth enveloped his parti-colored rags, his destitution, his loneliness, the essential desolation of his futile wanderings. For months —for years—his life hadn't been worth a day's purchase; and there he was gallantly, thoughtlessly alive, to all appearance indestructible solely by the virtue of his few years and of his unreflecting audacity. I was seduced into something like admiration—like envy. Glamour urged him on, glamour kept him unscathed. He surely wanted nothing from the wilderness but space to breathe in and to push on through. His need was to exist, and to move onwards at the greatest possible risk, and with a maximum of privation. If the absolutely pure, uncalculating, unpractical spirit of adventure had ever ruled a human being, it ruled this be-patched youth. I almost envied him the possession of this modest and clear flame. It seemed to have consumed all thought of self so completely, that even while he was talking to you, you forgot that it was he —the man before your eyes—who had gone through these things. I did not envy him his devotion to Kurtz, though. He had not meditated over it. It came to him and he accepted it with a sort of eager fatalism. I must say that to me it appeared about the most dangerous thing in every way he had come upon so far.

"They had come together unavoidably, like two ships becalmed near each other, and lay rubbing sides at last. I suppose Kurtz wanted an audience, because on a certain occasion, when encamped in the forest, they had talked all night, or more probably Kurtz had talked. 'We talked of everything,' he said, quite transported at the recollection. 'I forgot there was such a thing as sleep. The night did not seem to last an hour. Everything! Everything! . . . Of love, too.' 'Ah, he talked to you of love!' I said, much amused. 'It isn't what you think,' he cried, almost passionately. 'It was in general. He made me see things—things.'

"He threw his arms up. We were on deck at the time, and the headman of my wood-cutters, lounging near by, turned upon him his heavy and glittering eyes. I looked around, and I don't know why, but I assure you that never, never before, did this land, this river, this jungle, the very arch of this blazing sky, appear to me so hopeless and so dark, so impenetrable to human thought, so pitiless to human weakness. 'And, ever since, you have been with him, of course?' I said.

"On the contrary. It appears their intercourse had been very much broken by various causes. He had, as he informed me proudly, managed to nurse Kurtz through two illnesses (he alluded to it as you would to some risky feat), but as a rule Kurtz wandered alone far in the depths of the forest. 'Very often coming to this station, I had to wait days and days before he would turn up,' he said. 'Ah, it was worth waiting for!—sometimes.' 'What was he doing? exploring or what?' I asked. 'Oh, yes, of course'; he had discovered lots of villages, a lake, too—he did not know exactly in what direction; it was dangerous to inquire too much—but mostly his expeditions had been for ivory. 'But he had no goods to trade with by that time,' I objected. 'There's a good lot of cartridges left even yet,' he answered, looking away. 'To speak plainly, he raided the country,' I said. He nodded. 'Not alone, surely!' He muttered something about the villages round that lake. 'Kurtz got the tribe to follow him, did he?' I suggested. He fidgeted a little. 'They adored him,' he said. The tone of these words was so extraordinary that I looked at him searchingly. It was curious to see his mingled eagerness and reluctance to speak of Kurtz. The man filled his life, occupied his thoughts, swayed his emotions. 'What can you expect?' he burst out; 'he came to them with thunder and lightning, you know—and they had never seen anything like it—and very terrible. He could be very terrible. You can't judge Mr. Kurtz as you would an ordinary man. No, no, no! Now—just to give you an idea—I don't mind telling you, he wanted to shoot me, too, one day—but I don't judge him.' 'Shoot you!' I cried. 'What for?' 'Well, I had a small lot of ivory the chief of that village near my house gave me. You see I used to shoot game for them. Well, he wanted it, and wouldn't hear reason. He declared he would shoot me unless I gave him the ivory and then cleared out of the country, because he could do so, and had a fancy for it, and there was nothing on earth to prevent him killing whom he jolly well pleased. And it was true, too. I gave him the ivory. What did I care! But I didn't clear out. No, no. I couldn't leave him. I had to be careful, of course, till we got friendly again for a time. He had his second illness then. Afterwards I had to keep out of the way; but I didn't mind. He was living for the most part in those villages on the lake. When he came down to the river, sometimes he would take to me, and sometimes it was better for me to be careful. This man suffered too much. He hated all this, and somehow he couldn't get away. When I had a chance I begged him to try and leave while there was time; I offered to go back with him. And he would say yes, and then he would remain; go off on another ivory hunt; disappear for weeks; forget himself amongst these people—forget himself—you know.' 'Why! he's mad,' I said. He protested indignantly. Mr. Kurtz couldn't be mad. If I had heard him talk, only two days ago, I wouldn't dare hint at such a thing. . . . I had taken up my binoculars while we talked, and was looking at the shore, sweeping the limit of the forest at each side and at the back of the house. The consciousness of there being people in that bush, so silent, so quiet—as silent and quiet as the ruined house on the hill—made me uneasy. There was no sign on the face of nature of this amazing tale that was not so much told as suggested to me in desolate exclamations, completed by shrugs, in interrupted phrases, in hints ending in deep sighs. The woods were unmoved, like a mask—heavy, like the closed door of a prison—they looked with their air of hidden knowledge, of patient expectation, of unapproachable silence. The Russian was explaining to me that it was only lately that Mr. Kurtz had come down to the river, bringing along with him all the fighting men of that lake tribe. He had been absent for several months—getting himself adored, I suppose—and had come down unexpectedly, with the intention to all appearance of making a raid either across the river or down stream. Evidently the appetite for more ivory had got the better of the—what shall I say?—less material aspirations. However he had got much worse suddenly. 'I heard he was lying helpless, and so I came up—took my chance,' said the Russian. 'Oh, he is bad, very bad.' I directed my glass to the house. There were no signs of life, but there was the ruined roof, the long mud wall peeping above the grass, with three little square window-holes, no two of the same size; all this brought within reach of my hand, as it were. And then I made a brusque movement, and one of the remaining posts of that vanished fence leaped up in the field of my glass. You remember I told you I had been struck at the distance by certain attempts at ornamentation, rather remarkable in the ruinous aspect of the place. Now I had suddenly a nearer view, and its first result was to make me throw my head back as if before a blow. Then I went carefully from post to post with my glass, and I saw my mistake. These round knobs were not ornamental but symbolic; they were expressive and puzzling, striking and disturbing—food for thought and also for vultures if there had been any looking down from the sky; but at all events for such ants as were industrious enough to ascend the pole. They would have been even more impressive, those heads on the stakes, if their faces had not been turned to the house. Only one, the first I had made out, was facing my way. I was not so shocked as you may think. The start back I had given was really nothing but a movement of surprise. I had expected to see a knob of wood there, you know. I returned deliberately to the first I had seen— and there it was, black, dried, sunken, with closed eyelids,—a head that seemed to sleep at the top of that pole, and with the shrunken dry lips showing a narrow white line of the teeth, was smiling, too, smiling continuously at some endless and jocose dream of that eternal slumber.

"I am not disclosing any trade secrets. In fact, the manager said afterwards that Mr. Kurtz's methods had ruined the district. I have no opinion on that point, but I want you clearly to understand that there was nothing exactly profitable in these heads being there. They only showed that Mr. Kurtz lacked restraint in the gratification of his various lusts, that there was something wanting in him—some small matter which, when the pressing need arose, could not be found under his magnificent eloquence. Whether he knew of this deficiency himself I can't say. I think the knowledge came to him at last—only at the very last. But the wilderness had found him out early, and had taken on him a terrible vengeance for the fantastic invasion. I think it had whispered to him things about himself which he did not know, things of which he had no conception till he took counsel with this great solitude—and the whisper had proved irresistibly fascinating. It echoed loudly within him because he was hollow at the core. . . . I put down the glass, and the head that had appeared near enough to be spoken to seemed at once to have leaped away from me into inaccessible distance.

"The admirer of Mr. Kurtz was a bit crestfallen. In a hurried indistinct voice he began to assure me he had not dared to take these—say, symbols—down. He was not afraid of the natives; they would not stir till Mr. Kurtz gave the word. His ascendancy was extraordinary. The camps of these people surrounded the place, and the chiefs came every day to see him. They would crawl. . . . 'I don't want to know anything of the ceremonies used when approaching Mr. Kurtz,' I shouted. Curious, this feeling that came over me that such details would be more intolerable than those heads drying on the stakes under Mr. Kurtz's windows. After all, that was only a savage sight, while I seemed at one bound to have been transported into some lightless region of subtle horrors, where pure, uncomplicated savagery was a positive relief, being something that had a right to exist—obviously —in the sunshine. The young man looked at me with surprise. I suppose it did not occur to him that Mr. Kurtz was no idol of mine. He forgot I hadn't heard any of these splendid monologues on, what was it? on love, justice, conduct of life—or what not. If it had come to crawling before Mr. Kurtz, he crawled as much as the veriest savage of them all. I had no idea of the conditions, he said: these heads were the heads of rebels. I shocked him excessively by laughing. Rebels! What would be the next definition I was to hear? There had been enemies, criminals, workers—and these were rebels. Those rebellious heads looked very subdued to me on their sticks. 'You don't know how such a life tries a man like Kurtz,' cried Kurtz's last disciple. 'Well, and you?' I said. 'I! I! I am a simple man. I have no great thoughts. I want nothing from anybody. How can you compare me to . . . ?' His feelings were too much for speech, and suddenly he broke down. 'I don't understand,' he groaned. 'I've been doing my best to keep him alive, and that's enough. I had no hand in all this. I have no abilities. There hasn't been a drop of medicine or a mouthful of invalid food for months here. He was shamefully abandoned. A man like this, with such ideas. Shamefully! Shamefully! I—I—haven't slept for the last ten nights. . . .'

"His voice lost itself in the calm of the evening. The long shadows of the forest had slipped downhill while we talked, had gone far beyond the ruined hovel, beyond the symbolic row of stakes. All this was in the gloom, while we down there were yet in the sunshine, and the stretch of the river abreast of the clearing glittered in a still and dazzling splendor, with a murky and overshadowed bend above and below. Not a living soul was seen on the shore. The bushes did not rustle.

"Suddenly round the corner of the house a group of men appeared, as though they had come up from the ground. They waded waist-deep in the grass, in a compact body, bearing an improvised stretcher in their midst. Instantly, in the emptiness of the landscape, a cry arose whose shrillness pierced the still air like a sharp arrow flying straight to the very heart of the land; and, as if by enchantment, streams of human beings—of naked human beings—with spears in their hands, with bows, with shields, with wild glances and savage movements, were poured into the clearing by the dark-faced and pensive forest. The bushes shook, the grass swayed for a time, and then everything stood still in attentive immobility.

" 'Now, if he does not say the right thing to them we are all done for,' said the Russian at my elbow. The knot of men with the stretcher had stopped, too, halfway to the steamer, as if petrified. I saw the man on the stretcher sit up, lank and with an uplifted arm, above the shoulders of the bearers. 'Let us hope that the man who can talk so well of love in general will find some particular reason to spare us this time,' I said. I resented bitterly the absurd danger of our situation, as if to be at the mercy of that atrocious phantom had been a dishonoring necessity. I could not hear a sound, but through my glasses I saw the thin arm extended commandingly, the lower jaw moving, the eyes of that apparition shining darkly far in its bony head that nodded with grotesque jerks. Kurtz—Kurtz—that means short in German—don't it? Well, the name was as true as everything else in his life—and death. He looked at least seven feet long. His covering had fallen off, and his body emerged from it pitiful and appalling as from a winding-sheet. I could see the cage of his ribs all astir, the bones of his arm waving. It was as though an animated image of death carved out of old ivory had been shaking its hand with menaces at a motionless crowd of men made of dark and glittering bronze. I saw him open his mouth wide—it gave him a weirdly voracious aspect, as though he had wanted to swallow all the air, all the earth, all the men before him. A deep voice reached me faintly. He must have been shouting. He fell back suddenly. The stretcher shook as the bearers staggered forward again, and almost at the same time I noticed that the crowd of savages was vanishing without any perceptible movement of retreat, as if the forest that had ejected these beings so suddenly had drawn them in again as the breath is drawn in a long aspiration.

"Some of the pilgrims behind the stretcher carried his arms—two shotguns, a heavy rifle, and a light revolver-carbine—the thunderbolts of that pitiful Jupiter. The manager bent over him murmuring as he walked beside his head. They laid him down in one of the little cabins—just a room for a bedplace and a camp-stool or two, you know. We had brought his belated correspondence, and a lot of torn envelopes and open letters littered his bed. His hand roamed feebly amongst these papers. I was struck by the fire of his eyes and the composed languor of his expression. It was not so much the exhaustion of disease. He did not seem in pain. This shadow looked satiated and calm, as though for the moment it had had its fill of all the emotions.

"He rustled one of the letters, and looking straight in my face said, 'I am glad.' Somebody had been writing to him about me. These special recommendations were turning up again. The volume of tone he emitted without effort, almost without the trouble of moving his lips, amazed me. A voice! a voice! It was grave, profound, vibrating, while the man did not seem capable of a whisper. However, he had enough strength in him—factitious no doubt—to very nearly make an end of us, as you shall hear directly.

"The manager appeared silently in the doorway; I stepped out at once and he drew the curtain after me. The Russian, eyed curiously by the pilgrims, was staring at the shore. I followed the direction of his glance.

"Dark human shapes could be made out in the distance, flitting indistinctly against the gloomy border of the forest, and near the river two bronze figures, leaning on tall spears, stood in the sunlight under fantastic headdresses of spotted skins, war-like and still in statuesque repose. And from right to left along the lighted shore moved a wild and gorgeous apparition of a woman.

"She walked with measured steps, draped in striped and fringed cloths, treading the earth proudly, with a slight jingle and flash of barbarous ornaments. She carried her head high; her hair was done in the shape of a helmet; she had brass leggings to the knee, brass wire gauntlets to the elbow, a crimson spot on her tawny cheek, innumerable necklaces of glass beads on her neck; bizarre things, charms, gifts of witch-men, that hung about her, glittered and trembled at every step. She must have had the value of several elephant tusks upon her. She was savage and superb, wild-eyed and magnificent; there was something ominous and stately in her deliberate progress. And in the hush that had fallen suddenly upon the whole sorrowful land, the immense wilderness, the colossal body of the fecund and mysterious life seemed to look at her, pensive, as though it had been looking at the image of its own tenebrous and passionate soul.

"She came abreast of the steamer, stood still, and faced us. Her long shadow fell to the water's edge. Her face had a tragic and fierce aspect of wild sorrow and of dumb pain mingled with the fear of some struggling, half-shaped resolve. She stood looking at us without a stir, and like the wilderness itself, with an air of brooding over an inscrutable purpose. A whole minute passed, and then she made a step forward. There was a low jingle, a glint of yellow metal, a sway of fringed draperies, and she stopped as if her heart had failed her. The young fellow by my side growled. The pilgrims murmured at my back. She looked at us all as if her life had depended upon the unswerving steadiness of her glance. Suddenly she opened her bared arms and threw them up rigid above her head, as though in an uncontrollable desire to touch the sky, and at the same time the swift shadows darted out on the earth, swept around on the river, gathering the steamer into a shadowy embrace. A formidable silence hung over the scene.

"She turned away slowly, walked on, following the bank, and passed into the bushes to the left. Once only her eyes gleamed back at us in the dusk of the thickets before she disappeared.

" 'If she had offered to come aboard I really think I would have tried to shoot her,' said the man of patches, nervously. 'I have been risking my life every day for the last fortnight to keep her out of the house. She got in one day and kicked up a row about those miserable rags I picked up in the storeroom to mend my clothes with. I wasn't decent. At least it must have been that, for she talked like a fury to Kurtz for an hour, pointing at me now and then. I don't understand the dialect of this tribe. Luckily for me, I fancy Kurtz felt too ill that day to care, or there would have been mischief. I don't understand. . . . No—it's too much for me. Ah, well, it's all over now.'

"At this moment I heard Kurtz's deep voice behind the curtain: 'Save me!—save the ivory, you mean. Don't tell me. Save *me!* Why, I've had to save you. You are interrupting my plans now. Sick! Sick! Not so sick as you would like to believe. Never mind. I'll carry my ideas out yet—I will return. I'll show you what can be done. You with your little peddling notions—you are interfering with me. I will return. I . . .'

"The manager came out. He did me the honor to take me under the arm and lead me aside. 'He is very low, very low,' he said. He considered it necessary to sigh, but neglected to be consistently sorrowful. 'We have done all we could for him—haven't we? But there is no disguising the fact, Mr. Kurtz has done more harm than good to the Company. He did not see the time was not ripe for vigorous action. Cautiously, cautiously—that's my principle. We must be cautious yet. The district is closed to us for a time. Deplorable! Upon the whole, the trade will suffer. I don't deny there is a remarkable quantity of ivory—mostly fossil. We must save it, at all events—but look how precarious the position is—and why? Because the method is unsound.' 'Do you,' said I, looking at the shore, 'call it "unsound method"?' 'Without doubt,' he exclaimed, hotly. 'Don't you?' . . . 'No method at all,' I murmured after a while. 'Exactly,' he exulted. 'I anticipated this. Shows a complete want of judgment. It is my duty to point it out in the proper quarter.' 'Oh,' said I, 'that fellow—what's his name?—the brick-maker, will make a readable report for you.' He appeared confounded for a moment. It seemed to me I had never breathed an atmosphere so vile, and I turned mentally to Kurtz for relief—positively for relief. 'Nevertheless I think Mr. Kurtz is a remarkable man,' I said with emphasis. He started, dropped on me a cold heavy glance, said very quietly, 'he *was*,' and turned his back on me. My hour of favor was over; I found myself lumped along with Kurtz as a partisan of methods for which the time was not ripe: I was unsound! Ah! but it was something to have at least a choice of nightmares.

"I had turned to the wilderness really, not to Mr. Kurtz, who,

I was ready to admit, was as good as buried. And for a moment it seemed to me as if I also were buried in a vast grave full of unspeakable secrets. I felt an intolerable weight oppressing my breast, the smell of the damp earth, the unseen presence of victorious corruption, the darkness of an impenetrable night. . . . The Russian tapped me on the shoulder. I heard him mumbling and stammering something about 'brother seaman—couldn't conceal—knowledge of matters that would affect Mr. Kurtz's reputation.' I waited. For him evidently Mr. Kurtz was not in his grave; I suspect that for him Mr. Kurtz was one of the immortals. 'Well!' said I at last, 'speak out. As it happens, I am Mr. Kurtz's friend—in a way.'

"He stated with a good deal of formality that had we not been 'of the same profession,' he would have kept the matter to himself without regard to consequences. 'He suspected there was an active ill will towards him on the part of these white men that—' 'You are right,' I said, remembering a certain conversation I had overheard. 'The manager thinks you ought to be hanged.' He showed a concern at this intelligence which amused me at first. 'I had better get out of the way quietly,' he said, earnestly. 'I can do no more for Kurtz now, and they would soon find some excuse. What's to stop them? There's a military post three hundred miles from here.' 'Well, upon my word,' said I, 'perhaps you had better go if you have any friends amongst the savages near by.' 'Plenty,' he said. 'They are simple people—and I want nothing, you know.' He stood biting his lip, then: 'I don't want any harm to happen to these whites here, but of course I was thinking of Mr. Kurtz's reputation—but you are a brother seaman and—' 'All right,' said I, after a time. 'Mr. Kurtz's reputation is safe with me.' I did not know how truly I spoke.

"He informed me, lowering his voice, that it was Kurtz who had ordered the attack to be made on the steamer. 'He hated sometimes the idea of being taken away—and then again . . . But I don't understand these matters. I am a simple man. He thought it would scare you away—that you would give it up, thinking him dead. I could not stop him. Oh, I had an awful time of it this last month.' 'Very well,' I said. 'He is all right now.' 'Ye-e-es,' he muttered, not very convinced apparently. 'Thanks,' said I; 'I shall keep my eyes open.' 'But quiet—eh?' he urged, anxiously. 'It would be awful for his reputation if anybody here—'

I promised a complete discretion with great gravity. 'I have a canoe and three black fellows waiting not very far. I am off. Could you give me a few Martini-Henry cartridges?' I could, and did, with proper secrecy. He helped himself, with a wink at me, to a handful of my tobacco. 'Between sailors—you know —good English tobacco.' At the door of the pilot-house he turned round—'I say, haven't you a pair of shoes you could spare?' He raised one leg. 'Look.' The soles were tied with knotted strings sandal-wise under his bare feet. I rooted out an old pair, at which he looked with admiration before tucking them under his left arm. One of his pockets (bright red) was bulging with cartridges, from the other (dark blue) peeped 'Towson's Inquiry,' etc., etc. He seemed to think himself excellently well equipped for a re-newed encounter with the wilderness. 'Ah! I'll never, never meet such a man again. You ought to have heard him recite poetry— his own, too, it was, he told me. Poetry!' He rolled his eyes at the recollection of these delights. 'Oh, he enlarged my mind!' 'Good-by,' said I. He shook hands and vanished in the night. Sometimes I ask myself whether I had ever really seen him— whether it was possible to meet such a phenomenon! . . .

"When I woke up shortly after midnight his warning came to my mind with its hint of danger that seemed, in the starred darkness, real enough to make me get up for the purpose of having a look round. On the hill a big fire burned, illuminating fitfully a crooked corner of the station-house. One of the agents with a picket of a few of our blacks, armed for the purpose, was keeping guard over the ivory; but deep within the forest, red gleams that wavered, that seemed to sink and rise from the ground amongst confused columnar shapes of intense blackness, showed the exact position of the camp where Mr. Kurtz's adorers were keeping their uneasy vigil. The monotonous beating of a big drum filled the air with muffled shocks and a lingering vibration. A steady droning sound of many men chanting each to himself some weird incantation came out from the black, flat wall of the woods as the humming of bees comes out of a hive, and had a strange narcotic effect upon my half-awake senses. I believe I dozed off leaning over the rail, till an abrupt burst of yells, an overwhelming outbreak of a pent-up and mysterious frenzy, woke me up in a bewildered wonder. It was cut short all at once, and the low droning went on with an effect of audible and soothing silence. I glanced casually into the little cabin. A light was burning within, but Mr. Kurtz was not there.

"I think I would have raised an outcry if I had believed my eyes. But I didn't believe them at first—the thing seemed so impossible. The fact is I was completely unnerved by a sheer blank fright, pure abstract terror, unconnected with any distinct shape of physical danger. What made this emotion so overpowering was—how shall I define it?—the moral shock I received, as if something altogether monstrous, intolerable to thought and odious to the soul, had been thrust upon me unexpectedly. This lasted of course the merest fraction of a second, and then the usual sense of commonplace, deadly danger, the possibility of a sudden onslaught and massacre, or something of the kind, which I saw impending, was positively welcome and composing. It pacified me, in fact, so much, that I did not raise an alarm.

"There was an agent buttoned up inside an ulster and sleeping on a chair on deck within three feet of me. The yells had not awakened him; he snored very slightly; I left him to his slumbers and leaped ashore. I did not betray Mr. Kurtz—it was ordered I should never betray him—it was written I should be loyal to the nightmare of my choice. I was anxious to deal with this shadow by myself alone,—and to this day I don't know why I was so jealous of sharing with anyone the peculiar blackness of that experience.

"As soon as I got on the bank I saw a trail—a broad trail through the grass. I remember the exultation with which I said to myself, 'He can't walk—he is crawling on all-fours—I've got him.' The grass was wet with dew. I strode rapidly with clenched fists. I fancy I had some vague notion of falling upon him and giving him a drubbing. I don't know. I had some imbecile thoughts. The knitting old woman with the cat obtruded herself upon my memory as a most improper person to be sitting at the other end of such an affair. I saw a row of pilgrims squirting lead in the air out of Winchesters held to the hip. I thought I would never get back to the steamer, and imagined myself living alone and unarmed in the woods to an advanced age. Such silly things—you know. And I remember I confounded the beat of the drum with the beating of my heart, and was pleased at its calm regularity.

"I kept to the track though—then stopped to listen. The night was very clear; a dark blue space, sparkling with dew and star-light, in which black things stood very still. I thought I could see a kind of motion ahead of me. I was strangely cocksure of every-thing that night. I actually left the track and ran in a wide semi-circle (I verily believe chuckling to myself) so as to get in front of that stir, of that motion I had seen—if indeed I had seen any-thing. I was circumventing Kurtz as though it had been a boyish game.

"I came upon him, and, if he had not heard me coming, I would have fallen over him, too, but he got up in time. He rose, unsteady, long, pale, indistinct, like a vapor exhaled by the earth, and swayed slightly, misty and silent before me; while at my back the fires loomed between the trees, and the murmur of many voices issued from the forest. I had cut him off cleverly; but when actually confronting him I seemed to come to my senses, I saw the danger in its right proportion. It was by no means over yet. Suppose he began to shout? Though he could hardly stand, there was still plenty of vigor in his voice. 'Go away—hide yourself,' he said, in that profound tone. It was very awful. I glanced back. We were within thirty yards from the nearest fire. A black figure stood up, strode on long black legs, waving long black arms, across the glow. It had horns—antelope horns, I think—on its head. Some sorcerer, some witchman, no doubt: it looked fiend-like enough. 'Do you know what you are doing?' I whispered. 'Perfectly,' he answered, raising his voice for that single word: it sounded to me far off and yet loud, like a hail through a speaking-trumpet. If he makes a row we are lost, I thought to myself. This clearly was not a case for fisticuffs, even apart from the very natural aversion I had to beat that Shadow—this wandering and tormented thing. 'You will be lost,' I said—'utterly lost.' One gets sometimes such a flash of inspiration, you know. I did say the right thing, though indeed he could not have been more irretrievably lost than he was at this very moment, when the foundations of our intimacy were being laid—to endure—to endure—even to the end—even beyond.

" 'I had immense plans,' he muttered irresolutely. 'Yes,' said I; 'but if you try to shout I'll smash your head with—' There was not a stick or a stone near. 'I will throttle you for good,' I cor-rected myself. 'I was on the threshold of great things,' he pleaded, in a voice of longing, with a wistfulness of tone that made my blood run cold. 'And now for this stupid scoundrel—' 'Your success in Europe is assured in any case,' I affirmed, steadily. I did not want to have the throttling of him, you understand—and indeed it would have been very little use for any practical purpose. I tried to break the spell—the heavy, mute spell of the wilderness— that seemed to draw him to its pitiless breast by the awakening of forgotten and brutal instincts, by the memory of gratified and monstrous passions. This alone, I was convinced, had driven him out to the edge of the forest, to the bush, towards the gleam of fires, the throb of drums, the drone of weird incantations; this alone had beguiled his unlawful soul beyond the bounds of permitted aspirations. And, don't you see, the terror of the position was not in being knocked on the head—though I had a very lively sense of that danger, too—but in this, that I had to deal with a being to whom I could not appeal in the name of anything high or low. I had, even like the niggers, to invoke him—himself —his own exalted and incredible degradation. There was nothing either above or below him, and I knew it. He had kicked himself loose of the earth. Confound the man! he had kicked the very earth to pieces. He was alone, and I before him did not know whether I stood on the ground or floated in the air. I've been telling you what we said—repeating the phrases we pronounced—but what's the good? They were common everyday words—the familiar, vague sounds exchanged on every waking day of life. But what of that? They had behind them, to my mind, the terrific suggestiveness of words heard in dreams, of phrases spoken in nightmares. Soul! If anybody had ever struggled with a soul, I am the man. And I wasn't arguing with a lunatic either. Believe me or not, his intelligence was perfectly clear—concentrated, it is true, upon himself with horrible intensity, yet clear; and therein was my only chance—barring, of course, the killing him there and then, which wasn't so good, on account of unavoidable noise. But his soul was mad. Being alone in the wilderness, it had looked within itself, and, by heavens! I tell you, it had gone mad. I had —for my sins, I suppose—to go through the ordeal of looking into it myself. No eloquence could have been so withering to one's belief in mankind as his final burst of sincerity. He struggled with himself, too. I saw it,—I heard it. I saw the inconceivable mystery of a soul that knew no restraint, no faith, and no fear, yet struggling blindly with itself. I kept my head pretty well; but when I had him at last stretched on the couch, I wiped my forehead, while my legs shook under me as though I had carried half a ton on my back down that hill. And yet I had only supported him, his bony arm clasped round my neck—and he was not much heavier than a child.

"When next day we left at noon, the crowd, of whose presence behind the curtain of trees I had been acutely conscious all the time, flowed out of the woods again, filled the clearing, covered the slope with a mass of naked, breathing, quivering, bronze bodies. I steamed up a bit, then swung downstream, and two thousand eyes followed the evolutions of the splashing, thumping, fierce river-demon beating the water with its terrible tail and breathing black smoke into the air. In front of the first rank, along the river, three men, plastered with bright red earth from head to foot, strutted to and fro restlessly. When we came abreast again, they faced the river, stamped their feet, nodded their horned heads, swayed their scarlet bodies; they shook towards the fierce river-demon a bunch of black feathers, a mangy skin with a pendent tail—something that looked like a dried gourd; they shouted periodically together strings of amazing words that resembled no sounds of human language; and the deep murmurs of the crowd, interrupted suddenly, were like the responses of some satanic litany.

"We had carried Kurtz into the pilot-house: there was more air there. Lying on the couch, he stared through the open shutter. There was an eddy in the mass of human bodies, and the woman with helmeted head and tawny cheeks rushed out to the very brink of the stream. She put out her hands, shouted something, and all that wild mob took up the shout in a roaring chorus of articulated, rapid, breathless utterance.

" 'Do you understand this?' I asked.

"He kept on looking out past me with fiery, longing eyes, with a mingled expression of wistfulness and hate. He made no answer, but I saw a smile, a smile of indefinable meaning, appear on his colorless lips that a moment after twitched convulsively. 'Do I not?' he said slowly, gasping, as if the words had been torn out of him by a supernatural power.

"I pulled the string of the whistle, and I did this because I saw the pilgrims on deck getting out their rifles with an air of anticipating a jolly lark. At the sudden screech there was a movement of abject terror through that wedged mass of bodies. 'Don't! don't you frighten them away,' cried someone on deck disconsolately. I pulled the string time after time. They broke and ran, they leaped, they crouched, they swerved, they dodged the flying terror of the sound. The three red chaps had fallen flat, face down on the shore, as though they had been shot dead. Only the barbarous and superb woman did not so much as flinch, and stretched tragically her bare arms after us over the somber and glittering river.

"And then that imbecile crowd down on the deck started their little fun, and I could see nothing more for smoke.

"The brown current ran swiftly out of the heart of darkness, bearing us down towards the sea with twice the speed of our upward progress; and Kurtz's life was running swiftly, too, ebbing, ebbing out of his heart into the sea of inexorable time. The manager was very placid, he had no vital anxieties now, he took us both in with a comprehensive and satisfied glance: the 'affair' had come off as well as could be wished. I saw the time approaching when I would be left alone of the party of 'unsound method.' The pilgrims looked upon me with disfavor. I was, so to speak, numbered with the dead. It is strange how I accepted this unforeseen partnership, this choice of nightmares forced upon me in the tenebrous land invaded by these mean and greedy phantoms.

"Kurtz discoursed. A voice! a voice! It rang deep to the very last. It survived his strength to hide in the magnificent folds of eloquence the barren darkness of his heart. Oh, he struggled! he struggled! The wastes of his weary brain were haunted by shadowy images now—images of wealth and fame revolving obsequiously round his unextinguishable gift of noble and lofty expression. My Intended, my station, my career, my ideas—these were the subjects for the occasional utterances of elevated sentiments. The shade of the original Kurtz frequented the bedside of the hollow sham, whose fate it was to be buried presently in the mold of primeval earth. But both the diabolic love and the unearthly hate of the mysteries it had penetrated fought for the possession of that soul satiated with primitive emotions, avid of lying fame, of sham distinction, of all the appearances of success and power.

"Sometimes he was contemptibly childish. He desired to have kings meet him at railway stations on his return from some ghastly Nowhere, where he intended to accomplish great things. 'You show them you have in you something that is really profitable, and then there will be no limits to the recognition of your ability,' he would say. 'Of course you must take care of the motives—right motives—always.' The long reaches that were like one and the same reach, monotonous bends that were exactly alike, slipped past the steamer with their multitude of secular trees looking patiently after this grimy fragment of another world, the forerunner of change, of conquest, of trade, of massacres, of blessings. I looked ahead—piloting. 'Close the shutter,' said Kurtz suddenly one day; 'I can't bear to look at this.' I did so. There was a silence. 'Oh, but I will wring your heart yet!' he cried at the invisible wilderness.

"We broke down—as I had expected—and had to lie up for repairs at the head of an island. This delay was the first thing that shook Kurtz's confidence. One morning he gave me a packet of papers and a photograph—the lot tied together with a shoe-string. 'Keep this for me,' he said. 'This noxious fool' (meaning the manager) 'is capable of prying into my boxes when I am not looking.' In the afternoon I saw him. He was lying on his back with closed eyes, and I withdrew quietly, but I heard him mutter, 'Live rightly, die, die. . . .' I listened. There was nothing more. Was he rehearsing some speech in his sleep, or was it a fragment of a phrase from some newspaper article? He had been writing for the papers and meant to do so again, 'for the furthering of my ideas. It's a duty.'

"His was an impenetrable darkness. I looked at him as you peer down at a man who is lying at the bottom of a precipice where the sun never shines. But I had not much time to give him, because I was helping the engine-driver to take to pieces the leaky cylinders, to straighten a bent connecting-rod, and in other such matters. I lived in an infernal mess of rust, filings, nuts, bolts, spanners, hammers, ratchet-drills—things I abominate, because I don't get on with them. I tended the little forge we fortunately had aboard; I toiled wearily in a wretched scrap-heap—unless I had the shakes too bad to stand,

"One evening coming in with a candle I was startled to hear him say a little tremulously, 'I am lying here in the dark waiting for death.' The light was within a foot of his eyes. I forced myself to murmur, 'Oh, nonsense!' and stood over him as if transfixed.

"Anything approaching the change that came over his features I have never seen before, and hope never to see again. Oh, I wasn't touched. I was fascinated. It was as though a veil had been rent. I saw on that ivory face the expression of somber pride, of ruthless power, of craven terror—of an intense and hopeless despair. Did he live his life again in every detail of desire, temptation, and surrender during that supreme moment of complete knowledge? He cried in a whisper at some image, at some vision—he cried out twice, a cry that was no more than a breath—

" 'The horror! The horror!'

"I blew the candle out and left the cabin. The pilgrims were dining in the mess-room, and I took my place opposite the manager, who lifted his eyes to give me a questioning glance, which I successfully ignored. He leaned back, serene, with that peculiar smile of his sealing the unexpressed depths of his meanness. A continuous shower of small flies streamed upon the lamp, upon the cloth, upon our hands and faces. Suddenly the manager's boy put his insolent black head in the doorway, and said in a tone of scathing contempt—

" 'Mistah Kurtz—he dead.'

"All the pilgrims rushed out to see. I remained, and went on with my dinner. I believe I was considered brutally callous. However, I did not eat much. There was a lamp in there—light, don't you know—and outside it was so beastly, beastly dark. I went no more near the remarkable man who had pronounced a judgment upon the adventures of his soul on this earth. The voice was gone. What else had been there? But I am of course aware that next day the pilgrims buried something in a muddy hole.

"And then they very nearly buried me.

"However, as you see, I did not go to join Kurtz there and then. I did not. I remained to dream the nightmare out to the end, and to show my loyalty to Kurtz once more. Destiny. My destiny! Droll thing life is—that mysterious arrangement of merciless logic for a futile purpose. The most you can hope from it is some knowledge of yourself—that comes too late—a crop of unextinguishable regrets. I have wrestled with death. It is the most unexciting contest you can imagine. It takes place in an impalpable grayness, with nothing underfoot, with nothing around, without spectators, without clamor, without glory, without the great desire of victory, without the great fear of defeat, in a sickly atmosphere of tepid skepticism, without much belief in your own right, and still less in that of your adversary. If such is the form of ultimate wisdom, then life is a greater riddle than some of us think it to be. I was within a hair's breadth of the last opportunity for pronouncement, and I found with humiliation that probably I would have nothing to say. This is the reason why I affirm that Kurtz was a remarkable man. He had something to say. He said it. Since I had peeped over the edge myself, I understand better the meaning of his stare, that could not see the flame of the candle, but was wide enough to embrace the whole universe, piercing enough to penetrate all the hearts that beat in the darkness. He had summed up—he had judged. 'The horror!' He was a remarkable man. After all, this was the expression of some sort of belief; it had candor, it had conviction, it had a vibrating note of revolt in its whisper, it had the appalling face of a glimpsed truth—the strange commingling of desire and hate. And it is not my own extremity I remember best—a vision of grayness without form filled with physical pain, and a careless contempt for the evanescence of all things—even of this pain itself. No! It is his extremity that I seem to have lived through. True, he had made that last stride, he had stepped over the edge, while I had been permitted to draw back my hesitating foot. And perhaps in this is the whole difference; perhaps all the wisdom, and all truth, and all sincerity, are just compressed into that inappreciable moment of time in which we step over the threshold of the invisible. Perhaps! I like to think my summing-up would not have been a word of careless contempt. Better his cry—much better. It was an affirmation, a moral victory paid for by innumerable defeats, by abominable terrors, by abominable satisfactions. But it was a victory! That is why I have remained loyal to Kurtz to the last, and even beyond, when a long time after I heard once more, not his own choice, but the echo of his magnificent eloquence thrown to me from a soul as translucently pure as a cliff of crystal.

"No, they did not bury me, though there is a period of time

which I remember mistily, with a shuddering wonder, like a passage through some inconceivable world that had no hope in it and no desire. I found myself back in the sepulchral city resenting the sight of people hurrying through the streets to filch a little money from each other, to devour their infamous cookery, to gulp their unwholesome beer, to dream their insignificant and silly dreams. They trespassed upon my thoughts. They were intruders whose knowledge of life was to me an irritating pretense, because I felt so sure they could not possibly know the things I knew. Their bearing, which was simply the bearing of commonplace individuals going about their business in the assurance of perfect safety, was offensive to me like the outrageous flauntings of folly in the face of a danger it is unable to comprehend. I had no particular desire to enlighten them, but I had some difficulty in restraining myself from laughing in their faces, so full of stupid importance. I daresay I was not very well at that time. I tottered about the streets—there were various affairs to settle—grinning bitterly at perfectly respectable persons. I admit my behavior was inexcusable, but then my temperature was seldom normal in these days. My dear aunt's endeavors to 'nurse up my strength' seemed altogether beside the mark. It was not my strength that wanted nursing, it was my imagination that wanted soothing. I kept the bundle of papers given me by Kurtz, not knowing exactly what to do with it. His mother had died lately, watched over, as I was told, by his Intended. A clean-shaved man, with an official manner and wearing gold-rimmed spectacles, called on me one day and made inquiries, at first circuitous, afterwards suavely pressing, about what he was pleased to denominate certain 'documents.' I was not surprised, because I had had two rows with the manager on the subject out there. I had refused to give up the smallest scrap out of that package, and I took the same attitude with the spectacled man. He became darkly menacing at last, and with much heat argued that the Company had the right to every bit of information about its 'territories.' And said he, 'Mr. Kurtz's knowledge of unexplored regions must have been necessarily extensive and peculiar—owing to his great abilities and to the deplorable circumstances in which he had been placed: therefore—' I assured him Mr. Kurtz's knowledge, however extensive, did not bear upon the problems of commerce or administration. He invoked then the name of science. 'It would be an incalculable loss if,' etc., etc. I offered him the report on the 'Suppression of Savage Customs,' with the postscriptum torn off. He took it up eagerly, but ended by sniffing at it with an air of contempt. 'This is not what we had a right to expect,' he remarked. 'Expect nothing else,' I said. 'There are only private letters.' He withdrew upon some threat of legal proceedings, and I saw him no more; but another fellow, calling himself Kurtz's cousin, appeared two days later, and was anxious to hear all the details about his dear relative's last moments. Incidentally he gave me to understand that Kurtz had been essentially a great musician. 'There was the making of an immense success,' said the man, who was an organist, I believe, with lank gray hair flowing over a greasy coat-collar. I had no reason to doubt his statement; and to this day I am unable to say what was Kurtz's profession, whether he ever had any—which was the greatest of his talents. I had taken him for a painter who wrote for the papers, or else for a journalist who could paint—but even the cousin (who took snuff during the interview) could not tell me what he had been—exactly. He was a universal genius—on that point I agreed with the old chap, who thereupon blew his nose noisily into a large cotton handkerchief and withdrew in senile agitation, bearing off some family letters and memoranda without importance. Ultimately a journalist anxious to know something of the fate of his 'dear colleague' turned up. This visitor informed me Kurtz's proper sphere ought to have been politics 'on the popular side.' He had furry straight eyebrows, bristly hair cropped short, an eye-glass on a broad ribbon, and, becoming expansive, confessed his opinion that Kurtz really couldn't write a bit—'but heavens! how that man could talk. He electrified large meetings. He had faith—don't you see?—he had the faith. He could get himself to believe anything—anything. He would have been a splendid leader of an extreme party.' 'What party?' I asked. 'Any party,' answered the other. 'He was an—an—extremist.' Did I not think so? I assented. Did I know, he asked, with a sudden flash of curiosity, 'what it was that had induced him to go out there?' 'Yes,' said I, and forthwith handed him the famous Report for publication, if he thought fit. He glanced through it hurriedly, mumbling all the time, judged 'it would do,' and took himself off with this plunder.

"Thus I was left at last with a slim packet of letters and the girl's portrait. She struck me as beautiful—I mean she had a beautiful expression. I know that the sunlight can be made to lie, too, yet one felt that no manipulation of light and pose could have conveyed the delicate shade of truthfulness upon those features. She seemed ready to listen without mental reservation, without suspicion, without a thought for herself. I concluded I would go and give her back her portrait and those letters myself. Curiosity? Yes; and also some other feeling perhaps. All that had been Kurtz's had passed out of my hands: his soul, his body, his station, his plans, his ivory, his career. There remained only his memory and his Intended—and I wanted to give that up, too, to the past, in a way—to surrender personally all that remained of him with me to that oblivion which is the last word of our common fate. I don't defend myself. I had no clear perception of what it was I really wanted. Perhaps it was an impulse of unconscious loyalty, or the fulfillment of one of those ironic necessities, that lurk in the facts of human existence. I don't know. I can't tell. But I went.

"I thought his memory was like the other memories of the dead that accumulate in every man's life—a vague impress on the brain of shadows that had fallen on it in their swift and final passage; but before the high and ponderous door, between the tall houses of a street as still and decorous as a well-kept alley in a cemetery, I had a vision of him on the stretcher, opening his mouth voraciously, as if to devour all the earth with all its mankind. He lived then before me; he lived as much as he had ever lived—a shadow insatiable of splendid appearances, of frightful realities; a shadow darker than the shadow of the night, and draped nobly in the folds of a gorgeous eloquence. The vision seemed to enter the house with me—the stretcher, the phantom-bearers, the wild crowd of obedient worshipers, the gloom of the forests, the glitter of the reach between the murky bends, the beat of the drum, regular and muffled like the beating of a heart—the heart of a conquering darkness. It was a moment of triumph for the wilderness, an invading and vengeful rush which, it seemed to me, I would have to keep back alone for the salvation of another soul. And the memory of what I had heard him say afar there, with the horned shapes stirring at my back, in the glow of fires, within the patient woods, those broken phrases came back to me, were heard again in their ominous and terrifying simplicity. I remembered his abject pleading, his abject threats, the colossal scale of his vile desires, the meanness, the torment, the tempestuous anguish of his soul. And later on I seemed to see his collected languid manner, when he said one day, 'This lot of ivory now is really mine. The Company did not pay for it. I collected it myself at a very great personal risk. I am afraid they will try to claim it as theirs though. H'm. It is a difficult case. What do you think I ought to do—resist? Eh? I want no more than justice.' . . . He wanted no more than justice—no more than justice. I rang the bell before a mahogany door on the first floor, and while I waited he seemed to stare at me out of the glassy panel—stare with that wide and immense stare embracing, condemning, loathing all the universe. I seemed to hear the whispered cry, 'The horror! The horror!'

"The dusk was falling. I had to wait in a lofty drawing-room with three long windows from floor to ceiling that were like three luminous and bedraped columns. The bent gilt legs and backs of the furniture shone in indistinct curves. The tall marble fireplace had a cold and monumental whiteness. A grand piano stood massively in a corner; with dark gleams on the flat surfaces like a somber and polished sarcophagus. A high door opened—closed. I rose.

"She came forward, all in black, with a pale head, floating towards me in the dusk. She was in mourning. It was more than a year since his death, more than a year since the news came; she seemed as though she would remember and mourn forever. She took both my hands in hers and murmured, 'I had heard you were coming.' I noticed she was not very young—I mean not girlish. She had a mature capacity for fidelity, for belief, for suffering. The room seemed to have grown darker, as if all the sad light of the cloudy evening had taken refuge on her forehead. This fair hair, this pale visage, this pure brow, seemed surrounded by an ashy halo from which the dark eyes looked out at me. Their glance was guileless, profound, confident, and trustful. She carried her sorrowful head as though she were proud of that sorrow, as though she would say, I—I alone know how to mourn him as he deserves. But while we were still shaking hands, such a look of awful desolation came upon her face that I perceived she was one of those creatures that are not the playthings of Time. For her he had died only yesterday. And, by Jove! the impression was so powerful that for me, too, he seemed to have died only yesterday—nay, this very minute. I saw her and him in the same instant of time—his death and her sorrow—I saw her sorrow in the very moment of his death. Do you understand? I saw them together—I heard them together. She had said, with a deep catch of the breath, 'I have survived' while my strained ears seemed to hear distinctly, mingled with her tone of despairing regret, the summing up whisper of his eternal condemnation. I asked myself what I was doing there, with a sensation of panic in my heart as though I had blundered into a place of cruel and absurd mysteries not fit for a human being to behold. She motioned me to a chair. We sat down. I laid the packet gently on the little table, and she put her hand over it. . . . 'You knew him well,' she murmured, after a moment of mourning silence.

" 'Intimacy grows quickly out there,' I said. 'I knew him as well as it is possible for one man to know another.'

" 'And you admired him,' she said. 'It was impossible to know him and not to admire him. Was it?'

" 'He was a remarkable man,' I said, unsteadily. Then before the appealing fixity of her gaze, that seemed to watch for more words on my lips, I went on, 'It was impossible not to—'

" 'Love him,' she finished eagerly, silencing me into an appalled dumbness. 'How true! how true! But when you think that no one knew him so well as I! I had all his noble confidence. I knew him best.'

" 'You knew him best,' I repeated. And perhaps she did. But with every word spoken the room was growing darker, and only her forehead, smooth and white, remained illumined by the unextinguishable light of belief and love.

" 'You were his friend,' she went on. 'His friend,' she repeated, a little louder. 'You must have been, if he had given you this, and sent you to me. I feel I can speak to you—and oh! I must speak. I want you—you have heard his last words—to know I have been worthy of him. . . . It is not pride. . . . Yes! I am proud to know I understood him better than any one on earth—he told me so himself. And since his mother died I have had no one—no one—to—to—'

"I listened. The darkness deepened. I was not even sure he had given me the right bundle. I rather suspect he wanted me to take care of another batch of his papers which, after his death, I saw the manager examining under the lamp. And the girl talked, easing her pain in the certitude of my sympathy; she talked as thirsty men drink. I had heard that her engagement with Kurtz had been disapproved by her people. He wasn't rich enough or something. And indeed I don't know whether he had not been a pauper all his life. He had given me some reason to infer that it was his impatience of comparative poverty that drove him out there.

" '. . . Who was not his friend who had heard him speak once?' she was saying. 'He drew men towards him by what was best in them.' She looked at me with intensity. 'It is the gift of the great,' she went on, and the sound of her low voice seemed to have the accompaniment of all the other sounds, full of mystery, desolation, and sorrow, I had ever heard—the ripple of the river, the soughing of the trees swayed by the wind, the murmurs of the crowds, the faint ring of incomprehensible words cried from afar, the whisper of a voice speaking from beyond the threshold of an eternal darkness. 'But you have heard him! You know!' she cried.

" 'Yes, I know,' I said with something like despair in my heart, but bowing my head before the faith that was in her, before that great and saving illusion that shone with an unearthly glow in the darkness, in the triumphant darkness from which I could not have defended her—from which I could not even defend myself.

" 'What a loss to me—to us!'—she corrected herself with beautiful generosity; then added in a murmur, 'To the world.' By the last gleams of twilight I could see the glitter of her eyes, full of tears—of tears that would not fall.

" 'I have been very happy—very fortunate—very proud,' she went on. 'Too fortunate. Too happy for a little while. And now I am unhappy for—for life.'

"She stood up; her fair hair seemed to catch all the remaining light in a glimmer of gold. I rose, too.

" 'And of all this,' she went on, mournfully, 'of all his promise, and of all his greatness, of his generous mind, of his noble heart, nothing remains—nothing but a memory. You and I—'

" 'We shall always remember him,' I said, hastily.

" 'No!' she cried. 'It is impossible that all this should be lost—that such a life should be sacrificed to leave nothing—but sorrow. You know what vast plans he had. I knew of them, too—I could not perhaps understand—but others knew of them. Something must remain. His words, at least, have not died.'

" 'His words will remain,' I said.

" 'And his example,' she whispered to herself. 'Men looked up to him—his goodness shone in every act. His example—'

" 'True,' I said; 'his example, too. Yes, his example. I forgot that.'

" 'But I do not. I cannot—I cannot believe—not yet. I cannot believe that I shall never see him again, that nobody will see him again, never, never, never.'

"She put out her arms as if after a retreating figure, stretching them black and with clasped pale hands across the fading and narrow sheen of the window. Never see him! I saw him clearly enough then. I shall see this eloquent phantom as long as I live, and I shall see her, too, a tragic and familiar Shade, resembling in this gesture another one, tragic also, and bedecked with power-less charms, stretching bare brown arms over the glitter of the infernal stream, the stream of darkness. She said suddenly very low, 'He died as he lived.'

" 'His end,' said I, with dull anger stirring in me, 'was in every way worthy of his life.'

" 'And I was not with him,' she murmured. My anger subsided before a feeling of infinite pity.

" 'Everything that could be done—' I mumbled.

" 'Ah, but I believed in him more than anyone on earth—more than his own mother, more than—himself. He needed me! Me! I would have treasured every sigh, every word, every sign, every glance.'

"I felt like a chill grip on my chest. 'Don't,' I said, in a muffled voice.

" 'Forgive me. I—I have mourned so long in silence—in silence. . . . You were with him—to the last? I think of his loneliness. Nobody near to understand him as I would have understood. Perhaps no one to hear. . . .'

" 'To the very end,' I said, shakily. 'I heard his very last words. . . .' I stopped in a fright.

" 'Repeat them,' she murmured in a heart-broken tone. 'I want —I want—something—something—to—live with.'

"I was on the point of crying at her, 'Don't you hear them?' The dusk was repeating them in a persistent whisper all around us, in a whisper that seemed to swell menacingly like the first whisper of a rising wind. 'The horror! The horror!'

" 'His last word—to live with,' she insisted. 'Don't you under-stand I loved him—I loved him—I loved him!'

"I pulled myself together and spoke slowly.

" 'The last word he pronounced was—your name.'

"I heard a light sigh and then my heart stood still, stopped dead short by an exulting and terrible cry, by the cry of incon-

ceivable triumph and of unspeakable pain. 'I knew it—I was sure!'
. . . She knew. She was sure. I heard her weeping; she had hidden her face in her hands. It seemed to me that the house would collapse before I could escape, that the heavens would fall upon my head. But nothing happened. The heavens do not fall for such a trifle. Would they have fallen, I wonder, if I had rendered Kurtz that justice which was his due? Hadn't he said he wanted only justice? But I couldn't. I could not tell her. It would have been too dark—too dark altogether. . . ."

Marlow ceased, and sat apart, indistinct and silent, in the pose of a meditating Buddha. Nobody moved for a time. "We have lost the first of the ebb," said the Director, suddenly. I raised my head. The offing was barred by a black bank of clouds, and the tranquil waterway leading to the uttermost ends of the earth flowed somber under an overcast sky—seemed to lead into the heart of an immense darkness.

F. SCOTT FITZGERALD

Babylon Revisited

"And where's Mr. Campbell?" Charlie asked.

"Gone to Switzerland. Mr. Campbell's a pretty sick man, Mr. Wales."

"I'm sorry to hear that. And George Hardt?" Charlie inquired.

"Back in America, gone to work."

"And where is the Snow Bird?"

"He was in here last week. Anyway, his friend, Mr. Schaeffer, is in Paris."

Two familiar names from the long list of a year and a half ago. Charlie scribbled an address in his notebook and tore out the page.

"If you see Mr. Schaeffer, give him this," he said. "It's my brother-in-law's address. I haven't settled on a hotel yet."

He was not really disappointed to find Paris was so empty. But the stillness in the Ritz bar was strange and portentous. It was not an American bar any more—he felt polite in it, and not as if he owned it. It had gone back into France. He felt the stillness from the moment he got out of the taxi and saw the doorman, usually in a frenzy of activity at this hour, gossiping with a *chasseur* [1] by the servants' entrance.

Passing through the corridor, he heard only a single, bored voice in the once-clamorous women's room. When he turned into the bar he travelled the twenty feet of green carpet with his eyes fixed straight ahead by old habit; and then, with his foot firmly on the rail, he turned and surveyed the room, encountering only a single pair of eyes that fluttered up from a newspaper in the corner. Charlie asked for the head barman, Paul, who in the latter days of the bull market had come to work in his own custom-built car —disembarking, however, with due nicety at the nearest corner. But Paul was at his country house today and Alix giving him information.

"No, no more," Charlie said, "I'm going slow these days."

Alix congratulated him: "You were going pretty strong a couple of years ago."

"I'll stick to it all right," Charlie assured him. "I've stuck to it for over a year and a half now."

"How do you find conditions in America?"

"I haven't been to America for months. I'm in business in Prague, representing a couple of concerns there. They don't know about me down there."

Alix smiled.

"Remember the night of George Hardt's bachelor dinner here?" said Charlie. "By the way, what's become of Claude Fessenden?"

Alix lowered his voice confidentially: "He's in Paris, but he doesn't come here any more. Paul doesn't allow it. He ran up a bill of thirty thousand francs, charging all his drinks and his lunches, and usually his dinner, for more than a year. And when Paul finally told him he had to pay, he gave him a bad check."

Alix shook his head sadly.

[1] *Chasseur.* A hotel employee.

"I don't understand it, such a dandy fellow. Now he's all bloated up—" He made a plump apple of his hands.

Charlie watched a group of strident queens installing themselves in a corner.

"Nothing affects them," he thought. "Stocks rise and fall, people loaf or work, but they go on forever." The place oppressed him. He called for the dice and shook with Alix for the drink.

"Here for long, Mr. Wales?"

"I'm here for four or five days to see my little girl."

"Oh-h! You have a little girl?"

Outside, the fire-red, gas-blue, ghost-green signs shone smokily through the tranquil rain. It was late afternoon and the streets were in movement; the *bistros* [2] gleamed. At the corner of the Boulevard des Capucines he took a taxi. The Place de la Concorde moved by in pink majesty; they crossed the logical Seine, and Charlie felt the sudden provincial quality of the Left Bank.

Charlie directed his taxi to the Avenue de l'Opera, which was out of his way. But he wanted to see the blue hour spread over the magnificent façade, and imagine that the cab horns, playing endlessly the first few bars of *La Plus que Lente*,[3] were the trumpets of the Second Empire. They were closing the iron grill in front of Brentano's Book-store, and people were already at dinner behind the trim little bourgeois hedge of Duval's. He had never eaten at a really cheap restaurant in Paris. Five-course dinner, four francs fifty, eighteen cents, wine included. For some odd reason he wished that he had.

As they rolled on to the Left Bank and he felt its sudden provincialism, he thought, "I spoiled this city for myself. I didn't realize it, but the days came along one after another, and then two years were gone, and everything was gone, and I was gone."

He was thirty-five, and good to look at. The Irish mobility of his face was sobered by a deep wrinkle between his eyes. As he rang his brother-in-law's bell in the Rue Palatine, the wrinkle deepened till it pulled down his brows; he felt a cramping sensation in his belly. From behind the maid who opened the door darted a lovely little girl of nine who shrieked "Daddy!" and flew up, struggling like a fish, into his arms. She pulled his head around

[2] *Bistros.* Cafés.
[3] *La Plus que Lente.* The title of a Debussy piano composition.

by one ear and set her cheek against his.

"My old pie," he said.

"Oh, daddy, daddy, daddy, daddy, dads, dads, dads!"

She drew him into the salon, where the family waited, a boy and girl his daughter's age, his sister-in-law and her husband. He greeted Marion with his voice pitched carefully to avoid either feigned enthusiasm or dislike, but her response was more frankly tepid, though she minimized her expression of unalterable distrust by directing her regard toward his child. The two men clasped hands in a friendly way and Lincoln Peters rested his for a moment on Charlie's shoulder.

The room was warm and comfortably American. The three children moved intimately about, playing through the yellow oblongs that led to other rooms; the cheer of six o'clock spoke in the eager smacks of the fire and the sounds of French activity in the kitchen. But Charlie did not relax; his heart sat up rigidly in his body and he drew confidence from his daughter, who from time to time came close to him, holding in her arms the doll he had brought.

"Really extremely well," he declared in answer to Lincoln's question. "There's a lot of business there that isn't moving at all, but we're doing even better than ever. In fact, damn well. I'm bringing my sister over from America next month to keep house for me. My income last year was bigger than it was when I had money. You see, the Czechs—"

His boasting was for a specific purpose; but after a moment, seeing a faint restiveness in Lincoln's eye, he changed the subject:

"Those are fine children of yours, well brought up, good manners."

"We think Honoria's a great little girl too."

Marion Peters came back from the kitchen. She was a tall woman with worried eyes, who had once possessed a fresh American loveliness. Charlie had never been sensitive to it and was always surprised when people spoke of how pretty she had been. From the first there had been an instinctive antipathy between them.

"Well, how do you find Honoria?" she asked.

"Wonderful. I was astonished how much she's grown in ten

months. All the children are looking well."

"We haven't had a doctor for a year. How do you like being back in Paris?"

"It seems very funny to see so few Americans around."

"I'm delighted," Marion said vehemently. "Now at least you can go into a store without their assuming you're a millionaire. We've suffered like everybody, but on the whole it's a good deal pleasanter."

"But it was nice while it lasted," Charlie said. "We were a sort of royalty, almost infallible, with a sort of magic around us. In the bar this afternoon"—he stumbled, seeing his mistake—"there wasn't a man I knew."

She looked at him keenly. "I should think you'd have had enough of bars."

"I only stayed a minute. I take one drink every afternoon, and no more."

"Don't you want a cocktail before dinner?" Lincoln asked.

"I take only one drink every afternoon, and I've had that."

"I hope you keep to it," said Marion.

Her dislike was evident in the coldness with which she spoke, but Charlie only smiled; he had larger plans. Her very aggressiveness gave him an advantage, and he knew enough to wait. He wanted them to initiate the discussion of what they knew had brought him to Paris.

At dinner he couldn't decide whether Honoria was most like him or her mother. Fortunate if she didn't combine the traits of both that had brought them to disaster. A great wave of protectiveness went over him. He thought he knew what to do for her. He believed in character; he wanted to jump back a whole generation and trust in character again as the eternally valuable element. Everything wore out.

He left soon after dinner, but not to go home. He was curious to see Paris by night with clearer and more judicious eyes than those of other days. He bought a *strapontin* [4] for the Casino and watched Josephine Baker go through her chocolate arabesques.

After an hour he left and strolled toward Montmartre, up the Rue Pigalle into the Place Blanche. The rain had stopped and there

[4] *Strapontin.* Seat.

were a few people in evening clothes disembarking from taxis in front of cabarets, and *cocottes*[5] prowling singly or in pairs, and many Negroes. He passed a lighted door from which issued music, and stopped with the sense of familiarity; it was Bricktop's, where he had parted with so many hours and so much money. A few doors farther on he found another ancient rendezvous and incautiously put his head inside. Immediately an eager orchestra burst into sound, a pair of professional dancers leaped to their feet and a maître d'hôtel swooped toward him, crying, "Crowd just arriving, sir!" But he withdrew quickly.

"You have to be damn drunk," he thought.

Zelli's was closed, the bleak and sinister cheap hotels surrounding it were dark; up in the Rue Blanche there was more light and a local, colloquial French crowd. The Poet's Cave had disappeared, but the two great mouths of the Café of Heaven and the Café of Hell still yawned—even devoured, as he watched, the meagre contents of a tourist bus—a German, a Japanese, and an American couple who glanced at him with frightened eyes.

So much for the effort and ingenuity of Montmartre. All the catering to vice and waste was on an utterly childish scale, and he suddenly realized the meaning of the word "dissipate"—to dissipate into thin air; to make nothing out of something. In the little hours of the night every move from place to place was an enormous human jump, an increase of paying for the privilege of slower and slower motion.

He remembered thousand-franc notes given to an orchestra for playing a single number, hundred-franc notes tossed to a doorman for calling a cab.

But it hadn't been given for nothing.

It had been given, even the most wildly squandered sum, as an offering to destiny that he might not remember the things most worth remembering, the things that now he would always remember—his child taken from his control, his wife escaped to a grave in Vermont.

In the glare of a *brasserie*[6] a woman spoke to him. He bought her some eggs and coffee, and then, eluding her encouraging stare, gave her a twenty-franc note and took a taxi to his hotel.

[5] *Cocottes.* Prostitutes.
[6] *Brasserie.* Restaurant.

II

He woke upon a fine fall day—football weather. The depression of yesterday was gone and he liked the people on the streets. At noon he sat opposite Honoria at Le Grand Vatel, the only restaurant he could think of not reminiscent of champagne dinners and long luncheons that began at two and ended in a blurred and vague twilight.

"Now, how about vegetables? Oughtn't you to have some vegetables?"

"Well, yes."

"Here's *épinards* [7] and *chou-fleur* [8] and carrots and *haricots*." [9]

"I'd like *chou-fleur*."

"Wouldn't you like to have two vegetables?"

"I usually only have one at lunch."

The waiter was pretending to be inordinately fond of children. *"Qu'elle est mignonne la petite! Elle parle exactement comme une française."* [10]

"How about dessert? Shall we wait and see?"

The waiter disappeared. Honoria looked at her father expectantly.

"What are we going to do?"

"First, we're going to that toy store in the Rue Saint-Honoré and buy you anything you like. And then we're going to the vaudeville at the Empire."

She hesitated. "I like it about the vaudeville, but not the toy store."

"Why not?"

"Well, you brought me this doll." She had it with her. "And I've got lots of things. And we're not rich any more, are we?"

"We never were. But today you are to have anything you want."

"All right," she agreed resignedly.

When there had been her mother and a French nurse he had been inclined to be strict; now he extended himself, reached out

[7] *Epinards.* Spinach.
[8] *Chou-fleur.* Cauliflower.
[9] *Haricots.* Beans.
[10] *"Qu'elle est mignonne la petite! Elle parle exactement comme une française."* What a pretty little girl. She talks exactly like a French girl.

for a new tolerance; he must be both parents to her and not shut any of her out of communication.

"I want to get to know you," he said gravely. "First let me introduce myself. My names is Charles J. Wales, of Prague."

"Oh, daddy!" her voice cracked with laughter.

"And who are you, please?" he persisted, and she accepted a rôle immediately: "Honoria Wales, Rue Palatine, Paris."

"Married or single?"

"No, not married. Single."

He indicated the doll. "But I see you have a child, madame."

Unwilling to disinherit it, she took it to her heart and thought quickly: "Yes, I've been married, but I'm not married now. My husband is dead."

He went on quickly, "And the child's name?"

"Simone. That's after my best friend at school."

"I'm very pleased that you're doing so well at school."

"I'm third this month," she boasted. "Elsie"—that was her cousin—"is only about eighteenth, and Richard is about at the bottom."

"You like Richard and Elsie, don't you?"

"Oh, yes. I like Richard quite well and I like her all right."

Cautiously and casually he asked: "And Aunt Marion and Uncle Lincoln—which do you like best?"

"Oh, Uncle Lincoln, I guess."

He was increasingly aware of her presence. As they came in, a murmur of ". . . adorable" followed them, and now the people at the next table bent all their silences upon her, staring as if she were something no more conscious than a flower.

"Why don't I live with you?" she asked suddenly. "Because mamma's dead?"

"You must stay here and learn more French. It would have been hard for daddy to take care of you so well."

"I don't really need much taking care of any more. I do everything for myself."

Going out of the restaurant, a man and a woman unexpectedly hailed him! "Well, the old Wales!"

"Hello there, Lorraine. . . . Dunc."

Sudden ghosts out of the past: Duncan Schaeffer, a friend from college. Lorraine Quarrles, a lovely, pale blonde of thirty; one of a crowd who had helped them make months into days in the lavish times of three years ago.

"My husband couldn't come this year," she said, in answer to his question. "We're poor as hell. So he gave me two hundred a month and told me I could do my worst on that. . . . This your little girl?"

"What about coming back and sitting down?" Duncan asked.

"Can't do it." He was glad for an excuse. As always, he felt Lorraine's passionate, provocative attraction, but his own rhythm was different now.

"Well, how about dinner?" she asked.

"I'm not free. Give me your address and let me call you."

"Charlie, I believe you're sober," she said judicially. "I honestly believe he's sober, Dunc. Pinch him and see if he's sober."

Charlie indicated Honoria with his head. They both laughed.

"What's your address?" said Duncan sceptically.

He hesitated, unwilling to give the name of his hotel.

"I'm not settled yet. I'd better call you. We're going to see the vaudeville at the Empire."

"There! That's what I want to do," Lorraine said. "I want to see some clowns and acrobats and jugglers. That's just what we'll do, Dunc."

"We've got to do an errand first," said Charlie. "Perhaps we'll see you there."

"All right, you snob. . . . Good-by, beautiful little girl."

"Good-by."

Honoria bobbed politely.

Somehow, an unwelcome encounter. They liked him because he was functioning, because he was serious; they wanted to see him, because he was stronger than they were now, because they wanted to draw a certain sustenance from his strength.

At the Empire, Honoria proudly refused to sit upon her father's folded coat. She was already an individual with a code of her own, and Charlie was more and more absorbed by the desire of putting a little of himself into her before she crystallized utterly. It was hopeless to try to know her in so short a time.

Between the acts they came upon Duncan and Lorraine in the lobby where the band was playing.

"Have a drink?"

"All right, but not up at the bar. We'll take a table."

"The perfect father."

Listening abstractedly to Lorraine, Charlie watched Honoria's eyes leave their table, and he followed them wistfully about the room, wondering what they saw. He met her glance and she smiled.

"I liked that lemonade," she said.

What had she said? What had he expected? Going home in a taxi afterward, he pulled her over until her head rested against his chest .

"Darling, do you ever think about your mother?"

"Yes, sometimes," she answered vaguely.

"I don't want you to forget her. Have you got a picture of her?"

"Yes, I think so. Anyhow, Aunt Marion has. Why don't you want me to forget her?"

"She loved you very much."

"I loved her too."

They were silent for a moment.

"Daddy, I want to come and live with you," she said suddenly.

His heart leaped; he had wanted it to come like this.

"Aren't you perfectly happy?"

"Yes, but I love you better than anybody. And you love me better than anybody, don't you, now that mummy's dead?"

"Of course I do. But you won't always like me best, honey. You'll grow up and meet somebody your own age and go marry him and forget you ever had a daddy."

"Yes, that's true," she agreed tranquilly.

He didn't go in. He was coming back at nine o'clock and he wanted to keep himself fresh and new for the thing he must say then.

"When you're safe inside, just show yourself in that window."

"All right. Good-by, dads, dads, dads, dads."

He waited in the dark street until she appeared, all warm and glowing, in the window above and kissed her fingers out into the night.

III

They were waiting, Marion sat behind the coffee service in a dignified black dinner dress that just faintly suggested mourning.

Lincoln was walking up and down with the animation of one who had already been talking. They were as anxious as he was to get into the question. He opened it almost immediately:

"I suppose you know what I want to see you about—why I really came to Paris."

Marion played with the black stars on her necklace and frowned.

"I'm awfully anxious to have a home," he continued. "And I'm awfully anxious to have Honoria in it. I appreciate your taking in Honoria for her mother's sake, but things have changed now" —he hesitated and then continued more forcibly—"changed radically with me, and I want to ask you to reconsider the matter. It would be silly for me to deny that about three years ago I was acting badly—"

Marion looked up at him with hard eyes.

"—but all that's over. As I told you, I haven't had more than a drink a day for over a year, and I take that drink deliberately, so that the idea of alcohol won't get too big in my imagination. You see the idea?"

"No," said Marion succinctly.

"It's a sort of stunt I set myself. It keeps the matter in proportion."

"I get you," said Lincoln. "You don't want to admit it's got any attraction for you."

"Something like that. Sometimes I forget and don't take it. But I try to take it. Anyhow, I couldn't afford to drink in my position. The people I represent are more than satisfied with what I've done, and I'm bringing my sister over from Burlington to keep house for me, and I want awfully to have Honoria too. You know that even when her mother and I weren't getting along well we never let anything that happened touch Honoria. I know she's fond of me and I know I'm able to take care of her and—well, there you are. How do you feel about it?"

He knew that now he would have to take a beating. It would last an hour or two hours, and it would be difficult, but if he modulated his inevitable resentment to the chastened attitude of the reformed sinner, he might win his point in the end.

Keep your temper, he told himself. You don't want to be justified. You want Honoria.

Lincoln spoke first: "We've been talking it over ever since we got your letter last month. We're happy to have Honoria here. She's a dear little thing, and we're glad to be able to help her, but of course that isn't the question—"

Marion interrupted suddenly. "How long are you going to stay sober, Charlie?" she asked.

"Permanently, I hope."

"How can anybody count on that?"

"You know I never did drink heavily until I gave up business and came over here with nothing to do. Then Helen and I began to run around with—"

"Please leave Helen out of it. I can't bear to hear you talk about her like that."

He stared at her grimly; he had never been certain how fond of each other the sisters were in life.

"My drinking only lasted about a year and a half—from the time we came over until I—collapsed."

"It was time enough."

"It was time enough," he agreed.

"My duty is entirely to Helen," she said. "I try to think what she would have wanted me to do. Frankly, from the night you did that terrible thing you haven't really existed for me. I can't help that. She was my sister."

"Yes."

"When she was dying she asked me to look out for Honoria. If you hadn't been in a sanitarium then, it might have helped matters."

He had no answer.

"I'll never in my life be able to forget the morning when Helen knocked at my door, soaked to the skin and shivering, and said you'd locked her out."

Charlie gripped the sides of the chair. This was more difficult than he expected; he wanted to launch out into a long expostulation and explanation, but he only said: "The night I locked her out—" and she interrupted, "I don't feel up to going over that again."

After a moment's silence Lincoln said. "We're getting off the subject. You want Marion to set aside her legal guardianship and give you Honoria. I think the main point for her is whether she has confidence in you or not."

"I don't blame Marion," Charlie said slowly, "but I think she can have entire confidence in me. I had a good record up to three years ago. Of course, it's within human possibilities I might go wrong any time. But if we wait much longer I'll lose Honoria's childhood and my chance for a home." He shook his head, "I'll simply lose her, don't you see?"

"Yes, I see," said Lincoln.

"Why didn't you think of all this before?" Marion asked.

"I suppose I did, from time to time, but Helen and I were getting along badly. When I consented to the guardianship, I was flat on my back in a sanitarium and the market had cleaned me out. I knew I'd acted badly, and I thought if it would bring any peace to Helen, I'd agree to anything. But now it's different. I'm functioning, I'm behaving damn well, so far as—"

"Please don't swear at me," Marion said.

He looked at her, startled. With each remark the force of her dislike became more and more apparent. She had built up all her fear of life into one wall and faced it toward him. This trivial reproof was possibly the result of some trouble with the cook several hours before. Charlie became increasingly alarmed at leaving Honoria in this atmosphere of hostility against himself; sooner or later it would come out, in a word here, a shake of the head there, and some of that distrust would be irrevocably implanted in Honoria. But he pulled his temper down out of his face and shut it up inside him; he had a point, for Lincoln realized the absurdity of Marion's remark and asked her lightly since when she had objected to the word "damn."

"Another thing," Charlie said: "I'm able to give her certain advantages now. I'm going to take a French governess to Prague with me. I've got a lease on a new apartment—"

He stopped, realizing that he was blundering. They couldn't be expected to accept with equanimity the fact that his income was again twice as large as their own.

"I suppose you can give her more luxuries than we can," said Marion. "When you were throwing away money we were living along watching every ten francs. . . . I suppose you'll start doing it again."

"Oh, no," he said. "I've learned. I worked hard for ten years, you know—until I got lucky in the market, like so many people.

Terribly lucky. It didn't seem any use working any more, so I quit. It won't happen again."

There was a long silence. All of them felt their nerves straining, and for the first time in a year Charlie wanted a drink. He was sure now that Lincoln Peters wanted him to have his child.

Marion shuddered suddenly; part of her saw that Charlie's feet were planted on the earth now, and her own maternal feeling recognized the naturalness of his desire; but she had lived for a long time with a prejudice—a prejudice founded on a curious disbelief in her sister's happiness, and which, in the shock of one terrible night, had turned to hatred for him. It had all happened at a point in her life where the discouragement of ill health and adverse circumstances made it necessary for her to believe in tangible villainy and a tangible villain.

"I can't help what I think!" she cried out suddenly. "How much you were responsible for Helen's death, I don't know. It's something you'll have to square with your own conscience."

An electric current of agony surged through him; for a moment he was almost on his feet, an unuttered sound echoing in his throat. He hung on to himself for a moment, another moment.

"Hold on there," said Lincoln uncomfortably. "I never thought you were responsible for that."

"Helen died of heart trouble," Charlie said dully.

"Yes, heart trouble." Marion spoke as if the phrase had another meaning for her.

Then, in the flatness that followed her outburst, she saw him plainly and she knew he had somehow arrived at control over the situation. Glancing at her husband, she found no help from him, and as abruptly as if it were a matter of no importance, she threw up the sponge.

"Do what you like!" she cried, springing up from her chair. "She's your child. I'm not the person to stand in your way. I think if it were my child I'd rather see her—" She managed to check herself. "You two decide it. I can't stand this. I'm sick. I'm going to bed."

She hurried from the room; after a moment Lincoln said:

"This has been a hard day for her. You know how strongly she feels—" His voice was almost apologetic: "When a woman gets an idea in her head."

"Of course."

"It's going to be all right. I think she sees now that you—can provide for the child, and so we can't very well stand in your way or Honoria's way."

"Thank you, Lincoln."

"I'd better go along and see how she is."

"I'm going."

He was still trembling when he reached the street, but a walk down the Rue Bonaparte to the quais set him up, and as he crossed the Seine, fresh and new by the quai lamps, he felt exultant. But back in his room he couldn't sleep. The image of Helen haunted him. Helen whom he had loved so until they had senselessly begun to abuse each other's love, tear it into shreds. On that terrible February night that Marion remembered so vividly, a slow quarrel had gone on for hours. There was a scene at the Florida, and then he attempted to take her home, and then she kissed young Webb at a table; after that there was what she had hysterically said. When he arrived home alone he turned the key in the lock in wild anger. How could he know she would arrive an hour later alone, that there would be a snowstorm in which she wandered about in slippers, too confused to find a taxi? Then the aftermath, her escaping pneumonia by a miracle, and all the attendant horror. They were "reconciled," but that was the beginning of the end, and Marion, who had seen with her own eyes and who imagined it to be one of many scenes from her sister's martyrdom, never forgot.

Going over it again brought Helen nearer, and in the white, soft light that steals upon half sleep near morning he found himself talking to her again. She said that he was perfectly right about Honoria and that she wanted Honoria to be with him. She said she was glad he was being good and doing better. She said a lot of other things—very friendly things—but she was in a swing in a white dress, and swinging faster and faster all the time, so that at the end he could not hear clearly all that she said.

IV

He woke up feeling happy. The door of the world was open again. He made plans, vistas, futures for Honoria and himself, but suddenly he grew sad, remembering all the plans he and Helen had made. She had not planned to die. The present was the thing—work to do and someone to love. But not to love too much, for he knew the injury that a father can do to a daughter or a mother to a son by attaching them too closely: afterward, out in the world, the child would seek in the marriage partner the same blind tenderness and, failing probably to find it, turn against love and life.

It was another bright, crisp day. He called Lincoln Peters at the bank where he worked and asked if he could count on taking Honoria when he left for Prague. Lincoln agreed that there was no reason for delay. One thing—the legal guardianship. Marion wanted to retain that a while longer. She was upset by the whole matter, and it would oil things if she felt that the situation was still in her control for another year. Charlie agreed, wanting only the tangible, visible child.

Then the question of a governess. Charlie sat in a gloomy agency and talked to a cross Bernaise and to a buxom Breton peasant, neither of whom he could have endured. There were others whom he would see tomorrow.

He lunched with Lincoln Peters at Griffons, trying to keep down his exultation.

"There's nothing quite like your own child," Lincoln said. "But you understand how Marion feels too."

"She's forgotten how hard I worked for seven years there," Charlie said. "She just remembers one night."

"There's another thing." Lincoln hesitated. "While you and Helen were tearing around Europe throwing money away, we were just getting along. I didn't touch any of the prosperity because I never got ahead enough to carry anything but my insurance. I think Marion felt there was some kind of injustice in it—you not even working toward the end, and getting richer and richer."

"It went just as quick as it came," said Charlie.

"Yes, a lot of it stayed in the hands of *chasseurs* and saxophone players and maîtres d'hôtel—well, the big party's over now. I just said that to explain Marion's feeling about those crazy years. If you drop in about six o'clock tonight before Marion's too tired, we'll settle the details on the spot."

Back at his hotel, Charlie found a *pneumatique* [11] that had been redirected from the Ritz bar where Charlie had left his address for the purpose of finding a certain man.

DEAR CHARLIE: You were so strange when we saw you the other day that I wondered if I did something to offend you. If so, I'm not conscious of it. In fact, I have thought about you too much for the last year, and it's always been in the back of my mind that I might see you if I came over here. We *did* have such good times that crazy spring, like the night you and I stole the butcher's tricycle, and the time we tried to call on the president and you had the old derby rim and the wire cane. Everybody seems so old lately, but I don't feel old a bit. Couldn't we get together some time today for old time's sake? I've got a vile hangover for the moment, but will be feeling better this afternoon and will look for you about five in the sweatshop at the Ritz.

Always devotedly,

LORRAINE.

His first feeling was one of awe that he had actually, in his mature years, stolen a tricycle and pedalled Lorraine all over the Étoile between the small hours and dawn. In retrospect it was a nightmare. Locking out Helen didn't fit in with any other act of his life, but the tricycle incident did—it was one of many. How many weeks or months of dissipation to arrive at that condition of utter irresponsibility?

He tried to picture how Lorraine had appeared to him then— very attractive; Helen was unhappy about it, though she said nothing. Yesterday, in the restaurant, Lorraine had seemed trite, blurred, worn away. He emphatically did not want to see her, and he was glad Alix had not given away his hotel address. It was a relief to think, instead, of Honoria, to think of Sundays spent with her and saying good morning to her and knowing she was there in his house at night, drawing her breath in the darkness.

At five he took a taxi and bought presents for all the Peters— a piquant cloth doll, a box of Roman soldiers, flowers for Marion, big linen handkerchiefs for Lincoln.

He saw, when he arrived in the apartment, that Marion had accepted the inevitable. She greeted him now as though he were a recalcitrant member of the family rather than a menacing out-

[11] *Pneumatique.* Express letter.

sider. Honoria had been told she was going; Charlie was glad to see that her tact made her conceal her excessive happiness. Only on his lap did she whisper her delight and the question "When?" before she slipped away with the other children.

He and Marion were alone for a minute in the room, and on a impulse he spoke out boldly:

"Family quarrels are bitter things. They don't go according to any rules. They're not like aches or wounds; they're more like splits in the skin that won't heal because there's not enough material. I wish you and I could be on better terms."

"Some things are hard to forget," she answered. "It's a question of confidence." There was no answer to this and presently she asked, "When do you propose to take her?"

"As soon as I can get a governess. I hoped the day after tomorrow."

"That's impossible. I've got to get her things in shape. Not before Saturday."

He yielded. Coming back into the room, Lincoln offered him a drink.

"I'll take my daily whisky," he said.

It was warm here, it was a home, people together by a fire. The children felt very safe and important; the mother and father were serious, watchful. They had things to do for the children more important than his visit here. A spoonful of medicine was, after all, more important than the strained relations between Marion and himself. They were not dull people, but they were very much in the grip of life and circumstances. He wondered if he couldn't do something to get Lincoln out of his rut at the bank.

A long peal at the door-bell; the *bonne à toute faire* [12] passed through and went down the corridor. The door opened upon another long ring, and then voices, and the three in the salon looked up expectantly; Richard moved to bring the corridor within his range of vision, and Marion rose. Then the maid came back along the corridor, closely followed by the voices, which developed under the light into Duncan Schaeffer and Lorraine Quarrles.

They were gay, they were hilarious, they were roaring with laughter. For a moment Charlie was astounded; unable to understand how they ferreted out the Peters' address.

[12] *Bonne à toute faire.* Maid.

"Ah-h-h!" Duncan wagged his finger roguishly at Charlie. "Ah-h-h!"

They both slid down another cascade of laughter. Anxious and at a loss, Charlie shook hands with them quickly and presented them to Lincoln and Marion. Marion nodded, scarcely speaking. She had drawn back a step toward the fire; her little girl stood beside her, and Marion put an arm about her shoulder.

With growing annoyance at the intrusion, Charlie waited for them to explain themselves. After some concentration Duncan said:

"We came to invite you out to dinner. Lorraine and I insist that all this shishi, cagy business 'bout your address got to stop."

Charlie came closer to them, as if to force them backward down the corridor.

"Sorry, but I can't. Tell me where you'll be and I'll phone you in half an hour."

This made no impression. Lorraine sat down suddenly on the side of a chair, and focusing her eyes on Richard, cried, "Oh, what a nice little boy! Come here, little boy." Richard glanced at his mother, but did not move. With a perceptible shrug of her shoulders, Lorraine turned back to Charlie:

"Come and dine. Sure your cousins won' mine. See you so sel'om. Or solemn."

"I can't," said Charlie sharply. "You two have dinner and I'll phone you."

Her voice became suddenly unpleasant. "All right, we'll go. But I remember once when you hammered on my door at four A.M. I was enough of a good sport to give you a drink. Come on, Dunc."

Still in slow motion, with blurred, angry faces, with uncertain feet, they retired along the corridor.

"Good night," Charlie said.

"Good night!" responded Lorraine emphatically.

When he went back into the salon Marion had not moved, only now her son was standing in the circle of her other arm. Lincoln was still swinging Honoria back and forth like a pendulum from side to side.

"What an outrage!" Charlie broke out. "What an absolute outrage!"

Neither of them answered. Charlie dropped into an armchair, picked up his drink, set it down again and said:

"People I haven't seen for two years having the colossal nerve—"

He broke off. Marion had made the sound "Oh!" in one swift, furious breath, turned her body from him with a jerk and left the room.

Lincoln set down Honoria carefully.

"You children go in and start your soup," he said, and when they obeyed, he said to Charlie:

"Marion's not well and she can't stand shocks. That kind of people make her really physically sick."

"I didn't tell them to come here. They wormed your name out of somebody. They deliberately—"

"Well, it's too bad. It doesn't help matters. Excuse me a minute."

Left alone, Charlie sat tense in his chair. In the next room he could hear the children eating, talking in monosyllables, already oblivious to the scene between their elders. He heard a murmur of conversation from a farther room and then the ticking bell of a telephone receiver picked up, and in a panic he moved to the other side of the room and out of earshot.

In a minute Lincoln came back. "Look here, Charlie. I think we'd better call off dinner for tonight. Marion's in bad shape."

"Is she angry with me?"

"Sort of," he said, almost roughly. "She's not strong and—"

"You mean she's changed her mind about Honoria?"

"She's pretty bitter right now. I don't know. You phone me at the bank tomorrow."

"I wish you'd explain to her I never dreamed these people would come here. I'm just as sore as you are."

"I couldn't explain anything to her now."

Charlie got up. He took his coat and hat and started down the corridor. Then he opened the door of the dining room and said in a strange voice, "Good night, children."

Honoria rose and ran around the table to hug him.

"Good night, sweetheart," he said vaguely, and then trying to make his voice more tender, trying to conciliate something, "Good night, dear children."

●

V

Charlie went directly to the Ritz bar with the furious idea of finding Lorraine and Duncan, but they were not there, and he realized that in any case there was nothing he could do. He had not touched his drink at the Peters', and now he ordered a whisky-and-soda. Paul came over to say hello.

"It's a great change," he said sadly. "We do about half the business we did. So many fellows I hear about back in the States lost everything, maybe not in the first crash, but then in the second. Your friend George Hardt lost every cent, I hear. Are you back in the States?"

"No. I'm in business in Prague."

"I heard that you lost a lot in the crash."

"I did," and he added grimly, "but I lost everything I wanted in the boom."

"Selling short."

"Something like that."

Again the memory of those days swept over him like a nightmare—the people they had met traveling; then people who couldn't add a row of figures or speak a coherent sentence. The little man Helen had consented to dance with at the ship's party, who had insulted her ten feet from the table; the women and girls carried screaming with drink or drugs out of public places—

—The men who locked their wives out in the snow, because the snow of twenty-nine wasn't real snow. If you didn't want it to be snow, you just paid some money.

He went to the phone and called the Peters' apartment; Lincoln answered.

"I called up because this thing is on my mind. Has Marion said anything definite?"

"Marion's sick," Lincoln answered shortly. "I know this thing isn't altogether your fault, but I can't have her go to pieces about it. I'm afraid we'll have to let it slide for six months; I can't take the chance of working her up to this state again."

"I see."

"I'm sorry, Charlie."

He went back to his table. His whisky glass was empty, but he shook his head when Alix looked at it questioningly. There wasn't much he could do now except send Honoria some things; he would send her a lot of things tomorrow. He thought rather angrily that this was just money—he had given so many people money. . . .

"No, no more," he said to another waiter. "What do I owe you?"

He would come back some day; they couldn't make him pay forever. But he wanted his child, and nothing was much good now, beside that fact. He wasn't young any more, with a lot of nice thoughts and dreams to have by himself. He was absolutely sure Helen wouldn't have wanted him to be so alone.

MARY McCARTHY

Artists in Uniform

> The Colonel went out sailing,
> He spoke with Turk and Jew . . .

"Pour it on Colonel," cried the young man in the Dacron suit excitedly, making his first sortie into the club-car conversation. His face was white as Roquefort and of a glistening, cheese-like texture; he had a shock of tow-colored hair, badly cut and greasy, and a snub nose with large gray pores. Under his darting eyes were two black craters. He appeared to be under some intense nervous strain and had sat the night before in the club car drinking bourbon with beer chasers and leafing magazines which he frowningly tossed aside, like cards into a discard heap. This morning he had come in late, with a hangdog, hangover look, and had been sitting tensely forward on a settee, smoking cigarettes and following the conversation with little twitches of the nose and quivers of the body, as a dog follows a human conversation, veering its mistrustful eyeballs from one speaker to another and raising its head eagerly at its master's voice. The Colonel's voice, rich and light and plausible, had in fact abruptly risen and swollen, as he pronounced his last sentence. "I can tell you one thing," he said harshly. "They weren't named Ryan or Murphy!"

A sort of sigh, as of consummation, ran through the club car. "Pour it on, Colonel, give it to them, Colonel, that's right, Colonel," urged the young man in a transport of admiration. The Colonel fingered his collar and modestly smiled. He was a thin, hawklike, black-haired handsome man with a bright blue bloodshot eye and a well-pressed, well-tailored uniform that did not show the effects of the heat—the train, westbound for St. Louis, was passing through Indiana, and, as usual in a heat-wave, the air-conditioning had not met the test. He wore the Air Force insignia, and there was something in his light-boned, spruce figure and keen, knifelike profile that suggested a classic image of the aviator, ready to cut, piercing, into space. In base fact, however, the Colonel was in procurement, as we heard him tell the mining engineer who had just bought him a drink. From several silken hints that parachuted into the talk, it was patent to us that the Colonel was a man who knew how to enjoy this earth and its pleasures: he led, he gave us to think, a bachelor's life of abstemious dissipation and well-rounded sensuality. He had accepted the engineer's drink with a mere nod of the glass in acknowledgment, like a genial Mars quaffing a libation; there was clearly no prospect of his buying a second in return, not if the train were to travel from here to the Mojave Desert. In the same way, an understanding had arisen that I, the only woman in the club car, had become the Colonel's perquisite; it was taken for granted, without an invitation's being issued, that I was to lunch with him in St. Louis, where we each had a wait between trains—my plans for seeing the city in a taxicab were dished.

From the beginning, as we eyed each other over my volume of Dickens ("*The Christmas Carol?*" suggested the Colonel, opening relations), I had guessed that the Colonel was of Irish stock, and this, I felt, gave me an advantage, for he did not suspect the same of me; strangely so, for I am supposed to have the map of Ireland written on my features. In fact, he had just wagered, with a jaunty, sidelong grin at the mining engineer, that my people "came from Boston from way back," and that I—narrowed glance, running, like steel measuring-tape, up and down my form—was a professional sculptress. I might have laughed this off, as a crudely bad guess like his *Christmas Carol*, if I had not seen the engineer nodding gravely, like an idol, and the peculiar young man bobbing his head up and down in mute applause and agreement. I was wearing a bright apple-green raw silk blouse and a dark-green rather full raw silk skirt, plus a pair of pink glass earrings; my hair was done up in a bun. It came to me, for the first time, with a sort of dawning horror, that I had begun, in the course of years, without ever guessing it, to look irrevocably Bohemian. Refracted from the three men's eyes was a strange vision of myself as an artist, through and through, stained with my occupation like the dyer's hand. All I lacked, apparently, was a pair of sandals. My sick heart sank to my Ferragamo shoes; I had always particularly preened myself on being an artist in disguise. And it was not only a question of personal vanity—it seemed to me that the writer or intellectual had a certain missionary usefulness in just such accidental gatherings as this, if he spoke not as an intellectual but as a normal member of the public. Now, thanks to the Colonel, I slowly became aware that my contributions to the club-car conversation were being watched and assessed as coming from *a certain quarter*. My costume, it seemed, carefully assembled as it had been at an expensive shop, was to these observers simply a uniform that blazoned a caste and allegiance just as plainly as the Colonel's khaki and eagles. "*Gardez*," I said to myself. But, as the conversation grew tenser and I endeavored to keep cool, I began to writhe within myself, and every time I looked down, my contrasting greens seemed to be growing more and more lurid and taking on an almost menacing light, like leaves just before a storm that lift their bright undersides as the air becomes darker. We had been speaking, of course, of Russia, and I had mentioned a study that had been made at Harvard of political attitudes among Iron Curtain refugees. Suddenly, the Colonel had smiled. "They're pretty Red at Harvard, I'm given to understand," he observed in a comfortable tone, while the young man twitched and quivered urgently. The eyes of all the men settled on me and waited. I flushed as I saw myself reflected. The wood-land greens of my dress were turning to their complementary red, like a color-experiment in psychology or a traffic light changing. Down at the other end of the club car, a man looked up from his paper. I pulled myself together. "Set your mind at rest, Colonel," I remarked dryly. "I know Harvard very well and they're conservative to the point of dullness. The only thing crimson is the football team." This disparagement had its effect. "So . . . ?" queried the Colonel. "I thought there was some pro-fessor. . . ." I shook my head. "Absolutely not. There used to be a few fellow-travelers, but they're very quiet these days, when they haven't absolutely recanted. The general atmosphere is more anti-Communist than the Vatican." The Colonel and the mining engineer exchanged a thoughtful stare and seemed to agree that the Delphic oracle that had just pronounced knew whereof it spoke. "Glad to hear it," said the Colonel. The engineer frowned and shook his fat wattles; he was a stately, gray-haired, plump man with small hands and feet and the pampered, finical tidiness of a small-town widow. "There's so much hearsay these days," he exclaimed vexedly. "You don't know *what* to believe."

I reopened my book with an air of having closed the subject and read a paragraph three times over. I exulted to think that I had made a modest contribution to sanity in our times, and I imag-ined my words pyramiding like a chain letter—the Colonel tell-ing a fellow-officer on the veranda of a club in Texas, the engi-neer halting a works-superintendent in a Colorado mine shaft: "I met a woman on the train who claims . . . Yes, absolutely. . . ." Of course, I did not know Harvard as thoroughly as I pretended, but I forgave myself by thinking it was the convention of such club-car symposia in our positivistic country to speak from the horse's mouth.

Meanwhile, across the aisle, the engineer and the Colonel con-tinued their talk in slightly lowered voices. From time to time, the Colonel's polished index-fingernail scratched his burnished black head and his knowing blue eye forayed occasionally toward me. I saw that still I was a doubtful quantity to them, a move-ment in the bushes, a noise, a flicker, that was figuring in their crenelated thought as "she." The subject of Reds in our colleges had not, alas, been finished; they were speaking now of another university and a woman faculty-member who had been issuing

Communist statements. This story somehow, I thought angrily, had managed to appear in the newspapers without my knowledge, while these men were conversant with it; I recognized a big chink in the armor of my authority. Looking up from my book, I began to question them sharply, as though they were reporting some unheard-of natural phenomenon. "When?" I demanded. "Where did you see it? What was her name?" This request for the professor's name was a headlong attempt on my part to buttress my position, the implication being that the identities of all university professors were known to me and that if I were but given the name I could promptly clarify the matter. To admit that there was a single Communist in our academic system whose activities were hidden from me imperiled, I instinctively felt, all the small good I had done here. Moreover, in the back of my mind, I had a supreme confidence that these men were wrong: the story, I supposed, was some tattered piece of misinformation they had picked up from a gossip column. Pride, as usual, preceded my fall. To the Colonel, the demand for the name was not specific but generic: what *kind* of name was the question he presumed me to be asking. "Oh," he said slowly with a luxurious yawn, "Finkelstein or Fishbein or Feinstein." He lolled back in his seat with a side glance at the engineer, who deeply nodded. There was a voluptuary pause, as the implication sank in. I bit my lip, regarding this as a mere diversionary tactic. "Please!" I said impatiently. "Can't you remember exactly?" The Colonel shook his head and then his spare cheekbones suddenly reddened and he looked directly at me. "I can tell you one thing," he exclaimed irefully. "They weren't named Ryan or Murphy."

The Colonel went no further; it was quite unnecessary. In an instant, the young man was at his side, yapping excitedly and actually picking at the military sleeve. The poor thing was transformed, like some creature in a fairy tale whom a magic word releases from silence. "That's right, Colonel," he happily repeated. "I know them. *I* was at Harvard in the business school, studying accountancy. I left. I couldn't take it." He threw a poisonous glance at me, and the Colonel, who had been regarding him somewhat doubtfully, now put on an alert expression and inclined an ear for his confidences. The man at the other end of the car folded his newspaper solemnly and took a seat by the young man's side. "They're all Reds, Colonel," said the young man.

"They teach it in the classroom. I came back here to Missouri. It made me sick to listen to the stuff they handed out. If you didn't hand it back, they flunked you. Don't let anybody tell you different." "You are wrong," I said coldly and closed my book and rose. The young man was still talking eagerly, and the three men were leaning forward to catch his every gasping word, like three astute detectives over a dying informer, when I reached the door and cast a last look over my shoulder at them. For an instant, the Colonel's eye met mine, and I felt his scrutiny processing my green back as I tugged open the door and met a blast of hot air, blowing my full skirt wide. Behind me, in my fancy, I saw four sets of shrugging brows.

In my own car, I sat down, opposite two fat nuns, and tried to assemble my thoughts. I ought to have spoken, I felt, and yet what could I have said? It occurred to me that the four men had perhaps not realized why I had left the club car with such abruptness: was it possible that they thought I was a Communist, who feared to be unmasked? I spurned this possibility, and yet it made me uneasy. For some reason, it troubled my *amour-propre* to think of my anti-Communist self living on, so to speak, green in their collective memory as a Communist or fellow-traveler. In fact, though I did not give a fig for the men, I hated the idea, while a few years ago I should have counted it a great joke. This, it seemed to me, was a measure of the change in the social climate. I had always scoffed at the notion of liberals "living in fear" of political demagoguery in America, but now I had to admit that if I was not fearful, I was at least uncomfortable in the supposition that anybody, anybody whatever, could think of me, precious me, as a Communist. A remoter possibility was, of course, that back there my departure was being ascribed to Jewishness, and this too annoyed me. I am in fact a quarter Jewish, and though I did not "hate" the idea of being taken for a Jew, I did not precisely like it, particularly under these circumstances. I wished it to be clear that I had left the club car for intellectual and principled reasons; I wanted those men to know that it was not I, but my principles, that had been offended. To let them conjecture that I had left because I was Jewish would imply that only a Jew could be affronted by an anti-Semitic outburst: a terrible idea. Aside from anything else, it voided the whole concept of transcendence, which was very close to my heart, the concept that man is more than his circumstances, more even than himself.

However you looked at the episode, I said to myself nervously, I had not acquitted myself well. I ought to have done or said something concrete and unmistakable. From this, I slid glassily to the thought that those men ought to be punished, the Colonel, in particular, who occupied a responsible position. In a minute, I was framing a businesslike letter to the Chief of Staff, deploring the Colonel's conduct as unbecoming to an officer and identifying him by rank and post, since unfortunately I did not know his name. Earlier in the conversation, he had passed some comments on "Harry" that bordered positively on treason, I said to myself triumphantly. A vivid image of the proceedings against him presented itself to my imagination: the long military tribunal with a row of stern soldierly faces glaring down at the Colonel. I myself occupied only an inconspicuous corner of this tableau, for, to tell the truth, I did not relish the role of the witness. Perhaps it would be wiser to let the matter drop . . . ? We were nearing St. Louis now; the Colonel had come back into my car, and the young accountant had followed him, still talking feverishly. I pretended not to see them and turned to the two nuns, as if for sanctuary from this world and its hatreds and revenges. Out of the corner of my eye, I watched the Colonel, who now looked wry and restless; he shrank against the window as the young man made a place for himself amid the Colonel's smart luggage and continued to express his views in a pale breathless voice. I smiled to think that the Colonel was paying the piper. For the Colonel, anit-Semitism was simply an aspect of urbanity, like a knowledge of hotels or women. This frantic psychopath of an accountant was serving him as a nemesis, just as the German people had been served by their psychopath, Hitler. Colonel, I adjured him, you have chosen, between him and me; measure the depth of your error and make the best of it! No intervention on my part was now necessary; justice had been meted out. Nevertheless, my heart was still throbbing violently, as if I were on the verge of some dangerous action. What was I to do, I kept asking myself, as I chatted with the nuns, if the Colonel were to hold me to that lunch? And I slowly and apprehensively revolved this question, just as though it were a matter of the most serious import. It seemed to me that if I did not lunch with him— and I had no intention of doing so—I had the dreadful obligation of telling him why.

He was waiting for me as I descended the car steps. "Aren't you coming to lunch with me?" he called out and moved up to take my elbow. I began to tremble with audacity. "No," I said firmly, picking up my suitcase and draping an olive-green linen duster over my arm. "I can't lunch with you." He quirked a wiry black eyebrow. "Why not?" he said. "I understood it was all arranged." He reached for my suitcase. "No," I said, holding on to the suitcase. "I can't." I took a deep breath. "I have to tell you. I think you should be *ashamed* of yourself, Colonel, for what you said in the club car." The Colonel stared; I mechanically waved for a red-cap, who took my bag and coat and went off. The Colonel and I stood facing each other on the emptying platform. "What do you mean?" he inquired in a low, almost clandestine tone. "Those anti-Semitic remarks," I muttered, resolutely. "You ought to be *ashamed*." The Colonel gave a quick, relieved laugh. "Oh, come now," he protested. "I'm sorry," I said. "I can't have lunch with anybody who feels that way about the Jews." The Colonel put down his attaché case and scratched the back of his lean neck. "Oh, come now," he repeated, with a look of amusement. "You're not Jewish, are you?" "No," I said quickly. "Well, then . . ." said the Colonel, spreading his hands in a gesture of bafflement. I saw that he was truly surprised and slightly hurt by my criticism, and this made me feel wretchedly embarrassed and even apologetic, on my side, as though I had called attention to some physical defect in him, of which he himself was unconscious. "But I might have been," I stammered. "You had no way of knowing. You oughtn't to talk like that." I recognized, too late, that I was strangely reducing the whole matter to a question of etiquette: "Don't start anti-Semitic talk before making sure there are no Jews present." "Oh, hell," said the Colonel, easily. "I can tell a Jew." "No, you can't," I retorted, thinking of my Jewish grandmother, for by Nazi criteria I was Jewish. "Of course I can," he insisted. "So can you." We had begun to walk down the platform side by side, disputing with a restrained passion that isolated us like a pair of lovers. All at once, the Colonel halted, as though struck with a thought. "What *are* you, anyway?" he said meditatively, regarding my dark hair, green blouse, and pink earrings. Inside myself, I began to laugh. "Oh," I said gaily, playing out the trump I had been saving, "I'm Irish, like you, Colonel." "How did you know?" he said amazedly. I laughed aloud. "I can tell an Irishman," I taunted. The Colonel frowned. "What's your family name?" he said brusquely. "Mc-Carthy." He lifted an eyebrow, in defeat, and then quickly took note of my wedding ring. "That your maiden name?" I nodded. Under this peremptory questioning, I had the peculiar sensation that I get when I am lying; I began to feel that "McCarthy" was a nom de plume, a coinage of my artistic personality. But the Colo-nel appeared to be satisfied. "Hell," he said, "come on to lunch, then. With a fine name like that, you and I should be friends." I still shook my head, though by this time we were pacing outside the station restaurant; my baggage had been checked in a locker; sweat was running down my face and I felt exhausted and hun-gry. I knew that I was weakening and I wanted only an excuse to yield and go inside with him. The Colonel seemed to sense this. "Hell," he conceded. "You've got me wrong. I've got nothing against the Jews. Back there in the club car, I was just stating a simple fact: you won't find an Irishman sounding off for the Commies. You can't deny that, can you?"

His voice rose persuasively; he took my arm. In the heat, I wilted and we went into the air-conditioned cocktail lounge. The Colonel ordered two old-fashioneds. The room was dark as a cave and produced, in the midst of the hot midday, a hallucinated feel-ing, as though time had ceased, with the weather, and we were in eternity together. As the Colonel prepared to relax, I made a tre-mendous effort to guide the conversation along rational, purpos-ive lines; my only justification for being here would be to con-vert the Colonel. "There *have* been Irishmen associated with the Communist party," I said suddenly, when the drinks came. "I can think of two." "Oh, hell," said the Colonel, "every race and na-tion has its traitors. What I mean is, you won't find them in num-bers. You've got to admit that the Communists in this country are 90 per cent Jewish." "But the Jews in this country aren't 90 per cent Communist," I retorted.

As he stirred his drink, restively, I began to try to show him the reasons why the Communist movement in America had at-tracted such a large number, relatively, of Jews: how the Com-munists had been anti-Nazi when nobody else seemed to care what happened to the Jews in Germany; how the Communists still capitalized on a Jewish fear of fascism; how many Jews had become, after Buchenwald, traumatized by this fear. . . .

But the Colonel was scarcely listening. An impatient frown rested on his jaunty features. "I don't get it," he said slowly. "Why should you be for them, with a name like yours?" "I'm *not* for the Communists," I cried. "I'm just trying to explain to you—" "For the Jews," the Colonel interrupted, irritable now himself. "I've heard of such people but I never met one before." "I'm not 'for' them," I protested. "You don't understand. I'm not for *any* race or nation. I'm against those who are against them." This word, *them*, with a sort of slurring circle drawn round it, was beginning to sound ugly to me. Automatically, in arguing with him, I seemed to have slipped into the Colonel's style of thought. It occurred to me that defense of the Jews could be a subtle and safe form of anti-Semitism, an exercise of patronage: as a rational Gentile, one could feel superior both to the Jews and the anti-Semites. There could be no doubt that the Jewish question evoked a curious stealthy lust or concupiscence. I could feel it now vibrating between us over the dark table. If I had been a good person, I should unquestionably have got up and left.

"I don't get it," repeated the Colonel. "How were you brought up? Were your people this way too?" It was manifest that an odd reversal had taken place; each of us regarded the other as "abnormal" and was attempting to understand the etiology of a disease. "Many of my people think just as you do," I said, smiling coldly. "It seems to be a sickness to which the Irish are prone. Perhaps it's due to the potato diet," I said sweetly, having divined that the Colonel came from a social stratum somewhat lower than my own.

But the Colonel's hide was tough. "You've got me wrong," he reiterated, with an almost plaintive laugh. "I don't dislike the Jews. I've got a lot of Jewish friends. Among themselves, they think just as I do, mark my words. I tell you what it is," he added ruminatively, with a thoughtful prod of his muddler, "I draw a distinction between a kike and a Jew." I groaned. "Colonel, I've never heard an anti-Semite who didn't draw that distinction. You know what Otto Kahn said? 'A kike is a Jewish gentleman who has just left the room.'" Tht Colonel did not laugh. "I don't hold it against some of them," he persisted, in a tone of pensive justice. "It's not their fault if they were born that way. That's what I tell them, and they respect me for my honesty. I've had a lot of discussions; in procurement, you have to do business with them, and the Jews are the first to admit that you'll find more chiselers among their race than among the rest of mankind." "It's not a race," I interjected wearily, but the Colonel pressed on. "If I deal with a Jewish manufacturer, I can't bank on his word. I've seen it again and again, every damned time. When I deal with a Gentile, I can trust him to make delivery as promised. That's the difference between the two races. They're just a different breed. They don't have standards of honesty, even among each other." I sighed, feeling unequal to arguing the Colonel's personal experience.

"Look," I said, "you may be dealing with an industry where the Jewish manufacturers are the most recent comers and feel they have to cut corners to compete with the established firms. I've heard that said about Jewish cattle-dealers, who are supposed to be extra sharp. But what I think, really, is that you notice it when a Jewish firm fails to meet an agreement and don't notice it when it's a Yankee." "Hah," said the Colonel. "They'll tell you what I'm telling you themselves, if you get to know them and go into their homes. You won't believe it, but some of my best friends are Jews," he said, simply and thoughtfully, with an air of originality. "They may be *your* best friends, Colonel," I retorted, "but you are not theirs. I defy you to tell me that you talk to them as you're talking now." "Sure," said the Colonel, easily. "More or less." "They must be very queer Jews you know," I observed tartly, and I began to wonder whether there indeed existed a peculiar class of Jews whose function in life was to be "friends" with such people as the Colonel. It was difficult to think that all the anti-Semites who made the Colonel's assertion were the victims of a cruel self-deception.

A dispirited silence followed. I was not one of those liberals who believed that the Jews, alone among peoples, possessed no characteristics whatever of a distinguishing nature—this would mean they had no history and no culture, a charge which should be leveled against them only by an anti-Semite. Certainly, types of Jews could be noted and patterns of Jewish thought and feeling: Jewish humor, Jewish rationality, and so on, not that every Jew reflected every attribute of Jewish life or history. But somehow, with the Colonel, I dared not concede that there was such a thing as a Jew: I saw the sad meaning of the assertion that a Jew was a person whom other people thought was Jewish.

Hopeless, however, to convey this to the Colonel. The desolate truth was that the Colonel was extremely stupid, and it came to me, as we sat there, glumly ordering lunch, that for extremely stupid people anti-Semitism was a form of intellectuality, the sole form of intellectuality of which they were capable. It represented, in a rudimentary way, the ability to make categories, to generalize. Hence a thing I had noted before but never understood: the fact that anti-Semitic statements were generally delivered in an atmosphere of profundity. Furrowed brows attended these speculative distinctions between a kike and a Jew, these little empirical laws that you can't know one without knowing them all. To arrive, indeed, at the idea of a Jew was, for these grouping minds, an exercise in Platonic thought, a discovery of essence, and to be able to add the great corollary, "Some of my best friends are Jews," was to find the philosopher's cleft between essence and existence. From this, it would seem, followed the querulous obstinacy with which the anti-Semite clung to his concept; to be deprived of this intellectual tool by missionaries of tolerance would be, for persons like the Colonel, the equivalent of Western man's losing the syllogism: a lapse into animal darkness. In the club car, we had just witnessed an example: the Colonel with his anti-Semitic observation had come to the mute young man like the paraclete, bearing the gift of tongues.

Here in the bar, it grew plainer and plainer that the Colonel did not regard himself as an anti-Semite but merely as a heavy thinker. The idea that I considered him anti-Semitic sincerely outraged his feelings. "Prejudice" was the last trait he could have imputed to himself. He looked on me, almost respectfully, as a "Jew lover," a kind of being he had heard of but never actually encountered, like a centaur or a Siamese twin, and the interest of relating this prodigy to the natural state of mankind overrode any personal distaste. There I sat, the exception which was "proving" or testing the rule, and he kept pressing me for details of my history that might explain my deviation in terms of the norm. On my side, of course, I had become fiercely resolved that he would learn nothing from me that would make it possible for him to dismiss my anti-anti-Semitism as the product of special circumstances: I was stubbornly sitting on the fact of my Jewish grandmother like a hen on a golden egg. I was bent on making *him* see himself as a monster, a deviation, a heretic from Church and State. Unfortunately, the Colonel, owing perhaps to his military training, had not the glimmering of an idea of what democracy meant; to him, it was simply a slogan that was sometimes useful in war. The notion of an ordained inequality was to him "scientific."

"Honestly," he was saying in lowered tones, as our drinks were taken away and the waitress set down my sandwich and his corned-beef hash, "don't you, brought up the way you were, feel about them the way I do? Just between ourselves, isn't there a sort of inborn feeling of horror that the very word, Jew, suggests?" I shook my head, roundly. The idea of an *innate* anti-Semitism was in keeping with the rest of the Colonel's thought, yet it shocked me more than anything he had yet said. "No," I sharply replied. "It doesn't evoke any feeling one way or the other." "Honest Injun?" said the Colonel. "Think back; when you were a kid, didn't the word, Jew, make you feel sick?" There was a dreadful sincerity about this that made me answer in an almost kindly tone. "No, truthfully, I assure you. When we were children, we learned to call the old-clothes man a sheeny, but that was just a dirty word to us, like 'Hun' that we used to call after workmen we thought were Germans."

"I don't get it," pondered the Colonel, eating a pickle. "There must be something wrong with you. Everybody is born with that feeling. It's natural; it's part of nature." "On the contrary," I said. "It's something very unnatural that you must have been taught as a child." "It's not something you're *taught*," he protested. "You must have been," I said. "You simply don't remember it. In any case, you're a man now; you must rid yourself of that feeling. It's psychopathic, like that horrible young man on the train." "You thought he was crazy?" mused the Colonel, in an idle, dreamy tone. I shrugged my shoulders. "Of course. Think of his color. He was probably just out of a mental institution. People don't get that tattletale gray except in prison or mental hospitals." The Colonel suddenly grinned. "You might be right," he said. "He was quite a case." He chuckled.

I leaned forward. "You know, Colonel," I said quickly, "anti-Semitism is contrary to the Church's teaching. God will make you do penance for hating the Jews. Ask your priest; he'll tell you I'm right. You'll have a long spell in Purgatory, if you don't rid yourself of this sin. It's a deliberate violation of Christ's commandment, 'Love thy neighbor.' The Church holds that the Jews have a sacred place in God's design. Mary was a Jew and Christ was a Jew. The Jews are under God's special protection. The Church teaches that the millennium can't come until the conversion of the Jews; therefore, the Jews must be preserved that the Divine Will may be accomplished. Woe to them that harm them, for they controvert God's Will!" In the course of speaking, I had swept myself away with the solemnity of the doctrine. The Great Reconciliation between God and His chosen people, as envisioned by the Evangelist, had for me at that moment a piercing, majestic beauty, like some awesome Tintoretto. I saw a noble spectacle of blue sky, thronged with gray clouds, and a vast white desert, across which God and Israel advanced to meet each other, while below in hell the demons of disunion shrieked and gnashed their teeth.

"Hell," said the Colonel, jovially. "I don't believe in all that. I lost my faith when I was a kid. I saw that all this God stuff was a lot of bushwa." I gazed at him in stupefaction. His confidence had completely returned. The blue eyes glittered debonairly; the eagles glittered; the narrow polished head cocked and listened to itself like a trilling bird. I was up against an air man with a bird's-eye view, a man who believed in nothing but the law of kind: the epitome of godless materialism. "You still don't hold with that bunk?" the Colonel inquired in an undertone, with an expression of stealthy curiosity. "No," I confessed, sad to admit to a meeting of minds. "You know what got me?" exclaimed the Colonel. "That birth-control stuff. Didn't it kill you?" I made a neutral sound. "I was beginning to play around," said the Colonel, with a significant beam of the eye, "and I just couldn't take that guff. When I saw through the birth-control talk, I saw through the whole thing. They claimed it was against nature, but I claim, if that's so, an operation's against nature. I told my old man that when he was having his kidney stones out. You ought to have heard him yell!" A rich, reminiscent satisfaction dwelt in the Colonel's face.

This period of his life, in which he had thrown off the claims of the spiritual and adopted a practical approach, was evidently one of those "turning points" to which a man looks back with pride. He lingered over the story of his break with church and parents with a curious sort of heat, as though the flames of old sexual conquests stirred within his body at the memory of those old quarrels. The looks he rested on me, as a sharer of that experience, grew more and more lickerish and assaying. "What got *you* down?" he finally inquired, settling back in his chair and pushing his coffee cup aside. "Oh," I said wearily, "it's a long story. You can read it when it's published." "You're an author?" cried the Colonel, who was really very slow-witted. I nodded, and the Colonel regarded me afresh. "What do you write? Love stories?" He gave a half-wink. "No," I said. "Various things. Articles. Books. Highbrowish stories." A suspicion darkened in the Colonel's sharp face. "That McCarthy," he said. "Is that your pen name?" "Yes," I said, "but it's my real name too. It's the name I write under *and* my maiden name." The Colonel digested this thought. "Oh," he concluded.

A new idea seemed to visit him. Quite cruelly, I watched it take possession. He was thinking of the power of the press and the indiscretions of other military figures, who had been rewarded with demotion. The consciousness of the uniform he wore appeared to seep uneasily into his body. He straightened his shoulders and called thoughtfully for the check. We paid in silence, the Colonel making no effort to forestall my dive into my pocketbook. I should not have let him pay in any case, but it startled me that he did not try to do so, if only for reasons of vanity. The whole business of paying, apparently, was painful to him; I watched his facial muscles contract as he pocketed the change and slipped two dimes for the waitress onto the table, not daring quite to hide them under the coffee cup—he had short-changed me on the bill and the tip, and we both knew it. We walked out into the steaming station and I took my baggage out of the checking locker. The Colonel carried my suitcase and we strolled along without speaking. Again, I felt horribly embarrassed for him. He was meditative, and I supposed that he too was mortified by his meanness about the tip.

"Don't get me wrong," he said suddenly, setting the suitcase down and turning squarely to face me, as though he had taken a big decision. "I may have said a few things back there about the Jews getting what they deserved in Germany." I looked at him in surprise; actually, he had not said that to me. Perhaps he had let it drop in the club car. "But that doesn't mean I approve of Hitler." "I should hope not," I said. "What I mean is," and the Colonel, "that they probably gave the Germans a lot of provocation, but that doesn't excuse what Hitler did." "No," I said, somewhat ironically, but the Colonel was unaware of anything satiric in the air. His face was grave and determined; he was sorting out his philosophy for the record. "I mean, I don't approve of his methods," he finally stated. "No," I agreed. "You mean, you don't approve of the gas chamber." The Colonel shook his head very severely. "Absolutely not! That was terrible." He shuddered and drew out a handkerchief and slowly wiped his brow. "For God's sake," he said, "don't get me wrong. I think they're human beings." "Yes," I assented, and we walked along to my track. The Colonel's spirits lifted, as though, having stated his credo, he had both got himself in line with public policy and achieved an autonomous thought. "I mean," he resumed, "you may not care for them, but that's not the same as killing them, in cold blood, like that." "No, Colonel," I said.

He swung my bag onto the car's platform and I climbed up behind it. He stood below, smiling, with upturned face. "I'll look for your article," he cried, as the train whistle blew. I nodded, and the Colonel waved, and I could not stop myself from waving back at him and even giving him the corner of a smile. After all, I said to myself, looking down at him, the Colonel was "a human being." There followed one of those inane intervals in which one prays for the train to leave. We both glanced at our watches. "See you some time," he called. "What's your married name?" "Broadwater," I called back. The whistle blew again. "Brodwater?" shouted the Colonel, with a dazed look of unbelief and growing enlightenment; he was not the first person to hear it as a Jewish name, on the model of Goldwater. "B-r-o-a-d," I began, automatically, but then I stopped. I disdained to spell it out for him; the victory was his. "One of the chosen, eh?" his brief grimace commiserated. For the last time, and in the final fullness of understanding, the hawk eye patrolled the green dress, the duster, and the earrings; the narrow flue of his nostril contracted as he curtly turned away. The train commenced to move.

DYLAN THOMAS

A Story

If you can call it a story. There's no real beginning or
end and there's very little in the middle. It is all about
a day's outing, by charabanc, to Porthcawl, which, of course, the
charabanc never reached, and it happened when I was so high and
much nicer.

I was staying at the time with my uncle and his wife. Although
she was my aunt, I never thought of her as anything but the wife
of my uncle, partly because he was so big and trumpeting and red-
hairy and used to fill every inch of the hot little house like an old
buffalo squeezed into an airing cupboard, and partly because she
was so small and silk and quick and made no noise at all as she
whisked about on padded paws, dusting the china dogs, feeding
the buffalo, setting the mousetraps that never caught her; and
once she sleaked out of the room, to squeak in a nook or nibble
in the hayloft, you forgot she had ever been there.

But there he was, always, a steaming hulk of an uncle, his braces
straining like hawsers, crammed behind the counter of the tiny
shop at the front of the house, and breathing like a brass band; or
guzzling and blustery in the kitchen over his gutsy supper, too big
for everything except the great black boats of his boots. As he ate,
the house grew smaller; he billowed out over the furniture, the
loud check meadow of his waistcoat littered, as though after a
picnic, with cigarette ends, peelings, cabbage stalks, birds' bones,
gravy; and the forest fire of his hair crackled among the hooked
hams from the ceiling. She was so small she could hit him only if
she stood on a chair; and every Saturday night at half-past ten
he would lift her up, under his arm, onto a chair, in the kitchen

Reprinted from QUITE EARLY ONE MORNING by Dylan Thomas,
by permission of New Directions. Copyright 1954 by New Directions.

so that she could hit him on the head with whatever was handy, which was always a china dog. On Sundays, and when pickled, he sang high tenor, and had won many cups.

The first I heard of the annual outing was when I was sitting one evening on a bag of rice behind the counter, under one of my uncle's stomachs, reading an advertisement for sheepdip, which was all there was to read. The shop was full of my uncle, and when Mr. Benjamin Franklyn, Mr. Weazley, Noah Bowen, and Will Sentry came in, I thought it would burst. It was like all being together in a drawer that smelled of cheese and turps, and twist tobacco and sweet biscuits and snuff and waistcoat. Mr. Benjamin Franklyn said that he had collected enough money for the charabanc and twenty cases of pale ale and a pound apiece over that he would distribute among the members of the outing when they first stopped for refreshment, and he was about sick and tired, he said, of being followed by Will Sentry.

"All day long, wherever I go," he said, "he's after me like a collie with one eye. I got a shadow of my own *and* a dog. I don't need no Tom, Dick or Harry pursuing me with his dirty muffler on."

Will Sentry blushed, and said, "It's only oily. I got a bicycle."

"A man has no privacy at all," Mr. Franklyn went on. "I tell you he sticks so close I'm afraid to go out the back in case I sit in his lap. It's a wonder to me," he said, "he don't follow me into bed at night."

"Wife won't let," Will Sentry said.

And that started Mr. Franklyn off again, and they tried to soothe him down by saying, "Don't you mind Will Sentry." "No harm in old Will." "He's only keeping an eye on the money, Benjie."

"Aren't I honest?" asked Mr. Franklyn in surprise. There was no answer for some time; then Noah Bowen said, "You know what the committee is. Ever since Bob the Fiddle they don't feel safe with a new treasurer."

"Do you think *I'm* going to drink the outing funds, like Bob the Fiddle did?" said Mr. Franklyn.

"You *might*," said my uncle, slowly.

"I resign," said Mr. Franklyn.

"Not with our money you won't," Will Sentry said.

"Who put the dynamite in the salmon pool?" said Mr. Weazley, but nobody took any notice of him. And, after a time, they all began to play cards in the thickening dusk of the hot, cheesy shop, and my uncle blew and bugled whenever he won, and Mr. Weazley grumbled like a dredger, and I fell to sleep on the gravy-scented mountain meadow of uncle's waistcoat.

On Sunday evening, after Bethesda, Mr. Franklyn walked into the kitchen where my uncle and I were eating sardines from the tin with spoons because it was Sunday and his wife would not let us play draughts. She was somewhere in the kitchen, too. Perhaps she was inside the grandmother clock, hanging from the weights and breathing. Then, a second later, the door opened again and Will Sentry edged into the room, twiddling his hard, round hat. He and Mr. Franklyn sat down on the settee, stiff and mothballed and black in their chapel and funeral suits.

"I brought the list," said Mr. Franklyn. "Every member fully paid. You ask Will Sentry."

My uncle put on his spectacles, wiped his whiskery mouth with a handkerchief big as a Union Jack, laid down his spoon of sardines, took Mr. Franklyn's list of names, removed the spectacles so that he could read, and then ticked the names off one by one.

"Enoch Davies. Aye. He's good with his fists. You never know. Little Gerwain. Very melodious bass. Mr. Cadwalladwr. That's right. He can tell opening time better than my watch. Mr. Weazley. Of course. He's been to Paris. Pity he suffers so much in the charabanc. Stopped us nine times last year between the Beehive and the Red Dragon. Noah Bowen. Ah, very peaceable. He's got a tongue like a turtledove. Never a argument with Noah Bowen. Jenkins Loughor. Keep him off economics. It cost us a plateglass window. And ten pints for the Sergeant. Mr. Jervis. Very tidy."

"He tried to put a pig in the charra," Will Sentry said.

"Live and let live," said my uncle.

Will Sentry blushed.

"Sinbad the Sailor's Arms. Got to keep in with him. Old O. Jones."

"Why old O. Jones?" said Will Sentry.

"Old O. Jones always goes," said my uncle.

I looked down at the kitchen table. The tin of sardines was gone. By Gee, I said to myself, Uncle's wife is quick as a flash.

"Cuthbert Johnny Fortnight. Now there's a card," said my uncle.

"He whistles after women," Will Sentry said.

"So do you," said Mr. Benjamin Franklyn, "in your mind."

My uncle at last approved the whole list, pausing only to say, when he came across one name, "If we weren't a Christian community, we'd chuck that Bob the Fiddle in the sea."

"We can do that in Porthcawl," said Mr. Franklyn, and soon after that he went, Will Sentry no more than an inch behind him, their Sunday-bright boots squeaking on the kitchen cobbles.

And then, suddenly, there was my uncle's wife standing in front of the dresser, with a china dog in one hand. By Gee, I said to myself again, did you ever see such a woman, if that's what she is. The lamps were not lit yet in the kitchen and she stood in a wood of shadows, with the plates on the dresser behind her shining—like pink and white eyes.

"If you go on that outing on Saturday, Mr. Thomas," she said to my uncle in her small, silk voice, "I'm going home to my mother's."

Holy Mo, I thought, she's got a mother. Now that's one old bald mouse of a hundred and five I won't be wanting to meet in a dark lane.

"It's me or the outing, Mr. Thomas."

I would have made my choice at once, but it was almost half a minute before my uncle said, "Well, then, Sarah, it's the outing, my love." He lifted her up, under his arm, onto a chair in the kitchen, and she hit him on the head with the china dog. Then he lifted her down again, and then I said good night.

For the rest of the week my uncle's wife whisked quiet and quick round the house with her darting duster, my uncle blew and bugled and swole, and I kept myself busy all the time being up to no good. And then at breakfast time on Saturday morning, the morning of the outing, I found a note on the kitchen table. It said, "There's some eggs in the pantry. Take your boots off before you go to bed." My uncle's wife had gone, as quick as a flash.

When my uncle saw the note, he tugged out the flag of his handkerchief and blew such a hubbub of trumpets that the plates on the dresser shook. "It's the same every year," he said. And then he looked at me. "But this year it's different. *You'll* have to

come on the outing, too, and what the members will say I dare
not think."

The charabanc drew up outside, and when the members of
the outing saw my uncle and me squeeze out of the shop together,
both of us cat-licked and brushed in our Sunday best, they snarled
like a zoo.

"Are you bringing a *boy?*" asked Mr. Benjamin Franklyn as
we climbed into the charabanc. He looked at me with horror.

"Boys is nasty," said Mr. Weazley.

"He hasn't paid his contributions," Will Sentry said.

"No room for boys. Boys get sick in charabancs."

"So do you, Enoch Davies," said my uncle.

"Might as well bring *women.*"

The way they said it, women were worse than boys.

"Better than bringing grandfathers."

"Grandfathers is nasty, too," said Mr. Weazley.

"What can we do with him when we stop for refreshments?"

"I'm a grandfather," said Mr. Weazley.

"Twenty-six minutes to opening time," shouted an old man
in a panama hat, not looking at a watch. They forgot me at once.

"Good old Mr. Cadwalladwr," they cried, and the charabanc
started off down the village street.

A few cold women stood at their doorways, grimly watching
us go. A very small boy waved goodbye, and his mother boxed his
ears. It was a beautiful August morning.

We were out of the village, and over the bridge, and up the
hill toward Steeplehat Wood when Mr. Franklyn, with his list of
names in his hand, called out loud, "Where's old O. Jones?"

"Where's old O.?"

"We've left old O. behind."

"Can't go without old O."

And though Mr. Weazley hissed all the way, we turned and
drove back to the village, where, outside the Prince of Wales,
old O. Jones was waiting patiently and alone with a canvas bag.

"I didn't want to come at all," old O. Jones said as they hoisted
him into the charabanc and clapped him on the back and pushed
him on a seat and stuck a bottle in his hand, "but I always go."
And over the bridge and up the hill and under the deep green
wood and along the dusty road we wove, slow cows and ducks

flying by, until "Stop the bus!" Mr. Weazley cried, "I left my teeth on the mantelpiece."

"Never you mind," they said, "you're not going to bite no-body," and they gave him a bottle with a straw.

"I might want to smile," he said.

"Not you," they said.

"What's the time, Mr. Cadwalladwr?"

"Twelve minutes to go," shouted back the old man in the panama, and they all began to curse him.

The charabanc pulled up outside the Mountain Sheep, a small, unhappy public house with a thatched roof like a wig with ring-worm. From a flagpole by the Gents fluttered the flag of Siam. I knew it was the flag of Siam because of cigarette cards. The land-lord stood at the door to welcome us, simpering like a wolf. He was a long, lean, black-fanged man with a greased love-curl and pouncing eyes. "What a beautiful August day!" he said, and touched his love-curl with a claw. That was the way he must have welcomed the Mountain Sheep before he ate it, I said to myself. The members rushed out, bleating, and into the bar.

"You keep an eye on the charra," my uncle said, "see nobody steals it now."

"There's nobody to steal it," I said, "except some cows," but my uncle was gustily blowing his bugle in the bar. I looked at the cows opposite, and they looked at me. There was nothing else for us to do. Forty-five minutes passed, like a very slow cloud. The sun shone down on the lonely road, the lost, unwanted boy, and the lake-eyed cows. In the dark bar they were so happy they were breaking glasses. A Shoni-Onion Breton man, with a beret and a necklace of onions, bicycled down the road and stopped at the door.

"*Quelle un grand matin, monsieur,*" [1] I said.

"There's French, boy bach!" he said.

I followed him down the passage, and peered into the bar. I could hardly recognize the members of the outing. They had all changed color. Beetroot, rhubarb and puce, they hollered and rollicked in that dark, damp hole like enormous ancient bad boys, and my uncle surged in the middle, all red whiskers and bellies. On the floor was broken glass and Mr. Weazley.

---

[1] "*Quelle un grand matin, monsieur.*" "What a fine morning, sir."

"Drinks all round," cried Bob the Fiddle, a small, absconding man with bright blue eyes and a plump smile.

"Who's been robbing the orphans?"

"Who sold his little babby to the gyppoes?"

"Trust old Bob, he'll let you down."

"You will have your little joke," said Bob the Fiddle, smiling like a razor, "but I forgive you, boys."

Out of the fug and babel I heard: "Where's old O. Jones?" "Where are you, old O.?" "He's in the kitchen cooking his dinner." "He never forgets his dinner time." "Good old O. Jones." "Come out and fight." "No, not now, later." "No, now when I'm in a temper." "Look at Will Sentry, he's proper snobbled." "Look at his willful feet." "Look at Mr. Weazley lording it on the floor."

Mr. Weazley got up, hissing like a gander. "That boy pushed me down deliberate," he said, pointing to me at the door, and I slunk away down the passage and out to the mild, good cows.

Time clouded over, the cows wondered, I threw a stone at them and they wandered, wondering, away. Then out blew my uncle, ballooning, and one by one the members lumbered after him in a grizzle. They had drunk the Mountain Sheep dry. Mr. Weazley had won a string of onions that the Shoni-Onion man had raffled in the bar.

"What's the good of onions if you left your teeth on the mantelpiece?" he said. And when I looked through the back window of the thundering charabanc, I saw the pub grow smaller in the distance. And the flag of Siam, from the flagpole by the Gents, fluttered now at half mast.

The Blue Bull, the Dragon, the Star of Wales, the Twll in the Wall, the Sour Grapes, the Shepherd's Arms, the Bells of Aberdovey: I had nothing to do in the whole wild August world but remember the names where the outing stopped and keep an eye on the charabanc. And whenever it passed a public house, Mr. Weazley would cough like a billy goat and cry, "Stop the bus, I'm dying of breath." And back we would all have to go.

Closing time meant nothing to the members of that outing. Behind locked doors, they hymned and rumpused all the beautiful afternoon. And, when a policeman entered the Druid's Tap by the back door, and found them all choral with beer, "Sssh!" said

Noah Bowen, "the pub is shut."

"Where do you come from?" he said in his buttoned, blue voice.

They told him.

"I got a auntie there," the policeman said. And very soon he was singing "Asleep in the Deep."

Off we drove again at last, the charabanc bouncing with tenors and flagons, and came to a river that rushed along among willows.

"Water!" they shouted.

"Porthcawl!" sang my uncle.

"Where's the donkeys?" said Mr. Weazley.

And out they lurched, to paddle and whoop in the cool, white, winding water. Mr. Franklyn, trying to polka on the slippery stones, fell in twice. "Nothing is simple," he said with dignity as he oozed up the bank.

"It's cold!" they cried.

"It's lovely!"

"It's smooth as a moth's nose!"

"It's *better* than Porthcawl!"

And dusk came down warm and gentle on thirty wild, wet, pickled, splashing men without a care in the world at the end of the world in the west of Wales. And, "Who goes there?" called Will Sentry to a wild duck flying.

They stopped at the Hermit's Nest for a rum to keep out the cold. "I played for Aberavon in 1898," said a stranger to Enoch Davies.

"Liar," said Enoch Davies.

"I can show the photos," said the stranger.

"Forged," said Enoch Davies.

"And I'll show you my cap at home."

"Stolen."

"I got friends to prove it," the stranger said in a fury.

"Bribed," said Enoch Davies.

On the way home, through the simmering moonsplashed dark, old O. Jones began to cook his supper on a primus stove in the middle of the charabanc. Mr. Weazley coughed himself blue in the smoke. "Stop the bus!" he cried, "I'm dying of breath." We all climbed down into the moonlight. There was not a public house in sight. So they carried out the remaining cases, and the primus stove, and old O. Jones himself, and took them into a field, and sat down in a circle in the field and drank and sang while old O. Jones cooked sausage and mash and the moon flew above us. And there I drifted to sleep against my uncle's mountainous waistcoat, and, as I slept, "Who goes there?" called out Will Sentry to the flying moon.

FRANK O'CONNOR

My Oedipus Complex

Father was in the army all through the war—the first war, I mean—so, up to the age of five, I never saw much of him, and what I saw did not worry me. Sometimes I woke and there was a big figure in khaki peering down at me in the candlelight. Sometimes in the early morning I heard the slamming of the front door and the clatter of nailed boots down the cobbles of the lane. These were Father's entrances and exits. Like Santa Claus he came and went mysteriously.

In fact, I rather liked his visits, though it was an uncomfortable squeeze between Mother and him when I got into the big bed in the early morning. He smoked, which gave him a pleasant musty smell, and shaved, an operation of astounding interest. Each time he left a trail of souvenirs—model tanks and Gurkha knives with handles made of bullet cases, and German helmets and cap badges and button-sticks, and all sorts of military equipment—carefully stowed away in a long box on top of the wardrobe, in case they ever came in handy. There was a bit of the magpie about Father; he expected everything to come in handy. When his back was turned, Mother let me get a chair and rummage through his treasures. She didn't seem to think so highly of them

Reprinted from THE STORIES OF FRANK O'CONNOR by Frank O'Connor, by permission of Alfred A. Knopf, Inc. Copyright 1950, 1952 by Frank O'Connor.

as he did.

The war was the most peaceful period of my life. The window of my attic faced southeast. My mother had curtained it, but that had small effect. I always woke with the first light and, with all the responsibilities of the previous day melted, feeling myself rather like the sun, ready to illumine and rejoice. Life never seemed so simple and clear and full of possibilities as then. I put my feet out from under the clothes—I called them Mrs. Left and Mrs. Right—and invented dramatic situations for them in which they discussed the problems of the day. At least Mrs. Right did; she was very demonstrative, but I hadn't the same control of Mrs. Left, so she mostly contented herself with nodding agreement.

They discussed what Mother and I should do during the day, what Santa Claus should give a fellow for Christmas, and what steps should be taken to brighten the home. There was that little matter of the baby, for instance. Mother and I could never agree about that. Ours was the only house in the terrace without a new baby, and Mother said we couldn't afford one till Father came back from the war because they cost seventeen and six. That showed how simple she was. The Geneys up the road had a baby, and everyone knew they couldn't afford seventeen and six. It was probably a cheap baby, and Mother wanted something really good, but I felt she was too exclusive. The Geneys' baby would have done us fine.

Having settled my plans for the day, I got up, put a chair under the attic window, and lifted the frame high enough to stick out my head. The window overlooked the front gardens of the terrace behind ours, and beyond these it looked over a deep valley to the tall, red-brick houses terraced up the opposite hillside, which were all still in shadow, while those at our side of the valley were all lit up, though with long strange shadows that made them seem unfamiliar; rigid and painted.

After that I went into Mother's room and climbed into the big bed. She woke and I began to tell her of my schemes. By this time, though I never seem to have noticed it, I was petrified in my nightshirt, and I thawed as I talked until, the last frost melted, I fell asleep beside her and woke again only when I heard her below in the kitchen, making the breakfast.

After breakfast we went into town; heard Mass at St. Augustine's and said a prayer for Father, and did the shopping. If the afternoon was fine we either went for a walk in the country or a visit to Mother's great friend in the convent, Mother St. Dominic. Mother had them all praying for Father, and every night, going to bed, I asked God to send him back safe from the war to us. Little, indeed, did I know what I was praying for!

One morning, I got into the big bed, and there, sure enough, was Father in his usual Santa Claus manner, but later, instead of uniform, he put on his best blue suit, and Mother was as pleased as anything. I saw nothing to be pleased about, because, out of uniform, Father was altogether less interesting, but she only beamed, and explained that our prayers had been answered, and off we went to Mass to thank God for having brought Father safely home.

The irony of it! That very day when he came in to dinner he took off his boots and put on his slippers, donned the dirty old cap he wore about the house to save him from colds, crossed his legs, and began to talk gravely to Mother, who looked anxious. Naturally, I disliked her looking anxious, because it destroyed her good looks, so I interrupted him.

"Just a moment, Larry!" she said gently.

This was only what she said when we had boring visitors, so I attached no importance to it and went on talking.

"Do be quiet, Larry!" she said impatiently. "Don't you hear me talking to Daddy?"

This was the first time I had heard those ominous words, "talking to Daddy," and I couldn't help feeling that if this was how God answered prayers, he couldn't listen to them very attentively.

"Why are you talking to Daddy?" I asked with as great a show of indifference as I could muster.

"Because Daddy and I have business to discuss. Now, don't interrupt again!"

In the afternoon, at Mother's request, Father took me for a walk. This time we went into town instead of out the country, and I thought at first, in my usual optimistic way, that it might be an improvement. It was nothing of the sort. Father and I had quite different notions of a walk in town. He had no proper interest in trams, ships, and horses, and the only thing that seemed to divert him was talking to fellows as old as himself. When I wanted to stop he simply went on, dragging me behind him by the hand; when he wanted to stop I had no alternative but to do the same. I noticed that it seemed to be a sign that he wanted to stop for a long time whenever he leaned against a wall. The second time I saw him do it I got wild. He seemed to be settling himself forever. I pulled him by the coat and trousers, but, unlike Mother who, if you were too persistent, got into a wax and said: "Larry, if you don't behave yourself, I'll give you a good slap," Father had an extraordinary capacity for amiable inattention. I sized him up and wondered would I cry, but he seemed to be too remote to be annoyed even by that. Really, it was like going for a walk with a mountain! He either ignored the wrenching and pummeling entirely, or else glanced down with a grin of amusement from his peak. I had never met anyone so absorbed in himself as he seemed.

At teatime, "talking to Daddy" began again, complicated this time by the fact that he had an evening paper, and every few minutes he put it down and told Mother something new out of it. I felt this was foul play. Man for man, I was prepared to compete with him any time for Mother's attention, but when he had it all made up for him by other people it left me no chance. Several times I tried to change the subject without success.

"You must be quiet while Daddy is reading, Larry," Mother said impatiently.

It was clear that she either genuinely liked talking to Father better than talking to me, or else that he had some terrible hold on her which made her afraid to admit the truth.

"Mummy," I said that night when she was tucking me up, "do you think if I prayed hard God would send Daddy back to the war?"

She seemed to think about that for a moment.

"No, dear," she said with a smile. "I don't think he would."

"Why wouldn't he, Mummy?"

"Because there isn't a war any longer, dear."

"But, Mummy, couldn't God make another war, if He liked?"

"He wouldn't like to, dear. It's not God who makes wars, but bad people."

"Oh!" I said.

I was disappointed about that. I began to think that God wasn't quite what he was cracked up to be.

Next morning I woke at my usual hour, feeling like a bottle of champagne. I put out my feet and invented a long conversation in which Mrs. Right talked of the trouble she had with her own father till she put him in the Home. I didn't quite know what the Home was but it sounded like the right place for Father. Then I got my chair and stuck my head out of the attic window. Dawn was just breaking, with a guilty air that made me feel I had caught it in the act. My head bursting with stories and schemes, I stumbled in next door, and in the half-darkness scrambled into the big bed. There was no room at Mother's side so I had to get between her and Father. For the time being I had forgotten about him, and for several minutes I sat bolt upright, racking my brains to know what I could do with him. He was taking up more than his fair share of the bed, and I couldn't get comfortable, so I gave him several kicks that made him grunt and stretch. He made room all right, though. Mother waked and felt for me. I settled back comfortably in the warmth of the bed with my thumb in my mouth.

"Mummy!" I hummed, loudly and contentedly.

"Sssh! dear," she whispered. "Don't wake Daddy!"

This was a new development, which threatened to be even more serious than "talking to Daddy." Life without my early-morning conferences was unthinkable.

"Why?" I asked severely.

"Because poor Daddy is tired."

This seemed to me a quite inadequate reason, and I was sickened by the sentimentality of her "poor Daddy." I never liked that sort of gush; it always struck me as insincere.

"Oh!" I said lightly. Then in my most winning tone: "Do you know where I want to go with you today, Mummy?"

"No, dear," she sighed.

"I want to go down the Glen and fish for thornybacks with my new net, and then I want to go out to the Fox and Hounds, and—"

"Don't-wake-Daddy!" she hissed angrily, clapping her hand across my mouth.

But it was too late. He was awake, or nearly so. He grunted and reached for the matches. Then he stared incredulously at his watch.

"Like a cup of tea, dear?" asked Mother in a meek, hushed voice I had never heard her use before. It sounded almost as though she were afraid.

"Tea?" he exclaimed indignantly. "Do you know what the time is?"

"And after that I want to go up the Rathcooney Road," I said loudly, afraid I'd forget something in all those interruptions.

"Go to sleep at once, Larry!" she said sharply.

I began to snivel. I couldn't concentrate, the way that pair went on, and smothering my early-morning schemes was like burying a family from the cradle.

Father said nothing, but lit his pipe and sucked it, looking out into the shadows without minding Mother or me. I knew he was mad. Every time I made a remark Mother hushed me irritably. I was mortified. I felt it wasn't fair; there was even something sinister in it. Every time I had pointed out to her the waste of making two beds when we could both sleep in one, she had told me it was healthier like that, and now here was this man, this stranger sleeping with her without the least regard for her health!

He got up early and made tea but though he brought Mother a cup he brought none for me.

"Mummy," I shouted, "I want a cup of tea, too."

"Yes, dear," she said patiently. "You can drink from Mummy's saucer."

That settled it. Either Father or I would have to leave the house. I didn't want to drink from Mother's saucer; I wanted to be treated as an equal in my own home, so, just to spite her, I drank it all and left none for her. She took that quietly, too.

But that night when she was putting me to bed she said gently:

"Larry, I want you to promise me something."

"What is it?" I asked.

"Not to come in and disturb poor Daddy in the morning. Promise?"

"Poor Daddy" again! I was becoming suspicious of everything involving that quite impossible man.

"Why?" I asked.

"Because poor Daddy is worried and tired and he doesn't sleep well."

"Why doesn't he, Mummy?"

"Well, you know, don't you, that while he was at the war Mummy got the pennies from the Post Office?"

"From Miss MacCarthy?"

"That's right. But now, you see, Miss MacCarthy hasn't any more pennies, so Daddy must go out and find us some. You know what would happen if he couldn't?"

"No," I said, "tell us."

"Well, I think we might have to go out and beg for them like the poor old woman on Fridays. We wouldn't like that, would we?"

"No," I agreed. "We wouldn't."

"So you'll promise not to come in and wake him?"

"Promise."

Mind you, I meant that. I knew pennies were a serious matter, and I was all against having to go out and beg like the old woman on Fridays. Mother laid out all my toys in a complete ring round the bed so that, whatever way I got out, I was bound to fall over one of them.

When I woke I remembered my promise all right. I got up and sat on the floor and played—for hours, it seemed to me. Then I got my chair and looked out the attic window for more hours. I wished it was time for Father to wake; I wished someone would make me a cup of tea. I didn't feel in the least like the sun; instead, I was bored and so very, very cold! I simply longed for the warmth and depth of the big featherbed.

At last I could stand it no longer. I went into the next room. As there was still no room at Mother's side I climbed over her and she woke with a start.

"Larry," she whispered, gripping my arm very tightly, "what did you promise?"

"But I did, Mummy," I wailed, caught in the very act. "I was quiet for ever so long."

"Oh, dear, and you're perished!" she said sadly, feeling me all over. "Now, if I let you stay will you promise not to talk?"

"But I want to talk, Mummy," I wailed.

"That has nothing to do with it," she said with a firmness that was new to me. "Daddy wants to sleep. Now, do you understand that?"

I understood it only too well. I wanted to talk, he wanted to sleep—whose house was it, anyway?

"Mummy," I said with equal firmness, "I think it would be healthier for Daddy to sleep in his own bed."

That seemed to stagger her, because she said nothing for a while.

"Now, once for all," she went on, "you're to be perfectly quiet or go back to your own bed. Which is it to be?"

The injustice of it got me down. I had convicted her out of her own mouth of inconsistency and unreasonableness, and she hadn't even attempted to reply. Full of spite, I gave Father a kick, which she didn't notice but which made him grunt and open his eyes in alarm.

"What time is it?" he asked in a panic-stricken voice, not looking at Mother but at the door, as if he saw someone there.

"It's early yet," she replied soothingly. "It's only the child. Go to sleep again. . . . Now, Larry," she added, getting out of bed, "you've wakened Daddy and you must go back."

This time, for all her quiet air, I knew she meant it, and knew that my principal rights and privileges were as good as lost unless I asserted them at once. As she lifted me, I gave a screech, enough to wake the dead, not to mind Father. He groaned.

"That damn child! Doesn't he ever sleep?"

"It's only a habit, dear," she said quietly, though I could see she was vexed.

"Well, it's time he got out of it," shouted Father, beginning to heave in the bed. He suddenly gathered all the bedclothes about him, turned to the wall, and then looked back over his shoulder with nothing showing only two small, spiteful, dark eyes. The man looked very wicked.

To open the bedroom door, Mother had to let me down, and I broke free and dashed for the farthest corner, screeching. Father sat bolt upright in bed.

"Shut up, you little puppy!" he said in a choking voice.

I was so astonished that I stopped screeching. Never, never had anyone spoken to me in that tone before. I looked at him incredulously and saw his face convulsed with rage. It was only then that I fully realized how God had codded me, listening to my prayers for the safe return of this monster.

"Shut up, you!" I bawled, beside myself.

"What's that you said?" shouted Father, making a wild leap out of the bed.

"Mick, Mick!" cried Mother. "Don't you see the child isn't used to you?"

"I see he's better fed than taught," snarled Father, waving his arms wildly. "He wants his bottom smacked."

All his previous shouting was as nothing to these obscene words referring to my person. They really made my blood boil.

"Smack your own!" I screamed hysterically. "Smack your own! Shut up! Shut up!"

At this he lost his patience and let fly at me. He did it with the lack of conviction you'd expect of a man under Mother's horrified eyes, and it ended up as a mere tap, but the sheer indignity of being struck at all by a stranger, a total stranger who had cajoled his way back from the war into our big bed as a result of my innocent intercession, made me completely dotty. I shrieked and shrieked, and danced in my bare feet, and Father, looking awkward and hairy in nothing but a short grey army shirt, glared down at me like a mountain out for murder. I think it must have been then that I realized he was jealous too. And there stood Mother in her nightdress, looking as if her heart was broken between us. I hoped she felt as she looked. It seemed to me that she deserved it all.

From that morning out my life was a hell. Father and I were enemies, open and avowed. We conducted a series of skirmishes against one another, he trying to steal my time with Mother and I his. When she was sitting on my bed, telling me a story, he took to looking for some pair of old boots which he alleged he had left behind him at the beginning of the war. While he talked to Mother I played loudly with my toys to show my total lack of concern. He created a terrible scene one evening when he came in from work and found me at his box, playing with his regimental badges, Gurkha knives and button-sticks. Mother got up and took the box from me.

"You mustn't play with Daddy's toys unless he lets you, Larry," she said severely. "Daddy doesn't play with yours."

For some reason Father looked at her as if she had struck him and then turned away with a scowl.

"Those are not toys," he growled, taking down the box again to see had I lifted anything. "Some of those curios are very rare and valuable."

But as time went on I saw more and more how he managed to alienate Mother and me. What made it worse was that I couldn't grasp his method or see what attraction he had for Mother. In every possible way he was less winning than I. He had a common accent and made noises at his tea. I thought for a while that it might be the newspapers she was interested in, so I made up bits of news of my own to read to her. Then I thought it might be the smoking, which I personally thought attractive, and took his pipes and went round the house dribbling into them till he caught me. I even made noises at my tea, but Mother only told me I was disgusting. It all seemed to hinge round that unhealthy habit of sleeping together, so I made a point of dropping into their bedroom and nosing round, talking to myself, so that they wouldn't know I was watching them, but they were never up to anything that I could see. In the end it beat me. It seemed to depend on being grown-up and giving people rings, and I realized I'd have to wait.

But at the same time I wanted him to see that I was only waiting, not giving up the fight. One evening when he was being particularly obnoxious, chattering away well above my head, I let him have it.

"Mummy," I said, "do you know what I'm going to do when I grow up?"

"No, dear," she replied. "What?"

"I'm going to marry you," I said quietly.

Father gave a great guffaw out of him, but he didn't take me in. I knew it must only be pretence. And Mother, in spite of everything, was pleased. I felt she was probably relieved to know that one day Father's hold on her would be broken.

"Won't that be nice?" she said with a smile.

"It'll be very nice," I said confidently. "Because we're going to have lots and lots of babies."

"That's right, dear," she said placidly. "I think we'll have one soon, and then you'll have plenty of company."

I was no end pleased about that because it showed that in spite of the way she gave in to Father she still considered my wishes.

Besides, it would put the Geneys in their place.

It didn't turn out like that, though. To begin with, she was very preoccupied—I suppose about where she would get the seventeen and six—and though Father took to staying out late in the evenings it did me no particular good. She stopped taking me for walks, became as touchy as blazes, and smacked me for nothing at all. Sometimes I wished I'd never mentioned the confounded baby—I seemed to have a genius for bringing calamity on myself.

And calamity it was! Sonny arrived in the most appalling hulla-baloo—even that much he couldn't do without a fuss—and from the first moment I disliked him. He was a difficult child—so far as I was concerned he was always difficult—and demanded far too much attention. Mother was simply silly about him, and couldn't see when he was only showing off. As company he was worse than useless. He slept all day, and I had to go round the house on tiptoe to avoid waking him. It wasn't any longer a question of not waking Father. The slogan now was "Don't-wake-Sonny!" I couldn't understand why the child wouldn't sleep at the proper time, so whenever Mother's back was turned I woke him. Sometimes to keep him awake I pinched him as well. Mother caught me at it one day and gave me a most unmerciful flaking.

One evening, when Father was coming in from work, I was playing trains in the front garden. I let on not to notice him; instead, I pretended to be talking to myself, and said in a loud voice: "If another bloody baby comes into this house, I'm going out."

Father stopped dead and looked at me over his shoulder.

"What's that you said?" he asked sternly.

"I was only talking to myself," I replied, trying to conceal my panic. "It's private."

He turned and went in without a word. Mind you, I intended it as a solemn warning, but its effect was quite different. Father started being quite nice to me. I could understand that, of course. Mother was quite sickening about Sonny. Even at mealtimes she'd get up and gawk at him in the cradle with an idiotic smile, and tell Father to do the same. He was always polite about it, but he looked so puzzled you could see he didn't know what she was talking about. He complained of the way Sonny cried at night, but she only got cross and said that Sonny never cried except when there was something up with him—which was a flaming lie, because Sonny never had anything up with him, and only cried for attention. It was really painful to see how simple-minded she was. Father wasn't attractive, but he had a fine intelligence. He saw through Sonny, and now he knew that I saw through him as well.

One night I woke with a start. There was someone beside me in the bed. For one wild moment I felt sure it must be Mother, having come to her senses and left Father for good, but then I heard Sonny in convulsions in the next room, and Mother saying: "There! There! There!" and I knew it wasn't she. It was Father. He was lying beside me, wide awake, breathing hard and apparently as mad as hell.

After a while it came to me what he was mad about. It was his turn now. After turning me out of the big bed, he had been turned out himself. Mother had no consideration now for anyone but that poisonous pup, Sonny. I couldn't help feeling sorry for Father. I had been through it all myself, and even at that age I was magnanimous. I began to stroke him down and say: "There! There!" He wasn't exactly responsive.

"Aren't you asleep either?" he snarled.

"Ah, come on and put your arm around us, can't you?" I said, and he did, in a sort of way. Gingerly, I suppose, is how you'd describe it. He was very bony but better than nothing.

At Christmas he went out of his way to buy me a really nice model railway.

KATHERINE ANNE PORTER

The Grave

The Grandfather, dead for more than thirty years, had been twice disturbed in his long repose by the constancy and possessiveness of his widow. She removed his bones first to Louisiana and then to Texas as if she had set out to find her own burial place, knowing well she would never return to the places she had left. In Texas she set up a small cemetery in a corner of her first farm, and as the family connection grew, and oddments of relations came over from Kentucky to settle, it contained at last about twenty graves. After the Grandmother's death, part of her land was to be sold for the benefit of certain of her children, and the cemetery happened to lie in the part set aside for sale. It was necessary to take up the bodies and bury them again in the family plot in the big new public cemetery, where the Grandmother had been buried. At last her husband was to lie beside her for eternity, as she had planned.

The family cemetery had been a pleasant small neglected garden of tangled rose bushes and ragged cedar trees and cypress, the simple flat stones rising out of uncropped sweet-smelling wild grass. The graves were lying open and empty one burning day when Miranda and her brother Paul, who often went together to hunt rabbits and doves, propped their twenty-two Winchester rifles carefully against the rail fence, climbed over and explored among the graves. She was nine years old and he was twelve.

They peered into the pits all shaped alike with such purposeful accuracy, and looking at each other with pleased adventurous eyes, they said in solemn tones: "These were graves!" trying by words to shape a special, suitable emotion in their minds, but they felt nothing except an agreeable thrill of wonder: they were seeing a new sight, doing something they had not done before. In them both there was also a small disappointment at the entire commonplaceness of the actual spectacle. Even if it had once contained a coffin for years upon years, when the coffin was gone a grave was just a hole in the ground. Miranda leaped into the pit that had held her grandfather's bones. Scratching around aimlessly and pleasurably as any young animal, she scooped up a lump of earth and weighed it in her palm. It had a pleasantly sweet, corrupt smell, being mixed with cedar needles and small leaves, and as the crumbs fell apart, she saw a silver dove no larger than a hazel nut, with spread wings and a neat fan-shaped tail. The breast had a deep round hollow in it. Turning it up to the fierce sunlight, she saw that the inside of the hollow was cut in little whorls. She scrambled out, over the pile of loose earth that had fallen back into one end of the grave, calling to Paul that she had found something, he must guess what . . . His head appeared smiling over the rim of another grave. He waved a closed hand at her. "I've got something too!" They ran to compare treasures, making a game of it, so many guesses each, all wrong, and a final showdown with opened palms. Paul had found a thin wide gold ring carved with intricate flowers and leaves. Miranda was smitten at sight of the ring and wished to have it. Paul seemed more impressed by the dove. They made a trade, with some little bickering. After he had got the dove in his hand, Paul said, "Don't you know what this is? This is a screw head for a *coffin!* . . . . I'll bet nobody else in the world has one like this!"

Miranda glanced at it without covetousness. She had the gold ring on her thumb; it fitted perfectly. "Maybe we ought to go now," she said, "maybe one of the niggers 'll see us and tell somebody." They knew the land had been sold, the cemetery was no longer theirs, and they felt like trespassers. They climbed back over the fence, slung their rifles loosely under their arms—they had been shooting at targets with various kinds of firearms since they were seven years old—and set out to look for the rabbits and doves or whatever small game might happen along. On these expeditions Miranda always followed at Paul's heels along the path, obeying instructions about handling her gun when going through fences, learning how to stand it up properly so it would not slip and fire unexpectedly; how to wait her time for a shot and not just bang away in the air without looking, spoiling shots for Paul, who really could hit things if given a chance. Now and then, in her excitement at seeing birds whizz up suddenly before her face, or a rabbit leap across her very toes, she lost her head, and almost without sighting she flung her rifle up and pulled the trigger. She hardly ever hit any sort of mark. She had no proper sense of hunting at all. Her brother would be often completely disgusted with her. "You don't care whether you get your bird or not," he said. "That's no way to hunt." Miranda could not understand his indignation. She had seen him smash his hat and yell with fury when he had missed his aim. "What I like about shooting," said Miranda, with exasperating inconsequence, "is pulling the trigger and hearing the noise."

"Then, by golly," said Paul, "whyn't you go back to the range and shoot at bulls-eyes?"

"I'd just as soon," said Miranda, "only like this, we walk around more."

"Well, you just stay behind and stop spoiling my shots," said Paul, who, when he made a kill, wanted to be certain he had made it. Miranda, who alone brought down a bird once in twenty rounds, always claimed as her own any game they got when they fired at the same moment. It was tiresome and unfair and her brother was sick of it.

"Now, the first dove we see, or the first rabbit, is mine," he told her. "And the next will be yours. Remember that and don't get smarty."

"What about snakes?" asked Miranda idly. "Can I have the first snake?"

Waving her thumb gently and watching her gold ring glitter, Miranda lost interest in shooting. She was wearing her summer roughing outfit: dark blue overalls, a light blue shirt, a hired-man's straw hat, and thick brown sandals. Her brother had the same outfit except his was a sober hickory-nut color. Ordinarily Miranda preferred her overalls to any other dress, though it was making rather a scandal in the countryside, for the year was 1903, and in the back country the law of female decorum had teeth in it. Her father had been criticized for letting his girls dress like boys and go careering around astride barebacked horses. Big sister Maria, the really independent and fearless one, in spite of her rather affected ways, rode at a dead run with only a rope knotted around her horse's nose. It was said the motherless family was running down, with the Grandmother no longer there to hold it together. It was known that she had discriminated against her son Harry in her will, and that he was in straits about money. Some of his old neighbors reflected with vicious satisfaction that now he would probably not be so stiffnecked, nor have any more high-stepping horses either. Miranda knew this, though she could not say how. She had met along the road old women of the kind who smoked corn-cob pipes, who had treated her grandmother with most sincere respect. They slanted their gummy old eyes side-ways at the granddaughter and said, "Ain't you ashamed of yoself, Missy? It's aginst the Scriptures to dress like that. Whut yo Pappy thinkin about?" Miranda, with her powerful social sense, which was like a fine set of antennae radiating from every pore of her skin, would feel ashamed because she knew well it was rude and ill-bred to shock anybody, even bad-tempered old crones, though she had faith in her father's judgment and was perfectly comfortable in the clothes. Her father had said, "They're just what you need, and they'll save your dresses for school. . . ." This sounded quite simple and natural to her. She had been brought up in rigorous economy. Wastefulness was vulgar. It was also a sin. These were truths; she had heard them repeated many times and never once disputed.

Now the ring, shining with the serene purity of fine gold on her rather grubby thumb, turned her feelings against her overalls and sockless feet, toes sticking through the thick brown leather straps. She wanted to go back to the farmhouse, take a good cold bath, dust herself with plenty of Maria's violet talcum powder—provided Maria was not present to object, of course—put on the thinnest, most becoming dress she owned, with a big sash, and sit in a wicker chair under the trees. . . . These things were not all she wanted, of course; she had vague stirrings of desire for luxury and a grand way of living which could not take precise form in her imagination but were founded on family legend of past wealth and leisure. These immediate comforts were what she could have, and she wanted them at once. She lagged rather far behind Paul, and once she thought of just turning back without a word and going home. She stopped, thinking that Paul would never do that to her, and so she would have to tell him. When a rabbit leaped, she let Paul have it without dispute. He killed it with one shot.

When she came up with him, he was already kneeling, examining the wound, the rabbit trailing from his hands. "Right through the head," he said complacently, as if he had aimed for it. He took out his sharp, competent bowie knife and started to skin the body. He did it very cleanly and quickly. Uncle Jimbilly knew how to prepare the skins so that Miranda always had fur coats for her dolls, for though she never cared much for her dolls she liked seeing them in fur coats. The children knelt facing each other over the dead animal. Miranda watched admiringly while her brother stripped the skin away as if he were taking off a glove. The flayed flesh emerged dark scarlet, sleek, firm; Miranda with thumb and finger felt the long fine muscles with the silvery flat strips binding them to the joints. Brother lifted the oddly bloated belly. "Look," he said, in a low amazed voice. "It was going to have young ones."

Very carefully he slit the thin flesh from the center ribs to the flanks, and a scarlet bag appeared. He slit again and pulled the bag open, and there lay a bundle of tiny rabbits, each wrapped in a thin scarlet veil. The brother pulled these off and there they were, dark gray, their sleek wet down lying in minute even ripples, like a baby's head just washed, their unbelievably small delicate ears folded close, their little blind faces almost featureless.

Miranda said, "Oh, I want to *see*," under her breath. She looked and looked—excited but not frightened, for she was accustomed to the sight of animals killed in hunting—filled with pity and astonishment and a kind of shocked delight in the wonderful little creatures for their own sakes, they were so pretty. She touched one of them ever so carefully. "Ah, there's blood running over them," she said and began to tremble without knowing why. Yet she wanted most deeply to see and to know. Having seen, she felt at once as if she had known all along. The very memory of her former ignorance faded, she had always known just this. No one had ever told her anything outright, she had been rather unobservant of the animal life around her because she was so accustomed to animals. They seemed simply disorderly and unaccountably rude in their habits, but altogether natural and not very interesting. Her brother had spoken as if he had known about everything all along. He may have seen all this before. He had never said a word to her, but she knew now a part at least of what he knew. She understood a little of the secret, formless intuitions in her own mind and body, which had been clearing up, taking form, so gradually and so steadily she had not realized that she was learning what she had to know. Paul said cautiously, as if he were talking about something forbidden: "They were just about ready to be born." His voice dropped on the last word. "I know," said Miranda, "like kittens. I know, like babies." She was quietly and terribly agitated, standing again with her rifle under her arm, looking down at the bloody heap. "I don't want the skin," she said, "I won't have it." Paul buried the young rabbits again in their mother's body, wrapped the skin around her, carried her to a clump of sage bushes, and hid her away. He came out again at once and said to Miranda, with an eager friendliness, a confidential tone quite unusual in him, as if he were taking her into an important secret on equal terms: "Listen now. Now you listen to me, and don't ever forget. Don't you ever tell a living soul that you saw this. Don't tell a soul. Don't tell Dad because I'll get into trouble. He'll say I'm leading you into things you ought not to do. He's always saying that. So now don't you go and forget and blab out sometime the way you're always doing. . . . Now, that's a secret. Don't you tell."

Miranda never told, she did not even wish to tell anybody. She thought about the whole worrisome affair with confused unhappiness for a few days. Then it sank quietly into her mind and was heaped over by accumulated thousands of impressions, for nearly twenty years. One day she was picking her path among the puddles and crushed refuse of a market street in a strange city of a strange country, when without warning, plain and clear in its true colors as if she looked through a frame upon a scene that had not stirred nor changed since the moment it happened, the episode of that far-off day leaped from its burial place before her mind's eye. She was so reasonlessly horrified she halted suddenly staring, the scene before her eyes dimmed by the vision back of them. An Indian vendor had held up before her a tray of dyed sugar sweets, in the shapes of all kinds of small creatures: birds, baby chicks, baby rabbits, lambs, baby pigs. They were in gay colors and smelled of vanilla, maybe. . . . It was a very hot day and the smell in the market, with its piles of raw flesh and wilting flowers, was like the mingled sweetness and corruption she had smelled that other day in the empty cemetery at home: the day she had remembered always until now vaguely as the time she and her brother had found treasure in the opened graves. Instantly upon this thought the dreadful vision faded, and she saw clearly her brother, whose childhood face she had forgotten, standing again in the blazing sunshine, again twelve years old, a pleased sober smile in his eyes, turning the silver dove over and over in his hands.

JOHN UPDIKE

A Sense of Shelter

Snow fell against the high school all day, wet big-flaked snow that did not accumulate well. Sharpening two pencils, William looked down on a parking lot that was a blackboard in reverse; car tires had cut smooth arcs of black into its white, and where the school buses had backed around, there were handsome pairs of arabesque V's. The snow, though at moments it whirled opaquely, could not quite bleach these scars away. The temperature must be exactly 32°. The window was open a crack, and a canted pane of glass lifted outdoor air into his face, coating the cedarwood smell of pencil shavings with the transparent odor of the wet window sill. With each revolution of the handle his knuckles came within a fraction of an inch of the tilted glass, and the faint chill this proximity breathed on them sharpened his already acute sense of shelter.

The sky behind the shreds of snow was stone-colored. The

murk inside the high classroom gave the air a solidity that limited
the overhead radiance to its own vessels; six globes of dull incan-
descence floated on the top of a thin sea. The feeling the gloom
gave him was not gloomy, it was joyous: he felt they were all
sealed in, safe; the colors of cloth were dyed deeper, the sound of
whispers was made more distinct, the smells of tablet paper and
wet shoes and varnish and face powder pierced him with a vivid
sense of possession. These were his classmates sealed in, his, the
stupid as well as the clever, the plain as well as the lovely, his
enemies as well as his friends, his. He felt like a king and seemed
to move to his seat between the bowed heads of subjects that
loved him less than he loved them. His seat was sanctioned by
tradition; for twelve years he had sat at the rear of classrooms,
William Young, flanked by Marsha Wyckoff and Andy Zimmer-
man. Once there had been two Zimmermans, but one went to
work in his father's greenhouse, and in some classes—Latin and
Trig—there were none, and William sat at the edge of the class
as if on the lip of a cliff, and Marsha Wyckoff became Marvin
Wolf or Sandra Wade, but it was always the same desk, whose
surface altered from hour to hour but from whose blue-stained
ink-hole his mind could extract, like a chain of magician's handkerchiefs, a continuity of years. As a senior he was a kind of king,
and as a teacher's pet another kind, a puppet king, who had gathered in appointive posts and even, when the moron vote split
between two football heroes, some elective ones. He was not
popular, he had never had a girl, his intense friends of childhood
had drifted off into teams and gangs, and in large groups—when
the whole school, for instance, went in the fall to the beautiful,
dung-and-cotton-candy-smelling county fair—he was always an
odd man, without a seat on the bus home. But exclusion is itself
a form of inclusion. He even had a nickname: Mip, because he
stuttered. Taunts no longer much frightened him; he had come
late into his inheritance of size, but this summer it had arrived,
and he at last stood equal with his enormous, boisterous parents,
and had to unbutton his shirt cuffs to get his wrists through them,
and discovered he could pick up a basketball with one hand. So,
his long legs blocking two aisles, he felt regal even in size and,
almost trembling with happiness under the high globes of light
beyond whose lunar glow invisible snowflakes were drowning

on the gravel roof of his castle, believed that the long delay of unpopularity had been merely a consolidation, that he was at last strong enough to make his move. Today he must tell Mary Landis he loved her.

He had loved her since, a fat-faced toughie with freckles and green eyes, she deftly stole his rubber-lined schoolbag on the walk back from second grade along Jewett Street and outran him— simply had better legs. The superior speed a boy was supposed to have failed to come; his kidneys burned with panic. In front of the grocery store next to her home she stopped and turned. She was willing to have him catch up. This humiliation on top of the rest was too much to bear. Tears broke in his throat; he spun around and ran home and threw himself on the floor of the front parlor, where his grandfather, feet twiddling, perused the newspaper and soliloquized all morning. In time the letter slot rustled, and the doorbell rang, and his mother and Mary exchanged the schoolbag and polite apologies. Their gentle voices had been to him, lying there on the carpet with his head wrapped in his arms, indistinguishable. Mother had always liked Mary. From when she had been a tiny girl dancing along the hedge on the end of an older sister's arm, Mother had liked her. Out of all the children that flocked, similar as pigeons, around the neighborhood, Mother's heart had reached out with claws and fastened on Mary. He never took the schoolbag to school again, had refused to touch it. He supposed it was still in the attic, still faintly smelling of pink rubber.

The buzzer sounded the two-minute signal. In the middle of the classroom Mary Landis stood up, a Monitor badge pinned to her belt. She wore a lavender sweater with the sleeves pushed up to expose her forearms, a delicately cheap effect. Wild stories were told about her; perhaps it was merely his knowledge of these that put the hardness in her face. Her eyes in their shape seemed braced for squinting and their green was frosted. Her freckles had faded. William thought she laughed less this year; now that she was in the Secretarial Course and he in the College Preparatory, he saw her in only one class a day, this one, English. She stood a second, eclipsed at the thighs by Jack Stephens' shoulders, looking back at the room with a stiff glance, as if she had seen the same faces too many times before. Her habit of perfect posture emphasized the angularity she had grown into; there was a nervous edge, a boxiness in her bones, that must have been waiting all along under the childish fat. Her eye sockets were deeply indented and her chin had a prim square set that seemed defiant to him. Her brown skirt was snug and straight; she had less hips than bosom, and thin, athletic legs. Her pronged chest poised, she sauntered up the aisle and encountered a leg thrown in her path. She stared down until it withdrew; she was used to such attentions. As she went out the door, somebody she saw in the hall made her smile, a wide smile full of warmth and short white teeth, and love scooped at his heart. He would tell her.

In another minute, the second bell rasped. Shuffling through the perfumed crowds to his next class, he crooned to himself, in the slow, over-enunciated manner of the Negro vocalist who had brought the song back this year,

> "Lah-vender blue, dilly dilly,
> Lavendih greeh-een;
> *Eef* I were king, dilly dilly,
> You would: be queen."

The song gave him an exultant sliding sensation that intertwined with the pleasures of his day. He knew all the answers, he had done all the work, the teachers called upon him only to rebuke the ignorance of the others. In Trig and Soc Sci both it was this way. In gym, the fourth hour of the morning, he, who was always picked near the last, startled his side by excelling at volleyball, leaping like a madman, shouting like a bully. The ball felt light as a feather against his big bones. His hair wet from the shower, he walked in the icy air to Luke's Luncheonette, where he ate three hamburgers in a booth with three juniors. There was Barry Kruppman, a tall, thyroid-eyed boy who came on the school bus from the country town of Bowsville and was an amateur hypnotist and occultist; he told them about a Portland, Oregon, businessman who under hypnosis had been taken back through sixteen reincarnations to the condition of an Egyptian concubine in the household of a high priest of Isis. There was his friend Lionel Griffin, a pudgy simp whose blond hair stood out above his ears in two slick waxed wings. He was supposed to be a fairy, and in fact did seem most excited by the transvestite aspect of the soul's transmigration. And there was Lionel's girl, Virginia, a drab little mystery who chain-smoked Herbert Tareytons and never said anything. She had sallow skin, and Lionel kept jabbing her and shrieking. William would rather have sat with members of his own class, who filled the other booths, but he would have had to force himself on them. These juniors admired him and welcomed his company. He asked, "Wuh-well, was he ever a c-c-c-cockroach, like Archy?"

Kruppman's face grew intense; his furry lids dropped down over the bulge of his eyes, and when they drew back, his pupils were as small and hard as BBs. "That's the really interesting thing. There was this gap, see, between his being a knight under Charlemagne and then a sailor on a ship putting out from Macedonia— that's where Yugoslavia is now—in the time of Nero; there was this gap when the only thing the guy would do was walk around the office snarling and growling, see, like this." Kruppman worked his blotched ferret face up into a snarl and Griffin shrieked. "He tried to bite one of the assistants and they think that for six hundred years"—the uncanny, unhealthy seriousness of his whisper hushed Griffin momentarily—"for six hundred years he just was a series of wolves. Probably in the German forests. You see, when he was in Macedonia"—his whisper barely audible—"he murdered a woman."

Griffin squealed with pleasure and cried, "Oh, Kruppman! Kruppman, how you do go on!" and jabbed Virginia in the arm so hard a Herbert Tareyton jumped from her hand and bobbled across the Formica table.

The crowd at the soda bar had thinned and when the door to the outside opened he saw Mary come in and stand there for a second where the smoke inside and the snow outside swirled together. The mixture made a kind of—Kruppman's ridiculous story had put the phrase in his head—wolf-weather, and she was just a gray shadow against it. She bought a pack of cigarettes from Luke and went out again, a kerchief around her head, the pneumatic thing above the door hissing behind her. For a long time, always in fact, she had been at the center of whatever gang was the best one: in the second grade the one that walked home up Jewett Street together, and in the sixth grade the one that went bicycling as far away as the quarry and the Rentschler estate and played touch football Saturday afternoons, and in the ninth grade the one that went roller-skating at Candlebridge Park with the tenth-grade boys, and in the eleventh grade the one that held parties lasting past midnight and that on Sundays drove in caravans as far as Philadelphia and back. And all the while there had been a succession of boy friends, first Jack Stephens and Fritz March in their class and then boys a grade ahead and then Barrel Lord, who was a senior when they were sophomores and whose name was in the newspapers all football season, and then this last summer someone out of the school altogether, a man she met while working as a waitress in the city of Alton. So this year her weekends were taken up, and the party gang carried on as if she had never existed, and nobody saw her much except in school and when she stopped by in Luke's to buy a pack of cigarettes. Her silhouette against the big window had looked wan, her head hooded, her face nibbled by light, her fingers fiddling on the glassy counter with her coins. He yearned to reach out, to comfort her, but he was wedged deep in the shrill booths, between the jingling guts of the pinball machine and the hillbilly joy of the jukebox. The impulse left him with a disagreeable feeling. He had loved her too long to want to pity her; it endangered the investment of worship on which he had not yet realized any return.

The two hours of the school afternoon held Latin and a study hall. In study hall, while the five people at the table with him played ticktacktoe and sucked cough drops and yawned, he did all his homework for the next day. He prepared thirty lines of Vergil, Aeneas in the Underworld. The study hall was a huge low room in the basement of the building; its coziness crept into Tartarus. On the other side of the fudge-colored wall the circular saw in the woodworking shop whined and gasped and then whined again; it bit off pieces of wood with a rising, terrorized ınflection—bzzzzzup! He solved ten problems in trigonometry. His mind cut neatly through their knots and separated them, neat stiff squares of correctness, one by one from the long but finite plank of problems that connected Plane with Solid Geometry. Lastly, as the snow on a ragged slant drifted down into the cement pits outside the steel-mullioned windows, he read a short story by Edgar Allan Poe. He closed the book softly on the pleasing sonority of its final note of horror, gazed at the red, wet, menthol-scented inner membrane of Judy Whipple's yawn, rimmed with flaking pink lipstick, and yielded his conscience to the snug sense of his work done, of the snow falling, of the warm minutes that walked through their shelter so slowly. The perforated acoustic tiling above his head seemed the lining of a long tube that would go all the way: high school merging into college, college into graduate school, graduate school into teaching at a college—section man, assistant, associate, *full* professor, possessor of a dozen languages and a thousand books, a man brilliant in his forties, wise in his fifties, renowned in his sixties, revered in his seventies, and then retired, sitting in a study lined with acoustical books until the time for the last transition from silence to silence, and he would die, like Tennyson, with a copy of "Cymbeline" beside him on the moon-drenched bed.

After school he had to go to Room 101 and cut a sports cartoon into a stencil for the school paper. He liked the building best when it was nearly empty. Then the janitors went down the halls sowing seeds of red wax and making an immaculate harvest with broad brooms, gathering all the fluff and hairpins and wrappers and powder that the animals had dropped that day. The basketball team thumped in the hollow gymnasium; the cheerleaders rehearsed behind drawn curtains on the stage. In Room 101 two giggly typists with stripes bleached into their hair banged away between mistakes. At her desk Mrs. Gregory, the faculty sponsor, wearily passed her pencil through misspelled news copy. William took the shadow box from the top of the filing cabinet and the styluses and shaders from their drawer and the typed stencils from the closet where they hung, like fragile blue scarves, on hooks. "B-BALLERS BOW, 57-42," was the headline. He drew a tall b-baller bowing to a stumpy pagan idol, labeled "W" for victorious Weiserton High, and traced it in the soft blue wax with a fine loop stylus. His careful breath grazed his fingers. His eyebrows frowned while his heart throbbed happily on the giddy prattle of the typists. The shadow box was simply a plastic frame holding a pane of glass and lifted at one end by two legs so the light bulb, fitted in a tin tray, could slide under; it was like a primitive lean to sheltering a fire. As he worked, his eyes smarting, he mixed himself up with the light bulb, felt himself burning under a slanting roof upon which a huge hand scratched. The glass grew hot; the danger in the job was pulling the softened wax with your damp hand, distorting or tearing the typed letters. Sometimes the center of an o stuck to your skin like a bit of blue confetti. But he was expert and cautious. He returned the things to their places feeling airily tall, heightened by Mrs. Gregory's appreciation, which she expressed by keeping her back turned, in effect saying that other staff members were undependable but William did not need to be watched.

In the hall outside Room 101 only the shouts of a basketball scrimmage reverberated; the chant of the cheerleaders had been silenced. Though he had done everything, he felt reluctant to leave. Neither of his parents would be home yet. Since the death of his grandfather, both worked in Alton, and this building was as much his home. He knew all its nooks. On the second floor of the annex, beyond the art room, there was a strange, narrow boys' lavatory that no one ever seemed to use. It was here one time that Barry Kruppman tried to hypnotize him and thus cure his stuttering. Kruppman's voice purred and his irises turned tiny in the bulging whites, and for a moment William felt himself lean backward involuntarily, but he was distracted by the bits of bloodshot pink in the corners of these portentous eyes; the folly of giving up his will to an intellectual inferior occurred to him; he refused to let go and go under, and perhaps therefore his stuttering had continued.

The frosted window at the end of the long room cast a watery light on the green floor and made the porcelain urinals shine like slices of moon. The semiopacity of this window gave great denseness to the room's feeling of secrecy. William washed his hands with close attention, enjoying the lavish amount of powdered soap provided for him in this castle. He studied his face in the mirror, making infinitesimal adjustments to attain the absolutely most flattering angle, and then put his hands below his throat to get their strong, long-fingered beauty into the picture. As he walked toward the door he sang, closing his eyes and gasping as if he were a real Negro whose entire career depended upon this recording,

> "Who—told me so, dilly dilly,
> Who told me soho?"

Aii told myself, dilly dilly,
I told: me so."

When he emerged into the hall it was not empty: one girl walked down its varnished perspective toward him, Mary Landis, in a heavy brown coat, with a scarf on her head and books in her arms. Her locker was up here, on the second floor of the annex. His own was in the annex basement. A ticking sensation that existed neither in the medium of sound nor of light crowded against his throat. She flipped the scarf back from her hair and in a conversational voice that carried well down the clean planes of the hall said, "Hi, Billy." The name came from way back, when they were both children, and made him feel small but brave.

"Hi. How are you?"

"Fine." Her smile broadened.

What was so funny? Was she really, as it seemed, pleased to see him? "Du-did you just get through cheer-cheer-cheerleading?"

"Yes. Thank God. *Oh* she's so awful. She makes us do the same stupid locomotives for every cheer; I told her, no wonder nobody cheers any more."

"This is M-M-Miss Potter?" He blushed, feeling that he made an ugly face in getting past the "M." When he got caught in the middle of a sentence the constriction was somehow worse. He admired the way words poured up her throat, distinct and petulant.

"Yes, Potbottom Potter," she said. "She's just aching for a man and takes it out on us. I wish she would get one. Honestly, Billy, I have half a mind to quit. I'll be so glad when June comes, I'll never set foot in this idiotic building again."

Her lips, pale with the lipstick worn off, crinkled bitterly. Her face, foreshortened from the height of his eyes, looked cross as a cat's. He was a little shocked that poor Miss Potter and this kind, warm school stirred her to what he had to take as actual anger; this grittiness in her was the first abrasive texture he had struck today. Couldn't she see around teachers, into their fatigue, their poverty, their fear? It had been so long since he had spoken to her, he didn't know how insensitive she had become. "Don't quit," he brought out of his mouth at last. "It'd be n-n-nuh—it'd be nothing without you."

He pushed open the door at the end of the hall for her and as she passed under his arm she looked up and said, "Why, aren't you sweet."

The stair well, all asphalt and iron, smelled of galoshes. It felt more private than the hall, more specially theirs; there was something magical in its shifting multiplicity of planes as they descended that lifted the spell on his tongue, so that words came as quickly as his feet pattered on the steps.

"No I mean it," he said, "you're really a beautiful cheerleader. But then you're beautiful period."

"I have skinny legs."

"Who told you that?"

"Somebody."

"Well, *he* wasn't very sweet."

"No."

"Why do you hate this poor old school?"

"Now, Billy. You know you don't care about this junky place any more than I do."

"I love it. It breaks my heart to hear you say you want to get out, because then I'll never see you again."

"You don't care, do you?"

"Why *sure* I care you *know*"—their feet stopped; they had reached bottom, the first-floor landing, two brass-barred doors and a grimy radiator—"I've always li-loved you."

"You don't mean that."

"I do too. It's ridiculous but there it is. I wanted to tell you today and now I have."

He expected her to go out of the door in derision but instead she showed a willingness to discuss this awkward matter. He should have realized before this that women enjoy being talked to. "It's a very silly thing to say," she asserted tentatively.

"I don't see why," he said, fairly bold now that he couldn't seem more ridiculous, and yet picking his words with a certain strategic care. "It's not *that* silly to love somebody, I mean what the hell. Probably what's silly is not to do anything about it for umpteen years but then I never had an opportunity, I thought."

He set his books down on the radiator and she set hers down beside his. "What kind of opportunity were you waiting for?"

"Well, see, that's it; I didn't know." He wished, in a way, she'd go out the door. But she had propped herself against the wall and plainly expected him to keep talking. "Yuh-you were such a queen and I was such a nothing and I just didn't really want to presume." It wasn't very interesting; he was puzzled that she seemed to be interested. Her face had grown quite stern, the mouth very small and thoughtful, and he made a gesture with his hands intended to release her from the bother of thinking about it; after all, it was just a disposition of his heart, nothing permanent or expensive; maybe it was just his mother's idea anyway. Half in impatience to close the account, he asked, "Will you marry me?"

"You don't want to marry me," she said. "You're going to go on and be a great man."

He blushed in pleasure; is this how she saw him, is this how they all saw him, as worthless now but in time a great man? "No, I'm not," he said, "but anyway, you're great now. You're so pretty, Mary."

"Oh, Billy," she said, "if you were me for just one day you'd hate it."

She said this rather blankly, watching his eyes; he wished her voice had shown more misery. In his world of closed surfaces a panel, carelessly pushed, had opened, and he hung in this openness paralyzed, unable to think what to say. Nothing he could think of quite fitted the abruptly immense context. The radiator cleared its throat; its heat made, in the intimate volume just on this side of the doors on whose windows the snow beat limply, a provocative snugness; he supposed he should try, and stepped forward, his hands lifting toward her shoulders. Mary sidestepped between him and the radiator and put the scarf back on, lifting the cloth like a broad plaid halo above her head and then wrapping it around her chin and knotting it so she looked, in her red galoshes and bulky coat, like a peasant woman in a European movie. With her thick hair swathed, her face seemed pale and chunky, and when she recradled the books in her arms her back bent humbly under the point of the kerchief. "It's too hot in here," she said. "I have to wait for somebody." The disconnectedness of the two statements seemed natural in the fragmented atmosphere his stops and starts had produced. She bucked the brass bar with her shoulder and the door slammed open; he followed her into the weather.

"For the person who thinks your legs are too skinny?"

"Uh-huh." As she looked up at him a snowflake caught on the lashes of one eye. She jerkily rubbed that cheek on the shoulder of her coat and stamped a foot, splashing slush. Cold water gathered on the back of his shirt. He put his hands in his pockets and pressed his arms against his sides to keep from shivering.

"Thuh-then you wo-wo-won't marry me?" His wise instinct told him the only way back was by going forward, through absurdity.

"We don't know each other," she said.

"My God," he said. "Why not? I've known you since I was two."

"What do you know about me?"

This awful seriousness of hers; he must dissolve it. "That you're not a virgin." But instead of making her laugh, this made her face go dead and turned it away. Like beginning to kiss her, it had been a mistake; in part, he felt grateful for his mistakes. They were like loyal friends, who are nevertheless embarrassing. "What do you know about *me?*" he asked, setting himself up for a finishing insult but dreading it. He hated the stiff feel of his smile between his cheeks; glimpsed, as if the snow were a mirror, how hateful he looked.

"That you're basically very nice."

Her returning good for evil blinded him to his physical discomfort, set him burning with regret. "Listen," he said, "I did love you. Let's at least get that straight."

"You never loved anybody," she said. "You don't know what it is."

"O.K.," he said. "Pardon me."

"You're excused."

"You better wait in the school," he said. "He's-eez-eez going to be a long time."

She didn't answer and walked a little distance, toeing out in the childish way common to the women of the county, along the slack cable that divided the parking lot from the softball field. One bicycle, rusted as if it had been there for years, leaned in the rack, its fenders supporting thin crescents of white.

The warmth inside the door felt heavy, like a steamed towel laid against his face. William picked up his books and ran his pencil along the black ribs of the radiator before going down the stairs to his locker in the annex basement. The shadows were thick at the foot of the steps; suddenly it felt late, he must hurry and get home. He had the irrational fear they were going to lock him in. The cloistered odors of paper, sweat, and, from the woodshop at the far end of the basement hall, sawdust were no longer delightful to him. The tall green double lockers appeared to study him through the three air slits near their tops. When he opened his locker, and put his books on his shelf, below Marvin Wolf's, and removed his coat from his hook, his self seemed to crawl into the long dark space thus made vacant, the ugly, humiliated, educable self. In answer to a flick of his great hand the steel door weightlessly slammed shut, and through the length of his body he felt so clean and free he smiled. Between now and the happy future predicted for him he had nothing, almost literally nothing, to do.

DORIS LESSING

The Day Stalin Died

That day began badly for me with a letter from my aunt in Bournemouth. She reminded me that I had promised to take my cousin Jessie to be photographed at four that afternoon. So I had; and forgotten all about it. Having arranged to meet Bill at four, I had to telephone him to put it off. Bill was a film writer from the United States who, having had some trouble with an un-American Activities Committee, was blacklisted, could no longer earn his living, and was trying to get a permit to live in Britain. He was looking for someone to be a secretary to him. His wife had always been his secretary; but he was divorcing her after twenty years of marriage on the grounds that they had nothing in common. I planned to introduce him to Beatrice.

Beatrice was an old friend from South Africa whose passport had expired. Having been named as a communist, she knew that once she went back she would not get out again, and she wanted to stay another six months in Britain. But she had no money. She needed a job. I imagined that Bill and Beatrice might have a good deal in common; but later it turned out that they disapproved of each other. Beatrice said that Bill was corrupt, because he wrote sexy comedies for TV under another name and acted in bad films. She did not think his justification, namely, that a guy has to eat, had anything in its favor. Bill, for his part, had never been able to stand political women. But I was not to know about the incompatibility of my two dear friends; and I spent an hour following Bill through one switchboard after another, until at last I got him in some studio where he was rehearsing for a film about Lady Hamilton. He said it was quite all right, because he had forgotten about the appointment in any case. Beatrice did not have a telephone, so I sent her a telegram.

That left the afternoon free for cousin Jessie. I was just settling down to work when comrade Jean rang up to say she wanted to see me during lunch hour. Jean was for many years my self-appointed guide or mentor toward a correct political viewpoint. Perhaps it would be more accurate to say she was one of several self-appointed guides. It was Jean who, the day after I had my first volume of short stories published, took the morning off work to come and see me, in order to explain that one of the stories, I forget which, gave an incorrect analysis of the class struggle. I remember thinking at the time that there was a good deal in what she said.

When she arrived that day at lunch time, she had her sandwiches with her in a paper bag, but she accepted some coffee, and said she hoped I didn't mind her disturbing me, but she had been very upset by something she had been told I had said.

It appeared that a week before, at a meeting, I had remarked that there seemed to be evidence for supposing that a certain amount of dirty work must be going on in the Soviet Union. I would be the first to admit that this remark savored of flippancy.

Jean was a small, brisk woman with glasses, the daughter of a Bishop, whose devotion to the working class was proved by thirty years of work in the Party. Her manner toward me was always patient and kindly. "Comrade," she said, "intellectuals like yourself are under greater pressure from the forces of capitalist corruption than any other type of party cadre. It is not your fault. But you must be on your guard."

I said I thought I had been on my guard; but nevertheless I could not help feeling that there were times when the capitalist press, no doubt inadvertently, spoke the truth.

Jean tidily finished the sandwich she had begun, adjusted her spectacles, and gave me a short lecture about the necessity for unremitting vigilance on the part of the working class. She then said she must go, because she had to be at her office at two. She said that the only way an intellectual with my background could hope to attain to a correct working-class viewpoint was to work harder in the Party; to mix continually with the working class; and in this way my writing would gradually become a real weapon in the class struggle. She said, further, that she would send me the verbatim record of the Trials in the thirties, and if I read this, I would find my present vacillating attitude toward Soviet justice much improved. I said I had read the verbatim records a long time ago; and I always did think they sounded unconvincing. She said that I wasn't to worry; a really sound working-class attitude would develop with time.

With this she left me. I remember that, for one reason and another, I was rather depressed.

I was just settling down to work again when the telephone rang. It was Cousin Jessie, to say she could not come to my flat as arranged, because she was buying a dress to be photographed in. Could I meet her outside the dress shop in twenty minutes? I therefore abandoned work for the afternoon and took a taxi.

On the way the taxi man and I discussed the cost of living, the conduct of the government, and discovered that we had everything in common. Then he began telling me about his only daughter, aged eighteen, who wanted to marry his best friend, aged forty five. He did not hold with this; had said so; and thereby lost daughter and friend at one blow. What made it worse was that he had just read an article on psychology in the woman's magazine his wife took, from which he had suddenly gathered that his daughter was fatherfixated. "I felt real bad when I read that," he said. "It's a terrible thing to come on suddenlike, a thing like that." He drew up smartly outside the dress shop and I got out.

"I don't see why you should take it to heart," I said. "I wouldn't be at all surprised if we weren't all fatherfixated."

"That's not the way to talk," he said, holding out his hand for the fare. He was a small, bitter-looking man, with a head like a lemon or like a peanut, and his small blue eyes were brooding and bitter. "My old woman's been saying to me for years that I favored our Hazel too much. What gets me is, she might have been in the right of it."

"Well," I said, "look at it this way. It's better to love a child too much than too little."

"Love?" he said. "Love, is it? Precious little love or anything else these days if you ask me, and Hazel left home three months ago with my mate George and not so much as a postcard to say where or how."

"Life's pretty difficult for everyone," I said, "what with one thing and another."

"You can say that," he said.

This conversation might have gone on for some time, but I saw my cousin Jessie standing on the pavement watching us. I said goodby to the taxi man and turned, with some apprehension, to face her.

"I saw you," she said. "I saw you arguing with him. It's the only thing to do. They're getting so damned insolent these days. My principle is, tip them sixpence regardless of the distance, and if they argue, let them have it. Only yesterday I had one shouting at my back all down the street because I gave him sixpence. But we've got to stand up to them."

My cousin Jessie is a tall girl, broad-shouldered, aged about twenty-five. But she looks eighteen. She has light brown hair which she wears falling loose around her face, which is round and young and sharp-chinned. Her wide, light blue eyes are virginal and fierce. She is altogether like the daughter of a Viking, particularly when battling with bus conductors, taxi men, and porters. She and my Aunt Emma carry on permanent guerrilla warfare with the lower orders; an entertainment I begrudge neither of them, because their lives are dreary in the extreme. Besides, I believe their antagonists enjoy it. I remember once, after a set-to between Cousin Jessie and a taxi driver, when she had marched smartly off, shoulders swinging, he chuckled appreciatively and said: "That's a real old-fashioned type, that one. They don't make them like that these days."

"Have you bought your dress?" I asked.

"I've got it on," she said.

Cousin Jessie always wears the same outfit: a well-cut suit, a round-necked jersey, and a string of pearls. She looks very nice in it.

"Then we might as well go and get it over," I said.

"Mummy is coming, too," she said. She looked at me aggressively.

"Oh well," I said.

"But I told her I would *not* have her with me while I was buying my things. I told her to come and pick me up here. I will *not* have her choosing my clothes for me."

"Quite right," I said.

My Aunt Emma was coming toward us from the tearoom at the corner, where she had been biding her time. She is a very large woman, and she wears navy blue and pearls and white gloves like a policeman on traffic duty. She has a big, heavy-jowled, sorrowful face; and her bulldog eyes are nearly always fixed in disappointment on her daughter.

"There!" she said as she saw Jessie's suit. "You might just as well have had me with you."

"What do you mean?" said Jessie quickly.

"I went in to Renée's this morning and told them you were coming, and I asked them to show you that suit. And you've bought it. You see, I do know your tastes as I know my own."

Jessie lifted her sharp battling chin at her mother, who dropped her eyes in modest triumph and began poking at the pavement with the point of her umbrella.

"I think we'd better get started," I said.

Aunt Emma and Cousin Jessie, sending off currents of angry electricity into the air all around them, fell in beside me, and we proceeded up the street.

"We can get a bus at the top," I said.

"Yes, I think that would be better," said Aunt Emma. "I don't think I could face the insolence of another taxi driver today."

"No," said Jessie, "I couldn't either."

We went to the top of the bus, which was empty, and sat side by side along the two seats at the very front.

"I hope this man of yours is going to do Jessie justice," said Aunt Emma.

"I hope so too," I said. Aunt Emma believes that every writer lives in a whirl of photographers, press conferences, and publishers' parties. She thought I was the right person to choose a photographer. I wrote to say I wasn't. She wrote back to say it was the least I could do. "It doesn't matter in the slightest anyway," said Jessie, who always speaks in short, breathless, battling sentences, as from an unassuageably painful inner integrity that she doesn't expect anyone else to understand.

It seems that at the boarding house where Aunt Emma and Jessie live, there is an old inhabitant who has a brother who is a TV producer. Jessie had been acting in *Quiet Wedding* with the local Reps. Aunt Emma thought that if there was a nice photograph of Jessie, she could show it to the TV producer when he came to tea with his brother at the boarding house, which he was expected to do any weekend now; and if Jessie proved to be photogenic, the TV producer would whisk her off to London to be a TV star.

What Jessie thought of this campaign I did not know. I never did know what she thought of her mother's plans for her future. She might conform or she might not; but it was always with the same fierce and breathless integrity of indifference.

"If you're going to take that attitude, dear," said Aunt Emma, "I really don't think it's fair to the photographer."

"Oh, Mummy!" said Jessie.

"There's the conductor," said Aunt Emma, smiling bitterly. "I'm not paying a penny more than I did last time. The fare from Knightsbridge to Little Duchess Street is threepence."

"The fares have gone up," I said.

"Not a penny more," said Aunt Emma.

But it was not the conductor. It was two middle-aged people, who steadied each other at the top of the stair and then sat down, not side by side, but one in front of the other. I thought this was odd, particularly as the woman leaned forward over the man's shoulder and said in a loud parrot voice: "Yes, and if you turn my goldfish out of doors once more, I'll tell the landlady to turn *you* out. I've warned you before."

The man, in appearance like a damp, gray, squashed felt hat, looked in front of him and nodded with the jogging of the bus.

She said, "And there's fungus on my fish. You needn't think I don't know where it came from."

Suddenly he remarked in a high insistent voice, "There are all those little fishes in the depths of the sea, all those little fishes. We explode all these bombs at them, and we're not going to be forgiven for that, are we, we're not going to be forgiven for blowing up the poor little fishes."

She said, in an amiable voice, "I hadn't thought of that," and she left her seat behind him and sat in the same seat with him.

I had known that the afternoon was bound to get out of control at some point; but this conversation upset me. I was relieved when Aunt Emma restored normality by saying: "*There.* There never used to be people like *that.* It's the Labor Government."

"Oh, Mummy," said Jessie, "I'm not in the mood for politics this afternoon."

We had arrived at the place we wanted, and we got down off the bus. Aunt Emma gave the bus conductor ninepence for the three of us, which he took without comment. "And they're inefficient as well," she said.

It was drizzling and rather cold. We proceeded up the street, our heads together under Aunt Emma's umbrella.

Then I saw a newsboard with the item: Stalin Is Dying. I stopped and the umbrella went jerking up the pavement without me. The newspaperman was an old acquaintance. I said to him, "What's this, another of your sales boosters?" He said: "The old boy's had it, if you ask me. Well, the way he's lived—the way I look at it, he's had it coming to him. Must have the constitution of a bulldozer." He folded up a paper and gave it to me. "The way I look at it is that it doesn't do anyone any good to live that sort of life. Sedentary. Reading reports and sitting at meetings.

That's why I like this job—there's plenty of fresh air."

A dozen paces away Aunt Emma and Jessie were standing facing me, huddled together under the wet umbrella. "What's the matter, dear?" shouted Aunt Emma. "Can't you see, she's buying a newspaper," said Jessie crossly.

The newspaperman said, "It's going to make quite a change, with *him* gone. Not that I hold much with the goings-on out there. But they aren't used to democracy much, are they? What I mean is, if people aren't used to something, they don't miss it."

I ran through the drizzle to the umbrella. "Stalin's dying," I said.

"How do you know?" said Aunt Emma suspiciously.

"It says so in the newspaper."

"They said he was sick this morning, but I expect it's just propaganda. I won't believe it till I see it."

"Oh don't be silly, Mummy. How can you *see* it?" said Jessie.

We went on up the street. Aunt Emma said: "What do you think, would it have been better if Jessie had bought a nice pretty afternoon dress?"

"Oh, Mummy," said Jessie, "can't you see she's upset? It's the same for her as it would be for us if Churchill was dead."

"Oh, my *dear!*" said Aunt Emma, shocked, stopping dead. An umbrella spoke scraped across Jessie's scalp, and she squeaked. "Do put that umbrella down now. Can't you see it's stopped raining?" she said, irritably, rubbing her head.

Aunt Emma pushed and bundled at the umbrella until it collapsed, and Jessie took it and rolled it up. Aunt Emma, flushed and frowning, looked dubiously at me. "Would you like a nice cup of tea?" she said.

"Jessie's going to be late," I said. The photographer's door was just ahead.

"I do hope this man's going to get Jessie's expression," said Aunt Emma. "There's never been one yet that got her *look*."

Jessie went crossly ahead of us up some rather plushy stairs in a hallway with mauve and gold striped wallpaper. At the top there was a burst of Stravinsky as Jessie masterfully opened a door and strode in. We followed her into what seemed to be a drawing room, all white and gray and gold. The *Rites of Spring* tinkled a baby chandelier overhead; and there was no point in speaking until our host, a charming young man in a black velvet jacket, switched off the machine, which he did with an apologetic smile.

"I do hope this is the right place," said Aunt Emma. "I have brought my daughter to be photographed."

"Of course it's the right place," said the young man. "How delightful of you to come!" He took my Aunt Emma's white-gloved hands in his own and seemed to press her down on to a large sofa; a pressure to which she responded with a confused blush. Then he looked at me. I sat down quickly on another divan, a long way from Aunt Emma. He looked professionally at Jessie, smiling. She was standing on the carpet, hands linked behind her back, like an admiral on the job, frowning at him.

"You don't look at all relaxed," he said to her gently. "It's really no use at all, you know, unless you are really relaxed all over."

"I'm perfectly relaxed," said Jessie. "It's my cousin here who isn't relaxed."

I said, "I don't see that it matters whether I'm relaxed or not, because it's not me who is going to be photographed." A book fell off the divan beside me on the floor. It was *Prancing Nigger* by Ronald Firbank. Our host dived for it, anxiously.

"Do you read our Ron?" he asked.

"From time to time," I said.

"Personally I never read anything else," he said. "As far as I am concerned he said the last word. When I've read him all through, I begin again at the beginning and read him through again. I don't see that there's any point in anyone ever writing another word after Firbank."

This remark discouraged me, and I did not feel inclined to say anything.

"I think we could all do with a nice cup of tea," he said. "While I'm making it, would you like the gramophone on again?"

"I can't stand modern music," said Jessie.

"We can't all have the same tastes," he said. He was on his way to a door at the back, when it opened and another young man came in with a tea tray. He was as light and lithe as the first, with the same friendly ease of manner. He was wearing black jeans and a purple sweater, and his hair looked like two irregular glossy black wings on his head.

"Ah, bless you, dear!" said our host to him. Then, to us: "Let me introduce my friend and assistant, Jackie Smith. My name you know. Now if we all have a nice cup of tea, I feel that our vibrations might become just a *little* more harmonious."

All this time Jessie was standing-at-ease on the carpet. He handed her a cup of tea. She nodded toward me, saying, "Give it to her." He took it back and gave it to me. "What's the matter, dear?" he asked. "Aren't you feeling well?"

"I am perfectly well," I said, reading the newspaper.

"Stalin is dying," said Aunt Emma. "Or so they would like us to believe."

"Stalin?" said our host.

"That man in Russia," said Aunt Emma.

"Oh, you mean old Uncle Joe. Bless him."

Aunt Emma started. Jessie looked gruffly incredulous.

Jackie Smith came and sat down beside me and read the newspaper over my shoulder. "Well, well," he said. "Well, well, well, well." Then he giggled and said: "Nine doctors. If there were fifty doctors I still wouldn't feel very safe, would you?"

"No, not really," I said.

"Silly old nuisance," said Jackie Smith. "Should have bumped him off years ago. Obviously outlived his usefulness at the end of the war, wouldn't you think?"

"It seems rather hard to say," I said.

Our host, a teacup in one hand, raised the other in a peremptory gesture, "I don't like to hear that kind of thing," he said. "I really don't. God knows, if there's one thing I make a point of never knowing a thing about, it's politics, but during the war Uncle Joe and Roosevelt were absolutely my pin-up boys. But absolutely!"

Here Cousin Jessie, who had neither sat down nor taken a cup of tea, took a stride forward and said angrily: "Look, do you think we could get this *damned* business over with?" Her virginal pink cheeks shone with emotion, and her eyes were brightly unhappy.

"But, my *dear!*" said our host, putting down his cup. "But of course. If you feel like that, of course."

He looked at his assistant, Jackie, who reluctantly laid down the newspaper and pulled the cords of a curtain, revealing an alcove full of cameras and equipment. Then they both thoughtfully examined Jessie. "Perhaps it would help," said our host, "if you could give me an idea what you want it for? Publicity? Dust jackets? Or just for your lucky friends?"

"I don't know and I don't care," said Cousin Jessie.

Aunt Emma stood up and said: "I would like you to catch her expression. It's just a little *look* of hers. . . ."

Jessie clenched her fists at her.

"Aunt Emma," I said, "don't you think it would be a good idea if you and I went out for a little?"

"But my *dear*. . . ."

But our host had put his arm around her and was easing her to the door. "There's a duck," he was saying. "You do want me to make a good job of it, don't you? And I never could really do my best, even with the most sympathetic lookers-on."

Again Aunt Emma went limp, blushing. I took his place at her side and took her to the door. As we shut it, I heard Jackie Smith saying: "Music, do you think?" And Jessie: "I loathe music." And Jackie again: "We do rather find music helps, you know. . . ."

The door shut and Aunt Emma and I stood at the landing window, looking into the street.

"Has that young man done *you*?" she asked.

"He was recommended to me," I said.

Music started up from the room behind us. Aunt Emma's foot tapped on the floor. "Gilbert and Sullivan," she said. "Well, she can't say she loathes that. But I suppose she would, just to be difficult."

I lit a cigarette. *The Pirates of Penzance* abruptly stopped.

"Tell me, dear," said Aunt Emma, suddenly roguish, "about all the exciting things you are doing."

Aunt Emma always says this; and always I try hard to think of portions of my life suitable for presentation to Aunt Emma. "What have you been doing today, for instance?" I considered Bill; I considered Beatrice, I considered comrade Jean.

"I had lunch," I said, "with the daughter of a Bishop."

"Did you, dear?" she said doubtfully.

Music again: Cole Porter. "That doesn't sound right to me,"

said Aunt Emma. "It's modern, isn't it?" The music stopped. The door opened. Cousin Jessie stood there, shining with determination. "It's no good," she said. "I'm sorry, Mummy, but I'm not in the mood."

"But we won't be coming up to London again for another four months."

Our host and his assistant appeared behind cousin Jessie. Both were smiling rather bravely. "Perhaps we had better all forget about it," said Jackie Smith.

Our host said, "Yes, we'll try again later, when everyone is really themselves."

Jessie turned to the two young men and thrust out her hand at them. "I'm very sorry," she said, with her fierce virgin sincerity. "I am really terribly sorry."

Aunt Emma went forward, pushed aside Jessie, and shook their hands. "I must thank you both," she said, "for the tea."

Jackie Smith waved my newspaper over the three heads. "You've forgotten this," he said.

"Never mind, you can keep it," I said.

"Oh, bless you, now I can read all the gory details." The door shut on their friendly smiles.

"Well," said Aunt Emma, "I've never been more ashamed."

"I don't care," said Jessie fiercely. "I really couldn't care less."

We descended into the street. We shook each other's hands. We kissed each other's cheeks. We thanked each other. Aunt Emma and Cousin Jessie waved at a taxi. I got on a bus.

When I got home, the telephone was ringing. It was Beatrice. She said she had got my telegram, but she wanted to see me in any case. "Did you know Stalin was dying?" I said.

"Yes, of course. Look, it's absolutely essential to discuss this business on the Copper Belt."

"Why is it?"

"If we don't tell people the truth about it, who is going to?"

"Oh, well, I suppose so," I said.

She said she would be over in an hour. I set out my typewriter and began to work. The telephone rang. It was comrade Jean. "Have you heard the news?" she said. She was crying.

Comrade Jean had left her husband when he became a member of the Labor Party at the time of the Stalin-Hitler Pact, and ever since then had been living in bed-sitting rooms on bread, butter, and tea, with a portrait of Stalin over her bed.

"Yes, I have," I said.

"It's awful," she said sobbing. "Terrible. They've murdered him."

"Who had? How do you know?" I said.

"He's been murdered by capitalist agents," she said. "It's perfectly obvious."

"He was 73," I said.

"People don't die just like *that*," she said.

"They do at 73," I said.

"We will have to pledge ourselves to be worthy of him," she said.

"Yes," I said, "I suppose we will."

FLANNERY O'CONNOR

The Artificial Nigger

Mr. Head awakened to discover that the room was full of moonlight. He sat up and stared at the floor boards—the color of silver—and then at the ticking on his pillow, which might have been brocade, and after a second, he saw half of the moon five feet away in his shaving mirror, paused as if it were waiting for his permission to enter. It rolled forward and cast a dignifying light on everything. The straight chair against the wall looked stiff and attentive as if it were awaiting an order and Mr. Head's trousers, hanging to the back of it, had an almost noble air, like the garment some great man had just flung to his servant, but the face on the moon was a grave one. It gazed across the room and out the window where it floated over the horse stall and appeared to contemplate itself with the look of a young man who sees his old age before him.

Mr. Head could have said to it that age was a choice blessing and that only with years does a man enter into that calm understanding of life that makes him a suitable guide for the young. This, at least, had been his own experience.

He sat up and grasped the iron posts at the foot of his bed and raised himself until he could see the face on the alarm clock which sat on an overturned bucket beside the chair. The hour was two in the morning. The alarm on the clock did not work but he was not dependent on any mechanical means to awaken him. Sixty years had not dulled his responses; his physical reactions, like his moral ones, were guided by his will and strong character, and these could be seen plainly in his features. He had a long tube-like face with a long rounded open jaw and a long depressed nose. His eyes were alert but quiet, and in the miraculous moonlight they had a look of composure and of ancient wisdom as if they belonged to one of the great guides of men. He might have been Vergil summoned in the middle of the night to go to Dante, or better, Raphael, awakened by a blast of God's light to fly to the side of Tobias. The only dark spot in the room was Nelson's pallet, underneath the shadow of the window.

Nelson was hunched over on his side, his knees under his chin and his heels under his bottom. His new suit and hat were in the boxes that they had been sent in and these were on the floor at the foot of the pallet where he could get his hands on them as soon as he woke up. The slop jar, out of the shadow and made snow-white in the moonlight, appeared to stand guard over him like a small personal angel. Mr. Head lay back down, feeling entirely confident that he could carry out the moral mission of the coming day. He meant to be up before Nelson and to have the breakfast cooking by the time he awakened. The boy was always irked when Mr. Head was the first up. They would have to leave the house at four to get to the railroad junction by five-thirty. The train was to stop for them at five forty-five and they had to be there on time for this train was stopping merely to accommodate them.

This would be the boy's first trip to the city though he claimed it would be his second because he had been born there. Mr. Head had tried to point out to him that when he was born he didn't have the intelligence to determine his whereabouts but this had made no impression on the child at all and he continued to insist that this was to be his second trip. It would be Mr. Head's third trip. Nelson had said, "I will've already been there twict and I ain't but ten."

Mr. Head had contradicted him.

"If you ain't been there in fifteen years, how you know you'll be able to find your way about?" Nelson had asked. "How you know it hasn't changed some?"

"Have you ever," Mr. Head had asked, "seen me lost?"

Nelson certainly had not but he was a child who was never satisfied until he had given an impudent answer and he replied, "It's nowhere around here to get lost at."

"The day is going to come," Mr. Head prophesied, "when you'll find you ain't as smart as you think you are." He had been thinking about this trip for several months but it was for the most part in moral terms that he conceived it. It was to be a lesson that the boy would never forget. He was to find out from it that he had no cause for pride merely because he had been born in a city. He was to find out that the city is not a great place. Mr. Head meant him to see everything there is to see in a city so that he would be content to stay at home for the rest of his life. He fell asleep thinking how the boy would at last find out that he was not as smart as he thought he was.

He was awakened at three-thirty by the smell of fatback frying and he leaped off his cot. The pallet was empty and the clothes boxes had been thrown open. He put on his trousers and ran into the other room. The boy had a corn pone on cooking and had fried the meat. He was sitting in the half-dark at the table, drinking cold coffee out of a can. He had on his new suit and his new gray hat pulled low over his eyes. It was too big for him but they had ordered it a size large because they expected his head to grow. He didn't say anything but his entire figure suggested satisfaction at having arisen before Mr. Head.

Mr. Head went to the stove and brought the meat to the table in the skillet. "It's no hurry," he said. "You'll get there soon enough and it's no guarantee you'll like it when you do neither," and he sat down across from the boy whose hat teetered back slowly to reveal a fiercely expressionless face, very much the same shape as the old man's. They were grandfather and grandson but they looked enough alike to be brothers and brothers not too far apart in age, for Mr. Head had a youthful expression by daylight, while the boy's look was ancient, as if he knew everything already and would be pleased to forget it.

Mr. Head had once had a wife and daughter and when the wife died, the daughter ran away and returned after an interval with Nelson. Then one morning, without getting out of bed, she died and left Mr. Head with sole care of the year-old child. He had made the mistake of telling Nelson that he had been born in Atlanta. If he hadn't told him that, Nelson couldn't have insisted that this was going to be his second trip.

"You may not like it a bit," Mr. Head continued. "It'll be full of niggers."

The boy made a face as if he could handle a nigger.

"All right," Mr. Head said. "You ain't ever seen a nigger."

"You wasn't up very early," Nelson said.

"You ain't ever seen a nigger," Mr. Head repeated. "There hasn't been a nigger in this county since we run that one out twelve years ago and that was before you were born." He looked at the boy as if he were daring him to say he had ever seen a Negro.

"How you know I never saw a nigger when I lived there before?" Nelson asked. "I probably saw a lot of niggers."

"If you seen one you didn't know what he was," Mr. Head said, completely exasperated. "A six-month-old child don't know a nigger from anybody else."

"I reckon I'll know a nigger if I see one," the boy said and got up and straightened his slick sharply creased gray hat and went outside to the privy.

They reached the junction some time before the train was due to arrive and stood about two feet from the first set of tracks. Mr. Head carried a paper sack with some biscuits and a can of sardines in it for their lunch. A coarse-looking orange-colored sun coming up behind the east range of mountains was making the sky a dull red behind them, but in front of them it was still gray and they faced a gray transparent moon, hardly stronger than a thumbprint and completely without light. A small tin switch box and a black fuel tank were all there was to mark the place as a junction; the tracks were double and did not converge again until they were hidden behind the bends at either end of the clearing. Trains passing appeared to emerge from a tunnel of trees and, hit for a second by the cold sky, vanish terrified into the woods again. Mr. Head had had to make special arrangements with the ticket agent to have this train stop and he was secretly afraid it would not, in which case, he knew Nelson would say, "I never thought no train was going to stop for you." Under the useless morning moon the tracks looked white and fragile. Both the old man and the child stared ahead as if they were awaiting an apparition.

Then suddenly, before Mr. Head could make up his mind to turn back, there was a deep warning bleat and the train appeared, gliding very slowly, almost silently around the bend of trees about two hundred yards down the track, with one yellow front light shining. Mr. Head was still not certain it would stop and he felt it would make an even bigger idiot of him if it went by slowly. Both he and Nelson, however, were prepared to ignore the train if it passed them.

The engine charged by, filling their noses with the smell of hot metal and then the second coach came to a stop exactly where they were standing. A conductor with the face of an ancient bloated bulldog was on the step as if he expected them, though he did not look as if it mattered one way or the other to him if they got on or not. "To the right," he said.

Their entry took only a fraction of a second and the train was already speeding on as they entered the quiet car. Most of the travelers were still sleeping, some with their heads hanging off the chair arms, some stretched across two seats, and some sprawled out with their feet in the aisle. Mr. Head saw two unoccupied seats and pushed Nelson toward them. "Get in there by the winder," he said in his normal voice which was very loud at this hour of the morning. "Nobody cares if you sit there because it's nobody in it. Sit right there."

"I heard you," the boy muttered. "It's no use in you yelling," and he sat down and turned his head to the glass. There he saw a pale ghost-like face scowling at him beneath the brim of a pale ghost-like hat. His grandfather, looking quickly too, saw a different ghost, pale but grinning, under a black hat.

Mr. Head sat down and settled himself and took out his ticket and started reading aloud everything that was printed on it. People began to stir. Several woke up and stared at him. "Take off your hat," he said to Nelson and took off his own and put it on his knee. He had a small amount of white hair that had turned tobacco-colored over the years and this lay flat across the back of his head. The front of his head was bald and creased. Nelson took off his hat and put it on his knee and they waited for the conductor to come ask for their tickets.

The man across the aisle from them was spread out over two seats, his feet propped on the window and his head jutting into the aisle. He had on a light blue suit and a yellow shirt unbuttoned at the neck. His eyes had just opened and Mr. Head was ready to introduce himself when the conductor came up from behind and growled, "Tickets."

When the conductor had gone, Mr. Head gave Nelson the return half of his ticket and said, "Now put that in your pocket and don't lose it or you'll have to stay in the city."

"Maybe I will," Nelson said as if this were a reasonable suggestion.

Mr. Head ignored him. "First time this boy has ever been on a train," he explained to the man across the aisle, who was sitting up now on the edge of his seat with both feet on the floor.

Nelson jerked his hat on again and turned angrily to the window.

"He's never seen anything before," Mr. Head continued. "Ignorant as the day he was born, but I mean for him to get his fill once and for all."

The boy leaned forward, across his grandfather and toward the stranger. "I was born in the city," he said. "I was born there. This is my second trip." He said it in a high positive voice but the man across the aisle didn't look as if he understood. There were heavy purple circles under his eyes.

Mr. Head reached across the aisle and tapped him on the arm. "The thing to do with a boy," he said sagely, "is to show him all it is to show. Don't hold nothing back."

"Yeah," the man said. He gazed down at his swollen feet and

lifted the left one about ten inches from the floor. After a minute he put it down and lifted the other. All through the car people began to get up and move about and yawn and stretch. Separate voices could be heard here and there and then a general hum. Suddenly Mr. Head's serene expression changed. His mouth almost closed and a light, fierce and cautious both, came into his eyes. He was looking down the length of the car. Without turning, he caught Nelson by the arm and pulled him forward. "Look," he said.

A huge coffee-colored man was coming slowly forward. He had on a light suit and a yellow satin tie with a ruby pin in it. One of his hands rested on his stomach which rode majestically under his buttoned coat, and in the other he held the head of a black walking stick that he picked up and set down with a deliberate outward motion each time he took a step. He was proceeding very slowly, his large brown eyes gazing over the heads of the passengers. He had a small white mustache and white crinkly hair. Behind him there were two young women, both coffee-colored, one in a yellow dress and one in a green. Their progress was kept at the rate of his and they chatted in low throaty voices as they followed him.

Mr. Head's grip was tightening insistently on Nelson's arm. As the procession passed them, the light from a sapphire ring on the brown hand that picked up the cane reflected in Mr. Head's eye, but he did not look up nor did the tremendous man look at him. The group proceeded up the rest of the aisle and out of the car. Mr. Head's grip on Nelson's arm loosened. "What was that?" he asked.

"A man," the boy said and gave him an indignant look as if he were tired of having his intelligence insulted.

"What kind of a man?" Mr. Head persisted, his voice expressionless.

"A fat man," Nelson said. He was beginning to feel that he had better be cautious.

"You don't know what kind?" Mr. Head said in a final tone.

"An old man," the boy said and had a sudden foreboding that he was not going to enjoy the day.

"That was a nigger," Mr. Head said and sat back.

Nelson jumped up on the seat and stood looking backward to

the end of the car but the Negro had gone.

"I'd of thought you'd know a nigger since you seen so many when you was in the city on your first visit," Mr. Head continued. "That's his first nigger," he said to the man across the aisle.

The boy slid down into the seat. "You said they were black," he said in an angry voice. "You never said they were tan. How do you expect me to know anything when you don't tell me right?"

"You're just ignorant is all," Mr. Head said and he got up and moved over in the vacant seat by the man across the aisle.

Nelson turned backward again and looked where the Negro had disappeared. He felt that the Negro had deliberately walked down the aisle in order to make a fool of him and he hated him with a fierce raw fresh hate; and also, he understood now why his grandfather disliked them. He looked toward the window and the face there seemed to suggest that he might be inadequate to the day's exactions. He wondered if he would even recognize the city when they came to it.

After he had told several stories, Mr. Head realized that the man he was talking to was asleep and he got up and suggested to Nelson that they walk over the train and see the parts of it. He particularly wanted the boy to see the toilet so they went first to the men's room and examined the plumbing. Mr. Head demonstrated the ice-water cooler as if he had invented it and showed Nelson the bowl with the single spigot where the travelers brushed their teeth. They went through several cars and came to the diner.

This was the most elegant car in the train. It was painted a rich egg-yellow and had a wine-colored carpet on the floor. There were wide windows over the tables and great spaces of the rolling view were caught in miniature in the sides of the coffee pots and in the glasses. Three very black Negroes in white suits and aprons were running up and down the aisle, swinging trays and bowing and bending over the travelers eating breakfast. One of them rushed up to Mr. Head and Nelson and said, holding up two fingers, "Space for two!" but Mr. Head replied in a loud voice, "We eaten before we left!"

The waiter wore large brown spectacles that increased the size of his eye whites. "Stan' aside then please," he said with an airy wave of the arm as if he were brushing aside flies.

Neither Nelson nor Mr. Head moved a fraction of an inch. "Look," Mr. Head said.

The near corner of the diner, containing two tables, was set off from the rest by a saffron-colored curtain. One table was set but empty but at the other, facing them, his back to the drape, sat the tremendous Negro. He was speaking in a soft voice to the two women while he buttered a muffin. He had a heavy sad face and his neck bulged over his white collar on either side. "They rope them off," Mr. Head explained. Then he said, "Let's go see the kitchen," and they walked the length of the diner but the black waiter was coming fast behind them.

"Passengers are not allowed in the kitchen!" he said in a haughty voice. "Passengers are NOT allowed in the kitchen!"

Mr. Head stopped where he was and turned. "And there's good reason for that," he shouted into the Negro's chest, "because the cockroaches would run the passengers out!"

All the travelers laughed and Mr. Head and Nelson walked out, grinning. Mr. Head was known at home for his quick wit and Nelson felt a sudden keen pride in him. He realized the old man would be his only support in the strange place they were approaching. He would be entirely alone in the world if he were ever lost from his grandfather. A terrible excitement shook him and he wanted to take hold of Mr. Head's coat and hold on like a child.

As they went back to their seats they could see through the passing windows that the countryside was becoming speckled with small houses and shacks and that a highway ran alongside the train. Cars sped by on it, very small and fast. Nelson felt that there was less breath in the air than there had been thirty minutes ago. The man across the aisle had left and there was no one near for Mr. Head to hold a conversation with so he looked out the window, through his own reflection, and read aloud the names of the buildings they were passing. "The Dixie Chemical Corp!" he announced. "Southern Maid Flour! Dixie Doors! Southern Belle Cotton Products! Patty's Peanut Butter! Southern Mammy Cane Syrup!"

"Hush up!" Nelson hissed.

All over the car people were beginning to get up and take their luggage off the overhead racks. Women were putting on their coats and hats. The conductor stuck his head in the car and snarled, "Firstoppppmry," and Nelson lunged out of his sitting position, trembling. Mr. Head pushed him down by the shoulder.

"Keep your seat," he said in dignified tones. "The first stop is on the edge of town. The second stop is at the main railroad station." He had come by this knowledge on his first trip when he had got off at the first stop and had had to pay a man fifteen cents to take him into the heart of town. Nelson sat back down, very pale. For the first time in his life, he understood that his grandfather was indispensable to him.

The train stopped and let off a few passengers and glided on as if it had never ceased moving. Outside, behind rows of brown rickety houses, a line of blue buildings stood up, and beyond them a pale rose-gray sky faded away to nothing. The train moved into the railroad yard. Looking down, Nelson saw lines and lines of silver tracks multiplying and criss-crossing. Then before he could start counting them, the face in the window started out at him, gray but distinct, and he looked the other way. The train was in the station. Both he and Mr. Head jumped up and ran to the door. Neither noticed that they had left the paper sack with the lunch in it on the seat.

They walked stiffly through the small station and came out of a heavy door into the squall of traffic. Crowds were hurrying to work. Nelson didn't know where to look. Mr. Head leaned against the side of the building and glared in front of him.

Finally Nelson said, "Well, how do you see what all it is to see?"

Mr. Head didn't answer. Then as if the sight of people passing had given him the clue, he said, "You walk," and started off down the street. Nelson followed, steadying his hat. So many sights and sounds were flooding in on him that for the first block he hardly knew what he was seeing. At the second corner, Mr. Head turned and looked behind him at the station they had left, a putty-colored terminal with a concrete dome on top. He thought that if he could keep the dome always in sight, he would be able to get back in the afternoon to catch the train again.

As they walked along, Nelson began to distinguish details and take note of the store windows, jammed with every kind of equipment—hardware, drygoods, chicken feed, liquor. They passed one that Mr. Head called his particular attention to where you walked in and sat on a chair with your feet upon two rests and let a Negro polish your shoes. They walked slowly and stopped and stood at the entrances so he could see what went on in each place but they did not go into any of them. Mr. Head was determined not to go into any city store because on his first trip here, he had got lost in a large one and had found his way out only after many people had insulted him.

They came in the middle of the next block to a store that had a weighing machine in front of it and they both in turn stepped up on it and put in a penny and received a ticket. Mr. Head's ticket said, "You weigh 120 pounds. You are upright and brave and all your friends admire you." He put the ticket in his pocket, surprised that the machine should have got his character correct but his weight wrong, for he had weighed on a grain scale not long before and knew he weighed 110. Nelson's ticket said, "You weigh 98 pounds. You have a great destiny ahead of you but beware of dark women." Nelson did not know any women and he weighed only 68 pounds but Mr. Head pointed out that the machine had probably printed the number upside down, meaning the 9 for a 6.

They walked on and at the end of five blocks the dome of the terminal sank out of sight and Mr. Head turned to the left. Nelson could have stood in front of every store window for an hour if there had not been another more interesting one next to it. Suddenly he said, "I was born here!" Mr. Head turned and looked at him with horror. There was a sweaty brightness about his face. "This is where I come from!" he said.

Mr. Head was appalled. He saw the moment had come for drastic action. "Lemme show you one thing you ain't seen yet," he said and took him to the corner where there was a sewer entrance. "Squat down," he said, "and stick you head in there," and he held the back of the boy's coat while he got down and put his head in the sewer. He drew it back quickly, hearing a gurgling in the depths under the sidewalk. Then Mr. Head explained the sewer system, how the entire city was underlined with it, how it contained all the drainage and was full of rats and how a man could slide into it and be sucked along down endless pitchblack tunnels. At any minute any man in the city might be sucked into the sewer and never heard from again. He described it so well that Nelson was for some seconds shaken. He connected the sewer passages with the entrance to hell and understood for the first time how the world was put together in its lower parts. He drew away from the curb.

Then he said, "Yes, but you can stay away from the holes," and his face took on that stubborn look that was so exasperating to his grandfather. "This is where I come from!" he said.

Mr. Head was dismayed but he only muttered, "You'll get your fill," and they walked on. At the end of two more blocks he turned to the left, feeling that he was circling the dome; and he was correct for in a half-hour they passed in front of the railroad station again. At first Nelson did not notice that he was seeing the same stores twice but when they passed the one where you put your feet on the rests while the Negro polished your shoes, he perceived that they were walking in a circle.

"We done been here!" he shouted. "I don't believe you know where you're at!"

"The direction just slipped my mind for a minute," Mr. Head said and they turned down a different street. He still did not intend to let the dome get too far away and after two blocks in their new direction, he turned to the left. This street contained two and three-story wooden dwellings. Anyone passing on the sidewalk could see into the rooms and Mr. Head, glancing through one window, saw a woman lying on an iron bed, looking out, with a sheet pulled over her. Her knowing expression shook him. A fierce-looking boy on a bicycle came driving down out of nowhere and he had to jump to the side to keep from being hit. "It's nothing to them if they knock you down," he said. "You better keep closer to me."

They walked on for some time on streets like this before he remembered to turn again. The houses they were passing now were all unpainted and the wood in them looked rotten; the street between was narrower. Nelson saw a colored man. Then another. Then another. "Niggers live in these houses," he observed.

"Well come on and we'll go somewheres else," Mr. Head said. "We didn't come to look at niggers," and they turned down another street but they continued to see Negroes everywhere. Nelson's skin began to prickle and they stepped along at a faster pace in order to leave the neighborhood as soon as possible. There were colored men in their undershirts standing in the doors and colored women rocking on the sagging porches. Colored children played in the gutters and stopped what they were doing to look at them. Before long they began to pass rows of stores with colored customers in them but they didn't pause at the entrances of these. Black eyes in black faces were watching them from every direction. "Yes," Mr. Head said, "this is where you were born—right here with all these niggers."

Nelson scowled. "I think you done got us lost," he said.

Mr. Head swung around sharply and looked for the dome. It was nowhere in sight. "I ain't got us lost either," he said. "You're just tired of walking."

"I ain't tired, I'm hungry," Nelson said. "Give me a biscuit."

They discovered then that they had lost the lunch.

"You were the one holding the sack," Nelson said. "I would have kepaholt of it."

"If you want to direct this trip, I'll go on by myself and leave you right here," Mr. Head said and was pleased to see the boy turn white. However, he realized they were lost and drifting farther every minute from the station. He was hungry himself and beginning to be thirsty and since they had been in the colored neighborhood, they had both begun to sweat. Nelson had on his shoes and he was unaccustomed to them. The concrete sidewalks were very hard. They both wanted to find a place to sit down but this was impossible and they kept on walking, the boy muttering under his breath, "First you lost the sack and then you lost the way," and Mr. Head growling from time to time, "Anybody wants to be from this nigger heaven can be from it!"

By now the sun was well forward in the sky. The odor of dinners cooking drifted out to them. The Negroes were all at their doors to see them pass. "Whyn't you ast one of these niggers the way?" Nelson said. "You got us lost."

"This is where you were born," Mr. Head said. "You can ast one yourself if you want to."

Nelson was afraid of the colored men and he didn't want to be laughed at by the colored children. Up ahead he saw a large colored woman leaning in a doorway that opened onto the sidewalk. Her hair stood straight out from her head for about four inches all around and she was resting on bare brown feet that turned pink at the sides. She had on a pink dress that showed her exact shape. As they came abreast of her, she lazily lifted one hand to her head and her fingers disappeared into her hair.

Nelson stopped. He felt his breath drawn up by the woman's dark eyes. "How do you get back to town?" he said in a voice that did not sound like his own.

After a minute she said, "You in town now," in a rich low tone that made Nelson feel as if a cool spray had been turned on him.

"How do you get back to the train?" he said in the same reed-like voice.

"You can catch you a car," she said.

He understood she was making fun of him but he was too paralyzed even to scowl. He stood drinking in every detail of her. His eyes traveled up from her great knees to her forehead and then made a triangular path from the glistening sweat on her neck down and across her tremendous bosom and over her bare arm back to where her fingers lay hidden in her hair. He suddenly wanted her to reach down and pick him up and draw him against her and then he wanted to feel her breath on his face. He wanted to look down and down into her eyes while she held him tighter and tighter. He had never had such a feeling before. He felt as if he were reeling down through a pitchblack tunnel.

"You can go a block down yonder and catch you a car take you to the railroad station, Sugarpie," she said.

Nelson would have collapsed at her feet if Mr. Head had not pulled him roughly away. "You act like you don't have any sense!" the old man growled.

They hurried down the street and Nelson did not look back at the woman. He pushed his hat sharply forward over his face which was already burning with shame. The sneering ghost he had seen in the train window and all the foreboding feelings he had on the way returned to him and he remembered that his ticket from the scale had said to beware of dark women and that his grandfather's had said he was upright and brave. He took hold of the old man's hand, a sign of dependence that he seldom showed.

They headed down the street toward the car tracks where a long yellow rattling trolley was coming. Mr. Head had never boarded a streetcar and he let that one pass. Nelson was silent. From time to time his mouth trembled slightly but his grandfather, occupied with his own problems, paid him no attention. They stood on the corner and neither looked at the Negroes who were passing, going about their business just as if they had been white, except that most of them stopped and eyed Mr. Head and Nelson. It occurred to Mr. Head that since the streetcar ran on tracks, they could simply follow the tracks. He gave Nelson a slight push and explained that they would follow the tracks on into the railroad station, walking, and they set off.

Presently to their great relief they began to see white people again and Nelson sat down on the sidewalk against the wall of a building. "I got to rest myself some," he said. "You lost the sack and the direction. You can just wait on me to rest myself."

"There's the tracks in front of us," Mr. Head said. "All we got to do is keep them in sight and you could have remembered the sack as good as me. This is where you were born. This is your old home town. This is your second trip. You ought to know how to do," and he squatted down and continued in this vein but the boy, easing his burning feet out of his shoes, did not answer.

"And standing there grinning like a chim-pan-zee while a nigger woman gives you direction. Great Gawd!" Mr. Head said.

"I never said I was nothing but born here," the boy said in a shaky voice. "I never said I would or wouldn't like it. I never said I wanted to come. I only said I was born here and I never had nothing to do with that. I want to go home. I never wanted to come in the first place. It was all your big idea. How you know you ain't following the tracks in the wrong direction?"

This last had occurred to Mr. Head too. "All these people are white," he said.

"We ain't passed here before," Nelson said. This was a neighborhood of brick buildings that might have been lived in or might not. A few empty automobiles were parked along the curb and there was an occasional passerby. The heat of the pavement came up through Nelson's thin suit. His eyelids began to droop, and after a few minutes his head tilted forward. His shoulders twitched once or twice and then he fell over on his side and lay sprawled in an exhausted fit of sleep.

Mr. Head watched him silently. He was very tired himself but they could not both sleep at the same time and he could not have slept anyway because he did not know where he was. In a few minutes Nelson would wake up, refreshed by his sleep and very cocky, and would begin complaining that he had lost the sack and the way. You'd have a mighty sorry time if I wasn't here, Mr. Head thought; and then another idea occurred to him. He looked at the sprawled figure for several minutes; presently he stood up. He justified what he was going to do on the grounds that it is sometimes necessary to teach a child a lesson he won't forget, particularly when the child is always reasserting his position with some new impudence. He walked without a sound to the corner about twenty feet away and sat down on a covered garbage can in the alley where he could look out and watch Nelson wake up alone.

The boy was dozing fitfully, half conscious of vague noises and black forms moving up from some dark part of him into the light. His face worked in his sleep and he had pulled his knees up under his chin. The sun shed a dull dry light on the narrow street; everything looked like exactly what it was. After a while Mr. Head, hunched like an old monkey on the garbage can lid, decided that if Nelson didn't wake up soon, he would make a loud noise by bamming his foot against the can. He looked at his watch and discovered that it was two o'clock. Their train left at six and the possibility of missing it was too awful for him to think of. He kicked his foot backwards on the can and a hollow boom reverberated in the alley.

Nelson shot up onto his feet with a shout. He looked where his grandfather should have been and stared. He seemed to whirl several times and then, picking up his feet and throwing his head back, he dashed down the street like a wild maddened pony. Mr. Head jumped off the can and galloped after but the child was almost out of sight. He saw a streak of gray disappearing diagonally a block ahead. He ran as fast as he could, looking both ways down every intersection, but without sight of him again. Then as he passed the third intersection, completely winded, he saw about half a block down the street a scene that stopped him altogether. He crouched behind a trash box to watch and get his bearings.

Nelson was sitting with both legs spread out and by his side lay an elderly woman, screaming. Groceries were scattered about the sidewalk. A crowd of women had already gathered to see justice done and Mr. Head distinctly heard the old woman on the pavement shout, "You've broken my ankle and your daddy'll pay for it! Every nickel! Police! Police!" Several of the women were plucking at Nelson's shoulder but the boy seemed too dazed to get up.

Something forced Mr. Head from behind the trash box and forward, but only at a creeping pace. He had never in his life been accosted by a policeman. The women were milling around Nelson as if they might suddenly all dive on him at once and tear him to pieces, and the old woman continued to scream that her ankle was broken and to call for an officer. Mr. Head came on so slowly that he could have been taking a backward step after each forward one, but when he was about ten feet away, Nelson saw him and sprang. The child caught him around the hips and clung panting against him.

The women all turned on Mr. Head. The injured one sat up and shouted, "You sir! You'll pay every penny of my doctor's bill that your boy has caused. He's a juve-nile delinquent! Where is an officer? Somebody take this man's name and address!"

Mr. Head was trying to detach Nelson's fingers from the flesh in the back of his legs. The old man's head had lowered itself into his collar like a turtle's; his eyes were glazed with fear and caution.

"Your boy has broken my ankle!" the old woman shouted. "Police!"

Mr. Head sensed the approach of the policeman from behind. He stared straight ahead at the women who were massed in their fury like a solid wall to block his escape. "This is not my boy," he said. "I never seen him before."

He felt Nelson's fingers fall out of his flesh.

The women dropped back, staring at him with horror, as if they were so repulsed by a man who would deny his own image and likeness that they could not bear to lay hands on him. Mr.

Head walked on, through a space they silently cleared, and left Nelson behind. Ahead of him he saw nothing but a hollow tunnel that had once been the street.

The boy remained standing where he was, his neck craned forward and his hands hanging by his sides. His hat was jammed on his head so that there were no longer any creases in it. The injured woman got up and shook her fist at him and the others gave him pitying looks, but he didn't notice any of them. There was no policeman in sight.

In a minute he began to move mechanically, making no effort to catch up with his grandfather but merely following at about twenty paces. They walked on for five blocks in this way. Mr. Head's shoulders were sagging and his neck hung forward at such an angle that it was not visible from behind. He was afraid to turn his head. Finally he cut a short hopeful glance over his shoulder. Twenty feet behind him, he saw two small eyes piercing into his back like pitchfork prongs.

The boy was not of a forgiving nature but this was the first time he had ever had anything to forgive. Mr. Head had never disgraced himself before. After two more blocks, he turned and called over his shoulder in a high desperately gay voice, "Let's us go get us a Co' Cola somewheres!"

Nelson, with a dignity he had never shown before, turned and stood with his back to his grandfather.

Mr. Head began to feel the depth of his denial. His face as they walked on became all hollows and bare ridges. He saw nothing they were passing but he perceived that they had lost the car tracks. There was no dome to be seen anywhere and the afternoon was advancing. He knew that if dark overtook them in the city, they would be beaten and robbed. The speed of God's justice was only what he expected for himself, but he could not stand to think that his sins would be visited upon Nelson and that even now, he was leading the boy to his doom.

They continued to walk on block after block through an endless section of small brick houses until Mr. Head almost fell over a water spigot sticking up about six inches off the edge of a grass plot. He had not had a drink of water since early morning but felt he did not deserve it now. Then he thought that Nelson would be thirsty and they would both drink and be brought together. He squatted down and put his mouth to the nozzle and turned a cold stream of water into his throat. Then he called out in the high desperate voice, "Come on and getcher some water!"

This time the child stared through him for nearly sixty seconds. Mr. Head got up and walked on as if he had drunk poison. Nelson, though he had not had water since some he had drunk out of a paper cup on the train, passed by the spigot, disdaining to drink where his grandfather had. When Mr. Head realized this, he lost all hope. His face in the waning afternoon light looked ravaged and abandoned. He could feel the boy's steady hate, traveling at an even pace behind him and he knew that (if by some miracle they escaped being murdered in the city) it would continue just that way for the rest of his life. He knew that now he was wandering into a black strange place where nothing was like it had ever been before, a long old age without respect and an end that would be welcome because it would be the end.

As for Nelson, his mind had frozen around his grandfather's treachery as if he were trying to preserve it intact to present at the final judgment. He walked without looking to one side or the other, but every now and then his mouth would twitch and this was when he felt, from some remote place inside himself, a black mysterious form reach up as if it would melt his frozen vision in one hot grasp.

The sun dropped down behind a row of houses and hardly noticing, they passed into an elegant suburban section where mansions were set back from the road by lawns with birdbaths on them. Here everything was entirely deserted. For blocks they didn't pass even a dog. The big white houses were like partially submerged icebergs in the distance. There were no sidewalks, only drives, and these wound around and around in endless ridiculous circles. Nelson made no move to come nearer to Mr. Head. The old man felt that if he saw a sewer entrance he would drop down into it and let himself be carried away; and he could imagine the boy standing by, watching with only a slight interest, while he disappeared.

A loud bark jarred him to attention and he looked up to see a fat man approaching with two bulldogs. He waved both arms like someone shipwrecked on a desert island. "I'm lost!" he called.

"I'm lost and can't find my way and me and this boy have got to catch this train and I can't find the station. Oh Gawd I'm lost! Oh hep me Gawd I'm lost!"

The man, who was bald-headed and had on golf knickers, asked him what train he was trying to catch and Mr. Head began to get out his tickets, trembling so violently he could hardly hold them. Nelson had come up to within fifteen feet and stood watching.

"Well," the fat man said, giving him back the tickets, "you won't have time to get back to town to make this but you can catch it at the suburb stop. That's three blocks from here," and he began explaining how to get there.

Mr. Head stared as if he were slowly returning from the dead and when the man had finished and gone off with the dogs jumping at his heels, he turned to Nelson and said breathlessly, "We're going to get home!"

The child was standing about ten feet away, his face bloodless under the gray hat. His eyes were triumphantly cold. There was no light in them, no feeling, no interest. He was merely there, a small figure, waiting. Home was nothing to him.

Mr. Head turned slowly. He felt he knew now what time would be like without seasons and what heat would be like without light and what man would be like without salvation. He didn't care if he never made the train and if it had not been for what suddenly caught his attention, like a cry out of the gathering dusk, he might have forgotten there was a station to go to.

He had not walked five hundred yards down the road when he saw, within reach of him, the plaster figure of a Negro sitting bent over on a low yellow brick fence that curved around a wide lawn. The Negro was about Nelson's size and he was pitched forward at an unsteady angle because the putty that held him to the wall had cracked. One of his eyes was entirely white and he held a piece of brown watermelon.

Mr. Head stood looking at him silently until Nelson stopped at a little distance. Then as the two of them stood there, Mr. Head breathed, "An artificial nigger!"

It was not possible to tell if the artificial Negro were meant to be young or old; he looked too miserable to be either. He was meant to look happy because his mouth was stretched up at the corners but the chipped eye and the angle he was cocked at gave him a wild look of misery instead.

"An artificial nigger!" Nelson repeated in Mr. Head's exact tone.

The two of them stood there with their necks forward at almost the same angle and their shoulders curved in almost exactly the same way and their hands trembling identically in their pockets. Mr. Head looked like an ancient child and Nelson like a miniature old man. They stood gazing at the artificial Negro as if they were faced with some great mystery, some monument to another's victory that brought them together in their common defeat. They could both feel it dissolving their differences like an action of mercy. Mr. Head had never known before what mercy felt like because he had been too good to deserve any, but he felt he knew now. He looked at Nelson and understood that he must say something to the child to show that he was still wise and in the look the boy returned he saw a hungry need for that assurance. Nelson's eyes seemed to implore him to explain once and for all the mystery of existence.

Mr. Head opened his lips to make a lofty statement and heard himself say, "They ain't got enough real ones here. They got to have an artificial one."

After a second, the boy nodded with a strange shivering about his mouth, and said, "Let's go home before we get ourselves lost again."

Their train glided into the suburb stop just as they reached the station and they boarded it together, and ten minutes before it was due to arrive at the junction, they went to the door and stood ready to jump off if it did not stop; but it did, just as the moon, restored to its full splendor, sprang from a cloud and flooded the clearing with light. As they stepped off, the sage grass was shivering gently in shades of silver and the clinkers under their feet glittered with a fresh black light. The treetops, fencing the junction like the protecting walls of a garden, were darker than the sky which was hung with gigantic white clouds illuminated like lanterns.

Mr. Head stood very still and felt the action of mercy touch him again but this time he knew that there were no words in the world that could name it. He understood that it grew out of agony, which is not denied to any man and which is given in strange ways to children. He understood it was all a man could carry into death to give his Maker and he suddenly burned with shame that he had so little of it to take with him. He stood appalled, judging himself with the thoroughness of God, while the action of mercy covered his pride like a flame and consumed it. He had never thought himself a great sinner before but he saw now that his true depravity had been hidden from him lest it cause him despair. He realized that he was forgiven for sins from the beginning of time, when he had conceived of his own heart the sin of Adam, until the present, when he had denied poor Nelson. He saw that no sin was too monstrous for him to claim as his own, and since God loved in proportion as He forgave, he felt ready at that instant to enter Paradise.

Nelson, composing his expression under the shadow of his hat brim, watched him with a mixture of fatigue and suspicion, but as the train glided past them and disappeared like a frightened serpent into the woods, even his face lightened and he muttered, "I'm glad I've went once, but I'll never go back again!"

Part Two

INTRODUCTION

The stories of this second group might be described—
if we can forget the theater's use of the term—as
comedies of manners. Of this form, Henry James is the great
master in American literature, though his kind of comedy of
manners is not the only one. It was James' conviction that "proc-
esses, periods, intervals, stages, degrees, connexions, may be easily enough and barely enough named, may be unconvincingly
stated, in fiction, to the deep discredit of the writer, but it remains the very deuce to *represent* them . . . even though the
novelist who doesn't represent, and represent 'all the time,' is
lost. . . ." Comedies of manners are thus committed to the representation, as James calls it, of everything that happens in the
story. But James' principle of representation has to do with the
means, not the ends, and we must not conclude from it that comedies of manners are not just as much concerned with the meaning of what happens as any other kind of story. Comedies of
manners are written in the way they are because their authors are
convinced, as James put it, "of the perfect dependence of the
'moral' sense of a work of art on the amount of felt life concerned in producing it." With good writers of comedies of manners, that moral sense will be as profound as it is with good writers of any other kind of story.

What James meant by his remarks is made clear for us even by
so brief a comedy of manners as Thurber's *A Couple of Hamburgers*. Thurber barely names the things the husband and wife

do to annoy one another and never states why they do them. What he does is *show* us what they do, without giving it a name, in such a way that we can understand why they do it. We are never told that the husband prides himself on sticking to the language he grew up with and considers more modern phrases affected and namby-pamby, that he delights in the good old American expressions that go back even before his youth, that he loves timeworn popular songs of a particular gruesomeness and enjoys singing them loudly. Nor are we told that a part of his pleasure in these habits comes from his knowledge that they annoy his wife, who thinks they make him appear odd and no credit to her among "decent" people. It is the husband's feeling that this attitude is conventional and second-rate, that his interests are really superior to hers. We are not told that the wife has a series of apparently irrational prejudices about what makes a good place to eat—a belief that diners with nicknames are always run by Greeks and therefore bad, and that diners which sit at an angle to the road are cheap and poor—or that behind these rather impressionistic standards lies a real feeling for good food ("he knew she loved good coffee") and clean, attractive surroundings that makes her scorn her husband's cruder tastes. We are not told any of these things. We are made to see and hear what the husband and wife do and say because of them.

Out of the details of what they do and say Thurber gradually builds up the conflict between them. This conflict is unobtrusively framed by the problem of the "funny noise" in the car. The wife is ignorantly but decisively anxious about what she hears and describes it in absurd terms that give her husband a chance to laugh at her with overconfident assurance—*he* is the authority on cars—that leaves him badly exposed at the end of the story; singing loudly the songs he knows his wife hates, he fails to hear the now unquestionably ominous noises his wife hears. "She relaxed against the back of the seat, content to wait."

It is useful to compare *A Couple of Hamburgers* with Lawrence's *The White Stocking* in Part Three of this book. The two stories are about the same thing, the battle of the sexes. But what Lawrence asks us to think about are the powerful, buried feelings that underlie this battle, feelings that cannot be shown. What Thurber does is to show us an actual engagement in the battle, the clash of arms. Hamlet says of the plot of land that Fortinbras and his twenty thousand men are prepared to die for that it is

> a plot
> Whereon the numbers cannot try the cause,
> Which is not tomb and continent enough
> To hide the slain.

There is a similar absurdity about the triviality of the things Thurber's husband and wife quarrel over and the intensity of their feelings. Their quarrel is comic, as absurd as Fortinbras and his army. Nevertheless, like them, Thurber's husband and wife are serious. The things they quarrel over are only the visible occasions, the straws, as Hamlet calls them, over which they fight when "honor's at the stake"; for what is really in conflict between this husband and wife are the fundamental natures of men and women. The struggle between them can be as deadly as it is precisely because men and women need one another so badly.

These fundamental natures cannot be shown; all that ever appears on the human scene are their expressions in conduct, in the attitudes and manners of the combatants. These are the things we see and hear in actual life, and therefore these are the things the writer of comedies of manners seeks to make us see and hear in his stories. For him the true image of an experience—and therefore the most immediate and vivid representation of it—is a representation of what men and women actually do and say when they have that experience. That is what he makes his story out of, trusting that if he makes it true, his reader will think, yes, that is the way people are, and they are that way because, deep down in them are feelings I cannot describe except in the vaguest terms, but that I know from my own experience are there: I know what this writer means.

It would weaken a story like *A Couple of Hamburgers* if the author tried to describe directly the feelings that lie beneath such actions or if he intruded into his story with explanatory comments of his own. Thurber never tells us what his characters are really fighting about. If what they say and do is not well enough selected to makes us understand that, no explanation is going to make it real for us. Even in stories like Hemingway's *The Gambler, the Nun, and the Radio*, where Mr. Frazer appears to be stating the moral of the story in his meditation about "the opium of the people," it turns out that his meditation does not represent the story's full meaning at all.

The ideal of writers like James and Thurber and Hemingway is to have their characters think, speak, and act in such a way that the reader will understand without explanation what the story means. It seems to them that stories written in this way are as near to actual life as fiction can get. This is the way life itself presents to us such meaning as it has; in life, as in these stories, we see people act, hear them talk, and are sometimes aware of what they are thinking and feeling. But we never know directly what they think and feel.

Nevertheless, stories of this kind are, of course, "imitations" of life, not life itself. Their authors never intend them to be incoherent, full of irrelevancies, or chaotic, as actual life often is, or at least seems to be. As much as any other writers, these intend that everything in a story shall be relevant to what they feel the story means. But if they are to make us see what the story means without intruding on it to tell us, they must concentrate on the aspect of life that will most help them to do so. This aspect is manners, and the more fully developed and carefully shaded the manners of a community are, the more useful they will be.

This does not invariably mean, as it is sometimes said to mean, that comedies of manners must be written about wealthy and tightly knit social groups, which have time for the luxury of elaborate etiquettes, or about extraordinarily intelligent people who have the talent to play a complicated game of manners. Comedies of manners can be written about such people, and very good ones—like Edith Wharton's—have been. But they need not be. The people in the stories by Thurber and Roth in this book are ordinary people, not evidently extremely wealthy, certainly not members of a leisure class, and not extravagantly intellectual. But these stories convey their meanings by a representation of manners, by the gestures of ordinary husbands and wives, sergeants and privates, quite as completely as do James' stories. Nor are Hemingway's characters unusually rich or intellectual—indeed, Hemingway has often been accused of creating characters with no intelligence at all. What matters in all these stories is that the characters come from religious or social groups, professions or trades with highly developed and intricate codes of manners of their own (Hemingway liked to write about bullfighters, prize fighters, and soldiers as well as gamblers).

Brilliant comedies of manners have, of course, been written about intelligent people who have lived their lives in wealthy societies where manners are elaborate and subtle. Henry James' stories are about such people. But James is not writing these stories because he admires wealthy people. In fact, part of the moral of that strange ghost story, *The Jolly Corner*, is that Spencer Brydon has been saved from something like damnation, which living in the acquisitive business world of New York would have exposed him to, by living instead in London, where people are less acquisitive and finer. But in James' stories even London, in so far as it is wealthy and elegant, is subject to strong implicit criticism. In *The Lesson of the Master*, we first feel that St. George's great talent has been frustrated by his first wife's social ambition, and we sympathize with his efforts to prevent Paul Overt from marrying Miss Fancourt and perhaps suffering the same fate. This development is, incidentally, by no means complimentary to London's best society, in which all these people move. But then we discover that St. George is marrying Miss Fancourt, and in the great scene at the end of the story, we are, like Paul Overt, indignant at what appears to be his double-dealing. But St. George's conscience appears to be quite clear: "Of course I have [stopped writing]," he tells Paul. "It's too late. Didn't I tell you?" If that is true, if it is impossible, however great one's talent and one's belief in serious art, to start again after living some years as an English gentleman, then the best society of London is even worse than we had supposed, for it has not simply frustrated St. George, it has corrupted him, destroyed what had once been great seriousness and integrity.

What really counts in James—what he cared about—is the marvelous range and subtlety of the moral dilemmas he is able to dramatize in his stories because he is working with characters of considerable intelligence (whatever their moral shortcomings may be) who live in a highly cultivated and gregarious society (however corrupting it may be). James is interested in the range and subtlety of manners in this society, not the wealth and snobbishness, just as Hemingway is interested in the completeness and

definition of manners among his gamblers and prize fighters—
who are, incidentally, also sometimes snobbish and overcon-
cerned about money. In both cases, these artists are dealing with
societies that permit them to say what they want to by a representation of manners alone, but that ought not to fool us into
thinking that all they have to say is that the manners of their
chosen society are interesting.

HENRY JAMES

The Tone of Time

I was too pleased with what it struck me that, as an old, old friend, I had done for her, not to go to her that very afternoon with the news. I knew she worked late, as in general I also did; but I sacrificed for her sake a good hour of the February daylight. She was in her studio, as I had believed she would be, where her card ("Mary J. Tredick"—not Mary Jane, but Mary Juliana) was manfully on the door; a little tired, a little old and a good deal spotted, but with her ugly spectacles taken off, as soon as I appeared, to greet me. She kept on, while she scraped her palette and wiped her brushes, the big stained apron that covered her from head to foot and that I have often enough before seen her retain in conditions giving the measure of her renunciation of her desire to dazzle. Every fresh reminder of this brought home to me that she had given up everything but her work, and that there had been in her history some reason. But I was as far from the reason as ever. She had given up too much; this was just why one wanted to lend her a hand. I told her, at any rate, that I had a lovely job for her.

"To copy something I do like?"

Her complaint, I knew, was that people only gave orders, if they gave them at all, for things she did not like. But this wasn't a case of copying—not at all, at least, in the common sense. "It's for a portrait—quite in the air."

"Ah, you do portraits yourself!"

"Yes, and you know how. My trick won't serve for this. What's wanted is a pretty picture."

Reprinted from THE BETTER SORT by Henry James, by permission of Paul R. Reynolds & Son, 599 Fifth Avenue, New York 17, New York.

"Then of whom?"

"Of nobody. That is of anybody. Anybody you like."

She naturally wondered. "Do you mean I'm myself to choose my sitter?"

"Well, the oddity is that there is to *be* no sitter."

"Whom then is the picture to represent?"

"Why, a handsome, distinguished, agreeable man, of not more than forty, clean-shaven, thoroughly well-dressed, and a perfect gentleman."

She continued to stare. "And I'm to find him myself?"

I laughed at the term she used. "Yes, as you 'find' the canvas, the colours and the frame." After which I immediately explained. "I've just had the 'rummest' visit, the effect of which was to make me think of you. A lady, unknown to me and unintroduced, turned up at my place at three o'clock. She had come straight, she let me know, without preliminaries, on account of one's high reputation —the usual thing—and of her having admired one's work. Of course I instantly saw—I mean I saw it as soon as she named her affair—that she hadn't understood my work at all. What am I good for in the world but just the impression of the given, the presented case? I can do but the face I see."

"And do you think I can do the face I don't?"

"No, but you see so many more. You see them in fancy and memory, and they've come out, for you, from all the museums you've haunted and all the great things you've studied. I *know* you'll be able to see the one my visitor wants and to give it— what's the *crux* of the business—the tone of time."

She turned the question over. "What does she want it for?"

"Just *for* that—for the tone of time. And, except that it's to hang over her chimney, she didn't tell me. I've only my idea that it's to represent, to symbolise, as it were, her husband, who's not alive and who perhaps never was. This is exactly what will give you a free hand."

"With nothing to go by—no photographs or other portraits?"

"Nothing."

"She only proposes to describe him?"

"Not even; she wants the picture itself to do that. Her only condition is that he be a *très-bel homme*." [1]

---

[1] *Très-bel homme.* Very handsome man.

She had begun at last, a little thoughtfully, to remove her apron. "Is she French?"

"I don't know. I give it up. She calls herself Mrs. Bridgenorth."

Mary wondered. "*Connais pas!* [2] I never heard of her."

"You wouldn't."

"You mean it's not her real name?"

I hesitated. "I mean that she's a very downright fact, full of the implication that she'll pay a downright price. It's clear to me that you can ask what you like; and it's therefore a chance that I can't consent to your missing." My friend gave no sign either way, and I told my story. "She's a woman of fifty, perhaps of more, who has been pretty, and who still presents herself, with her grey hair a good deal powdered, as I judge, to carry it off, extraordinarily well. She was a little frightened and a little free; the latter because of the former. But she did uncommonly well, I thought, considering the oddity of her wish. This oddity she quite admits; she began indeed by insisting on it so in advance that I found myself expecting I didn't know what. She broke at moments into French, which was perfect, but no better than her English, which isn't vulgar; not more at least than that of everybody else. The things people *do* say, and the way they say them, to artists! She wanted immensely, I could see, not to fail of her errand, not to be treated as absurd; and she was extremely grateful to me for meeting her so far as I did. She was beautifully dressed and she came in a brougham."

My listener took it in; then, very quietly, "Is she respectable?" she inquired.

"Ah, there you are!" I laughed; "and how you always pick the point right out, even when one has endeavoured to diffuse a specious glamour! She's extraordinary," I pursued after an instant; "and just what she wants of the picture, I think, is to make her a little less so."

"Who is she, then? What is she?" my companion simply went on.

It threw me straightway back on one of my hobbies. "Ah, my dear, what is so interesting as life? What is, above all, so stupendous as London? There's everything in it, everything in the world, and nothing too amazing not some day to pop out at you.

[2] *Connais pas!* I don't know her.

What is a woman, faded, preserved, pretty, powdered, vague, odd, dropping on one without credentials, but with a carriage and very good lace? What is such a person but a person who *may* have had adventures, and have made them, in one way or another pay? They're, however, none of one's business; it's scarcely on the cards that one should ask her. I should like, with Mrs. Bridgenorth, to see a fellow ask! She goes in for propriety, the real thing. If I suspect her of being the creation of her own talents, she has clearly, on the other hand, seen a lot of life. Will you meet her?" I next demanded.

My hostess waited. "No."

"Then you won't try?"

"Need I meet her to try?" And the question made me guess that, so far as she had understood, she began to feel herself a little taken. "It seems strange," she none the less mused, "to attempt to please her on such a basis. To attempt," she presently added, "to please her at all. It's your idea that she's not married?" she, with this, a trifle inconsequentially asked.

"Well," I replied, "I've only had an hour to think of it, but I somehow already see the scene. Not immediately, not the day after, or even perhaps the year after the thing she desires is set up there, but in due process of time and on convenient opportunity, the transfiguration will occur. 'Who is that awfully handsome man?' 'That? Oh, that's an old sketch of my dear dead husband.' Because I told her—insidiously sounding her—that she would want it to look old, and that the tone of time is exactly what you're full of."

"I believe I am," Mary sighed at last.

"Then put on your hat." I had proposed to her on my arrival to come out to tea with me, and it was when left alone in the studio while she went to her room that I began to feel sure of the success of my errand. The vision that had an hour before determined me grew deeper and brighter for her while I moved about and looked at her things. There were more of them there on her hands than one liked to see; but at least they sharpened my confidence, which was pleasant for me in view of that of my visitor, who had accepted without reserve my plea for Miss Tredick. Four or five of her copies of famous portraits—ornaments of great public and private collections—were on the walls, and to see them again together was to feel at ease about my guarantee. The mellow manner of them was what I had had in my mind in saying, to excuse myself to Mrs. Bridgenorth, "Oh, my things, you know, look as if they had been painted tomorrow!" It made no difference that Mary's Vandykes and Gainsboroughs were reproductions and replicas, for I had known her more than once to amuse herself with doing the thing quite, as she called it, off her own bat. She had copied so bravely so many brave things that she had at the end of her brush an extraordinary bag of tricks. She had always replied to me that such things were mere clever humbug, but mere clever humbug was what our client happened to want. The thing was to let her have it—one could trust her for the rest. And at the same time that I mused in this way I observed to myself that there was already something more than, as the phrase is, met the eye in such response as I felt my friend had made. I had touched, without intention, more than one spring; I had set in motion more than one impulse. I found myself indeed quite certain of this after she had come back in her hat and her jacket. She was different—her idea had flowered; and she smiled at me from under her tense veil, while she drew over her firm, narrow hands a pair of fresh gloves, with a light distinctly new. "Please tell your friend that I'm greatly obliged to both of you and that I take the order."

"Good. And to give him all his good looks?"

"It's just to do *that* that I accept. I shall make him supremely beautiful—and supremely base."

"Base?" I just demurred.

"The finest gentleman you'll ever have seen, and the worst friend."

I wondered, as I was startled; but after an instant I laughed for joy. "Ah well, so long as he's not mine! I see we *shall* have him," I said as we went, for truly I had touched a spring. In fact I had touched *the* spring.

It rang, more or less, I was presently to find, all over the place. I went, as I had promised, to report to Mrs. Bridgenorth on my mission, and though she declared herself much gratified at the success of it I could see she a little resented the apparent absence of any desire on Miss Tredick's part for a preliminary conference. "I only thought she might have liked just to see me, and have imagined I might like to see *her*."

But I was full of comfort. "You'll see her when it's finished. You'll see her in time to thank her."

"And to pay her, I suppose," my hostess laughed, with an asperity that was, after all, not excessive. "Will she take very long?"

I thought. "She's so full of it that my impression would be that she'll do it off at a heat."

"She *is* full of it then?" she asked; and on hearing to what tune, though I told her but half, she broke out with admiration. "You artists are the most extraordinary people!" It was almost with a bad conscience that I confessed we indeed were, and while she said that what she meant was that we seemed to understand everything, and I rejoined that this was also what *I* meant, she took me into another room to see the place for the picture—a proceeding of which the effect was singularly to confirm the truth in question. The place for the picture—in her own room, as she called it, a boudoir at the back, overlooking the general garden of the approved modern row and, as she said, only just wanting that touch—proved exactly the place (the space of a large panel in the white woodwork over the mantel) that I had spoken of to my friend. She put it quite candidly, "Don't you see what it will do?" and looked at me, wonderfully, as for a sign that I could sympathetically take from her what she didn't literally say. She said it, poor woman, so very nearly that I had no difficulty whatever. The portrait, tastefully enshrined there, of the finest gentleman one should ever have seen, would do even more for herself than it would do for the room.

I may as well mention at once that my observation of Mrs. Bridgenorth was not in the least of a nature to unseat me from the hobby I have already named. In the light of the impression she made on me life seemed quite as prodigious and London quite as amazing as I had ever contended, and nothing could have been more in the key of that experience than the manner in which everything was vivid between us and nothing expressed. We remained on the surface with the tenacity of shipwrecked persons clinging to a plank. Our plank was our concentrated gaze at Mrs. Bridgenorth's mere present. We allowed her past to exist for us only in the form of the prettiness that she had gallantly rescued from it and to which a few scraps of its identity still adhered. She was amiable, gentle, consistently proper. She gave me more than anything else the sense, simply, of waiting. She was like a house so freshly and successfully "done up" that you were surprised it wasn't occupied. She was waiting for something to happen—for somebody to come. She was waiting, above all, for Mary Tredick's work. She clearly counted that it would help her.

I had foreseen the fact—the picture was produced at a heat; rapidly, directly, at all events, for the sort of thing it proved to be. I left my friend alone at first, left the ferment to work, troubling her with no questions and asking her for no news; two or three weeks passed, and I never went near her. Then at last, one afternoon as the light was failing, I looked in. She immediately knew what I wanted. "Oh yes, I'm doing him."

"Well," I said, "I've respected your intensity, but I *have* felt curious."

I may not perhaps say that she was never so sad as when she laughed, but it's certain that she always laughed when she was sad. When, however, poor dear, for that matter, was she, secretly, not? Her little gasps of mirth were the mark of her worst moments. But why should she have one of these just now? "Oh, I know your curiosity!" she replied to me; and the small chill of her amusement scarcely met it. "He's coming out, but I can't show him to you yet. I must muddle it through in my own way. It has insisted on being, after all, a 'likeness,'" she added. "But nobody will ever know."

"Nobody?"

"Nobody *she* sees."

"Ah, she doesn't, poor thing," I returned, "seem to see anybody!"

"So much the better. I'll risk it." On which I felt I should have to wait, though I had suddenly grown impatient. But I still hung about, and while I did so she explained. "If what I've done is really a portrait, the condition itself prescribed it. If I was to do the most beautiful man in the world I could do but one."

We looked at each other; then I laughed. "It can scarcely be *me!* But you're getting," I asked, "the great thing?"

"The infamy? Oh yes, please God."

It took away my breath a little, and I even for the moment scarce felt at liberty to press. But one could always be cheerful.

"What I meant is the tone of time."

"Getting it, my dear man? Didn't I get it long ago? Don't I *show* it—the tone of time?" she suddenly, strangely sighed at me, with something in her face I had never yet seen. "I can't give it to him more than—for all these years—he was to have given it to *me*."

I scarce knew what smothered passion, what remembered wrong, what mixture of joy and pain my words had accidentally quickened. Such an effect of them could only become, for me, an instant pity, which, however, I brought out but indirectly. "It's the tone," I smiled, "in which you're speaking now."

This served, unfortunately, as something of a check. "I didn't mean to speak now." Then with her eyes on the picture, "I've said everything there. Come back," she added, "in three days. He'll be all right."

He was indeed when at last I saw him. She had produced an extraordinary thing—a thing wonderful, ideal, for the part it was to play. My only reserve, from the first, was that it was too fine for its part, that something much less "sincere" would equally have served Mrs. Bridgenorth's purpose, and that relegation to that lady's "own room"—whatever charm it was to work there— might only mean for it cruel obscurity. The picture is before me now, so that I could describe it if description availed. It represents a man of about five-and-thirty, seen only as to the head and shoulders, but dressed, the observer gathers, in a fashion now almost antique and which was far from contemporaneous with the date of the work. His high, slightly narrow face, which would be perhaps too aquiline but for the beauty of the forehead and the sweetness of the mouth, has a charm that even, after all these years, still stirs my imagination. His type has altogether a distinction that you feel to have been firmly caught and yet not vulgarly emphasised. The eyes are just too near together, but they are, in a wondrous way, both careless and intense, while lip, cheek, and chin, smooth and clear, are admirably drawn. Youth is still, you see, in all his presence, the joy and pride of life, the perfection of a high spirit and the expectation of a great fortune, which he takes for granted with unconscious insolence. Nothing has ever happened to humiliate or disappoint him, and if my fancy doesn't run away with me the whole presentation of him is a guarantee that he will die without having suffered. He is so handsome in short, that you can scarcely say what he means, and so happy that you can scarcely guess what he feels.

It is of course, I hasten to add, an appreciably feminine rendering, light, delicate, vague, imperfectly synthetic—insistent and evasive, above all, in the wrong places; but the composition, none the less, is beautiful and the suggestion infinite. The grandest air of the thing struck me in fact, when first I saw it, as coming from the high artistic impertinence with which it offered itself as painted about 1850. It would have been a rare flower of refinement for that dark day. The "tone"—that of such a past as it pretended to—was there almost to excess, a brown bloom into which the image seemed mysteriously to retreat. The subject of it looks at me now across more years and more knowledge, but what I felt at the moment was that he managed to be at once a triumphant trick and a plausible evocation. He hushed me, I remember, with so many kinds of awe that I shouldn't have dreamt of asking who he was. All I said, after my first incoherences of wonder at my friend's practised skill, was: "And you've arrived at this truth without documents?"

"It depends on what you call documents."

"Without notes, sketches, studies?"

"I destroyed them years ago."

"Then you once had them?"

She just hung fire. "I once had everything."

It told me both more and less than I had asked; enough at all events to make my next question, as I uttered it, sound even to myself a little foolish. "So that it's all memory?"

From where she stood she looked once more at her work; after which she jerked away and, taking several steps, came back to me with something new—whatever it was I had already seen—in her air and answer. "It's all *hate!*" she threw at me, and then went out of the room. It was not till she had gone that I quite understood why. Extremely affected by the impression visibly made on me, she had burst into tears but had wished me not to see them. She left me alone for some time with her wonderful subject, and I again, in her absence, made things out. He was dead—he had been dead for years; the sole humiliation, as I have called it, that he was to know had come to him in that form. The canvas held and cherished him, in any case, as it only holds the dead. She had suffered from him, it came to me, the worst that a woman can suffer, and the wound he had dealt her, though hidden, had never effectually healed. It had bled again while she worked. Yet when she at last reappeared there was but one thing to say. "The beauty, heaven knows, I see. But I don't see what you call the infamy."

She gave him a last look—again she turned away. "Oh, he was like that."

"Well, whatever he was like," I remember replying, "I wonder you can bear to part with him. Isn't it better to let her see the picture first here?"

As to this she doubted. "I don't think I want her to come."

I wondered. "You continue to object so to meet her?"

"What good will it do? It's quite impossible I should alter him for her."

"Oh, she won't want *that!*" I laughed. "She'll adore him as he is."

"Are you quite sure of your idea?"

"That he's to figure as Mr. Bridgenorth? Well, if I hadn't been from the first, my dear lady, I should be now. Fancy, with the chance, her *not* jumping at him! Yes, he'll figure as Mr. Bridgenorth."

"Mr. Bridgenorth!" she echoed, making the sound, with her small, cold laugh, grotesquely poor for him. He might really have been a prince, and I wondered if he hadn't been. She had, at all events, a new notion. "Do you mind my having it taken to your place and letting her come to see it there?" Which—as I immediately embraced her proposal, deferring to her reasons, whatever they were—was what was speedily arranged.

II

The next day therefore I had the picture in charge, and on the following Mrs. Bridgenorth, whom I had notified, arrived. I had placed it, framed and on an easel, well in evidence, and I have never forgotten the look and the cry that, as she became aware of it, leaped into her face and from her lips. It was an extraordinary moment, all the more that it found me quite unprepared—so extraordinary that I scarce knew at first what had happened. By the time I really perceived, moreover, more things had happened than one, so that when I pulled myself together it was to face the situation as a whole. She had recognised on the instant the subject; that came first and was irrepressibly vivid in her. Her recognition had, for the length of a flash, lighted for her the possibility that the stroke had been directed. That came second, and she flushed with it as with a blow in the face. What came third—and it was what was really most wondrous—was the quick instinct of getting both her strange recognition and her blind suspicion well in hand. She couldn't control, however, poor woman, the strong colour in her face and the quick tears in her eyes. She could only glare at the canvas, gasping, grimacing, and try to gain time. Whether in surprise or in resentment she intensely reflected, feeling more than anything else how little she might prudently show; and I was conscious even at the moment that nothing of its kind could have been finer than her effort to swallow her shock in ten seconds.

How many seconds she took I didn't measure; enough, assuredly, for me also to profit. I gained more time than she, and the greatest oddity doubtless was my own private maneuver—the quickest calculation that, acting from a mere confused instinct, I had ever made. If she had known the great gentleman represented there and yet had determined on the spot to carry herself as ignorant, all my loyalty to Mary Tredick came to the surface in a prompt counter-move. What gave me opportunity was the red in her cheek. "Why, you've known him!"

I saw her ask herself for an instant if she mightn't successfully make her startled state pass as the mere glow of pleasure—her natural greeting to her acquisition. She was pathetically, yet at the same time almost comically, divided. Her line was so to cover her tracks that every avowal of a past connection was a danger; but it also concerned her safety to learn, in the light of our astounding coincidence, how far she already stood exposed. She meanwhile begged the question. She smiled through her tears. "He's too magnificent!"

But I gave her, as I say, all too little time. "Who is he? Who *was* he?"

It must have been my look still more than my words that determined her. She wavered but an instant longer, panted, laughed, cried again, and then, dropping into the nearest seat, gave herself up so completely that I was almost ashamed. "Do you think I'd tell you his *name?*" The burden of the backward years—all the effaced and ignored—lived again, almost like an accent unlearned but freshly breaking out at a touch, in the very sound of the words. These perceptions she, however, the next thing showed me, were a game at which two could play. She had to look at me but an instant. "Why, you really *don't* know it!"

I judged best to be frank. "I don't know it."

"Then how does *she?*"

"How do you?" I laughed. "I'm a different matter."

She sat a minute turning things round, staring at the picture. "The likeness, the likeness!" It was almost too much.

"It's so true?"

"Beyond everything."

I considered. "But a resemblance to a known individual—that wasn't what you wanted."

She sprang up at this in eager protest. "Ah, no one else would see it."

I showed again, I fear, my amusement. "No one but you and she?"

"It's her doing *him!*" She was held by her wonder. "Doesn't she, on your honour, know?"

"That his is the very head you would have liked if you had dared? Not a bit. How *should* she? She knows nothing—on my honour."

Mrs. Bridgenorth continued to marvel. "She just painted him for the kind of face—?"

"That corresponds with my description of what you wished? Precisely."

"But *how*—after so long? From memory? As a friend?"

"As a reminiscence—yes. Visual memory, you see, in our uncanny race, is wonderful. As the ideal thing, simply, for your purpose. You *are* then suited?" I, after an instant added.

She had again been gazing, and at this turned her eyes on me; but I saw she couldn't speak, couldn't do more at least than sound, unutterably, "Suited!" so that I was positively not surprised when suddenly—just as Mary had done, the power to produce this effect seeming a property of the model—she burst into tears. I feel no harsher in relating it, however I may appear, than I did at the moment, but it is a fact that while she just wept I literally had a fresh inspiration on behalf of Miss Tredick's interests. I knew exactly, moreover, before my companion had recovered herself, what she would next ask me; and I consciously brought this appeal on in order to have it over. I explained that I had not the least idea of the identity of our artist's sitter, to which she had given me no clue. I had nothing but my impression that she had known him—known him well; and, from whatever material she had worked, the fact of his having also been known to Mrs. Bridgenorth was a coincidence pure and simple. It partook of the nature of prodigy, but such prodigies did occur. My visitor listened with avidity and credulity. She was so far reassured. Then I saw her question come. "Well, if she doesn't dream he was ever anything to me—or what he will be now—I'm going to ask you, as a very particular favour, never to tell her. She will want to know of course exactly how I've been struck. You'll naturally say that I'm delighted, but may I exact from you that you say nothing else?"

There was supplication in her face, but I had to think. "There are conditions I must put to you first, and one of them is also a question, only more frank than yours. Was this mysterious personage—frustrated by death—to have married you?"

She met it bravely. "Certainly, if he had lived."

I was only amused at an artlessness in her "certainly." "Very good. But why do you wish the coincidence—"

"Kept from her?" She knew exactly why. "Because if she suspects it she won't let me have the picture. Therefore," she added with decision, "you must let me pay for it on the spot."

"What do you mean by on the spot?"

"I'll send you a cheque as soon as I get home."

"Oh," I laughed, "let us understand. Why do you consider she won't let you have the picture?"

She made me wait a little for this, but when it came it was perfectly lucid. "Because she'll then see how much more I must want it."

"How much less—wouldn't it be rather, since the bargain was, as the more convenient thing, not for a likeness?"

"Oh," said Mrs. Bridgenorth with impatience, "the likeness will take care of itself. She'll put this and that together." Then she brought out her real apprehension. "She'll be jealous."

"Oh!" I laughed. But I was startled.

"She'll hate me!"

I wondered. "But I don't think she liked him."

"Don't think?" She stared at me, with her echo, over all that might be in it, then seemed to find little enough. "I *say!*"

It was almost comically the old Mrs. Bridgenorth. "But I gather from her that he was bad."

"Then what was *she?*"

I barely hesitated. "What were *you?*"

"That's my own businesss." And she turned again to the picture. "He was good enough for her to do *that* of him."

I took it in once more. "Artistically speaking, for the way it's done, it's one of the most curious things I've ever seen."

"It's a grand treat!" said poor Mrs. Bridgenorth more simply.

It was, it *is* really; which is exactly what made the case so interesting. "Yet I feel somehow that, as I say, it wasn't done with love."

It was wonderful how she understood. "It was done with rage."

"Then what have you to fear?"

She knew again perfectly. "What happened when he made *me* jealous. So much," she declared, "that if you'll give me your word for silence—"

"Well?"

"Why, I'll double the money."

"Oh," I replied, taking a turn about in the excitement of our concurrence, "that's exactly what—to do a still better stroke for her—it had just come to *me* to propose!"

"It's understood then, on your oath, as a gentleman?" She was so eager that practically this settled it, though I moved to and fro a little while she watched me in suspense. It vibrated all round us that she had gone out to the thing in a stifled flare, that a whole close relation had in the few minutes revived. We know it of the truly amiable person that he will strain a point for another that he wouldn't strain for himself. The stroke to put in for Mary was positively prescribed. The work represented really much more than had been covenanted, and if the purchaser chose so to value it this was her own affair. I decided. "If it's understood also on *your* word."

We were so at one that we shook hands on it. "And when may I send?"

"Well, I shall see her this evening. Say early tomorrow."

"Early tomorrow." And I went with her to her brougham, into which, I remember, as she took leave, she expressed regret that she mightn't then and there have introduced the canvas for removal. I consoled her with remarking that she couldn't have got it in—which was not quite true.

I saw Mary Tredick before dinner, and though I was not quite ideally sure of my present ground with her I instantly brought out my news. "She's so delighted that I felt I must in conscience do something still better for you. She's not to have it on the original terms. I've put up the price."

Mary wondered. "But to what?"

"Well, to four hundred. If you say so, I'll try even for five."

"Oh, she'll never give that."

"I beg your pardon."

"After the agreement?" She looked grave. "I don't like such leaps and bounds."

"But, my dear child, they're yours. You contracted for a decorative trifle, and you've produced a breathing masterpiece."

She thought. "Is that what she calls it?" Then, as having to think too, I hesitated, "What does she know?" she pursued.

"She knows she wants it."

"So much as that?"

At this I had to brace myself a little. "So much that she'll send me the cheque this afternoon, and that you'll have mine by the first post in the morning."

"Before she has received the picture?"

"Oh, she'll send for it tomorrow." And as I was dining out and had still to dress, my time was up. Mary came with me to the door, where I repeated my assurance. "You shall receive my cheque by the first post." To which I added: "If it's little enough for a lady so much in need to pay for *any* husband, it isn't worth mentioning as the price of such a one as you've given her!"

I was in a hurry, but she held me. "Then you've felt your idea confirmed?"

"My idea?"

"That that's what I *have* given her?"

I suddenly fancied I had perhaps gone too far; but I had kept my cab and was already in it. "Well, put it," I called with excess of humour over the front, "that you've, at any rate, given *him* a wife!"

When on my return from dinner that night I let myself in, my first care, in my dusty studio, was to make light for another look at Mary's subject. I felt the impulse to bid him good night, but, to my astonishment, he was no longer there. His place was a void—he had already disappeared. I saw, however, after my first surprise, what had happened—saw it moreover, frankly, with some relief. As my servants were in bed I could ask no questions, but it was clear that Mrs. Bridgenorth, whose note, containing its cheque, lay on my table, had been after all unable to wait. The note, I found, mentioned nothing but the enclosure; but it had come by hand, and it was her silence that told the tale. Her messenger had been instructed to "act"; he had come with a vehicle, he had transferred to it canvas and frame. The prize was now therefore landed and the incident closed. I didn't altogether, the next morning, know why, but I had slept the better for the sense of these things, and as soon as my attendant came in I asked for details. It was on this that his answer surprised me. "No, sir, there was no man; she came herself. She had only a four-wheeler, but I helped her, and we got it in. It was a squeeze, sir, but she *would* take it."

I wondered. "She had a four-wheeler? and not her servant?"

"No, no, sir. She came, as you may say, single-handed."

"And not even in her brougham, which would have been larger."

My man, with his habit, weighed it. "But *have* she a brougham, sir?"

"Why, the one she was here in yesterday."

Then light broke. "Oh, *that* lady! It wasn't her, sir. It was Miss Tredick."

Light broke, but darkness a little followed it—a darkness that, after breakfast, guided my steps back to my friend. There, in its own first place, I met her creation; but I saw it would be a different thing meeting *her*. She immediately put down on a table, as if she had expected me, the cheque I had sent her overnight. "Yes, I've brought it away. And I can't take the money."

I found myself in despair. "You want to keep him?"

"I don't understand what has happened."

"You just back out?"

"I don't understand," she repeated, "what has happened." But what I had already perceived was, on the contrary, that she very nearly, that she in fact quite remarkably, did understand. It was as if in my zeal I had given away my case, and I felt that my test was coming. She had been thinking all night with intensity, and Mrs. Bridgenorth's generosity, coupled with Mrs. Bridgenorth's promptitude, had kept her awake. Thence, for a woman nervous and critical, imaginations, visions, questions. "Why, in writing me last night, did you take for granted it was *she* who had swooped down? Why," asked Mary Tredick, "should she swoop?"

Well, if I could drive a bargain for Mary, I felt I could *a fortiori* [3] lie for her. "Because it's her way. She does swoop. She's impatient and uncontrolled. And it's affectation for you to pretend," I said with diplomacy, "that you see no reason for her falling in love—"

"Falling in love?" She took me straight up.

"With that gentleman. Certainly. What woman wouldn't? What woman didn't? I really don't see, you know, your right to back out."

"I won't back out," she presently returned, "if you'll answer me a question. Does she know the man represented?" Then as I hung fire: "It has come to me that she must. It would account for so much. For the strange way I feel," she went on, "and for the extraordinary sum you've been able to extract from her."

It was a pity, and I flushed with it, besides wincing at the word she used. But Mrs. Bridgenorth and I, between us, had clearly made the figure too high. "You think that, if she *had* guessed, I would naturally work it to 'extract' more?"

She turned away from me on this and, looking blank in her trouble, moved vaguely about. Then she stopped. "I see him set up there. I hear her say it. What you said she would make him pass for."

I believe I foolishly tried—though only for an instant—to look as if I didn't remember what I had said. "Her husband?"

"He wasn't."

[3] *A fortiori.* For a still stronger reason.

The next minute I had risked it. "Was he yours?"

I don't know what I had expected, but I found myself surprised at her mere pacific headshake. "No."

"Then why mayn't he have been—?"

"Another woman's? Because he died, to my absolute knowledge, unmarried." She spoke as quietly. "He had known many women, and there was one in particular with whom he became—and too long remained—ruinously intimate. She tried to make him marry her, and he was very near it. Death, however, saved him. But she was the reason—"

"Yes?" I feared again from her a wave of pain, and I went on while she kept it back. "Did you know her?"

"She was one I wouldn't." Then she brought it out. "She was the reason he failed me." Her successful detachment somehow said all, reduced me to a flat, kind "Oh!" that marked my sense of her telling me, against my expectation, more than I knew what to do with. But it was just while I wondered how to turn her confidence that she repeated, in a changed voice, her challenge of a moment before. "Does she know the man represented?"

"I haven't the least idea." And having so acquitted myself I added, with what strikes me now as futility: "She certainly—yesterday—didn't name him."

"Only recognised him?"

"If she did she brilliantly concealed it."

"So that you got nothing from her?"

It was a question that offered me a certain advantage. "I thought you accused me of getting too much."

She gave me a long look, and I now saw everything in her face. "It's very nice—what you're doing for me, and you do it handsomely. It's beautiful—beautiful, and I thank you with all my heart. But I know."

"And what do you know?"

She went about now preparing her usual work. "What he must have been to her."

"You mean she was the person?"

"Well," she said, putting on her old spectacles, "she was one of them."

"And you accept so easily the astounding coincidence—?"

"Of my finding myself, after years, in so extraordinary a rela-

tion with her? What do you call easily? I've passed a night of
torment."

"But what put it into your head—?"

"That I had so blindly and strangely given him back to her?
You put it—yesterday."

"And how?"

"I can't tell you. You didn't in the least mean to—on the contrary. But you dropped the seed. The plant, after you had gone,"
she said with a businesslike pull at her easel, "the plant began
to grow. I *saw* them there—in your studio—face to face."

"You were jealous?" I laughed.

She gave me through her glasses another look, and they seemed,
from this moment, in their queerness, to have placed her quite on
the other side of the gulf of time. She was firm there; she was
settled; I couldn't get at her now. "I see she told you I *would*
be." I doubtless kept down too little my start at it, and she
immediately pursued. "You say I accept the coincidence, which
is of course prodigious. But such things happen. Why shouldn't
I accept it if you do?"

"*Do* I?" I smiled.

She began her work in silence, but she presently exclaimed:
"I'm glad I didn't meet her!"

"I don't yet see why you wouldn't."

"Neither do I. It was an instinct."

"Your instincts"—I tried to be ironic—"are miraculous."

"They *have* to be, to meet such accidents. I must ask you
kindly to tell her, when you return her gift, that now I have
done the picture I find I must after all keep it for myself."

"Giving no reason?"

She painted away. "She'll know the reason."

Well, by this time I knew it too; I knew so many things that
I feared my resistance was weak. If our wonderful client hadn't
been his wife in fact, she was not to be helped to become his
wife in fiction. I knew almost more than I can say, more at any
rate than I could then betray. He had been bound in common
mercy to stand by my friend, and he had basely forsaken her.
This indeed brought up the obscure, into which I shyly gazed.
"Why, even granting your theory, should you grudge her the
portrait? It was painted in bitterness."

"Yes. Without that—!"

"It wouldn't have come? Precisely. Is it in bitterness, then, you'll keep it?"

She looked up from her canvas. "In what would *you* keep it?"

It made me jump. "Do you mean I *may?*" Then I had my idea. "I'd give you her price for it!"

Her smile through her glasses was beautiful. "And afterwards make it over to her? You shall have it when I die." With which she came away from her easel, and I saw that I was staying her work and should properly go. So I put out my hand to her. "It took—whatever you will!—to paint it," she said, "but I shall keep it in joy." I could answer nothing now—had to cease to pretend; the thing was in her hands. For a moment we stood there, and I had again the sense, melancholy and final, of her being, as it were, remotely glazed and fixed into what she had done. "He's taken from me, and for all those years he's kept. Then she herself, by a prodigy—!" She lost herself again in the wonder of it.

"Unwittingly gives him back?"

She fairly, for an instant over the marvel, closed her eyes. "Gives him back."

Then it was I saw how he would be kept! But it was the end of my vision. I could only write, ruefully enough, to Mrs. Bridgenorth, whom I never met again, but of whose death—preceding by a couple of years Mary Tredick's—I happened to hear. This is an old man's tale. I have inherited the picture, in the deep beauty of which, however, darkness still lurks. No one, strange to say, has ever recognised the model, but everyone asks his name. I don't even know it.

HENRY JAMES

The Jolly Corner

"Every one asks me what I 'think' of everything,"
said Spencer Brydon; "and I make answer as I can—
begging or dodging the question, putting them off with any
nonsense. It wouldn't matter to any of them really," he went on,
"for, even were it possible to meet in that stand-and-deliver way
so silly a demand on so big a subject, my 'thoughts' would still
be almost altogether about something that concerns only myself."
He was talking to Miss Staverton, with whom for a couple of
months now he had availed himself of every possible occasion
to talk; this disposition and this resource, this comfort and support, as the situation in fact presented itself, having promptly
enough taken the first place in the considerable array of rather
unattenuated surprises attending his so strangely belated return
to America. Everything was somehow a surprise; and that might
be natural when one had so long and so consistently neglected
everything, taken pains to give surprises so much margin for play.
He had given them more than thirty years—thirty-three, to be
exact; and they now seemed to him to have organised their performance quite on the scale of that licence. He had been twenty-
three on leaving New York—he was fifty-six today: unless indeed
he were to reckon as he had sometimes, since his repatriation,
found himself feeling; in which case he would have lived longer
than is often allotted to man. It would have taken a century, he
repeatedly said to himself, and said also to Alice Staverton, it
would have taken a longer absence and a more averted mind than
those even of which he had been guilty, to pile up the differences,

Reprinted from THE NOVELS AND TALES OF HENRY JAMES
by Henry James, by permission of Paul R. Reynolds & Son, 599 Fifth Avenue, New York 17, New York.

the newnesses, the queernesses, above all the bignesses, for the better or the worse, that at present assaulted his vision wherever he
looked.

The great fact all the while however had been the incalculabil-
ity: since he *had* supposed himself, from decade to decade, to
be allowing, and in the most liberal and intelligent manner, for
brilliancy of change. He actually saw that he had allowed for
nothing; he missed what he would have been sure of finding, he
found what he would never have imagined. Proportions and
values were upside-down; the ugly things he had expected, the
ugly things of his far-away youth, when he had too promptly
waked up to a sense of the ugly—these uncanny phenomena placed
him rather, as it happened, under the charm; whereas the "swagger" things, the modern, the monstrous, the famous things, those
he had more particularly, like thousands of ingenuous enquirers
every year, come over to see, were exactly his sources of dismay.
They were as so many set traps for displeasure, above all for reaction, of which his restless tread was constantly pressing the
spring. It was interesting, doubtless, the whole show, but it would
have been too disconcerting hadn't a certain finer truth saved the
situation. He had distinctly not, in this steadier light, come over
all for the monstrosities; he had come, not only in the last analysis
but quite on the face of the act, under an impulse with which they
had nothing to do. He had come—putting the thing pompously—
to look at his "property," which he had thus for a third of a
century not been within four thousand miles of; or, expressing
it less sordidly, he had yielded to the humour of seeing again
his house on the jolly corner, as he usually, and quite fondly,
described it—the one in which he had first seen the light, in which
various members of his family had lived and had died, in which the
holidays of his overschooled boyhood had been passed and the
few social flowers of his chilled adolescence gathered, and which,
alienated then for so long a period, had, through the successive
deaths of his two brothers and the termination of old arrangements, come wholly into his hands. He was the owner of another,
not quite so "good"—the jolly corner having been, from far back,
superlatively extended and consecrated; and the value of the pair
represented his main capital, with an income consisting, in these
later years, of their respective rents which (thanks precisely to

their original excellent type) had never been depressingly low. He could live in "Europe," as he had been in the habit of living, on the product of these flourishing New York leases, and all the better since, that of the second structure, the mere number in its long row, having within a twelvemonth fallen in, renovation at a high advance had proved beautifully possible.

These were items of property indeed, but he had found himself since his arrival distinguishing more than ever between them. The house within the street, two bristling blocks westward, was already in course of reconstruction as a tall mass of flats; he had acceded, some time before, to overtures for this conversion—in which, now that it was going forward, it had been not the least of his astonishments to find himself able, on the spot, and though without a previous ounce of such experience, to participate with a certain intelligence, almost with a certain authority. He had lived his life with his back so turned to such concerns and his face addressed to those of so different an order that he scarce knew what to make of this lively stir, in a compartment of his mind never yet penetrated, of a capacity for business and a sense for construction. These virtues, so common all round him now, had been dormant in his own organism—where it might be said of them perhaps that they had slept the sleep of the just. At present, in the splendid autumn weather—the autumn at least was a pure boon in the terrible place—he loafed about his "work" undeterred, secretly agitated; not in the least "minding" that the whole proposition, as they said, was vulgar and sordid, and ready to climb ladders, to walk the plank, to handle materials and look wise about them, to ask questions, in fine, and challenge explanations and really "go into" figures.

It amused, it verily quite charmed him; and, by the same stroke, it amused, and even more, Alice Staverton, though perhaps charming her perceptibly less. She wasn't however going to be better off for it, as *he* was—and so astonishingly much: nothing was now likely, he knew, ever to make her better off than she found herself, in the afternoon of life, as the delicately frugal possessor and tenant of the small house in Irving Place to which she had subtly managed to cling through her almost unbroken New York career. If he knew the way to it now better than to any other address among the dreadful multiplied numberings which seemed to him to reduce the whole place to some vast ledger-page, overgrown, fantastic, of ruled and criss-crossed lines and figures—if he had formed, for his consolation, that habit, it was really not a little because of the charm of his having encountered and recognised, in the vast wilderness of the wholesale, breaking through the mere gross generalisation of wealth and force and success, a small still scene where items and shades, all delicate things, kept the sharpness of the notes of a high voice perfectly trained, and where economy hung about like the scent of a garden. His old friend lived with one maid and herself dusted her relics and trimmed her lamps and polished her silver; she stood off, in the awful modern crush, when she could, but she sallied forth and did battle when the challenge was really to "spirit," the spirit she after all confessed to, proudly and a little shyly, as to that of the better time, that of *their* common, their quite far-away and antediluvian social period and order. She made use of the street-cars when need be, the terrible things that people scrambled for as the panic-stricken at sea scramble for the boats; she affronted, inscrutably, under stress, all the public concussions and ordeals; and yet, with that slim mystifying grace of her appearance, which defied you to say if she were a fair young woman who looked older through trouble, or a fine smooth older one who looked young through successful indifference; with her precious reference, above all, to memories and histories into which he could enter, she was as exquisite for him as some pale pressed flower (a rarity to begin with), and, failing other sweetnesses, she was a sufficient reward of his effort. They had communities of knowledge, "their" knowledge (this discriminating possessive was always on her lips) of presences of the other age, presences all overlaid, in his case, by the experience of a man and the freedom of a wanderer, overlaid by pleasure, by infidelity, by passages of life that were strange and dim to her, just by "Europe" in short, but still unobscured, still exposed and cherished, under that pious visitation of the spirit from which she had never been diverted.

She had come with him one day to see how his "apartment-house" was rising; he had helped her over gaps and explained to her plans, and while they were there had happened to have, before her, a brief but lively discussion with the man in charge, the representative of the building-firm that had undertaken his work.

He had found himself quite "standing-up" to his personage over a failure on the latter's part to observe some detail of one of their noted conditions, and had so lucidly urged his case that, besides ever so prettily flushing, at the time, for sympathy in his triumph, she had afterwards said to him (though to a slightly greater effect of irony) that he had clearly for too many years neglected a real gift. If he had but stayed at home he would have anticipated the inventor of the sky-scraper. If he had but stayed at home he would have discovered his genius in time really to start some new variety of awful architectural hare and run it till it burrowed in a gold-mine. He was to remember these words, while the weeks elapsed, for the small silver ring they had sounded over the queerest and deepest of his own lately most disguised and most muffled vibrations.

It had begun to be present to him after the first fortnight, it had broken out with the oddest abruptness, this particular wanton wonderment: it met him there—and this was the image under which he himself judged the matter, or at least, not a little, thrilled and flushed with it—very much as he might have been met by some strange figure, some unexpected occupant, at a turn of one of the dim passages of an empty house. The quaint analogy quite hauntingly remained with him, when he didn't indeed rather improve it by a still intenser form: that of his opening a door behind which he would have made sure of finding nothing, a door into a room shuttered and void, and yet so coming, with a great suppressed start, on some quite erect confronting presence, something planted in the middle of the place and facing him through the dusk. After that visit to the house in construction he walked with his companion to see the other and always so much the better one, which in the eastward direction formed one of the corners, the "jolly" one precisely, of the street now so generally dishonoured and disfigured in its westward reaches, and of the comparatively conservative Avenue. The Avenue still had pretensions, as Miss Staverton said, to decency; the old people had mostly gone, the old names were unknown, and here and there an old association seemed to stray, all vaguely, like some very aged person, out too late, whom you might meet and feel the impulse to watch or follow, in kindness, for safe restoration to shelter.

They went in together, our friends; he admitted himself with his key, as he kept no one there, he explained, preferring, for his reasons, to leave the place empty, under a simple arrangement with a good woman living in the neighbourhood and who came for a daily hour to open windows and dust and sweep. Spencer Brydon had his reasons and was growingly aware of them; they seemed to him better each time he was there, though he didn't name them all to his companion, any more than he told her as yet how often, how quite absurdly often, he himself came. He only let her see for the present, while they walked through the great blank rooms, that absolute vacancy reigned and that, from top to bottom, there was nothing but Mrs. Muldoon's broomstick, in a corner, to tempt the burglar. Mrs. Muldoon was then on the premises, and she loquaciously attended the visitors, preceding them from room to room and pushing back shutters and throwing up sashes—all to show them, as she remarked, how little there was to see. There was little indeed to see in the great gaunt shell where the main dispositions and the general apportionment of space, the style of an age of ampler allowances, had nevertheless for its master their honest pleading message, affecting him as some good old servant's, some lifelong retainer's appeal for a character, or even for a retiring-pension; yet it was also a remark of Mrs. Muldoon's that, glad as she was to oblige him by her noonday round, there was a request she greatly hoped he would never make of her. If he should wish her for any reason to come in after dark she would just tell him, if he "plased," that he must ask it of somebody else.

The fact that there was nothing to see didn't militate for the worthy woman against what one *might* see, and she put it frankly to Miss Staverton that no lady could be expected to like, could she? "craping up to thim top storeys in the ayvil hours." The gas and the electric light were off the house, and she fairly evoked a gruesome vision of her march through the great grey rooms—so many of them as there were too!—with her glimmering taper. Miss Staverton met her honest glare with a smile and the profession that she herself certainly would recoil from such an adventure. Spencer Brydon meanwhile held his peace—for the moment; the question of the "evil" hours in his old home had already become too grave for him. He had begun some time since to "crape," and he knew just why a packet of candles addressed to that pursuit had been stowed by his own hand, three weeks before, at the back of a drawer of the fine old sideboard that occupied, as a "fixture," the deep recess in the dining-room. Just now he laughed at his companions—quickly however changing the subject; for the reason that, in the first place, his laugh struck him even at that moment as starting the odd echo, the conscious human resonance (he scarcely knew how to qualify it) that sounds made while he was there alone sent back to his ear or his fancy; and that, in the second, he imagined Alice Staverton for the instant on the point of asking him, with a divination, if he ever so prowled. There were divinations he was unprepared for, and he had at all events averted enquiry by the time Mrs. Muldoon had left them, passing on to other parts.

There was happily enough to say, on so consecrated a spot, that could be said freely and fairly; so that a whole train of declarations was precipitated by his friend's having herself broken out, after a yearning look around: "But I hope you don't mean they want you to pull *this* to pieces!" His answer came, promptly, with his re-awakened wrath: it was of course exactly what they wanted, and what they were "at" him for, daily, with the iteration of people who couldn't for their life understand a man's liability to decent feelings. He had found the place, just as it stood and beyond what he could express, an interest and a joy. There were values other than the beastly rent-values, and in short, in short—! But it was thus Miss Staverton took him up. "In short you're to make so good a thing of your sky-scraper that, living in luxury on *those* ill-gotten gains, you can afford for a while to be sentimental here!" Her smile had for him, with the words, the particular mild irony with which he found half her talk suffused; an irony without bitterness and that came, exactly, from her having so much imagination—not, like the cheap sarcasms with which one heard most people, about the world of "society," bid for the reputation of cleverness, from nobody's really having any. It was agreeable to him at this very moment to be sure that when he had answered, after a brief demur, "Well yes: so, precisely, you may put it!" her imagination would still do him justice. He explained that even if never a dollar were to come to him from the other house he would nevertheless cherish this one; and he dwelt, further, while they lingered and wandered, on the fact of the stupefaction he was already exciting, the positive mystification he felt himself create.

234 · HENRY JAMES

He spoke of the value of all he read into it, into the mere sight
of the walls, mere shapes of the room, mere sound of the floors,
mere feel, in his hand, of the old silver-plated knobs of the several
mahogany doors, which suggested the pressure of the palms of the
dead; the seventy years of the past in fine that these things represented, the annals of nearly three generations, counting his grandfather's, the one that had ended there, and the impalpable ashes
of his long-extinct youth, afloat in the very air like microscopic
motes. She listened to everything; she was a woman who answered
intimately but who utterly didn't chatter. She scattered abroad
therefore no cloud of words; she could assent, she could agree,
above all she could encourage, without doing that. Only at the last
she went a little further than he had done himself. "And then how
do you know? You may still, after all, want to live here." It rather
indeed pulled him up, for it wasn't what he had been thinking, at
least in her sense of the words. "You mean I may decide to stay on
for the sake of it?"

"Well, *with* such a home—!" But quite beautifully, she had
too much tact to dot so monstrous an *i*, and it was precisely an
illustration of the way she didn't rattle. How could any one—of
any wit—insist on any one else's "wanting" to live in New York?

"Oh," he said, "I *might* have lived here (since I had my opportunity early in life); I might have put in here all these years.
Then everything would have been different enough—and, I dare
say, 'funny' enough. But that's another matter. And then the
beauty of it—I mean of my perversity, of my refusal to agree to
a 'deal'—is just in the total absence of a reason. Don't you see
that if I had a reason about the matter at all it would *have* to be
the other way, and would then be inevitably a reason of dollars?
There are no reasons here *but* of dollars. Let us therefore have
none whatever—not the ghost of one."

They were back in the hall then for departure, but from where
they stood the vista was large, through an open door, into the
great square main saloon, with its almost antique felicity of brave
spaces between windows. Her eyes came back from that reach and
met his own a moment. "Are you very sure the 'ghost' of one
doesn't, much rather, serve—?"

He had a positive sense of turning pale. But it was as near as
they were then to come. For he made answer, he believed, between

a glare and a grin: "Oh ghosts—of course the place must swarm with them! I should be ashamed of it if it didn't. Poor Mrs. Muldoon's right, and it's why I haven't asked her to do more than look in."

Miss Staverton's gaze again lost itself, and things she didn't utter, it was clear, came and went in her mind. She might even for the minute, off there in the fine room, have imagined some element dimly gathering. Simplified like the death-mask of a handsome face, it perhaps produced for her just then an effect akin to the stir of an expression in the "set" commemorative plaster. Yet whatever her impression may have been she produced instead a vague platitude. "Well, if it were only furnished and lived in—!"

She appeared to imply that in case of its being still furnished he might have been a little less opposed to the idea of a return. But she passed straight into the vestibule, as if to leave her words behind her, and the next moment he had opened the house-door and was standing with her on the steps. He closed the door and, while he re-pocketed his key, looking up and down, they took in the comparatively harsh actuality of the Avenue, which reminded him of the assault of the outer light of the Desert on the traveller emerging from an Egyptian tomb. But he risked before they stepped into the street his gathering answer to her speech. "For me it *is* lived in. For me it *is* furnished." At which it was easy for her to sigh "Ah yes—!" all vaguely and discreetly; since his parents and his favourite sister, to say nothing of other kin, in numbers, had run their course and met their end there. That represented, within the walls, ineffaceable life.

It was a few days after this that, during an hour passed with her again, he had expressed his impatience of the too flattering curiosity—among the people he met—about his appreciation of New York. He had arrived at none at all that was socially producible, and as for that matter of his "thinking" (thinking the better or the worse of anything there) he was wholly taken up with one subject of thought. It was mere vain egoism, and it was moreover, if she liked, a morbid obsession. He found all things come back to the question of what he personally might have been, how he might have led his life and "turned out," if he had not so, at the outset, given it up. And confessing for the first time

to the intensity within him of this absurd speculation—which but
proved also, no doubt, the habit of too selfishly thinking—he
affirmed the impotence there of any other source of interest, any
other native appeal. "What would it have made of me, what would
it have made of me? I keep for ever wondering, all idiotically; as
if I could possibly know! I see what it has made of dozens of
others, those I meet, and it positively aches within me, to the point
of exasperation, that it would have made something of me as well.
Only I can't make out *what*, and the worry of it, the small rage of
curiosity never to be satisfied, brings back what I remember to
have felt, once or twice, after judging best, for reasons, to burn
some important letter unopened. I've been sorry, I've hated it—
I've never known what was in the letter. You may of course say
it's a trifle—!"

"I don't say it's a trifle," Miss Staverton gravely interrupted.

She was seated by her fire, and before her, on his feet and restless, he turned to and fro between this intensity of his idea and a
fitful and unseeing inspection, through his single eye-glass, of the
dear little old objects on her chimney-piece. Her interruption
made him for an instant look at her harder. "I shouldn't care if
you did!" he laughed, however; "and it's only a figure, at any
rate, for the way I now feel. *Not* to have followed my perverse
young course—and almost in the teeth of my father's curse, as I
may say; not to have kept it up, so, 'over there,' from that day to
this, without a doubt or a pang; not, above all, to have liked it,
to have loved it, so much, loved it, no doubt, with such an abysmal
conceit of my own preference: some variation from *that*, I say,
must have produced some different effect for my life and for my
'form.' I should have stuck here—if it had been possible; and I
was too young, at twenty-three, to judge, *pour deux sous*, whether
it *were* possible. If I had waited I might have seen it was, and
then I might have been, by staying here, something nearer to one
of these types who have been hammered so hard and made so
keen by their conditions. It isn't that I admire them so much—
the question of any charm in them, or of any charm, beyond that
of the rank money-passion, exerted by their conditions *for* them,
has nothing to do with the matter: it's only a question of what
fantastic, yet perfectly possible, development of my own nature
I mayn't have missed. It comes over me that I had then a strange

alter ego deep down somewhere within me, as the full-blown flower is in the small tight bud, and that I just took the course, I just transferred him to the climate, that blighted him for once and for ever."

"And you wonder about the flower," Miss Staverton said. "So do I, if you want to know; and so I've been wondering these several weeks. I believe in the flower," she continued, "I feel it would have been quite splendid, quite huge and monstrous."

"Monstrous above all!" her visitor echoed; "and I imagine, by the same stroke, quite hideous and offensive."

"You don't believe that," she returned; "if you did you wouldn't wonder. You'd know, and that would be enough for you. What you feel—and what I feel *for* you—is that you'd have had power."

"You'd have liked me that way?" he asked.

She barely hung fire. "How should I not have liked you?"

"I see. You'd have liked me, have preferred me, a billionaire!"

"How should I not have liked you?" she simply again asked.

He stood before her still—her question kept him motionless. He took it in, so much there was of it; and indeed his not otherwise meeting it testified to that. "I know at least what I am," he simply went on; "the other side of the medal's clear enough. I've not been edifying—I believe I'm thought in a hundred quarters to have been barely decent. I've followed strange paths and worshipped strange gods; it must have come to you again and again —in fact you've admitted to me as much—that I was leading, at any time these thirty years, a selfish frivolous scandalous life. And you see what it has made of me."

She just waited, smiling at him. "You see what it has made of *me*."

"Oh you're a person whom nothing can have altered. You were born to be what you are, anywhere, anyway: you've the perfection nothing else could have blighted. And you don't see how, without my exile, I shouldn't have been waiting till now—?" But he pulled up for the strange pang.

"The great thing to see," she presently said, "seems to me to be that it has spoiled nothing. It hasn't spoiled your being here at last. It hasn't spoiled this. It hasn't spoiled your speaking—" She also however faltered.

He wondered at everything her controlled emotion might mean. "Do you believe then—too dreadfully!—that I *am* as good as I might ever have been?"

"Oh no! Far from it!" With which she got up from her chair and was nearer to him. "But I don't care," she smiled.

"You mean I'm good enough?"

She considered a little. "Will you believe it if I say so? I mean will you let that settle your question for you?" And then as if making out in his face that he drew back from this, that he had some idea which, however absurd, he couldn't yet bargain away: "Oh you don't care either—but very differently: you don't care for anything but yourself."

Spencer Brydon recognised it—it was in fact what he had absolutely professed. Yet he importantly qualified. "*He* isn't myself. He's the just so totally other person. But I do want to see him," he added. "And I can. And I shall."

Their eyes met for a minute while he guessed from something in hers that she divined his strange sense. But neither of them otherwise expressed it, and her apparent understanding, with no protesting shock, no easy derision, touched him more deeply than anything yet, constituting for his stifled perversity, on the spot, an element that was like breatheable air. What she said however was unexpected. "Well, *I've* seen him."

"You—?"

"I've seen him in a dream."

"Oh a 'dream'—!" It let him down.

"But twice over," she continued. "I saw him as I see you now."

"You've dreamed the same dream—?"

"Twice over," she repeated. "The very same."

This did somehow a little speak to him, as it also gratified him. "You dream about me at that rate?"

"Ah about *him!*" she smiled.

His eyes again sounded her. "Then you know all about him." And as she said nothing more: "What's the wretch like?"

She hesitated, and it was as if he were pressing her so hard that, resisting for reasons of her own, she had to turn away. "I'll tell you some other time!"

II

It was after this that there was most of a virtue for him, most of a cultivated charm, most of a preposterous secret thrill, in the particular form of surrender to his obsession and of address to what he more and more believed to be his privilege. It was what in these weeks he was living for—since he really felt life to begin but after Mrs. Muldoon had retired from the scene and, visiting the ample house from attic to cellar, making sure he was alone, he knew himself in safe possession and, as he tacitly expressed it, let himself go. He sometimes came twice in the twenty-four hours; the moments he liked best were those of gathering dusk, of the short autumn twilight; this was the time of which, again and again, he found himself hoping most. Then he could, as seemed to him, most intimately wander and wait, linger and listen, feel his fine attention, never in his life before so fine, on the pulse of the great vague place: he preferred the lampless hour and only wished he might have prolonged each day the deep crepuscular spell. Later—rarely much before midnight, but then for a considerable vigil—he watched with his glimmering light; moving slowly, holding it high, playing it far, rejoicing above all, as much as he might, in open vistas, reaches of communication between rooms and by passages; the long straight chance or show, as he would have called it, for the revelation he pretended to invite. It was a practice he found he could perfectly "work" without exciting remark; no one was in the least the wiser for it; even Alice Staverton, who was moreover a well of discretion, didn't quite fully imagine.

He let himself in and let himself out with the assurance of calm proprietorship; and accident so far favoured him that, if a fat Avenue "officer" had happened on occasion to see him entering at eleven-thirty, he had never yet, to the best of his belief, been noticed as emerging at two. He walked there on the crisp November nights, arrived regularly at the evening's end; it was as easy to do this after dining out as to take his way to a club or to his hotel. When he left his club, if he hadn't been dining out, it was ostensibly to go to his hotel; and when he left his hotel, if he had spent a part of the evening there, it was ostensibly to go to his club. Everything was easy in fine; everything conspired and promoted: there was truly even in the strain of his experience something that glossed over, something that salved and simplified, all the rest of consciousness. He circulated, talked, renewed, loosely and pleasantly, old relations—met indeed, so far as he could, new expectations and seemed to make out on the whole that in spite of the career, of such different contacts, which he had spoken of to

Miss Staverton as ministering so little, for those who might have watched it, to edification, he was positively rather liked than not. He was a dim secondary social success—and all with people who had truly not an idea of him. It was all mere surface sound, this murmur of their welcome, this popping of their corks—just as his gestures of response were the extravagant shadows, emphatic in proportion as they meant little, of some game of *ombres chinoises*.[1] He projected himself all day, in thought, straight over the bristling line of hard unconscious heads and into the other, the real, the waiting life; the life that, as soon as he had heard behind him the click of his great house-door, began for him, on the jolly corner, as beguilingly as the slow opening bars of some rich music follows the tap of the conductor's wand.

He always caught the first effect of the steel point of his stick on the old marble of the hall pavement, large black-and-white squares that he remembered as the admiration of his childhood and that had then made in him, as he now saw, for the growth of an early conception of style. This effect was the dim reverberating tinkle as of some far-off bell hung who should say where?—in the depths of the house, of the past, of that mystical other world that might have flourished for him had he not, for weal or woe, abandoned it. On this impression he did ever the same thing; he put his stick noiselessly away in a corner—feeling the place once more in the likeness of some great glass bowl, all precious concave crystal, set delicately humming by the play of a moist finger round its edge. The concave crystal held, as it were, this mystical other world, and the indescribably fine murmur of its rim was the sigh there, the scarce audible pathetic wail to his strained ear, of all the old baffled forsworn possibilities. What he did therefore by this appeal of his hushed presence was to wake them into such measure of ghostly life as they might still enjoy. They were shy, all but unappeasably shy, but they weren't really sinister; at least they weren't as he had hitherto felt them—before they had taken the Form he so yearned to make them take, the Form he at moments saw himself in the light of fairly hunting on tiptoe, the points of his evening-shoes, from room to room and from storey to storey.

That was the essence of his vision—which was all rank folly,

[1] *ombres chinoises*. Galanty show; shadow play.

if one would, while he was out of the house and otherwise occupied, but which took on the last verisimilitude as soon as he was
placed and posted. He knew what he meant and what he wanted;
it was as clear as the figure on a cheque presented in demand for
cash. His *alter ego* "walked"—that was the note of his image of
him, while his image of his motive for his own odd pastime was the
desire to waylay him and meet him. He roamed, slowly, warily,
but all restlessly, he himself did—Mrs. Muldoon had been right,
absolutely, with her figure of their "craping"; and the presence
he watched for would roam restlessly too. But it would be as
cautious and as shifty; the conviction of its probable, in fact its
already quite sensible, quite audible evasion of pursuit grew for
him from night to night, laying on him finally a rigour to which
nothing in his life had been comparable. It had been the theory of
many superficially-judging persons, he knew, that he was wasting
that life in a surrender to sensations, but he had tasted of no pleasure so fine as his actual tension, had been introduced to no sport
that demanded at once the patience and the nerve of this stalking
of a creature more subtle, yet at bay perhaps more formidable,
than any beast of the forest. The terms, the comparisons, the very
practices of the chase positively came again into play; there were
even moments when passages of his occasional experience as a
sportsman, stirred memories, from his younger time, of moor and
mountain and desert, revived for him—and to the increase of his
keenness—by the tremendous force of analogy. He found himself at moments—once he had placed his single light on some
mantel-shelf or in some recess—stepping back into shelter or shade,
effacing himself behind a door or in an embrasure, as he had
sought of old the vantage of rock and tree; he found himself holding his breath and living in the joy of the instant, the supreme
suspense created by big game alone.

He wasn't afraid (though putting himself to the question as he
believed gentlemen on Bengal tiger-shoots or in close quarters
with the great bear of the Rockies had been known to confess to
having put it); and this indeed—since here at least he might be
frank!—because of the impression, so intimate and so strange,
that he himself produced as yet a dread, produced certainly a
strain, beyond the liveliest he was likely to feel. They fell for him
into categories, they fairly became familiar, the signs, for his own

perception, of the alarm his presence and his vigilance created; though leaving him always to remark, portentously, on his probably having formed a relation, his probably enjoying a consciousness, unique in the experience of man. People enough, first and last, had been in terror of apparitions, but who had ever before so turned the tables and become himself, in the apparitional world, an incalculable terror? He might have found this sublime had he quite dared to think of it; but he didn't too much insist, truly, on that side of his privilege. With habit and repetition he gained to an extraordinary degree the power to penetrate the dusk of distances and the darkness of corners, to resolve back into their innocence the treacheries of uncertain light, the evil-looking forms taken in the gloom by mere shadows, by accidents of the air, by shifting effects of perspective; putting down his dim luminary he could still wander on without it, pass into other rooms and, only knowing it was there behind him in case of need, see his way about, visually project for his purpose a comparative clearness. It made him feel, this acquired faculty, like some monstrous stealthy cat; he wondered if he would have glared at these moments with large shining yellow eyes, and what it mightn't verily be, for the poor hard-pressed *alter ego*, to be confronted with such a type.

He liked however the open shutters; he opened everywhere those Mrs. Muldoon had closed, closing them as carefully afterwards, so that she shouldn't notice: he liked—oh this he did like, and above all in the upper rooms!—the sense of the hard silver of the autumn stars through the window-panes, and scarcely less the flare of the street-lamps below, the white electric lustre which it would have taken curtains to keep out. This was human actual social; this was of the world he had lived in, and he was more at his ease certainly for the countenance, coldly general and impersonal, that all the while and in spite of his detachment it seemed to give him. He had support of course mostly in the rooms at the wide front and the prolonged side; it failed him considerably in the central shades and the parts at the back. But if he sometimes, on his rounds, was glad of his optical reach, so none the less often the rear of the house affected him as the very jungle of his prey. The place was there more subdivided; a large "extension" in particular, where small rooms for servants had been multiplied, abounded in nooks and corners, in closets and passages, in the ramifications especially of an ample back staircase over which he leaned, many a time, to look far down—not deterred from his gravity even while aware that he might, for a spectator, have figured some solemn simpleton playing at hide-and-seek. Outside in fact he might himself make that ironic *rapprochement;* but with the walls, and in spite of the clear windows, his consistency was proof against the cynical light of New York.

It had belonged to that idea of the exasperated consciousness of his victim to become a real test for him; since he had quite put it to himself from the first that, oh distinctly! he could "cultivate" his whole perception. He had felt it as above all open to cultivation—which indeed was but another name for his manner of spending his time. He was bringing it on, bringing it to perfection, by practice; in consequence of which it had grown so fine that he was now aware of impressions, attestations of his general postulate, that couldn't have broken upon him at once. This was the case more specifically with a phenomenon at last quite frequent for him in the upper rooms, the recognition—absolutely unmistakeable, and by a turn dating from a particular hour, his resumption of his campaign after a diplomatic drop, a calculated absence of three nights—of his being definitely followed, tracked at a distance carefully taken and to the express end that he should the less confidently, less arrogantly, appear to himself merely to pursue. It worried, it finally quite broke him up, for it proved, of all the conceivable impressions, the one least suited to his book. He was kept in sight while remaining himself—as regards the essence of his position—sightless, and his only recourse then was in abrupt turns, rapid recoveries of ground. He wheeled about, retracing his steps, as if he might so catch in his face at least the stirred air of some other quick revolution. It was indeed true that his fully dislocalised thought of these maneuvres recalled to him Pantaloon, at the Christmas farce, buffeted and tricked from behind by ubiquitous Harlequin; but it left intact the influence of the conditions themselves each time he was re-exposed to them, so that in fact this association, had he suffered it to become constant, would on a certain side have ministered to his intenser gravity. He had made, as I have said, to create on the premises the baseless sense of a reprieve, his three absences; and the result of the third was to confirm the after-effect of the second.

On his return, that night—the night succeeding his last intermission—he stood in the hall and looked up the staircase with a certainty more intimate than any he had yet known. "He's *there*, at the top, and waiting—not, as in general, falling back for disappearance. He's holding his ground, and it's the first time—which is a proof, isn't it? that something has happened for him." So Brydon argued with his hand on the banister and his foot on the lowest stair; in which position he felt as never before the air chilled by his logic. He himself turned cold in it, for he seemed of a sudden to know what now was involved. "Harder pressed?—yes, he takes it in, with its thus making clear to him that I've come, as they say, 'to stay.' He finally doesn't like and can't bear it, in the sense, I mean, that his wrath, his menaced interest, now balances with his dread. I've hunted him till he has 'turned': that, up there, is what has happened—he's the fanged or the antlered animal brought at last to bay." There came to him, as I say—but determined by an influence beyond my notation!—the acuteness of this certainty; under which however the next moment he had broken into a sweat that he would as little have consented to attribute to fear as he would have dared immediately to act upon it for enterprise. It marked none the less a prodigious thrill, a thrill that represented sudden dismay, no doubt, but also represented, and with the selfsame throb, the strangest, the most joyous, possibly the next minute almost the proudest, duplication of consciousness.

"He has been dodging, retreating, hiding, but now, worked up to anger, he'll fight!"—this intense impression made a single mouthful, as it were, of terror and applause. But what was wondrous was that the applause, for the felt fact, was so eager, since, if it was his other self he was running to earth, this ineffable identity was thus in the last resort not unworthy of him. It bristled there—somewhere near at hand, however unseen still—as the hunted thing, even as the trodden worm of the adage *must* at last bristle; and Brydon at this instant tasted probably of a sensation more complex than had ever before found itself consistent with sanity. It was as if it would have shamed him that a character so associated with his own should triumphantly succeed in just

skulking, should to the end not risk the open, so that the drop of
this danger was, on the spot, a great lift of the whole situation. Yet
with another rare shift of the same subtlety he was already trying
to measure by how much more he himself might now be in peril of
fear; so rejoicing that he could, in another form, actively inspire
that fear, and simultaneously quaking for the form in which he
might passively know it.

The apprehension of knowing it must after a little have grown
in him, and the strangest moment of his adventure perhaps, the
most memorable or really most interesting, afterwards, of his
crisis, was the lapse of certain instants of concentrated conscious
combat, the sense of a need to hold on to something, even after the
manner of a man slipping and slipping on some awful incline;
the vivid impulse, above all, to move, to act, to charge, somehow
and upon something—to show himself, in a word, that he wasn't
afraid. The state of "holding-on" was thus the state to which he
was momentarily reduced; if there had been anything, in the great
vacancy, to seize, he would presently have been aware of having
clutched it as he might under a shock at home have clutched the
nearest chair-back. He had been surprised at any rate—of this
he *was* aware—into something unprecedented since his original
appropriation of the place; he had closed his eyes, held them
tight, for a long minute, as with that instinct of dismay and that
terror of vision. When he opened them the room, the other con-
tiguous rooms, extraordinarily, seemed lighter—so light, almost,
that at first he took the change for day. He stood firm, however
that might be, just where he had paused; his resistance had helped
him—it was as if there were something he had tided over. He
knew after a little what this was—it had been in the imminent
danger of flight. He had stiffened his will against going; without
this he would have made for the stairs, and it seemed to him that,
still with his eyes closed, he would have descended them, would
have known how, straight and swiftly, to the bottom.

Well, as he had held out, here he was—still at the top, among
the more intricate upper rooms and with the gauntlet of the others,
of all the rest of the house, still to run when it should be his time
to go. He would go at his time—only at his time: didn't he go
every night very much at the same hour? He took out his watch
—there was light for that: it was scarcely a quarter past one, and

he had never withdrawn so soon. He reached his lodgings for the most part at two—with his walk of a quarter of an hour. He would wait for the last quarter—he wouldn't stir till then; and he kept his watch there with his eyes on it, reflecting while he held it that this deliberate wait, a wait with an effort, which he recognised, would serve perfectly for the attestation he desired to make. It would prove his courage—unless indeed the latter might most be proved by his budging at last from his place. What he mainly felt now was that, since he hadn't originally scuttled, he had his dignities—which had never in his life seemed so many—all to preserve and to carry aloft. This was before him in truth as a physical image, an image almost worthy of an age of greater romance. That remark indeed glimmered for him only to glow the next instant with a finer light, since what age of romance, after all, could have matched either the state of his mind or, "objectively," as they said, the wonder of his situation? The only difference would have been that, brandishing his dignities over his head as in a parchment scroll, he might then—that is in the heroic time—have proceeded downstairs with a drawn sword in his other grasp.

At present, really, the light he had set down on the mantel of the next room would have to figure his sword; which utensil, in the course of a minute, he had taken the requisite number of steps to possess himself of. The door between the rooms was open, and from the second another door opened to a third. These rooms, as he remembered, gave all three upon a common corridor as well, but there was a fourth, beyond them, without issue save through the preceding. To have moved, to have heard his step again, was appreciably a help; though even in recognising this he lingered once more a little by the chimney-piece on which his light had rested. When he next moved, just hesitating where to turn, he found himself considering a circumstance that, after his first and comparatively vague apprehension of it, produced in him the start that often attends some pang of recollection, the violent shock of having ceased happily to forget. He had come into sight of the door in which the brief chain of communication ended and which he now surveyed from the nearer threshold, the one not directly facing it. Placed at some distance to the left of this point, it would have admitted him to the last room of the four, the room without other approach or egress, had it not, to his intimate conviction, been closed *since* his former visitation, the matter probably of a quarter of an hour before. He stared with all his eyes at the wonder of the fact, arrested again where he stood and again holding his breath while he sounded its sense. Surely it had been *subsequently* closed—that is it had been on his previous passage indubitably open!

He took it full in the face that something had happened between—that he couldn't not have noticed before (by which he meant on his original tour of all the rooms that evening) that such a barrier had exceptionally presented itself. He had indeed since that moment undergone an agitation so extraordinary that it might have muddled for him any earlier view; and he tried to convince himself that he might perhaps then have gone into the room and, inadvertently, automatically, on coming out, have drawn the door after him. The difficulty was that this exactly was what he never did; it was against his whole policy, as he might have said, the essence of which was to keep vistas clear. He had them from the first, as he was well aware, quite on the brain: the strange apparition, at the far end of one of them, of his baffled "prey" (which had become by so sharp an irony so little the term now to apply!) was the form of success his imagination had most cherished, projecting into it always a refinement of beauty. He had known fifty times the start of perception that had afterwards dropped; had fifty times gasped to himself "There!" under some fond brief hallucination. The house, as the case stood, admirably lent itself; he might wonder at the taste, the native architecture of the particular time, which could rejoice so in the multiplication of doors—the opposite extreme to the modern, the actual almost complete proscription of them; but it had fairly contributed to provoke this obsession of the presence encountered telescopically, as he might say, focussed and studied in diminishing perspective and as by a rest for the elbow.

It was with these considerations that his present attention was charged—they perfectly availed to make what he saw portentous. He *couldn't*, by any lapse, have blocked that aperture; and if he hadn't, if it was unthinkable, why what else was clear but that there had been another agent? Another agent?—he had been catching, as he felt, a moment back, the very breath of him; but when had he been so close as in this simple, this logical, this completely personal act? It was so logical, that is, that one might have *taken* it for personal; yet for what did Brydon take it, he asked himself, while, softly panting, he felt his eyes almost leave their sockets. Ah this time at last they *were*, the two, the opposed projections of him, in presence; and this time, as much as one would, the question of danger loomed. With it rose, as not before, the question of courage—for what he knew the blank face of the door to say to him was "Show us how much you have!" It stared, it glared back at him with that challenge; it put to him the two alternatives: should he just push it open or not? Oh to have this consciousness was to *think*—and to think, Brydon knew, as he stood there, was, with the lapsing moments, not to have acted! Not to have acted—that was the misery and the pang—was even still not to act; was in fact *all* to feel the thing in another, in a new and terrible way. How long did he pause and how long did he debate? There was presently nothing to measure it; for his vibration had already changed—as just by the effect of its intensity. Shut up there, at bay, defiant, and with the prodigy of the thing palpably proveably *done*, thus giving notice like some stark signboard—under that accession of accent the situation itself had turned; and Brydon at last remarkably made up his mind on what it had turned to.

It had turned altogether to a different admonition; to a supreme hint, for him, of the value of Discretion! This slowly dawned, no doubt—for it could take its time; so perfectly, on his threshold, had he been stayed, so little as yet had he either advanced or retreated. It was the strangest of all things that now when, by his taking ten steps and applying his hand to a latch, or even his shoulder and his knee, if necessary, to a panel, all the hunger of his prime need might have been met, his high curiosity crowned, his unrest assuaged—it was amazing, but it was also exquisite and rare, that insistence should have, at a touch, quite dropped from him. Discretion—he jumped at that; and yet not, verily, at such a pitch, because it saved his nerves or his skin, but because, much more valuably, it saved the situation. When I say he "jumped" at it I feel the consonance of this term with the fact that—at the end indeed of I know not how long—he did move again, he crossed straight to the door. He wouldn't touch it—it seemed now that he might *if* he would: he would only just wait there a little, to show, to prove, that he wouldn't. He had thus another station, close to the thin partition by which revelation was denied him; but with his eyes bent and his hands held off in a mere intensity of stillness. He listened as if there had been something to hear, but this attitude, while it lasted, was his own communication. "If you won't then—good: I spare you and I give up. You affect me as by the appeal positively for pity: you convince me that for reasons rigid and sublime—what do I know?—we both of us should have suffered. I respect them then, and, though moved and privileged as, I believe, it has never been given to man, I retire, I renounce—never, on my honour, to try again. So rest for ever— and let *me!*"

That, for Brydon was the deep sense of this last demonstration —solemn, measured, directed, as he felt it to be. He brought it to a close, he turned away; and now verily he knew how deeply he had been stirred. He retraced his steps, taking up his candle, burnt, he observed, well-nigh to the socket, and marking again, lighten it as he would, the distinctness of his footfall; after which, in a moment, he knew himself at the other side of the house. He did here what he had not yet done at these hours—he opened half a casement, one of those in the front, and let in the air of the night, a thing he would have taken at any time previous for a sharp rupture of his spell. His spell was broken now, and it didn't matter—broken by his concession and his surrender, which made it idle henceforth that he should ever come back. The empty street —its other life so marked even by the great lamplit vacancy—was within call, within touch; he stayed there as to be in it again, high above it though he was still perched; he watched as for some com- forting common fact, some vulgar human note, the passage of a scavenger or a thief, some night-bird however base. He would have blessed that sign of life; he would have welcomed positively the slow approach of his friend the policeman, whom he had hitherto only sought to avoid, and was not sure that if the patrol had come into sight he mightn't have felt the impulse to get into relation with it, to hail it, on some pretext, from his fourth floor.

The pretext that wouldn't have been too silly or too compro- mising, the explanation that would have saved his dignity and kept his name, in such a case, out of the papers, was not definite to him: he was so occupied with the thought of recording his Discretion— as an effect of the vow he had just uttered to his intimate adversary

—that the importance of this loomed large and something had overtaken all ironically his sense of proportion. If there had been a ladder applied to the front of the house, even one of the vertiginous perpendiculars employed by painters and roofers and sometimes left standing overnight, he would have managed somehow, astride of the window-sill, to compass by outstretched leg and arm that mode of descent. If there had been some such uncanny thing as he had found in his room at hotels, a workable fire-escape in the form of notched cable or a canvas shoot, he would have availed himself of it as a proof—well, of his present delicacy. He nursed that sentiment, as the question stood, a little in vain, and even—at the end of he scarce knew, once more, how long— found it, as by the action on his mind of the failure of response of the outer world, sinking back to vague anguish. It seemed to him he had waited an age for some stir of the great grim hush; the life of the town was itself under a spell—so unnaturally, up and down the whole prospect of known and rather ugly objects, the blankness and the silence lasted. Had they ever, he asked himself, the hard-faced houses, which had begun to look livid in the dim dawn, had they ever spoken so little to any need of his spirit? Great built voids, great crowded stillnesses put on, often, in the heart of cities, for the small hours, a sort of sinister mask, and it was of this large collective negation that Brydon presently became conscious—all the more that the break of day was, almost incredibly, now at hand, proving to him what a night he had made of it.

He looked again at his watch, saw what had become of his time-values (he had taken hours for minutes—not, as in other tense situations, minutes for hours) and the strange air of the streets was but the weak, the sullen flush of a dawn in which everything was still locked up. His choked appeal from his own open window had been the sole note of life, and he could but break off at last as for a worse despair. Yet while so deeply demoralised he was capable again of an impulse denoting—at least by his present measure—extraordinary resolution; of retracing his steps to the spot where he had turned cold with the extinction of his last pulse of doubt as to there being in the place another presence than his own. This required an effort strong enough to sicken him; but he had his reason, which over-mastered for the moment everything else. There was the whole of the rest of the house to traverse, and how should he screw himself to that if the door he had seen closed were at present open? He could hold to the idea that the closing had practically been for him an act of mercy, a chance offered him to descend, depart, get off the ground and never again profane it. This conception held together, it worked; but what it meant for him depended now clearly on the amount of forbearance his recent action, or rather his recent inaction, had engendered. The image of the "presence," whatever it was, waiting there for him to go —this image had not yet been so concrete for his nerves as when he stopped short of the point at which certainty would have come to him. For, with all his resolution, or more exactly with all his dread, he did stop short—he hung back from really seeing. The risk was too great and his fear too definite: it took at this moment an awful specific form.

He knew—yes, as he had never known anything—that, *should* he see the door open, it would all too abjectly be the end of him. It would mean that the agent of his shame—for his shame was the deep abjection—was once more at large and in general possession; and what glared him thus in the face was the act that this would determine for him. It would send him straight about to the window he had left open, and by that window, be long ladder and dangling rope as absent as they would, he saw himself uncontrollably insanely fatally take his way to the street. The hideous chance of this he at least could avert; but he could only avert it by recoiling in time from assurance. He had the whole house to deal with, this fact was still there; only he now knew that uncertainty alone could start him. He stole back from where he had checked himself —merely to do so was suddenly like safety—and, making blindly for the greater staircase, left gaping rooms and sounding passages behind. Here was the top of the stairs, with a fine large dim descent and three spacious landings to mark off. His instinct was all for mildness, but his feet were harsh on the floors, and, strangely, when he had in a couple of minutes become aware of this, it counted somehow for help. He couldn't have spoken, the tone of his voice would have scared him, and the common conceit or resource of "whistling in the dark" (whether literally or figuratively) have appeared basely vulgar; yet he liked none the less to hear himself go, and when he had reached his first landing—

taking it all with no rush, but quite steadily—that stage of success drew from him a gasp of relief.

The house, withal, seemed immense, the scale of space again inordinate; the open rooms to no one of which his eyes deflected, gloomed in their shuttered state like mouths of caverns; only the high skylight that formed the crown of the deep well created for him a medium in which he could advance, but which might have been, for queerness of colour, some watery under-world. He tried to think of something noble, as that his property was really grand, a splendid possession; but this nobleness took the form too of the clear delight with which he was finally to sacrifice it. They might come in now, the builders, the destroyers—they might come as soon as they would. At the end of two flights he had dropped to another zone, and from the middle of the third, with only one more left, he recognised the influence of the lower windows, of half-drawn blinds, of the occasional gleam of street-lamps, of the glazed spaces of the vestibule. This was the bottom of the sea, which showed an illumination of its own and which he even saw paved—when at a given moment he drew up to sink a long look over the banisters—with the marble squares of his childhood. By that time indubitably he felt, as he might have said in a commoner cause, better; it had allowed him to stop and draw breath, and the ease increased with the sight of the old black-and-white slabs. But what he most felt was that now surely, with the element of impunity pulling him as by hard firm hands, the case was settled for what he might have seen above had he dared that last look. The closed door, blessedly remote now, was still closed—and he had only in short to reach that of the house.

He came down further, he crossed the passage forming the access to the last flight; and if here again he stopped an instant it was almost for the sharpness of the thrill of assured escape. It made him shut his eyes—which opened again to the straight slope of the remainder of the stairs. Here was impunity still, but impunity almost excessive; inasmuch as the side-lights and the high fan-tracery of the entrance were glimmering straight into the hall; an appearance produced, he the next instant saw, by the fact that the vestibule gaped wide, that the hinged halves of the inner door had been thrown far back. Out of that again the *question* sprang at him, making his eyes, as he felt, half-start from his head, as they had done, at the top of the house, before the sign of the other door. If he had left that one open, hadn't he left this one closed, and wasn't he now in *most* immediate presence of some inconceivable occult activity? It was as sharp, the question, as a knife in his side, but the answer hung fire still and seemed to lose itself in the vague darkness to which the thin admitted dawn, glimmering archwise over the whole outer door, made a semicircular margin, a cold silvery nimbus that seemed to play a little as he looked—to shift and expand and contract.

It was as if there had been something within it, protected by indistinctness and corresponding in extent with the opaque surface behind, the painted panels of the last barrier to his escape, of which the key was in his pocket. The indistinctness mocked him even while he stared, affected him as somehow shrouding or challenging certitude, so that after faltering an instant on his step he let himself go with the sense that here *was* at last something to meet, to touch, to take, to know—something all unnatural and dreadful, but to advance upon which was the condition for him either of liberation or of supreme defeat. The penumbra, dense and dark, was the virtual screen of a figure which stood in it as still as some image erect in a niche or as some black-vizored sentinel guarding a treasure. Brydon was to know afterwards, was to recall and make out, the particular thing he had believed during the rest of his descent. He saw, in its great grey glimmering margin, the central vagueness diminish, and he felt it to be taking the very form toward which, for so many days, the passion of his curiosity had yearned. It gloomed, it loomed, it was something, it was somebody, the prodigy of a personal presence.

Rigid and conscious, spectral yet human, a man of his own substance and stature waited there to measure himself with his power to dismay. This only could it be—this only till he recognised, with his advance, that what made the face dim was the pair of raised hands that covered it and in which, so far from being offered in defiance, it was buried as for dark deprecation. So Brydon, before him, took him in; with every fact of him now, in the higher light, hard and acute—his planted stillness, his vivid truth, his grizzled bent head and white masking hands, his queer actuality of evening-dress, of dangling double eye-glass, of gleaming silk lappet and white linen, of pearl button and gold watch-guard and polished shoe. No portrait by a great modern master could have presented him with more intensity, thrust him out of his frame with more art, as if there had been "treatment," of the consummate sort, in his every shade and salience. The revulsion, for our friend, had become, before he knew it, immense—this drop, in the act of apprehension, to the sense of his adversary's inscrutable maneuvre. That meaning at least, while he gaped, it offered him; for he could but gape at his other self in this other anguish, gape as a proof that *he*, standing there for the achieved, the enjoyed, the triumphant life, couldn't be faced in his triumph. Wasn't the proof in the splendid covering hands, strong and completely spread?—so spread and so intentional that, in spite of a special verity that surpassed every other, the fact that one of these hands had lost two fingers, which were reduced to stumps, as if accidentally shot away, the face was effectually guarded and saved.

"Saved," though, *would* it be?—Brydon breathed his wonder till the very impunity of his attitude and the very insistence of his eyes produced, as he felt, a sudden stir which showed the next instant as a deeper portent, while the head raised itself, the betrayal of a braver purpose. The hands, as he looked, began to move, to open; then, as if deciding in a flash, dropped from the face and left it uncovered and presented. Horror, with the sight, had leaped into Brydon's throat, gasping there in a sound he couldn't utter; for the bared identity was too hideous as *his*, and his glare was the passion of his protest. The face, *that* face, Spencer Brydon's?—he searched it still, but looking away from it in dismay and denial, falling straight from his height of sublimity. It was unknown, inconceivable, awful, disconnected from any possibility—! He had been "sold," he inwardly moaned, stalking such game as this: the presence before him was a presence, the horror within him a horror, but the waste of his nights had been only grotesque and the success of his adventure an irony. Such an identity fitted his at *no* point, made its alternative monstrous. A thousand times yes, as it came upon him nearer now—the face was the face of a stranger. It came upon him nearer now, quite as one of those expanding fantastic images projected by the magic lantern of childhood; for the stranger, whoever he might be, evil, odious, blatant, vulgar, had advanced as for aggression, and he knew himself give ground. Then harder pressed still, sick with the force of his shock, and falling back as under the hot breath and the roused passion of a life larger than his own, a rage of personality before which his own collapsed, he felt the whole vision turn to darkness and his very feet give way. His head went round; he was going; he had gone.

III

What had next brought him back, clearly—though after how long?—was Mrs. Muldoon's voice, coming to him from quite near, from so near that he seemed presently to see her as kneeling on the ground before him while he lay looking up at her; himself not wholly on the ground, but half-raised and upheld—conscious, yes, of tenderness of support and, more particularly, of a head pillowed in extraordinary softness and faintly refreshing fragrance. He considered, he wondered, his wit but half at his service; than another face intervened, bending more directly over him, and he finally knew that Alice Staverton had made her lap an ample and perfect cushion to him, and that she had to this end seated herself on the lowest degree of the staircase, the rest of his long person remaining stretched on his old black-and-white slabs. They were cold, these marble squares of his youth; but *he* somehow was not, in this rich return of consciousness—the most wonderful hour, little by little, that he had ever known, leaving him, as it did, so gratefully, so abysmally passive, and yet as with a treasure of intelligence waiting all round him for quiet appropriation; dissolved, he might call it, in the air of the place and producing the golden glow of a late autumn afternoon. He had come back, yes—come back from further away than any man but himself had ever travelled; but it was strange how with this sense what he had come back *to* seemed really the great thing, and as if his prodigious journey had been all for the sake of it. Slowly but surely his consciousness grew, his vision of his state thus completing itself: he had been miraculously *carried* back—lifted and carefully borne as from where he had been picked up, the uttermost end of an interminable grey passage. Even with this he was suffered to rest, and what had now brought him to knowledge was the break in the long mild motion.

It had brought him to knowledge, to knowledge—yes, this was the beauty of his state; which came to resemble more and more

that of a man who has gone to sleep on some news of a great inheritance, and then, after dreaming it away, after profaning it with
matters strange to it, has waked up again to serenity of certitude
and has only to lie and watch it grow. This was the drift of his
patience—that he had only to let it shine on him. He must
moreover, with intermissions, still have been lifted and borne;
since why and how else should he have known himself, later on,
with the afternoon glow intenser, no longer at the foot of his
stairs—situated as these now seemed at that dark other end of his
tunnel—but on a deep window-bench of his high saloon, over
which had been spread, couch-fashion, a mantel of soft stuff lined
with grey fur that was familiar to his eyes and that one of his
hands kept fondly feeling as for its pledge of truth. Mrs. Muldoon's face had gone, but the other, the second he had recognised,
hung over him in a way that showed how he was still propped and
pillowed. He took it all in, and the more he took it the more it
seemed to suffice: he was as much at peace as if he had had food
and drink. It was the two women who had found him, on Mrs.
Muldoon's having plied, at her usual hour, her latch-key—and on
her having above all arrived while Miss Staverton still lingered
near the house. She had been turning away, all anxiety, from
worrying the vain bell-handle—her calculation having been of
the hour of the good woman's visit; but the latter, blessedly, had
come up while she was still there, and they had entered together.
He had then lain, beyond the vestibule, very much as he was
lying now—quite, that is, as he appeared to have fallen, but all
so wondrously without bruise or gash; only in a depth of stupor.
What he most took in, however, at present, with the steadier clear-
ance, was that Alice Staverton had for a long unspeakable moment
not doubted he was dead.

"It must have been that I *was*." He made it out as she held him.
"Yes—I can only have died. You brought me literally to life.
Only," he wondered, his eyes rising to her, "only, in the name of
all the benedictions, how?"

It took her but an instant to bend her face and kiss him, and
something in the manner of it, and in the way her hands clasped
and locked his head while he felt the cool charity and virtue of
her lips, something in all this beatitude somehow answered everything. "And now I keep you," she said.

"Oh keep me, keep me!" he pleaded while her face still hung over him: in response to which it dropped again and stayed close, clingingly close. It was the seal of their situation—of which he tasted the impress for a long blissful moment in silence. But he came back. "Yet how did you know—?"

"I was uneasy. You were to have come, you remember—and you had sent no word."

"Yes, I remember—I was to have gone to you at one today." It caught on to their "old" life and relation—which were so near and so far. "I was still out there in my strange darkness—where was it, what was it? I must have stayed there so long." He could but wonder at the depth and the duration of his swoon.

"Since last night?" she asked with a shade of fear for her possible indiscretion.

"Since this morning—it must have been: the cold dim dawn of today. Where have I been," he vaguely wailed, "where have I been?" He felt her hold him close, and it was as if this helped him now to make in all security his mild moan. "What a long dark day!"

All in her tenderness she had waited a moment. "In the cold dim dawn?" she quavered.

But he had already gone on piecing together the parts of the whole prodigy. "As I didn't turn up you came straight—?"

She barely cast about. "I went first to your hotel—where they told me of your absence. You had dined out last evening and hadn't been back since. But they appeared to know you had been at your club."

"So you had the idea of *this*—?"

"Of what?" she asked in a moment.

"Well—of what has happened."

"I believed at least you'd have been here. I've known, all along," she said, "that you've been coming."

" 'Known' it—?"

"Well, I've believed it. I said nothing to you after that talk we had a month ago—but I felt sure. I knew you *would*," she declared.

"That I'd persist, you mean?"

"That you'd see him."

"Ah but I didn't!" cried Brydon with his long wail. "There's somebody—an awful beast; whom I brought, too horribly, to bay. But it's not me."

At this she bent over him again, and her eyes were in his eyes. "No—it's not you." And it was as if, while her face hovered, he might have made out in it, hadn't it been so near, some particular meaning blurred by a smile. "No, thank heaven," she repeated— "it's not you! Of course it wasn't to have been."

"Ah but it *was,*" he gently insisted. And he stared before him now as he had been staring for so many weeks. "I was to have known myself."

"You couldn't!" she returned consolingly. And then reverting, and as if to account further for what she had herself done, "But it wasn't only *that,* that you hadn't been at home," she went on. "I waited till the hour at which we had found Mrs. Muldoon that day of my going with you; and she arrived, as I've told you, while, failing to bring any one to the door, I lingered in my despair on the steps. After a little, if she hadn't come, by such a mercy, I should have found means to hunt her up. But it wasn't," said Alice Staverton, as if once more with her fine intention—"it wasn't only that."

His eyes, as he lay, turned back to her. "What more then?"

She met it, the wonder she had stirred. "In the cold dim dawn, you say? Well, in the cold dim dawn of this morning I too saw you."

"Saw *me*—?"

"Saw *him,*" said Alice Staverton. "It must have been at the same moment."

He lay an instant taking it in—as if he wished to be quite reasonable. "At the same moment?"

"Yes—in my dream again, the same one I've named to you. He came back to me. Then I knew it for a sign. He had come to you."

At this Brydon raised himself; he had to see her better. She helped him when she understood his movement, and he sat up, steadying himself beside her there on the window-bench and with his right hand grasping her left. "*He* didn't come to me."

"You came to yourself," she beautifully smiled.

"Ah I've come to myself now—thanks to you, dearest. But this brute, with his awful face—this brute's a black stranger. He's none of *me,* even as I *might* have been," Brydon sturdily declared.

But she kept the clearness that was like the breath of infallibility. "Isn't the whole point that you'd have been different?"

He almost scowled for it. "As different as *that*—?"

Her look again was more beautiful to him than the things of this world. "Haven't you exactly wanted to know *how* different? So this morning," she said, "you appeared to me."

"Like *him?*"

"A black stranger!"

"Then how did you know it was I?"

"Because, as I told you weeks ago, my mind, my imagination, had worked so over what you might, what you mightn't have been—to show you, you see, how I've thought of you. In the midst of that you came to me—that my wonder might be answered. So I knew," she went on; "and believed that, since the question held you too so fast, as you told me that day, you too would see for yourself. And when this morning I again saw I knew it would be because you had—and also then, from the first moment, because you somehow wanted me. *He* seemed to tell me of that. So why," she strangely smiled, "shouldn't I like him?"

It brought Spencer Brydon to his feet. "You 'like' that horror—?"

"I *could* have liked him. And to me," she said, "he was no horror. I had accepted him."

" 'Accepted'—?" Brydon oddly sounded.

"Before, for the interest of his difference—yes. And as *I* didn't disown him, as *I* knew him—which you at last, confronted with him in his difference, so cruelly didn't, my dear—well, he must have been, you see, less dreadful to me. And it may have pleased him that I pitied him."

She was beside him on her feet, but still holding his hand—still with her arm supporting him. But though it all brought for him thus a dim light, "You 'pitied' him?" he grudgingly, resentfully asked.

"He has been unhappy; he has been ravaged," she said.

"And haven't I been unhappy? Am not I—you've only to look at me!—ravaged?"

"Ah I don't say I like him *better*," she granted after a thought. "But he's grim, he's worn—and things have happened to him. He doesn't make shift, for sight, with your charming monocle."

"No"—it struck Brydon: "I couldn't have sported mine 'down-town.' They'd have guyed me there."

"His great convex pince-nez—I saw it, I recognised the kind —is for his poor ruined sight. And his poor right hand—!"

"Ah!" Brydon winced—whether for his proved identity or for his lost fingers. Then, "He has a million a year," he lucidly added. "But he hasn't you."

"And he isn't—no, he isn't—*you!*" she murmured as he drew her to his breast.

HENRY JAMES

The Lesson of the Master

He had been told the ladies were at church, but this was corrected by what he saw from the top of the steps —they descended from a great height in two arms, with a circular sweep of the most charming effect—at the threshold of the door which, from the long bright gallery, overlooked the immense lawn. Three gentlemen, on the grass, at a distance, sat under the great trees, while the fourth figure showed a crimson dress that told as a "bit of colour" amid the fresh rich green. The servant had so far accompanied Paul Overt as to introduce him to this view, after asking him if he wished first to go to his room. The young man declined that privilege, conscious of no disrepair from so short and easy a journey and always liking to take at once a general perceptive possession of a new scene. He stood there a little with his eyes on the group and on the admirable picture, the wide grounds of an old country house near London— that only made it better—on a splendid Sunday in June. "But that lady, who's *she?*" he said to the servant before the man left him.

"I think she's Mrs. St. George, sir."

"Mrs. St. George, the wife of the distinguished—" Then Paul Overt checked himself, doubting if a footman would know.

"Yes, sir—probably, sir," said his guide, who appeared to wish to intimate that a person staying at Summersoft would naturally be, if only by alliance, distinguished. His tone, however, made poor Overt himself feel for the moment scantly so.

"And the gentlemen?" Overt went on.

"Well, sir, one of them's General Fancourt."

"Ah, yes, I know; thank you." General Fancourt was distinguished, there was no doubt of that, for something he had done, or perhaps even hadn't done—the young man couldn't remember which—some years before in India. The servant went away, leaving the glass doors open into the gallery, and Paul Overt remained at the head of the wide double staircase, saying to himself that the place was sweet and promised a pleasant visit, while he leaned on the balustrade of fine old ironwork which, like all the other details, was of the same period as the house. It all went together and spoke in one voice—a rich English voice of the early part of the eighteenth century. It might have been church-time on a summer's day in the reign of Queen Anne: the stillness was too perfect to be modern, the nearness counted so as distance, and there was something so fresh and sound in the originality of the large smooth house, the expanse of beautiful brickwork that showed for pink rather than red and that had been kept clear of messy creepers by the law under which a woman with a rare complexion disdains a veil. When Paul Overt became aware that the people under the trees had noticed him he turned back through the open doors into the great gallery which was the pride of the place. It marched across from end to end and seemed—with its bright colours, its high panelled windows, its faded flowered chintzes, its quickly-recognised portraits and pictures, the blue-and-white china of its cabinets and the attenuated festoons and rosettes of its ceiling—a cheerful, upholstered avenue into the other century.

Our friend was slightly nervous; that went with his character as a student of fine prose, went with the artist's general disposition to vibrate; and there was a particular thrill in the idea that Henry St. George might be a member of the party. For the young aspirant he had remained a high literary figure, in spite of the lower range of production to which he had fallen after his three first great successes, the comparative absence of quality in his later work. There had been moments when Paul Overt almost shed tears for this; but now that he was near him—he had never met him—he was conscious only of the fine original source and of his own immense debt. After he had taken a turn or two up and down the gallery he came out again and descended the steps. He was but slenderly supplied with a certain social boldness—it was really a weakness in him—so that, conscious of a want of acquaintance with the four persons in the distance, he gave way to motions recommended by their not committing him to a positive approach. There was a fine English awkwardness in this—he felt that too as he sauntered vaguely and obliquely across the lawn, taking an independent line. Fortunately there was an equally fine English directness in the way one of the gentlemen presently rose and made as if to "stalk" him, though with an air of conciliation and reassurance. To this demonstration Paul Overt instantly responded, even if the gentleman were not his host. He was tall, straight and elderly and had, like the great house itself, a pink smiling face, and into the bargain a white moustache. Our young man met him halfway while he laughed and said: "Er—Lady Watermouth told us you were coming; she asked me just to look after you." Paul Overt thanked him, liking him on the spot, and turned round with him to walk towards the others. "They've all gone to church—all except us," the stranger continued as they went; "we're just sitting here—it's so jolly." Overt pronounced it jolly indeed: it was such a lovely place. He mentioned that he was having the charming impression for the first time.

"Ah, you've not been here before?" said his companion. "It's a nice little place—not much to *do*, you know." Overt wondered what he wanted to "do"—he felt that he himself was doing so much. By the time they came to where the others sat he had recognised his initiator for a military man and—such was the turn of Overt's imagination—he had found him thus still more sympathetic. He would naturally have a need for action, for deeds at variance with the pacific pastoral scene. He was evidently so good-natured, however, that he accepted the inglorious hour for what it was worth. Paul Overt shared it with him and with his companions for the next twenty minutes; the latter looked at him and he looked at them without knowing much who they were, while the talk went on without much telling him even what it meant. It seemed indeed to mean nothing in particular; it wandered, with casual pointless pauses and short terrestrial flights, amid names of persons and places—names which, for our friend, had no great power of evocation. It was all sociable and slow, as was right and natural of a warm Sunday morning.

His first attention was given to the question, privately considered, of whether one of the two younger men would be Henry St. George. He knew many of his distinguished contemporaries by their photographs, but had never, as happened, seen a portrait of the great misguided novelist. One of the gentlemen was unimaginable—he was too young; and the other scarcely looked clever enough, with such mild, undiscriminating eyes. If those eyes were St. George's the problem presented by the ill-matched parts of his genius would be still more difficult of solution. Besides, the deportment of their proprietor was not, as regards the lady in the red dress, such as could be natural, toward the wife of his bosom, even to a writer accused by several critics of sacrificing too much to manner. Lastly, Paul Overt had a vague sense that if the gentleman with the expressionless eyes bore the name that had set his heart beating faster (he also had contradictory, conventional whiskers—the young admirer of the celebrity had never in a mental vision seen *his* face in so vulgar a frame) he would have given him a sign of recognition or of friendliness, would have heard of him a little, would know something about "Ginistrella," would have an impression of how that fresh fiction had caught the eye of real criticism. Paul Overt had a dread of being grossly proud, but even morbid modesty might view the authorship of "Ginistrella" as constituting a degree of identity. His soldierly friend became clear enough: he was "Fancourt," but was also "the General"; and he mentioned to the new visitor in the course of a few moments that he had but lately returned from twenty years' service abroad.

"And now you remain in England?" the young man asked.

"Oh, yes; I've bought a small house in London."

"And I hope you like it," said Overt, looking at Mrs. St. George.

"Well, a little house in Manchester Square—there's a limit to the enthusiasm *that* inspires."

"Oh, I meant being home again—being back in Piccadilly."

"My daughter likes Piccadilly—that's the main thing. She's

very fond of art and music and literature and all that kind of thing. She missed it in India and she finds it in London, or she hopes she'll find it. Mr. St. George has promised to help her— he has been awfully kind to her. She has gone to church—she's fond of that too—but they'll all be back in a quarter of an hour. You must let me introduce you to her—she'll be so glad to know you. I daresay she has read every blest word you've written."

"I shall be delighted—I haven't written so very many," Overt pleaded, feeling, and without resentment, that the General at least was vagueness itself about that. But he wondered a little why, expressing this friendly disposition, it didn't occur to the doubtless eminent soldier to pronounce the word that would put him in relation with Mrs. St. George. If it was a question of introductions Miss Fancourt—apparently as yet unmarried—was far away, while the wife of his illustrious confrère was almost between them. This lady struck Paul Overt as altogether pretty, with a surprising juvenility and a high smartness of aspect, something that—he could scarcely have said why—served for mystification. St. George certainly had every right to a charming wife, but he himself would never have imagined the important little woman in the aggressively Parisian dress the partner for life, the *alter ego,* of a man of letters. That partner in general, he knew, that second self, was far from presenting herself in a single type: observation had taught him that she was not inveterately, not necessarily plain. But he had never before seen her look so much as if her prosperity had deeper foundations than an ink-spotted study-table littered with proof-sheets. Mrs. St. George might have been the wife of a gentleman who "kept" books rather than wrote them, who carried on great affairs in the City and made better bargains than those that poets mostly make with publishers. With this she hinted at a success more personal—a success peculiarly stamping the age in which society, the world of conversation, is a great drawing-room with the City for its antechamber. Overt numbered her years at first as some thirty, and then ended by believing that she might approach her fiftieth. But she somehow in this case juggled away the excess and the difference—you only saw them in a rare glimpse, like the rabbit in the conjurer's sleeve. She was extraordinarily white, and her every element and item was pretty; her eyes, her ears, her hair, her

voice, her hands, her feet—to which her relaxed attitude in her
wicker chair gave a great publicity—and the numerous ribbons
and trinkets with which she was bedecked. She looked as if she
had put on her best clothes to go to church and then had decided
they were too good for that and had stayed at home. She told
a story of some length about the shabby way Lady Jane had
treated the Duchess, as well as an anecdote in relation to a purchase she had made in Paris—on her way back from Cannes; made
for Lady Egbert, who had never refunded the money. Paul Overt
suspected her of a tendency to figure great people as larger than
life, until he noticed the manner in which she handled Lady Egbert, which was so sharply mutinous that it reassured him. He
felt he should have understood her better if he might have met
her eye; but she scarcely so much as glanced at him. "Ah, here
they come—all the good ones!" she said at last; and Paul Overt
admired at his distance the return of the churchgoers—several
persons, in couples and threes, advancing in a flicker of sun and
shade at the end of a large green vista formed by the level grass
and the overarching boughs.

"If you mean to imply that *we're* bad, I protest," said one of
the gentlemen—"after making one's self agreeable all the morning!"

"Ah, if they've found you agreeable—!" Mrs. St. George gaily
cried. "But if we're good the others are better."

"They must be angels then," said the amused General.

"Your husband was an angel, the way he went off at your
bidding," the gentleman who had first spoken declared to Mrs.
St. George.

"At my bidding?"

"Didn't you make him go to church?"

"I never made him do anything in my life but once—when I
made him burn up a bad book. That's all!" At her "That's all!"
our young friend broke into an irrepressible laugh; it lasted only
a second, but it drew her eyes to him. His own met them, though
not long enough to help him to understand her; unless it were a
step towards this that he saw on the instant how the burnt book
—the way she alluded to it!—would have been one of her husband's finest things.

"A bad book?" her interlocutor repeated.

"I didn't like it. He went to church because your daughter went," she continued to General Fancourt. "I think it my duty to call your attention to his extraordinary demonstrations to your daughter."

"Well, if you don't mind them I don't!" the General laughed.

"*Il s'attache à ses pas.*[1] But I don't wonder—she's so charming."

"I hope she won't make him burn any books!" Paul Overt ventured to exclaim.

"If she'd make him write a few it would be more to the purpose," said Mrs. St. George. "He has been of a laziness of late—!"

Our young man stared—he was so struck with the lady's phraseology. Her "Write a few" seemed to him almost as good as her "That's all." Didn't she, as the wife of a rare artist, know what it was to produce *one* perfect work of art? How in the world did she think they were turned off? His private conviction was that, admirably as Henry St. George wrote, he had written for the last ten years, and especially for the last five, only too much, and there was an instant during which he felt inwardly solicited to make this public. But before he had spoken a diversion was affected by the return of the absentees. They strolled up dispersedly—there were eight or ten of them—and the circle under the trees rearranged itself as they took their place in it. They made it much larger, so that Paul Overt could feel—he was always feeling that sort of thing, as he said to himself—that if the company had already been interesting to watch the interest would now become intense. He shook hands with his hostess, who welcomed him without many words, in the manner of a woman able to trust him to understand and conscious that so pleasant an occasion would in every way speak for itself. She offered him no particular facility for sitting by her, and when they had all subsided again he found himself still next General Fancourt, with an unknown lady on his other flank.

"That's my daughter—that one opposite," the General said to him without loss of time. Overt saw a tall girl, with magnificent red hair, in a dress of pretty grey-green tint and of a limp silken texture, a garment that clearly shirked every modern effect. It had therefore somehow the stamp of the latest thing, so that our beholder quickly took her for nothing if not contemporaneous.

[1] *Il s'attache à ses pas.* He follows her around closely.

"She's very handsome—very handsome," he repeated while he considered her. There was something noble in her head, and she appeared fresh and strong.

Her good father surveyed her with complacency, remarking soon: "She looks too hot—that's her walk. But she'll be all right presently. Then I'll make her come over and speak to you."

"I should be sorry to give you that trouble. If you were to take me over *there*—!" the young man murmured.

"My dear sir, do you suppose I put myself out that way? I don't mean for you, but for Marian," the General added.

"*I* would put myself out for her soon enough," Overt replied; after which he went on: "Will you be so good as to tell me which of those gentlemen is Henry St. George?"

"The fellow talking to my girl. By Jove, he *is* making up to her—they're going off for another walk."

"Ah, is that he—really?" Our friend felt a certain surprise, for the personage before him seemed to trouble a vision which had been vague only while not confronted with the reality. As soon as the reality dawned, the mental image, retiring with a sigh, became substantial enough to suffer a slight wrong. Overt, who had spent a considerable part of his short life in foreign lands, made now, but not for the first time, the reflexion that whereas in those countries he had almost always recognised the artist and the man of letters by his personal "type," the mould of his face, the character of his head, the expression of his figure, and even the indications of his dress, so in England this identification was as little as possible a matter of course, thanks to the greater conformity, the habit of sinking the profession instead of advertising it, the general diffusion of the air of the gentleman—the gentleman committed to no particular set of ideas. More than once, on returning to his own country, he had said to himself about people met in society: "One sees them in this place and that, and one even talks with them; but to find out what they *do* one would really have to be a detective." In respect to several individuals whose work he was the opposite of "drawn to"—perhaps he was wrong—he found himself adding, "No wonder they conceal it—when it's so bad!" He noted that oftener than in France and in Germany his artist looked like a gentleman—that is, like an English one— while, certainly outside a few exceptions, his gentleman didn't

look like an artist. St. George was not one of the exceptions;
that circumstance he definitely apprehended before the great man
had turned his back to walk off with Miss Fancourt. He certainly
looked better behind than any foreign man of letters—showed for
beautifully correct in his tall black hat and his superior frock
coat. Somehow, all the same, these very garments—he wouldn't
have minded them so much on a weekday—were disconcerting
to Paul Overt, who forgot for the moment that the head of the
profession was not a bit better dressed than himself. He had caught
a glimpse of a regular face, a fresh colour, a brown moustache,
and a pair of eyes surely never visited by a fine frenzy, and he
promised himself to study these denotements on the first occasion.
His superficial sense was that their owner might have passed for
a lucky stockbroker—a gentleman driving eastward every morning from a sanitary suburb in a smart dogcart. That carried out
the impression already derived from his wife. Paul's glance, after
a moment, travelled back to this lady, and he saw how her own
had followed her husband as he moved off with Miss Fancourt.
Overt permitted himself to wonder a little if she were jealous
when another woman took him away. Then he made out that
Mrs. St. George wasn't glaring at the indifferent maiden. Her
eyes rested but on her husband, and with unmistakable serenity.
That was the way she wanted him to be—she liked his conventional uniform. Overt longed to hear more about the book she
had induced him to destroy.

II

As they all came out from luncheon General Fancourt took
hold of him with an "I say, I want you to know my girl!" as if the
idea had just occurred to him and he hadn't spoken of it before.
With the other hand he possessed himself all paternally of the
young lady. "You know all about him. I've seen you with his
books. She reads everything—everything!" he went on to Paul.
The girl smiled at him and then laughed at her father. The General turned away and his daughter spoke—"Isn't papa delightful?"

"He is indeed, Miss Fancourt."

"As if I read you because I read 'everything'!"

"Oh, I don't mean for saying that," said Paul Overt. "I liked
him from the moment he began to be kind to me. Then he prom-

ised me this privilege."

"It isn't for you he means it—it's for me. If you flatter yourself that he thinks of anything in life but me you'll find you're mistaken. He introduces everyone. He thinks me insatiable."

"You speak just like him," laughed our youth.

"Ah, but sometimes I want to"—and the girl coloured. "I don't read everything—I read very little. But I *have* read you."

"Suppose we go into the gallery," said Paul Overt. She pleased him greatly, not so much because of this last remark—though that of course was not too disconcerting—as because, seated opposite to him at luncheon, she had given him for half an hour the impression of her beautiful face. Something else had come with it—a sense of generosity, of an enthusiasm which, unlike many enthusiasms, was not all manner. That was not spoiled for him by his seeing that the repast had placed her again in familiar contact with Henry St. George. Sitting next her this celebrity was also opposite our young man, who had been able to note that he multiplied the attentions lately brought by his wife to the General's notice. Paul Overt had gathered as well that this lady was not in the least discomposed by these fond excesses and that she gave every sign of an unclouded spirit. She had Lord Masham on one side of her and on the other the accomplished Mr. Mulliner, editor of the new high-class lively evening paper which was expected to meet a want felt in circles increasingly conscious that Conservatism must be made amusing, and unconvinced when assured by those of another political colour that it was already amusing enough. At the end of an hour spent in her company Paul Overt thought her still prettier than at the first radiation, and if her profane allusions to her husband's work had not still rung in his ears he should have liked her—so far as it could be a question of that in connexion with a woman to whom he had not yet spoken and to whom probably he should never speak if it were left to her. Pretty women were a clear need to his genius, and for the hour it was Miss Fancourt who supplied the want. If Overt had promised himself a closer view the occasion was now of the best, and it brought consequences felt by the young man as important. He saw more in St. George's face, which he liked the better for its not having told its whole story in the first three minutes. That story came out as one read, in short instalments—it was excusable that one's analogies should be somewhat professional—and the text was a style considerably involved, a language not easy to translate at sight. There were shades of meaning in it and a vague perspective of history which receded as you advanced. Two facts Paul had particularly heeded. The first of these was that he liked the measured mask much better at inscrutable rest than in social agitation; its almost convulsive smile above all displeased him (as much as any impression from that source could), whereas the quiet face had a charm that grew in proportion as stillness settled again. The change to the expression of gaiety excited, he made out, very much the private protest of a person sitting gratefully in the twilight when the lamp is brought in too soon. His second reflexion was that, though generally adverse to the flagrant use of ingratiating arts by a man of age "making up" to a pretty girl, he was not in this case too painfully affected: which seemed to prove either that St. George had a light hand or the air of being younger than he was, or else that Miss Fancourt's own manner somehow made everything right.

Overt walked with her into the gallery, and they strolled to the end of it, looking at the pictures, the cabinets, the charming vista, which harmonised with the prospect of the summer afternoon, resembling it by a long brightness, with great divans and old chairs that figured hours of rest. Such a place as that had the added merit of giving those who came into it plenty to talk about. Miss Fancourt sat down with her new acquaintance on a flowered sofa, the cushions of which, very numerous, were tight ancient cubes of many sizes, and presently said: "I'm so glad to have a chance to thank you."

"To thank me—?" He had to wonder.

"I liked your book so much. I think it splendid."

She sat there smiling at him, and he never asked himself which book she meant; for after all he had written three or four. That seemed a vulgar detail, and he wasn't even gratified by the idea of the pleasure she told him—her handsome bright face told him —he had given her. The feeling she appealed to, or at any rate the feeling she excited, was something larger, something that had little to do with any quickened pulsation of his own vanity. It was responsive admiration of the life she embodied, the young purity and richness of which appeared to imply that real success was to resemble *that*, to live, to bloom, to present the perfection of a fine type, not to have hammered out headachy fancies with a bent back at an ink-stained table. While her grey eyes rested on him—there was a widish space between these, and the division of her rich-coloured hair, so thick that it ventured to be smooth, made a free arch above them—he was almost ashamed of that exercise of the pen which it was her present inclination to commend. He was conscious he should have liked better to please her in some other way. The lines of her face were those of a woman grown, but the child lingered on in her complexion and in the sweetness of her mouth. Above all she was natural—that was indubitable now; more natural than he had supposed at first, perhaps on account of her esthetic toggery, which was conventionally unconventional, suggesting what he might have called a tortuous spontaneity. He had feared that sort of thing in other cases, and his fears had been justified; for, though he was an artist to the essence, the modern reactionary nymph, with the brambles of the woodland caught in her folds and a look as if the satyrs had toyed with her hair, made him shrink, not as a man of starch and patent leather, but as a man potentially himself a poet or even a faun. The girl was really more candid than her costume, and the best proof of it was her supposing her liberal character suited by any uniform. This was a fallacy, since if she was draped as a pessimist he was sure she liked the taste of life. He thanked her for her appreciation—aware at the same time that he didn't appear to thank her enough and that she might think him ungracious. He was afraid she would ask him to explain something he had written, and he always winced at that—perhaps too timidly—for to his own ear the explanation of a work of art sounded fatuous. But he liked her so much as to feel a confidence that in the long run he should be able to show her he wasn't rudely evasive. Moreover, she surely wasn't quick to take offence, wasn't irritable; she could be trusted to wait. So when he said to her, "Ah, don't talk of anything I've done, don't talk of it *here;* there's another man in the house who's the actuality!"—when he uttered this short sincere protest it was with the sense that she would see in the words neither mock humility nor the impatience of a successful man bored with praise.

"You mean Mr. St. George—isn't he delightful?"

Paul Overt met her eyes, which had a cool morning light that would have half-broken his heart if he hadn't been so young. "Alas, I don't know him. I only admire him at a distance."

"Oh, you *must* know him—he wants so to talk to you," returned Miss Fancourt, who evidently had the habit of saying the things that, by her quick calculation, would give people pleasure. Paul saw how she would always calculate on everything's being simple between others.

"I shouldn't have supposed he knew anything about me," he professed.

"He does then—everything. And if he didn't I should be able to tell him."

"To tell him everything?" our friend smiled.

"You talk just like the people in your book," she answered.

"Then they must all talk alike."

She thought a moment, not a bit disconcerted. "Well, it must be so difficult. Mr. St. George tells me it *is*—terribly. I've tried too—and I find it so. I've tried to write a novel."

"Mr. St. George oughtn't to discourage you," Paul went so far as to say.

"You do much more—when you wear that expression."

"Well, after all, why try to be an artist?" the young man pursued. "It's so poor—so poor!"

"I don't know what you mean," said Miss Fancourt, who looked grave.

"I mean as compared with being a person of action—as living your works."

"But what's art but an intense life—if it be real?" she asked. "I think it's the only one—everything else is so clumsy!" Her companion laughed, and she brought out with her charming serenity what next struck her. "It's so interesting to meet so many celebrated people."

"So I should think—but surely it isn't new to you."

"Why, I've never seen anyone—anyone: living always in Asia."

The way she talked of Asia somehow enchanted him. "But doesn't that continent swarm with great figures? Haven't you administered provinces in India and had captive rajahs and tributary princes chained to your car?"

It was as if she didn't care even *should* he amuse himself at her cost. "I was with my father, after I left school to go out there. It was delightful being with him—we're alone together in the world, he and I—but there was none of the society I like best. One never heard of a picture—never of a book, except bad ones."

"Never of a picture? Why, wasn't all life a picture?"

She looked over the delightful place where they sat. "Nothing to compare to this. I adore England!" she cried.

It fairly stirred in him the sacred chord. "Ah, of course I don't deny that we must do something with her, poor old dear, yet!"

"She hasn't been touched, really," said the girl.

"Did Mr. St. George say that?"

There was a small and, as he felt, harmless spark of irony in his question; which, however, she answered very simply, not noticing the insinuation. "Yes, he says England hasn't been touched —not considering all there is," she went on eagerly. "He's so interesting about our country. To listen to him makes one want so to do something."

"It would make *me* want to," said Paul Overt, feeling strongly, on the instant, the suggestion of what she said and that of the emotion with which she said it, and well aware of what an incentive, on St. George's lips, such a speech might be.

"Oh, you—as if you hadn't! I should like so to hear you talk together," she added ardently.

"That's very genial of you; but he'd have it all his own way. I'm prostrate before him."

She had an air of earnestness. "Do you think, then, he's so perfect?"

"Far from it. Some of his later books seem to me of a queerness—!"

"Yes, yes—he knows that."

Paul Overt stared. "That they seem to me of a queerness—?"

"Well, yes, or at any rate that they're not what they should be. He told me he didn't esteem them. He has told me such wonderful things—he's so interesting."

There was a certain shock for Paul Overt in the knowledge that the fine genius they were talking of had been reduced to so explicit a confession and had made it, in his misery, to the first comer; for though Miss Fancourt was charming what was she after all but an immature girl encountered at a country-house? Yet precisely this was part of the sentiment he himself had just expressed: he would make way completely for the poor peccable great man, not because he didn't read him clear, but altogether because he did. His consideration was half composed of tenderness for superficialities which he was sure their perpetrator judged privately, judged more ferociously than anyone, and which represented some tragic intellectual secret. He would have his reasons for his psychology *à fleur de peau*,[2] and these reasons could only be cruel ones, such as would make him dearer to those who already were fond of him. "You excite my envy. I have my reserves, I discriminate—but I love him," Paul said in a moment. "And seeing him for the first time this way is a great event for me."

"How momentous—how magnificent!" cried the girl. "How delicious to bring you together!"

"*Your* doing it—that makes it perfect," our friend returned.

"He's as eager as you," she went on. "But it's so odd you shouldn't have met."

"It's not really so odd as it strikes you. I've been out of England so much—made repeated absences all these last years."

She took this in with interest. "And yet you write of it as well as if you were always here."

"It's just the being away perhaps. At any rate the best bits, I suspect, are those that were done in dreary places abroad."

"And why were they dreary?"

"Because they were health-resorts—where my poor mother was dying."

"Your poor mother?"—she was all sweet wonder.

"We went from place to place to help her to get better. But she never did. To the deadly Riviera (I hate it!), to the high Alps, to Algiers, and far away—a hideous journey—to Colorado."

"And she isn't better?" Miss Fancourt went on.

"She died a year ago."

"Really?—like mine! Only that's years since. Some day you must tell me about your mother," she added.

He could at first, on this, only gaze at her. "What right things you say! If you say them to St. George I don't wonder he's in bondage."

²*À fleur de peau.* Skin deep.

It pulled her up for a moment. "I don't know what you mean. He doesn't make speeches and professions at all—he isn't ridiculous."

"I'm afraid you consider, then, that I am."

"No, I don't"—she spoke it rather shortly. And then she added: "He understands—understands everything."

The young man was on the point of saying jocosely: "And I don't—is that it?" But these words, in time, changed themselves to others slightly less trivial. "Do you suppose he understands his wife?"

Miss Fancourt made no direct answer, but after a moment's hesitation put in: "Isn't she charming?"

"Not in the least!"

"Here he comes. Now you must know him," she went on. A small group of visitors had gathered at the other end of the gallery and had been there overtaken by Henry St. George, who strolled in from a neighbouring room. He stood near them a moment, not falling into the talk but taking up an old miniature from a table and vaguely regarding it. At the end of a minute he became aware of Miss Fancourt and her companion in the distance; whereupon, laying down his miniature, he approached them with the same procrastinating air, his hands in his pockets and his eyes turned, right and left, to the pictures. The gallery was so long that this transit took some little time, especially as there was a moment when he stopped to admire the fine Gainsborough. "He says Mrs. St. George has been the making of him," the girl continued in a voice slightly lowered.

"Ah, he's often obscure!" Paul laughed.

"Obscure?" she repeated as if she heard it for the first time. Her eyes rested on her other friend, and it wasn't lost upon Paul that they appeared to send out great shafts of softness. "He's going to speak to us!" she fondly breathed. There was a sort of rapture in her voice, and our friend was startled. "Bless my soul, does she care for him like *that?*—is she in love with him?" he mentally inquired. "Didn't I tell you he was eager?" she had meanwhile asked of him.

"It's eagerness dissimulated," the young man returned as the subject of their observation lingered before his Gainsborough. "He edges toward us shyly. Does he mean that she saved him by burning that book?"

"That book? what book did she burn?" The girl quickly turned her face to him.

"Hasn't he told you, then?"

"Not a word."

"Then he doesn't tell you everything!" Paul had guessed that she pretty much supposed he did. The great man had now resumed his course and come nearer; in spite of which his more qualified admirer risked a profane observation. "St. George and the Dragon is what the anecdote suggests!"

His companion, however, didn't hear it; she smiled at the dragon's adversary. "He *is* eager—he is!" she insisted.

"Eager for you—yes."

But meanwhile she had called out: "I'm sure you want to know Mr. Overt. You'll be great friends, and it will always be delightful to me to remember I was here when you first met and that I had something to do with it."

There was a freshness of intention in the words that carried them off; nevertheless our young man was sorry for Henry St. George, as he was sorry at any time for any person publicly invited to be responsive and delightful. He would have been so touched to believe that a man he deeply admired should care a straw for him that he wouldn't play with such a presumption if it were possibly vain. In a single glance of the eye of the pardonable master he read—having the sort of divination that belonged to his talent—that this personage had ever a store of friendly patience, which was part of his rich outfit, but was versed in no printed page of a rising scribbler. There was even a relief, a simplification, in that: liking him so much already for what he had done, how could one have liked him any more for a perception which must at the best have been vague? Paul Overt got up, trying to show his compassion, but at the same instant he found himself encompassed by St. George's happy personal art—a manner of which it was the essence to conjure away false positions. It all took place in a moment. Paul was conscious that he knew him now, conscious of his handshake and of the very quality of his hand; of his face, seen nearer and consequently seen better, of a general fraternising assurance, and in particular of the circumstance that St. George didn't dislike him (as yet at least) for being imposed by a charming but too gushing girl, attractive enough without such danglers. No irritation at any rate was reflected in the voice with which he questioned Miss Fancourt as to some project of a walk—a general walk of the company round the park. He had soon said something to Paul about a talk—"We must have a tremendous lot of talk; there are so many things, aren't there?"— but our friend could see this idea wouldn't in the present case take very immediate effect. All the same he was extremely happy, even after the matter of the walk had been settled—the three presently passed back to the other part of the gallery, where it was discussed with several members of the party; even when, after they had all gone out together, he found himself for half an hour conjoined with Mrs. St. George. Her husband had taken the advance with Miss Fancourt, and this pair were quite out of sight. It was the prettiest of rambles for a summer afternoon— a grassy circuit, of immense extent, skirting the limit of the park within. The park was completely surrounded by its old mottled but perfect red wall, which, all the way on their left, constituted in itself an object of interest. Mrs. St. George mentioned to him the surprising number of acres thus enclosed, together with numerous other facts relating to the property and the family, and the family's other properties: she couldn't too strongly urge on him the importance of seeing their other houses. She ran over the names of these and rang the changes on them with the facility of practice, making them appear an almost endless list. She had received Paul Overt very amiably on his breaking ground with her by the mention of his joy in having just made her husband's acquaintance, and struck him as so alert and so accommodating a little woman that he was rather ashamed of his *mot* [3] about her to Miss Fancourt; though he reflected that a hundred other people, on a hundred occasions, would have been sure to make it. He got on with Mrs. St. George, in short, better than he expected; but this didn't prevent her suddenly becoming aware that she was faint with fatigue and must take her way back to the house by the shortest cut. She professed that she hadn't the strength of a kitten and was a miserable wreck; a character he had been too preoccupied to discern in her while he wondered in what sense she could be held to have been the making of her husband. He had

[3] *Mot.* Remark.

arrived at a glimmering of the answer when she announced that she must leave him, though this perception was of course provisional. While he was in the very act of placing himself at her disposal for the return, the situation underwent a change; Lord Masham had suddenly turned up, coming back to them, overtaking them, emerging from the shrubbery—Overt could scarcely have said how he appeared—and Mrs. St. George had protested that she wanted to be left alone and not to break up the party. A moment later she was walking off with Lord Masham. Our friend fell back and joined Lady Watermouth, to whom he presently mentioned that Mrs. St. George had been obliged to renounce the attempt to go further.

"She oughtn't to have come out at all," her ladyship rather grumpily remarked.

"Is she so very much of an invalid?"

"Very bad indeed." And his hostess added with still greater austerity: "She oughtn't really to come to one!" He wondered what was implied by this, and presently gathered that it was not a reflexion on the lady's conduct or her moral nature: it only represented that her strength was not equal to her aspirations.

III

The smoking-room at Summersoft was on the scale of the rest of the place—high light commodious and decorated with such refined old carvings and mouldings that it seemed rather a bower for ladies who should sit at work at fading crewels than a parliament of gentlemen smoking strong cigars. The gentlemen mustered there in considerable force on the Sunday evening, collecting mainly at one end, in front of one of the cool fair fireplaces of white marble, the entablature of which was adorned with a delicate little Italian "subject." There was another in the wall that faced it, and, thanks to the mild summer night, a fire in neither; but a nucleus for aggregation was furnished on one side by a table in the chimney-corner laden with bottles, decanters and tall tumblers. Paul Overt was a faithless smoker; he would puff a cigarette for reasons with which tobacco had nothing to do. This was particularly the case on the occasion of which I speak; his motive was the vision of a little direct talk with Henry St. George. The "tremendous" communion of which the great man had held out

hopes to him earlier in the day had not yet come off, and this saddened him considerably, for the party was to go its several ways
immediately after breakfast on the morrow. He had, however,
the disappointment of finding that apparently the author of
"Shadowmere" was not disposed to prolong his vigil. He wasn't
among the gentlemen assembled when Paul entered, nor was he
one of those who turned up, in bright habiliments, during the
next ten minutes. The young man waited a little, wondering if
he had only gone to put on something extraordinary; this would
account for his delay as well as contribute further to Overt's impression of his tendency to do the approved superficial thing. But
he didn't arrive—he must have been putting on something more
extraordinary than was probable. Our hero gave him up, feeling
a little injured, a little wounded, at this loss of twenty coveted
words. He wasn't angry, but he puffed his cigarette sighingly,
with the sense of something rare possibly missed. He wandered
away with his regret and moved slowly round the room, looking
at the old prints on the walls. In this attitude he presently felt a
hand on his shoulder and a friendly voice in his ear: "This is good.
I hoped I should find you. I came down on purpose." St. George
was there without a change of dress and with a fine face—his
graver one—to which our young man all in a flutter responded.
He explained that it was only for the Master—the idea of a little
talk—that he had sat up, and that, not finding him, he had been
on the point of going to bed.

"Well, you know, I don't smoke—my wife doesn't let me,"
said St. George, looking for a place to sit down. "It's very good
for me—very good for me. Let us take that sofa."

"Do you mean smoking's good for you?"

"No, no—her not letting me. It's a great thing to have a wife
who's so sure of all the things one can do without. One might
never find them out one's self. She doesn't allow me to touch a
cigarette." They took possession of a sofa at a distance from the
group of smokers, and St. George went on: "Have you got one
yourself?"

"Do you mean a cigarette?"

"Dear no—a wife!"

"No; and yet I'd give up my cigarette for one."

"You'd give up a good deal more than that," St. George returned. "However, you'd get a great deal in return. There's a something to be said for wives," he added, folding his arms and crossing his outstretched legs. He declined tobacco altogether and sat there without returning fire. His companion stopped smoking, touched by his courtesy; and after all they were out of the fumes, their sofa was in a faraway corner. It would have been a mistake, St. George went on, a great mistake for them to have separated without a little chat; "for I know all about you," he said, "I know you're very remarkable. You've written a very distinguished book."

"And how do you know it?" Paul asked.

"Why, my dear fellow, it's in the air, it's in the papers, it's everywhere." St. George spoke with the immediate familiarity of a confrère—a tone that seemed to his neighbour the very rustle of the laurel. "You're on all men's lips and, what's better, on all women's. And I've just been reading your book."

"Just? You hadn't read it this afternoon," said Overt.

"How do you know that?"

"I think you should know how I know it," the young man laughed.

"I suppose Miss Fancourt told you."

"No indeed—she led me rather to suppose you had."

"Yes—that's much more what she'd do. Doesn't she shed a rosy glow over life? But you didn't believe her?" asked St. George.

"No, not when you came to us there."

"Did I pretend? did I pretend badly?" But without waiting for an answer to this St. George went on: "You ought always to believe such a girl as that—always, always. Some women are meant to be taken with allowances and reserves; but you must take *her* just as she is."

"I like her very much," said Paul Overt.

Something in his tone appeared to excite on his companion's part a momentary sense of the absurd; perhaps it was the air of deliberation attending this judgment. St. George broke into a laugh to reply. "It's the best thing you can do with her. She's a rare young lady! In point of fact, however, I confess I hadn't read you this afternoon."

"Then you see how right I was in this particular case not to believe Miss Fancourt."

"How right? how can I agree to that when I lost credit by it?"

"Do you wish to pass exactly for what she represents you? Certainly you needn't be afraid," Paul said.

"Ah, my dear young man, don't talk about passing—for the likes of me! I'm passing away—nothing else than that. She has a better use for her young imagination (isn't it fine?) than in 'representing' in any way such a weary wasted used-up animal!" The Master spoke with a sudden sadness that produced a protest on Paul's part; but before the protest could be uttered he went on, reverting to the latter's striking novel: "I had no idea you were so good—one hears of so many things. But you're surprisingly good."

"I'm going to be surprisingly better," Overt made bold to reply.

"I see that, and it's what fetches me. I don't see so much else— as one looks about—that's going to be surprisingly better. They're going to be consistently worse—most of the things. It's so much easier to be worse—heaven knows I've found it so. I'm not in a great glow, you know, about what's breaking out all over the place. But you *must* be better, you really must keep it up. I haven't, of course. It's very difficult—that's the devil of the whole thing, keeping it up. But I see you'll be able to. It will be a great disgrace if you don't."

"It's very interesting to hear you speak of yourself; but I don't know what you mean by your allusions to your having fallen off," Paul Overt observed with pardonable hypocrisy. He liked his companion so much now that the fact of any decline of talent or of care had ceased for the moment to be vivid to him.

"Don't say that—don't say that," St. George returned gravely, his head resting on the top of the sofa-back and his eyes on the ceiling. "You know perfectly what I mean. I haven't read twenty pages of your book without seeing that you can't help it."

"You make me very miserable," Paul ecstatically breathed.

"I'm glad of that, for it may serve as a kind of warning. Shocking enough it must be, especially to a young fresh mind, full of faith—the spectacle of a man meant for better things sunk at my age in such dishonour." St. George, in the same contemplative attitude, spoke softly but deliberately, and without perceptible emotion. His tone indeed suggested an impersonal lucidity that was practically cruel—cruel to himself—and made his young friend lay an argumentative hand on his arm. But he went on while his eyes seemed to follow the graces of the eighteenth-century ceiling: "Look at me well, take my lesson to heart—for it *is* a lesson. Let that good come of it at least that you shudder with your pitiful impression, and that this may help to keep you straight in the future. Don't become in your old age what I have in mine—the depressing, the deplorable illustration of the worship of false gods!"

"What do you mean by your old age?" the young man asked.

"It has made me old. But I like your youth."

Paul answered nothing—they sat for a minute in silence. They heard the others going on about the governmental majority. Then "What do you mean by false gods?" he inquired.

His companion had no difficulty whatever in saying, "The idols of the market; money and luxury and 'the world'; placing one's children and dressing one's wife; everything that drives one to the short and easy way. Ah, the vile things they make one do!"

"But surely one's right to want to place one's children."

"One has no business to have any children," St. George placidly declared. "I mean, of course, if one wants to do anything good."

"But aren't they an inspiration—an incentive?"

"An incentive to damnation, artistically speaking."

"You touch on very deep things—things I should like to discuss with you," Paul said. "I should like you to tell me volumes about yourself. This is a great feast for *me!*"

"Of course it is, cruel youth. But to show you I'm still not incapable, degraded as I am, of an act of faith, I'll tie my vanity to the stake for you and burn it to ashes. You must come and see me—you must come and see us," the Master quickly substituted. "Mrs. St. George is charming; I don't know whether you've had any opportunity to talk to her. She'll be delighted to see you; she likes great celebrities, whether incipient or predominant. You must come and dine—my wife will write to you. Where are you to be found?"

"This is my little address"—and Overt drew out his pocket-book and extracted a visiting-card. On second thoughts, however, he kept it back, remarking that he wouldn't trouble his friend to take charge of it but would come and see him straightway in London and leave it at his door if he should fail to obtain entrance.

"Ah, you'll probably fail; my wife's always out—or when she isn't out is knocked up from having *been* out. You must come and dine—though that won't do much good either, for my wife insists on big dinners." St. George turned it over further, but then went on: "You must come down and see us in the country, that's the best way; we've plenty of room and it isn't bad."

"You've a house in the country?" Paul asked enviously.

"Ah, not like this! But we have a sort of place we go to—an hour from Euston. That's one of the reasons."

"One of the reasons?"

"Why my books are so bad."

"You must tell me all the others!" Paul longingly laughed.

His friend made no direct rejoinder to this, but spoke again abruptly. "Why have I never seen you before?"

The tone of the question was singularly flattering to our hero, who felt it to imply the great man's now perceiving he had for years missed something. "Partly, I suppose, because there has been no particular reason why you should see me. I haven't lived in the world—in your world. I've spent many years out of England, in different places abroad."

"Well, please don't do it any more. You must do England—there's such a lot of it."

"Do you mean I must write about it?"—and Paul struck the note of the listening candour of a child.

"Of course you must. And tremendously well, do you mind? That takes off a little of my esteem for this thing of yours—that it goes on abroad. Hang 'abroad'! Stay at home and do things here—do subjects we can measure."

"I'll do whatever you tell me," Overt said, deeply attentive. "But pardon me if I say I don't understand how you've been reading my book," he added. "I've had you before me all the afternoon, first in that long walk, then at tea on the lawn, till we went to dress for dinner, and all the evening at dinner and in this place."

St. George turned his face about with a smile. "I gave it but a quarter of an hour."

"A quarter of an hour's immense, but I don't understand where you put it in. In the drawing-room after dinner you weren't reading—you were talking to Miss Fancourt."

"It comes to the same thing, because we talked about 'Ginistrella.' She described it to me—she lent me her copy."

"Lent it to you?"

"She travels with it."

"It's incredible," Paul blushed.

"It's glorious for you, but it also turned out very well for me. When the ladies went off to bed she kindly offered to send the book down to me. Her maid brought it to me in the hall, and I went to my room with it. I hadn't thought of coming here, I do that so little. But I don't sleep early, I always have to read an hour or two. I sat down to your novel on the spot, without undressing, without taking off anything but my coat. I think that's a sign my curiosity had been strongly aroused about it. I read a quarter of an hour, as I tell you, and even in a quarter of an hour I was greatly struck."

"Ah, the beginning isn't very good—it's the whole thing!" said Overt, who had listened to this recital with extreme interest. "And you laid down the book and came after me?" he asked.

"That's the way it moved me. I said to myself, 'I see it's off his own bat, and he's there, by the way, and the day's over, and I haven't said twenty words to him.' It occurred to me that you'd probably be in the smoking-room and that it wouldn't be too late to repair my omission. I wanted to do something civil to you, so I put on my coat and came down. I shall read your book again when I go up."

Our friend faced round in his place—he was touched as he had scarce ever been by the picture of such a demonstration in his favour. "You're really the kindest of men. *Cela s'est passé comme ça?* [4]—and I've been sitting here with you all this time and never apprehended it and never thanked you!"

"Thank Miss Fancourt—it was she who wound me up. She has made me feel as if I had read your novel."

"She's an angel from heaven!" Paul declared.

"She is indeed. I've never seen anyone like her. Her interest in

---

[4] *Cela s'est passé comme ça?* It happened that way?

literature's touching—something quite peculiar to herself; she takes it all so seriously. She feels the arts and she wants to feel them more. To those who practise them it's almost humiliating— her curiosity, her sympathy, her good faith. How can anything be as fine as she supposes it?"

"She's a rare organisation," the younger man sighed.

"The richest I've ever seen—an artistic intelligence really of the first order. And lodged in such a form!" St. George exclaimed.

"One would like to represent such a girl as that," Paul continued.

"Ah, there it is—there's nothing like life!" said his companion. "When you're finished, squeezed dry and used up and you think the sack's empty, you're still appealed to, you still get touches and thrills, the idea springs up—out of the lap of the actual—and shows you there's always something to be done. But I shan't do it—she's not for me!"

"How do you mean, not for you?"

"Oh, it's all over—she's for you, if you like."

"Ah, much less!" said Paul. "She's not for a dingy little man of letters; she's for the world, the bright rich world of bribes and rewards. And the world will take hold of her—it will carry her away."

"It will try—but it's just a case in which there may be a fight. It would be worth fighting, for a man who had it in him, with youth and talent on his side."

These words rang not a little in Paul Overt's consciousness— they held him briefly silent. "It's a wonder she has remained as she is; giving herself away so—with so much to give away."

"Remaining, you mean, so ingenuous—so natural? Oh, she doesn't care a straw—she gives away because she overflows. She has her own feelings, her own standards; she doesn't keep remembering that she must be proud. And then she hasn't been here long enough to be spoiled; she has picked up a fashion or two, but only the amusing ones. She's a provincial—a provincial genius," St. George went on; "her very blunders are charming, her mistakes are interesting. She has come back from Asia with all sorts of excited curiosities and unappeased appetites. She's first-rate herself and she expends herself on the second-rate. She's life herself and she takes a rare interest in imitations. She mixes all things up, but there are none in regard to which she hasn't perceptions. She sees things in a perspective—as if from the top of the Himalayas—and she enlarges everything she touches. Above all she exaggerates—to herself, I mean. She exaggerates you and me!"

There was nothing in that description to allay the agitation caused in our younger friend by such a sketch of a fine subject. It seemed to him to show the art of St. George's admired hand, and he lost himself in gazing at the vision—this hovered there before him—of a woman's figure which should be part of the glory of a novel. But at the end of a moment the thing had turned into smoke, and out of the smoke—the last puff of a big cigar—proceeded the voice of General Fancourt, who had left the others and come and planted himself before the gentlemen on the sofa. "I suppose that when you fellows get talking you sit up half the night."

"Half the night?—*jamais de la vie!* [5] I follow a hygiene"—and St. George rose to his feet.

"I see—you're hothouse plants," laughed the General. "That's the way you produce your flowers."

"I produce mine between ten and one every morning—I bloom with a regularity!" St. George went on.

"And with a splendour!" added the polite General, while Paul noted how little the author of "Shadowmere" minded, as he phrased it to himself, when addressed as a celebrated storyteller. The young man had an idea *he* should never get used to that; it would always make him uncomfortable—from the suspicion that people would think they had to—and he would want to prevent it. Evidently his great colleague had toughened and hardened—had made himself a surface. The group of men had finished their cigars and taken up their bedroom candlesticks; but before they all passed out Lord Watermouth invited the pair of guests who had been so absorbed together to "have" something. It happened that they both declined; upon which General Fancourt said: "Is that the hygiene? You don't water the flowers?"

"Oh, I should drown them!" St. George replied; but, leaving the room still at his young friend's side, he added whimsically, for the latter's benefit, in a lower tone: "My wife doesn't let me."

"Well, I'm glad I'm not one of you fellows!" the General richly

[5] *Jamais de la vie!* Never!

concluded.

The nearness of Summersoft to London had this consequence, chilling to a person who had had a vision of sociability in a railway carriage, that most of the company, after breakfast, drove back to town, entering their own vehicles, which had come out to fetch them, while their servants returned by train with their luggage. Three or four young men, among whom was Paul Overt, also availed themselves of the common convenience; but they stood in the portico of the house and saw the others roll away. Miss Fancourt got into a victoria with her father after she had shaken hands with our hero and said, smiling in the frankest way in the world, "I *must* see you more. Mrs. St. George is so nice; she has promised to ask us both to dinner together." This lady and her husband took their places in a perfectly appointed brougham —she required a closed carriage—and as our young man waved his hat to them in response to their nods and flourishes he reflected that, taken together, they were an honourable image of success, of the material rewards and the social credit of literature. Such things were not the full measure, but he nevertheless felt a little proud for literature.

IV

Before a week had elapsed he met Miss Fancourt in Bond Street, at a private view of the works of a young artist in "black-and-white" who had been so good as to invite him to the stuffy scene. The drawings were admirable, but the crowd in the one little room was so dense that he felt himself up to his neck in a sack of wool. A fringe of people at the outer edge endeavoured by curving forward their backs and presenting, below them, a still more convex surface of resistance to the pressure of the mass, to preserve an interval between their noses and the glazed mounts of the pictures; while the central body, in the comparative gloom projected by a wide horizontal screen hung under the skylight and allowing only a margin for the day, remained upright, dense, and vague, lost in the contemplation of its own ingredients. This contemplation sat especially in the sad eyes of certain female heads, surmounted with hats of strange convolution and plumage, which rose on long necks above the others. One of the heads, Paul perceived, was much the most beautiful of the collection, and his next discovery was that it belonged to Miss Fancourt. Its beauty was enhanced by the glad smile she sent him across surrounding obstructions, a smile that drew him to her as fast as he could make his way. He had seen for himself at Summersoft that the last thing her nature contained was an affectation of indifference; yet even with this circumspection he took a fresh satisfaction in her not having pretended to await his arrival with composure. She smiled as radiantly as if she wished to make him hurry, and as soon as he came within earshot she broke out in her voice of joy: "He's here —he's here; he's coming back in a moment!"

"Ah, your father?" Paul returned as she offered him her hand.

"Oh, dear no, this isn't in my poor father's line. I mean Mr. St. George. He has just left me to speak to someone—he's coming back. It's he who brought me—wasn't it charming?"

"Ah that gives him a pull over me—I couldn't have 'brought' you, could I?"

"If you had been so kind as to propose it—why not you as well as he?" the girl returned with a face that, expressing no cheap coquetry, simply affirmed a happy fact.

"Why he's a *père de famille*.[6] They've privileges," Paul explained. And then quickly: "Will you go to see places with *me*?" he asked.

"Anything you like," she smiled. "I know what you mean, that girls have to have a lot of people—!" Then she broke off: "I don't know; I'm free. I've always been like that—I can go about with anyone. I'm so glad to meet you," she added with a sweet distinctness that made those near her turn around.

"Let me at least repay that speech by taking you out of this squash," her friend said. "Surely people aren't happy here!"

"No, they're awfully *mornes*,[7] aren't they? But I'm very happy indeed and I promised Mr. St. George to remain on this spot till he comes back. He's going to take me away. They send him invitations for things of this sort—more than he wants. It was so kind of him to think of me."

"They also send me invitations of this kind—more than *I* want. And if thinking of *you* will do it—!" Paul went on.

"Oh, I delight in them—everything that's life, everything that's

---

[6] *Père de famille.* The father of a family.
[7] *Mornes.* Mournful.

London!"

"They don't have private views in Asia, I suppose," he laughed. "But what a pity that for this year, even in this gorged city, they're pretty well over."

"Well, next year will do, for I hope you believe we're going to be friends always. Here he comes!" Miss Fancourt continued before Paul had time to respond.

He made out St. George in the gaps of the crowd, and this perhaps led to his hurrying a little to say: "I hope that doesn't mean I'm to wait till next year to see you."

"No, no—aren't we to meet at dinner on the twenty-fifth?" she panted with an eagerness as happy as his own.

"That's almost next year. Is there no means of seeing you before?"

She stared with all her brightness. "Do you mean you'd *come?*"

"Like a shot, if you'll be so good as to ask me!"

"On Sunday then—this next Sunday?"

"What have I done that you should doubt it?" the young man asked with delight.

Miss Fancourt turned instantly to St. George, who had now joined them, and announced triumphantly: "He's coming on Sunday—this next Sunday!"

"Ah, my day—my day too!" said the famous novelist, laughing, to their companion.

"Yes, but not yours only. You shall meet in Manchester Square; you shall talk—you shall be wonderful!"

"We don't meet often enough," St. George allowed, shaking hands with his disciple. "Too many things—ah, too many things! But we must make it up in the country in September. You won't forget you've promised me that?"

"Why, he's coming on the twenty-fifth—you'll see him then," said the girl.

"On the twenty-fifth?" St. George asked vaguely.

"We dine with you; I hope you haven't forgotten. He's dining out that day," she added gaily to Paul.

"Oh, bless me, yes—that's charming! And you're coming? My wife didn't tell me," St. George said to him. "Too many things—too many things!" he repeated.

"Too many people—too many people!" Paul exclaimed, giving ground before the penetration of an elbow.

"You oughtn't to say that. They all read you."

"Me? I should like to see them! Only two or three at most," the young man returned.

"Did you ever hear anything like that? He knows, haughtily, how good he is!" St. George declared, laughing, to Miss Fancourt. "They read *me*, but that doesn't make me like them any better. Come away from them, come away!" And he led the way out of the exhibition.

"He's going to take me to the Park," Miss Fancourt observed to Overt with elation as they passed along the corridor that led to the street.

"Ah, does he go there?" Paul asked, taking the fact for a somewhat unexpected illustration of St. George's *moeurs*.[8]

"It's a beautiful day—there'll be a great crowd. We're going to look at the people, to look at types," the girl went on. "We shall sit under the trees; we shall walk by the Row."

"I go once a year—on business," said St. George, who had overheard Paul's question.

"Or with a country cousin, didn't you tell me? I'm the country cousin!" she continued over her shoulder to Paul as their friend drew her toward a hansom to which he had signalled. The young man watched them get in; he returned, as he stood there, the friendly wave of the hand with which, ensconced in the vehicle beside her, St. George took leave of him. He even lingered to see the vehicle start away and lose itself in the confusion of Bond Street. He followed it with his eyes; it put to him embarrassing things. "She's not for *me*!" the great novelist had said emphatically at Summersoft; but his manner of conducting himself toward her appeared not quite in harmony with such a conviction. How could he have behaved differently if she *had* been for him? An indefinite envy rose in Paul Overt's heart as he took his way on foot alone; a feeling addressed alike, strangely enough, to each of the occupants of the hansom. How much he should like to rattle about London with such a girl! How much he should like to go and look at "types" with St. George!

The next Sunday at four o'clock he called in Manchester Square, where his secret wish was gratified by his finding Miss

[8] *Moeurs.* Habits.

Fancourt alone. She was in a large bright friendly occupied room, which was painted red all over, draped with the quaint cheap florid stuffs that are represented as coming from southern and eastern countries, where they are fabled to serve as the counterpanes of the peasantry, and bedecked with pottery of vivid hues, ranged on casual shelves, and with many water-colour drawings from the hand (as the visitor learned) of the young lady herself, commemorating with a brave breadth the sunsets, the mountains, the temples and palaces of India. He sat an hour—more than an hour, two hours—and all the while no one came in. His hostess was so good as to remark, with her liberal humanity, that it was delightful they weren't interrupted: it was so rare in London, especially at that season, that people got a good talk. But luckily now, of a fine Sunday, half the world went out of town, and that made it better for those who didn't go, when these others were in sympathy. It was the defect of London—one of two or three, the very short list of those she recognised in the teeming worldcity she adored—that there were too few good chances for talk: you never had time to carry anything far.

"Too many things, too many things!" Paul said, quoting St. George's exclamation of a few days before.

"Ah, yes, for him there are too many—his life's too complicated."

"Have you seen it *near?* That's what I should like to do; it might explain some mysteries," the visitor went on. She asked him what mysteries he meant, and he said: "Oh, peculiarities of his work, inequalities, superficialities. For one who looks at it from the artistic point of view it contains a bottomless ambiguity."

She became at this, on the spot, all intensity. "Ah, do describe that more—it's so interesting. There are no such suggestive questions. I'm so fond of them. He thinks he's a failure—fancy!" she beautifully wailed.

"That depends on what his ideal may have been. With his gifts it ought to have been high. But till one knows what he really proposed to himself—! Do *you* know by chance?" the young man broke off.

"Oh, he doesn't talk to me about himself. I can't make him. It's too provoking."

Paul was on the point of asking what, then, he did talk about, but discretion checked it and he said instead: "Do you think he's unhappy at home?"

She seemed to wonder. "At home?"

"I mean in his relations with his wife. He has a mystifying little way of alluding to her."

"Not to me," said Marian Fancourt with her clear eyes. "That wouldn't be right, would it?" she asked gravely.

"Not particularly so; I'm glad he doesn't mention her to you. To praise her might bore you, and he has no business to do anything else. Yet he knows you better than me."

"Ah, but he respects *you!*" the girl cried as with envy.

Her visitor stared a moment, then broke into a laugh. "Doesn't he respect you?"

"Of course, but not in the same way. He respects what you've done—he told me so the other day."

Paul drank it in, but retained his faculties. "When you went to look at types?"

"Yes—we found so many: he has such an observation of them! He talked a great deal about your book. He says it's really important."

"Important! Ah the grand creature!"—and the author of the work in question groaned for joy.

"He was wonderfully amusing, he was inexpressibly droll, while we walked about. He sees everything; he has so many comparisons and images, and they're always exactly right. *C'est d'un trouvé,* [9] as they say!"

"Yes, with his gifts, such things as he ought to have done!" Paul sighed.

"And don't you think he *has* done them?"

Ah, it was just the point. "A part of them, and of course even that part's immense. But he might have been one of the greatest. However, let us not make this an hour of qualifications. Even as they stand," our friend earnestly concluded, "his writings are a mine of gold."

To this proposition she ardently responded, and for half an hour the pair talked over the Master's principal productions. She knew them well—she knew them even better than her visitor, who was struck with her critical intelligence and with something large

[9] *C'est d'un trouvé.* They are perfectly selected.

and bold in the movement in her mind. She said things that startled him and that evidently had come to her directly; they weren't picked-up phrases—she placed them too well. St. George had been right about her being first-rate, about her not being afraid to gush, not remembering that she must be proud. Suddenly something came back to her, and she said: "I recollect that he did speak of Mrs. St. George to me once. He said, apropos of something or other, that she didn't care for perfection."

"That's a great crime in an artist's wife," Paul returned.

"Yes, poor thing!" and the girl sighed with a suggestion of many reflexions, some of them mitigating. But she presently added: "Ah perfection, perfection—how one ought to go in for it! I wish *I* could."

"Every one can in his way," her companion opined.

"In *his* way, yes—but not in hers. Women are so hampered —so condemned! Yet it's a kind of dishonour if you don't, when you want to *do* something, isn't it?" Miss Fancourt pursued, dropping one train in her quickness to take up another, an accident that was common with her. So these two young persons sat discussing high themes in their eclectic drawing-room, in their London "season"—discussing, with extreme seriousness, the high theme of perfection. It must be said in extenuation of this eccentricity that they were interested in the business. Their tone had truth and their emotion beauty; they weren't posturing for each other or for someone else.

The subject was so wide that they found themselves reducing it; the perfection to which for the moment they agreed to confine their speculations was that of the valid, the exemplary work of art. Our young woman's imagination, it appeared, had wandered far in that direction, and her guest had the rare delight of feeling in their conversation a full interchange. This episode will have lived for years in his memory and even in his wonder; it had the quality that fortune distils in a single drop at a time—the quality that lubricates many ensuing frictions. He still, whenever he likes, has a vision of the room, the bright red sociable talkative room with the curtains that, by a stroke of successful audacity, had the note of vivid blue. He remembers where certain things stood, the particular book open on the table and the almost intense odour of the flowers placed, at the left, somewhere behind him.

These facts were the fringe, as it were, of a fine special agitation which had its birth in those two hours and of which perhaps the main sign was in its leading him inwardly and repeatedly to breathe, "I had no idea there was any one like this—I had no idea there was any one like this!" Her freedom amazed him and charmed him—it seemed so to simplify the practical question. She was on the footing of an independent personage—a motherless girl who had passed out of her teens and had a position and responsibilities, who wasn't held down to the limitations of a little miss. She came and went with no dragged duenna, she received people alone, and, though she was totally without hardness, the question of protection or patronage had no relevancy in regard to her. She gave such an impression of the clear and the noble combined with the easy and the natural that in spite of her eminent modern situation she suggested no sort of sisterhood with the "fast" girl. Modern she was indeed, and made Paul Overt, who loved old colour, the golden glaze of time, think with some alarm of the muddled palette of the future. He couldn't get used to her interest in the arts he cared for; it seemed too good to be real—it was so unlikely an adventure to tumble into such a well of sympathy. One might stray into the desert easily—that was on the cards and that was the law of life; but it was too rare an accident to stumble on a crystal well. Yet if her aspirations seemed at one moment too extravagant to be real they struck him at the next as too intelligent to be false. They were both high and lame, and, whims for whims, he preferred them to any he had met in a like relation. It was probable enough she would leave them behind— exchange them for politics or "smartness" or mere prolific maternity, as was the custom of scribbling daubing educated flattered girls in an age of luxury and a society of leisure. He noted that the water-colours on the walls of the room she sat in had mainly the quality of being naïves, and reflected that naïveté in art is like a zero in a number: its importance depends on the figure it is united with. Meanwhile, however, he had fallen in love with her. Before he went away, at any rate, he said to her: "I thought St. George was coming to see you today, but he doesn't turn up."

For a moment he supposed she was going to cry "*Comment donc?* [10] Did you come here only to meet him?" But the next he

[10] *Comment donc?* Really now?

became aware of how little such a speech would have fallen in with any note of flirtation he had as yet perceived in her. She only replied: "Ah, yes, but I don't think he'll come. He recommended me not to expect him." Then she gaily but all gently added: "He said it wasn't fair to you. But I think I could manage two."

"So could I," Paul Overt returned, stretching the point a little to meet her. In reality his appreciation of the occasion was so completely an appreciation of the woman before him that another figure in the scene, even so esteemed a one as St. George, might for the hour have appealed to him vainly. He left the house wondering what the great man had meant by its not being fair to him; and, still more than that, whether he had actually stayed away from the force of that idea. As he took his course through the Sunday solitude of Manchester Square, swinging his stick and with a good deal of emotion fermenting in his soul, it appeared to him he was living in a world strangely magnanimous. Miss Fancourt had told him it was possible she should be away, and that her father should be, on the following Sunday, but that she had the hope of a visit from him in the other event. She promised to let him know should their absence fail, and then he might act accordingly. After he had passed into one of the streets that open from the Square he stopped, without definite intentions, looking sceptically for a cab. In a moment he saw a hansom roll through the place from the other side and come a part of the way toward him. He was on the point of hailing the driver when he noticed a "fare" within; then he waited, seeing the man prepare to deposit his passenger by pulling up at one of the houses. The house was apparently the one he himself had just quitted; at least he drew that inference as he recognised Henry St. George in the person who stepped out of the hansom. Paul turned off as quickly as if he had been caught in the act of spying. He gave up his cab—he preferred to walk; he would go nowhere else. He was glad St. George hadn't renounced his visit altogether—that would have been too absurd. Yes, the world was magnanimous, and even he himself felt so as, on looking at his watch, he noted but six o'clock, so that he could mentally congratulate his successor on having an hour still to sit in Miss Fancourt's drawing-room. He himself might use that hour for another visit, but by the time he reached the Marble Arch the idea of such a course had become incongruous to him. He passed beneath that architectural effort and walked into the Park till he had got upon the spreading grass. Here he continued to walk; he took his way across the elastic turf and came out by the Serpentine. He watched with a friendly eye the diversions of the London people, he bent a glance almost encouraging on the young ladies paddling their sweethearts about the lake and the guardsmen tickling tenderly with their bearskins the artificial flowers in the Sunday hats of their partners. He prolonged his meditative walk; he went into Kensington Gardens, he sat upon the penny chairs, he looked at the little sail-boats launched upon the round pond and was glad he had no engagement to dine. He repaired for this purpose, very late, to his club, where he found himself unable to order a repast and told the waiter to bring whatever there was. He didn't even observe what he was served with, and he spent the evening in the library of the establishment, pretending to read an article in an American magazine. He failed to discover what it was about; it appeared in a dim way to be about Marian Fancourt.

Quite late in the week she wrote to him that she was not to go into the country—it had only just been settled. Her father, she added, would never settle anything, but put it all on her. She felt her responsibility—she had to—and since she was forced this was the way she had decided. She mentioned no reasons, which gave our friend all the clearer field for bold conjecture about them. In Manchester Square on this second Sunday he esteemed his fortune less good, for she had three or four other visitors. But there were three or four compensations; perhaps the greatest of which was that, learning how her father had after all, at the last hour, gone out of town alone, the bold conjecture I just now spoke of found itself becoming a shade more bold. And then her presence was her presence, and the personal red room was there and was full of it, whatever phantoms passed and vanished, emitting incomprehensible sounds. Lastly, he had the resource of staying till every one had come and gone and of believing this grateful to her, though she gave no particular sign. When they were alone together he came to his point. "But St. George did come—last Sunday. I saw him as I looked back."

"Yes, but it was the last time."

"The last time?"

"He said he would never come again."

Paul Overt stared. "Does he mean he wishes to cease to see you?"

"I don't know what he means," the girl bravely smiled. "He won't at any rate see me here."

"And pray why not?"

"I haven't the least idea," said Marian Fancourt, whose visitor found her more perversely sublime than ever yet as she professed this clear helplessness.

v

"Oh, I say, I want you to stop a little," Henry St. George said to him at eleven o'clock the night he dined with the head of the profession. The company—none of it indeed *of* the profession—had been numerous and was taking its leave; our young man, after bidding good-night to his hostess, had put out his hand in farewell to the master of the house. Besides drawing from the latter the protest I have cited, this movement provoked a further priceless word about their chance now to have a talk, their going into his room, his having still everything to say. Paul Overt was all delight at this kindness; nevertheless he mentioned in weak jocose qualification the bare fact that he had promised to go to another place which was at a considerable distance.

"Well, then, you'll break your promise, that's all. You quite awful humbug!" St. George added in a tone that confirmed our young man's ease.

"Certainly I'll break it—but it was a real promise."

"Do you mean to Miss Fancourt? You're following her?" his friend asked.

He answered by a question. "Oh, is *she* going?"

"Base impostor!" his ironic host went on. "I've treated you handsomely on the article of that young lady: I won't make another concession. Wait three minutes—I'll be with you." He gave himself to his departing guests, accompanied the long-trained ladies to the door. It was a hot night, the windows were open, the sound of the quick carriages and of the linkmen's call came into the house. The affair had rather glittered; a sense of festal things was in the heavy air: not only the influence of that particular entertainment, but the suggestion of the wide hurry of pleasure which in London on summer nights fills so many of the happier quarters of the complicated town. Gradually Mrs. St. George's drawing-room emptied itself; Paul was left alone with his hostess, to whom he explained the motive of his waiting. "Ah, yes, some intellectual, some *professional*, talk," she leered; "at this season doesn't one miss it? Poor dear Henry, I'm so glad!" The young man looked out of the window a moment, at the called hansoms that lurched up, at the smooth broughams that rolled away. When he turned round Mrs. St. George had disappeared; her husband's voice rose to him from below—he was laughing and talking, in the portico, with some lady who awaited her carriage. Paul had solitary possession, for some minutes, of the warm deserted rooms where the covered tinted lamplight was soft, the seats had been pushed about, and the odour of flowers lingered. They were large, they were pretty, they contained objects of value; everything in the picture told of a "good house." At the end of five minutes a servant came in with a request from the Master that he would join him downstairs; upon which, descending, he followed his conductor through a long passage to an apartment thrown out, in the rear of the habitation, for the special requirements, as he guessed, of a busy man of letters.

St. George was in his shirt-sleeves in the middle of a large high room—a room without windows, but with a wide skylight at the top, that of a place of exhibition. It was furnished as a library, and the serried bookshelves rose to the ceiling, a surface of incomparable tone produced by dimly gilt "backs" interrupted here and there by the suspension of old prints and drawings. At the end furthest from the door of admission was a tall desk, of great extent, at which the person using it could write only in the erect posture of a clerk in a counting-house; and stretched from the entrance to this structure was a wide plain band of crimson cloth, as straight as a garden path and almost as long, where, in his mind's eye, Paul at once beheld the Master pace to and fro during vexed hours—hours, that is, of admirable composition. The servant gave him a coat, an old jacket with a hang of experience, from a cupboard in the wall, retiring afterwards with the garment he had taken off. Paul Overt welcomed the coat; it was a coat for talk, it promised confidences—having visibly received so many—and had tragic literary elbows. "Ah, we're practical—we're practical!"

St. George said as he saw his visitor look the place over. "Isn't it a good big cage for going round and round? My wife invented it and she locks me up here every morning."

Our young man breathed—by way of tribute—with a certain oppression. "You don't miss a window—a place to look out?"

"I did at first awfully; but her calculation was just. It saves time, it has saved me many months in these ten years. Here I stand, under the eye of day—in London of course, very often, it's rather a bleared old eye—walled in to my trade. I can't get away—so the room's a fine lesson in concentration. I've learnt the lesson, I think; look at that big bundle of proof and acknowledge it." He pointed to a fat roll of papers, on one of the tables, which had not been undone.

"Are you bringing out another—?" Paul asked in a tone the fond deficiencies of which he didn't recognise till his companion burst out laughing, and indeed scarce even then.

"You humbug, you humbug!"—St. George appeared to enjoy caressing him, as it were, with that opprobrium. "Don't I know what you think of them?" he asked, standing there with his hands in his pockets and with a new kind of smile. It was as if he were going to let his young votary see him all now.

"Upon my word in that case you know more than I do!" the latter ventured to respond, revealing a part of the torment of being able neither clearly to esteem nor distinctly to renounce him.

"My dear fellow," said the more and more interesting Master, "don't imagine I talk about my books specifically; they're not a decent subject—*il ne manquerait plus que ça!* [11] I'm not so bad as you may apprehend. About myself, yes, a little, if you like; though it wasn't for that I brought you down here. I want to ask you something—very much indeed; I value this chance. Therefore sit down. We're practical, but there *is* a sofa, you see—for she does humour my poor bones so far. Like all really great administrators and disciplinarians she knows when wisely to relax." Paul sank into the corner of a deep leathern couch, but his friend remained standing and explanatory. "If you don't mind, in this room, this is my habit. From the door to the desk and from the desk to the door. That shakes up my imagination gently; and don't you see what a good thing it is that there's no window for her to fly

[11] *Il ne manquerait plus que ça!* That would be the last straw!

out of? The eternal standing as I write (I stop at that bureau and put it down, when anything comes, and so we go on) was rather wearisome at first, but we adopted it with an eye to the long run: you're in better order—if your legs don't break down!—and you can keep it up for more years. Oh, we're practical—we're practical!" St. George repeated, going to the table and taking up all mechanically the bundle of proofs. But, pulling off the wrapper, he had a change of attention that appealed afresh to our hero. He lost himself a moment, examining the sheets of his new book, while the younger man's eyes wandered over the room again.

"Lord, what good things I should do if I had such a charming place as this to do them in!" Paul reflected. The outer world, the world of accident and ugliness, was so successfully excluded, and within the rich protecting square, beneath the patronising sky, the dream-figures, the summoned company, could hold their particular revel. It was a fond prevision of Overt's rather than an observation on actual data, for which occasions had been too few, that the Master thus more closely viewed would have the quality, the charming gift, of flashing out, all surprisingly, in personal intercourse and at moments of suspended or perhaps even of diminished expectation. A happy relation with him would be a thing proceeding by jumps, not by traceable stages.

"Do you read them—really?" he asked, laying down the proofs on Paul's inquiring of him how soon the work would be published. And when the young man answered, "Oh, yes, always," he was moved to mirth again by something he caught in his manner of saying that. "You go to see your grandmother on her birthday —and very proper it is, especially as she won't last for ever. She has lost every faculty and every sense; she neither sees, nor hears, nor speaks; but all customary pieties and kindly habits are respectable. Only you're strong if you *do* read 'em. *I* couldn't, my dear fellow. You *are* strong, I know; and that's just a part of what I wanted to say to you. You're very strong indeed. I've been going into your other things—they've interested me immensely. Some one ought to have told me about them before—some one I could believe. But whom can one believe? You're wonderfully on the right road—it's awfully decent work. Now do you mean to keep it up?—that's what I want to ask you."

"Do I mean to do others?" Paul asked, looking up from his

sofa at his erect inquisitor and feeling partly like a happy little boy when the schoolmaster is gay, and partly like some pilgrim of old who might have consulted a world-famous oracle. St. George's own performance had been infirm, but as an adviser he would be infallible.

"Others—others? Ah, the number won't matter; one other would do, if it were really a further step—a throb of the same effort. What I mean is, have you it in your heart to go in for some sort of decent perfection?"

"Ah, decency, ah, perfection—!" the young man sincerely sighed. "I talked of them the other Sunday with Miss Fancourt."

It produced on the Master's part a laugh of odd acrimony. "Yes, they'll 'talk' of them as much as you like! But they'll do little to help one to them. There's no obligation of course; only you strike me as capable," he went on. "You must have thought it all over. I can't believe you're without a plan. That's the sensation you give me, and it's so rare that it really stirs one up—it makes you remarkable. If you haven't a plan, if you *don't* mean to keep it up, surely you're within your rights; it's nobody's business, no one can force you, and not more than two or three people will notice you don't go straight. The others—*all* the rest, every blest soul in England, will think you do—will think you *are* keeping it up: upon my honour they will! I shall be one of the two or three who know better. Now the question is whether you can do it for two or three. Is that the stuff you're made of?"

It locked his guest a minute as in closed throbbing arms. "I could do it for one, if you were the one."

"Don't say that; I don't deserve it; it scorches me," he protested with eyes suddenly grave and glowing. "The 'one' is of course one's self, one's conscience, one's idea, the singleness of one's aim. I think of that pure spirit as a man thinks of a woman he has in some detested hour of his youth loved and forsaken. She haunts him with reproachful eyes, she lives for ever before him. As an artist, you know, I've married for money." Paul stared and even blushed a little, confounded by this avowal; whereupon his host, observing the expression of his face, dropped a quick laugh and pursued: "You don't follow my figure. I'm not speaking of my dear wife, who had a small fortune—which, however, was not my bribe. I fell in love with her, as many other people have done.

I refer to the mercenary muse whom I led to the altar of literature. Don't, my boy, put your nose into *that* yoke. The awful jade will lead you a life!"

Our hero watched him, wondering and deeply touched. "Haven't you been happy!"

"Happy? It's a kind of hell."

"There are things I should like to ask you," Paul said after a pause.

"Ask me anything in all the world. I'd turn myself inside out to save you."

"To 'save' me?" he quavered.

"To make you stick to it—to make you see it through. As I said to you the other night at Summersoft, let my example be vivid to you."

"Why, your books are not so bad as that," said Paul, fairly laughing and feeling that if ever a fellow had breathed the air of art—!

"So bad as what?"

"Your talent's so great that it's in everything you do, in what's less good as well as in what's best. You've some forty volumes to show for it—forty volumes of wonderful life, of rare observation, of magnificent ability."

"I'm very clever, of course I know that"—but it was a thing, in fine, this author made nothing of. "Lord, what rot they'd all be if I hadn't been! I'm a successful charlatan," he went on—"I've been able to pass off my system. But do you know what it is? It's *carton-pierre*." [12]

"*Carton-pierre?*" Paul was struck, and gaped.

"Lincrusta-Walton!"

"Ah, don't say such things—you make me bleed!" the younger man protested. "I see you in a beautiful fortunate home, living in comfort and honour."

"Do you call it honour?"—his host took him up with an intonation that often comes back to him. "That's what I want *you* to go in for. I mean the real thing. This is brummagem."

---

[12] *Carton-pierre*. A patented mixture of cardboard, chalk, oil, etc., which hardens into something like stone. *Lincrusta-Walton* is a patent material, canvas stiffened with linseed oil and stamped with a design, for use on walls and ceilings.

"Brummagem?" Paul ejaculated while his eyes wandered, by a movement natural at the moment, over the luxurious room.

"Ah, they make it so well today—it's wonderfully deceptive!"

Our friend thrilled with the interest and perhaps even more with the pity of it. Yet he wasn't afraid to seem to patronise when he could still so far envy. "Is it deceptive that I find you living with every appearance of domestic felicity—blest with a devoted, accomplished wife, with children whose acquaintance I haven't yet had the pleasure of making, but who *must* be delightful young people, from what I know of their parents?"

St. George smiled as for the candour of his question. "It's all excellent, my dear fellow—heaven forbid I should deny it. I've made a great deal of money; my wife has known how to take care of it, to use it without wasting it, to put a good bit of it by, to make it fructify. I've got a loaf on the shelf; I've got everything in fact but the great thing."

"The great thing?" Paul kept echoing.

"The sense of having done the best—the sense which is the real life of the artist and the absence of which is his death, of having drawn from his intellectual instrument the finest music that nature had hidden in it, of having played it as it should be played. He either does that or he doesn't—and if he doesn't he isn't worth speaking of. Therefore, precisely, those who really know *don't* speak of him. He may still hear a great chatter, but what he hears most is the incorruptible silence of Fame. I've squared her, you may say, for my little hour—but what's my little hour? Don't imagine for a moment," the Master pursued, "that I'm such a cad as to have brought you down here to abuse or to complain of my wife to you. She's a woman of distinguished qualities, to whom my obligations are immense; so that, if you please, we'll say nothing about her. My boys—my children are all boys—are straight and strong, thank God, and have no poverty of growth about them, no penury of needs. I receive periodically the most satisfactory attestation from Harrow, from Oxford, from Sandhurst—oh, we've done the best for them!—of their eminence as living thriving consuming organisms."

"It must be delightful to feel that the son of one's loins is at Sandhurst," Paul remarked enthusiastically.

"It is—it's charming. Oh, I'm a patriot!"

The young man then could but have the greater tribute of questions to pay. "Then what did you mean—the other night at Summersoft—by saying that children are a curse?"

"My dear youth, on what basis are we talking?" and St. George dropped upon the sofa at a short distance from him. Sitting a little sideways he leaned back against the opposite arm with his hands raised and interlocked behind his head. "On the supposition that a certain perfection's possible and even desirable—isn't it so? Well, all I say is that one's children interfere with perfection. One's wife interferes. Marriage interferes."

"You think, then, the artist shouldn't marry?"

"He does so at his peril—he does so at his cost."

"Not even when his wife's in sympathy with his work?"

"She never is—she can't be! Women haven't a conception of such things."

"Surely they on occasion work themselves," Paul objected.

"Yes, very badly indeed. Oh, of course, often, they think they understand, they think they sympathise. Then it is they're most dangerous. Their idea is that you shall do a great lot and get a great lot of money. Their great nobleness and virtue, their exemplary conscientiousness as British females, is in keeping you up to that. My wife makes all my bargains with my publishers for me, and has done so for twenty years. She does it consummately well—that's why I'm really pretty well off. Aren't you the father of their innocent babes, and will you withhold from them their natural sustenance? You asked me the other night if they're not an immense incentive. Of course they are—there's no doubt of that!"

Paul turned it over: it took, from eyes he had never felt open so wide, so much looking at. "For myself I've an idea I need incentives."

"Ah, well, then, *n'en parlons plus!*" [13] his companion handsomely smiled.

"*You* are an incentive, I maintain," the young man went on. "You don't affect me in the way you'd apparently like to. Your great success is what I see—the pomp of Ennismore Gardens!"

"Success?"—St. George's eyes had a cold fine light. "Do you call it success to be spoken of as you'd speak of me if you were

[13] *N'en parlons plus.* Let's not say anything more about it.

sitting here with another artist—a young man intelligent and sincere like yourself? Do you call it success to make you blush—as you *would* blush!—if some foreign critic (some fellow, of course I mean, who should know what he was talking about and should have shown you he did, as foreign critics like to show it) were to say to you: 'He's the one, in this country, whom they consider the most perfect, isn't he?' Is it success to be the occasion of a young Englishman's having to stammer as you would have to stammer at such a moment for old England? No, no; success is to have made people wriggle to another tune. Do try it!"

Paul continued all gravely to glow. "Try what?"

"Try to do some really good work."

"Oh, I want to, heaven knows!"

"Well, you can't do it without sacrifices—don't believe that for a moment," the Master said. "I've made none. I've had everything. In other words, I've missed everything."

"You've had the full rich masculine human general life, with all the responsibilities and duties and burdens and sorrows and joys—all the domestic and social initiations and complications. They must be immensely suggestive, immensely amusing," Paul anxiously submitted.

"Amusing?"

"For a strong man—yes."

"They've given me subjects without number, if that's what you mean; but they've taken away at the same time the power to use them. I've touched a thousand things, but which one of them have I turned into gold? The artist has to do only with that —he knows nothing of any baser metal. I've led the life of the world, with my wife and my progeny; the clumsy conventional expensive materialised vulgarised brutalised life of London. We've got everything handsome, even a carriage—we're perfect Philistines and prosperous hospitable eminent people. But, my dear fellow, don't try to stultify yourself and pretend you don't know what we *haven't* got. It's bigger than all the rest. Between artists —come!" the Master wound up. "You know as well as you sit there that you'd put a pistol ball into your brains if you had written my books!"

It struck his listener that the tremendous talk promised by him at Summersoft had indeed come off, and with a promptitude, a fulness, with which the latter's young imagination had scarcely reckoned. His impression fairly shook him and he throbbed with the excitement of such deep soundings and such strange confidences. He throbbed indeed with the conflict of his feelings—bewilderment and recognition and alarm, enjoyment and protest and assent, all commingled with tenderness (and a kind of shame in the participation) for the sores and bruises exhibited by so fine a creature, and with the sense of the tragic secret nursed under his trappings. The idea of *his*, Paul Overt's, becoming the occasion of such an act of humility made him flush and pant, at the same time that his consciousness was in certain directions too much alive not to swallow—and not intensely to taste—every offered spoonful of the revelation. It had been his odd fortune to blow upon the deep waters, to make them surge and break in waves of strange eloquence. But how couldn't he give out a passionate contradiction of his host's last extravagance, how couldn't he enumerate to him the parts of his work he loved, the splendid things he had found in it, beyond the compass of any other writer of the day? St. George listened a while, courteously; then he said, laying his hand on his visitor's: "That's all very well; and if your idea's to do nothing better, there's no reason you shouldn't have as many good things as I—as many human and material appendages, as many sons or daughters, a wife with as many gowns, a house with as many servants, a stable with as many horses, a heart with as many aches." The Master got up when he had spoken thus—he stood a moment—near the sofa, looking down on his agitated pupil. "Are you possessed of any property?" it occurred to him to ask.

"None to speak of."

"Oh, well then there's no reason why you shouldn't make a goodish income—if you set about it the right way. Study *me* for that—study me well. You may really have horses."

Paul sat there some minutes without speaking. He looked straight before him—he turned over many things. His friend had wandered away, taking up a parcel of letters from the table where the roll of proofs had lain. "What was the book Mrs. St. George made you burn—the one she didn't like?" our young man brought out.

"The book she made me burn—how did you know that?" The

Master looked up from his letters quite without the facial convulsion the pupil had feared.

"I heard her speak of it at Summersoft."

"Ah, yes—she's proud of it. I don't know—it was rather good."

"What was it about?"

"Let me see." And he seemed to make an effort to remember. "Oh, yes—it was about myself." Paul gave an irrepressible groan for the disappearance of such a production, and the elder man went on: "Oh, but *you* should write it—*you* should do me." And he pulled up—from the restless motion that had come upon him; his fine smile a generous glare. "There's a subject, my boy: no end of stuff in it!"

Again Paul was silent, but it was all tormenting. "Are there no women who really understand—who can take part in a sacrifice?"

"How can they take part? They themselves are the sacrifice. They're the idol and the altar and the flame."

"Isn't there even *one* who sees further?" Paul continued.

For a moment St. George made no answer; after which, having torn up his letters, he came back to the point all ironic. "Of course I know the one you mean. But not even Miss Fancourt."

"I thought you admired her so much."

"It's impossible to admire her more. Are you in love with her?" St. George asked.

"Yes," Paul Overt presently said.

"Well, then, give it up."

Paul stared. "Give up my 'love'?"

"Bless me, no. Your idea." And then as our hero but still gazed: "The one you talked with her about. The idea of a decent perfection."

"She'd help it—she'd help it!" the young man cried.

"For about a year—the first year, yes. After that she'd be as a millstone round its neck."

Paul frankly wondered. "Why, she has a passion for the real thing, for good work—for everything you and I care for most."

" 'You and I' is charming my dear fellow!" his friend laughed. "She has it indeed, but she'd have a still greater passion for her children—and very proper too. She'd insist on everything's being made comfortable, advantageous, propitious for them. That isn't the artist's business."

"The artist—the artist! Isn't he a man all the same?"

St. George had a grand grimace. "I mostly think not. You know as well as I what he has to do: the concentration, the finish, the independence he must strive for from the moment he begins to wish his work really decent. Ah, my young friend, his relations to women, and especially to the one he's most intimately concerned with, is at the mercy of the damning fact that whereas he can in the nature of things have but one standard, they have about fifty. That's what makes them so superior," St. George amusingly added. "Fancy an artist with a change of standards as you'd have a change of shirts or of dinner plates. To *do* it—to do it and make it divine—is the only thing he has to think about. 'Is it done or not?' is his only question. Not 'Is it done as well as a proper solicitude for my dear little family will allow?' He has nothing to do with the relative—he has only to do with the absolute; and a dear little family may represent a dozen relatives."

"Then you don't allow him the common passions and affections of men?" Paul asked.

"Hasn't he a passion, an affection, which includes all the rest? Besides, let him have all the passions he likes—if he only keeps his independence. He must be able to be poor."

Paul slowly got up. "Why, then, did you advise me to make up to her?"

St. George laid a hand on his shoulder. "Because she'd make a splendid wife! And I hadn't read you then."

The young man had a strained smile. "I wish you had left me alone!"

"I didn't know that wasn't good enough for you," his host returned.

"What a false position, what a condemnation of the artist, that he's a mere disfranchised monk and can produce his effect only by giving up personal happiness. What an arraignment of art!" Paul went on with a trembling voice.

"Ah, you don't imagine by chance that I'm defending art? 'Arraignment'—I should think so! Happy the societies in which it hasn't made its appearance, for from the moment it comes they have a consuming ache, they have an incurable corruption, in their breast. Most assuredly is the artist in a false position! But I thought we were taking him for granted. Pardon me," St. George continued: " 'Ginistrella' made me!"

Paul stood looking at the floor—one o'clock struck, in the stillness, from a neighbouring church-tower. "Do you think she'd ever look at me?" he put to his friend at last.

"Miss Fancourt—as a suitor? Why shouldn't I think it? That's why I've tried to favour you—I've had a little chance or two of bettering your opportunity."

"Forgive my asking you, but do you mean by keeping away yourself?" Paul said with a blush.

"I'm an old idiot—my place isn't there," St. George stated gravely.

"I'm nothing yet, I've no fortune; and there must be so many others," his companion pursued.

The Master took this considerably in, but made little of it. "You're a gentleman and a man of genius. I think you might do something."

"But if I must give that up—the genius?"

"Lots of people, you know, think I've kept mine," St. George wonderfully grinned.

"You've a genius for mystification!" Paul declared, but grasping his hand gratefully in attenuation of this judgment.

"Poor, dear boy, I do worry you! But try, try, all the same. I think your chances are good and you'll win a great prize."

Paul held fast the other's hand a minute; he looked into the strange deep face. "No, I *am* an artist—I can't help it!"

"Ah, show it then!" St. George pleadingly broke out. "Let me see before I die the thing I most want, the thing I yearn for: a life in which the passion—ours—is really intense. If you can be rare don't fail of it! Think what it is—how it counts—how it lives!"

They had moved to the door and he had closed both his hands over his companion's. Here they paused again and our hero breathed deep. "I want to live!"

"In what sense?"

"In the greatest."

"Well, then, stick to it—see it through."

"With your sympathy—your help?"

"Count on that—you'll be a great figure to me. Count on my highest appreciation, my devotion. You'll give me satisfaction—

if that has any weight with you!" After which, as Paul appeared still to waver, his host added: "Do you remember what you said to me at Summersoft?"

"Something infatuated, no doubt!"

"'I'll do anything in the world you tell me.' You said that."

"And you hold me to it?"

"Ah, what am I?" the Master expressively sighed.

"Lord, what things I shall have to do!" Paul almost moaned as he departed.

VI

"It goes on too much abroad—hang abroad!" These or something like them had been the Master's remarkable words in relation to the action of "Ginistrella"; and yet, though they had made a sharp impression on the author of that work, like almost all spoken words from the same source, he a week after the conversation I have noted left England for a long absence and full of brave intentions. It is not a perversion of the truth to pronounce that encounter the direct cause of his departure. If the oral utterance of the eminent writer had the privilege of moving him deeply it was especially on his turning it over at leisure, hours and days later, that it appeared to yield him its full meaning and exhibit its extreme importance. He spent the summer in Switzerland and, having in September begun a new task, determined not to cross the Alps till he should have made a good start. To this end he returned to a quiet corner he knew well, on the edge of the Lake of Geneva and within sight of the towers of Chillon: a region and a view for which he had an affection that sprang from old associations and was capable of mysterious revivals and refreshments. Here he lingered late, till the snow was on the nearer hills, almost down to the limit to which he could climb when his stint, on the shortening afternoons, was performed. The autumn was fine, the lake was blue, and his book took form and direction. These felicities, for the time, embroidered his life, which he suffered to cover him with its mantle. At the end of six weeks he felt he had learnt St. George's lesson by heart, had tested and proved its doctrine. Nevertheless he did a very inconsistent thing: before crossing the Alps he wrote to Marian Fancourt. He was aware of the perversity of this act, and it was only as a luxury, an amusement, the reward of a strenuous autumn, that he justified it. She had asked of him no such favour when, shortly before he left London, three days after their dinner in Ennismore Gardens, he went to take leave of her. It was true she had had no ground—he hadn't named his intention of absence. He had kept his counsel for want of due assurance: it was that particular visit that was, the next thing, to settle the matter. He had paid the visit to see how much he really cared for her, and quick departure, without so much as an explicit farewell, was the sequel to this inquiry, the answer to which had created within him a deep yearning. When he wrote her from Clarens he noted that he owed her an explanation (more than three months after!) for not having told her what he was doing.

She replied now briefly but promptly, and gave him a striking piece of news: that of the death, a week before, of Mrs. St. George. This exemplary woman had succumbed, in the country, to a violent attack of inflammation of the lungs—he would remember that for a long time she had been delicate. Miss Fancourt added that she believed her husband was overwhelmed by the blow; he would miss her too terribly—she had been everything in life to him. Paul Overt, on this, immediately wrote to St. George. He would from the day of their parting have been glad to remain in communication with him, but had hitherto lacked the right excuse for troubling so busy a man. Their long nocturnal talk came back to him in every detail, but this was no bar to an expression of proper sympathy with the head of the profession, for hadn't that very talk made it clear that the late accomplished lady was the influence that ruled his life? What catastrophe could be more cruel than the extinction of such an influence? This was to be exactly the tone taken by St. George in answering his young friend upwards of a month later. He made no allusion of course to their important discussion. He spoke of his wife as frankly and generously as if he had quite forgotten that occasion, and the feeling of deep bereavement was visible in his words. "She took everything off my hands—off my mind. She carried on our life with the greatest art, the rarest devotion, and I was free, as few men can have been, to drive my pen, to shut myself up with my trade. This was a rare service—the highest she could have rendered me. Would I could have acknowledged it more fitly!"

A certain bewilderment, for our hero, disengaged itself from these remarks: they struck him as a contradiction, a retraction, strange on the part of a man who hadn't the excuse of witlessness. He had certainly not expected his correspondent to rejoice in the death of his wife, and it was perfectly in order that the rupture of a tie of more than twenty years should have left him sore. But if she had been so clear a blessing what in the name of consistency had the dear man meant by turning *him* upside down that night— by dosing him to that degree, at the most sensitive hour of his life, with the doctrine of renunciation? If Mrs. St. George was an irreparable loss, then her husband's inspired advice had been a bad joke and renunciation was a mistake. Overt was on the point of rushing back to London to show that, for his part, he was perfectly willing to consider it so, and he went so far as to take the manuscript of the first chapters of his new book out of his table-drawer and insert it into a pocket of his portmanteau. This led to his catching a glimpse of certain pages he hadn't looked at for months, and that accident, in turn, to his being struck with the high promise they revealed—a rare result of such retrospections, which it was his habit to avoid as much as possible: they usually brought home to him that the glow of composition might be a purely subjective and misleading emotion. On this occasion a certain belief in himself disengaged itself whimsically from the serried erasures of his first draft, making him think it best after all to pursue his present trial to the end. If he could write so well under the rigour of privation it might be a mistake to change the conditions before that spell had spent itself. He would go back to London of course, but he would go back only when he should have finished his book. This was the vow he privately made, restoring his manuscript to the table-drawer. It may be added that it took him a long time to finish his book, for the subject was as difficult as it was fine, and he was literally embarrassed by the fulness of his notes. Something within him warned him he must make it supremely good—otherwise he should lack, as regards his private behaviour, a handsome excuse. He had a horror of this deficiency and found himself as firm as need be on the question of the lamp and the file. He crossed the Alps at last and spent the winter, the spring, the ensuing summer, in Italy, where still, at the end of a twelvemonth, his task was unachieved. "Stick to it—

see it through": this general injunction of St. George's was good also for the particular case. He applied it to the utmost, with the result that when in its slow order the summer had come round again he felt he had given all that was in him. This time he put his papers into his portmanteau, with the address of his publisher attached, and took his way northward.

He had been absent from London for two years; two years which, seeming to count as more, had made such a difference in his own life—through the production of a novel far stronger, he believed, than "Ginistrella"—that he turned out into Piccadilly, the morning after his arrival, with a vague expectation of changes, of finding great things had happened. But there were few transformations in Piccadilly—only three or four big red houses where there had been low black ones—and the brightness of the end of June peeped through the rusty railings of the Green Park and glittered in the varnish of the rolling carriages as he had seen it in other, more cursory Junes. It was a greeting he appreciated; it seemed friendly and pointed, added to the exhilaration of his finished book, of his having his own country and the huge oppressive amusing city that suggested everything, that contained everything, under his hand again. "Stay at home and do things here—do subjects we can measure," St. George had said; and now it struck him he should ask nothing better than to stay at home for ever. Late in the afternoon he took his way to Manchester Square, looking out for a number he hadn't forgotten. Miss Fancourt, however, was not at home, so that he turned rather dejectedly from the door. His movement brought him face to face with a gentleman just approaching it and recognised on another glance as Miss Fancourt's father. Paul saluted this personage, and the General returned the greeting with his customary good manner—a manner so good, however, that you could never tell whether it meant he placed you. The disappointed caller felt the impulse to address him; then, hesitating, became both aware of having no particular remark to make, and convinced that though the old soldier remembered him he remembered him wrong. He therefore went his way without computing the irresistible effect his own evident recognition would have on the General, who never neglected a chance to gossip. Our young man's face was expressive, and observation seldom let it pass. He hadn't taken ten steps before he heard himself called after with a friendly semi-articulate "Er—I beg your pardon!" He turned round and the General, smiling at him from the porch, said: "Won't you come in? I won't leave you the advantage of me!" Paul declined to come in, and then felt regret, for Miss Fancourt, so late in the afternoon, might return at any moment. But her father gave him no second chance; he appeared mainly to wish not to have struck him as ungracious. A further look at the visitor had recalled something, enough at least to enable him to say: "You've come back, you've come back?" Paul was on the point of replying that he had come back the night before, but he suppressed, the next instant, this strong light on the immediacy of his visit and, giving merely a general assent, alluded to the young lady he deplored not having found. He had come late in the hope she would be in. "I'll tell her —I'll tell her," said the old man; and then he added quickly, gallantly: "You'll be giving us something new? It's a long time, isn't it?" Now he remembered him right.

"Rather long. I'm very slow," Paul explained. "I met you at Summersoft a long time ago."

"Oh, yes—with Henry St. George. I remember very well. Before his poor wife—" General Fancourt paused a moment, smiling a little less. "I daresay you know."

"About Mrs. St. George's death? Certainly—I heard at the time."

"Oh, no, I mean—I mean he's to be married."

"Ah, I've not heard that!" But just as Paul was about to add "To whom?" the General crossed his intention.

"When did you come back? I know you've been away—by my daughter. She was very sorry. You ought to give her something new."

"I came back last night," said our young man, to whom something had occurred which made his speech for the moment a little thick.

"Ah, most kind of you to come so soon. Couldn't you turn up at dinner?"

"At dinner?" Paul just mechanically repeated, not liking to ask whom St. George was going to marry, but thinking only of that.

"There are several people, I believe. Certainly St. George. Or afterwards if you like better. I believe my daughter expects—" He appeared to notice something in the visitor's raised face (on his steps he stood higher) which led him to interrupt himself, and the interruption gave him a momentary sense of awkwardness, from which he sought a quick issue. "Perhaps, then, you haven't heard she's to be married."

Paul gaped again. "To be married?"

"To Mr. St. George—it has just been settled. Odd marriage, isn't it?" Our listener uttered no opinion on this point: he only continued to stare. "But I daresay it will do—she's so awfully literary!" said the General.

Paul had turned very red. "Oh, it's a surprise—very interesting, very charming! I'm afraid I can't dine—so many thanks!"

"Well, you must come to the wedding!" cried the General. "Oh, I remember that day at Summersoft. He's a great man, you know."

"Charming—charming!" Paul stammered for retreat. He shook hands with the general and got off. His face was red and he had the sense of its growing more and more crimson. All the evening at home—he went straight to his rooms and remained there dinnerless—his cheek burned at intervals as if it had been smitten. He didn't understand what had happened to him, what trick had been played him, what treachery practised. "None, none," he said to himself. "I've nothing to do with it. I'm out of it—it's none of my business." But that bewildered murmur was followed again and again by the incongruous ejaculation: "Was it a plan—was it a plan?" Sometimes he cried to himself, breathless, "Have I been duped, sold, swindled?" If at all, he was an absurd, an abject victim. It was as if he hadn't lost her till now. He had renounced her, yes; but that was another affair—that was a closed but not a locked door. Now he seemed to see the door quite slammed in his face. Did he expect her to wait—was she to give him his time like that: two years at a stretch? He didn't know what he had expected—he only knew what he hadn't. It wasn't this—it wasn't this. Mystification bitterness and wrath rose and boiled in him when he thought of the deference, the devotion, the credulity with which he had listened to St. George. The evening wore on and the light was long, but even when it had darkened he remained without a lamp. He had flung himself on the sofa, where he lay through the hours with his eyes either closed or gazing at the gloom, in the attitude of a man teaching himself to bear something, to bear having been made a fool of. He had made it too easy—that idea

passed over him like a hot wave. Suddenly, as he heard eleven
o'clock strike, he jumped up, remembering what General Fancourt had said about his coming after dinner. He'd go—he'd see
her at least; perhaps he should see what it meant. He felt as if some
of the elements of a hard sum had been given him and the others
were wanting: he couldn't do his sum till he had got all his
figures.

He dressed and drove quickly, so that by half-past eleven he
was at Manchester Square. There were a good many carriages at
the door—a party was going on; a circumstance which at the last
gave him a slight relief, for now he would rather see her in a crowd.
People passed him on the staircase; they were going away, going
"on" with the hunted herdlike movement of London society at
night. But sundry groups remained in the drawing-room, and it
was some minutes, as she didn't hear him announced, before he
discovered and spoke to her. In this short interval he had seen
St. George talking to a lady before the fireplace; but he at once
looked away, feeling unready for an encounter, and therefore
couldn't be sure the author of "Shadowmere" noticed him. At all
events he didn't come over; though Miss Fancourt did as soon as
she saw him—she almost rushed at him, smiling rustling radiant
beautiful. He had forgotten what her head, what her face offered
to the sight; she was in white, there were gold figures on her dress
and her hair was a casque of gold. He saw in a single moment
that she was happy, happy with an aggressive splendour. But she
wouldn't speak to him of that, she would speak only of himself.

"I'm so delighted; my father told me. How kind of you to
come!" She struck him as so fresh and brave, while his eyes moved
over her, that he said to himself irresistibly: "Why to *him*, why
not to youth, to strength, to ambition, to a future? Why, in her
rich young force, to failure, to abdication, to superannuation?" In
his thought at that sharp moment he blasphemed even against all
that had been left of his faith in the peccable master. "I'm so sorry
I missed you," she went on. "My father told me. How charming
of you to have come so soon!"

"Does that surprise you?" Paul Overt asked.

"The first day? No, from you—nothing that's nice." She was
interrupted by a lady who bade her good-night, and he seemed
to read that it cost her nothing to speak to him in that tone; it
was her old liberal lavish way, with a certain added amplitude that

time had brought; and if this manner began to operate on the
spot, at such a juncture in her history, perhaps in the other days
too it had meant just as little or as much—a mere mechanical
charity, with the difference now that she was satisfied, ready to give
but in want of nothing. Oh, she was satisfied—and why shouldn't
she be? Why shouldn't she have been surprised at his coming the
first day—for all the good she had ever got from him? As the lady
continued to hold her attention Paul turned from her with a
strange irritation in his complicated artistic soul and a sort of
disinterested disappointment. She was so happy that it was almost
stupid—a disproof of the extraordinary intelligence he had formerly found in her. Didn't she know how bad St. George could
be, hadn't she recognised the awful thinness—? If she didn't she
was nothing, and if she did why such an insolence of serenity?
This question expired as our young man's eyes settled at last on
the genius who had advised him in a great crisis. St. George was
still before the chimney-piece, but now he was alone—fixed, waiting, as if he meant to stop after every one—and he met the clouded
gaze of the young friend so troubled as to the degree of his right
(the right his resentment would have enjoyed) to regard himself
as a victim. Somehow the ravage of the question was checked by
the Master's radiance. It was as fine in its way as Marian Fancourt's, it denoted the happy human being; but also it represented
to Paul Overt that the author of "Shadowmere" had now definitely
ceased to count—ceased to count as a writer. As he smiled a welcome across the place he was almost *banal*, was almost smug. Paul
fancied that for a moment he hesitated to make a movement, as if,
for all the world, he *had* his bad conscience; then they had already
met in the middle of the room and had shaken hands—expressively,
cordially on St. George's part. With which they had passed back
together to where the elder man had been standing, while St.
George said: "I hope you're never going away again. I've been
dining here; the General told me." He was handsome, he was
young, he looked as if he had still a great fund of life. He bent
the friendliest, most unconfessing eyes on his disciple of a couple
of years before; asked him about everything, his health, his plans,
his late occupations, the new book. "When will it be out—soon,
soon, I hope? Splendid, eh? That's right; you're a comfort, you're
a luxury! I've read you all over again these last six months." Paul
waited to see if he'd tell him what the General had told him in
the afternoon and what Miss Fancourt, verbally, at least, of course

hadn't. But as it didn't come out he at last put the question, "Is it true, the great news I hear—that you're to be married?"

"Ah, you *have* heard it, then?"

"Didn't the General tell you?" Paul asked.

The Master's face was wonderful. "Tell me what?"

"That he mentioned it to me this afternoon?"

"My dear fellow, I don't remember. We've been in the midst of people. I'm sorry, in that case, that I lose the pleasure, myself, of announcing to you a fact that touches me so nearly. It *is* a fact, strange as it may appear. It has only just become one. Isn't it ridiculous?" St. George made this speech without confusion, but on the other hand, so far as our friend could judge, without latent impudence. It struck his interlocutor that, to talk so comfortably and coolly, he must simply have forgotten what had passed between them. His next words, however, showed he hadn't, and they produced, as an appeal to Paul's own memory, an effect which would have been ludicrous if it hadn't been cruel. "Do you recall the talk we had at my house that night, into which Miss Fancourt's name entered? I've often thought of it since."

"Yes; no wonder you said what you did"—Paul was careful to meet his eyes.

"In the light of the present occasion? Ah, but there was no light then. How could I have foreseen this hour?"

"Didn't you think it probable?"

"Upon my honour, no," said Henry St. George. "Certainly I owe you that assurance. Think how my situation has changed."

"I see—I see," our young man murmured.

His companion went on as if, now that the subject had been broached, he was, as a person of imagination and tact, quite ready to give every satisfaction—being both by his genius and his method so able to enter into everything another might feel. "But it's not only that; for honestly, at my age, I never dreamed—a widower with big boys and with so little else! It has turned out differently from anything one could have dreamed, and I'm fortunate beyond all measure. She has been so free, and yet she consents. Better than any one else perhaps—for I remember how you liked her before you went away, and how she liked you—you can intelligently congratulate me."

"She has been so free!" Those words made a great impression on Paul Overt, and he almost writhed under that irony in them as to which it so little mattered whether it was designed or casual. Of course she had been free, and appreciably perhaps by his own act; for wasn't the Master's allusion to her having liked him a part of the irony too? "I thought that by your theory you disapproved of a writer's marrying."

"Surely—surely. But you don't call me a writer?"

"You ought to be ashamed," said Paul.

"Ashamed of marrying again?"

"I won't say that—but ashamed of your reasons."

The elderly man beautifully smiled. "You must let me judge of them, my good friend."

"Yes; why not? For you judged wonderfully of mine."

The tone of these words appeared suddenly, for St. George, to suggest the unsuspected. He stared as if divining a bitterness. "Don't you think I've been straight?"

"You might have told me at the time perhaps."

"My dear fellow, when I say I couldn't pierce futurity—!"

"I mean afterwards."

The Master wondered. "After my wife's death?"

"When this idea came to you."

"Ah, never, never! I wanted to save you, rare and precious as you are."

Poor Overt looked hard at him. "Are you marrying Miss Fancourt to save me?"

"Not absolutely, but it adds to the pleasure. I shall be the making of you," St. George smiled. "I was greatly struck, after our talk, with the brave, devoted way you quitted the country, and still more perhaps with your force of character in remaining abroad. You're very strong—you're wonderfully strong."

Paul tried to sound his shining eyes; the strange thing was that he seemed sincere—not a mocking fiend. He turned away, and as he did so heard the Master say something about his giving them all the proof, being the joy of his old age. He faced him again, taking another look. "Do you mean to say you've stopped writing?"

"My dear fellow, of course I have. It's too late. Didn't I tell you?"

"I can't believe it!"

"Of course you can't—with your own talent! No, no; for the rest of my life I shall only read *you*."

"Does she know that—Miss Fancourt?"

"She will—she will." Did he mean this, our young man wondered, as a covert intimation that the assistance he should derive from that young lady's fortune, moderate as it was, would make the difference of putting it in his power to cease to work ungratefully an exhausted vein? Somehow, standing there in the ripeness of his successful manhood, he didn't suggest that any of his veins were exhausted. "Don't you remember the moral I offered myself to you that night as pointing?" St. George continued. "Consider at any rate the warning I am at present."

This was too much—he *was* the mocking fiend. Paul turned from him with a mere nod for good-night and the sense in a sore heart that he might come back to him and his easy grace, his fine way of arranging things, some time in the far future, but he couldn't fraternise with him now. It was necessary to his soreness to believe for the hour in the intensity of his grievance—all the more cruel for its not being a legal one. It was doubtless in the attitude of hugging this wrong that he descended the stairs without taking leave of Miss Fancourt, who hadn't been in view at the moment he quitted the room. He was glad to get out into the honest dusky unsophisticating night, to move fast, to take his way home on foot. He walked a long time, going astray, paying no attention. He was thinking of too many other things. His steps recovered their direction, however, and at the end of an hour he found himself before his door in the small inexpensive empty street. He lingered, questioned himself still before going in, with nothing around and above him but moonless blackness, a bad lamp or two, and a few far-away dim stars. To these last faint features he raised his eyes; he had been saying to himself that he should have been "sold" indeed, diabolically sold, if now, on his new foundation, at the end of a year, St. George were to put forth something of his prime quality—something of the type of "Shadowmere" and finer than his finest. Greatly as he admired his talent Paul literally hoped such an incident wouldn't occur; it seemed to him just then that he shouldn't be able to bear it. His late adviser's words were still in his ears—"You're very strong, wonderfully strong." Was he really? Certainly he would have to be, and it might a little serve for revenge. *Is* he? the reader may ask in turn, if his interest has followed the perplexed young man so far. The best answer to that perhaps is that he's doing his best, but that it's too soon to say. When the new book came out in the autumn Mr. and Mrs. St. George found it really magnificent. The former still has published nothing, but Paul doesn't even yet feel safe. I may say for him, however, that if this event were to occur he would really be the very first to appreciate it: which is perhaps a proof that the Master was essentially right and that nature had dedicated him to intellectual, not to personal passion.

EDITH WHARTON

Roman Fever

From the table at which they had been lunching two American ladies of ripe but well-cared-for middle age moved across the lofty terrace of the Roman restaurant and, leaning on its parapet, looked first at each other, and then down on the outspread glories of the Palatine and the Forum, with the same expression of vague but benevolent approval.

As they leaned there a girlish voice echoed up gaily from the stairs leading to the court below. "Well, come along, then," it cried, not to them but to an invisible companion, "and let's leave the young things to their knitting"; and a voice as fresh laughed back: "Oh, look here, Babs, not actually *knitting*—" "Well, I mean figuratively," rejoined the first. "After all, we haven't left our poor parents much else to do . . ." and at that point the turn of the stairs engulfed the dialogue.

The two ladies looked at each other again, this time with a tinge of smiling embarrassment, and the smaller and paler one shook her head and coloured slightly.

"Barbara!" she murmured, sending an unheard rebuke after the mocking voice in the stairway.

The other lady, who was fuller, and higher in colour, with a small determined nose supported by vigorous black eyebrows, gave a good-humoured laugh. "That's what our daughters think of us!"

Her companion replied by a deprecating gesture. "Not of us individually. We must remember that. It's just the collective modern idea of Mothers. And you see—" Half guiltily she drew from her handsomely mounted black hand-bag a twist of crimson silk run through by two fine knitting needles. "One never knows," she murmured. "The new system has certainly given us a good deal of time to kill; and sometimes I get tired just looking—even at this." Her gesture was now addressed to the stupendous scene at their feet.

The dark lady laughed again, and they both relapsed upon the view, contemplating it in silence, with a sort of diffused serenity which might have been borrowed from the spring effulgence of the Roman skies. The luncheon-hour was long past, and the two had their end of the vast terrace to themselves. At this opposite extremity a few groups, detained by a lingering look at the outspread city, were gathering up guide-books and fumbling for tips. The last of them scattered, and the two ladies were alone on the air-washed height.

"Well, I don't see why we shouldn't just stay here," said Mrs. Slade, the lady of the high colour and energetic brows. Two derelict basket-chairs stood near, and she pushed them into the angle of the parapet, and settled herself in one, her gaze upon the Palatine. "After all, it's still the most beautiful view in the world."

"It always will be, to me," assented her friend Mrs. Ansley, with so slight a stress on the "me" that Mrs. Slade, though she noticed it, wondered if it were not merely accidental, like the random underlinings of old-fashioned letter-writers.

"Grace Ansley was always old-fashioned," she thought; and added aloud, with a retrospective smile: "It's a view we've both been familiar with for a good many years. When we first met here we were younger than our girls are now. You remember?"

"Oh, yes, I remember," murmured Mrs. Ansley, with the same undefinable stress.—"There's that head-waiter wondering," she interpolated. She was evidently far less sure than her companion of herself and of her rights in the world.

"I'll cure him of wondering," said Mrs. Slade, stretching her hand toward a bag as discreetly opulent-looking as Mrs. Ansley's. Signing to the head-waiter, she explained that she and her friend were old lovers of Rome, and would like to spend the end of the afternoon looking down on the view—that is, if it did not disturb the service? The head-waiter, bowing over her gratuity, assured her that the ladies were most welcome, and would be still more so if they would condescend to remain for dinner. A full moon night, they would remember. . . .

Mrs. Slade's black brows drew together, as though references to the moon were out-of-place and even unwelcome. But she smiled away her frown as the head-waiter retreated. "Well, why not? We might do worse. There's no knowing, I suppose, when the girls will be back. Do you even know back from *where?* I don't!"

Mrs. Ansley again coloured slightly. "I think those young Italian aviators we met at the Embassy invited them to fly to Tarquinia for tea. I suppose they'll want to wait and fly back by moonlight."

"Moonlight—moonlight! What a part it still plays. Do you suppose they're as sentimental as we were?"

"I've come to the conclusion that I don't in the least know what they are," said Mrs. Ansley. "And perhaps we didn't know much more about each other."

"No; perhaps we didn't."

Her friend gave her a shy glance. "I never should have supposed you were sentimental, Alida."

"Well, perhaps I wasn't." Mrs. Slade drew her lids together in retrospect; and for a few moments the two ladies, who had been intimate since childhood, reflected how little they knew each other. Each one, of course, had a label ready to attach to the other's name; Mrs. Delphin Slade, for instance, would have told herself, or any one who asked her, that Mrs. Horace Ansley, twenty-five years ago, had been exquisitely lovely—no, you wouldn't believe it, would you? . . . though, of course, still charming, distinguished . . . Well, as a girl she had been exquisite; far more beautiful than her daughter Barbara, though certainly Babs, according to the new standards at any rate, was more effective—had more edge, as they say. Funny where she got it, with those two nullities as parents. Yes; Horace Ansley was—well, just the duplicate of his wife. Museum specimens of old New York. Good-looking, irreproachable, exemplary. Mrs. Slade and Mrs. Ansley had lived opposite each other—actually as well as figuratively—for years. When the drawing-room curtains in No. 20 East 73rd Street were renewed, No. 23, across the way, was always aware of it. And of all the movings, buyings, travels, anniversaries, illnesses—the tame chronicle of an estimable pair. Little of it escaped Mrs. Slade. But she had grown bored with it by the time her husband made his big *coup* in Wall Street, and when they bought in upper Park Avenue had already begun to think: "I'd rather live opposite a speak-easy for a change; at least one might see it raided." The idea of seeing Grace raided was so amusing that (before the move) she launched it at a woman's lunch. It made a hit, and went the rounds—she sometimes wondered if it had crossed the street, and reached Mrs. Ansley. She hoped not, but didn't much mind. Those were the days when respectability was at a discount, and it did the irreproachable no harm to laugh at them a little.

A few years later, and not many months apart, both ladies lost their husbands. There was an appropriate exchange of wreaths and condolences, and a brief renewal of intimacy in the half-shadow of their mourning; and now, after another interval, they had run across each other in Rome, at the same hotel, each of them the modest appendage of a salient daughter. The similarity of their lot had again drawn them together, lending itself to mild jokes, and the mutual confession that, if in old days it must have been tiring to "keep up" with daughters, it was now, at times, a little dull not to.

No doubt, Mrs. Slade reflected, she felt her unemployment more than poor Grace ever would. It was a big drop from being the wife of Delphin Slade to being his widow. She had always regarded herself (with a certain conjugal pride) as his equal in social gifts, as contributing her full share to the making of the exceptional couple they were: but the difference after his death was irremediable. As the wife of the famous corporation lawyer, always with an international case or two on hand, every day brought its exciting and unexpected obligation: the impromptu entertaining of eminent colleagues from abroad, the hurried dashes on legal business to London, Paris or Rome, where the entertaining was so handsomely reciprocated; the amusement of hearing in her wake: "What, that handsome woman with the good clothes and eyes is Mrs. Slade—*the* Slade's wife? Really? Generally the wives of celebrities are such frumps."

Yes; being *the* Slade's widow was a dullish business after that. In living up to such a husband all her faculties had been engaged; now she had only her daughter to live up to, for the son who seemed to have inherited his father's gifts had died suddenly in boyhood. She had fought through that agony because her husband was there, to be helped and to help; now, after the father's death, the thought of the boy had become unbearable. There was nothing left but to mother her daughter; and dear Jenny was such a perfect daughter that she needed no excessive mothering. "Now with Babs Ansley I don't know that I *should* be so quiet," Mrs. Slade sometimes half-enviously reflected; but Jenny, who was younger than her brilliant friend, was that rare accident, an extremely pretty girl who somehow made youth and prettiness seem as safe as their absence. It was all perplexing—and to Mrs. Slade a little boring. She wished that Jenny would fall in love— with the wrong man, even; that she might have to be watched, out-maneuvered, rescued. And instead, it was Jenny who watched her mother, kept her out of draughts, made sure that she had taken her tonic . . .

Mrs. Ansley was much less articulate than her friend, and her mental portrait of Mrs. Slade was slighter, and drawn with fainter touches. "Alida Slade's awfully brilliant; but not as brilliant as she thinks," would have summed it up; though she would have added, for the enlightenment of strangers, that Mrs. Slade had been an extremely dashing girl; much more so than her daughter, who was pretty, of course, and clever in a way, but had none of her mother's—well, "vividness," some one had once called it. Mrs. Ansley would take up current words like this, and cite them in quotation marks, as unheard-of audacities. No; Jenny was not like her mother. Sometimes Mrs. Ansley thought Alida Slade was disappointed; on the whole she had had a sad life. Full of failures and mistakes; Mrs. Ansley had always been rather sorry for her . . .

So these two ladies visualized each other, each through the wrong end of her little telescope.

II

For a long time they continued to sit side by side without speaking. It seemed as though, to both, there was a relief in laying down their somewhat futile activities in the presence of the vast Memento Mori which faced them. Mrs. Slade sat quite still, her eyes fixed on the golden slope of the Palace of the Cæsars, and after a while Mrs. Ansley ceased to fidget with her bag, and she too sank into meditation. Like many intimate friends, the two ladies had never before had occasion to be silent together, and Mrs. Ansley was slightly embarrassed by what seemed, after so many years, a new stage in their intimacy, and one with which she did not yet know how to deal.

Suddenly the air was full of that deep clangour of bells which periodically covers Rome with a roof of silver. Mrs. Slade glanced at her wrist-watch. "Five o'clock already," she said, as though surprised.

Mrs. Ansley suggested interrogatively: "There's bridge at the Embassy at five." For a long time Mrs. Slade did not answer. She appeared to be lost in contemplation, and Mrs. Ansley thought the remark had escaped her. But after a while she said, as if speaking out of a dream: "Bridge, did you say? Not unless you want to . . . But I don't think I will, you know."

"Oh, no," Mrs. Ansley hastened to assure her. "I don't care to at all. It's so lovely here; and so full of old memories, as you say." She settled herself in her chair, and almost furtively drew forth her knitting. Mrs. Slade took sideway note of this activity, but her own beautifully cared-for hands remained motionless on her knee.

"I was just thinking," she said slowly, "what different things Rome stands for to each generation of travellers. To our grandmothers, Roman fever; to our mothers, sentimental dangers—how we used to be guarded!—to our daughters, no more dangers than the middle of Main Street. They don't know it—but how much they're missing!"

The long golden light was beginning to pale, and Mrs. Ansley lifted her knitting a little closer to her eyes. "Yes; how we were guarded!"

"I always used to think," Mrs. Slade continued, "that our

mothers had a much more difficult job than our grandmothers. When Roman fever stalked the streets it must have been comparatively easy to gather in the girls at the danger hour; but when you and I were young, with such beauty calling us, and the spice of disobedience thrown in, and no worse risk than catching cold during the cool hour after sunset, the mothers used to be put to it to keep us in—didn't they?"

She turned again toward Mrs. Ansley, but the latter had reached a delicate point in her knitting. "One, two, three—slip two; yes, they must have been," she assented, without looking up.

Mrs. Slade's eyes rested on her with a deepened attention. "She can knit—in the face of *this!* How like her . . ."

Mrs. Slade leaned back, brooding, her eyes ranging from the ruins which faced her to the long green hollow of the Forum, the fading glow of the church fronts beyond it, and the outlying immensity of the Colosseum. Suddenly she thought: "It's all very well to say that our girls have done away with sentiment and moonlight. But if Babs Ansley isn't out to catch that young aviator—the one who's a Marchese—then I don't know anything. And Jenny has no chance beside her. I know that too. I wonder if that's why Grace Ansley likes the two girls to go everywhere together? My poor Jenny as a foil—!" Mrs. Slade gave a hardly audible laugh, and at the sound Mrs. Ansley dropped her knitting.

"Yes—?"

"I—oh, nothing. I was only thinking how your Babs carries everything before her. That Campolieri boy is one of the best matches in Rome. Don't look so innocent, my dear—you know he is. And I was wondering, ever so respectfully, you understand . . . wondering how two such exemplary characters as you and Horace had managed to produce anything quite so dynamic." Mrs. Slade laughed again, with a touch of asperity.

Mrs. Ansley's hands lay inert across her needles. She looked straight out at the great accumulated wreckage of passion and splendour at her feet. But her small profile was almost expressionless. At length she said: "I think you overrate Babs, my dear."

Mrs. Slade's tone grew easier. "No; I don't. I appreciate her. And perhaps envy you. Oh, my girl's perfect; if I were a chronic invalid I'd—well, I think I'd rather be in Jenny's hands. There must be times . . . but there! I always wanted a brilliant daughter . . . and never quite understood why I got an angel instead."

Mrs. Ansley echoed her laugh in a faint murmur. "Babs is an angel too."

"Of course—of course! But she's got rainbow wings. Well, they're wandering by the sea with their young men; and here we sit . . . and it all brings back the past a little too acutely."

Mrs. Ansley had resumed her knitting. One might almost have imagined (if one had known her less well, Mrs. Slade reflected) that, for her also, too many memories rose from the lengthening shadows of those august ruins. But no; she was simply absorbed in her work. What was there for her to worry about? She knew that Babs would almost certainly come back engaged to the extremely eligible Campolieri. "And she'll sell the New York house, and settle down near them in Rome, and never be in their way . . . she's much too tactful. But she'll have an excellent cook, and just the right people in for bridge and cocktails . . . and a perfectly peaceful old age among her grandchildren."

Mrs. Slade broke off this prophetic flight with a recoil of self-disgust. There was no one of whom she had less right to think unkindly than of Grace Ansley. Would she never cure herself of envying her? Perhaps she had begun too long ago.

She stood up and leaned against the parapet, filling her troubled eyes with the tranquillizing magic of the hour. But instead of tranquillizing her the sight seemed to increase her exasperation. Her gaze turned toward the Colosseum. Already its golden flank was drowned in purple shadow, and above it the sky curved crystal clear, without light or colour. It was the moment when afternoon and evening hang balanced in mid-heaven.

Mrs. Slade turned back and laid her hand on her friend's arm. The gesture was so abrupt that Mrs. Ansley looked up, startled.

"The sun's set. You're not afraid, my dear?"

"Afraid—?"

"Of Roman fever or pneumonia? I remember how ill you were that winter. As a girl you had a very delicate throat, hadn't you?"

"Oh, we're all right up here. Down below, in the Forum, it does get deathly cold, all of a sudden . . . but not here."

"Ah, of course you know because you had to be so careful." Mrs. Slade turned back to the parapet. She thought: "I must make one more effort not to hate her." Aloud she said: "Whenever I look at the Forum from up here, I remember that story about a great-aunt of yours, wasn't she? A dreadfully wicked great-aunt?"

"Oh, yes; Great-aunt Harriet. The one who was supposed to have sent her young sister out to the Forum after sunset to gather a night-blooming flower for her album. All our great-aunts and grandmothers used to have albums of dried flowers."

Mrs. Slade nodded. "But she really sent her because they were in love with the same man—"

"Well, that was the family tradition. They said Aunt Harriet confessed it years afterward. At any rate, the poor little sister caught the fever and died. Mother used to frighten us with the story when we were children."

"And you frightened *me* with it, that winter when you and I were here as girls. The winter I was engaged to Delphin."

Mrs. Ansley gave a faint laugh. "Oh, did I? Really frightened you? I don't believe you're easily frightened."

"Not often; but I was then. I was easily frightened because I was too happy. I wonder if you know what that means?"

"I—yes . . ." Mrs. Ansley faltered.

"Well, I suppose that was why the story of your wicked aunt made such an impression on me. And I thought: 'There's no more Roman fever, but the Forum is deathly cold after sunset—especially after a hot day. And the Colosseum's even colder and damper'."

"The Colosseum—?"

"Yes. It wasn't easy to get in, after the gates were locked for the night. Far from easy. Still, in those days it could be managed; it was managed, often. Lovers met there who couldn't meet elsewhere. You knew that?"

"I—I daresay. I don't remember."

"You don't remember? You don't remember going to visit some ruins or other one evening, just after dark, and catching a bad chill? You were supposed to have gone to see the moon rise. People always said that expedition was what caused your illness."

There was a moment's silence; then Mrs. Ansley rejoined: "Did they? It was all so long ago."

"Yes. And you got well again—so it didn't matter. But I suppose it struck your friends—the reason given for your illness, I mean—because everybody knew you were so prudent on account of your throat, and your mother took such care of you . . . You *had* been out late sightseeing, hadn't you, that night?"

"Perhaps I had. The most prudent girls aren't always prudent. What made you think of it now?"

Mrs. Slade seemed to have no answer ready. But after a moment she broke out: "Because I simply can't bear it any longer—!"

Mrs. Ansley lifted her head quickly. Her eyes were wide and very pale. "Can't bear what?"

"Why—your not knowing that I've always known why you went."

"Why I went—?"

"Yes. You think I'm bluffing, don't you? Well, you went to meet the man I was engaged to—and I can repeat every word of the letter that took you there."

While Mrs. Slade spoke Mrs. Ansley had risen unsteadily to her feet. Her bag, her knitting and gloves, slid in a panic-stricken heap to the ground. She looked at Mrs. Slade as though she were looking at a ghost.

"No, no—don't," she faltered out.

"Why not? Listen, if you don't believe me. 'My one darling, things can't go on like this. I must see you alone. Come to the Colosseum immediately after dark tomorrow. There will be somebody to let you in. No one whom you need fear will suspect'—but perhaps you've forgotten what the letter said?"

Mrs. Ansley met the challenge with an unexpected composure. Steadying herself against the chair she looked at her friend, and replied: "No, I know it by heart too."

"And the signature? 'Only *your* D.S.' Was that it? I'm right, am I? That was the letter that took you out that evening after dark?"

Mrs. Ansley was still looking at her. It seemed to Mrs. Slade that a slow struggle was going on behind the voluntarily controlled mask of her small quiet face. "I shouldn't have thought she had herself so well in hand," Mrs. Slade reflected, almost resentfully. But at this moment Mrs. Ansley spoke. "I don't know how you knew. I burnt that letter at once."

"Yes; you would, naturally—you're so prudent!" The sneer was open now. "And if you burnt the letter you're wondering how on earth I know what was in it. That's it, isn't it?"

Mrs. Slade waited, but Mrs. Ansley did not speak.

"Well, my dear, I know what was in that letter because I wrote it!"

"You wrote it?"

"Yes."

The two women stood for a minute staring at each other in the last golden light. Then Mrs. Ansley dropped back into her chair. "Oh," she murmured, and covered her face with her hands.

Mrs. Slade waited nervously for another word or movement. None came, and at length she broke out: "I horrify you."

Mrs. Ansley's hands dropped to her knee. The face they uncovered was streaked with tears. "I wasn't thinking of you. I was thinking—it was the only letter I ever had from him!"

"And I wrote it. Yes; I wrote it! But I was the girl he was engaged to. Did you happen to remember that?"

Mrs. Ansley's head dropped again. "I'm not trying to excuse myself . . . I remembered . . ."

"And still you went?"

"Still I went."

Mrs. Slade stood looking down on the small bowed figure at her side. The flame of her wrath had already sunk, and she wondered why she had ever thought there would be any satisfaction in inflicting so purposeless a wound on her friend. But she had to justify herself.

"You do understand? I found out—and I hated you, hated you. I knew you were in love with Delphin—and I was afraid; afraid of you, of your quiet ways, your sweetness . . . your . . . well, I wanted you out of the way, that's all. Just for a few weeks; just till I was sure of him. So in a blind fury I wrote that letter . . . I don't know why I'm telling you now."

"I suppose," said Mrs. Ansley slowly, "it's because you've always gone on hating me."

"Perhaps. Or because I wanted to get the whole thing off my mind." She paused. "I'm glad you destroyed the letter. Of course I never thought you'd die."

Mrs. Ansley relapsed into silence, and Mrs. Slade, leaning above her, was conscious of a strange sense of isolation, of being cut off from the warm current of human communion. "You think me a monster!"

"I don't know . . . It was the only letter I had, and you say he didn't write it?"

"Ah, how you care for him still!"

"I cared for that memory," said Mrs. Ansley.

Mrs. Slade continued to look down on her. She seemed physically reduced by the blow—as if, when she got up, the wind might scatter her like a puff of dust. Mrs. Slade's jealousy suddenly leapt up again at the sight. All these years the woman had been living on that letter. How she must have loved him, to treasure the mere memory of its ashes! The letter of the man her friend was engaged to. Wasn't it she who was the monster?

"You tried your best to get him away from me, didn't you? But you failed; and I kept him. That's all."

"Yes. That's all."

"I wish now I hadn't told you. I'd no idea you'd feel about it as you do; I thought you'd be amused. It all happened so long ago, as you say; and you must do me the justice to remember that I had no reason to think you'd ever taken it seriously. How could I, when you were married to Horace Ansley two months afterward? As soon as you could get out of bed your mother rushed you off to Florence and married you. People were rather surprised —they wondered at its being done so quickly; but I thought I knew. I had an idea you did it out of *pique*—to be able to say you'd got ahead of Delphin and me. Girls have such silly reasons for doing the most serious things. And your marrying so soon convinced me that you'd never really cared."

"Yes, I suppose it would," Mrs. Ansley assented.

The clear heaven overhead was emptied of all its gold. Dusk spread over it, abruptly darkening the Seven Hills. Here and there lights began to twinkle through the foliage at their feet. Steps were coming and going on the deserted terrace—waiters looking out of the doorway at the head of the stairs, then reappearing with trays and napkins and flasks of wine. Tables were moved, chairs straightened. A feeble string of electric lights flickered out. Some vases of faded flowers were carried away, and brought back replenished. A stout lady in a dust-coat suddenly appeared, asking in broken Italian if any one had seen the elastic band which held together her tattered Baedeker. She poked with her stick under the table at which she had lunched, the waiters assisting.

The corner where Mrs. Slade and Mrs. Ansley sat was still shadowy and deserted. For a long time neither of them spoke. At length Mrs. Slade began again: "I suppose I did it as a sort of joke—"

"A joke?"

"Well, girls are ferocious sometimes, you know. Girls in love especially. And I remember laughing to myself all that evening at the idea that you were waiting around there in the dark, dodging out of sight, listening for every sound, trying to get in—. Of course I was upset when I heard you were so ill afterward."

Mrs. Ansley had not moved for a long time. But now she turned slowly toward her companion. "But I didn't wait. He'd arranged everything. He was there. We were let in at once," she said.

Mrs. Slade sprang up from her leaning position. "Delphin there? They let you in?— Ah, now you're lying!" she burst out with violence.

Mrs. Ansley's voice grew clearer, and full of surprise. "But of course he was there. Naturally he came—"

"Came? How did he know he'd find you there? You must be raving!"

Mrs. Ansley hesitated, as though reflecting. "But I answered the letter. I told him I'd be there. So he came."

Mrs. Slade flung her hands up to her face. "Oh, God—you answered! I never thought of your answering . . ."

"It's odd you never thought of it, if you wrote the letter."

"Yes. I was blind with rage."

Mrs. Ansley rose, and drew her fur scarf about her. "It is cold here. We'd better go . . . I'm sorry for you," she said, as she clasped the fur about her throat.

The unexpected words sent a pang through Mrs. Slade. "Yes; we'd better go." She gathered up her bag and cloak. "I don't know why you should be sorry for me," she muttered.

Mrs. Ansley stood looking away from her toward the dusky secret mass of the Colosseum. "Well—because I didn't have to wait that night."

Mrs. Slade gave an unquiet laugh. "Yes; I was beaten there. But I oughtn't to begrudge it to you, I suppose. At the end of all these years. After all, I had everything; I had him for twenty-five years.

And you had nothing but that one letter that he didn't write."

Mrs. Ansley was again silent. At length she turned toward the door of the terrace. She took a step, and turned back, facing her companion.

"I had Barbara," she said, and began to move ahead of Mrs. Slade toward the stairway.

ERNEST HEMINGWAY

The Gambler, The Nun, and The Radio

They brought them in around midnight and then, all night long, every one along the corridor heard the Russian.

"Where is he shot?" Mr. Frazer asked the night nurse.

"In the thigh, I think."

"What about the other one?"

"Oh, he's going to die, I'm afraid."

"Where is he shot?"

"Twice in the abdomen. They only found one of the bullets."

They were both beet workers, a Mexican and a Russian, and they were sitting drinking coffee in an all-night restaurant when some one came in the door and started shooting at the Mexican. The Russian crawled under a table and was hit, finally, by a stray shot fired at the Mexican as he lay on the floor with two bullets in his abdomen. That was what the paper said.

The Mexican told the police he had no idea who shot him. He believed it to be an accident.

First published under the title "Give Us A Prescription, Doctor". Copyright 1933 Charles Scribner's Sons; renewal copyright © 1961 Ernest Hemingway. Reprinted with the permission of Charles Scribner's Sons from WINNER TAKE NOTHING by Ernest Hemingway.

"An accident that he fired eight shots at you and hit you twice, there?"

"*Si, señor*," said the Mexican, who was named Cayetano Ruiz.

"An accident that he hit me at all, the *cabron*," he said to the interpreter.

"What does he say?" asked the detective sergeant, looking across the bed at the interpreter.

"He says it was an accident."

"Tell him to tell the truth, that he is going to die," the detective said.

"Na," said Cayetano. "But tell him that I feel very sick and would prefer not to talk so much."

"He says that he is telling the truth," the interpreter said. Then speaking confidently, to the detective, "He don't know who shot him. They shot him in the back."

"Yes," said the detective. "I understand that, but why did the bullets all go in the front?"

"Maybe he is spinning around," said the interpreter.

"Listen," said the detective, shaking his finger almost at Cayetano's nose, which projected, waxen yellow, from his dead-man's face in which his eyes were alive as a hawk's. "I don't give a damn who shot you, but I've got to clear this thing up. Don't you want the man who shot you to be punished? Tell him that," he said to the interpreter.

"He says to tell who shot you."

"*Mandarlo al carajo*,"[1] said Cayetano, who was very tired.

"He says he never saw the fellow at all," the interpreter said. "I tell you straight they shot him in the back."

"Ask him who shot the Russian."

"Poor Russian," said Cayetano. "He was on the floor with his head enveloped in his arms. He started to give cries when they shot him and he is giving cries ever since. Poor Russian."

"He says some fellow that he doesn't know. Maybe the same fellow that shot him."

"Listen," the detective said. "This isn't Chicago. You're not a gangster. You don't have to act like a moving picture. It's all right to tell who shot you. Anybody would tell who shot them.

[1] *"Mandarlo al carajo."* "Tell him to go to hell."

That's all right to do. Suppose you don't tell me who he is and he shoots somebody else. Suppose he shoots a woman or a child. You can't let him get away with that. You tell him," he said to Mr. Frazer. "I don't trust that damn interpreter."

"I am very reliable," the interpreter said. Cayetano looked at Mr. Frazer.

"Listen, *amigo*," said Mr. Frazer. "The policeman says that we are not in Chicago but in Hailey, Montana. You are not a bandit and this has nothing to do with the cinema."

"I believe him," said Cayetano softly. "*Ya lo creo.*"

"One can, with honor, denounce one's assailant. Every one does it here, he says. He says what happens if after shooting you, this man shoots a woman or a child?"

"I am not married," Cayetano said.

"He says any woman, any child."

"The man is not crazy," Cayetano said.

"He says you should denounce him," Mr. Frazer finished.

"Thank you," Cayetano said. "You are of the great translators. I speak English, but badly. I understand it all right. How did you break your leg?"

"A fall off a horse."

"What bad luck. I am very sorry. Does it hurt much?"

"Not now. At first, yes."

"Listen, *amigo*," Cayetano began, "I am very weak. You will pardon me. Also I have much pain; enough pain. It is very possible that I die. Please get this policeman out of here because I am very tired." He made as though to roll to one side; then held himself still.

"I told him everything exactly as you said and he said to tell you, truly, that he doesn't know who shot him and that he is very weak and wishes you would question him later on," Mr. Frazer said.

"He'll probably be dead later on."

"That's quite possible."

"That's why I want to question him now."

"Somebody shot him in the back, I tell you," the interpreter said.

"Oh, for Chrisake," the detective sergeant said, and put his notebook in his pocket.

Outside in the corridor the detective sergeant stood with the interpreter beside Mr. Frazer's wheeled chair.

"I suppose you think somebody shot him in the back too?"

"Yes," Frazer said. "Somebody shot him in the back. What's it to you?"

"Don't get sore," the sergeant said. "I wish I could talk spick."

"Why don't you learn?"

"You don't have to get sore. I don't get any fun out of asking that spick questions. If I could talk spick it would be different."

"You don't need to talk Spanish," the interpreter said. "I am a very reliable interpreter."

"Oh, for Chrisake," the sergeant said. "Well, so long. I'll come up and see you."

"Thanks. I'm always in."

"I guess you are all right. That was bad luck all right. Plenty bad luck."

"It's coming along good now since he spliced the bone."

"Yes, but it's a long time. A long, long time."

"Don't let anybody shoot you in the back."

"That's right," he said. "That's right. Well, I'm glad you're not sore."

"So long," said Mr. Frazer.

Mr. Frazer did not see Cayetano again for a long time, but each morning Sister Cecilia brought news of him. He was so uncomplaining she said and he was very bad now. He had peritonitis and they thought he could not live. Poor Cayetano, she said. He had such beautiful hands and such a fine face and he never complains. The odor, now, was really terrific. He would point toward his nose with one finger and smile and shake his head, she said. He felt badly about the odor. It embarrassed him, Sister Cecilia said. Oh, he was such a fine patient. He always smiled. He wouldn't go to confession to Father but he promised to say his prayers, and not a Mexican had been to see him since he had been brought in. The Russian was going out at the end of the week. I could never feel anything about the Russian, Sister Cecilia said. Poor fellow, he suffered too. It was a greased bullet and dirty and the wound infected, but he made so much noise and then I always like the bad ones. That Cayetano, he's a bad one. Oh, he must really be a bad one, a thoroughly bad one, he's so fine and deli-cately made and he's never done any work with his hands. He's not a beet worker. I know he's not a beet worker. His hands are as smooth and not a callous on them. I know he's a bad one of some sort. I'm going down and pray for him now. Poor Cayetano, he's having a dreadful time and he doesn't make a sound. What did they have to shoot him for? Oh, that poor Cayetano! I'm going right down and pray for him.

She went right down and prayed for him.

In that hospital a radio did not work very well until it was dusk. They said it was because there was so much ore in the ground or something about the mountains, but anyway it did not work well at all until it began to get dark outside; but all night it worked beautifully and when one station stopped you could go farther west and pick up another. The last one that you could get was Seattle, Washington, and due to the difference in time, when they signed off at four o'clock in the morning it was five o'clock in the morning in the hospital; and at six o'clock you could get the morning revellers in Minneapolis. That was on account of the difference in time, too, and Mr. Frazer used to like to think of the morning revellers arriving at the studio and picture how they would look getting off a street car before daylight in the morning carry-ing their instruments. Maybe that was wrong and they kept their instruments at the place they revelled, but he always pictured them with their instruments. He had never been in Minneapolis and believed he probably would never go there, but he knew what it looked like that early in the morning.

Out of the window of the hospital you could see a field with tumbleweed coming out of the snow, and a bare clay butte. One morning the doctor wanted to show Mr. Frazer two pheasants that were out there in the snow, and pulling the bed toward the window, the reading light fell off the iron bedstead and hit Mr. Frazer on the head. This does not sound so funny now but it was very funny then. Every one was looking out the window, and the doctor, who was a most excellent doctor, was pointing at the pheasants and pulling the bed toward the window, and then, just as in a comic section, Mr. Frazer was knocked out by the leaded base of the lamp hitting the top of his head. It seemed the antithesis of healing or whatever people were in the hospital for, and every one thought it was very funny, as a joke on Mr. Frazer and on the doctor. Everything is much simpler in a hospital, including the jokes.

From the other window, if the bed was turned, you could see the town, with a little smoke above it, and the Dawson mountains looking like real mountains with the winter snow on them. Those were the two views since the wheeled chair had proved to be premature. It is really best to be in bed if you are in a hospital; since two views, with time to observe them, from a room the temperature of which you control, are much better than any number of views seen for a few minutes from hot, empty rooms that are waiting for some one else, or just abandoned, which you are wheeled in and out of. If you stay long enough in a room the view, whatever it is, acquires a great value and becomes very important and you would not change it, not even by a different angle. Just as, with the radio, there are certain things that you become fond of, and you welcome them and resent the new things. The best tunes they had that winter were "Sing Something Simple," "Singsong Girl," and "Little White Lies." No other tunes were as satisfactory, Mr. Frazer felt. "Betty Co-ed" was a good tune too, but the parody of the words which came unavoidably into Mr. Frazer's mind, grew so steadily and increasingly obscene that there being no one to appreciate it, he finally abandoned it and let the song go back to football.

About nine o'clock in the morning they would start using the X-ray machine, and then the radio, which, by then, was only getting Hailey, became useless. Many people in Hailey who owned radios protested about the hospital's X-ray machine which ruined their morning reception, but there was never any action taken, although many felt it was a shame the hospital could not use their machine at a time when people were not using their radios.

About the time when it became necessary to turn off the radio Sister Cecilia came in.

"How's Cayetano, Sister Cecilia?" Mr. Frazer asked.

"Oh, he's very bad."

"Is he out of his head?"

"No, but I'm afraid he's going to die."

"How are you?"

"I'm very worried about him, and do you know absolutely no one has come to see him? He could die just like a dog for all those Mexicans care. They're really dreadful."

"Do you want to come up and hear the game this afternoon?"

"Oh, no," she said. "I'd be too excited. I'll be in the chapel praying."

"We ought to be able to hear it pretty well," Mr. Frazer said. "They're playing out on the coast and the difference in time will bring it late enough so we can get it all right."

"Oh, no. I couldn't do it. The world series nearly finished me. When the Athletics were at bat I was praying right out loud: 'Oh, Lord, direct their batting eyes! Oh, Lord, may he hit one! Oh, Lord, may he hit safely!' Then when they filled the bases in the third game, you remember, it was too much for me. 'Oh, Lord, may he hit it out of the lot! Oh, Lord, may he drive it clean over the fence!' Then you know when the Cardinals would come to bat it was simply dreadful. 'Oh, Lord, may they not see it! Oh, Lord, don't let them even catch a glimpse of it! Oh, Lord, may they fan!' And this game is even worse. It's Notre Dame. Our Lady. No, I'll be in the chapel. For Our Lady. They're playing for Our Lady. I wish you'd write something sometime for Our Lady. You could do it. You know you could do it, Mr. Frazer."

"I don't know anything about her that I could write. It's mostly been written already," Mr. Frazer said. "You wouldn't like the way I write. She wouldn't care for it either."

"You'll write about her sometime," Sister said. "I know you will. You must write about Our Lady."

"You'd better come up and hear the game."

"It would be too much for me. No, I'll be in the chapel doing what I can."

That afternoon they had been playing about five minutes when a probationer came into the room and said, "Sister Cecilia wants to know how the game is going?"

"Tell her they have a touchdown already."

In a little while the probationer came into the room again.

"Tell her they're playing them off their feet," Mr. Frazer said.

A little later he rang the bell for the nurse who was on floor duty. "Would you mind going down to the chapel or sending word down to Sister Cecilia that Notre Dame has them fourteen to nothing at the end of the first quarter and that it's all right. She can stop praying."

In a few minutes Sister Cecilia came into the room. She was very excited. "What does fourteen to nothing mean? I don't know anything about this game. That's a nice safe lead in baseball. But I don't know anything about football. It may not mean a thing. I'm going right back down to the chapel and pray until it's finished."

"They have them beaten," Frazer said. "I promise you. Stay and listen with me."

"No. No. No. No. No. No. No," she said. "I'm going right down to the chapel to pray."

Mr. Frazer sent down word whenever Notre Dame scored, and finally, when it had been dark a long time, the final result.

"How's Sister Cecilia?"

"They're all at chapel," she said.

The next morning Sister Cecilia came in. She was very pleased and confident.

"I knew they couldn't beat Our Lady," she said. "They couldn't. Cayetano's better too. He's much better. He's going to have visitors. He can't see them yet, but they are going to come and that will make him feel better and know he's not forgotten by his own people. I went down and saw that O'Brien boy at Police Headquarters and told him that he's got to send some Mexicans up to see poor Cayetano. He's going to send some this afternoon. Then that poor man will feel better. It's wicked the way no one has come to see him."

That afternoon about five o'clock three Mexicans came into the room.

"Can one?" asked the biggest one, who had very thick lips and was quite fat.

"Why not?" Mr. Frazer answered. "Sit down, gentlemen. Will you take something?"

"Many thanks," said the big one.

"Thanks," said the darkest and smallest one.

"Thanks, no," said the thin one. "It mounts to my head." He

tapped his head.

The nurse brought some glasses. "Please give them the bottle," Frazer said. "It is from Red Lodge," he explained.

"That of Red Lodge is the best," said the big one. "Much better than that of Big Timber."

"Clearly," said the smallest one, "and costs more too."

"In Red Lodge it is of all prices," said the big one.

"How many tubes has the radio?" asked the one who did not drink.

"Seven."

"Very beautiful," he said. "What does it cost?"

"I don't know," Mr. Frazer said. "It is rented."

"You gentlemen are friends of Cayetano?"

"No," said the big one. "We are friends of he who wounded him."

"We were sent here by the police," the smallest one said.

"We have a little place," the big one said. "He and I," indicating the one who did not drink. "He has a little place too," indicating the small, dark one. "The police tell us we have to come—so we come."

"I am very happy you have come."

"Equally," said the big one.

"Will you have another little cup?"

"Why not?" said the big one.

"With your permission," said the smallest one.

"Not me," said the thin one. "It mounts to my head."

"It is very good," said the smallest one.

"Why not try some," Mr. Frazer asked the thin one. "Let a little mount to your head."

"Afterwards comes the headache," said the thin one.

"Could you not send friends of Cayetano to see him?" Frazer asked.

"He has no friends."

"Every man has friends."

"This one, no."

"What does he do?"

"He is a card-player."

"Is he good?"

"I believe it."

"From me," said the smallest one, "he won one hundred and eighty dollars. Now there is no longer one hundred and eighty dollars in the world."

"From me," said the thin one, "he won two hundred and eleven dollars. Fix yourself on that figure."

"I never played with him," said the fat one.

"He must be very rich," Mr. Frazer suggested.

"He is poorer than we," said the little Mexican. "He has no more than the shirt on his back."

"And that shirt is of little value now," Mr. Frazer said. "Perforated as it is."

"Clearly."

"The one who wounded him was a card-player?"

"No, a beet worker. He has had to leave town."

"Fix yourself on this," said the smallest one. "He was the best guitar player ever in this town. The finest."

"What a shame."

"I believe it," said the biggest one. "How he could touch the guitar."

"There are no good guitar players left?"

"Not the shadow of a guitar player."

"There is an accordion player who is worth something," the thin man said.

"There are a few who touch various instruments," the big one said. "You like music?"

"How would I not?"

"We will come one night with music? You think the sister would allow it? She seems very amiable."

"I am sure she would permit it when Cayetano is able to hear it."

"Is she a little crazy?" asked the thin one.

"Who?"

"That sister."

"No," Mr. Frazer said. "She is a fine woman of great intelligence and sympathy."

"I distrust all priests, monks, and sisters," said the thin one.

"He had bad experiences when a boy," the smallest one said.

"I was acolyte," the thin one said proudly. "Now I believe in nothing. Neither do I go to mass."

"Why? Does it mount to your head?"

"No," said the thin one. "It is alcohol that mounts to my head. Religion is the opium of the poor."

"I thought marijuana was the opium of the poor," Frazer said.

"Did you ever smoke opium?" the big one asked.

"No."

"Nor I," he said. "It seems very bad. One commences and cannot stop. It is a vice."

"Like religion," said the thin one.

"This one," said the smallest Mexican, "is very strong against religion."

"It is necessary to be very strong against something," Mr. Frazer said politely.

"I respect those who have faith even though they are ignorant," the thin one said.

"Good," said Mr. Frazer.

"What can we bring you?" asked the big Mexican. "Do you lack for anything?"

"I would be glad to buy some beer if there is good beer."

"We will bring beer."

"Another *copita* [2] before you go?"

"It is very good."

"We are robbing you."

"I can't take it. It goes to my head. Then I have a bad headache and sick at the stomach."

"Good-by, gentlemen."

"Good-by and thanks."

They went out and there was supper and then the radio, turned to be as quiet as possible and still be heard, and the stations finally signed off in this order: Denver, Salt Lake City, Los Angeles, and Seattle. Mr. Frazer received no picture of Denver from the radio. He could see Denver from the *Denver Post*, and correct the picture from *The Rocky Mountain News*. Nor did he ever have any feel of Salt Lake City or Los Angeles from what he heard from those places. All he felt about Salt Lake City was that it was clean, but dull, and there were too many ballrooms mentioned in too many big hotels for him to see Los Angeles. He could not feel it for the ballrooms. But Seattle he came to know very well, the taxicab company with the big white cabs (each cab equipped

[2] *Copita*. Little glass.

with radio itself) he rode in every night out to the roadhouse on the Canadian side where he followed the course of parties by the musical selections they phoned for. He lived in Seattle from two o'clock on, each night, hearing the pieces that all the different people asked for, and it was as real as Minneapolis, where the revellers left their beds each morning to make that trip down to the studio. Mr. Frazer grew very fond of Seattle, Washington.

The Mexicans came and brought beer but it was not good beer. Mr. Frazer saw them but he did not feel like talking, and when they went he knew they would not come again. His nerves had become tricky and he disliked seeing people while he was in this condition. His nerves went bad at the end of five weeks, and while he was pleased they lasted that long yet he resented being forced to make the same experiment when he already knew the answer. Mr. Frazer had been through all this before. The only thing which was new to him was the radio. He played it all night long, turned so low he could barely hear it, and he was learning to listen to it without thinking.

Sister Cecilia came into the room about ten o'clock in the morning on that day and brought the mail. She was very handsome, and Mr. Frazer liked to see her and to hear her talk, but the mail, supposedly coming from a different world, was more important. However, there was nothing in the mail of any interest.
"You look *so* much better," she said. "You'll be leaving us soon."
"Yes," Mr. Frazer said. "You look very happy this morning."
"Oh, I am. This morning I feel as though I might be a saint."
Mr. Frazer was a little taken aback at this.
"Yes," Sister Cecilia went on. "That's what I want to be. A saint. Ever since I was a little girl I've wanted to be a saint. When I was a girl I thought if I renounced the world and went into the convent I would be a saint. That was what I wanted to be and that was what I thought I had to do to be one. I expected I would be a saint. I was absolutely sure I would be one. For just a moment I thought I was one. I was so happy and it seemed so simple and easy. When I awoke in the morning I expected I would be a saint, but I wasn't. I've never become one. I wanted so to be one. All I want is to be a saint. That is all I've ever wanted. And this morning

I feel as though I might be one. Oh, I hope I will get to be one."

"You'll be one. Everybody gets what they want. That's what they always tell me."

"I don't know now. When I was a girl it seemed so simple. I knew I would be a saint. Only I believed it took time when I found it did not happen suddenly. Now it seems almost impossible."

"I'd say you had a good chance."

"Do you really think so? No, I don't want just to be encouraged. Don't just encourage me. I want to be a saint. I want so to be a saint."

"Of course you'll be a saint," Mr. Frazer said.

"No, probably I won't be. But, oh, if I could only be a saint! I'd be perfectly happy."

"You're three to one to be a saint."

"No, don't encourage me. But, oh, if I could only be a saint! If I could only be a saint!"

"How's your friend Cayetano?"

"He's going to get well but he's paralyzed. One of the bullets hit the big nerve that goes down through his thigh and that leg is paralyzed. They only found it out when he got well enough so that he could move."

"Maybe the nerve will regenerate."

"I'm praying that it will," Sister Cecilia said. "You ought to see him."

"I don't feel like seeing anybody."

"You know you'd like to see him. They could wheel him in here."

"All right."

They wheeled him in, thin, his skin transparent, his hair black and needing to be cut, his eyes very laughing, his teeth bad when he smiled.

"*Hola, amigo! Que tal!*" [3]

"As you see," said Mr. Frazer. "And thou?"

"Alive and with the leg paralyzed."

"Bad," Mr. Frazer said. "But the nerve can regenerate and be as good as new."

[3] "*Hola, amigo! Que tal!*" "Hello, friend! How are you?"

"So they tell me."

"What about the pain?"

"Not now. For a while I was crazy with it in the belly. I thought the pain alone would kill me."

Sister Cecilia was observing them happily.

"She tells me you never made a sound," Mr. Frazer said.

"So many people in the ward," the Mexican said deprecatingly. "What class of pain do you have?"

"Big enough. Clearly not as bad as yours. When the nurse goes out I cry an hour, two hours. It rests me. My nerves are bad now."

"You have the radio. If I had a private room and a radio I would be crying and yelling all night long."

"I doubt it."

"*Hombre, si.* It's very healthy. But you cannot do it with so many people."

"At least," Mr. Frazer said, "the hands are still good. They tell me you make your living with the hands."

"And the head," he said, tapping his forehead. "But the head isn't worth as much."

"Three of your countrymen were here."

"Sent by the police to see me."

"They brought some beer."

"It probably was bad."

"It was bad."

"Tonight, sent by the police, they come to serenade me." He laughed, then tapped his stomach. "I cannot laugh yet. As musicians they are fatal."

"And the one who shot you?"

"Another fool. I won thirty-eight dollars from him at cards. That is not to kill about."

"The three told me you win much money."

"And am poorer than the birds."

"How?"

"I am a poor idealist. I am the victim of illusions." He laughed, then grinned and tapped his stomach. "I am a professional gambler but I like to gamble. To really gamble. Little gambling is all crooked. For real gambling you need luck. I have no luck."

"Never?"

"Never. I am completely without luck. Look, this *cabron* who shoots me just now. Can he shoot? No. The first shot he fires into nothing. The second is intercepted by a poor Russian. That would seem to be luck. What happens? He shoots me twice in the belly. He is a lucky man. I have no luck. He could not hit a horse if he were holding the stirrup. All luck."

"I thought he shot you first and the Russian after."

"No, the Russian first, me after. The paper was mistaken."

"Why didn't you shoot him?"

"I never carry a gun. With my luck, if I carried a gun I would be hanged ten times a year. I am a cheap card player, only that." He stopped, then continued. "When I make a sum of money I gamble and when I gamble I lose. I have passed at dice for three thousand dollars and crapped out for the six. With good dice. More than once."

"Why continue?"

"If I live long enough the luck will change. I have bad luck now for fifteen years. If I ever get any good luck I will be rich." He grinned. "I am a good gambler, really I would enjoy being rich."

"Do you have bad luck with all games?"

"With everything and with women." He smiled again, showing his bad teeth.

"Truly?"

"Truly."

"And what is there to do?"

"Continue, slowly, and wait for luck to change."

"But with women?"

"No gambler has luck with women. He is too concentrated. He works nights. When he should be with the woman. No man who works nights can hold a woman if the woman is worth anything."

"You are a philosopher."

"No, *hombre*. A gambler of the small towns. One small town, then another, another, then a big town, then start over again."

"Then shot in the belly."

"The first time," he said. "That has only happened once."

"I tire you talking?" Mr Frazer suggested.

"No," he said. "I must tire you."

"And the leg?"

"I have no great use for the leg. I am all right with the leg or not. I will be able to circulate."

"I wish you luck, truly, and with all my heart," Mr. Frazer said.

"Equally," he said. "And that the pain stops."

"It will not last, certainly. It is passing. It is of no importance."

"That it passes quickly."

"Equally."

That night the Mexicans played the accordion and other instruments in the ward and it was cheerful and the noise of the inhalations and exhalations of the accordion, and of the bells, the traps, and the drum came down the corridor. In that ward there was a rodeo rider who had come out of the chutes on Midnight on a hot dusty afternoon with the big crowd watching, and now, with a broken back, was going to learn to work in leather and to cane chairs when he got well enough to leave the hospital. There was a carpenter who had fallen with a scaffolding and broken both ankles and both wrists. He had lit like a cat but without a cat's resiliency. They could fix him up so that he could work again but it would take a long time. There was a boy from a farm, about sixteen years old, with a broken leg that had been badly set and was to be rebroken. There was Cayetano Ruiz, a small-town gambler with a paralyzed leg. Down the corridor Mr. Frazer could hear them all laughing and merry with the music made by the Mexicans who had been sent by the police. The Mexicans were having a good time. They came in, very excited, to see Mr. Frazer and wanted to know if there was anything he wanted them to play, and they came twice more to play at night of their own accord.

The last time they played Mr. Frazer lay in his room with the door open and listened to the noisy, bad music and could not keep from thinking. When they wanted to know what he wished played, he asked for the Cucaracha, which has the sinister lightness and deftness of so many of the tunes men have gone to die to. They played noisily and with emotion. The tune was better than most of such tunes, to Mr. Frazer's mind, but the effect was all the same.

In spite of this introduction of emotion, Mr. Frazer went on thinking. Usually he avoided thinking all he could, except when he was writing, but now he was thinking about those who were playing and what the little one had said.

Religion is the opium of the people. He believed that, that dyspeptic little joint-keeper. Yes, and music is the opium of the people. Old mount-to-the-head hadn't thought of that. And now economics is the opium of the people; along with patriotism the opium of the people in Italy and Germany. What about sexual intercourse; was that an opium of the people? Of some of the people. Of some of the best people. But drink was a sovereign opium of the people, oh, an excellent opium. Although some prefer the radio, another opium of the people, a cheap one he had just been using. Along with these went gambling, an opium of the people if there ever was one, one of the oldest. Ambition was another, an opium of the people, along with a belief in any new form of government. What you wanted was the minimum of government, always less government. Liberty, what we believed in, now the name of a MacFadden publication. We believed in that although they had not found a new name for it yet. But what was the real one? What was the real, the actual, opium of the people? He knew it very well. It was gone just a little way around the corner in that well-lighted part of his mind that was there after two or more drinks in the evening; that he knew was there (it was not really there of course). What was it? He knew very well. What was it? Of course; bread was the opium of the people. Would he remember that and would it make sense in the daylight? Bread is the opium of the people.

"Listen," Mr. Frazer said to the nurse when she came. "Get that little thin Mexican in here, will you, please?"

"How do you like it?" the Mexican said at the door.

"Very much."

"It is a historic tune," the Mexican said. "It is the tune of the real revolution."

"Listen," said Mr. Frazer. "Why should the people be operated on without an anesthetic?"

"I do not understand."

"Why are not all the opiums of the people good? What do you want to do with the people?"

"They should be rescued from ignorance."

"Don't talk nonsense. Education is an opium of the people. You ought to know that. You've had a little."

"You do not believe in education?"

"No," said Mr. Frazer. "In knowledge, yes."

"I do not follow you."

"Many times I do not follow myself with pleasure."

"You want to hear the Cucaracha another time?" asked the Mexican worriedly.

"Yes," said Mr. Frazer. "Play the Cucaracha another time. It's better than the radio."

Revolution, Mr. Frazer thought, is no opium. Revolution is a catharsis; an ecstasy which can only be prolonged by tyranny. The opiums are for before and for after. He was thinking well, a little too well.

They would go now in a little while, he thought, and they would take the Cucaracha with them. Then he would have a little spot of the giant killer and play the radio, you could play the radio so that you could hardly hear it.

JAMES THURBER

A Couple of Hamburgers

It had been raining for a long time, a slow, cold rain falling out of iron-colored clouds. They had been driving since morning and they still had a hundred and thirty miles to go. It was about three o'clock in the afternoon. "I'm getting hungry," she said. He took his eyes off the wet, winding road for a fraction of a second and said, "We'll stop at a dog-wagon." She shifted her position irritably. "I wish you wouldn't call them *dog*-wagons," she said. He pressed the klaxon button and went around a slow car. "That's what they are," he said. "Dog-wagons." She waited a few seconds. "*Decent* people call them *diners*," she told him, and added, "Even if you call them diners, I don't like them." He speeded up a hill. "They have better stuff than most

Permission the author; © 1935 The New Yorker Magazine, Inc.

restaurants," he said. "Anyway, I want to get home before dark and it takes too long in a restaurant. We can stay our stomachs with a couple of hamburgers." She lighted a cigarette and he asked her to light one for him. She lighted one deliberately and handed it to him. "I wish you wouldn't say 'stay our stomachs,' " she said. "You know I hate that. It's like 'sticking to your ribs.' You say that all the time." He grinned. "Good old American expressions, both of them," he said. "Like sow belly. Old pioneer term, sow belly." She sniffed. "My ancestors were pioneers, too. You don't have to be vulgar just because you were a pioneer." "Your ancestors never got as far west as mine did," he said. "The real pioneers traveled on their sow belly and got somewhere." He laughed loudly at that. She looked out at the wet trees and signs and telephone poles going by. They drove on for several miles without a word; he kept chortling every now and then.

"What's that funny sound?" she asked, suddenly. It invariably made him angry when she heard a funny sound. "What funny sound?" he demanded. "You're always hearing funny sounds." She laughed briefly. "That's what you said when the bearing burned out," she reminded him. "You'd never have noticed it if it hadn't been for me." "I noticed it, all right," he said. "Yes," she said. "When it was too late." She enjoyed bringing up the subject of the burned-out bearing whenever he got to chortling. "It was too late when *you* noticed it, as far as that goes," he said. Then, after a pause, "Well, what does it sound like *this* time? All engines make a noise running, you know." "I know all about that," she answered. "It sounds like—it sounds like a lot of safety pins being jiggled around in a tumbler." He snorted. "That's your imagination. Nothing gets the matter with a car that sounds like a lot of safety pins. I happen to know that." She tossed away her cigarette. "Oh, sure," she said. "You always happen to know everything." They drove on in silence.

"I want to stop somewhere and get something to *eat!*" she said loudly. "All right, all right!" he said. "I been watching for a dog-wagon, haven't I? There hasn't been any. I can't make you a dog-wagon." The wind blew rain in on her and she put up the window on her side all the way. "I won't stop at just any old diner," she said. "I won't stop unless it's a cute one." He looked around at her. "Unless it's a *what* one?" he shouted. "You know what I mean," she said. "I mean a decent, clean one where they don't slosh things at you. I hate to have a lot of milky coffee sloshed at me." "All right," he said. "We'll find a cute one, then. You pick it out. I wouldn't know. I might find one that was cunning but not cute." That struck him as funny and he began to chortle again. "Oh, shut up," she said.

Five miles farther along they came to a place called Sam's Diner. "Here's one," he said, slowing down. She looked it over. "I don't want to stop there," she said. "I don't like the ones that have nick-names." He brought the car to a stop at one side of the road. "Just what's the matter with the ones that have nicknames?" he asked with edgy, mock interest. "They're always Greek ones," she told him. "They're always Greek ones," he repeated after her. He set his teeth firmly together and started up again. After a time, "Good old Sam, the Greek," he said, in a singsong. "Good old Connecticut Sam Beardsley, the Greek." "You didn't see his name," she snapped. "Winthrop, then," he said. "Old Samuel Cabot Winthrop, the Greek dog-wagon man." He was getting hungry.

On the outskirts of the next town she said, as he slowed down, "It looks like a factory kind of town." He knew that she meant she wouldn't stop there. He drove on through the place. She lighted a cigarette as they pulled out into the open again. He slowed down and lighted a cigarette for himself. "Factory kind of town than *I* am!" he snarled. It was ten miles before they came to another town. "Torrington," he growled. "Happen to know there's a dog-wagon here because I stopped in it once with Bob Combs. Damn cute place, too, if you ask me." "I'm not asking you anything," she said, coldly. "You think you're *so* funny. I think I know the one you mean," she said, after a moment. "It's right in the town and it sits at an angle from the road. They're never so good, for some reason." He glared at her and almost ran up against the curb. "What the hell do you mean 'sits at an angle from the road'?" he cried. He was very hungry now. "Well, it isn't silly," she said, calmly. "I've noticed the ones that sit at an angle. They're cheaper, because they fitted them into funny little pieces of ground. The big ones parallel to the road are the best." He drove right through Torrington, his lips compressed. "Angle from the *road*, for God's sake!" he snarled, finally. She was looking out her window.

On the outskirts of the next town there was a diner called The Elite Diner. "This looks—" she began. "I see it, I see it!" he said. "It doesn't happen to look any cuter to me than any goddam—" She cut him off. "Don't be such a sorehead, for Lord's sake," she said. He pulled up and stopped beside the diner, and turned on her. "Listen," he said, grittingly, "I'm going to put down a couple of hamburgers in this place even if there isn't one single inch of chintz or cretonne in the whole—" "Oh, be still," she said. "You're just hungry and mean like a child. Eat your old hamburgers, what do I care?" Inside the place they sat down on stools and the counterman walked over to them, wiping up the counter top with a cloth as he did so. "What'll it be, folks?" he said. "Bad day, ain't it? Except for ducks." "I'll have a couple of—" began the husband, but his wife cut in. "I just want a pack of cigarettes," she said. He turned around slowly on his stool and stared at her as she put a dime and a nickel in the cigarette machine and ejected a package of Lucky Strikes. He turned to the counterman again. "I want a couple of hamburgers," he said. "With mustard and lots of onion. *Lots* of onion!" She hated onions. "I'll wait for you in the car," she said. He didn't answer and she went out.

He finished his hamburgers and his coffee slowly. It was terrible coffee. Then he went out to the car and got in and drove off, slowly humming "Who's Afraid of the Big Bad Wolf?" After a mile or so, "Well," he said, "what was the matter with the Elite Diner, milady?" "Didn't you *see* that cloth the man was wiping the counter with?" she demanded. "Ugh!" She shuddered. "I didn't happen to want to eat any of the counter," he said. He laughed at that comeback. "You didn't even notice it," she said. "You never notice anything. It was filthy." "I noticed they had some damn fine coffee in there," he said. "It was swell." He knew she loved good coffee. He began to hum his tune again; then he whistled it; then he began to sing it. She did not show her annoyance, but she knew that he knew she was annoyed. "Will you be kind enough to tell me what time it is?" she asked. "Big *bad* wolf, big *bad* wolf—five minutes o' five—tum-dee-*doo*-dee-dum-m-m." She settled back in her seat and took a cigarette from her case and tapped it on the case. "I'll wait till we get home," she said. "If you'll be kind enough to speed up a little." He drove on at the same speed. After a time he gave up the "Big Bad Wolf" and there was deep silence for two miles. Then suddenly he began to sing, very loudly, "*H*-A-double-R-*I*-G-A-*N spells Harrr-i-gan*—" She gritted her teeth. She hated that worse than any of his songs except "Barney Google." He would go on to "Barney Google" pretty soon, she knew. Suddenly she leaned slightly forward. The straight line of her lips began to curve up ever so slightly. She heard the safety pins in the tumbler again. Only now they were louder, more insistent, ominous. He was singing too loud to hear them. "Is a *name* that *shame* has never been con-*nec*-ted with—*Harrr*-i-gan, that's *me!*" She relaxed against the back of the seat, content to wait.

PHILIP ROTH

Defender of the Faith

In May of 1945, only a few weeks after the fighting had ended in Europe, I was rotated back to the States, where I spent the remainder of the war with a training company at Camp Crowder, Missouri. Along with the rest of the Ninth Army, I had been racing across Germany so swiftly during the late winter and spring that when I boarded the plane, I couldn't believe its destination lay to the west. My mind might inform me otherwise, but there was an inertia of the spirit that told me we were flying to a new front, where we would disembark and continue our push eastward—eastward until we'd circled the globe,

Reprinted from GOODBYE COLUMBUS by Philip Roth, by permission of Houghton Mifflin Company. Copyright 1959 by Philip Roth.

marching through villages along whose twisting, cobbled streets crowds of the enemy would watch us take possession of what, up to then, they'd considered their own. I had changed enough in two years not to mind the trembling of the old people, the crying of the very young, the uncertainty and fear in the eyes of the once arrogant. I had been fortunate enough to develop an infantryman's heart, which, like his feet, at first aches and swells but finally grows horny enough for him to travel the weirdest paths without feeling a thing.

Captain Paul Barrett was my C.O. in Camp Crowder. The day I reported for duty, he came out of his office to shake my hand. He was short, gruff, and fiery, and—indoors or out—he wore his polished helmet liner pulled down to his little eyes. In Europe, he had received a battlefield commission and a serious chest wound, and he'd been returned to the States only a few months before. He spoke easily to me, and at the evening formation he introduced me to the troops. "Gentlemen," he said, "Sergeant Thurston, as you know, is no longer with this company. Your new first sergeant is Sergeant Nathan Marx, here. He is a veteran of the European theatre, and consequently will expect to find a company of soldiers here, and not a company of *boys*."

I sat up late in the orderly room that evening, trying half-heartedly to solve the riddle of duty rosters, personnel forms, and morning reports. The Charge of Quarters slept with his mouth open on a mattress on the floor. A trainee stood reading the next day's duty roster, which was posted on the bulletin board just inside the screen door. It was a warm evening, and I could hear radios playing dance music over in the barracks. The trainee, who had been staring at me whenever he thought I wouldn't notice, finally took a step in my direction.

"Hey, Sarge—we having a G.I. party tomorrow night?" he asked. A G.I. party is a barracks cleaning.

"You usually have them on Friday nights?" I asked him.

"Yes," he said, and then he added mysteriously, "That's the whole thing."

"Then you'll have a G.I. party."

He turned away, and I heard him mumbling. His shoulders were moving, and I wondered if he was crying.

"What's your name, soldier?" I asked.

He turned, not crying at all. Instead, his green-speckled eyes, long and narrow, flashed like fish in the sun. He walked over to me and sat on the edge of my desk. He reached out a hand. "Sheldon," he said.

"Stand on your feet, Sheldon."

Getting off the desk, he said, "Sheldon Grossbart." He smiled at the familiarity into which he'd led me.

"You against cleaning the barracks Friday night, Grossbart?" I said. "Maybe we shouldn't have G.I. parties. Maybe we should get a maid." My tone startled me. I felt I sounded like every top sergeant I had ever known.

"No, Sergeant." He grew serious, but with a seriousness that seemed to be only the stifling of a smile. "It's just—G.I. parties on Friday night, of all nights."

He slipped up onto the corner of the desk again—not quite sitting, but not quite standing, either. He looked at me with those speckled eyes flashing, and then made a gesture with his hand. It was very slight—no more than a movement back and forth of the wrist—and yet it managed to exclude from our affairs everything else in the orderly room, to make the two of us the center of the world. It seemed, in fact, to exclude everything even about the two of us except our hearts.

"Sergeant Thurston was one thing," he whispered, glancing at the sleeping C.Q., "but we thought that with you here things might be a little different."

"We?"

"The Jewish personnel."

"Why?" I asked, harshly. "What's on your mind?" Whether I was still angry at the "Sheldon" business, or now at something else, I hadn't time to tell, but clearly I was angry.

"We thought you—Marx, you know, like Karl Marx. The Marx Brothers. Those guys are all—M-a-r-x. Isn't that how *you* spell it, Sergeant?"

"M-a-r-x."

"Fishbein said—" He stopped. "What I mean to say, Sergeant—" His face and neck were red, and his mouth moved but no words came out. In a moment, he raised himself to attention, gazing down at me. It was as though he had suddenly decided he could expect no more sympathy from me than from Thurston, the reason being that I was of Thurston's faith, and not his. The young man had managed to confuse himself as to what my faith really was, but I felt no desire to straighten him out. Very simply, I didn't like him.

When I did nothing but return his gaze, he spoke, in an altered tone. "You see, Sergeant," he explained to me, "Friday nights, Jews are supposed to go to services."

"Did Sergeant Thurston tell you you couldn't go to them when there was a G.I. party?"

"No."

"Did he say you had to stay and scrub the floors?"

"No, Sergeant."

"Did the Captain say you had to stay and scrub the floors?"

"That isn't it, Sergeant. It's the other guys in the barracks." He leaned toward me. "They think we're goofing off. But we're not. That's when Jews go to services, Friday night. We have to."

"Then go."

"But the other guys make accusations. They have no right."

"That's not the Army's problem, Grossbart. It's a personal problem you'll have to work out yourself."

"But it's un*fair*."

I got up to leave. "There's nothing I can do about it," I said.

Grossbart stiffened and stood in front of me. "But this is a matter of *religion*, sir."

"Sergeant," I said.

"I mean 'Sergeant,'" he said, almost snarling.

"Look, go see the chaplain. You want to see Captain Barrett, I'll arrange an appointment."

"No, no. I don't want to make trouble, Sergeant. That's the first thing they throw up to you. I just want my rights!"

"Damn it, Grossbart, stop whining. You have your rights. You can stay and scrub floors or you can go to shul—"

The smile swam in again. Spittle gleamed at the corners of his mouth. "You mean church, Sergeant."

"I mean shul, Grossbart!"

I walked past him and went outside. Near me, I heard the scrunching of a guard's boots on gravel. Beyond the lighted windows of the barracks, young men in T shirts and fatigue pants were sitting on their bunks, polishing their rifles. Suddenly there was a light rustling behind me. I turned and saw Grossbart's dark frame fleeing back to the barracks, racing to tell his Jewish friends that they were right—that, like Karl and Harpo, I was one of them.

The next morning, while chatting with Captain Barrett, I recounted the incident of the previous evening. Somehow, in the telling, it must have seemed to the Captain that I was not so much explaining Grossbart's position as defending it. "Marx, I'd fight side by side with a nigger if the fella proved to me he was a man. I pride myself," he said, looking out the window, "that I've got an open mind. Consequently, Sergeant, nobody gets special treatment here, for the good *or* the bad. All a man's got to do is prove himself. A man fires well on the range, I give him a weekend pass. He scores high in P.T., he gets a weekend pass. He *earns* it." He turned from the window and pointed a finger at me. "You're a Jewish fella, am I right, Marx?"

"Yes, sir."

"And I admire you. I admire you because of the ribbons on your chest. I judge a man by what he shows me on the field of battle, Sergeant. It's what he's got *here*," he said, and then, though I expected he would point to his heart, he jerked a thumb toward the buttons straining to hold his blouse across his belly. "Guts," he said.

"O.K., sir. I only wanted to pass on to you how the men felt."

"Mr. Marx, you're going to be old before your time if you worry about how the men feel. Leave that stuff to the chaplain—that's his business, not yours. Let's us train these fellas to shoot straight. If the Jewish personnel feels the other men are accusing them of goldbricking—well, I just don't know. Seems awfully funny that suddenly the Lord is calling so loud in Private Grossman's ear he's just got to run to church."

"Synagogue," I said.

"Synagogue is right, Sergeant. I'll write that down for handy reference. Thank you for stopping by."

That evening, a few minutes before the company gathered outside the orderly room for the chow formation, I called the C.Q., Corporal Robert LaHill, in to see me. LaHill was a dark, burly fellow whose hair curled out of his clothes wherever it could. He had a glaze in his eyes that made one think of caves and dinosaurs. "LaHill," I said, "when you take the formation, remind the men that they're free to attend church services *whenever* they are held, provided they report to the orderly room before they leave the area."

LaHill scratched his wrist, but gave no indication that he'd heard or understood.

"LaHill," I said, "*church*. You remember? Church, priest, Mass, confession."

He curled one lip into a kind of smile; I took it for a signal that for a second he had flickered back up into the human race.

"Jewish personnel who want to attend services this evening are to fall out in front of the orderly room at 1900," I said. Then, as an afterthought, I added, "By order of Captain Barrett."

A little while later, as the day's last light—softer than any I had seen that year—began to drop over Camp Crowder, I heard LaHill's thick, inflectionless voice outside my window: "Give me your ears, troopers. Toppie says for me to tell you that at 1900 hours all Jewish personnel is to fall out in front, here, if they want to attend the Jewish Mass."

At seven o'clock, I looked out the orderly-room window and saw three soldiers in starched khakis standing on the dusty quadrangle. They looked at their watches and fidgeted while they whispered back and forth. It was getting dimmer, and, alone on the otherwise deserted field, they looked tiny. When I opened the door, I heard the noises of the G.I. party coming from the surrounding barracks—bunks being pushed to the walls, faucets pounding water into buckets, brooms whisking at the wooden floors, cleaning the dirt away for Saturday's inspection. Big puffs of cloth moved round and round on the windowpanes. I walked outside, and the moment my foot hit the ground I thought I heard Grossbart call to the others, " 'Ten-*hut!*' " Or maybe, when they all three jumped to attention, I imagined I heard the command.

Grossbart stepped forward. "Thank you, sir," he said.

" 'Sergeant,' Grossbart," I reminded him. "You call officers 'sir.' I'm not an officer. You've been in the Army three weeks—you know that."

He turned his palms out at his sides to indicate that, in truth, he and I lived beyond convention. "Thank you, anyway," he said.

"Yes," a tall boy behind him said. "Thanks a lot."

And the third boy whispered, "Thank you," but his mouth barely fluttered, so that he did not alter by more than a lip's movement his posture of attention.

"For what?" I asked.

Grossbart snorted happily. "For the announcement. The Corporal's announcement. It helped. It made it—"

"Fancier." The tall boy finished Grossbart's sentence.

Grossbart smiled. "He means formal, sir. Public," he said to me. "Now it won't seem as though we're just taking off—goldbricking because the work has begun."

"It was by order of Captain Barrett," I said.

"Aaah, but you pull a little weight," Grossbart said. "So we thank you." Then he turned to his companions. "Sergeant Marx, I want you to meet Larry Fishbein."

The tall boy stepped forward and extended his hand. I shook it. "You from New York?" he asked.

"Yes."

"Me, too." He had a cadaverous face that collapsed inward from his cheekbone to his jaw, and when he smiled—as he did at the news of our communal attachment—revealed a mouthful of bad teeth. He was blinking his eyes a good deal, as though he were fighting back tears. "What borough?" he asked.

I turned to Grossbart. "It's five after seven. What time are services?"

"Shul," he said, smiling, "is in ten minutes. I want you to meet Mickey Halpern. This is Nathan Marx, our sergeant."

The third boy hopped forward. "Private Michael Halpern." He saluted.

"Salute officers, Halpern," I said. The boy dropped his hand, and, on its way down, in his nervousness, checked to see if his shirt pockets were buttoned.

"Shall I march them over, sir?" Grossbart asked. "Or are you coming along?"

From behind Grossbart, Fishbein piped up. "Afterward, they're having refreshments. A ladies' auxiliary from St. Louis, the rabbi told us last week."

"The chaplain," Halpern whispered.

362 · PHILIP ROTH

"You're welcome to come along," Grossbart said.

To avoid his plea, I looked away, and saw, in the windows of the barracks, a cloud of faces staring out at the four of us. "Hurry along, Grossbart," I said.

"O.K., then," he said. He turned to the others. "Double time, *march!*"

They started off, but ten feet away Grossbart spun around and, running backward, called to me, "Good *shabbus*,[1] sir!" And then the three of them were swallowed into the alien Missouri dusk.

Even after they had disappeared over the parade ground, whose green was now a deep blue, I could hear Grossbart singing the double-time cadence, and as it grew dimmer and dimmer, it suddenly touched a deep memory—as did the slant of the light—and I was remembering the shrill sounds of a Bronx playground where, years ago, beside the Grand Concourse, I had played on long spring evenings such as this. It was a pleasant memory for a young man so far from peace and home, and it brought so many recollections with it that I began to grow exceedingly tender about myself. In fact, I indulged myself in a reverie so strong that I felt as though a hand were reaching down inside me. It had to reach so very far to touch me! It had to reach past those days in the forests of Belgium, and past the dying I'd refused to weep over; past the nights in German farmhouses whose books we'd burned to warm us; past endless stretches when I had shut off all softness I might feel for my fellows, and had managed even to deny myself the posture of a conqueror—the swagger that I, as a Jew, might well have worn as my boots whacked against the rubble of Wesel, Münster, and Braunschweig.

But now one night noise, one rumor of home and time past, and memory plunged down through all I had anesthetized, and came to what I suddenly remembered was myself. So it was not altogether curious that, in search of more of me, I found myself following Grossbart's tracks to Chapel No. 3, where the Jewish services were being held.

I took a seat in the last row, which was empty. Two rows in front of me sat Grossbart, Fishbein, and Halpern, holding little white Dixie cups. Each row of seats was raised higher than the one in front of it, and I could see clearly what was going on. Fish-

[1] *Shabbus.* Sabbath.

bein was pouring the contents of his cup into Grossbart's, and Grossbart looked mirthful as the liquid made a purple arc between Fishbein's hand and his. In the glaring yellow light, I saw the chaplain standing on the platform at the front; he was chanting the first line of the responsive reading. Grossbart's prayer book remained closed on his lap; he was swishing the cup around. Only Halpern responded to the chant by praying. The fingers of his right hand were spread wide across the cover of his open book. His cap was pulled down low onto his brow, which made it round, like a *yarmulke*.[2] From time to time, Grossbart wet his lips at the cup's edge; Fishbein, his long yellow face a dying light bulb, looked from here to there, craning forward to catch sight of the faces down the row, then of those in front of him, then behind. He saw me, and his eyelids beat a tattoo. His elbow slid into Grossbart's side, his neck inclined toward his friend, he whispered something, and then, when the congregation next responded to the chant, Grossbart's voice was among the others. Fishbein looked into his book now, too; his lips, however, didn't move.

Finally, it was time to drink the wine. The chaplain smiled down at them as Grossbart swigged his in one long gulp, Halpern sipped, meditating, and Fishbein faked devotion with an empty cup. "As I look down amongst the congregation"—the chaplain grinned at the word—"this night, I see many new faces, and I want to welcome you to Friday-night services here at Camp Crowder. I am Major Leo Ben Ezra, your chaplain." Though an American, the chaplain spoke deliberately—syllable by syllable, almost—as though to communicate, above all, with the lip readers in his audience. "I have only a few words to say before we adjourn to the refreshment room, where the kind ladies of the Temple Sinai, St. Louis, Missouri, have a nice setting for you."

Applause and whistling broke out. After another momentary grin, the chaplain raised his hands, palms out, his eyes flicking upward a moment, as if to remind the troops where they were and Who Else might be in attendance. In the sudden silence that followed, I thought I heard Grossbart cackle, "Let the goyim clean the floors!" Were those the words? I wasn't sure, but Fishbein, grinning, nudged Halpern. Halpern looked dumbly at him, then went back to his prayer book, which had been occupying him all

[2] *Yarmulke.* Skullcap.

through the rabbi's talk. One hand tugged at the black kinky hair that stuck out under his cap. His lips moved.

The rabbi continued. "It is about the food that I want to speak to you for a moment. I know, I know, I know," he intoned, wearily, "how in the mouths of most of you the *trafe* ³ food tastes like ashes. I know how you gag, some of you, and how your parents suffer to think of their children eating foods unclean and offensive to the palate. What can I tell you? I can only say, close your eyes and swallow as best you can. Eat what you must to live, and throw away the rest. I wish I could help more. For those of you who find this impossible, may I ask that you try and try, but then come to see me in private. If your revulsion is so great, we will have to seek aid from those higher up."

A round of chatter rose and subsided. Then everyone sang "Ain Kelohainu;" after all those years, I discovered, I still knew the words. Then, suddenly, the service over, Grossbart was upon me. "Higher up? He means the General?"

"Hey, Shelly," Fishbein said, "he means God." He smacked his face and looked at Halpern. "How high can you go!"

"Sh-h-h!" Grossbart said. "What do you think, Sergeant?"

"I don't know," I said. "You better ask the chaplain."

"I'm going to. I'm making an appointment to see him in private. So is Mickey."

Halpern shook his head. "No, no, Sheldon—"

"You have rights, Mickey," Grossbart said. "They can't push us around."

"It's O.K.," said Halpern. "It bothers my mother, not me."

Grossbart looked at me. "Yesterday he threw up. From the hash. It was all ham and God knows what else."

"I have a cold—that was why," Halpern said. He pushed his *yarmulke* back into a cap.

"What about you, Fishbein?" I asked. "You kosher, too?"

He flushed. "A little. But I'll let it ride. I have a very strong stomach, and I don't eat a lot anyway." I continued to look at him, and he held up his wrist to reinforce what he'd just said; his watch strap was tightened to the last hole, and he pointed that out to me.

"But services are important to you?" I asked him.

He looked at Grossbart. "Sure, sir."

³ *Trafe.* Opposite of *kosher;* unfit to eat.

" 'Sergeant.' "

"Not so much at home," said Grossbart, stepping between us, "but away from home it gives one a sense of his Jewishness."

"We have to stick together," Fishbein said.

I started to walk toward the door; Halpern stepped back to make way for me.

"That's what happened in Germany," Grossbart was saying, loud enough for me to hear. "They didn't stick together. They let themselves get pushed around."

I turned. "Look, Grossbart. This is the Army, not summer camp."

He smiled. "So?"

Halpern tried to sneak off, but Grossbart held his arm.

"Grossbart, how old are you?" I asked.

"Nineteen."

"And you?" I said to Fishbein.

"The same. The same month, even."

"And what about him?" I pointed to Halpern, who had by now made it safely to the door.

"Eighteen," Grossbart whispered. "But like he can't tie his shoes or brush his teeth himself. I feel sorry for him."

"I feel sorry for all of us, Grossbart," I said, "but just act like a man. Just don't overdo it."

"Overdo what, sir?"

"The 'sir' business, for one thing. Don't overdo that," I said.

I left him standing there. I passed by Halpern, but he did not look at me. Then I was outside, but, behind, I heard Grossbart call, "Hey, Mickey, my *leben*,[4] come on back. Refreshments!"

"*Leben!*" My grandmother's word for me!

One morning a week later, while I was working at my desk, Captain Barrett shouted for me to come into his office. When I entered, he had his helmet liner squashed down so far on his head that I couldn't even see his eyes. He was on the phone, and when he spoke to me, he cupped one hand over the mouthpiece. "Who the hell is Grossbart?"

"Third platoon, Captain," I said. "A trainee."

"What's all this stink about food? His mother called a goddam

4 *Leben.* Darling.

congressman about the food." He uncovered his mouthpiece and slid his helmet up until I could see his bottom eyelashes. "Yes, sir," he said into the phone. "Yes, sir. I'm still here, sir. I'm asking Marx, here, right now—"

He covered the mouthpiece again and turned his head back toward me. "Lightfoot Harry's on the phone," he said, between his teeth. "This congressman calls General Lyman, who calls Colonel Sousa, who calls the Major, who calls me. They're just dying to stick this thing on me. Whatsa matter?" He shook the phone at me. "I don't feed the troops? What the hell is this?"

"Sir, Grossbart is strange—" Barrett greeted that with a mockingly indulgent smile. I altered my approach. "Captain, he's a very orthodox Jew, and so he's only allowed to eat certain foods."

"He throws up, the congressman said. Every time he eats something, his mother says, he throws up!"

"He's accustomed to observing the dietary laws, Captain."

"So why's his old lady have to call the White House?"

"Jewish parents, sir—they're apt to be more protective than you expect. I mean, Jews have a very close family life. A boy goes away from home, sometimes the mother is liable to get very upset. Probably the boy mentioned something in a letter, and his mother misinterpreted."

"I'd like to punch him one right in the mouth," the Captain said. "There's a goddam war on, and he wants a silver platter!"

"I don't think the boy's to blame, sir. I'm sure we can straighten it out by just asking him. Jewish parents worry—"

"*All* parents worry, for Christ's sake. But they don't get on their high horse and start pulling strings—"

I interrupted, my voice higher, tighter than before. "The home life, Captain, is very important—but you're right, it may sometimes get out of hand. It's a very wonderful thing, Captain, but because it's so close, this kind of thing . . ."

He didn't listen any longer to my attempt to present both myself and Lightfoot Harry with an explanation for the letter. He turned back to the phone. "Sir?" he said. "Sir—Marx, here, tells me Jews have a tendency to be pushy. He says he thinks we can settle it right here in the company. . . . Yes, sir. . . . I *will* call back, sir, soon as I can." He hung up. "Where are the men, Sergeant?"

"On the range."

With a whack on the top of his helmet, he crushed it down over his eyes again, and charged out of his chair. "We're going for a ride," he said.

The Captain drove, and I sat beside him. It was a hot spring day, and under my newly starched fatigues I felt as though my armpits were melting down onto my sides and chest. The roads were dry, and by the time we reached the firing range, my teeth felt gritty with dust, though my mouth had been shut the whole trip. The Captain slammed the brakes on and told me to get the hell out and find Grossbart.

I found him on his belly, firing wildly at the five-hundred-feet target. Waiting their turns behind him were Halpern and Fishbein. Fishbein, wearing a pair of rimless G.I. glasses I hadn't seen on him before, had the appearance of an old peddler who would gladly have sold you his rifle and the cartridges that were slung all over him. I stood back by the ammo boxes, waiting for Grossbart to finish spraying the distant targets. Fishbein straggled back to stand near me.

"Hello, Sergeant Marx," he said.

"How are you?" I mumbled.

"Fine, thank you. Sheldon's really a good shot."

"I didn't notice."

"I'm not so good, but I think I'm getting the hang of it now. Sergeant, I don't mean to, you know, ask what I shouldn't—" The boy stopped. He was trying to speak intimately, but the noise of the shooting forced him to shout at me.

"What is it?" I asked. Down the range, I saw Captain Barrett standing up in the jeep, scanning the line for me and Grossbart.

"My parents keep asking and asking where we're going," Fishbein said. "Everybody says the Pacific. I don't care, but my parents —if I could relieve their minds, I think I could concentrate more on my shooting."

"I don't know where, Fishbein. Try to concentrate anyway."

"Sheldon says you might be able to find out."

"I don't know a thing, Fishbein. You just take it easy, and don't let Sheldon—"

"*I'm* taking it easy, Sergeant. It's at home—"

Grossbart had finished on the line, and was dusting his fatigues with one hand. I called to him. "Grossbart, the Captain wants to see you."

He came toward us. His eyes blazed and twinkled. "Hi!"

"Don't point that goddam rifle!" I said.

"I wouldn't shoot you, Sarge." He gave me a smile as wide as a pumpkin, and turned the barrel aside.

"Damn you, Grossbart, this is no joke! Follow me."

I walked ahead of him, and had the awful suspicion that, behind me, Grossbart was *marching*, his rifle on his shoulder, as though he were a one-man detachment. At the jeep, he gave the Captain a rifle salute. "Private Sheldon Grossbart, sir."

"At ease, Grossman." The Captain sat down, slid over into the empty seat, and, crooking a finger, invited Grossbart closer.

"Bart, sir. Sheldon Gross*bart*. It's a common error." Grossbart nodded at me; *I* understood, he indicated. I looked away just as the mess truck pulled up to the range, disgorging a half-dozen K.P.'s with rolled-up sleeves. The mess sergeant screamed at them while they set up the chow-line equipment.

"Grossbart, your mama wrote some congressman that we don't feed you right. Do you know that?" the Captain said.

"It was my father, sir. He wrote to Representative Franconi that my religion forbids me to eat certain foods."

"What religion is that, Grossbart?"

"Jewish."

"'Jewish, *sir*,'" I said to Grossbart.

"Excuse me, sir. Jewish, sir."

"What have you been living on?" the Captain asked. "You've been in the Army a month already. You don't look to me like you're falling to pieces."

"I eat because I have to, sir. But Sergeant Marx will testify to the fact that I don't eat one mouthful more than I need in order to survive."

"Is that so, Marx?" Barrett asked.

"I've never seen Grossbart eat, sir," I said.

"But you heard the rabbi," Grossbart said. "He told us what to do, and I listened."

The Captain looked at me. "Well, Marx?"

"I still don't know what he eats and doesn't eat, sir."

Grossbart raised his arms to plead with me, and it looked for a moment as though he were going to hand me his weapon to hold. "But, Sergeant—"

"Look, Grossbart, just answer the Captain's questions," I said sharply.

Barrett smiled at me, and I resented it. "All right, Grossbart," he said. "What is it you want? The little piece of paper? You want out?"

"No, sir. Only to be allowed to live as a Jew. And for the others, too."

"What others?"

"Fishbein, sir, and Halpern."

"They don't like the way we serve, either?"

"Halpern throws up, sir. I've seen it."

"I thought *you* throw up."

"Just once, sir. I didn't know the sausage was sausage."

"We'll give menus, Grossbart. We'll show training films about the food, so you can identify when we're trying to poison you."

Grossbart did not answer. The men had been organized into two long chow lines. At the tail end of one, I spotted Fishbein—or, rather, his glasses spotted me. They winked sunlight back at me. Halpern stood next to him, patting the inside of his collar with a khaki handkerchief. They moved with the line as it began to edge up toward the food. The mess sergeant was still screaming at the K.P.s. For a moment, I was actually terrified by the thought that somehow the mess sergeant was going to become involved in Grossbart's problem.

"Marx," the Captain said, "you're a Jewish fella—am I right?"

I played straight man. "Yes, sir."

"How long you been in the Army? Tell this boy."

"Three years and two months."

"A year in combat, Grossbart. Twelve goddam months in combat all through Europe. I admire this man." The Captain snapped a wrist against my chest. "Do you hear him peeping about the food? Do you? I want an answer, Grossbart. Yes or no."

"No, sir."

"And why not? He's a Jewish fella."

"Some things are more important to some Jews than other things to other Jews."

Barrett blew up. "Look, Grossbart. Marx, here, is a good man—a goddam hero. When you were in high school, Sergeant Marx was killing Germans. Who does more for the Jews—you, by throwing up over a lousy piece of sausage, a piece of first-cut meat, or Marx, by killing those Nazi bastards? If I was a Jew, Grossbart, I'd kiss this man's feet. He's a goddam hero, and *he* eats what we give him. Why do you have to cause trouble is what I want to know! What is it you're buckin' for—a discharge?"

"No, sir."

"I'm talking to a wall! Sergeant, get him out of my way." Barrett swung himself back into the driver's seat. "I'm going to see the chaplain." The engine roared, the jeep spun around in a whirl of dust, and the Captain was headed back to camp.

For a moment, Grossbart and I stood side by side, watching the jeep. Then he looked at me and said, "I don't want to start trouble. That's the first thing they toss up to us."

When he spoke, I saw that his teeth were white and straight, and the sight of them suddenly made me understand that Grossbart actually did have parents—that once upon a time someone had taken little Sheldon to the dentist. He was their son. Despite all the talk about his parents, it was hard to believe in Grossbart as a child, an heir—as related by blood to anyone, mother, father, or, above all, to me. This realization led me to another.

"What does your father do, Grossbart?" I asked as we started to walk back toward the chow line.

"He's a tailor."

"An American?"

"Now, yes. A son in the Army," he said, jokingly.

"And your mother?" I asked.

He winked. "A *ballabusta*.[5] She practically sleeps with a dust-cloth in her hand."

"She's also an immigrant?"

"All she talks is Yiddish, still."

"And your father, too?"

"A little English. 'Clean,' 'Press,' 'Take the pants in.' That's the extent of it. But they're good to me."

"Then, Grossbart—" I reached out and stopped him. He turned toward me, and when our eyes met, his seemed to jump back, to

[5] *Ballabusta.* Good housekeeper.

shiver in their sockets. "Grossbart—you were the one who wrote that letter, weren't you?"

It took only a second or two for his eyes to flash happy again. "Yes." He walked on, and I kept pace. "It's what my father *would* have written if he had known how. It was his name, though. *He* signed it. He even mailed it. I sent it home. For the New York postmark."

I was astonished, and he saw it. With complete seriousness, he thrust his right arm in front of me. "Blood is blood, Sergeant," he said, pinching the blue vein in his wrist.

"What the hell *are* you trying to do, Grossbart?" I asked. "I've seen you eat. Do you know that? I told the Captain I don't know what you eat, but I've seen you eat like a hound at chow."

"We work hard, Sergeant. We're in training. For a furnace to work, you've got to feed it coal."

"Why did you say in the letter that you threw up all the time?"

"I was really talking about Mickey there. I was talking *for* him. He would never write, Sergeant, though I pleaded with him. He'll waste away to nothing if I don't help. Sergeant, I used my name— my father's name—but it's Mickey, and Fishbein, too, I'm watching out for."

"You're a regular Messiah, aren't you?"

We were at the chow line now.

"That's a good one, Sergeant," he said, smiling. "But who knows? Who can tell? Maybe you're the Messiah—a little bit. What Mickey says is the Messiah is a collective idea. He went to Yeshiva, Mickey, for a while. He says *together* we're the Messiah. Me a little bit, you a little bit. You should hear that kid talk, Sergeant, when he gets going."

"Me a little bit, you a little bit," I said. "You'd like to believe that, wouldn't you, Grossbart? That would make everything so clean for you."

"It doesn't seem too bad a thing to believe, Sergeant. It only means we should all *give* a little, is all."

I walked off to eat my rations with the other noncoms.

Two days later, a letter addressed to Captain Barrett passed over my desk. It had come through the chain of command—from the office of Congressman Franconi, where it had been received, to

General Lyman, to Colonel Sousa, to Major Lamont, now to
Captain Barrett. I read it over twice. It was dated May 14th, the
day Barrett had spoken with Grossbart on the rifle range.

DEAR CONGRESSMAN:
First let me thank you for your interest in behalf of my son,
Private Sheldon Grossbart. Fortunately, I was able to speak with
Sheldon on the phone the other night, and I think I've been able to
solve our problem. He is, as I mentioned in my last letter, a very
religious boy, and it was only with the greatest difficulty that I could
persuade him that the religious thing to do—what God Himself
would want Sheldon to do—would be to suffer the pangs of religious
remorse for the good of his country and all mankind. It took some
doing, Congressman, but finally he saw the light. In fact, what he
said (and I wrote down the words on a scratch pad so as never to
forget), what he said was "I guess you're right, Dad. So many millions of my fellow-Jews gave up their lives to the enemy, the least I
can do is live for a while minus a bit of my heritage so as to help
end this struggle and regain for all the children of God dignity and
humanity." That, Congressman, would make any father proud.
By the way, Sheldon wanted me to know—and to pass on to you—
the name of a soldier who helped him reach this decision: SER-
GEANT NATHAN MARX. Sergeant Marx is a combat veteran
who is Sheldon's first sergeant. This man has helped Sheldon over
some of the first hurdles he's had to face in the Army, and is in part
responsible for Sheldon's changing his mind about the dietary laws.
I know Sheldon would appreciate any recognition Marx could receive.
Thank you and good luck. I look forward to seeing your name on
the next election ballot.

Respectfully,
SAMUEL E. GROSSBART

Attached to the Grossbart communiqué was another, addressed
to General Marshall Lyman, the post commander, and signed by
Representative Charles E. Franconi of the House of Representatives. The communiqué informed General Lyman that Sergeant
Nathan Marx was a credit to the U.S. Army and the Jewish
people.
What was Grossbart's motive in recanting? Did he feel he'd
gone too far? Was the letter a strategic retreat—a crafty attempt
to strengthen what he considered our alliance? Or had he actually
changed his mind, via an imaginary dialogue between Grossbart
père and Grossbart fils? I was puzzled, but only for a few days—

that is, only until I realized that, whatever his reasons, he had actually decided to disappear from my life; he was going to allow himself to become just another trainee. I saw him at inspection, but he never winked; at chow formations, but he never flashed me a sign. On Sundays, with the other trainees, he would sit around watching the noncoms' softball team, for which I pitched, but not once did he speak an unnecessary word to me. Fishbein and Halpern retreated, too—at Grossbart's command, I was sure. Apparently he had seen that wisdom lay in turning back before he plunged over into the ugliness of privilege undeserved. Our separation allowed me to forgive him our past encounters, and, finally, to admire him for his good sense.

Meanwhile, free of Grossbart, I grew used to my job and my administrative tasks. I stepped on a scale one day, and discovered I had truly become a noncombatant; I had gained seven pounds. I found patience to get past the first three pages of a book. I thought about the future more and more, and wrote letters to girls I'd known before the war. I even got a few answers. I sent away to Columbia for a Law School catalogue. I continued to follow the war in the Pacific, but it was not my war. I thought I could see the end, and sometimes, at night, I dreamed that I was walking on the streets of Manhattan—Broadway, Third Avenue, 116th Street, where I had lived the three years I attended Columbia. I curled myself around these dreams and I began to be happy.

And then, one Saturday, when everybody was away and I was alone in the orderly room reading a month-old copy of the *Sporting News*, Grossbart reappeared.

"You a baseball fan, Sergeant?"

I looked up. "How are you?"

"Fine," Grossbart said. "They're making a soldier out of me."

"How are Fishbein and Halpern?"

"Coming along," he said. "We've got no training this afternoon. They're at the movies."

"How come you're not with them?"

"I wanted to come over and say hello."

He smiled—a shy regular-guy smile, as though he and I well knew that our friendship drew its sustenance from unexpected visits, remembered birthdays, and borrowed lawnmowers. At first it offended me, and then the feeling was swallowed by the general uneasiness I felt at the thought that everyone on the post was locked away in a dark movie theatre and I was here alone with Grossbart. I folded up my paper.

"Sergeant," he said, "I'd like to ask a favor. It is a favor, and I'm making no bones about it."

He stopped, allowing me to refuse him a hearing—which, of course, forced me into a courtesy I did not intend. "Go ahead."

"Well, actually it's two favors."

I said nothing.

"The first one's about these rumors. Everybody says we're going to the Pacific."

"As I told your friend Fishbein, I don't know," I said. "You'll just have to wait to find out. Like everybody else."

"You think there's a chance of any of us going East?"

"Germany?" I said. "Maybe."

"I meant New York."

"I don't think so, Grossbart. Offhand."

"Thanks for the information, Sergeant," he said.

"It's not information, Grossbart. Just what I surmise."

"It certainly would be good to be near home. My parents—you know." He took a step toward the door and then turned back. "Oh, the other thing. May I ask the other?"

"What is it?"

"The other thing is—I've got relatives in St. Louis, and they say they'll give me a whole Passover dinner if I can get down there. God, Sergeant, that'd mean an awful lot to me."

I stood up. "No passes during basic, Grossbart."

"But we're off from now till Monday morning, Sergeant. I could leave the post and no one would even know."

"I'd know. You'd know."

"But that's all. Just the two of us. Last night, I called my aunt, and you should have heard her. 'Come—come,' she said. 'I got gefilte fish, *chrain* [6]—the works!' Just a day, Sergeant. I'd take the blame if anything happened."

"The Captain isn't here to sign a pass."

"You could sign."

"Look, Grossbart—"

[6] *Chrain.* Horseradish.

"Sergeant, for two months, practically, I've been eating *trafe* till I want to die."

"I thought you'd made up your mind to live with it. To be minus a little bit of heritage."

He pointed a finger at me. "You!" he said. "That wasn't for you to read."

"I read it. So what?"

"That letter was addressed to a congressman."

"Grossbart, don't feed me any baloney. You *wanted* me to read it."

"Why are you persecuting me, Sergeant?"

"Are you kidding!"

"I've run into this before," he said, "but never from my own!"

"Get out of here, Grossbart! Get the hell out of my sight!"

He did not move. "Ashamed, that's what you are," he said. "So you take it out on the rest of us. They say Hitler himself was half a Jew. Hearing you, I wouldn't doubt it."

"What are you trying to do with me, Grossbart?" I asked him. "What are you after? You want me to give you special privileges, to change the food, to find out about your orders, to give you weekend passes."

"You even talk like a goy!" Grossbart shook his fist. "Is this just a weekend pass I'm asking for? Is a Seder sacred, or not?"

Seder! It suddenly occurred to me that Passover had been celebrated weeks before. I said so.

"That's right," he replied. "Who says no? A month ago—and I was in the field eating hash! And now all I ask is a simple favor. A Jewish boy I thought would understand. My aunt's willing to go out of her way—to make a Seder a month later. . . ." He turned to go, mumbling.

"Come back here!" I called. He stopped and looked at me. "Grossbart, why can't you be like the rest? Why do you have to stick out like a sore thumb?"

"Because I'm a Jew, Sergeant. I *am* different. Better, maybe not. But different."

"This is a war, Grossbart. For the time being *be* the same."

"I refuse."

"What?"

"I refuse. I can't stop being me, that's all there is to it." Tears

came to his eyes. "It's a hard thing to be a Jew. But now I understand what Mickey says—it's a harder thing to stay one." He raised
a hand sadly toward me. "Look at *you*."

"Stop crying!"

"Stop this, stop that, stop the other thing! *You* stop, Sergeant.
Stop closing your heart to your own!" And, wiping his face with
his sleeve, he ran out the door. "The least we can do for one another
—the least . . ."

An hour later, looking out of the window, I saw Grossbart
headed across the field. He wore a pair of starched khakis and
carried a little leather ditty bag. I went out into the heat of the
day. It was quiet; not a soul was in sight except, over by the mess
hall, four K.P.s sitting around a pan, sloped forward from their
waists, gabbing and peeling potatoes in the sun.

"Grossbart!" I called.

He looked toward me and continued walking.

"Grossbart, get over here!"

He turned and came across the field. Finally, he stood before me.

"Where are you going?" I asked.

"St. Louis. I don't care."

"You'll get caught without a pass."

"So I'll get caught without a pass."

"You'll go to the stockade."

"I'm *in* the stockade." He made an about-face and headed off.

I let him go only a step or two. "Come back here," I said, and he
followed me into the office, where I typed out a pass and signed
the Captain's name, and my own initials after it.

He took the pass and then, a moment later, reached out and
grabbed my hand. "Sergeant, you don't know how much this
means to me."

"O.K.," I said. "Don't get in any trouble."

"I wish I could show you how much this means to me."

"Don't do me any favors. Don't write any more congressmen
for citations."

He smiled. "You're right, I won't. But let me do something."

"Bring me a piece of that gefilte fish. Just get out of here."

"I will!" he said. "With a slice of carrot and a little horseradish.
I won't forget."

"All right. Just show your pass at the gate. And don't tell *any-*

body."

"I won't. It's a month late, but a good Yom Tov to you."

"Good Yom Tov, Grossbart," I said.

"You're a good Jew, Sergeant. You like to think you have a hard heart, but underneath you're a fine, decent man. I mean that."

Those last three words touched me more than any words from Grossbart's mouth had the right to. "All right, Grossbart," I said. "Now call me 'sir,' and get the hell out of here."

He ran out the door and was gone. I felt very pleased with myself; it was a great relief to stop fighting Grossbart, and it had cost me nothing. Barrett would never find out, and if he did, I could manage to invent some excuse. For a while, I sat at my desk comfortable in my decision. Then the screen door flew back and Grossbart burst in again. "Sergeant!" he said. Behind him I saw Fishbein and Halpern, both in starched khakis, both carrying ditty bags like Grossbart's.

"Sergeant, I caught Mickey and Larry coming out of the movies. I almost missed them."

"Grossbart—did I say tell no one?" I said.

"But my aunt said I could bring friends. That I should, in fact."

"*I'm* the Sergeant, Grossbart—not your aunt!"

Grossbart looked at me in disbelief. He pulled Halpern up by his sleeve. "Mickey, tell the Sergeant what this would mean to you."

Halpern looked at me and, shrugging, said, "A lot."

Fishbein stepped forward without prompting. "This would mean a great deal to me and my parents, Sergeant Marx."

"No!" I shouted.

Grossbart was shaking his head. "Sergeant, I could see you denying me, but how you can deny Mickey, a Yeshiva boy—that's beyond me."

"I'm not denying Mickey anything," I said. "You just pushed a little too hard, Grossbart. *You* denied him."

"I'll give him my pass, then," Grossbart said. "I'll give him my aunt's address and a little note. At least let him go."

In a second, he had crammed the pass into Halpern's pants pocket. Halpern looked at me, and so did Fishbein. Grossbart was at the door, pushing it open. "Mickey, bring me a piece of gefilte fish, at least," he said, and then he was outside again.

The three of us looked at one another, and then I said, "Halpern, hand that pass over."

He took it from his pocket and gave it to me. Fishbein had now moved to the doorway, where he lingered. He stood there for a moment with his mouth slightly open, and then he pointed to himself. "And me?" he asked.

His utter ridiculousness exhausted me. I slumped down in my seat and felt pulses knocking at the back of my eyes. "Fishbein," I said, "you understand I'm not trying to deny you anything, don't you? If it was my Army, I'd serve gefilte fish in the mess hall. I'd sell *kugel* [7] in the PX, honest to God."

Halpern smiled.

"You understand, don't you, Halpern?"

"Yes, Sergeant."

"And you, Fishbein? I don't want enemies. I'm just like you—I want to serve my time and go home. I miss the same things you miss."

"Then, Sergeant," Fishbein said, "why don't you come, too?"

"Where?"

"To St. Louis. To Shelly's aunt. We'll have a regular Seder. Play hide-the-matzo." He gave me a broad, black-toothed smile.

I saw Grossbart again, on the other side of the screen.

"Pst!" He waved a piece of paper. "Mickey, here's the address. Tell her I couldn't get away."

Halpern did not move. He looked at me, and I saw the shrug moving up his arms into his shoulders again. I took the cover off my typewriter and made out passes for him and Fishbein. "Go," I said. "The three of you."

I thought Halpern was going to kiss my hand.

That afternoon, in a bar in Joplin, I drank beer and listened with half an ear to the Cardinal game. I tried to look squarely at what I'd become involved in, and began to wonder if perhaps the struggle with Grossbart wasn't as much my fault as his. What was I that I had to *muster* generous feelings? Who was I to have been feeling so grudging, so tight-hearted? After all, I wasn't being asked to move the world. Had I a right, then, or a reason, to clamp down on Grossbart, when that meant clamping down on Halpern, too?

[7] *Kugel.* Pudding.

And Fishbein—that ugly, agreeable soul? Out of the many recollections of my childhood that had tumbled over me these past few days, I heard my grandmother's voice: "What are you making a *tsimmes?*" [8] It was what she would ask my mother when, say, I had cut myself while doing something I shouldn't have done, and her daughter was busy bawling me out. I needed a hug and a kiss, and my mother would moralize. But my grandmother knew—mercy overrides justice. I should have known it, too. Who was Nathan Marx to be such a penny pincher with kindness? Surely, I thought, the Messiah himself—if He should ever come—won't niggle over nickels and dimes. God willing, he'll hug and kiss.

The next day, while I was playing softball over on the parade ground, I decided to ask Bob Wright, who was noncom in charge of Classification and Assignment, where he thought our trainees would be sent when their cycle ended, in two weeks. I asked casually, between innings, and he said, "They're pushing them all into the Pacific. Shulman cut the orders on your boys the other day."

The news shocked me, as though I were the father of Halpern, Fishbein, and Grossbart.

That night, I was just sliding into sleep when someone tapped on my door. "Who is it?" I asked.

"Sheldon."

He opened the door and came in. For a moment, I felt his presence without being able to see him. "How was it?" I asked.

He popped into sight in the near-darkness before me. "Great, Sergeant." Then he was sitting on the edge of the bed. I sat up.

"How about you?" he asked. "Have a nice weekend?"

"Yes."

"The others went to sleep." He took a deep, paternal breath. We sat silent for a while, and a homey feeling invaded my ugly little cubicle; the door was locked, the cat was out, the children were safely in bed.

"Sergeant, can I tell you something? Personal?"

I did not answer, and he seemed to know why. "Not about me. About Mickey. Sergeant, I never felt for anybody like I feel for him. Last night I heard Mickey in the bed next to me. He was

[8] *Tsimmes.* A dish made with carrots, involving complicated preparation, hence "to make a *tsimmes*" means to make a fuss.

crying so, it could have broken your heart. Real sobs."

"I'm sorry to hear that."

"I had to talk to him to stop him. He held my hand, Sergeant—
he wouldn't let it go. He was almost hysterical. He kept saying if
he only knew where we were going. Even if he knew it *was* the
Pacific, that would be better than nothing. Just to know."

Long ago, someone had taught Grossbart the sad rule that only
lies can get the truth. Not that I couldn't believe in the fact of
Halpern's crying: his eyes *always* seemed red-rimmed. But, fact
or not, it became a lie when Grossbart uttered it. He was entirely
strategic. But then—it came with the force of indictment—so was
I! There are strategies of aggression, but there are strategies of
retreat as well. And so, recognizing that I myself had not been
without craft and guile, I told him what I knew. "It is the Pacific."

He let out a small gasp, which was not a lie. "I'll tell him. I wish
it was otherwise."

"So do I."

He jumped on my words. "You mean you think you could do
something? A change, maybe?"

"No, I couldn't do a thing."

"Don't you know anybody over at C. and A.?"

"Grossbart, there's nothing I can do," I said. "If your orders
are for the Pacific, then it's the Pacific."

"But Mickey—"

"Mickey, you, me—everybody, Grossbart. There's nothing to
be done. Maybe the war'll end before you go. Pray for a miracle."

"But—"

"Good night, Grossbart." I settled back, and was relieved to feel
the springs unbend as Grossbart rose to leave. I could see him
clearly now; his jaw had dropped, and he looked like a dazed prize-
fighter. I noticed for the first time a little paper bag in his hand.

"Grossbart," I smiled. "My gift?"

"Oh, yes, Sergeant. Here—from all of us." He handed me the
bag. "It's egg roll."

"Egg roll?" I accepted the bag and felt a damp grease spot on the
bottom. I opened it, sure that Grossbart was joking.

"We thought you'd probably like it. You know—Chinese egg
roll. We thought you'd probably have a taste for—"

"Your aunt served egg roll?"

"She wasn't home."

"Grossbart, she invited you. You told me she invited you and your friends."

"I know," he said. "I just reread the letter. *Next* week."

I got out of bed and walked to the window. "Grossbart," I said. But I was not calling to him.

"What?"

"What are you, Grossbart? Honest to God, what are you?"

I think it was the first time I'd asked him a question for which he didn't have an immediate answer.

"How can you do this to people?" I went on.

"Sergeant, the day away did us all a world of good. Fishbein, you should see him, he *loves* Chinese food."

"But the Seder," I said.

"We took second best, Sergeant."

Rage came charging at me. I didn't sidestep. "Grossbart, you're a liar!" I said. "You're a schemer and a crook. You've got no respect for anything. Nothing at all. Not for me, for the truth—not even for poor Halpern! You use us all—"

"Sergeant, Sergeant, I feel for Mickey. Honest to God, I do. I *love* Mickey. I try—"

"You try! You feel!" I lurched toward him and grabbed his shirt front. I shook him furiously. "Grossbart, get out! Get out and stay the hell away from me. Because if I see you, I'll make your life miserable. *You understand that?*"

"Yes."

I let him free, and when he walked from the room, I wanted to spit on the floor where he had stood. I couldn't stop the fury. It engulfed me, owned me, till it seemed I could only rid myself of it with tears or an act of violence. I snatched from the bed the bag Grossbart had given me and, with all my strength, threw it out the window. And the next morning, as the men policed the area around the barracks, I heard a great cry go up from one of the trainees, who had been anticipating only his morning handful of cigarette butts and candy wrappers. "Egg roll!" he shouted. "Holy Christ, Chinese goddam egg roll!"

A week later, when I read the orders that had come down from C. and A., I couldn't believe my eyes. Every single trainee was to

382 · PHILIP ROTH

be shipped to Camp Stoneman, California, and from there to the Pacific—every trainee but one. Private Sheldon Grossbart. He was to be sent to Fort Monmouth, New Jersey. I read the mimeographed sheet several times. Dee, Farrell, Fishbein, Fuselli, Fylypowicz, Glinicki, Gromke, Gucwa, Halpern, Hardy, Helebrandt, right down to Anton Zygadlo—all were to be headed West before the month was out. All except Grossbart. He had pulled a string, and I wasn't it. I lifted the phone and called C. and A.

The voice on the other end said smartly, "Corporal Shulman, sir."

"Let me speak to Sergeant Wright."

"Who is this calling, sir?"

"Sergeant Marx."

And, to my surprise, the voice said, "*Oh!*" Then, "Just a minute, Sergeant."

Shulman's "*Oh!*" stayed with me while I waited for Wright to come to the phone. Why "*Oh!*"? Who was Shulman? And then, so simply, I knew I'd discovered the string that Grossbart had pulled. In fact, I could hear Grossbart the day he'd discovered Shulman in the PX, or in the bowling alley, or maybe even at services. "Glad to meet you. Where you from? Bronx? Me, too. Do you know So-and-So? And So-and-So? Me, too! You work at C. and A.? Really? Hey, how's chances of getting East? Could you do something? Change something? Swindle, cheat, lie? We gotta help each other, you know. If the Jews in Germany . . ."

Bob Wright answered the phone. "How are you, Nate? How's the pitching arm?"

"Good. Bob, I wonder if you could do me a favor." I heard clearly my own words, and they so reminded me of Grossbart that I dropped more easily than I could have imagined into what I had planned. "This may sound crazy, Bob, but I got a kid here on orders to Monmouth who wants them changed. He had a brother killed in Europe, and he's hot to go to the Pacific. Says he'd feel like a coward if he wound up Stateside. I don't know, Bob—can anything be done? Put somebody else in the Monmouth slot?"

"Who?" he asked cagily.

"Anybody. First guy in the alphabet. I don't care. The kid just asked if something could be done."

"What's his name?"

"Grossbart, Sheldon."

Wright didn't answer.

"Yeah," I said. "He's a Jewish kid, so he thought I could help him out. You know."

"I guess I can do something," he finally said. "The Major hasn't been around here for weeks. Temporary duty to the golf course. I'll try, Nate, that's all I can say."

"I'd appreciate it, Bob. See you Sunday." And I hung up, perspiring.

The following day, the corrected orders appeared: Fishbein, Fuselli, Fylypowicz, Glinicki, Gromke, Grossbart, Gucwa, Halpern, Hardy . . . Lucky Private Harley Alton was to go to Fort Monmouth, New Jersey, where, for some reason or other, they wanted an enlisted man with infantry training.

After chow that night, I stopped back at the orderly room to straighten out the guard-duty roster. Grossbart was waiting for me. He spoke first.

"You son of a bitch!"

I sat down at my desk, and while he glared at me, I began to make the necessary alterations in the duty roster.

"What do you have against me?" he cried. "Against my family? Would it kill you for me to be near my father, God knows how many months he has left to him?"

"Why so?"

"His heart," Grossbart said. "He hasn't had enough troubles in a lifetime, you've got to add to them. I curse the day I ever met you, Marx! Shulman told me what happened over there. There's no limit to your anti-Semitism, is there? The damage you've done here isn't enough. You have to make a special phone call! You really want me dead!"

I made the last few notations in the duty roster and got up to leave. "Good night, Grossbart."

"You owe me an explanation!" He stood in my path.

"Sheldon, you're the one who owes explanations."

He scowled. "To *you?*"

"To me, I think so—yes. Mostly to Fishbein and Halpern."

"That's right, twist things around. I owe nobody nothing, I've done all I could do for them. Now I think I've got the right to watch out for myself."

"For each other we have to learn to watch out, Sheldon. You told me yourself."

"You call this watching out for me—what you did?"

"No. For all of us."

I pushed him aside and started for the door. I heard his furious breathing behind me, and it sounded like steam rushing from an engine of terrible strength.

"You'll be all right," I said from the door. And, I thought, so would Fishbein and Halpern be all right, even in the Pacific, if only Grossbart continued to see—in the obsequiousness of the one, the soft spirituality of the other—some profit for himself.

I stood outside the orderly room, and I heard Grossbart weeping behind me. Over in the barracks, in the lighted windows, I could see the boys in their T shirts sitting on their bunks talking about their orders, as they'd been doing for the past two days. With a kind of quiet nervousness, they polished shoes, shined belt buckles, squared away underwear, trying as best they could to accept their fate. Behind me, Grossbart swallowed hard, accepting his. And then, resisting with all my will an impulse to turn and seek pardon for my vindictiveness, I accepted my own.

J. F. POWERS

A Losing Game

Father Fabre, coming from the bathroom, stopped and knocked at the pastor's door—something about the door had said, Why not? No sound came from the room, but the pastor had a ghostly step and there he was, opening the door an inch, giving his new curate a glimpse of the green eyeshade he wore and of the chaos in which he dwelt. Father Fabre saw the radio in the unmade bed, the correspondence, pamphlets, the folding money, and all the rest of it—what the bishop, on an official visitation, barging into the room and then hurriedly backing out, had passed off to the attending clergy as "a little unfinished business."

"Yes? Yes?"

"How about that table you promised me?"

The pastor just looked at him.

"The one for my room, remember? Something to put my typewriter on."

"See what I can do."

The pastor had said that before. Father Fabre said, "I'm using the radiator now."

The pastor nodded, apparently granting him permission to continue using it.

Father Fabre put down the old inclination to give up. "I thought you said you'd fix me up, Father."

"See what I can do, Father."

"Now?"

"Busy now."

The pastor started to close the door, which was according to the rules of their little game, but Father Fabre didn't budge, which was not according to the rules.

"Tell you what I'll do, Father," he said. "I'll just look around in the basement and you won't have to bother. I know how busy you are." Father Fabre had a strange feeling that he was getting somewhere with the pastor. Everything he'd said so far had been right, but he had to keep it up. "Of course I'll need to know the combination." He saw the pastor buck and shudder at the idea of telling anyone the combination of the lock that preserved his treasures.

"Better go with you," the pastor said, feeling his throat.

Father Fabre nodded. This was what he'd had in mind all the time. While the pastor was inside his room looking for his collar (always a chance of meeting a parishioner on the stairs), Father Fabre relaxed and fell to congratulating himself. He had been tough and it had worked. The other thing had proved a waste of time.

After a bit, though, Father Fabre took another view of the situation, knowing as he did so that it was the right one, that the door hadn't just happened to shut after the pastor, that the man wasn't coming out. Oh, that was it. The pastor had won again. He was safe in his room again, secure in the knowledge that his curate wouldn't knock and start up the whole business again, not for a while anyway.

Father Fabre went away. Going downstairs, he told himself that though he had lost, he had extended the pastor as never before, and would get the best of him yet.

Father Fabre sensed John, the janitor, before he saw him sitting in the dark under the staircase, at one of his stations. He might be found in this rather episcopal chair, which was also a hall-tree, or on a box in the furnace room, or in the choir loft behind the organ, or in the visiting priest's confessional. There were probably other places which Father Fabre didn't know about. John moved around a lot, foxlike, killing time.

Father Fabre switched on the light. John pulled himself together and managed a smile, his glasses as always frosted over with dust so that he seemed to be watching you through basement windows.

"John, you know that lock on the door of the church basement?"

John nodded.

"It's not much of a lock. Think we can open it?"

John frowned.

"A tap on the side?"

John shook his head.

"No?"

"Sorry, Father."

"So." Father Fabre turned away.

"Will you need a hammer, Father?"

"Don't think I'll need one. Sure you won't come along?"

"Awful busy, Father." But John found time to get up and accompany Father Fabre to the iron staircase that led to the church basement. There they parted. Father Fabre snapped the light switch on the wall. He wasn't surprised when nothing happened. He left the door open for light. A half flight down, pausing, he hearkened to John's distant footsteps, rapidly climbing, and then he went winding down into the gloom. At the bottom he seated himself on a step and waited.

Soon he heard a slight noise above. Rounding the last turn, descending into view, was the pastor. "Oh, there you are," said Father Fabre, rising.

The pastor voiced no complaint—and why should he? He'd lost a trick, but Father Fabre had taken it honorably, according to the rules, in a manner worthy of the pastor himself.

Father Fabre was up on his toes, straining to see.

The pastor was fooling with something inside the fuse box on the wall, standing up to it, his back almost a shield against Father Fabre's eyes. Overhead a bulb lit up. So that was it, thought Father Fabre, coming down to earth—and to think that he'd always blamed the wiring for the way some of the lights didn't work around the church and rectory, recommending a general check-up, prophesying death by conflagration to the pastor. Father Fabre, rising again, saw the pastor screw in another fuse where none had been before. That would be the one controlling the basement lights.

The pastor dealt next with the door, dropping into a crouch to dial the lock.

Father Fabre leaned forward like an umpire for the pitch, but saw at once that it would be impossible to lift the combination. He scraped his foot in disgust, grinding a bit of fallen plaster. The pastor's fingers tumbled together. He seemed to be listening. After a moment, he began to dial again, apparently having to start all over.

"There," he said finally. He removed the lock, threw open the door, but before he went in, he stepped over to the fuse box. The overhead light went out. Father Fabre entered the basement, where he had been only once before, and not very far inside then. The pastor secured the door behind them. From a convenient clothes tree he removed a black cap and put it on—protection against the dust? Father Fabre hadn't realized that the pastor, who now looked like a burglar in an insurance ad, cared. The pastor glanced at him. Quickly Father Fabre looked away. He gazed around him in silence.

It was impossible to decide what it all meant. In the clothes tree alone, Father Fabre noted a cartridge belt, a canteen stenciled

388 · J. F. POWERS

with the letters U.S., a pair of snowshoes, an old bicycle tire of wrinkled red rubber, a beekeeper's veil. One of Father Fabre's first services to the pastor had been to help John carry two work-benches into the basement. At that time he had thought the pastor must have plans for a school in which manual training would be taught. Now he felt that the pastor had no plans at all for any of the furniture and junk. A few of the unemployed statues when seen at a distance, those with their arms extended, appeared to be trying to get the place straightened up, carrying things, but on closer examination they, too, proved to be preoccupied with a higher kind of order, and carrying crosiers.

The pastor came away from a rack containing billiard cues, ski poles, and guns.

"Here," he said, handing an air rifle to Father Fabre.

Father Fabre accepted the gun, tipped it, listening to the BB shot bowling up and down inside. "What's this for?"

"Rats."

"Couldn't kill a rat with this, could I?"

"Could."

But Father Fabre noticed that the pastor was arming himself with a .22 rifle. "What's that?" he asked covetously.

"This gun's not accurate," said the pastor. "From a shooting gallery."

"What's wrong with trapping 'em?"

"Too smart."

"How about poison?"

"Die in the walls."

The pastor moved off, bearing his gun in the way that was supposed to assure safety.

Father Fabre held his gun the same way and followed the pastor. He could feel the debris closing in, growing up behind him. The path ahead appeared clear only when he looked to either side. He trailed a finger in the dust on a table top, revealing the grain. He stopped. The wood was maple, he thought, maple oiled and aged to the color of saddle leather. There were little niches de-signed to hold glasses. The table was round, a whist table, it might be, and apparently sound. Here was a noble piece of furniture that would do wonders for his room. It could be used for his pur-poses, and more. That might be the trouble with it. The pastor was strong for temperance. It might not be enough for Father Fabre to deplore the little niches.

"Oh, Father."

The pastor retraced his steps.

"This might do," Father Fabre said grudgingly, careful not to betray a real desire. There was an awful glazed green urn thing in the middle of the table which Father Fabre feared would leave scratches or a ring. A thing like that, which might have spent its best days in a hotel, by the elevators, belonged on the floor. Father Fabre wanted to remove it from the table, but he controlled himself.

"Don't move," said the pastor. "Spider."

Father Fabre held still while the pastor brushed it off his back. "Thanks." Father Fabre relaxed and gazed upon the table again. He had to have it. He would have it.

But the pastor was moving on.

Father Fabre followed in his steps, having decided to say nothing just then, needing more time to think. The important thing was not to seem eager. "It isn't always what we want that's best for us," the pastor had said more than once. He loved to speak of Phil Mooney—a classmate of Father Fabre's—who had been offered a year of free study at a major secular university, but who had been refused permission by the bishop. Young Mooney, as the pastor said, had taken it so well . . . "This—how about this?" said Father Fabre. He had stopped before a nightstand, a little tall for typing. "I could saw the legs off some."

The pastor, who had paused, now went ahead again, faster.

Father Fabre lifted his gun and followed again, wondering if he'd abused the man's sensibilities, some article of the accumulator's creed. He saw a piano stool well suited to his strategy. This he could give up with good grace. "Now here's something," he said. "I wouldn't mind having this." He sounded as though he thought he could get it too.

The pastor glanced back and shook his head. "Belongs upstairs."

"Oh, I see," said Father Fabre submissively. There was no piano in the rectory, unless that, too, was in the pastor's room.

The pastor, obviously pleased with his curate's different tone, stopped to explain. "A lot of this will go upstairs when we're through remodeling."

Father Fabre forgot himself. "*Remodeling?*" he said, and tried to get the pastor to look him in the eye.

The pastor turned away.

Father Fabre, who was suddenly seeing his error, began to reflect upon it. There was no material evidence of remodeling, it was true, but he had impugned the pastor's good intentions. Was there a pastor worth his salt who didn't have improvements in mind, contractors and costs on the brain?

They moved deeper into the interior. Above them the jungle joined itself in places now. Father Fabre passed under the full length of a ski without taking notice of it until confronted by its triangular head, arching down at him. He shied away. Suddenly the pastor stopped. Father Fabre pulled up short, cradling his gun, which he'd been using as a cane. Something coiled on the trail?

"How's this?" said the pastor. He was trying the drawers of a pitiful old sideboard affair with its mirrors out and handles maimed, a poor, blind thing. "Like this?" he said. He seemed to have no idea what they were searching for.

"I need something to type on," Father Fabre said bluntly.

The pastor hit the trail again, somehow leaving the impression that Father Fabre was the one who was being difficult.

They continued to the uttermost end of the basement. Here they were confronted by a small mountain of pamphlets. In the bowels of the mountain something moved.

The pastor's hands shifted on his gun. "They're in there," he whispered, and drew back a pace. He waved Father Fabre to one side, raised the gun, and pumped lead into the pamphlets. *Sput-flub. Sput-flub. Sput-spong-spit.*

Father Fabre reached for his left leg, dropped to his knees, his gun clattering down under him. He grabbed up his trouser leg and saw the little hole bleeding in his calf. It hurt, but not as much as he would've thought.

The pastor came over to examine the leg. He bent down. "Just a flesh wound," he said, straightening up. "You're lucky."

"*Lucky!*"

"Tire there at the bottom of the pile. Absorbed most of the fire power. Bullet went through and ricocheted. You're lucky.

Here." The pastor was holding out his hand.

"Oh, no," said Father Fabre, and lowered his trouser leg over the wound.

The pastor seemed to be surprised that Father Fabre wouldn't permit him to pinch the bullet out with his dirty fingers.

Father Fabre stood up. The leg held him, but his walking would be affected. He thought he could feel some blood in his sock. "Afraid I'll have to leave you," he said. He glanced at the pastor, still seeking sympathy. And there it was, at last, showing in the pastor's face, some sympathy, and words were on the way—no, caught again in the log jam of the man's mind and needing a shove if they were to find their way down to the mouth, and so Father Fabre kept on looking at the pastor, shoving . . .

"Sorry it had to happen," muttered the pastor. Apparently that was going to be all. He was picking up Father Fabre's gun.

Painfully, Father Fabre began to walk. Sorry! That it *had* to happen! Anyone else, having fired a shot, would've been only too glad to assume the blame. What kind of man was this? This was a man of very few words, as everyone knew, and he had said he was sorry. How sorry then? Sorry enough?

Father Fabre stopped. "How about this?" he said, sounding as if he hadn't asked about the maple table before. It was a daring maneuver, but he was giving the pastor a chance to reverse himself without losing face, to redeem himself . . .

The pastor was shaking his head.

Father Fabre lost patience. He'd let the old burglar shoot him down and this was what he got for it. "Why not?" he demanded.

The pastor was looking down, not meeting Father Fabre's eye. "You don't have a good easy chair, do you?"

Father Fabre, half turning, saw what the pastor had in mind. There just weren't any words for the chair. Father Fabre regarded it stoically—the dust lying fallow in the little mohair furrows, the ruptured bottom—and didn't know what to say. It would be impossible to convey his true feelings to the pastor. The pastor really did think that this was a good easy chair. There was no way to get at the facts with him. But the proper study of curates is pastors. "It's *too* good," Father Fabre said, making the most of his opportunity. "If I ever sat down in a chair like that I might never get up again. No, it's not for me."

Oh, the pastor was pleased—the man was literally smiling. Of a self-denying nature himself, famous for it in the diocese, he saw the temptation that such a chair would be to his curate.

"No?" he said, and appeared, besides pleased, relieved.

"No, thanks," said Father Fabre briskly, and moved on. It might be interesting to see how far he could go with the man—but some other time. His leg seemed to be stiffening.

When they arrived back at the door, the pastor, in a manner that struck Father Fabre as too leisurely under the circumstances, racked the guns, hung up his cap, boxed the dust out of his knees and elbows, all the time gazing back where they'd been—not, Father Fabre thought, with the idea of returning to the rats as soon as he decently could, but with the eyes of a game conservationist looking to the future.

"I was thinking I'd better go to the hospital with this," said Father Fabre. He felt he ought to tell the pastor that he didn't intend to let the bullet remain in his leg.

He left the pastor to lock up, and limped out.

"Better take the car," the pastor called after him.

Father Fabre pulled up short. "*Thanks*," he said, and began to climb the stairs. The hospital was only a few blocks away, but it hadn't occurred to him that he might have walked there. He was losing every trick. Earlier he had imagined the pastor driving him to the hospital, and the scene there when they arrived—how it would be when the pastor's indifference to his curate's leg became apparent to the doctors and nurses, causing their hearts to harden against him. But all this the pastor had doubtless foreseen, and that was why he wasn't going along. The man was afraid of public opinion.

At the hospital, however, they only laughed when Father Fabre told them what had happened to him, and when, after they had taken the bullet out, he asked if they had to report the matter to the police. Just laughed at him. Only a flesh wound, they said. They didn't even want him to keep off the leg. It had been a mistake for him to ask. Laughed. Told him just to change his sock. But he arranged for the pastor to get the bill. And, on leaving, although he knew nothing would come of it, he said, "I thought you were required by law to report *all* gunshot cases."

When he returned to the rectory, the pastor and John were talking softly in the upstairs hall. They said nothing to him, which he thought strange, and so he said nothing to them. He was lucky, he guessed, that they hadn't laughed. He limped into his room, doubting whether John had even been told, and closed the door with a little bang. He turned and stood still. Then, after a few moments in which he realized why the pastor and John were in the hall, he limped over to the window—to the old mohair chair.

Ruefully, he recalled his false praise of the chair. How it had cost him! For the pastor had taken him at his word. After the shooting accident, the pastor must have been in no mood to give Father Fabre a table in which he seemed only half interested. Nothing would do then but that the wounded curate be compensated with the object of his only enthusiasm in the basement. No one knew better than the pastor where soft living could land a young priest, and yet there it was—luxury itself, procured by the pastor and dragged upstairs by his agent and now awaiting his curate's pleasure. And to think it might have been the maple table!

They clearly hadn't done a thing to the chair. The dust was all there, every grain intact. They were waiting for him, the pastor and John, waiting to see him sitting in it. He thought of disappointing them, of holing up as the pastor had earlier. But he just couldn't contend with the man any more that day. He didn't know how he'd ever be able to thank them. John for carrying it up from the basement, the pastor for the thing itself, but he limped over to the door to let them in. Oh, it was a losing game.

DAN JACOBSON

Beggar My Neighbour

Michael saw them for the first time when he was coming home from school one day. One moment the street had been empty, glittering in the light from the sun behind Michael's back, with no traffic on the roadway and apparently no pedestrians on the broad sandy pavement; the next moment these two were before him, their faces raised to his. They seemed to emerge directly in front of him, as if the light and shade of the glaring street had suddenly condensed itself into two little piccanins with large eyes set in their round, black faces.

'*Stukkie brood?*' the elder, a boy, said in a plaintive voice. A piece of bread. At Michael's school the slang term for any African child was just that: *stukkie brood*. That was what African children were always begging for.

'*Stukkie brood?*' the little girl said. She was wearing a soiled white dress that was so short it barely covered her loins; there seemed to be nothing at all beneath the dress. She wore no socks, no shoes, no cardigan, no cap or hat. She must have been about ten years old. The boy, who wore a torn khaki shirt and a pair of grey shorts much too large for him, was about Michael's age, about twelve, though he was a little smaller than the white boy. Like the girl, the African boy had no shoes or socks. Their limbs were painfully thin; their wrists and ankles stood out in knobs, and the skin over these protruding ones was rougher than elsewhere. The dirt on their skin showed up as a faint grayness against the black.

'I've got no bread,' the white boy said. He had halted in his surprise at the suddenness of their appearance before him. They must have been hiding behind one of the trees that were planted at intervals along the pavement. 'I don't bring bread from school.'

They did not move. Michael shifted his school case from one hand to the other and took a pace forward. Silently, the African children stood aside. As he passed them, Michael was conscious of the movement of their eyes; when he turned to look back he saw that they were standing still to watch him go. The boy was holding one of the girl's hands in his.

It was this that made the white child pause. He was touched by their dependence on one another, and disturbed by it too, as he had been by the way they had suddenly come before him, and by their watchfulness and silence after they had uttered their customary, begging request. Michael saw again how ragged and dirty they were, and thought of how hungry they must be. Surely he could give them a piece of bread. He was only three blocks from home.

He said, 'I haven't got any bread here. But if you come home with me, I'll see that you get some bread. Do you understand?'

They made no reply; but they obviously understood what he had said. The three children moved down the pavement, the two piccanins as silent as the shadows that slid over the rough sand ahead of them. The Africans walked a little behind Michael, and to one side of him. Once Michael asked them if they went to school, and the boy shook his head; when Michael asked them if they were brother and sister, the boy nodded.

When they reached Michael's house, he went inside and told Dora, the cook-girl, that there were two piccanins in the lane outside, and that he wanted her to cut some bread and jam for them. Dora grumbled that she was not supposed to look after every little beggar in town, and Michael answered her angrily, 'We've got lots of bread. Why shouldn't we give them some?' He was particularly indignant because he felt that Dora, being of the same race as the two outside, should have been even readier than he was to help them. When Dora was about to take the bread out to the back gate, where the piccanins waited, Michael stopped her. 'It's all right, Dora,' he said in a tone of reproof, 'I'll take it,' and he went out into the sunlight, carrying the plate in his hand.

396 · DAN JACOBSON

'*Stukkie brood*,' he called out to them. 'Here's your *stukkie brood*.'

The two children stretched their hands out eagerly, and Michael let them take the inch-thick slices from the plate. He was pleased to see that Dora had put a scraping of apricot jam on the bread. Each of the piccanins held the bread in both hands, as if afraid of dropping it. The girl's mouth worked a little, but she kept her eyes fixed on the white boy.

'What do you say?' Michael asked.

They replied in high, clear voices, 'Thank you, baas.'

'That's better. Now you can eat.' He wanted to see them eat it; he wanted to share their pleasure in satisfying their strained appetites. But without saying a word to him, they began to back away, side by side. They took a few paces, and then they turned and ran along the lane towards the main road they had walked down earlier. The little girl's dress fluttered behind her, white against her black body. At the corner they halted, looked back once, and then ran on, out of sight.

A few days later, at the same time and in the same place, Michael saw them again, on his way home from school. They were standing in the middle of the pavement, and he saw them from a long way off. They were obviously waiting for him to come. Michael was the first to speak, as he approached them.

'What? Another piece of bread?' he called out from a few yards away.

'Yes, baas,' they answered together. They turned immediately to join him as he walked by. Yet they kept a respectful pace or two behind.

'How did you know I was coming?'

'We know the baas is coming from school.'

'And how do you know that I'm going to give you bread?'

There was no reply; not even a smile from the boy, in response to Michael's. They seemed to Michael, as he glanced casually at them, identical in appearance to a hundred, a thousand, other piccanins, from the peppercorns on top of their heads to their wide, calloused, sand-grey feet.

When they reached the house, Michael told Dora, 'Those *stukkie broods* are waiting outside again. Give them something, and then they can go.'

Dora grumbled once again, but did as she was told. Michael did not go out with the bread himself; he was in a hurry to get back to work on a model car he was making, and was satisfied to see, out of his bedroom window, Dora coming from the back gate a few minutes later with an empty plate in her hand. Soon he had forgotten all about the two children. He did not go out of the house until a couple of hours had passed; by then it was dusk, and he took a torch with him to help him find a piece of wire for his model in the darkness of the lumber-shed. Handling the torch gave Michael a feeling of power and importance, and he stepped into the lane with it, intending to shine it about like a policeman on his beat. Immediately he opened the gate, he saw the two little piccanins standing in the half-light, just a few paces away from him.

'What are you doing here?' Michael exclaimed in surprise.

The boy answered, holding his head up, as if warning Michael to be silent. 'We were waiting to say thank you to the baas.'

'What!' Michael took a step towards them both, and they stood their ground, only shrinking together slightly.

For all the glare and glitter there was in the streets of Lynd-hurst by day, it was winter, midwinter; and once the sun had set a bitter chill came into the air, as swiftly as the darkness. The cold at night wrung deep notes from the contracting iron roofs of the houses, and froze the fish-ponds in all the fine gardens of the white suburbs. Already Michael could feel its sharp touch on the tips of his ears and fingers. And the two African children stood there barefoot, in a flimsy dress and torn shirt, waiting to thank him for the bread he had had sent out to them.

'You mustn't wait,' Michael said. In the half-darkness he saw the white dress on the girl more clearly than the boy's clothing; and he remembered the nakedness and puniness of her black thighs. He stretched his hand out, with the torch in it. 'Take it,' he said. The torch was in his hand, and there was nothing else that he could give to them. 'It's nice,' he said. 'It's a torch. Look.' He switched it on and saw in its beam of light a pair of startled eyes, darting desperately from side to side. 'You see how nice it is,' Michael said, turning the beam upwards, where it lost itself against the light that lingered in the sky. 'If you don't want it, you can sell it. Go on, take it.'

A hand came up and took the torch from him. Then the two children ran off, in the same direction they had taken on the first afternoon. When they reached the corner all the street lights came on, as if at a single touch, and the children stopped and stared at them, before running on. Michael saw the torch glinting in the boy's hand, and only then did it occur to him that despite their zeal to thank him for the bread they hadn't thanked him for the torch. The size of the gift must have surprised them into silence, Michael decided; and the thought of his own generosity helped to console him for the regret he couldn't help feeling when he saw the torch being carried away from him.

Michael was a lonely child. He had neither brothers nor sisters; both his parents worked during the day, and he had made few friends at school. But he was not by any means unhappy in his loneliness. He was used to it, in the first place; and then, because he was lonely, he was all the better able to indulge himself in his own fantasies. He played for hours, by himself, games of his own invention—games of war, of exploration, of seafaring, of scientific invention, of crime, of espionage, of living in a house beneath or above his real one. It was not long before the two African children, who were now accosting him regularly, appeared in some of his games, for their weakness, poverty, and dependence gave Michael ample scope to display in fantasy his kindness, generosity, courage and decisiveness. Sometimes in his games Michael saved the boy's life, and was thanked for it in broken English. Sometimes he saved the girl's, and then she humbly begged his pardon for having caused him so much trouble. Sometimes he was just too late to save the life of either, though he tried his best, and then there were affecting scenes of farewell.

But in real life, Michael did not play with the children at all: they were too dirty, too ragged, too strange, too persistent. Their persistence eventually drove Dora to tell Michael's mother about them; and his mother did her duty by telling Michael that on no account should he play with the children, nor should he give them anything of value.

'Play with them!' Michael laughed at the idea. And apart from bread and the torch he had given them nothing but a few old toys, a singlet or two, a pair of old canvas shoes. No one could begrudge them those gifts. And the truth was that Michael's mother begrudged the piccanins neither the old toys and clothes nor the bread. What she was anxious to do was simply to prevent her son playing with the piccanins, fearing that he would pick up germs, bad language, and 'kaffir ways' generally from them, if he did. Hearing both from Michael and Dora that he did not play with them at all, and that he had never even asked them into the back yard, let alone the house, Michael's mother was satisfied.

They came to Michael about once a week, meeting him as he walked back from school, or simply waiting for him outside the back gate. The spring winds had already blown the cold weather away, almost overnight, and still the children came. Their words of thanks varied neither in tone nor length, whatever Michael gave them; but they had revealed, in response to his questions, that the boy's name was Frans and the girl's name was Annie, that they lived in Green Point Location, and that their mother and father were both dead. During all this time Michael had not touched them, except for the fleeting contact of their hands when he passed a gift to them. Yet sometimes Michael wished that they were more demonstrative in their expressions of gratitude to him; he thought that they could, for instance, seize his hand and embrace it; or go down on their knees and weep, just once. As it was, he had to content himself with fantasies of how they spoke of him among their friends, when they returned to the tumbled squalor of Green Point Location; of how incredulous their friends must be to hear their stories about the kind white *klein-baas* who gave them food and toys and clothing.

One day Michael came out to them carrying a possession he particularly prized—an elaborate pen and pencil set which had been given to him for a recent birthday. He had no intention of giving the outfit to the African children, and he did not think that he would be showing off with it in front of them. He merely wanted to share his pleasure in it with someone who had not already seen it. But as soon as he noticed the way the children were looking at the open box, Michael knew the mistake he had made. 'This isn't for you,' he said abruptly. The children blinked soundlessly, staring from the box to Michael and back to the box again. 'You can just look at it,' Michael said. He held the box tightly in his hand, stretching it forward, the pen and the propelling pencils shining inside the velvet-lined case. The two heads of the children came together over the box; they stared deeply into it.

At last the boy lifted his head. 'It's beautiful,' he breathed out. As he spoke, his hand slowly came up towards the box.

'No,' Michael said, and snatched the box away.

'Baas?'

'No.' Michael retreated a little, away from the beseeching eyes, and the uplifted hand.

'Please, baas, for me?'

And his sister said, 'For me also, baas.'

'No, you can't have this.' Michael attempted to laugh, as if at the absurdity of the idea. He was annoyed with himself for having shown them the box, and at the same time shocked at them for having asked for it. It was the first time they had asked for anything but bread.

'Please, baas. It's nice.' The boy's voice trailed away on the last word, in longing; and then his sister repeated the word, like an echo, her own voice trailing away too. 'Ni-ice.'

'No! I won't give it to you! I won't give you anything if you ask for this. Do you hear?'

Their eyes dropped, their hands came together, they lowered their heads. Being sure now that they would not again ask for the box, Michael relented. He said, 'I'm going in now, and I'll tell Dora to bring you some bread.'

But Dora came to him in his room a few minutes later. 'The little kaffirs are gone.' She was holding the plate of bread in her hand. Dora hated the two children, and Michael thought there was some kind of triumph in her voice and manner as she made the announcement.

He went outside to see if she was telling the truth. The lane was empty. He went to the street, and looked up and down its length, but there was no sign of them there either. They were gone. He had driven them away. Michael expected to feel guilty; but to his own intense surprise he felt nothing of the kind. He was relieved that they were gone, and that was all.

When they reappeared a few days later, Michael felt scorn towards them for coming back after what had happened on the last occasion. He felt they were in his power. 'So you've come back?' he greeted them. 'You like your *stukkies brood*, hey? You're hungry, so today you'll wait, you won't run away.'

'Yes, baas,' they said, in their low voices.

Michael brought the bread out to them; when they reached for it he jokingly pulled the plate back and laughed at their surprise. Then only did he give them the bread.

'Thank you, baas.'

'Thank you, baas.'

They ate the bread in Michael's presence; watching them, he felt a little more kindly disposed towards them. 'All right, you can come another day, and there'll be some more bread for you.'

'Thank you, baas.'

'Thank you, baas.'

They came back sooner than Michael had expected them to. He gave them their bread and told them to go. They went off, but again did not wait for the usual five or six days to pass, before approaching him once more. Only two days had passed, yet here they were with their eternal request—'*Stukkie brood*, baas?'

Michael said, 'Why do you get hungry so quickly now?' But he gave them their bread.

When they appeared in his games and fantasies, Michael no longer rescued them, healed them, casually presented them with kingdoms and motor-cars. Now he ordered them about, sent them away on disastrous missions, picked them out to be shot for cowardice in the face of the enemy. And because something similar to these fantasies was easier to enact in the real world than his earlier fantasies, Michael soon was ordering them about unreasonably in fact. He deliberately left them waiting; he sent them away and told them to come back on days when he knew he would be in town; he told them there was no bread in the house. And when he did give them anything, it was bread only now; never old toys or articles of clothing.

So, as the weeks passed, Michael's scorn gave way to impatience and irritation, irritation to anger. And what angered him most was that the two piccanins seemed too stupid to realize what he now felt about them, and instead of coming less frequently, continued to appear more often than ever before. Soon they were coming almost every day, though Michael shouted at them and teased them, left them waiting for hours, and made them do tricks and sing songs for their bread. They did everything he told them to do; but they altogether ignored his instructions as to which days they should come. Invariably, they would be waiting for him, in the shade of one of the trees that grew alongside the main road from school, or standing at the gate behind the house with sand scuffed up about their bare toes. They were as silent as before; but more persistent, inexorably persistent. Michael took to walking home by different routes, but they were not to be so easily discouraged. They simply waited at the back gate, and whether he went into the house by the front or the back gate he could not avoid seeing their upright, unmoving figures.

Finally, he told them to go and never come back at all. Often he had been tempted to do this, but some shame or pride had always prevented him from doing it; he had always weakened previously, and named a date, a week or two weeks ahead, when they could come again. But now he shouted at them, 'It's finished! No more bread—nothing! Come on, *voetsak!* If you come back I'll tell the garden-boy to chase you away.'

From then on they came every day. They no longer waited right at the back gate, but squatted in the sand across the lane. Michael was aware of their eyes following him when he went by, but they did not approach him at all. They did not even get up from the ground when he passed. A few times he shouted at them to go, and stamped his foot, but he shrank from hitting them. He did not want to touch them. Once he sent out Jan, the garden-boy, to drive them away; but Jan, who had hitherto always shared Dora's views on the piccanins, came back muttering angrily and incomprehensibly to himself; and when Michael peeped into the lane he saw that they were still there. Michael tried to ignore them, to pretend he did not see them. He hated them now; even more, he began to dread them.

But he did not know how much he hated and feared the two piccanins until he fell ill with a cold, and lay feverish in bed for a few days. During those days the two children were constantly in his dreams, or in his half-dreams, for even as he dreamed he knew he was turning on his bed; he was conscious of the sun shining outside by day, and at night of the passage-light that had been left on inside the house. In these dreams he struck and struck again at the children with weapons he found in his hands; he fled in fear from them down lanes so thick with sand his feet could barely move through it; he committed lewd, cruel acts upon the bare-thighed girl, and her brother shrieked to tell the empty street of what he was doing. Michael struck out at him with a piece of heavy cast-iron guttering. Its edge dug sharply into Michael's hands as the blow fell, and when he lifted the weapon he saw the horror he had made of the side of the boy's head, and how the one remaining eyeball still stared unwinkingly at him.

Michael thought he was awake, and suddenly calm. The fever seemed to have left him. It was as though he had slept deeply, for days, after that last dream of violence; yet his impression was that he had woken directly from it. The bedclothes felt heavy on him, and he threw them off. The house was quite silent. He got out of bed and went to look at the clock in the kitchen: it was early afternoon. Dora and Jan were resting in their rooms across the yard, as they always did after lunch. Outside, the light of the sun was unremitting, a single golden glare. He walked back to his bedroom; there, he put on his dressing-gown and slippers, feeling the coolness inside his slippers on his bare feet. He went through the kitchen again, quietly, and on to the back stoep, and then across the back yard. The sun seemed to seize the back of his neck as firmly as a hand grasping, and its light was so bright he was aware of it only as a darkness beyond the little stretch of ground he looked down upon. He opened the back gate. Inevitably, as he had known they would be, the two were waiting.

He did not want to go beyond the gate in his pyjamas and dressing-gown, so, shielding his eyes from the glare with one hand, he beckoned them to him with the other. Together, in silence, they rose and crossed the lane. It seemed to take them a long time to come to him, but at last they stood in front of him, with their hands interlinked. Michael stared into their dark faces, and they stared into his.

'What are you waiting for?' he asked.

'For you.' First the boy answered; then the girl repeated, 'For you.'

Michael looked from the one to the other; and he remembered what he had been doing to them in his dreams. Their eyes were black to look into, deep black. Staring forward, Michael understood what he should have understood long before: that they came to him not in hope or appeal or even in reproach, but in hatred. What he felt towards them, they felt towards him; what he had done to them in his dreams, they did to him in theirs.

The sun, their staring eyes, his own fear came together in a sound that seemed to hang in the air of the lane—a cry, the sound of someone weeping. Then Michael knew that it was he who was crying. He felt the heat of the tears in his eyes, he felt the moisture running down his cheeks. And with the same fixity of decision that had been his in his dreams of violence and torture, Michael knew what he must do. He beckoned them forward, closer. They came. He stretched out his hands, he felt under his fingers the springy hair he had looked at so often before from the distance between himself and them; he felt the smooth skin of their faces; their frail, rounded shoulders, their hands. Their hands were in his, and he led them inside the gate.

He led them into the house, through the kitchen, down the passage, into his room, where they had never been before. They looked about at the pictures on the walls, the toys on top of the low cupboard, the twisted white sheets and tumbled blankets on the bed. They stood on both sides of him, and for the first time since he had met them, their lips parted into slow, grave smiles. And Michael knew that what he had to give them was not toys or clothes or bread, but something more difficult. Yet it was not difficult at all, for there was nothing else he could give them. He took the girl's face in his hands and pressed his lips to hers. He was aware of the darkness of her skin, and the smell of it, and of the faint movement of her lips, a single pulse that beat momentarily against his own. Then it was gone. He kissed the boy, too, and let them go. They came together, and grasped each other by the hand, staring at him.

'What do you want now?' he asked.

A last anxiety flickered in Michael and left him, as the boy slowly shook his head. He began to step back, pulling his sister with him; when he was through the door he turned his back on Michael and they walked away down the passage. Michael watched them go. At the door of the kitchen, on their way out of the house, they paused, turned once more, and lifted their hands, the girl copying the boy, in a silent, tentative gesture of farewell.

Michael did not follow them. He heard the back gate swing

open and then bang when it closed. He went wearily back to his bed, and as he fell upon it, his relief and gratitude that the bed should be there to receive him, changed suddenly into grief at the knowledge that he was already lying upon it—that he had never left it.

His cold grew worse, turned into bronchitis, kept him in bed for several weeks. But his dreams were no longer of violence; they were calm, spacious, and empty of people. As empty as the lane was, when he was at last allowed out of the house, and made his way there immediately, to see if the children were waiting for him.

He never saw them again, though he looked for them in the streets and lanes of the town. He saw a hundred, a thousand, children like them; but not the two he hoped to find.

JAMES AGEE

The Waiting

A few minutes before ten, the phone rang. Mary hurried to quiet it. "Hello?"

The voice was a man's, wiry and faint, a country voice. It was asking a question, but she could not hear it clearly.

"Hello?" she asked again. "Will you please talk a little louder? I can't hear. . . . I said I can't hear you! Will you talk a little louder, please? . . . Thank you."

Now, straining and impatient, she could hear, though the voice seemed still to come from a great distance.

"Is this Miz Jay Follet?"

"Yes; what is it?" (for there was a silence); "yes, this is she."

After further silence the voice said, "There's been a slight—your husband has been in a accident."

His head! she told herself.

"Yes," she said, in a caved-in voice.

At the same moment the voice said, "A serious accident."

"Yes," Mary said more clearly.

"What I wanted to ask, is there a man in his family, some kin, could come out? We'd appreciate it you could send a man out here, right away."

"Yes; yes, there's my brother. Where should he come to?"

"I'm out at Powell Station, at Brannick's blacksmith shop, bout twelve miles out the Ball Camp Pike."

"Brannick's bl—"

"B-r-a-n-n-i-c-k. It's right on the left of the Pike comin out just a little way this side, Knoxvul side of Bell's Bridge." She heard muttering, and another muttering voice. "Tell him he can't miss it. We'll keep the light on and a lantern out in front."

"Do you have a doctor?"

"How's that again, ma'am?"

"A doctor, do you have one? Should I send a doctor?"

"That's all right, ma'am. Just some man that's kin."

"He'll come right out just as fast as he can." Walter's auto, she thought. "Thank you very much for calling."

"That's all right, ma'am. I sure do hate to give you bad news."

"Good night."

"Goodbye, ma'am."

She found she was scarcely standing, she was all but hanging from the telephone. She stiffened her knees, leaned against the wall, and rang.

"Andrew?"

"Mary?" her brother said.

She drew a deep breath.

"Mary."

She drew another deep breath; she felt as if her lungs were not large enough.

"Mary?"

Dizzy, seeing gray, trying to control her shaking voice, she said, "Andrew, there's been an— A man just phoned, from Powell's Station, about twelve miles out towards La Follette, and he says—he says Jay—has met with a very serious accident. He wants—"

"Oh, my God, Mary!"

"He said they want some man of his family to come out just as soon as possible and—help bring him in, I guess."

"I'll call Walter Starr, he'll take me out."

"Yes, do, will you, Andrew?"

"Of course I will. Just a minute."

"What?"

"Aunt Hannah."

"May I speak to her when you're through?"

"Certainly. Where is he hurt, Mary?"

"He didn't say."

"Well, didn't you—no matter."

"No I didn't," she said, now realizing with surprise that she had not. "I guess because I was so sure. Sure it's his head, that is."

"Do they—shall I get Dr. Dekalb?"

"He says no; just you."

"I guess there's already a doctor there."

"I guess."

"I'll call Wa—wait, here's Aunt Hannah."

"Mary."

"Aunt Hannah, Jay is in a serious accident, Andrew has to go out. Would you come up and wait with me and get things ready just in case? Just in case he's well enough to be brought home and not the hospital?"

"Certainly, Mary. Of course I will."

"And will you tell Mama and Papa not to worry, not to come out, give them my love. We might as well just be calm as we can, till we know."

"Of course we must. I'll be right up."

"Thank you, Aunt Hannah."

She went into the kitchen and built a quick fire and put on a large kettle of water and a small kettle, for tea. The phone rang.

"Mary! Where do I go!"

"Why, Powell's Station, out the Pike towards—"

"I know, but exactly where? Didn't he say?"

"He said Brannick's blacksmith shop. B-r-a-n-n-i-c-k. Do you hear?"

"Yes. Brannick."

"He said they'll keep the lights on and you can't miss it. It's just to the left of the Pike just this side of Bell's Bridge. Just a little way this side."

"All right, Mary, Walter will come by here and we'll bring Aunt Hannah on our way."

"All right. Thank you, Andrew."

She put on more kindling and hurried into the downstairs bedroom. How do I know, she thought; he didn't even say; I didn't even ask. By the way he talks he may be— She whipped off the coverlet, folded it, and smoothed the pad. I'm just simply not going to think about it until I know more, she told herself. She hurried to the linen closet and brought clean sheets and pillowcases. He didn't say whether there was a doctor there or not. She spread a sheet, folded it under the foot of the mattress, pulled it smooth, and folded it under all around. Then she spread her palms along it; it was cold and smooth beneath her hands and it brought her great hope. O God, let him be well enough to come home where I can take care of him, where I can take *good* care of him. How good to rest! That's all right, ma'am. Just some man that's kin. She spread the top sheet. That's all right, ma'am. That can mean anything. It can mean there's a doctor there and although it's serious he has it in hand, under control, it isn't so dreadfully bad, although he did say it's serious, or it can . . . A light blanket, this weather. Two, case it turns cool. She hurried and got them, unaware whether she was making such noise as might wake the children and unaware that even in this swiftness she was moving, by force of habit, almost silently. Just some man that's kin. That means it's bad, or he'd ask for me. No, I'd have to stay with the children. But *he* doesn't know there are children. My place'd be home anyhow, getting things ready, he knows that. He didn't suggest getting anything ready. He knew I'd know. He is a man, wouldn't occur to him. She took the end of a pillow between her teeth and pulled the slip on and plumped it and put it in place. She took the end of the second pillow between her teeth and bit it so hard the roots of her teeth ached, and pulled the slip on and plumped it. Then she set the first pillow up on edge and set the second pillow on edge against it and plumped them both and smoothed them and stood away and looked at them with her head on one side, and for a moment she saw him sitting up in bed with a tray on his knees as he had sat when he strained his back, and he looked at her, almost but not quite smiling, and she could hear his voice, grouchy, pretending to be, for the fun of it. If it's his head, she remembered, perhaps he'll have to lie very flat.

How do I know? How do I know?

She left the pillows as they were, and turned down the bed on that side, next the window, and smoothed it. She carefully re-folded the second blanket and laid it on the lower foot of the bed—no, it would bother his poor feet. She hung it over the foot-board. She stood looking at the carefully made bed, and for a few seconds she was not sure where she was or why she was doing this. Then she remembered and said "oh," in a small, stupefied, soft voice. She opened the window, top and bottom, and when the curtains billowed she tied them back more tightly. She went to the hall closet and brought out the bedpan and rinsed and dried it and put it under the bed. She went to the medicine chest and took out the thermometer, shook it, washed it in cool water, dried it, and put it beside the bed in a tumbler of water. She saw that the hand towel which covered this table was dusty, and threw it into the dirty-clothes hamper, and replaced it with a fresh one, and replaced that with a dainty linen guest towel upon the border of which pansies and violets were embroidered. She saw that the front pillow had sagged a little, and set it right. She pulled down the shade. She turned out the light and dropped to her knees, facing the bed, and closed her eyes. She touched her forehead, her breastbone, her left shoulder and her right shoulder, and clasped her hands.

"O God, if it by Thy will," she whispered. She could not think of anything more. She made the sign of the Cross again, slowly, deeply, and widely upon herself, and she felt something of the shape of the Cross: strength and quiet.

"Thy will be done." And again she could think of nothing more. She got up from her knees and, without turning on the light or glancing towards the bed, went into the kitchen. The water for tea had almost boiled away. The water in the large kettle was scarcely tepid. The fire was almost out. While she was putting in more kindling, she heard them on the porch.

Hannah came in with her hands stretched out and Mary extended her own hands and took them and kissed her cheek while at the same instant they said "Mary" and "my dear"; then Hannah hurried to put her hat on the rack. Andrew stayed at the open door and did not speak but merely kept looking into Mary's eyes; his own eyes were as hard and bright as those of a bird and they spoke to her of a cold and bitter incredulity, as if he were accusing something or someone (even perhaps his sister) that it was useless beyond words to accuse. She felt that he was saying, "And you can still believe in that idiotic God of yours?" Walter Starr stayed back in the darkness; Mary could just see the large lenses of his glasses, and the darkness of his mustache and of his heavy shoulders.

"Come in, Walter," she said, and her voice was as overwarm as if she were coaxing a shy child.

"We can't stop," Andrew said sharply.

Walter came forward and took her hand, and gently touched her wrist with his other hand. "We shan't be long," he said.

"Bless you," Mary murmured, and so pressed his hand that her arm trembled.

He patted her trembling wrist four times rapidly, turned away saying, "Better be off, Andrew," and went towards his automobile. She could hear that he had left the engine running, and now she realized all the more clearly how grave matters were.

"Everything's ready here in case—you know—he's—well enough to be brought home," Mary told Andrew.

"Good. I'll phone, the minute I know. Anything."

"Yes, dear."

His eyes changed, and abruptly his hand reached out and caught her shoulder. "Mary, I'm so sorry," he said, almost crying.

"Yes, dear," she said again, and felt that it was a vacuous reply; but by the time this occurred to her, Andrew was getting into the automobile. She stood and watched until it had vanished and, turning to go in, found that Hannah was at her elbow.

"Let's have some tea," she said. "I've hot water all ready," she said over her shoulder as she hurried down the hall.

Let her, Hannah thought, following. By all means.

"Goodness no, it's boiled away! Sit down, Aunt Hannah, it'll be ready in a jiff." She hustled to the sink.

"Let me—" Hannah began; then knew better, and hoped that Mary had not heard.

"What?" She was drawing the water.

"Just let me know, if there's anything I can help with."

"Not a thing, thank you." She put the water on the stove.

"Goodness, sit down." Hannah took a chair by the table.

"Everything is ready that I can think of," Mary said. "That we can know about, yet." She sat at the opposite side of the table. "I've made up the downstairs bedroom" (she waved vaguely towards it), "where he stayed when his poor back was sprained, you remember." (Of course I do, Hannah thought; let her talk.) "It's better than upstairs. Near the kitchen and bathroom both and no stairs to climb, and of course if need be, that is, if he needs a nurse, night nursing, we can put her in the dining room and eat in the kitchen, or even set up a cot right in the room with him; put up a screen; or if she minds that, why she can just sleep on the living-room davenport and keep the door open between. Don't you think?"

"Certainly," Hannah said.

"I think I'll see if I can possibly get Celia, Celia Gunn, if she's available, or if she's on a case she can possibly leave; it'll be so much nicer for everyone to have someone around who is an old friend, really one of the family, rather than just a complete stranger, don't you think?"

Hannah nodded.

"Even though of course Jay doesn't specially— Of course she's really an old friend of mine, rather than Jay's. Still, I think it would be more, well, harmonious, don't you think?"

"Yes indeed."

"But I guess it's just as well to wait till we hear from Andrew, not—create any needless disturbance, I guess. After all, it's very possible he'll have to be taken straight to a hospital. The man *did* say it was serious, after all."

"I think you're wise to wait," Hannah said.

"How's that water?" Mary twisted in her chair to see. "Sakes alive, the watched pot." She got up and stuffed in more kindling, and brought down the box of tea. "I don't know's I really want any tea, anyway, but I think it's a good idea to drink something warm while we're waiting, don't you?"

"I'd like some," said Hannah, who wanted nothing.

"Good, then we'll have some. Just as soon as the water's ready." She sat down again. "I thought one light blanket would be enough on a night like this but I've another over the foot of the bed in case it should turn cool."

"That should be sufficient."

"Goodness knows," Mary said vaguely, and became silent. She looked at her hands, which lay loosely clasped on the table. Hannah found that she was watching Mary closely. In shame, she focussed her sad eyes a little away from her. She wondered. It was probably better for her not to face it if she could help until it had to be faced. If it had to be. Just quiet, she said to herself. Just be quiet.

"You know," Mary said slowly, "the queerest thing." She began slowly to turn and rub her clasped fingers among each other. Hannah waited. "When the man phoned," she said, gazing quietly upon her moving fingers, "and said Jay had been in a—serious accident" (and now Hannah realized that Mary was looking at her, and met her brilliant gray eyes), "I felt it just as certainly as I'm sitting here now: 'It's his head.' What do you think of that?" she asked, almost proudly.

Hannah looked away. What's one to say, she wondered. Yet Mary had spoken with such conviction that she herself was half convinced. She looked into an image of still water, clear and very deep, and even though it was dark, and she had not seen so clearly since her girlhood, she could see sand and twigs and dead leaves at the bottom of the water. She drew a deep breath and let it out in a long slow sigh and clucked her tongue once. "We never know," she murmured.

"Of course, we just have to wait," Mary said, after a long silence.

"Hyesss," Hannah said softly, sharply inhaling the first of the word, and trailing the sibilant to a hair.

Through their deep silence, at length, they began to be aware of the stumbling crackle of the water. When Mary got up for it, it had boiled half away.

"There's still plenty for two cups," she said, and prepared the strainer and poured them, and put on more water. She lifted the lid of the large kettle. Its sides, below the waterline, were richly beaded; from the bottom sprang a leisured spiral of bubbles so small they resembled white sand; the surface of the water slowly circled upon itself. She wondered what the water might possibly be good for.

"Just in case," she murmured.

Hannah decided not to ask her what she had said.

"There's Zu-Zus," Mary said, and got them from the cupboard. "Or would you like bread and butter? Or toast. I could toast some."

"Just tea, thank you."

"Help yourself to sugar and milk. Or lemon? Let's see, do I have le—"

"Milk, thank you."

"Me, too." Mary sat down again. "My, it's frightfully *hot* in here!" She got up and opened the door to the porch, and sat down again.

"I wonder what ti—" She glanced over her shoulder at the kitchen clock. "What time did they leave, do you know?"

"Walter came for us at quarter after ten. About twenty-five after, I should think."

"Let's see, Walter drives pretty fast, though not so fast as Jay, but he'd be driving faster than usual tonight, and it's just over twelve miles. That would be, supposing he goes thirty miles an hour, that's twelve miles in, let's see, six times four is twenty-four, six times five's thirty, twice twelve is twenty-four. Sakes alive, I was always dreadful at arithmetic. . . ."

"Say about half an hour, allowing for darkness, and Walter isn't familiar with those roads."

"Then we ought to be hearing pretty soon. Ten minutes. Fifteen at the outside."

"Yes, I should think."

"Maybe twenty, allowing for the roads, but that is a good road out that far, as roads go."

"Maybe."

"Why didn't he *tell* me!" Mary burst out.

"What is it?"

"Why didn't I *ask?*" She looked at her aunt in furious bewilderment. "I didn't even *ask! How* serious! *Where* is he hurt! Is he living or *dead!*"

There it is, Hannah said to herself. She looked back steadily into Mary's eyes.

"That we simply have to wait to find out," she said.

"Of *course* we have," Mary cried angrily. "That's what's so *unbearable!*" She drank half her tea at a gulp; it burned her painfully but she scarcely noticed. She continued to glare at her aunt.

Hannah could think of nothing to say.

"I'm sorry," Mary said. "You're perfectly right. I've just got to hold myself together, that's all."

"Never mind," Hannah said, and they fell silent.

Hannah knew that silence must itself be virtually unbearable for Mary, and that it would bring her face to face with likelihoods still harder to endure. But she has to, she told herself; and the sooner the better. But she found that she herself could not bear to be present and say nothing which might in some degree protect, and postpone. She was about to speak when Mary burst out: "In heaven's *name*, why didn't I ask him! *Why* didn't I? Didn't I *care?*"

"It was so sudden," Hannah said. "It was such a shock."

"You *would* think I'd *ask*, though! Wouldn't you?"

"You thought you knew. You told me you were sure it was his—in the head."

"But how *bad? What!*"

We both know, Hannah said to herself. But it's better if you bring yourself to say it. "It certainly wasn't because you didn't care, anyway," she said.

"No. No, it certainly wasn't that, but I think I do know what it was. I think, I think I must have been too afraid of what he would have to say."

Hannah looked into her eyes. Nod, she told herself. Say yes I imagine so. Just say nothing and it'll be just as terrible for her. She heard herself saying what she had intended to venture a while before, when Mary had interrupted her: "Do you understand why your father stayed home, and your mother?"

"Because I asked them not to come."

"Why did you?"

"Because if all of you come up here in a troop like that, it would be like assuming that—like assuming the very worst before we even know."

"That's why they stayed home. Your father said he knew you'd understand."

"Of course I do."

Neither of them spoke of another reason—her mother's deafness, which required them to bellow into an ear trumpet anything that they wanted to say to her.

"We just must try to keep from making any assumptions—*good* or bad," Hannah said.

"I know. I know we must. It's just, this waiting in the dark like this, it's just more than I can stand."

"We ought to hear very soon."

Mary glanced at the clock. "Almost any minute," she said.

She took a little tea.

"I just can't help wondering," she said, "why he didn't say *more*. 'A serious accident,' he said. Not a 'very' serious one. Just 'serious.' Though, goodness knows, that's serious enough. But why couldn't he *say?*"

"As your father says, it's ten to one he's just a plain damned fool," Hannah said.

"But it's such an *important* thing to say, and so *simple* to say, at least to give some general idea about. At least whether he could come home, or go to a hospital, or . . . He didn't say anything about an ambulance. An ambulance would mean hospital, almost for sure. And surely if he meant the—the *very* worst, he'd have just said so straight out and not leave us all on tenterhooks. I know it's just what we have no earthly business guessing about, good *or* bad, but really it does seem to me there's every good reason for hope, Aunt Hannah. It seems to me that if—"

The telephone rang; its sound frightened each of them as deeply as either had experienced in her lifetime. They looked at each other and got up and turned towards the hall. "I . . ." Mary said, waving her right hand at Hannah as if she would wave her out of existence.

Hannah stopped where she stood, bowed her head, closed her eyes, and made the sign of the Cross.

Mary lifted the receiver from its hook before the second ring, but for a moment she could neither put it to her ear, nor speak.

"God, *help me, help me*," she whispered. "Andrew?"

"Poll?"

"Papa!" Relief and fear were equal in her. "Have you heard anything?"

"You've heard?"

"No," she said. "*Have you heard from Andrew?*"

"No. Thought you might have by now."

"No. Not yet. Not yet."

"I must have frightened you."

"Never mind, Papa. It's all right."

"Sorry as hell, Poll. I shouldn't have phoned."

"Never mind."

"Let us know, quick's you hear anything."

"Of course I will, Papa. I promise. Of course I will."

"Shall we come up?"

"No, bless you, Papa, it's better not, yet. No use getting all worked up till we *know*, is there?"

"That's my girl!"

"My love to Mama."

"Hers to you. Mine, too, needless to say. You let us know."

"Certainly. Goodbye."

"Poll."

"Yes?"

"You know how I feel about this."

"I do, Papa, and thank you. There's no need to say it."

"Couldn't if I tried. Ever. And for Jay as much as you, and your mother, too. You understand."

"I do understand, Papa. Goodbye."

"It's only Papa," she said, and sat down, heavily.

"Thought Andrew had phoned."

"Yes . . ." She drank tea. "He scared me half out of my wits."

"He had no business phoning. He was a perfect fool to phone."

"I don't blame him. I think it's even worse for them, sitting down there, than for us here."

"I've no doubt it is hard."

"Papa feels things a lot more than he shows."

"I know. I'm glad you realize it."

"I realize how very much he really does think of Jay."

"Great—heavens, I should hope you do!"

"Well, for a long time there was no reason to be sure," Mary retorted with spirit. "Or Mama either." She waited a moment. "You and her, Aunt Hannah," she said. "You know that. You tried not to show it, but I knew and you knew I did. It's all right, it has been for a long time, but you do know that."

Hannah continued to meet her eyes. "Yes, it's true, Mary. There were all kinds of—terrible misgivings; and not without good reason, as you both came to know."

"Plenty of good reasons," Mary said. "But that didn't make it any easier for us."

"Not for any of us," Hannah said. "Particularly you and Jay, but your mother and father, too, you know. Anyone who loved you."

"I know. I *do* know, Aunt Hannah. I don't know how I got onto this track. There's nothing there to resent any more, or worry over, or be grieved by, for any of us, and hasn't been for a long time, thank God. Why on earth did I get *off* on such a tangent! Let's not say another word about it!"

"Just one word more, because I'm not sure you've ever quite known it. Have you ever realized how very highly your father *always* thought of Jay, right from the very beginning?"

Mary looked at her, sensitively and suspiciously. She thought carefully before she spoke. "I know he's *told* me so. But every time he told me, he was warning me, too. I know that, as time passed, he came to think a great deal of Jay."

"He thinks the world of him," Hannah rapped out.

"But, no, I never quite believed he really liked him, or respected him, from the first, and I never will. I think it was just some kind of soft soap."

"Is your father a man for soft soap?"

"No"—she smiled a little—"he certainly isn't, ordinarily. But what *am* I to make of it? Here he was praising Jay to the skies on the one hand and on the other, why practically in the same breath, telling me one reason after another why it would be plain foolhardiness to marry him. What would *you* think!"

"Can't you see that both things might be so—or that he might very sincerely have felt that both things were so, rather?"

Mary thought a moment. "I don't know, Aunt Hannah. No, I don't see quite how."

"You learned how yourself, Mary."

"Did I?"

"You learned there was a lot in what your father—in all our misgivings, but learning it never changed your essential opinion of him, did it? You found you could realize both things at once."

"That's true. Yes. I did."

"We had to learn more and more that was good. You had to learn more and more that wasn't so good."

Mary looked at her with smiling defiance. "All the same, blind as I began it," she said, "I was more right than Papa, wasn't I? It wasn't a *mistake*. Papa was right there'd be trouble—more than he'll ever know or any of you—but it *wasn't* a mistake. Was it?"

Don't *ask* me, child, *tell* me, Hannah thought. "Obviously not," she said.

Mary was quiet a few moments. Then she said, shyly and proudly, "In these past few months, Aunt Hannah, we've come to a—kind of harmoniousness that—that . . ." She began to shake her head. "I've no business talking about it." Her voice trembled. "Least of all right now!" She bit her lips together, shook her head again, and swallowed some tea noisily. "The way we've been talking," she blurted, her voice full of tea, "it's just like a post-mortem!" She struck her face into her hands and was shaken by tearless sobbing. Hannah subdued an impulse to go to her side. "God help her," she whispered. "God keep her." After a little while Mary looked up at her; her eyes were quiet and amazed. "If he dies," she said, "if he's dead, Aunt Hannah, I don't know what I'll do. I just don't know what I'll do."

"God help you," Hannah said; she reached across and took her hand. "God keep you." Mary's face was working. "You'll do well. Whatever it is, you'll do well. Don't you doubt it. Don't you fear." Mary subdued her crying. "It's well to be ready for the worst," Hannah continued. "But we mustn't forget, we don't know yet."

At the same instant, both looked at the clock.

"Certainly by very soon now, he should phone," Mary said. "Unless *he's* had an accident!" She laughed sharply.

"Oh soon, I'm sure," Hannah said. Long before now, she said to herself, if it were anything but the worst. She squeezed Mary's clasped hands, patted them, and withdrew her own hand, feeling there's so little comfort anyone can give, it'd better be saved for when it's needed most.

Mary did not speak, and Hannah could not think of a word to say. It was absurd, she realized, but along with everything else she felt almost a kind of social embarrassment about her speechlessness.

But after all, she thought, what *is* there to say! What earthly help am I, or anyone else?

She felt so heavy, all of a sudden, and so deeply tired that she wished she might lean her forehead against the edge of the table.

"We've simply got to wait," Mary said.

"Yes," Hannah sighed.

I'd better drink some tea, she thought, and did so. Lukewarm and rather bitter, somehow it made her feel even more tired.

They sat without speaking for fully two minutes.

"At least we're given the mercy of a little time," Mary said slowly, "awful as it is to have to wait. To try to prepare ourselves for whatever it may be." She was gazing studiously into her empty cup.

Hannah felt unable to say anything.

"Whatever it is," Mary went on, "it's already over and done with." She was speaking virtually without emotion; she was absorbed beyond feeling, Hannah became sure, in what she was beginning to find out and to face. Now she looked up at Hannah and they looked steadily into each other's eyes.

"One of three things," Mary said slowly. "Either he's badly hurt but he'll live, and at best even get thoroughly well, and at worst be a helpless cripple or an invalid or his mind impaired." Hannah wished that she might look away, but she knew that she must not. "Or he is so terribly hurt that he will die of it, maybe quite soon, maybe after a long, terrible struggle, maybe breathing his last at this very minute and wondering where I am, why I'm not beside him." She set her teeth for a moment and tightened her lips, and spoke again, evenly: "Or he was gone already when the man called and he couldn't bear to be the one to tell me, poor thing.

"One, or the other, or the other. And no matter what, there's not one thing in this world *or* the next that we can do or hope or guess at or wish or pray that can change it or help it one iota. Because whatever is, is. That's all. And all there is now is to be ready for it, strong enough for it, whatever it may be. That's all. That's all that matters. It's all that matters because it's all that's possible. Isn't that so?"

While she was speaking, she was with her voice, her eyes, and with each word opening in Hannah those all but forgotten hours, almost thirty years past, during which the cross of living had first nakedly borne in upon her being, and she had made the first beginnings of learning how to endure and accept it. *Your turn now, poor child*, she thought; she felt as if a prodigious page were being silently turned, and the breath of its turning touched her heart with cold and tender awe. Her soul is beginning to come of age, she thought; and within those moments she herself became much older, much nearer her own death, and was content to be. Her heart lifted up in a kind of pride in Mary, in every sorrow she could remember, her own or that of others (and the remembrances rushed upon her); in all existence and endurance. She wanted to cry out *Yes! Exactly! Yes. Yes. Begin to see. Your turn now*. She wanted to hold her niece at arm's length and to turn and admire this blossoming. She wanted to take her in her arms and groan unto God for what it meant to be alive. But chiefly she wanted to keep stillness and to hear the young woman's voice and to watch her eyes and her round forehead while she spoke, and to accept and experience this repetition of her own younger experience, which bore her high, and pierced like music.

"Isn't that so?" Mary repeated.

"That and much more," she said.

"You mean God's mercy?" Mary asked softly.

"Nothing of the kind," Hannah replied sharply. "What I mean, I'd best not try to say." (I've begun, though, she reflected; and I startled her, I hurt her, almost as if I'd spoken against God.) "Only because it's better if you learn it for yourself. *By* yourself."

"What do you mean?"

"Whatever we hear, learn, Mary, it's almost certain to be hard.

Tragically hard. You're beginning to know that and to face it, very bravely. What I mean is that this is only the beginning. You'll learn much more. Beginning very soon now."

"Whatever it is, I want so much to be *worthy* of it," Mary said, her eyes shining.

"Don't try too hard to be worthy of it, Mary. Don't think of it that way. Just do your best to endure it and let any question of worthiness take care of itself. That's more than enough."

"I feel so utterly unprepared. So little time to prepare *in*."

"I don't think it's a kind of thing that can be prepared for; it just has to be lived through."

There was a kind of ambition there, Hannah felt, a kind of pride or poetry, which was very mistaken and very dangerous. But she was not yet quite sure what she meant; and of all the times to become beguiled by such a matter, to try to argue it, or warn about it! She's so young, she told herself. She'll learn; poor soul, she'll learn.

Even while Hannah watched her, Mary's face became diffuse and humble. "*Oh, not yet,*" Hannah whispered desperately to herself. "*Not yet.*" But Mary said, shyly, "Aunt Hannah, can we kneel down for a minute?"

Not yet, she wanted to say. For the first time in her life she suspected how mistakenly prayer can be used, but she was unsure why. *What can I say,* she thought, almost in panic. *How can I judge?* She was waiting too long; Mary smiled at her, timidly, and in a beginning of bewilderment; and in compassion and self-doubt Hannah came around the table and they knelt side by side. We can be seen, Hannah realized; for the shades were up. *Let us,* she told herself angrily.

"In the name of the Father and of the Son and of the Holy Ghost, Amen," Mary said in a low voice.

"Amen," Hannah trailed.

They were silent and they could hear the ticking of the clock, the shuffling of the fire, and the yammering of the big kettle.

God is not here, Hannah said to herself; and made a small cross upon her breastbone, against her blasphemy.

"O God," Mary whispered, "strengthen me to accept Thy will, whatever it may be." Then she stayed silent.

God hear her, Hannah said to herself. God forgive me. God

forgive me.

What can I know of the proper time for her, she said to herself. God forgive me.

Yet she could not rid herself: Something mistaken, unbearably piteous, infinitely malign was at large within that faithfulness; she was helpless to forfend it or even to know its nature.

Suddenly there opened within her a chasm of infinite depth and from it flowed the paralyzing breath of eternal darkness.

I believe nothing. Nothing whatever.

"Our Father," she heard herself say, in a strange voice; and Mary, innocent of her terror, joined in the prayer. And as they continued, and Hannah heard more and more clearly than her own the young, warm, earnest, faithful, heartsick voice, her moment of terrifying unbelief became a remembrance, a temptation successfully resisted through God's grace.

Deliver us from evil, she repeated silently several times after their prayer was finished. But the malign was still there, as well as the mercifulness.

They got to their feet.

As it became with every minute and then with every flickering of the clock more and more clear that Andrew had had far more than enough time to get out there, and to telephone, Mary and her aunt talked less and less. For a little while after their prayer, in relief, Mary had talked quite volubly of matters largely irrelevant to the event; she had even made little jokes and had even laughed at them, without more than a small undertone of hysteria; and in all this Hannah had thought it best (and, for that matter, the only thing possible) to follow suit; but that soon faded away; nor was it to return; now they merely sat in quietness, each on her side of the kitchen table, their eyes cast away from each other, drinking tea for which they had no desire. Mary made a full fresh pot of tea, and they conversed a little about that, and she heated water with which to dilute it, and they discussed that briefly; but such little exchanges wore quickly down into silence. Mary, whispering "Excuse me," retired to the bathroom, affronted and humbled that one should have to obey such a call at such a time; she felt for a few moments as stupid and enslaved as a baby on its potty, and far more ungainly and vulgar; then with her wet hands planted in the basin of cold water she stared incredulously into her numb, reflected face, which seemed hardly real to her, until, with shame, she realized that at this of all moments she was mirror gazing.

Hannah, left alone, was grateful that we are animals; it was this silly, strenuous, good, humble cluttering of animal needs which saw us through sane, fully as much as prayer; and towards the end of these moments of solitude, with her mind free from the subtle deceptions of concern, she indulged herself in whispering, aloud, "He's dead. There's no longer the slightest doubt of it"; and began to sign herself with the Cross in prayer for the dead, but, sharply remembering *we do not know*, and feeling as if she had been on the verge of exercising malign power against him, deflected the intention of the gesture towards God's mercy upon him, in whatsoever condition he might now be.

When Mary returned, she put more wood on the fire, looked into the big kettle, saw that a third of the water had boiled away, and refilled it. Neither of them said anything about this, but each knew what the other was thinking, and after they had sat again in silence for well over ten minutes, Mary looked at her aunt, who, feeling the eyes upon her, looked into them; then Mary said, very quietly, "I only wish we'd hear now, because I am ready."

Hannah nodded, and felt: you really are. How good it is that you don't even want to touch my hand. And she felt something shining and majestic stand up within her darkness as if to say before God: Here she is and she is adequate to the worst and she has done it for herself, not through my help or even, particularly, through Yours. See to it that You appreciate her.

Mary went on, "It's just barely conceivable that the news is so much less bad than we'd expected that Andrew is simply too overjoyed with relief to bother to phone, and is bringing him straight home instead, for a wonderful surprise. That would be like him. If things were that way. And like Jay, if they were, if he were conscious enough to go right along with the surprise and enjoy it, and just *laugh* at how scared we've been." By her shining eyes, and her almost smiling face, she seemed almost to be believing this while she said it; almost to be sure that within another few minutes it would happen in just that way. But now she went on, "That's just barely conceivable, just about one chance in a million, and so long as there *is* that chance, so long as we don't absolutely know to the contrary, I'm not going to dismiss the possibility entirely from my mind. I'm not going to say he's dead, Aunt Hannah, till I know he is," she said as if defiantly.

"Certainly *not!*"

"But I'm all but certain he is, all the same," Mary said; and saying so, and meeting Hannah's eyes, she could not for a few moments remember what more she had intended to say. Then she remembered, and it seemed too paltry to speak of, and she waited until all that she saw in her mind was again clear and full of its own weight; then again she spoke. "I think what's very much more likely is that he was already dead when the man just phoned, and that he couldn't bear to tell me, and I don't blame him, I'm grateful he didn't. It ought to come from a man in the family, somebody—close to Jay, and to me. I think Andrew was pretty sure—what was up—when he went out, and had every intention not to leave us in midair this way. He meant to phone. But all the time he was hoping against hope, as we all were, and when—when he *saw* Jay—it was more than he could do to phone, and he knew it was more than I could stand to *hear* over a phone, even from him, and so he didn't, and I'm infinitely grateful he didn't. He must have known that as time kept—wearing on in this terrible way, we'd draw our own conclusions and have time to—time. And that's best. He wanted to be with me when I heard. And that's right. So do I. Straight from his lips. I think what he did—what he's doing, it's . . ."

Hannah saw that she was now nearer to breaking than at any time before, and she could scarcely resist her impulse to reach for her hand; she managed, with anguish, to forbid herself. After a moment Mary continued, quietly and in control, "What he's doing is to come in with Jay's poor body to the undertaker's, and soon now he'll come home to us and tell us."

Hannah continued to look into her gentle and ever more incredulous and shining eyes; she found that she could not speak and that she was nodding, as curtly, and rapidly, almost, as if she were palsied. She made herself stop nodding.

"That's what I think," Mary said, "and that's what I'm ready for. But I'm not going to say it, or accept it, or do my husband any such dishonor or danger—not until I know beyond recall that it's so."

They continued to gaze into each other's eyes—Hannah's eyes were burning because she felt she must not blink; and after some moments a long, crying groan broke from the younger woman and in a low and shaken voice she said, "Oh I do beseech my God that it not be so," and Hannah whispered, "So do I"; and again they became still, knowing little and seeing nothing except each other's suffering eyes; and it was thus that they were when they heard footsteps on the front porch. Hannah looked aside and downward; a long, breaking breath came from Mary; they drew back their chairs and started for the door.

Andrew did not bother to knock, but opened the door and closed it quietly behind him and, seeing their moving shadows near the kitchen threshold, walked quickly down the hall. They could not see his face in the dark hallway but by his tight, set way of walking they were virtually sure. They were all but blocking his way. Instead of going into the hall to meet him, they drew aside to let him into the kitchen. He did not hesitate with their own moment's hesitation but came straight on, his mouth a straight line and his eyes like splintered glass, and without saying a word he put his arms around his aunt so tightly that she gasped, and lifted her from the floor. "Mary," Hannah whispered, close to his ear; he looked; there she stood waiting, her eyes, her face, like that of an astounded child which might be pleading, Oh, don't hit me; and before he could speak he heard her say, thinly and gently, "He's dead, Andrew, isn't he?" and he could not speak, but nodded, and he became aware that he was holding his aunt's feet off the floor and virtually breaking her bones, and his sister said, in the same small and unearthly voice, "He was dead when you got there"; and again he nodded; and then he set Hannah down carefully on her feet and, turning to his sister, took her by her shoulders and said, more loudly than he had expected, "He was instantly killed," and he kissed her upon the mouth and they embraced, and without tears but with great violence he sobbed twice, his cheek against hers, while he stared downwards through her loose hair at her humbled back and at the changeful blinking of the linoleum.

Part Three

INTRODUCTION

Like the authors of the stories in the first group in this book, the authors represented in this third group are anxious to give due consideration to man's sentiments, to his subjective life, because they are convinced—as Lawrence is—that man's passional life is the significant one, or because their perception is—as is Katherine Mansfield's—so subjective that the objective world scarcely exists for them apart from some human feeling about it.

Because the writers of these two groups are similar, at least in their concern with the subjective life, they sometimes write stories that appear similar. There is a resemblance between John Updike's *A Sense of Shelter* and Sherwood Anderson's *The Egg*, for instance; yet these two stories, like all the stories in the two groups they represent, differ in an important way. Anderson is perfectly aware that, in the last scene of his story, the narrator's father is ludicrous, if we judge his conduct from the casual, common-sense point of view of Joe Kane, who felt that "the man who confronted him was mildly insane but harmless." By putting Joe Kane in the story, Anderson recognizes that, from the objective point of view, the narrator's father is absurd. But he gives very little weight to this objective judgment. What matters to him is not what the father is objectively, but what inner convictions he acts on, how *he* conceives what he does, and what he believes he is accomplishing. The more passionate the father becomes as he attempts to make the egg stand on end or to squeeze it through the neck of a bottle, the more he mutters and swears, the more we are made to feel the pathos of his determination to achieve the

427

kind of theatrical triumph he believes will make his restaurant a success. In all innocence and good will—we feel—he has given everything he has to this purpose, only to be ignored or laughed at when he fails.

Updike's story also deals closely with the feelings of its protagonist, giving us a minute and sympathetic account of the conception of reality and of himself with which William Young lives. Against William's long-cherished vision of Mary Landis and his feeling for her, an important part of William's conception of things, the story sets the view of a character who knows the reality of Mary Landis's situation and can measure the gap between it and William's conception of it. This character is Mary Landis herself, who has gone out into the world beyond the shelter of the high school and is now involved in a bitterly unhappy love affair with an older man. Our knowledge of this fact and the few brief but decisive comments Mary makes on William gives her view a weight and an authority that Joe Kane's view in Anderson's story never has.

In addition, Updike's treatment of William's own conception of experience—though never unsympathetic or satiric—emphasizes its inadequacy in a way Anderson's treatment of his hero's vision never does. William sees before him an untroubled progression through life as if life were an acoustically lined tube, like the high-school study hall, which will lead him painlessly to a full professorship and, ultimately, to a gracefully enacted death "like Tennyson, with a copy of 'Cymbeline' beside him on the moon-drenched bed." This is the image of a life lived from beginning to end within the protective shelter of the high-school world he has so far lived in. Just for a moment at the end of the story, when he makes real contact with Mary Landis, he steps out of that world with her, into the winter world beyond the high school's doors. But even as he does so, he is beginning to think of the blunders that alienate Mary as his "loyal friends" who will help him to escape from this cold world back into the shelter of the familiar high school: not quite consciously, he is trying to drive Mary away, frightened of what a commitment to her will require him to face. He succeeds, and escapes back into the warm, stuffy world of the high school where he is king of the castle. Once more, "in answer to a flick of his great hand the steel door [in

PART THREE Introduction · 429

reality the door of his locker] weightlessly slammed shut, and through the length of his body he felt so clean and free he smiled. Between now and the happy future predicted for him he had nothing, almost literally nothing, to do." He is safe again in his vision of an untroubled and painless future, protected from the reality into which he had, for a few steps, followed Mary Landis.

If the revealing moment in *The Egg* is the moment when the father kneels by his wife's bed and cries like a boy and we feel the sadness of the defeat of those longings—however grotesque their expression—that possessed his heart, the significant moment in Updike's story is the moment when Mary Landis makes us (though not William) see that William is hiding from reality in the familiar high-school world, content with his dream of a future: he has not truly lived at all ("You never loved anybody. You don't know what it is"). Like the other stories in Part One of this book, *A Sense of Shelter* will not, for all its understanding of its hero's feelings and its sympathy with them, deny for a moment the necessity for men to bring their feelings into accord with reality. But *The Egg*, though it does not say reality will adjust itself to the hero's desires, plainly implies that the hero's feelings count for more than reality and that, if life were reasonable—if people were as sensitive as they ought to be—reality would be adjusted to the hero's desires. Anderson's story makes us feel that the objective common sense of Joe Kane is likely to be right about how things will turn out but will miss the real meaning of things because it will fail to take into account the feelings of the hero. To writers of this third group of stories, what men feel is so important, and therefore so real, that the objective world visible to common sense does not—however often it may triumph over men's dreams—finally have a meaning.

In the simplest—though far from least valuable—form, this attitude expresses itself, as it does in *The Egg*, in a story that insists throughout on the conflict between the objective world and the central characters' feelings and ends with a passionate assertion of the tragedy of the central character's defeat by the world. This, to take a second example, is what happens in Joyce's *Araby*, which ends: "Gazing up into the darkness I saw myself as a creature driven and derided by vanity; and my eyes burned with anguish and anger." Or, to take a third example, it is what happens in *Pnin* when Pnin thinks: "I must not, I must not, oh it is idiotical, . . . as he felt—unaccountably, ridiculously, humiliatingly —his tear glands discharge their hot, infantine, uncontrollable fluid."

Kipling's *The Gardener* also asserts the power of feeling to create a significant reality. This story faintly suggests that Michael is Helen's illegitimate son; if he is, Helen's situation is precisely like Mrs. Scarsworth's. But what makes the man she thinks (mistakenly, see *John*, 20:15) the gardener call Michael her son is no mere matter of fact but the purity and intensity of her love, just as the quality of Mrs. Scarsworth's love will, we are sure, make the gardener call the man she is seeking her husband.

But the most persistent—if at times the most impatient—writer of this kind is D. H. Lawrence. Lawrence's stories are like an organism with a translucent skin. The surface is complete and solid; Lawrence had observed very acutely the lower-class life of the coal-mining community of Eastwood in Nottinghamshire, where he grew up, and in stories like *Odor of Chrysanthemums* he represents that life vividly. Even in stories like *The Shadow in the Rose Garden* his knowledge of class distinctions—that passionate pedantry of the British lower middle classes—is constantly at work. It is characteristic that the quarrel between husband and wife in this story should express itself in references to their differences in class. "You might as well be in pit as bed, on a morning like this," says the husband. "I shouldn't have thought the pit would occur to you, here," says the wife. Even the phrasing—"in pit," "I shouldn't have thought"—indicates their class origins.

When Elsie Whiston picks up her skirts to show "her pretty legs in the neat stockings," Teddy is "filled with unreasonable rage." She goes right on defying him, resenting him in some way she does not understand, behaving with an indifference that enrages him for reasons he cannot quite grasp. Yet Elsie is afraid of the crisis she is bringing on. When Teddy, knowing that he is "scarcely responsible for what he might do," goes outside, he is "unconscious with a black storm of rage." When Elsie finally drives him to strike her, she watches him approach her "transfixed in terror." When Teddy does strike her, he first feels a satisfaction of "his lust to see her bleed"; then he feels "shame and nausea"; and finally he is only "sick and tired of the responsibility of it, the violence, the shame." But a moment later he sees Elsie in an entirely different light, as "forlorn and pathetic," and "a great flash of anguish [goes] over his body." "I never meant—" she says; "My love—my little love—" he says. They do not understand themselves or each other, in any logical sense, any better then they ever have. But in each of them, deep, blind, powerful feelings have groped out toward the other, and they are again united in the only meaningful way in which, for Lawrence, people ever can be united. And despite Lawrence's almost belligerent insistence on the rational incoherence of the sequence of feelings that occurs in each character, that sequence has a coherence of its own, a psychological rightness, that is completely convincing.

It is this instinctive and—at Lawrence's best—almost infallible sense of how the buried life of the deep feelings moves that makes Lawrence a great writer. But we must never forget that he is a great writer wholly committed to what he himself calls the "Fantasia of the Unconscious." If we do forget that, we will make the mistake with him—as we may with all the writers in this group—of looking for an action built up out of the recognizable events of everyday life, which in the stories of writers like these is either not present at all or only insignificantly present. If we make that mistake, we will miss the drama of the powerful, often unconscious subjective life which is, most magnificently, present in these stories.

D. H. LAWRENCE

Odor of Chrysanthemums

The small locomotive engine, Number 4, came clanking, stumbling down from Selston with seven full wagons. It appeared round the corner with loud threats of speed, but the colt that it startled from among the gorse, which still flickered indistinctly in the raw afternoon, outdistanced it at a canter. A woman, walking up the railway line to Underwood, drew back into the hedge, held her basket aside, and watched the footplate of the engine advancing. The trucks thumped heavily past, one by one, with slow inevitable movement, as she stood insignificantly trapped between the jolting black wagons and the hedge; then they curved away toward the coppice where the withered oak leaves dropped noiselessly, while the birds, pulling at the scarlet hips beside the track, made off into the dusk that had already crept into the spinney. In the open, the smoke from the engine sank and cleaved to the rough grass. The fields were dreary and forsaken, and in the marshy strip that led to the whimsey, a reedy pit-pond, the fowls had already abandoned their run among the alders, to roost in the tarred fowl-house. The pit-bank loomed up beyond the pond, flames like red sores licking its ashy sides, in the afternoon's stagnant light. Just beyond rose the tapering chimneys and the clumsy black headstocks of Brinsley Colliery. The two wheels were spinning fast up against the sky, and the winding-engine rapped out its little spasms. The miners were being turned up.

The engine whistled as it came into the wide bay of railway lines beside the colliery, where rows of trucks stood in harbor.

Miners, single, trailing and in groups, passed like shadows diverging home. At the edge of the ribbed level of sidings squat a low cottage, three steps down from the cinder track. A large bony vine clutched at the house, as if to claw down the tiled roof. Round the bricked yard grew a few wintry primroses. Beyond, the long garden sloped down to a bush-covered brook course. There were some twiggy apple trees, winter-crack trees, and ragged cabbages. Beside the path hung dishevelled pink chrysanthemums, like pink cloths hung on bushes. A woman came stooping out of the felt-covered fowl-house, halfway down the garden. She closed and padlocked the door, then drew herself erect, having brushed some bits from her white apron.

She was a tall woman of imperious mien, handsome, with definite black eyebrows. Her smooth black hair was parted exactly. For a few moments she stood steadily watching the miners as they passed along the railway: then she turned toward the brook course. Her face was calm and set, her mouth was closed with disillusionment. After a moment she called:

"John!" There was no answer. She waited, and then said distinctly:

"Where are you?"

"Here!" replied a child's sulky voice from among the bushes. The woman looked piercingly through the dusk.

"Are you at that brook?" she asked sternly.

For answer the child showed himself before the raspberry-canes that rose like whips. He was a small, sturdy boy of five. He stood quite still, defiantly.

"Oh!" said the mother, conciliated. "I thought you were down at that wet brook—and you remember what I told you—"

The boy did not move or answer.

"Come, come on in," she said more gently, "it's getting dark. There's your grandfather's engine coming down the line!"

The lad advanced slowly, with resentful, taciturn movement. He was dressed in trousers and waistcoat of cloth that was too thick and hard for the size of the garments. They were evidently cut down from a man's clothes.

As they went slowly toward the house he tore at the ragged wisps of chrysanthemums and dropped the petals in handfuls along the path.

"Don't do that—it does look nasty," said his mother. He re-frained, and she, suddenly pitiful, broke off a twig with three or four wan flowers and held them against her face. When mother and son reached the yard her hand hesitated, and instead of laying the flower aside, she pushed it in her apron-band. The mother and son stood at the foot of the three steps looking across the bay of lines at the passing home of the miners. The trundle of the small train was imminent. Suddenly the engine loomed past the house and came to a stop opposite the gate.

The engine-driver, a short man with round gray beard, leaned out of the cab high above the woman.

"Have you got a cup of tea?" he said in a cheery, hearty fashion.

It was her father. She went in, saying she would mash. Directly, she returned.

"I didn't come to see you on Sunday," began the little gray-bearded man.

"I didn't expect you," said his daughter.

The engine-driver winced; then, reassuming his cheery, airy manner, he said:

"Oh, have you heard then? Well, and what do you think—?"

"I think it is soon enough," she replied.

At her brief censure the little man made an impatient gesture, and said coaxingly, yet with dangerous coldness:

"Well, what's a man to do? It's no sort of life for a man of my years, to sit at my own hearth like a stranger. And if I'm going to marry again it may as well be soon as late—what does it matter to anybody?"

The woman did not reply, but turned and went into the house. The man in the engine-cab stood assertive, till she returned with a cup of tea and a piece of bread and butter on a plate. She went up the steps and stood near the footplate of the hissing engine.

"You needn't 'a' brought me bread an' butter," said her father. "But a cup of tea"—he sipped appreciatively—"it's very nice." He sipped for a moment or two, then: "I hear as Walter's got another bout on," he said.

"When hasn't he?" said the woman bitterly.

"I heered tell of him in the 'Lord Nelson' braggin' as he was going to spend that b— afore he went: half a sovereign that was."

"When?" asked the woman.

"A' Sat'day night—I know that's true."

"Very likely," she laughed bitterly. "He gives me twenty-three shillings."

"Aye, it's a nice thing, when a man can do nothing with his money but make a beast of himself!" said the gray-whiskered man. The woman turned her head away. Her father swallowed the last of his tea and handed her the cup.

"Aye," he sighed, wiping his mouth. "It's a settler, it is—"

He put his hand on the lever. The little engine strained and groaned, and the train rumbled toward the crossing. The woman again looked across the metals. Darkness was settling over the spaces of the railway and trucks: the miners, in gray somber groups, were still passing home. The winding-engine pulsed hurriedly, with brief pauses. Elizabeth Bates looked at the dreary flow of men, then she went indoors. Her husband did not come.

The kitchen was small and full of firelight; red coals piled glowing up the chimney mouth. All the life of the room seemed in the white, warm hearth and the steel fender reflecting the red fire. The cloth was laid for tea; cups glinted in the shadows. At the back, where the lowest stairs protruded into the room, the boy sat struggling with a knife and a piece of whitewood. He was almost hidden in the shadow. It was half-past four. They had but to await the father's coming to begin tea. As the mother watched her son's sullen little struggle with the wood, she saw herself in his silence and pertinacity; she saw the father in her child's indifference to all but himself. She seemed to be occupied by her husband. He had probably gone past his home, slunk past his own door, to drink before he came in, while his dinner spoiled and wasted in waiting. She glanced at the clock, then took the potatoes to strain them in the yard. The garden and fields beyond the brook were closed in uncertain darkness. When she rose with the saucepan, leaving the drain steaming into the night behind her, she saw the yellow lamps were lit along the high road that went up the hill away beyond the space of the railway lines and the field.

Then again she watched the men trooping home, fewer now and fewer.

Indoors the fire was sinking and the room was dark red. The woman put her saucepan on the hob, and set a batter pudding near the mouth of the oven. Then she stood unmoving. Directly, grate-fully, came quick young steps to the door. Someone hung on the latch a moment, then a little girl entered and began pulling off her outdoor things, dragging a mass of curls, just ripening from gold to brown, over her eyes with her hat.

Her mother chid her for coming late from school, and said she would have to keep her at home the dark winter days.

"Why, mother, it's hardly a bit dark yet. The lamp's not lighted, and my father's not home."

"No, he isn't. But it's a quarter to five! Did you see anything of him?"

The child became serious. She looked at her mother with large, wistful blue eyes.

"No, mother, I've never seen him. Why? Has he come up an' gone past, to Old Brinsley? He hasn't, mother, 'cos I never saw him."

"He'd watch that," said the mother bitterly, "he'd take care as you didn't see him. But you may depend upon it, he's seated in the 'Prince o' Wales.' He wouldn't be this late."

The girl looked at her mother piteously.

"Let's have our teas, mother, should we?" said she.

The mother called John to table. She opened the door once more and looked out across the darkness of the lines. All was de-serted: she could not hear the winding-engines.

"Perhaps," she said to herself, "he's stopped to get some ripping done."

They sat down to tea. John, at the end of the table near the door, was almost lost in the darkness. Their faces were hidden from each other. The girl crouched against the fender slowly moving a thick piece of bread before the fire. The lad, his face a dusky mark on the shadow, sat watching her who was transfigured in the red glow.

"I do think it's beautiful to look in the fire," said the child.

"Do you?" said her mother. "Why?"

"It's so red, and full of little caves—and it feels so nice, and you can fair smell it."

"It'll want mending directly," replied the mother, "and then if your father comes he'll carry on and say there never is a fire when a man comes home sweating from the pit. A public-house is always warm enough."

There was silence till the boy said complainingly: "Make haste, our Annie."

"Well, I am doing! I can't make the fire do it no faster, can I?"

"She keeps wafflin' it about so's to make 'er slow," grumbled the boy.

"Don't have such an evil imagination, child," replied the mother.

Soon the room was busy in the darkness with the crisp sound of crunching. The mother ate very little. She drank her tea determinedly, and sat thinking. When she rose her anger was evident in the stern unbending of her head. She looked at the pudding in the fender, and broke out:

"It is a scandalous thing as a man can't even come home to his dinner! If it's crozzled up to a cinder I don't see why I should care. Past his very door he goes to get to a public-house, and here I sit with his dinner waiting for him—"

She went out. As she dropped piece after piece of coal on the red fire, the shadows fell on the walls, till the room was almost in total darkness.

"I canna see," grumbled the invisible John. In spite of herself, the mother laughed.

"You know the way to your mouth," she said. She set the dustpan outside the door. When she came again like a shadow on the hearth, the lad repeated, complaining sulkily:

"I canna see."

"Good gracious!" cried the mother irritably, "you're as bad as your father if it's a bit dusk!"

Nevertheless she took a paper spill from a sheaf on the mantelpiece and proceeded to light the lamp that hung from the ceiling in the middle of the room. As she reached up, her figure displayed itself just rounding with maternity.

"Oh, mother—!" exclaimed the girl.

"What?" said the woman, suspended in the act of putting the lamp glass over the flame. The copper reflector shone handsomely on her, as she stood with uplifted arm, turning to face her daughter.

"You've got a flower in your apron!" said the child, in a little rapture at this unusual event.

"Goodness me!" exclaimed the woman, relieved. "One would

think the house was afire." She replaced the glass and waited a moment before turning up the wick. A pale shadow was seen floating vaguely on the floor.

"Let me smell!" said the child, still rapturously, coming forward and putting her face to her mother's waist.

"Go along, silly!" said the mother, turning up the lamp. The light revealed their suspense so that the woman felt it almost unbearable. Annie was still bending at her waist. Irritably, the mother took the flowers out from her apron-band.

"Oh, mother—don't take them out!" Annie cried, catching her hand and trying to replace the sprig.

"Such nonsense!" said the mother, turning away. The child put the pale chrysanthemums to her lips, murmuring:

"Don't they smell beautiful!"

Her mother gave a short laugh.

"No," she said, "not to me. It was chrysanthemums when I married him, and chrysanthemums when you were born, and the first time they ever brought him home drunk, he'd got brown chrysanthemums in his buttonhole."

She looked at the children. Their eyes and their parted lips were wondering. The mother sat rocking in silence for some time. Then she looked at the clock.

"Twenty minutes to six!" In a tone of fine bitter carelessness she continued: "Eh, he'll not come now till they bring him. There he'll stick! But he needn't come rolling in here in his pit-dirt, for *I* won't wash him. He can lie on the floor— Eh, what a fool I've been, what a fool! And this is what I came here for, to this dirty hole, rats and all, for him to slink past his very door. Twice last week—he's begun now—"

She silenced herself, and rose to clear the table.

While for an hour or more the children played, subduedly intent, fertile of imagination, united in fear of the mother's wrath, and in dread of their father's home-coming, Mrs. Bates sat in her rocking-chair making a "singlet" of thick cream-colored flannel, which gave a dull wounded sound as she tore off the gray edge. She worked at her sewing with energy, listening to the children, and her anger wearied itself, lay down to rest, opening its eyes from time to time and steadily watching, its ears raised to listen. Sometimes even her anger quailed and shrank, and the mother suspended her sewing, tracing the footsteps that thudded along the sleepers outside; she would lift her head sharply to bid the children "hush," but she recovered herself in time, and the footsteps went past the gate, and the children were not flung out of their play-world.

But at last Annie sighed, and gave in. She glanced at her wagon of slippers, and loathed the game. She turned plaintively to her mother.

"Mother!"—but she was inarticulate.

John crept out like a frog from under the sofa. His mother glanced up.

"Yes," she said, "just look at those shirt-sleeves!"

The boy held them out to survey them, saying nothing. Then somebody called in a hoarse voice away down the line, and suspense bristled in the room, till two people had gone by outside, talking.

"It is time for bed," said the mother.

"My father hasn't come," wailed Annie plaintively. But her mother was primed with courage.

"Never mind. They'll bring him when he does come—like a log." She meant there would be no scene. "And he may sleep on the floor till he wakes himself. I know he'll not go to work to-morrow after this!"

The children had their hands and faces wiped with a flannel. They were very quiet. When they had put on their nightdresses, they said their prayers, the boy mumbling. The mother looked down at them, at the brown silken bush of intertwining curls in the nape of the girl's neck, at the little black head of the lad, and her heart burst with anger at their father who caused all three such distress. The children hid their faces in her skirts for comfort.

When Mrs. Bates came down, the room was strangely empty, with a tension of expectancy. She took up her sewing and stitched for some time without raising her head. Meantime her anger was tinged with fear.

II

The clock struck eight and she rose suddenly, dropping her sewing on her chair. She went to the stairfoot door, opened it, listening. Then she went out, locking the door behind her.

Something scuffled in the yard, and she started, though she knew it was only the rats with which the place was overrun. The night was very dark. In the great bay of railway lines, bulked with trucks, there was no trace of light, only away back she could see a few yellow lamps at the pit-top, and the red smear of the burning pit-bank on the night. She hurried along the edge of the track, then, crossing the converging lines, came to the stile by the white gates, whence she emerged on the road. Then the fear which had led her shrank. People were walking up to New Brinsley; she saw the lights in the houses; twenty yards further on were the broad windows of the "Prince of Wales," very warm and bright, and the loud voices of men could be heard distinctly. What a fool she had been to imagine that anything had happened to him! He was merely drinking over there at the "Prince of Wales." She faltered. She had never yet been to fetch him, and she never would go. So she continued her walk toward the long straggling line of houses, standing blank on the highway. She entered a passage between the dwellings.

"Mr. Rigley?—Yes! Did you want him? No, he's not in at this minute."

The raw-boned woman leaned forward from her dark scullery and peered at the other, upon whom fell a dim light through the blind of the kitchen window.

"Is it Mrs. Bates?" she asked in a tone tinged with respect.

"Yes. I wondered if your Master was at home. Mine hasn't come yet."

"'Asn't 'e! Oh, Jack's been 'ome an' 'ad 'is dinner an' gone out. 'E's just gone for 'alf an hour afore bedtime. Did you call at the 'Prince of Wales'?"

"No—"

"No, you didn't like—! It's not very nice." The other woman was indulgent. There was an awkward pause. "Jack never said nothink about—about your Mester," she said.

"No!—I expect he's stuck in there!"

Elizabeth Bates said this bitterly, and with recklessness. She knew that the woman across the yard was standing at her door listening, but she did not care. As she turned:

"Stop a minute! I'll just go an' ask Jack if 'e knows anythink," said Mrs. Rigley.

"Oh, no—I wouldn't like to put—!"

"Yes, I will, if you'll just step inside an' see as th' childer doesn't come downstairs and set theirselves afire."

Elizabeth Bates, murmuring a remonstrance, stepped inside. The other woman apologized for the state of the room.

The kitchen needed apology. There were little frocks and trousers and childish undergarments on the squab and on the floor, and a litter of playthings everywhere. On the black American cloth of the table were pieces of bread and cake, crusts, slops, and a teapot with cold tea.

"Eh, ours is just as bad," said Elizabeth Bates, looking at the woman, not at the house. Mrs. Rigley put a shawl over her head and hurried out, saying:

"I shanna be a minute."

The other sat, noting with faint disapproval the general untidiness of the room. Then she fell to counting the shoes of various sizes scattered over the floor. There were twelve. She sighed and said to herself, "No wonder!"—glancing at the litter. There came the scratching of two pairs of feet on the yard, and the Rigleys entered. Elizabeth Bates rose. Rigley was a big man, with very large bones. His head looked particularly bony. Across his temple was a blue scar, caused by a wound got in the pit, a wound in which the coal-dust remained blue like tattooing.

" 'Asna 'e come whoam yit?" asked the man, without any form of greeting, but with deference and sympathy. "I couldna say wheer 'e is—'e's non ower theer!"—he jerked his head to signify the "Prince of Wales."

" 'E's 'appen gone up to th' 'Yew,' " said Mrs. Rigley.

There was another pause. Rigley had evidently something to get off his mind:

"Ah left 'im finishin' a stint," he began. "Loose-all 'ad bin gone about ten minutes when we com'n away, an' I shouted, 'Are ter comin', Walt?' an' 'e said, 'Go on, Ah shanna be but a'ef a minnit,' so we com'n ter th' bottom, me an' Bowers, thinkin' as 'e wor just behint, an' 'ud come up i' th' next bantle—"

He stood perplexed, as if answering a charge of deserting his mate. Elizabeth Bates, now again certain of disaster, hastened to reassure him:

"I expect 'e's gone up to th' 'Yew Tree,' as you say. It's not the first time. I've fretted myself into a fever before now. He'll come home when they carry him."

"Ay, isn't it too bad!" deplored the other woman.

"I'll just step up to Dick's an' see if 'e *is* theer," offered the man, afraid of appearing alarmed, afraid of taking liberties.

"Oh, I wouldn't think of bothering you that far," said Elizabeth Bates, with emphasis, but he knew she was glad of his offer.

As they stumbled up the entry, Elizabeth Bates heard Rigley's wife run across the yard and open her neighbor's door. At this, suddenly all the blood in her body seemed to switch away from her heart.

"Mind!" warned Rigley. "Ah've said many a time as Ah'd fill up them ruts in this entry, sumb'dy 'll be breakin' their legs yit."

She recovered herself and walked quickly along with the miner.

"I don't like leaving the children in bed, and nobody in the house," she said.

"No, you dunna!" he replied courteously. They were soon at the gate of the cottage.

"Well, I shanna be many minnits. Dunna you be frettin' now, 'e'll be all right," said the butty.

"Thank you very much, Mr. Rigley," she replied.

"You're welcome!" he stammered, moving away. "I shanna be many minnits."

The house was quiet. Elizabeth Bates took off her hat and shawl, and rolled back the rug. When she had finished, she sat down. It was a few minutes past nine. She was startled by the rapid chuff of the winding-engine at the pit, and the sharp whirr of the brakes on the rope as it descended. Again she felt the painful sweep of her blood, and she put her hand to her side, saying aloud, "Good gracious!—it's only the nine o'clock deputy going down," rebuking herself.

She sat still, listening. Half an hour of this, and she was wearied out.

"What am I working myself up like this for?" she said pitiably to herself, "I s'll only be doing myself some damage."

She took out her sewing again.

At a quarter to ten there were footsteps. One person! She watched for the door to open. It was an elderly woman, in a black bonnet and a black woollen shawl—his mother. She was about sixty years old, pale, with blue eyes, and her face all wrinkled and lamentable. She shut the door and turned to her daughter-in-law peevishly.

"Eh, Lizzie, whatever shall we do, whatever shall we do!" she cried.

Elizabeth drew back a little, sharply.

"What is it, mother?" she said.

The elder woman seated herself on the sofa.

"I don't know, child, I can't tell you!"—she shook her head slowly. Elizabeth sat watching her, anxious and vexed.

"I don't know," replied the grandmother, sighing very deeply. "There's no end to my troubles, there isn't. The things I've gone through, I'm sure it's enough—" She wept without wiping her eyes, the tears running.

"But, mother," interrupted Elizabeth, "what do you mean? What is it?"

The grandmother slowly wiped her eyes. The fountains of her tears were stopped by Elizabeth's directness. She wiped her eyes slowly.

"Poor child! Eh, you poor thing!" she moaned. "I don't know what we're going to do, I don't—and you as you are—it's a thing, it is indeed!"

Elizabeth waited.

"Is he dead?" she asked, and at the words her heart swung violently, though she felt a slight flush of shame at the ultimate extravagance of the question. Her words sufficiently frightened the old lady, almost brought her to herself.

"Don't say so, Elizabeth! We'll hope it's not as bad as that; no, may the Lord spare us that, Elizabeth. Jack Rigley came just as I was sittin' down to a glass afore going to bed, an' 'e said, ' 'Appen you'll go down th' line, Mrs. Bates. Walt's had an accident. 'Appen you'll go an' sit wi' 'er till we can get him home.' I hadn't time to ask him a word afore he was gone. An' I put my bonnet on an' come straight down, Lizzie. I thought to myself, 'Eh, that poor blessed child, if anybody should come an' tell her of a sudden, there's no knowin' what'll 'appen to 'er.' You mustn't let it upset you, Lizzie—or you know what to expect. How long is it, six months—or is it five, Lizzie? Ay!"—the old woman shook her head—"time slips on, it slips on! Ay!"

Elizabeth's thoughts were busy elsewhere. If he was killed—would she be able to manage on the little pension and what she could earn?—she counted up rapidly. If he was hurt—they wouldn't take him to the hospital—how tiresome he would be to nurse!—but perhaps she'd be able to get him away from the drink and his hateful ways. She would—while he was ill. The tears offered to come to her eyes at the picture. But what sentimental luxury was this she was beginning? She turned to consider the children. At any rate she was absolutely necessary for them. They were her business.

"Ay!" repeated the old woman, "it seems but a week or two since he brought me his first wages. Ay—he was a good lad, Elizabeth, he was, in his way. I don't know why he got to be such a trouble, I don't. He was a happy lad at home, only full of spirits. But there's no mistake he's been a handful of trouble, he has! I hope the Lord'll spare him to mend his ways. I hope so, I hope so. You've had a sight o' trouble with him, Elizabeth, you have indeed. But he was a jolly enough lad wi' me, he was, I can assure you. I don't know how it is. . . ."

The old woman continued to muse aloud, a monotonous irritating sound, while Elizabeth thought concentratedly, startled once, when she heard the winding-engine chuff quickly, and the brakes skirr with a shriek. Then she heard the engine more slowly, and the brakes made no sound. The old woman did not notice. Elizabeth waited in suspense. The mother-in-law talked, with lapses into silence.

"But he wasn't your son, Lizzie, an' it makes a difference. Whatever he was, I remember him when he was little, an' I learned to understand him and to make allowances. You've got to make allowances for them—"

It was half-past ten, and the old woman was saying: "But it's trouble from beginning to end; you're never too old for trouble, never too old for that—" when the gate banged back, and there were heavy feet on the steps.

"I'll go, Lizzie, let me go," cried the old woman, rising. But Elizabeth was at the door. It was a man in pit-clothes.

"They're bringin' 'im, Missis," he said. Elizabeth's heart halted a moment. Then it surged on again, almost suffocating her.

"Is he—is it bad?" she asked.

The man turned away, looking at the darkness:

"The doctor says 'e'd been dead hours. 'E saw 'im i' th' lamp-cabin."

The old woman, who stood just behind Elizabeth, dropped into a chair, and folded her hands, crying: "Oh, my boy, my boy!"

"Hush!" said Elizabeth, with a sharp twitch of a frown. "Be still, mother, don't waken th' children: I wouldn't have them down for anything!"

The old woman moaned softly, rocking herself. The man was drawing away. Elizabeth took a step forward.

"How was it?" she asked.

"Well, I couldn't say for sure," the man replied, very ill at ease. " 'E wor finishin' a stint an' th' butties 'ad gone, an' a lot o' stuff come down atop 'n 'im."

"And crushed him?" cried the widow, with a shudder.

"No," said the man, "it fell at th' back of 'im. 'E wor under th' face, an' it niver touched 'im. It shut 'im in. It seems 'e wor smothered."

Elizabeth shrank back. She heard the old woman behind her cry:

"What?—what did 'e say it was?"

The man replied, more loudly: " 'E wor smothered!"

Then the old woman wailed aloud, and this relieved Elizabeth.

"Oh, mother," she said, putting her hand on the old woman, "don't waken th' children, don't waken th' children."

She wept a little, unknowing, while the old mother rocked herself and moaned. Elizabeth remembered that they were bringing him home, and she must be ready. "They'll lay him in the parlor," she said to herself, standing a moment pale and perplexed.

Then she lighted a candle and went into the tiny room. The air was cold and damp, but she could not make a fire, there was no fireplace. She set down the candle and looked round. The candlelight glittered on the luster-glasses, on the two vases that held some of the pink chrysanthemums, and on the dark mahogany. There was a cold, deathly smell of chrysanthemums in the room. Elizabeth stood looking at the flowers. She turned away, and calculated whether there would be room to lay him on the floor, between the couch and the chiffonier. She pushed the chairs aside. There would be room to lay him down and to step round him. Then she fetched the old red tablecloth, and another old cloth, spreading them down to save her bit of carpet. She shivered on leaving the parlor; so, from the dresser-drawer she took a clean shirt and put it at the fire to air. All the time her mother-in-law was rocking herself in the chair and moaning.

"You'll have to move from there, mother," said Elizabeth. "They'll be bringing him in. Come in the rocker."

The old mother rose mechanically, and seated herself by the fire, continuing to lament. Elizabeth went into the pantry for another candle, and there, in the little penthouse under the naked tiles, she heard them coming. She stood still in the pantry doorway, listening. She heard them pass the end of the house, and come awkwardly down the three steps, a jumble of shuffling footsteps and muttering voices. The old woman was silent. The men were in the yard.

Then Elizabeth heard Matthews, the manager of the pit, say: "You go in first, Jim. Mind!"

The door came open, and the two women saw a collier backing into the room, holding one end of a stretcher, on which they could see the nailed pit-boots of the dead man. The two carriers halted, the man at the head stooping to the lintel of the door.

"Wheer will you have him?" asked the manager, a short, white-bearded man.

Elizabeth roused herself and came from the pantry carrying the unlighted candle.

"In the parlor," she said.

"In there, Jim!" pointed the manager, and the carriers backed round into the tiny room. The coat with which they had covered the body fell off as they awkwardly turned through the two doorways, and the women saw their man, naked to the waist, lying stripped for work. The old woman began to moan in a low voice of horror.

"Lay th' stretcher at th' side," snapped the manager, "an' put 'im on th' cloths. Mind now, mind! Look you now—!"

One of the men had knocked off a vase of chrysanthemums. He stared awkwardly, then they set down the stretcher. Elizabeth did not look at her husband. As soon as she could get in the room, she went and picked up the broken vase and the flowers.

"Wait a minute!" she said.

The three men waited in silence while she mopped up the water with a duster.

"Eh, what a job, what a job, to be sure!" the manager was saying, rubbing his brow with trouble and perplexity. "Never knew such a thing in my life, never! He'd no business to ha' been left. I never knew such a thing in my life! Fell over him clean as a whistle, an' shut him in. Not four foot of space, there wasn't —yet it scarce bruised him."

He looked down at the dead man, lying prone, half naked, all grimed with coal-dust.

" ' 'Sphyxiated,' the doctor said. It *is* the most terrible job I've ever known. Seems as if it was done o' purpose. Clean over him, an' shut 'im in, like a mouse-trap"—he made a sharp, descending gesture with his hand.

The colliers standing by jerked aside their heads in hopeless comment.

The horror of the thing bristled upon them all.

Then they heard the girl's voice upstairs calling shrilly: "Mother, mother—who is it? Mother, who is it?"

Elizabeth hurried to the foot of the stairs and opened the door:

"Go to sleep!" she commanded sharply. "What are you shouting about? Go to sleep at once—there's nothing—"

Then she began to mount the stairs. They could hear her on the boards, and on the plaster floor of the little bedroom. They could hear her distinctly:

"What's the matter now?—what's the matter with you, silly thing?"—her voice was much agitated, with an unreal gentleness.

"I thought it was some men come," said the plaintive voice of the child. "Has he come?"

"Yes, they've brought him. There's nothing to make a fuss about. Go to sleep now, like a good child."

They could hear her voice in the bedroom, they waited whilst she covered the children under the bedclothes.

"Is he drunk?" asked the girl, timidly, faintly.

"No! No—he's not! He—he's asleep."

"Is he asleep downstairs?"

"Yes—and don't make a noise."

There was silence for a moment, then the men heard the frightened child again:

"What's that noise?"

"It's nothing, I tell you, what are you bothering for?"

The noise was the grandmother moaning. She was oblivious of everything, sitting on her chair rocking and moaning. The manager put his hand on her arm and bade her "Sh—sh!!"

The old woman opened her eyes and looked at him. She was shocked by this interruption, and seemed to wonder.

"What time is it?"—the plaintive thin voice of the child, sinking back unhappily into sleep, asked this last question.

"Ten o'clock," answered the mother more softly. Then she must have bent down and kissed the children.

Matthews beckoned to the men to come away. They put on their caps and took up the stretcher. Stepping over the body, they tiptoed out of the house. None of them spoke till they were far from the wakeful children.

When Elizabeth came down she found his mother alone on the parlor floor, leaning over the dead man, the tears dropping on him.

"We must lay him out," the wife said. She put on the kettle, then returning knelt at the feet, and began to unfasten the knotted leather laces. The room was clammy and dim with only one candle, so that she had to bend her face almost to the floor. At last she got off the heavy boots and put them away.

"You must help me now," she whispered to the old woman. Together they stripped the man.

When they arose, saw him lying in the naïve dignity of death, the women stood arrested in fear and respect. For a few moments they remained still, looking down, the old mother whimpering. Elizabeth felt countermanded. She saw him, how utterly inviolable he lay in himself. She had nothing to do with him. She could not accept it. Stooping, she laid her hand on him, in claim. He was still warm, for the mine was hot where he had died. His mother had his face between her hands, and was murmuring incoherently. The old tears fell in succession as drops from wet leaves; the mother was not weeping, merely her tears flowed. Elizabeth embraced the body of her husband, with cheek and lips. She seemed to be listening, inquiring, trying to get some connection. But she could not. She was driven away. He was impregnable.

She rose, went into the kitchen, where she poured warm water into a bowl, brought soap and flannel and a soft towel.

"I must wash him," she said.

Then the old mother rose stiffly, and watched Elizabeth as she carefully washed his face, carefully brushing the big blond moustache from his mouth with the flannel. She was afraid with a bottomless fear, so she ministered to him. The old woman, jealous, said:

"Let me wipe him!"—and she kneeled on the other side drying slowly as Elizabeth washed, her big black bonnet sometimes brushing the dark head of her daughter-in-law. They worked thus in silence for a long time. They never forgot it was death, and the touch of the man's dead body gave them strange emotions, different in each of the women; a great dread possessed them both, the mother felt the lie was given to her womb, she was denied; the wife felt the utter isolation of the human soul, the child within her was a weight apart from her.

At last it was finished. He was a man of handsome body, and his face showed no traces of drink. He was blond, full-fleshed, with fine limbs. But he was dead.

"Bless him," whispered his mother, looking always at his face, and speaking out of sheer terror. "Dear lad—bless him!" She spoke in a faint, sibilant ecstasy of fear and mother love.

Elizabeth sank down again to the floor, and put her face against his neck, and trembled and shuddered. But she had to draw away again. He was dead, and her living flesh had no place against his. A great dread and weariness held her: he was so unavailing. Her life was gone like his.

"White as milk he is, clear as a twelve-month baby, bless him, the darling!" the old mother murmured to herself. "Not a mark on him, clear and clean and white, beautiful as ever a child was made," she murmured with pride. Elizabeth kept her face hidden.

"He went peaceful, Lizzie—peaceful as sleep. Isn't he beautiful, the lamb? Ay—he must ha' made his peace, Lizzie. 'Appen he made it all right, Lizzie, shut in there. He'd have time. He wouldn't look like this if he hadn't made his peace. The lamb, the dear lamb. Eh, but he had a hearty laugh. I loved to hear it. He had the heartiest laugh, Lizzie, as a lad—"

Elizabeth looked up. The man's mouth was fallen back, slightly open under the cover of the moustache. The eyes, half shut, did not show glazed in the obscurity. Life with its smoky burning gone from him, had left him apart and utterly alien to her. And she knew what a stranger he was to her. In her womb was ice of fear, because of this separate stranger with whom she had been living as one flesh. Was this what it all meant—utter, intact separateness, obscured by heat of living? In dread she turned her face away. The fact was too deadly. There had been nothing between them, and yet they had come together, exchanging their nakedness repeatedly. Each time he had taken her, they had been two isolated beings, far apart as now. He was no more responsible than she. The child was like ice in her womb. For as she looked at the dead man, her mind, cold and detached, said clearly: "Who am I? What have I been doing? I have been fighting a husband who did not exist. *He* existed all the time. What wrong have I done? What was that I have been living with? There lies the reality, this man." And her soul died in her for fear: she knew she had never seen him, he had never seen her, they had met in the dark and had fought in the dark, not knowing whom they met nor whom they fought. And now she saw, and turned silent in seeing. For she had been wrong. She had said he was something he was not; she had felt familiar with him. Whereas he was apart all the while, living as she never lived, feeling as she never felt.

In fear and shame she looked at his naked body, that she had known falsely. And he was the father of her children. Her soul was torn from her body and stood apart. She looked at his naked body and was ashamed, as if she had denied it. After all, it was itself. It seemed awful to her. She looked at his face, and she turned her own face to the wall. For his look was other than hers, his way was not her way. She had denied him what he was— she saw it now. She had refused him as himself. And this had been her life, and his life. She was grateful to death, which restored the truth. And she knew she was not dead.

And all the while her heart was bursting with grief and pity for him. What had he suffered? What stretch of horror for this helpless man! She was rigid with agony. She had not been able to help him. He had been cruelly injured, this naked man, this other being, and she could make no reparation. There were the children—but the children belonged to life. This dead man had nothing to do with them. He and she were only channels through which life had flowed to issue in the children. She was a mother—but how awful she knew it now to have been a wife. And he, dead now, how awful he must have felt it to be a husband. She felt that in the next world he would be a stranger to her. If they met there, in the beyond, they would only be ashamed of what had been before. The children had come, for some mysterious reason, out of both of them. But the children did not unite them. Now he was dead, she knew how eternally he was apart from her, how eternally he had nothing more to do with her. She saw this episode of her life closed. They had denied each other in life. Now he had withdrawn. An anguish came over her. It was finished then: it had become hopeless between them long before he died. Yet he had been her husband. But how little!

"Have you got his shirt, 'Lizabeth?"

Elizabeth turned without answering, though she strove to weep and behave as her mother-in-law expected. But she could not, she was silenced. She went into the kitchen and returned with the garment.

"It is aired," she said, grasping the cotton shirt here and there to try. She was almost ashamed to handle him; what right had she or any one to lay hands on him; but her touch was humble on his body. It was hard work to clothe him. He was so heavy and inert. A terrible dread gripped her all the while: that he could be so heavy and utterly inert, unresponsive, apart. The horror of the distance between them was almost too much for her —it was so infinite a gap she must look across.

At last it was finished. They covered him with a sheet and left him lying, with his face bound. And she fastened the door of the little parlor, lest the children should see what was lying there. Then, with peace sunk heavy on her heart, she went about making tidy the kitchen. She knew she submitted to life, which was her immediate master. But from death, her ultimate master, she winced with fear and shame.

D. H. LAWRENCE

The Shadow in the Rose Garden

A rather small young man sat by the window of a pretty seaside cottage trying to persuade himself that he was reading the newspaper. It was about half-past eight in the morning. Outside, the glory roses hung in the morning sunshine like little bowls of fire tipped up. The young man looked at the table, then at the clock, then at his own big silver watch. An expression of stiff endurance came on to his face. Then he rose and reflected on the oil-paintings that hung on the walls of the room, giving careful but hostile attention to "The Stag at Bay." He tried the lid of the piano, and found it locked. He caught sight of his own face in a little mirror, pulled his brown moustache, and an alert interest sprang into his eyes. He was not ill-favored. He twisted his moustache. His figure was rather small, but alert and vigorous. As he turned from the mirror a look of self-commiseration mingled with his appreciation of his own physiognomy.

In a state of self-suppression, he went through into the garden. His jacket, however, did not look dejected. It was new, and had a smart and self-confident air, sitting upon a confident body. He contemplated the Tree of Heaven that flourished by the lawn, then sauntered on to the next plant. There was more promise in a crooked apple tree covered with brown-red fruit. Glancing round, he broke off an apple and, with his back to the house, took a clean, sharp bite. To his surprise the fruit was sweet. He took another. Then again he turned to survey the bedroom windows overlooking the garden. He started, seeing a woman's figure; but it was only his wife. She was gazing across to the sea, apparently ignorant of him.

The Shadow in the Rose Garden · 453

For a moment or two he looked at her, watching her. She was a good-looking woman, who seemed older than he, rather pale, but healthy, her face yearning. Her rich auburn hair was heaped in folds on her forehead. She looked apart from him and his world, gazing away to the sea. It irked her husband that she should continue abstracted and in ignorance of him; he pulled poppy fruits and threw them at the window. She started, glanced at him with a wild smile, and looked away again. Then almost immediately she left the window. He went indoors to meet her. She had a fine carriage, very proud, and wore a dress of soft white muslin.

"I've been waiting long enough," he said.

"For me or for breakfast?" she said lightly. "You know we said nine o'clock. I should have thought you could have slept after the journey."

"You know I'm always up at five, and I couldn't stop in bed after six. You might as well be in pit as in bed, on a morning like this."

"I shouldn't have thought the pit would occur to you, here."

She moved about examining the room, looking at the ornaments under glass covers. He, planted on the hearth-rug, watched her rather uneasily, and grudgingly indulgent. She shrugged her shoulders at the apartment.

"Come," she said, taking his arm, "let us go into the garden till Mrs. Coates brings the tray."

"I hope she'll be quick," he said, pulling his moustache. She gave a short laugh, and leaned on his arm as they went. He had lighted a pipe.

Mrs. Coates entered the room as they went down the steps. The delightful, erect old lady hastened to the window for a good view of her visitors. Her china-blue eyes were bright as she watched the young couple go down the path, he walking in an easy, confident fashion, with his wife on his arm. The landlady began talking to herself in a soft, Yorkshire accent.

"Just of a height they are. She wouldn't ha' married a man less than herself in stature, I think, though he's not her equal otherwise." Here her granddaughter came in, setting a tray on the table. The girl went to the old woman's side.

"He's been eating the apples, Gran'," she said.

"Has he, my pet? Well, if he's happy, why not?"

Outside, the young, well-favored man listened with impatience to the chink of the tea-cups. At last, with a sigh of relief, the couple came in to breakfast. After he had eaten for some time, he rested a moment and said:

"Do you think it's any better place than Bridlington?"

"I do," she said, "infinitely! Besides, I am at home here—it's not like a strange seaside place to me."

"How long were you here?"

"Two years."

He ate reflectively.

"I should ha' thought you'd rather go to a fresh place," he said at length.

She sat very silent, and then, delicately, put out a feeler.

"Why?" she said. "Do you think I shan't enjoy myself?"

He laughed comfortably, putting the marmalade thick on his bread.

"I hope so," he said.

She again took no notice of him.

"But don't say anything about it in the village, Frank," she said casually. "Don't say who I am, or that I used to live here. There's nobody I want to meet, particularly, and we should never feel free if they knew me again."

"Why did you come, then?"

" 'Why?' Can't you understand why?"

"Not if you don't want to know anybody."

"I came to see the place, not the people."

He did not say any more.

"Women," she said, "are different from men. I don't know why I wanted to come—but I did."

She helped him to another cup of coffee, solicitously.

"Only," she resumed, "don't talk about me in the village." She laughed shakily. "I don't want my past brought up against me, you know." And she moved the crumbs on the cloth with her finger-tip.

He looked at her as he drank his coffee; he sucked his moustache, and putting down his cup, said phlegmatically:

"I'll bet you've had a lot of past."

She looked with a little guiltiness, that flattered him, down at the tablecloth.

"Well," she said, caressive, "you won't give me away, who I am, will you?"

"No," he said, comforting, laughing. "I won't give you away." He was pleased.

She remained silent. After a moment or two she lifted her head, saying:

"I've got to arrange with Mrs. Coates, and do various things. So you'd better go out by yourself this morning—and we'll be in to dinner at one."

"But you can't be arranging with Mrs. Coates all morning," he said.

"Oh, well—then I've got some letters to write, and I must get that mark out of my skirt. I've got plenty of little things to do this morning. You'd better go out by yourself."

He perceived that she wanted to be rid of him, so that when she went upstairs, he took his hat and lounged out on to the cliffs, suppressedly angry.

Presently she too came out. She wore a hat with roses, and a long lace scarf hung over her white dress. Rather nervously, she put up her sunshade, and her face was half hidden in its colored shadow. She went along the narrow track of flag-stones that were worn hollow by the feet of the fishermen. She seemed to be avoiding her surroundings, as if she remained safe in the little obscurity of her parasol.

She passed the church, and went down the lane till she came to a high wall by the wayside. Under this she went slowly, stopping at length by an open doorway, which shone like a picture of light in the dark wall. There in the magic beyond the doorway, patterns of shadow lay on the sunny court, on the blue and white sea-pebbles of its paving, while a green lawn glowed beyond, where a bay tree glittered at the edges. She tiptoed nervously into the courtyard, glancing at the house that stood in shadow. The uncurtained windows looked black and soulless, the kitchen door stood open. Irresolutely she took a step forwards, and again forward, leaning, yearning, towards the garden beyond.

She had almost gained the corner of the house when a heavy step came crunching through the trees. A gardener appeared before her. He held a wicker tray on which were rolling great, dark red gooseberries, over-ripe. He moved slowly.

"The garden isn't open to-day," he said quietly to the attractive woman, who was poised for retreat.

For a moment she was silent with surprise. How should it be public at all?

"When is it open?" she asked, quick-witted.

"The rector lets visitors in on Fridays and Tuesdays."

She stood still, reflecting. How strange to think of the rector opening his garden to the public!

"But everybody will be at church," she said coaxingly to the man. "There'll be nobody here, will there?"

He moved, and the big gooseberries rolled.

"The rector lives at the new rectory," he said.

The two stood still. He did not like to ask her to go. At last she turned to him with a winning smile.

"Might I have *one* peep at the roses?" she coaxed, with pretty wilfulness.

"I don't suppose it would matter," he said, moving aside; "you won't stop long—"

She went forward, forgetting the gardener in a moment. Her face became strained, her movements eager. Glancing round, she saw all the windows giving on to the lawn were curtainless and dark. The house had a sterile appearance, as if it were still used, but not inhabited. A shadow seemed to go over her. She went across the lawn towards the garden, through an arch of crimson ramblers, a gate of color. There beyond lay the soft blue sea within the bay, misty with morning, and the farthest headland of black rock jutting dimly out between blue and blue of the sky and water. Her face began to shine, transfigured with pain and joy. At her feet the garden fell steeply, all a confusion of flowers, and away below was the darkness of tree-tops covering the beck.

She turned to the garden that shone with sunny flowers around her. She knew the little corner where was the seat beneath the yew tree. Then there was the terrace where a great host of flowers shone, and from this, two paths went down, one at each side of the garden. She closed her sunshade and walked slowly among the many flowers. All round were rose bushes, big banks of roses, then roses hanging and tumbling from pillars, or roses balanced on the standard bushes. By the open earth were many other flowers. If she lifted her head, the sea was upraised beyond, and the Cape.

Slowly she went down one path, lingering, like one who has gone back into the past. Suddenly she was touching some heavy crimson roses that were soft as velvet, touching them thoughtfully, without knowing, as a mother sometimes fondles the hand of her child. She leaned slightly forward to catch the scent. Then she wandered on in abstraction. Sometimes a flame-colored, scentless rose would hold her arrested. She stood gazing at it as if she could not understand it. Again the same softness of intimacy came over her, as she stood before a tumbling heap of pink petals. Then she wondered over the white rose, that was greenish, like ice, in the center. So, slowly, like a white, pathetic butterfly, she drifted down the path, coming at last to a tiny terrace all full of roses. They seemed to fill the place, a sunny, gay throng. She was shy of them, they were so many and so bright. They seemed to be conversing and laughing. She felt herself in a strange crowd. It exhilarated her, carried her out of herself. She flushed with excitement. The air was pure scent.

Hastily, she went to a little seat among the white roses, and sat down. Her scarlet sunshade made a hard blot of color. She sat quite still, feeling her own existence lapse. She was no more than a rose, a rose that could not quite come into blossom, but remained tense. A little fly dropped on her knee, on her white dress. She watched it, as if it had fallen on a rose. She was not herself.

Then she started cruelly as a shadow crossed her and a figure moved into her sight. It was a man who had come in slippers, unheard. He wore a linen coat. The morning was shattered, the spell vanished away. She was only afraid of being questioned. He came forward. She rose. Then, seeing him, the strength went from her and she sank on the seat again.

He was a young man, military in appearance, growing slightly stout. His black hair was brushed smooth and bright, his moustache was waxed. But there was something rambling in his gait. She looked up, blanched to the lips, and saw his eyes. They were black, and stared without seeing. They were not a man's eyes. He was coming towards her.

He stared at her fixedly, made an unconscious salute, and sat down beside her on the seat. He moved on the bench, shifted his feet, saying, in a gentlemanly, military voice:

"I don't disturb you—do I?"

She was mute and helpless. He was scrupulously dressed in dark clothes and a linen coat. She could not move. Seeing his hands, with the ring she knew so well upon the little finger, she felt as if she were going dazed. The whole world was deranged. She sat unavailing. For his hands, her symbols of passionate love, filled her with horror as they rested now on his strong thighs.

"May I smoke?" he asked intimately, almost secretly, his hand going to his pocket.

She could not answer, but it did not matter, he was in another world. She wondered, craving, if he recognized her—if he could recognize her. She sat pale with anguish. But she had to go through with it.

"I haven't got any tobacco," he said thoughtfully.

But she paid no heed to his words, only she attended to him. Could he recognize her, or was it all gone? She sat still in a frozen kind of suspense.

"I smoke John Cotton," he said, "and I must economize with it, it is expensive. You know, I'm not very well off while these lawsuits are going on."

"No," she said, and her heart was cold, her soul kept rigid.

He moved, made a loose salute, rose, and went away. She sat motionless. She could see his shape, the shape she had loved with all her passion: his compact, soldier's head, his fine figure now slackened. And it was not he. It only filled her with horror too difficult to know.

Suddenly he came again, his hand in his jacket pocket.

"Do you mind if I smoke?" he said. "Perhaps I shall be able to see things more clearly."

He sat down beside her again, filling a pipe. She watched his hands with the fine strong fingers. They had always inclined to tremble slightly. It surprised her, long ago, in such a healthy man. Now they moved inaccurately, and the tobacco hung raggedly out of the pipe.

"I have legal business to attend to. Legal affairs are always so uncertain. I tell my solicitor exactly, precisely what I want, but I can never get it done."

She sat and heard him talking. But it was not he. Yet those were the hands she had kissed, there were the glistening, strange black eyes that she had loved. Yet it was not he. She sat motionless with horror and silence. He dropped his tobacco-pouch, and groped for it on the ground. Yet she must wait to see if he would recognize her. Why could she not go? In a moment he rose.

"I must go at once," he said. "The owl is coming." Then he added confidentially: "His name isn't really the owl, but I call him that. I must go and see if he has come."

She rose too. He stood before her, uncertain. He was a handsome, soldierly fellow, and a lunatic. Her eyes searched him, and searched him, to see if he would recognize her, if she could discover him.

"You don't know me?" she asked, from the terror of her soul, standing alone.

He looked back at her quizzically. She had to bear his eyes. They gleamed on her, but with no intelligence. He was drawing nearer to her.

"Yes, I do know you," he said, fixed, intent, but mad, drawing his face nearer hers. Her horror was too great. The powerful lunatic was coming too near to her.

A man approached, hastening.

"The garden isn't open this morning," he said.

The deranged man stopped and looked at him. The keeper went to the seat and picked up the tobacco-pouch left lying there.

"Don't leave your tobacco, sir," he said, taking it to the gentleman in the linen coat.

"I was just asking this lady to stay to lunch," the latter said politely. "She is a friend of mine."

The woman turned and walked swiftly, blindly, between the sunny roses, out from the garden, past the house with the blank, dark windows, through the sea-pebbled courtyard to the street. Hastening and blind, she went forward without hesitating, not knowing whither. Directly she came to the house she went upstairs, took off her hat, and sat down on the bed. It was as if some membrane had been torn in two in her, so that she was not an entity that could think and feel. She sat staring across at the window, where an ivy spray waved slowly up and down in the sea wind. There was some of the uncanny luminousness of the sunlit sea in the air. She sat perfectly still, without any being. She only felt she might be sick, and it might be blood that was loose in her torn entrails. She sat perfectly still and passive.

After a time she heard the hard tread of her husband on the floor below, and, without herself changing, she registered his movement. She heard his rather disconsolate footsteps go out again, then his voice speaking, answering, growing cheery, and his solid tread drawing near.

He entered, ruddy, rather pleased, an air of complacency about his alert, sturdy figure. She moved stiffly. He faltered in his approach.

"What's the matter?" he asked, a tinge of impatience in his voice. "Aren't you feeling well?"

This was torture to her.

"Quite," she replied.

His brown eyes became puzzled and angry.

"What is the matter?" he said.

"Nothing."

He took a few strides, and stood obstinately, looking out of the window.

"Have you run up against anybody?" he asked.

"Nobody who knows me," she said.

His hands began to twitch. It exasperated him, that she was no more sensible of him than if he did not exist. Turning on her at length, driven, he asked:

"Something has upset you, hasn't it?"

"No, why?" she said, neutral. He did not exist for her, except as an irritant.

His anger rose, filling the veins of his throat.

"It seems like it," he said, making an effort not to show his anger, because there seemed no reason for it. He went away downstairs. She sat still on the bed, and with the residue of feeling left to her, she disliked him because he tormented her. The time went by. She could smell the dinner being served, the smoke of her husband's pipe from the garden. But she could not move. She had no being. There was a tinkle of the bell. She heard him come indoors. And then he mounted the stairs again. At every step her heart grew tight in her. He opened the door.

"Dinner is on the table," he said.

It was difficult for her to endure his presence, for he would interfere with her. She could not recover her life. She rose stiffly and went down. She could neither eat nor talk during the meal. She sat absent, torn, without any being of her own. He tried to go on as if nothing were the matter. But at last he became silent with fury. As soon as it was possible, she went upstairs again, and locked the bedroom door. She must be alone. He went with his pipe into the garden. All his suppressed anger against her who held herself superior to him filled and blackened his heart. Though he had not known it, yet he had never really won her, she had never loved him. She had taken him on sufferance. This had foiled him. He was only a laboring electrician in the mine, she was superior to him. He had always given way to her. But all the while, the injury and ignominy had been working in his soul because she did not hold him seriously. And now all his rage came up against her.

He turned and went indoors. The third time, she heard him mounting the stairs. Her heart stood still. He turned the catch and pushed the door—it was locked. He tried it again, harder. Her heart was standing still.

"Have you fastened the door?" he asked quietly, because of the landlady.

"Yes. Wait a minute."

She rose and turned the lock, afraid he would burst in. She felt hatred towards him, because he did not leave her free. He entered, his pipe between his teeth, and she returned to her old position on the bed. He closed the door and stood with his back to it.

"What's the matter?" he asked determinedly.

She was sick of him. She could not look at him.

"Can't you leave me alone?" she replied, averting her face from him.

He looked at her quickly, wincing with ignominy. Then he seemed to consider for a moment.

"There's something up with you, isn't there?" he asked definitely.

"Yes," she said, "but that's no reason why you should torment me."

"I don't torment you. What's the matter?"

"Why should you know?" she cried, in hate and desperation.

Something snapped. He started and caught his pipe as it fell from his mouth. Then he pushed forward the bitten-off mouthpiece with his tongue, took it from off his lips, and looked at it. Then he put out his pipe, and brushed the ash from his waistcoat. After which he raised his head.

"I want to know," he said. His face was greyish pale, and set uglily.

Neither looked at the other. She knew he was fired now. His heart was pounding heavily. She hated him, but she could not withstand him. Suddenly she lifted her head and turned on him.

"What right have you to know?" she asked.

He looked at her. She felt a pang of surprise for his tortured eyes and his fixed face. But her heart hardened swiftly. She had never loved him. She did not love him now.

But suddenly she lifted her head again swiftly, like a thing that tries to get free. She wanted to be free of it. It was not him so much, but it, something she had put on herself, that bound her so horribly. And having put the bond on herself, it was hardest to take it off. But now she hated everything and felt destructive. He stood with his back to the door, fixed, as if he would oppose her eternally, till she was extinguished. She looked at him. Her eyes were cold and hostile. His workman's hands spread on the panels of the door behind him.

"You know I used to live here?" she began, in a hard voice, as if wilfully to wound him. He braced himself against her, and nodded.

"Well, I was companion to Miss Birch of Torril Hall—she and the rector were friends, and Archie was the rector's son." There was a pause. He listened without knowing what was happening. He stared at his wife. She was squatted in her white dress on the bed, carefully folding and re-folding the hem of her skirt. Her voice was full of hostility.

"He was an officer—a sub-lieutenant—then he quarreled with his colonel and came out of the army. At any rate"—she plucked at her skirt hem, her husband stood motionless, watching her movements which filled his veins with madness—"he was awfully fond of me, and I was of him—awfully."

"How old was he?" asked the husband.

"When—when I first knew him? Or when he went away—?"

"When you first knew him."

"When I first knew him, he was twenty-six—he's thirty-one—

nearly thirty-two—because I'm twenty-nine, and he is nearly three years older—"

She lifted her head and looked at the opposite wall.

"And what then?" said her husband.

She hardened herself, and said callously:

"We were as good as engaged for nearly a year, though nobody knew—at least—they talked—but—it wasn't open. Then he went away—"

"He chucked you?" said the husband brutally, wanting to hurt her into contact with himself. Her heart rose wildly with rage. Then "Yes," she said, to anger him. He shifted from one foot to the other, giving a "Pah!" of rage. There was silence for a time.

"Then," she resumed, her pain giving a mocking note to her words, "he suddenly went out to fight in Africa, and almost the very day I first met you, I heard from Miss Birch he'd got sunstroke—and two months after, that he was dead—"

"That was before you took on with me?" said the husband.

There was no answer. Neither spoke for a time. He had not understood. His eyes were contracted uglily.

"So you've been looking at your old courting places!" he said. "That was what you wanted to go out by yourself for this morning."

Still she did not answer him anything. He went away from the door to the window. He stood with his hands behind him, his back to her. She looked at him. His hands seemed gross to her, the back of his head paltry.

At length, almost against his will, he turned round, asking:

"How long were you carrying on with him?"

"What do you mean?" she replied coldly.

"I mean how long were you carrying on with him?"

She lifted her head, averting her face from him. She refused to answer. Then she said:

"I don't know what you mean, by carrying on. I loved him from the first days I met him—two months after I went to stay with Miss Birch."

"And do you reckon he loved you?" he jeered.

"I know he did."

"How do you know, if he'd have no more to do with you?"

There was a long silence of hate and suffering.

"And how far did it go between you?" he asked at length, in a frightened, stiff voice.

"I hate your not-straightforward questions," she cried, beside herself with his baiting. "We loved each other, and we *were* lovers—we were. I don't care what *you* think: what have you got to do with it? We were lovers before I knew you—"

"Lovers—lovers," he said, white with fury. "You mean you had your fling with an army man, and then came to me to marry when you'd had done—"

She sat swallowing her bitterness. There was a long pause.

"Do you mean to say you used to go—the whole hogger?" he asked, still incredulous.

"Why, what else do you think I mean?" she cried brutally.

He shrank, and became white, impersonal. There was a long, paralyzed silence. He seemed to have gone small.

"You never thought to tell me all this before I married you," he said, with bitter irony, at last.

"You never asked me," she replied.

"I never thought there was any need."

"Well, then, you *should* think."

He stood with expressionless, almost child-like set face, revolving many thoughts, whilst his heart was mad with anguish.

Suddenly she added:

"And I saw him to-day," she said. "He is not dead, he's mad."

"Mad!" he said involuntarily.

"A lunatic," she said. It almost cost her her reason to utter the word. There was a pause.

"Did he know you?" asked the husband, in a small voice.

"No," she said.

He stood and looked at her. At last he had learned the width of the breach between them. She still squatted on the bed. He could not go near her. It would be violation to each of them to be brought into contact with the other. The thing must work itself out. They were both shocked so much, they were impersonal, and no longer hated each other. After some minutes he left her and went out.

D. H. LAWRENCE

The White Stocking

"I'm getting up, Teddilinks," said Mrs. Whiston, and she sprang out of bed briskly.

"What the Hanover's got you?" asked Whiston.

"Nothing. Can't I get up?" she replied animatedly.

It was about seven o'clock, scarcely light yet in the cold bedroom. Whiston lay still and looked at his wife. She was a pretty little thing, with her fleecy, short black hair all tousled. He watched her as she dressed quickly, flicking her small, delightful limbs, throwing her clothes about her. Her slovenliness and untidiness did not trouble him. When she picked up the edge of her petticoat, ripped off a torn string of white lace, and flung it on the dressing-table, her careless abandon made his spirit glow. She stood before the mirror and roughly scrambled together her profuse little mane of hair. He watched the quickness and softness of her young shoulders, calmly, like a husband, and appreciatively.

"Rise up," she cried, turning to him with a quick wave of her arm—"and shine forth."

They had been married two years. But still, when she had gone out of the room, he felt as if all his light and warmth were taken away, he became aware of the raw, cold morning. So he rose himself, wondering casually what had roused her so early. Usually she lay in bed as late as she could.

Whiston fastened a belt round his loins and went downstairs in shirt and trousers. He heard her singing in her snatchy fashion. The stairs creaked under his weight. He passed down the narrow little passage, which she called a hall, of the seven and sixpenny house which was his first home.

He was a shapely young fellow of about twenty-eight, sleepy now and easy with well-being. He heard the water drumming into the kettle, and she began to whistle. He loved the quick way she dodged the supper cups under the tap to wash them for breakfast. She looked an untidy minx, but she was quick and handy enough.

"Teddilinks," she cried.

"What?"

"Light a fire, quick."

She wore an old, sack-like dressing-jacket of black silk pinned across her breast. But one of the sleeves, coming unfastened, showed some delightful pink upper-arm.

"Why don't you sew your sleeve up?" he said, suffering from the sight of the exposed soft flesh.

"Where?" she cried, peering round. "Nuisance," she said, seeing the gap, then with light fingers went on drying the cups.

The kitchen was of fair size, but gloomy. Whiston poked out the dead ashes.

Suddenly a thud was heard at the door down the passage.

"I'll go," cried Mrs. Whiston, and she was gone down the hall.

The postman was a ruddy-faced man who had been a soldier. He smiled broadly, handing her some packages.

"They've not forgot you," he said impudently.

"No—lucky for them," she said, with a toss of the head. But she was interested only in her envelopes this morning. The postman waited inquisitively, smiling in an ingratiating fashion. She slowly, abstractedly, as if she did not know anyone was there, closed the door in his face, continuing to look at the addresses on her letters.

She tore open the thin envelope. There was a long, hideous, cartoon valentine. She smiled briefly and dropped it on the floor. Struggling with the string of a packet, she opened a white cardboard box, and there lay a white silk handkerchief packed neatly under the paper lace of the box, and her initial, worked in heliotrope, fully displayed. She smiled pleasantly, and gently put the box aside. The third envelope contained another white packet —apparently a cotton handkerchief neatly folded. She shook it out. It was a long white stocking, but there was a little weight in the toe. Quickly, she thrust down her arm, wriggling her fingers into the toe of the stocking, and brought out a small box. She peeped inside the box, then hastily opened a door on her left hand, and went into the little cold sitting-room. She had her lower lip caught earnestly between her teeth.

With a little flash of triumph, she lifted a pair of pearl ear-rings from the small box, and she went to the mirror. There, earnestly, she began to hook them through her ears, looking at herself sideways in the glass. Curiously concentrated and intent she seemed as she fingered the lobes of her ears, her head bent on one side.

Then the pearl ear-rings dangled under her rosy, small ears. She shook her head sharply, to see the swing of the drops. They went chill against her neck, in little, sharp touches. Then she stood still to look at herself, bridling her head in the dignified fashion. Then she simpered at herself. Catching her own eye, she could not help winking at herself and laughing.

She turned to look at the box. There was a scrap of paper with this posy:

"Pearls may be fair, but thou art fairer.
Wear these for me, and I'll love the wearer."

She made a grimace and a grin. But she was drawn to the mirror again, to look at her ear-rings.

Whiston had made the fire burn, so he came to look for her. When she heard him, she started round quickly, guiltily. She was watching him with intent blue eyes when he appeared.

He did not see much, in his morning-drowsy warmth. He gave her, as ever, a feeling of warmth and slowness. His eyes were very blue, very kind, his manner simple.

"What ha' you got?" he asked.

"Valentines," she said briskly, ostentatiously turning to show him the silk handkerchief. She thrust it under his nose. "Smell how good," she said.

"Who's that from?" he replied, without smelling.

"It's a valentine," she cried. "How do I know who it's from."

"I'll bet you know," he said.

"Ted!—I don't!" she cried, beginning to shake her head, then stopping because of the ear-rings.

He stood still a moment, displeased.

"They've no right to send you valentines now," he said.

"Ted!—Why not? You're not jealous, are you? I haven't the least idea who it's from. Look—there's my initial"—she pointed with an emphatic finger at the heliotrope embroidery—

> "E for Elsie,
> Nice little gelsie,"

she sang.

"Get out," he said. "You know who it's from."

"Truth, I don't," she cried.

He looked round, and saw the white stocking lying on a chair. "Is this another?" he said.

"No, that's a sample," she said. "There's only a comic." And she fetched in the long cartoon.

He stretched it out and looked at it solemnly.

"Fools!" he said, and went out of the room.

She flew upstairs and took off the ear-rings. When she returned, he was crouched before the fire blowing the coals. The skin of his face was flushed, and slightly pitted, as if he had had small-pox. But his neck was white and smooth and goodly. She hung her arms round his neck as he crouched there, and clung to him. He balanced on his toes.

"This fire's a slow-coach," he said.

"And who else is a slow-coach?" she said.

"One of us two, I know," he said, and he rose carefully. She remained clinging round his neck, so that she was lifted off her feet.

"Ha!—swing me," she cried.

He lowered his head, and she hung in the air, swinging from his neck, laughing. Then she slipped off.

"The kettle is singing," she sang, flying for the teapot. He bent down again to blow the fire. The veins in his neck stood out, his shirt collar seemed too tight.

> "Doctor Wyer,
> Blow the fire,
> Puff! puff! puff!"

she sang, laughing.

He smiled at her.

She was so glad because of her pearl ear-rings.

Over the breakfast she grew serious. He did not notice. She

became portentous in her gravity. Almost it penetrated through his steady good-humor to irritate him.

"Teddy!" she said at last.

"What?" he asked.

"I told you a lie," she said, humbly tragic.

His soul stirred uneasily.

"Oh aye?" he said casually.

She was not satisfied. He ought to be more moved.

"Yes," she said.

He cut a piece of bread.

"Was it a good one?" he asked.

She was piqued. Then she considered—*was* it a good one? Then she laughed.

"No," she said, "it wasn't up to much."

"Ah!" he said easily, but with a steady strength of fondness for her in his tone. "Get it out then."

It became a little more difficult.

"You know that white stocking," she said earnestly. "I told you a lie. It wasn't a sample. It was a valentine."

A little frown came on his brow.

"Then what did you invent it as a sample for?" he said. But he knew this weakness of hers. The touch of anger in his voice frightened her.

"I was afraid you'd be cross," she said pathetically.

"I'll bet you were vastly afraid," he said.

"I *was*, Teddy."

There was a pause. He was resolving one or two things in his mind.

"And who sent it?" he asked.

"I can guess," she said, "though there wasn't a word with it—except—"

She ran to the sitting-room and returned with a slip of paper.

"Pearls may be fair, but thou art fairer.
Wear these for me, and I'll love the wearer."

He read it twice, then a dull red flush came on his face.

"And *who* do you guess it is?" he asked, with a ringing of anger in his voice.

"I suspect it's Sam Adams," she said, with a little virtuous indignation.

Whiston was silent for a moment.

"Fool!" he said. "An' what's it got to do with pearls?—and how can he say 'wear these for me' when there's only one? He hasn't got the brain to invent a proper verse."

He screwed the slip of paper into a ball and flung it into the fire.

"I suppose he thinks it'll make a pair with the one last year," she said.

"Why, did he send one then?"

"Yes. I thought you'd be wild if you knew."

His jaw set rather sullenly.

Presently he rose, and went to wash himself, rolling back his sleeves and pulling open his shirt at the breast. It was as if his fine, clear-cut temples and steady eyes were degraded by the lower, rather brutal part of his face. But she loved it. As she whisked about, clearing the table, she loved the way in which he stood washing himself. He was such a man. She liked to see his neck glistening with water as he swilled it. It amused her and pleased her and thrilled her. He was so sure, so permanent, he had her so utterly in his power. It gave her a delightful, mischievous sense of liberty. Within his grasp, she could dart about excitingly.

He turned round to her, his face red from the cold water, his eyes fresh and very blue.

"You haven't been seeing anything of him, have you?" he asked roughly.

"Yes," she answered, after a moment, as if caught guilty. "He got into the tram with me, and he asked me to drink a coffee and a Benedictine in the Royal."

"You've got it off fine and glib," he said sullenly. "And did you?"

"Yes," she replied, with the air of a traitor before the rack.

The blood came up into his neck and face, he stood motionless, dangerous.

"It was cold, and it was such fun to go into the Royal," she said.

"You'd go off with a nigger for a packet of chocolate," he said, in anger and contempt, and some bitterness. Queer how he drew away from her, cut her off from him.

"Ted—how beastly!" she cried. "You know quite well—" She caught her lip, flushed, and the tears came to her eyes.

He turned away, to put on his necktie. She went about her work, making a queer pathetic little mouth, down which occasionally dripped a tear.

He was ready to go. With his hat jammed on his head, and his overcoat buttoned up to his chin, he came to kiss her. He would be miserable all the day if he went without. She allowed herself to be kissed. Her cheek was wet under his lips and his heart burned. She hurt him so deeply. And she felt aggrieved, and did not quite forgive him.

In a moment she went upstairs to her ear-rings. Sweet they looked nestling in the little drawer—sweet! She examined them with voluptuous pleasure, she threaded them in her ears, she looked at herself, she posed and postured and smiled and looked sad and tragic and winning and appealing, all in turn before the mirror. And she was happy, and very pretty.

She wore her ear-rings all morning, in the house. She was self-conscious, and quite brilliantly winsome, when the baker came, wondering if he would notice. All the tradesmen left her door with a glow in them, feeling elated, and unconsciously favoring the delightful little creature, though there had been nothing to notice in her behavior.

She was stimulated all the day. She did not think about her husband. He was the permanent basis from which she took these giddy little flights into nowhere. At night, like chickens and curses, she would come home to him, to roost.

Meanwhile Whiston, a traveller and confidential support of a small firm, hastened about his work, his heart all the while anxious for her, yearning for surety, and kept tense by not getting it.

II

She had been a warehouse girl in Adams's lace factory before she was married. Sam Adams was her employer. He was a bachelor of forty, growing stout, a man well dressed and florid, with a large brown moustache and thin hair. From the rest of his well-groomed, showy appearance, it was evident his baldness was a chagrin to him. He had a good presence, and some Irish blood in his veins.

His fondness for the girls, or the fondness of the girls for him, was notorious. And Elsie, quick, pretty, almost witty little thing

—she *seemed* witty, although, when her sayings were repeated, they were entirely trivial—she had a great attraction for him. He would come into the warehouse dressed in a rather sporting reefer coat, of fawn color, and trousers of fine black-and-white check, a cap with a big peak and a scarlet carnation in his button-hole, to impress her. She was only half impressed. He was too loud for her good taste. Instinctively perceiving this, he sobered down to navy blue. Then a well-built man, florid, with large brown whiskers, smart navy blue suit, fashionable boots, and manly hat, he was the irreproachable. Elsie was impressed.

But meanwhile Whiston was courting her, and she made splendid little gestures, before her bedroom mirror, of the constant-and-true sort.

"True, true till death—"

That was her song. Whiston was made that way, so there was no need to take thought for him.

Every Christmas Sam Adams gave a party at his house, to which he invited his superior work-people—not factory hands and la-borers, but those above. He was a generous man in his way, with a real warm feeling for giving pleasure.

Two years ago Elsie had attended this Christmas-party for the last time. Whiston had accompanied her. At that time he worked for Sam Adams.

She had been very proud of herself, in her close-fitting, full-skirted dress of blue silk. Whiston called for her. Then she tripped beside him, holding her large cashmere shawl across her breast. He strode with long strides, his trousers handsomely strapped under his boots, and her silk shoes bulging the pocket of his full-skirted overcoat.

They passed through the park gates, and her spirits rose. Above them the Castle Rock loomed grandly in the night, the naked trees stood still and dark in the frost, along the boulevard.

They were rather late. Agitated with anticipation, in the cloak-room she gave up her shawl, donned her silk shoes, and looked at herself in the mirror. The loose bunches of curls on either side her face danced prettily, her mouth smiled.

She hung a moment in the door of the brilliantly lighted room. Many people were moving within the blaze of lamps, under the crystal chandeliers, the full skirts of the women balancing and floating, the side-whiskers and white cravats of the men bowing above. Then she entered the light.

In an instant Sam Adams was coming forward, lifting both his arms in boisterous welcome. There was a constant red laugh on his face.

"Come late, would you," he shouted, "like royalty."

He seized her hands and led her forward. He opened his mouth wide when he spoke, and the effect of the warm, dark opening behind the brown whiskers was disturbing. But she was floating into the throng on his arm. He was very gallant.

"Now then," he said, taking her card to write down the dances, "I've got *carte blanche*, haven't I?"

"Mr. Whiston doesn't dance," she said.

"I am a lucky man!" he said, scribbling his initials. "I was born with an *amourette* [1] in my mouth."

He wrote on, quietly. She blushed and laughed, not knowing what it meant.

"Why, what is that?" she said.

"It's you, even littler than you are, dressed in little wings," he said.

"I should have to be pretty small to get in your mouth," she said.

"You think you're too big, do you!" he said easily.

He handed her her card, with a bow.

"Now I'm set up, my darling, for this evening," he said.

Then, quick, always at his ease, he looked over the room. She waited in front of him. He was ready. Catching the eye of the band, he nodded. In a moment, the music began. He seemed to relax, giving himself up.

"Now then, Elsie," he said, with a curious caress in his voice that seemed to lap the outside of her body in a warm glow, delicious. She gave herself to it. She liked it.

He was an excellent dancer. He seemed to draw her close in to him by some male warmth of attraction, so that she became all soft and pliant to him, flowing to his form, whilst he united her with him and they lapsed along in one movement. She was just carried in a kind of strong, warm flood, her feet moved of themselves, and only the music threw her away from him, threw her

[1] *Amourette*. A love affair.

back to him, to his clasp, in his strong form moving against her, rhythmically, deliciously.

When it was over, he was pleased and his eyes had a curious gleam which thrilled her and yet had nothing to do with her. Yet it held her. He did not speak to her. He only looked straight into her eyes with a curious, gleaming look that disturbed her fearfully and deliciously. But also there was in his look some of the automatic irony of the *roué*. It left her partly cold. She was not carried away.

She went, driven by an opposite, heavier impulse, to Whiston. He stood looking gloomy, trying to admit that she had a perfect right to enjoy herself apart from him. He received her with rather grudging kindliness.

"Aren't you going to play whist?" she asked.

"Aye," he said. "Directly."

"I do wish you could dance."

"Well, I can't," he said. "So you enjoy yourself."

"But I should enjoy it better if I could dance with you."

"Nay, you're all right," he said. "I'm not made that way."

"Then you ought to be!" she cried.

"Well, it's my fault, not yours. You enjoy yourself," he bade her. Which she proceeded to do, a little bit irked.

She went with anticipation to the arms of Sam Adams, when the time came to dance with him. It *was* so gratifying, irrespective of the man. And she felt a little grudge against Whiston, soon forgotten when her host was holding her near to him, in a delicious embrace. And she watched his eyes, to meet the gleam in them, which gratified her.

She was getting warmed right through, the glow was penetrating into her, driving away everything else. Only in her heart was a little tightness, like conscience.

When she got a chance, she escaped from the dancing-room to the card-room. There, in a cloud of smoke, she found Whiston playing cribbage. Radiant, roused, animated, she came up to him and greeted him. She was too strong, too vibrant a note in the quiet room. He lifted his head, and a frown knitted his gloomy forehead.

"Are you playing cribbage? Is it exciting? How are you getting on?" she chattered.

He looked at her. None of these questions needed answering, and he did not feel in touch with her. She turned to the cribbage-board.

"Are you white or red?" she asked.

"He's red," replied the partner.

"Then you're losing," she said, still to Whiston. And she lifted the red peg from the board. "One—two—three—four—five—six—seven—eight— Right up there you ought to jump—"

"Now put it back in its right place," said Whiston.

"Where was it?" she asked gaily, knowing her transgression. He took the little red peg away from her and stuck it in its hole.

The cards were shuffled.

"What a shame you're losing," said Elsie.

"You'd better cut for him," said the partner.

She did so hastily. The cards were dealt. She put her hand on his shoulder, looking at his cards.

"It's good," she cried, "isn't it?"

He did not answer, but threw down two cards. It moved him more strongly than was comfortable to have her hand on his shoulder, her curls dangling and touching his ears, whilst she was roused to another man. It made the blood flame over him.

At that moment Sam Adams appeared, florid and boisterous, intoxicated more with himself, with the dancing, than with wine. In his eye the curious, impersonal light gleamed.

"I thought I should find you here, Elsie," he cried boisterously, a disturbing, high note in his voice.

"What made you think so?" she replied, the mischief rousing in her.

The florid, well-built man narrowed his eyes to a smile.

"I should never look for you among the ladies," he said, with a kind of intimate, animal call to her. He laughed, bowed, and offered her his arm.

"Madam, the music waits."

She went almost helplessly, carried along with him, unwilling, yet delighted.

That dance was an intoxication to her. After the first few steps, she felt herself slipping away from herself. She almost knew she was going, she did not even want to go. Yet she must have chosen to go. She lay in the arm of the steady, close man with whom she was dancing, and she seemed to swim away out of contact with the room, into him. She had passed into another, denser element of him, an essential privacy. The room was all vague around her, like an atmosphere, like under sea, with a flow of ghostly, dumb movements. But she herself was held real against her partner, and it seemed she was connected with him, as if the movements of his body and limbs were her own movements, yet not her own movements—and oh, delicious! He also was given up, oblivious, concentrated, into the dance. His eye was unseeing. Only his large, voluptuous body gave off a subtle activity. His fingers seemed to search into her flesh. Every moment, and every moment, she felt she would give way utterly, and sink molten: the fusion point was coming when she would fuse down into perfect unconsciousness at his feet and knees. But he bore her round the room in the dance, and he seemed to sustain all her body with his limbs, his body, and his warmth seemed to come closer into her, nearer, till it would fuse right through her, and she would be as liquid to him, as an intoxication only.

It was exquisite. When it was over, she was dazed, and was scarcely breathing. She stood with him in the middle of the room as if she were alone in a remote place. He bent over her. She expected his lips on her bare shoulder, and waited. Yet they were not alone, they were not alone. It was cruel.

" 'Twas good, wasn't it, my darling?" he said to her, low and delighted. There was a strange impersonality about his low, exultant call that appealed to her irresistibly. Yet why was she aware of some part shut off in her? She pressed his arm, and he led her towards the door.

She was not aware of what she was doing, only a little grain of resistant trouble was in her. The man, possessed, yet with a superficial presence of mind, made way to the dining-room, as if to give her refreshment, cunningly working to his own escape with her. He was molten hot, filmed over with presence of mind, and bottomed with cold disbelief. In the dining-room was Whiston, carrying coffee to the plain, neglected ladies. Elsie saw him, but felt as if he could not see her. She was beyond his reach and ken. A sort of fusion existed between her and the large man at her side. She ate her custard, but an incomplete fusion all the while sustained and contained within the being of her employer.

But she was growing cooler. Whiston came up. She looked at him, and saw him with different eyes. She saw his slim, young man's figure real and enduring before her. That was he. But she was in the spell with the other man, fused with him, and she could not be taken away.

"Have you finished your cribbage?" she asked, with hasty evasion of him.

"Yes," he replied. "Aren't you getting tired of dancing?"

"Not a bit," she said.

"Not she," said Adams heartily. "No girl with any spirit gets tired of dancing. Have something else, Elsie. Come—sherry. Have a glass of sherry with us, Whiston."

Whilst they sipped the wine, Adams watched Whiston almost cunningly, to find his advantage.

"We'd better be getting back—there's the music," he said. "See the women get something to eat, Whiston, will you, there's a good chap."

And he began to draw away. Elsie was drifting helplessly with him. But Whiston put himself beside them, and went along with them. In silence they passed through to the dancing-room. There Adams hesitated, and looked round the room. It was as if he could not see.

A man came hurrying forward, claiming Elsie, and Adams went to his other partner. Whiston stood watching during the dance. She was conscious of him standing there observant of her, like a ghost, or a judgment, or a guardian angel. She was also conscious, much more intimately and impersonally, of the body of the other man moving somewhere in the room. She still belonged to him, but a feeling of distraction possessed her, and helplessness. Adams danced on, adhering to Elsie, waiting his time, with the persistence of cynicism.

The dance was over. Adams was detained. Elsie found herself beside Whiston. There was something shapely about him as he sat, about his knees and his distinct figure, that she clung to it. It was as if he had enduring form. She put her hand on his knee.

"Are you enjoying yourself?" he asked.

"*Ever* so," she replied, with a fervent, yet detached tone.

"It's going on for one o'clock," he said.

"Is it?" she answered. It meant nothing to her.

"Should we be going?" he said.

She was silent. For the first time for an hour or more an inkling of her normal consciousness returned. She resented it.

"What for?" she said.

"I thought you might have had enough," he said.

A slight soberness came over her, an irritation at being frustrated of her illusion.

"Why?" she said.

"We've been here since nine," he said.

There was no answer, no reason. It conveyed nothing to her. She sat detached from him. Across the room Sam Adams glanced at her. She sat there exposed for him.

"You don't want to be too free with Sam Adams," said Whiston cautiously, suffering. "You know what he is."

"How, free?" she asked.

"Why—you don't want to have too much to do with him."

She sat silent. He was forcing her into consciousness of her position. But he could not get hold of her feelings, to change them. She had a curious, perverse desire that he should not.

"I like him," she said.

"What do you find to like in him?" he said, with a hot heart.

"I don't know—but I like him," she said.

She was immutable. He sat feeling heavy and dulled with rage. He was not clear as to what he felt. He sat there unliving whilst she danced. And she, distracted, lost to herself between the opposing forces of the two men, drifted. Between the dances, Whiston kept near to her. She was scarcely conscious. She glanced repeatedly at her card, to see when she would dance again with Adams, half in desire, half in dread. Sometimes she met his steady, glaucous eye as she passed him in the dance. Sometimes she saw the steadiness of his flank as he danced. And it was always as if she rested on his arm, were borne along, up-borne by him, away from herself. And always there was present the other's antagonism. She was divided.

The time came for her to dance with Adams. Oh, the delicious closing of contact with him, of his limbs touching her limbs, his arm supporting her. She seemed to resolve. Whiston had not made himself real to her. He was only a heavy place in her consciousness.

But she breathed heavily, beginning to suffer from the closeness of strain. She was nervous. Adams also was constrained. A tightness, a tension was coming over them all. And he was exasperated, feeling something counteracting physical magnetism, feeling a will stronger with her than his own, intervening in what was becoming a vital necessity to him.

Elsie was almost lost to her own control. As she went forward with him to take her place at the dance, she stooped for her pocket handkerchief. The music sounded for quadrilles. Everybody was ready. Adams stood with his body near her, exerting his attraction over her. He was tense and fighting. She stooped for her pocket handkerchief, and shook it as she rose. It shook out and fell from her hand. With agony, she saw she had taken a white stocking instead of a handkerchief. For a second it lay on the floor, a twist of white stocking. Then, in an instant, Adams picked it up, with a little, surprised laugh of triumph.

"That'll do for me," he whispered—seeming to take possession of her. And he stuffed the stocking in his trousers pocket, and quickly offered her his handkerchief.

The dance began. She felt weak and faint, as if her will were turned to water. A heavy sense of loss came over her. She could not help herself any more. But it was peace.

When the dance was over, Adams yielded her up. Whiston came to her.

"What was it as you dropped?" Whiston asked.

"I thought it was my handkerchief—I'd taken a stocking by mistake," she said, detached and muted.

"And he's got it?"

"Yes."

"What does he mean by that?"

She lifted her shoulders.

"Are you going to let him keep it?" he asked.

"I don't let him."

There was a long pause.

"Am I to go and have it out with him?" he asked, his face flushed, his blue eyes going hard with opposition.

"No," she said, pale.

"Why?"

"No—I don't want you to say anything about it."

He sat exasperated and nonplussed.

"You'll let him keep it, then?" he asked.

She sat silent and made no form of answer.

"What do you mean by it?" he said, dark with fury. And he started up.

"No!" she cried. "Ted!" And she caught hold of him, sharply detaining him.

It made him black with rage.

"Why?" he said.

Then something about her mouth was pitiful to him. He did not understand, but he felt she must have her reasons.

"Then I'm not stopping here," he said. "Are you coming with me?"

She rose mutely, and they went out of the room. Adams had not noticed.

In a few moments they were in the street.

"What the hell do you mean?" he said, in a black fury.

She went at his side, in silence, neutral.

"That great hog, an' all," he added.

Then they went a long time in silence through the frozen, deserted darkness of the town. She felt she could not go indoors. They were drawing near her house.

"I don't want to go home," she suddenly cried in distress and anguish. "I don't want to go home."

He looked at her.

"Why don't you?" he said.

"I don't want to go home," was all she could sob.

He heard somebody coming.

"Well, we can walk a bit farther," he said.

She was silent again. They passed out of the town into the fields. He held her by the arm—they could not speak.

"What's a-matter?" he asked at length, puzzled.

She began to cry again.

At last he took her in his arms, to soothe her. She sobbed by herself, almost unaware of him.

"Tell me what's a-matter, Elsie," he said. "Tell me what's a-matter—my dear—tell me, then—"

He kissed her wet face, and caressed her. She made no response.

He was puzzled and tender and miserable.

At length she became quiet. Then he kissed her, and she put her arms round him, and clung to him very tight, as if for fear and anguish. He held her in his arms, wondering.

"Ted!" she whispered, frantic. "Ted!"

"What, my love?" he answered, becoming also afraid.

"Be good to me," she cried. "Don't be cruel to me."

"No, my pet," he said, amazed and grieved. "Why?"

"Oh, be good to me," she sobbed.

And he held her very safe, and his heart was white-hot with love for her. His mind was amazed. He could only hold her against his chest that was white-hot with love and belief in her. So she was restored at last.

III

She refused to go to her work at Adams's any more. Her father had to submit and she sent in her notice—she was not well. Sam Adams was ironical. But he had a curious patience. He did not fight.

In a few weeks, she and Whiston were married. She loved him with passion and worship, a fierce little abandon of love that moved him to the depths of his being, and gave him a permanent surety and sense of realness in himself. He did not trouble about himself any more: he felt he was fulfilled and now he had only the many things in the world to busy himself about. Whatever troubled him, at the bottom was surety. He had found himself in this love.

They spoke once or twice of the white stocking.

"Ah!" Whiston exclaimed. "What does it matter?"

He was impatient and angry, and could not bear to consider the matter. So it was left unresolved.

She was quite happy at first, carried away by her adoration of her husband. Then gradually she got used to him. He always was the ground of her happiness, but she got used to him, as to the air she breathed. He never got used to her in the same way.

Inside of marriage she found her liberty. She was rid of the responsibility of herself. Her husband must look after that. She was free to get what she could out of her time.

So that, when, after some months, she met Sam Adams, she was

482 · D. H. LAWRENCE

not quite as unkind to him as she might have been. With a young wife's new and exciting knowledge of men, she perceived he was in love with her, she knew he had always kept an unsatisfied desire for her. And, sportive, she could not help playing a little with this, though she cared not one jot for the man himself.

When Valentine's day came, which was near the first anniversary of her wedding day, there arrived a white stocking with a little amethyst brooch. Luckily Whiston did not see it, so she said nothing of it to him. She had not the faintest intention of having anything to do with Sam Adams, but once a little brooch was in her possession, it was hers, and she did not trouble her head for a moment how she had come by it. She kept it.

Now she had the pearl ear-rings. They were a more valuable and a more conspicuous present. She would have to ask her mother to give them to her, to explain their presence. She made a little plan in her head. And she was extraordinarily pleased. As for Sam Adams, even if he saw her wearing them, he would not give her away. What fun, if he saw her wearing his ear-rings! She would pretend she had inherited them from her grandmother, her mother's mother. She laughed to herself as she went down-town in the afternoon, the pretty drops dangling in front of her curls. But she saw no one of importance.

Whiston came home tired and depressed. All day the male in him had been uneasy, and this had fatigued him. She was curiously against him, inclined, as she sometimes was nowadays, to make mock of him and jeer at him and cut him off. He did not understand this, and it angered him deeply. She was uneasy before him.

She knew he was in a state of suppressed irritation. The veins stood out on the backs of his hands, his brow was drawn stiffly. Yet she could not help goading him.

"What did you do wi' that white stocking?" he asked, out of a gloomy silence, his voice strong and brutal.

"I put it in a drawer—why?" she replied flippantly.

"Why didn't you put it on the fire-back?" he asked harshly. "What are you hoarding it up for?"

"I'm not hoarding it up," she said. "I've got a pair."

He relapsed into gloomy silence. She, unable to move him, ran away upstairs, leaving him smoking by the fire. Again she tried on the ear-rings. Then another little inspiration came to her. She drew on the white stockings, both of them.

Presently she came down in them. Her husband still sat immovable and glowering by the fire.

"Look!" she said. "They'll do beautifully."

And she picked up her skirts to her knees, and twisted round, looking at her pretty legs in the neat stockings.

He filled with unreasonable rage, and took the pipe from his mouth.

"Don't they look nice?" she said. "One from last year and one from this, they just do. Save you buying a pair."

And she looked over her shoulders at her pretty calves, and at the dangling frills of her knickers.

"Put your skirts down and don't make a fool of yourself," he said.

"Why a fool of myself?" she asked.

And she began to dance slowly round the room, kicking up her feet half reckless, half jeering, in a ballet-dancer's fashion. Almost fearful, yet in defiance, she kicked up her legs at him, singing as she did so. She resented him.

"You little fool, ha' done with it," he said. "And you'll backfire them stockings, I'm telling you." He was angry. His face flushed dark, he kept his head bent. She ceased to dance.

"I shan't," she said. "They'll come in very useful."

He lifted his head and watched her, with lighted, dangerous eyes.

"You'll put 'em on the fire-back, I tell you," he said.

It was war now. She bent forward, in a ballet-dancer's fashion, and put her tongue between her teeth.

"I shan't backfire them stockings," she sang, repeating his words, "I shan't, I shan't, I shan't."

And she danced round the room doing a high kick to the tune of her words. There was a real biting indifference in her behavior.

"We'll see whether you will or not," he said, "trollops! You'd like Sam Adams to know you was wearing 'em, wouldn't you? That's what would please you."

"Yes, I'd like him to see how nicely they fit me, he might give me some more then."

And she looked down at her pretty legs.

He knew somehow that she *would* like Sam Adams to see how

pretty her legs looked in the white stockings. It made his anger go deep, almost to hatred.

"Yer nasty trolley," he cried. "Put yer petticoats down, and stop being so foul-minded."

"I'm not foul-minded," she said. "My legs are my own. And why shouldn't Sam Adams think they're nice?"

There was a pause. He watched her with eyes glittering to a point.

"Have you been havin' owt to do with him?" he asked.

"I've just spoken to him when I've seen him," she said. "He's not as bad as you would make out."

"Isn't he?" he cried, a certain wakefulness in his voice. "Them who has anything to do wi' him is too bad for me, I tell you."

"Why, what are you frightened of him for?" she mocked.

She was rousing all his uncontrollable anger. He sat glowering. Every one of her sentences stirred him up like a red-hot iron. Soon it would be too much. And she was afraid herself; but she was neither conquered nor convinced.

A curious little grin of hate came on his face. He had a long score against her.

"What am I frightened of him for?" he repeated automatically. "What am I frightened of him for? Why, for you, you stray-running little bitch."

She flushed. The insult went deep into her, right home.

"Well, if you're so dull—" she said, lowering her eyelids, and speaking coldly, haughtily.

"If I'm so dull I'll break your neck the first word you speak to him," he said, tense.

"Pf!" she sneered. "Do you think I'm frightened of you?" She spoke coldly, detached.

She was frightened, for all that, white round the mouth.

His heart was getting hotter.

"You *will* be frightened of me, the next time you have anything to do with him," he said.

"Do you think *you'd* ever be told—ha!"

Her jeering scorn made him go white-hot, molten. He knew he was incoherent, scarcely responsible for what he might do. Slowly, unseeing, he rose and went out of doors, stifled, moved to kill her.

He stood leaning against the garden fence, unable either to see or hear. Below him, far off, fumed the lights of the town. He stood still, unconscious with a black storm of rage, his face lifted to the night.

Presently, still unconscious of what he was doing, he went indoors again. She stood, a small, stubborn figure with tight-pressed lips and big, sullen, childish eyes, watching him, white with fear. He went heavily across the floor and dropped into his chair.

There was a silence.

"*You're* not going to tell me everything I shall do, and everything I shan't," she broke out at last.

He lifted his head.

"I tell you *this*," he said, low and intense. "Have anything to do with Sam Adams, and I'll break your neck."

She laughed, shrill and false.

"How I hate your word 'break your neck,'" she said, with a grimace of the mouth. "It sounds so common and beastly. Can't you say something else—"

There was a dead silence.

"And besides," she said, with a queer chirrup of mocking laughter, "what do you know about anything? He sent me an amethyst brooch and a pair of pearl ear-rings."

"He what?" said Whiston, in a suddenly normal voice. His eyes were fixed on her.

"Sent me a pair of pearl ear-rings, and an amethyst brooch," she repeated, mechanically, pale to the lips.

And her big, black, childish eyes watched him, fascinated, held in her spell.

He seemed to thrust his face and his eyes forward at her, as he rose slowly and came to her. She watched transfixed in terror. Her throat made a small sound, as she tried to scream.

Then, quick as lightning, the back of his hand struck her with a crash across the mouth, and she was flung back blinded against the wall. The shock shook a queer sound out of her. And then she saw him still coming on, his eyes holding her, his fist drawn back, advancing slowly. At any instant the blow might crash into her.

Mad with terror, she raised her hands with a queer clawing movement to cover her eyes and her temples, opening her mouth in a dumb shriek. There was no sound. But the sight of her slowly arrested him. He hung before her, looking at her fixedly, as she stood crouched against the wall with open, bleeding mouth, and wide-staring eyes, and two hands clawing over her temples. And his lust to see her bleed, to break her and destroy her, rose from an old source against her. It carried him. He wanted satisfaction.

But he had seen her standing there, a piteous, horrified thing, and he turned his face aside in shame and nausea. He went and sat heavily in his chair, and a curious ease, almost like sleep, came over his brain.

She walked away from the wall towards the fire, dizzy, white to the lips, mechanically wiping her small, bleeding mouth. He sat motionless. Then, gradually, her breath began to hiss, she shook, and was sobbing silently, in grief for herself. Without looking, he saw. It made his mad desire to destroy her come back.

At length he lifted his head. His eyes were glowing again, fixed on her.

"And what did he give them you for?" he asked, in a steady, unyielding voice.

Her crying dried up in a second. She also was tense.

"They came as valentines," she replied, still not subjugated, even if beaten.

"When, to-day?"

"The pearl ear-rings to-day—the amethyst brooch last year."

"You've had it a year?"

"Yes."

She felt that now nothing would prevent him if he rose to kill her. She could not prevent him any more. She was yielded up to him. They both trembled in the balance, unconscious.

"What have you had to do with him?" he asked, in a barren voice.

"I've not had anything to do with him," she quavered.

"You just kept 'em because they were jewellery?" he said.

A weariness came over him. What was the worth of speaking any more of it? He did not care any more. He was dreary and sick.

She began to cry again, but he took no notice. She kept wiping her mouth on her handkerchief. He could see it, the blood-mark. It made him only more sick and tired of the responsibility of it, the violence, the shame.

When she began to move about again, he raised his head once more from his dead, motionless position.

"Where are the things?" he said.

"They are upstairs," she quavered. She knew the passion had gone down in him.

"Bring them down," he said.

"I won't," she wept, with rage. "You're not going to bully me and hit me like that on the mouth."

And she sobbed again. He looked at her in contempt and compassion and in rising anger.

"Where are they?" he said.

"They're in the little drawer under the looking-glass," she sobbed.

He went slowly upstairs, struck a match, and found the trinkets. He brought them downstairs in his hand.

"These?" he said, looking at them as they lay in his palm.

She looked at them without answering. She was not interested in them any more.

He looked at the little jewels. They were pretty.

"It's none of their fault," he said to himself.

And he searched round slowly, persistently, for a box. He tied the things up and addressed them to Sam Adams. Then he went out in his slippers to post the little package.

When he came back she was still sitting crying.

"You'd better go to bed," he said.

She paid no attention. He sat by the fire. She still cried.

"I'm sleeping down here," he said. "Go you to bed."

In a few moments she lifted her tear-stained, swollen face and looked at him with eyes all forlorn and pathetic. A great flash of anguish went over his body. He went over, slowly, and very gently took her in his hands. She let herself be taken. Then as she lay against his shoulder, she sobbed aloud:

"I never meant—"

"My love—my little love—" he cried, in anguish of spirit, holding her in his arms.

VLADIMIR NABOKOV

Pnin

During the eight years Pnin had taught at Waindell
College he had changed his lodgings—for one reason or
another, mainly sonic—about every semester. The accumulation
of consecutive rooms in his memory now resembled those dis-
plays of grouped elbow chairs on show, and beds, and lamps, and
inglenooks which, ignoring all space-time distinctions, commingle
in the soft light of a furniture store beyond which it snows, and
the dusk deepens, and nobody really loves anybody. The rooms of
his Waindell period looked especially trim in comparison with one
he had had in uptown New York, midway between Tsentral Park
and Reeverside, on a block memorable for the waste paper along
the curb, the bright pat of dog dirt somebody had already slipped
upon, and a tireless boy pitching a ball against the steps of the
high brown porch; and even that room became positively dapper
in Pnin's mind (where a small ball still rebounded) when compared with the old, now dust-blurred lodgings of his long Central-
European, Nansen-passport period.

With age, however, Pnin had become choosy. Pretty fixtures
no longer sufficed. Waindell was a quiet townlet, and Waindellville, in a notch of the hills, was yet quieter; but nothing was quiet
enough for Pnin. There had been, at the start of his life here, that
studio in the thoughtfully furnished College Home for Single Instructors, a very nice place despite certain gregarious drawbacks
("Pingpong, Pnin?" "I don't any more play at games of infants"),
until workmen came and started to drill holes in the street—Brain-
pan Street, Pningrad—and patch them up again, and this went

on and on, in fits of shivering black zigzags and stunned pauses, for weeks, and it did not seem likely they would ever find again the precious tool they had entombed by mistake. There had been (to pick out here and there only special offenders) that room in the eminently hermetic-looking Duke's Lodge, Waindellville: a delightful *kabinet*,[1] above which, however, every evening, among crashing bathroom cascades and banging doors, two monstrous statues on primitive legs of stone would grimly tramp—shapes hard to reconcile with the slender build of his actual upstairs neighbors, who turned out to be the Starrs, of the Fine Arts Department ("I am Christopher, and this is Louise"), an angelically gentle couple keenly interested in Dostoevski and Shostakovich. There had been—in yet another rooming house—a still cozier bedroom-study, with nobody butting in for a free lesson in Russian; but as soon as the formidable Waindell winter began to penetrate the coziness by means of sharp little drafts, coming not only from the window but even from the closet and the base plugs, the room had developed something like a streak of madness or mystic delusion—namely, a tenacious murmur of music, more or less classical, oddly located in Pnin's silver-washed radiator. He tried to muffle it up with a blanket, as if it were a caged songbird, but the song persisted until Mrs. Thayer's old mother was removed to the hospital where she died, upon which the radiator switched to Canadian French.

He tried habitats of another type: rooms for rent in private houses which, although differing from each other in many respects (not all, for instance, were clapboard ones; a few were stucco, or at least partly stucco), had one generic characteristic in common: in their parlor or stair-landing bookcases Hendrik Willem van Loon and Dr. Cronin were inevitably present; they might be separated by a flock of magazines, or by some glazed and buxom historical romance, or even by Mrs. Garnett impersonating somebody (and in such houses there would be sure to hang somewhere a Toulouse-Lautrec poster), but you found the pair without fail, exchanging looks of tender recognition, like two old friends at a crowded party.

[1] *Kabinet*. Office.

II

He had returned for a spell to the College Home, but so had the pavement drillers, and there had cropped up other nuisances besides. At present Pnin was still renting the pink-walled, white-flounced second-floor bedroom in the Clements' house, and this was the first house he really liked and the first room he had occupied for more than a year. By now he had weeded out all trace of its former occupant; or so he thought, for he did not notice, and probably never would, a funny face scrawled on the wall just behind the headboard of the bed and some half-erased height-level marks penciled on the doorjamb, beginning from a four-foot altitude in 1940.

For more than a week now, Pnin had had the run of the house: Joan Clements had left by plane for a Western state to visit her married daughter, and a couple of days later, at the very beginning of his spring course in philosophy, Professor Clements, summoned by a telegram, had flown West too.

Our friend had a leisurely breakfast, pleasantly based on the milk that had not been discontinued, and at half-past nine prepared for his usual walk to the campus.

It warmed my heart, the Russian-intelligentski way he had of getting into his overcoat: his inclined head would demonstrate its ideal baldness, and his large, Duchess of Wonderland chin would firmly press against the crossed ends of his green muffler to hold it in place on his chest while, with a jerk of his broad shoulders, he contrived to get into both armholes at once; another heave and the coat was on.

He picked up his *portfel'* (briefcase), checked its contents, and walked out.

He was still at a newspaper's throw from his porch when he remembered a book the college library had urgently requested him to return, for the use of another reader. For a moment he struggled with himself; he still needed the volume; but kindly Pnin sympathized too much with the passionate clamor of another (unknown) scholar not to go back for the stout and heavy tome: It was Volume 18—mainly devoted to Tolstoyana—of *Sovetskiy Zolotoy Fond Literaturi* (Soviet Gold Fund of Literature), *Moskva-Leningrad, 1940.*

III

The organs concerned in the production of English speech sounds are the larynx, the velum, the lips, the tongue (that punchinello in the troupe), and, last but not least, the lower jaw; mainly upon its overenergetic and somewhat ruminant motion did Pnin rely when translating in class passages in the Russian grammar or some poem by Pushkin. If his Russian was music, his English was murder. He had enormous difficulty ("dzeefee-cooltsee" in Pninian English) with depalatization, never managing to remove the extra Russian moisture from *t*'s and *d*'s before the vowels he so quaintly softened. His explosive "hat" ("I never go in a hat even in winter") differed from the common American pronunciation of "hot" (typical of Waindell townspeople, for example) only by its briefer duration, and thus sounded very much like the German verb *hat* (has). Long *o*'s with him inevitably became short ones: his "no" sounded positively Italian, and this was accentuated by his trick of triplicating the simple negative ("May I give you a lift, Mr. Pnin?" "No-no-no, I have only two paces from here"). He did not possess (nor was he aware of this lack) any long *oo:* all he could muster when called upon to utter "noon" was the lax vowel of the German *"nun"* ("I have no classes in after*nun* on Tuesday. Today is Tuesday").

Tuesday—true; but what day of the month, we wonder. Pnin's birthday for instance fell on February 3, by the Julian calendar into which he had been born in St. Petersburg in 1898. He never celebrated it nowadays, partly because, after his departure from Russia, it sidled by in a Gregorian disguise (thirteen—no, twelve days late), and partly because during the academic year he existed mainly on a motuweth frisas basis.

On the chalk-clouded blackboard, which he wittily called the grayboard, he now wrote a date. In the crook of his arm he still felt the bulk of *Zol. Fond Lit.* The date he wrote had nothing to do with the day this was in Waindell:

December 26, 1829

He carefully drilled in a big white full stop, and added underneath:

3:03 P.M. St. Petersburg

Dutifully this was taken down by Frank Backman, Rose Balsamo, Frank Carroll, Irving D. Herz, beautiful, intelligent Marilyn Hohn, John Mead, Jr., Peter Volkov, and Allan Bradbury Walsh.

Pnin, rippling with mute mirth, sat down again at his desk: he had a tale to tell. That line in the absurd Russian grammar, "*Brozhu li ya vdol' ulits shumnïh* (Whether I wander along noisy streets)," was really the opening of a famous poem. Although Pnin was supposed in this Elementary Russian class to stick to language exercises ("*Mama, telefon! Brozhu li ya vdol' ulits shumnïh. Ot Vladivostoka do Vashingtona 5000 mil'.*"), he took every opportunity to guide his students on literary and historical tours.

In a set of eight tetrametric quatrains Pushkin described the morbid habit he always had—wherever he was, whatever he was doing—of dwelling on thoughts of death and of closely inspecting every passing day as he strove to find in its cryptogram a certain "future anniversary": the day and month that would appear, somewhere, sometime upon his tombstone.

" 'And where will fate send me,' imperative future, 'death,' " declaimed inspired Pnin, throwing his head back and translating with brave literality, " 'in fight, in travel, or in waves? Or will the neighboring dale'—*dolina*, same word, 'valley' we would now say —'accept my refrigerated ashes,' *poussière*, 'cold dust' perhaps more correct. 'And though it is indifferent to the insensible body . . .' "

Pnin went on to the end and then, dramatically pointing with the piece of chalk he still held, remarked how carefully Pushkin had noted the day and even the minute of writing down that poem.

"But," exclaimed Pnin in triumph, "he died on a quite, quite different day! He died—" The chair back against which Pnin was vigorously leaning emitted an ominous crack, and the class resolved a pardonable tension in loud young laughter.

(Sometime, somewhere—Petersburg? Prague?—one of the two musical clowns pulled out the piano stool from under the other, who remained, however, playing on, in a seated, though seatless, position, with his rhapsody unimpaired. Where? Circus Busch, Berlin!)

IV

Pnin did not bother to leave the classroom between his dismissed Elementary and the Advanced that was trickling in. The office where *Zol. Fond Lit.* now lay, partly enveloped in Pnin's green muffler, on the filing case, was on another floor, at the end of a resonant passage and next to the faculty lavatory. Till 1950 (this was 1953—how time flies!) he had shared an office in the German Department with Miller, one of the younger instructors, and then was given for his exclusive use Office R, which formerly had been a lumber room but had now been completely renovated. During the spring he had lovingly Pninized it. It had come with two ignoble chairs, a cork bulletin board, a can of floor wax forgotten by the janitor, and a humble pedestal desk of indeterminable wood. He wangled from the Administration a small steel file with an entrancing locking device. Young Miller, under Pnin's direction, embraced and brought over Pnin's part of a sectional bookcase. From old Mrs. McCrystal, in whose white frame house he had spent a mediocre winter (1949–50), Pnin purchased for three dollars a faded, once Turkish rug. With the help of the janitor he screwed onto the side of the desk a pencil sharpener—that highly satisfying, highly philosophical implement that goes ticonderoga-ticonderoga, feeding on the yellow finish and sweet wood, and ends up in a kind of soundlessly spinning ethereal void as we all must. He had other, even more ambitious plans, such as an armchair and a tall lamp. When, after a summer spent teaching in Washington, Pnin returned to his office, an obese dog lay asleep on his rug, and his furniture had been moved to a darker part of the office, so as to make room for a magnificent stainless-steel desk and a swivel chair to match, in which sat writing and smiling to himself the newly imported Austrian scholar, Dr. Bodo von Falternfels; and thenceforth, so far as Pnin was concerned, Office R had gone to seed.

V

At noon, as usual, Pnin washed his hands and head.

He picked up in Office R his overcoat, muffler, book, and brief case. Dr. Falternfels was writing and smiling; his sandwich was half unwrapped; his dog was dead. Pnin walked down the gloomy stairs and through the Museum of Sculpture. Humanities Hall, where, however, Ornithology and Anthropology also lurked, was connected with another brick building, Frieze Hall, which housed the dining rooms and the Faculty Club, by means of a rather rococo openwork gallery: it went up a slope, then turned sharply and wandered down toward a routine smell of potato chips and the sadness of balanced meals. In summer its trellis was alive with quivering flowers; but now through its nakedness an icy wind blew, and someone had placed a found red mitten upon the spout of the dead fountain that stood where one branch of the gallery led to the President's House.

President Poore, a tall, slow, elderly man wearing dark glasses, had started to lose his sight a couple of years before and was now almost totally blind. With solar regularity, however, he would be led every day by his niece and secretary to Frieze Hall; he came, a figure of antique dignity, moving in his private darkness to an invisible luncheon, and although everybody had long grown accustomed to his tragic entrance, there was invariably the shadow of a hush while he was being steered to his carved chair and while he groped for the edge of the table; and it was strange to see, directly behind him on the wall, his stylized likeness in a mauve double-breasted suit and mahogany shoes, gazing with radiant magenta eyes at the scrolls handed him by Richard Wagner, Dostoevski, and Confucius, a group that Oleg Komarov, of the Fine Arts Department, had painted a decade ago into Lang's celebrated mural of 1938, which carried all around the dining room a pageant of historical figures and Waindell faculty members.

Pnin, who wanted to ask his compatriot something, sat down beside him. This Komarov, a Cossack's son, was a very short man with a crew cut and a death's-head's nostrils. He and Serafima, his large, cheerful, Moscow-born wife, who wore a Tibetan charm on a long silver chain that hung down to her ample, soft belly, would throw Russki parties every now and then, with Russki hors d'oeuvres and guitar music and more or less phony folk songs—occasions at which shy graduate students would be taught vodka-drinking rites and other stale Russianisms; and after such feasts, upon meeting gruff Pnin, Serafima and Oleg (she raising her eyes to heaven, he covering his with one hand) would murmur in awed self-gratitude: *"Gospodi, skol'ko mï im dayom!* (My, what a lot we give them!)"—"them" being the benighted American people. Only another Russian could understand the reactionary and Soviet-ophile blend presented by the pseudo-colorful Komarovs, for whom an ideal Russia consisted of the Red Army, an anointed monarch, collective farms, anthroposophy, the Russian Church and the Hydro-Electric Dam. Pnin and Oleg Komarov were usually in a subdued state of war, but meetings were inevitable, and such of their American colleagues as deemed the Komarovs "grand people" and mimicked droll Pnin were sure the painter and Pnin were excellent friends.

It would be hard to say, without applying some very special tests, which of them, Pnin or Komarov, spoke the worse English; probably Pnin; but for reasons of age, general education, and a slightly longer stage of American citizenship, he found it possible to correct Komarov's frequent English interpolations, and Komarov resented this even more than he did Pnin's *antikvarnïy liberalizm*.[2]

"Look here, Komarov (*Poslushayte, Komarov*"—a rather discourteous manner of address)—said Pnin. "I cannot understand who else here might want this book; certainly none of my students; and if it is you, I cannot understand why you should want it anyway."

"I don't," answered Komarov, glancing at the volume. "Not interested," he added in English.

Pnin moved his lips and lower jaw mutely once or twice, wanted to say something, did not, and went on with his salad.

VI

This being Tuesday, he could walk over to his favorite haunt immediately after lunch and stay there till dinner time. No gallery connected Waindell College Library with any other buildings, but it was intimately and securely connected with Pnin's heart. He walked past the great bronze figure of the first president of the college, Alpheus Frieze, in sports cap and knickerbockers, holding by its horns the bronze bicycle he was eternally about to mount, judging by the position of his left foot, forever glued to the left pedal. There was snow on the saddle and snow in the absurd basket that recent pranksters had attached to the handle

---

[2] *Antikvarnïy liberalizm.* Outmoded liberalism.

bars. *"Huligani,"* ³ fumed Pnin, shaking his head—and slipped slightly on a flag of the path that meandered down a turfy slope among the leafless elms. Besides the big book under his right arm, he carried in his left hand his brief case, an old, Central European-looking, black *portfel'*, and this he swung rhythmically by its leathern grip as he marched to his books, to his scriptorium in the stacks, to his paradise of Russian lore.

An elliptic flock of pigeons, in circular volitation, soaring gray, flapping white, and then gray again, wheeled across the limpid, pale sky, above the College Library. A train whistled afar as mournfully as in the steppes. A skimpy squirrel dashed over a patch of sunlit snow, where a tree trunk's shadow, olive-green on the turf, became grayish blue for a stretch, while the tree itself, with a brisk, scrabbly sound, ascended, naked, into the sky, where the pigeons swept by for a third and last time. The squirrel, invisible now in a crotch, chattered, scolding the delinquents who would pot him out of his tree. Pnin, on the dirty black ice of the flagged path, slipped again, threw up one arm in an abrupt convulsion, regained his balance, and, with a solitary smile, stooped to pick up *Zol. Fond Lit.*, which lay wide open to a snapshot of a Russian pasture with Lyov Tolstoy trudging across it toward the camera and some long-maned horses behind him, their innocent heads turned toward the photographer too.

V boyu li, v stranstvii, v volnah? In fight, in travel, or in waves? Or on the Waindell campus? Gently champing his dentures, which retained a sticky layer of cottage cheese, Pnin went up the slippery library steps.

Like so many aging college people, Pnin had long ceased to notice the existence of students on the campus, in the corridors, in the library—anywhere, in brief, save in functional classroom concentrations. In the beginning, he had been much upset by the sight of some of them, their poor young heads on their forearms, fast asleep among the ruins of knowledge; but now, except for a girl's comely nape here and there, he saw nobody in the Reading Room.

Mrs. Thayer was at the circulation desk. Her mother and Mrs. Clements' mother had been first cousins.

"How are you today, Professor Pnin?"

"I am very well, Mrs. Fire."

³ *"Huligani."* Hooligans.

"Laurence and Joan aren't back yet, are they?"

"No. I have brought this book back because I received this card—"

"I wonder if poor Isabel will really get divorced."

"I have not heard. Mrs. Fire, permit me to ask—"

"I suppose we'll have to find you another room, if they bring her back with them."

"Mrs. Fire, permit me to ask something or other. This card which I received yesterday—could you maybe tell me who is the other reader?"

"Let me check."

She checked. The other reader proved to be Timofey Pnin; Volume 18 had been requested by him the Friday before. It was also true that this Volume 18 was already charged to this Pnin, who had had it since Christmas and now stood with his hands upon it, like an ancestral picture of a magistrate.

"It can't be!" cried Pnin. "I requested on Friday Volume 19, year 1947, not 18, year 1940."

"But look—you wrote Volume 18. Anyway, 19 is still being processed. Are you keeping this?"

"Eighteen, 19," muttered Pnin. "There is not great difference! I put the year correctly, *that* is important! Yes, I still need 18— and send to me a more effishant card when 19 available."

Growling a little, he took the unwieldy, abashed book to his favorite alcove and laid it down there, wrapped in his muffler.

They can't read, these women. The year was plainly inscribed.

As usual he marched to the Periodicals Room and there glanced at the news in the latest (Saturday, February 12—and this was Tuesday, O Careless Reader!) issue of the Russian-language daily published, since 1918, by an émigré group in Chicago. As usual, he carefully scanned the advertisements. Dr. Popov, photographed in his new white smock, promised elderly people new vigor and joy. A music corporation listed Russian phonograph records for sale, such as "Broken Life, a Waltz" and "The Song of a Front-Line Chauffeur." A somewhat Gogolian mortician praised his hearses de luxe, which were also available for picnics. Another Gogolian person, in Miami, offered "a two-room apartment for non-drinkers (*dlya trezvïh*), among fruit trees and flowers," while in Hammond a room was wistfully being let "in a small quiet family"—and for no special reason the reader suddenly saw, with passionate and ridiculous lucidity, his parents, Dr. Pavel Pnin and Valeria Pnin, he with a medical journal, she with a political review, sitting in two armchairs, facing each other in a small, cheerfully lighted drawing room on Galernaya Street, St. Petersburg, forty years ago.

He also perused the current item in a tremendously long and tedious controversy between three émigré factions. It had started by Faction A's accusing Faction B of inertia and illustrating it by the proverb, "He wishes to climb the fir tree but is afraid to scrape his shins." This had provoked an acid Letter to the Editor from "An Old Optimist," entitled "Fir Trees and Inertia" and beginning: "There is an old American saying 'He who lives in a glass house should not try to kill two birds with one stone.'" In the present issue, there was a two-thousand-word *feuilleton* [4] contributed by a representative of Faction C and headed "On Fir Trees, Glass Houses, and Optimism," and Pnin read this with great interest and sympathy.

He then returned to his carrell for his own research.

He contemplated writing a *Petite Histoire* of Russian culture, in which a choice of Russian Curiosities, Customs, Literary Anecdotes, and so forth would be presented in such a way as to reflect in miniature *la Grande Histoire*—Major Concatenations of Events. He was still at the blissful stage of collecting his material; and many good young people considered it a treat and an honor to see Pnin pull out a catalogue drawer from the comprehensive bosom of a card cabinet and take it, like a big nut, to a secluded corner and there make a quiet mental meal of it, now moving his lips in soundless comment, critical, satisfied, perplexed, and now lifting his rudimentary eyebrows and forgetting them there, left high upon his spacious brow where they remained long after all trace of displeasure or doubt had gone. He was lucky to be at Waindell. Sometimes in the nineties the eminent bibliophile and Slavist John Thurston Todd (his bearded bust presided over the drinking fountain), had visited hospitable Russia, and after his death the books he had amassed there quietly chuted into a remote stack.

[4] *Feuilleton.* An article appearing in a journal in a special section devoted to criticism, reviews, etc.

Wearing rubber gloves so as to avoid being stung by the *ameri-kanski* electricity in the metal of the shelving, Pnin would go to those books and gloat over them: obscure magazines of the Roaring Sixties in marbled boards; century-old historical monographs, their somnolent pages foxed with fungus spots; Russian classics in horrible and pathetic cameo bindings, whose molded profiles of poets reminded dewy-eyed Timofey of his boyhood, when he could idly palpate on the book cover Pushkin's slightly chafed side whisker or Zhukovski's smudgy nose.

Today from Kostromskoy's voluminous work (Moscow, 1855), on Russian myths—a rare book, not to be removed from the library—Pnin, with a not unhappy sigh, started to copy out a passage referring to the old pagan games that were still practiced at the time, throughout the woodlands of the Upper Volga, in the margins of Christian ritual. During a festive week in May— the so-called Green Week which graded into Whitsuntide— peasant maidens would make wreaths of buttercups and frog orchises; then, singing snatches of ancient love chants, they hung these garlands on riverside willows; and on Whitsunday the wreaths were shaken down into the river, where, unwinding, they floated like so many serpents while the maidens floated and chanted among them.

A curious verbal association struck Pnin at this point; he could not catch it by its mermaid tail but made a note on his index card and plunged back into Kostromskoy.

When Pnin raised his eyes again, it was dinnertime.

Doffing his spectacles, he rubbed with the knuckles of the hand that held them his naked and tired eyes and, still in thought, fixed his mild gaze on the window above, where, gradually, through his dissolving meditation, there appeared the violet-blue air of dusk, silver-tooled by the reflection of the fluorescent lights of the ceiling, and, among spidery black twigs, a mirrored row of bright book spines.

Before leaving the library, he decided to look up the correct pronunciation of "interested," and discovered that Webster, or at least the battered 1930 edition lying on a table in the Browsing Room, did not place the stress accent on the third syllable, as he did. He sought a list of errata at the back, failed to find one, and, upon closing the elephantine lexicon, realized with a pang that he had immured somewhere in it the index card with notes that he had been holding all this time. Must now search and search through 2500 thin pages, some torn! On hearing his interjection, suave Mr. Case, a lank, pink-faced librarian with sleek white hair and a bow tie, strolled up, took up the colossus by both ends, inverted it, and gave it a slight shake, whereupon it shed a pocket comb, a Christmas card, Pnin's notes, and a gauzy wraith of tissue paper, which descended with infinite listlessness to Pnin's feet and was replaced by Mr. Case on the Great Seals of the United States and Territories.

Pnin pocketed his index card and, while doing so, recalled without any prompting what he had not been able to recall a while ago:

. . . *plila i pela, pela i plila* . . .
. . . she floated and she sang, she sang and floated . . .

Of course! Ophelia's death! *Hamlet!* In good old Andrey Kroneberg's Russian translation, 1844—the joy of Pnin's youth, and of his father's and grandfather's young days! And here, as in the Kostromskoy passage, there is, we recollect, also a willow and also wreaths. But where to check properly? Alas, *"Gamlet" Vil'yama Shekspira* had not been acquired by Mr. Todd, was not represented in Waindell College Library, and whenever you were reduced to look up something in the English version, you never found this or that beautiful, noble, sonorous line that you remembered all your life from Kroneberg's text in Vengerov's splendid edition. Sad!

It was getting quite dark on the sad campus. Above the distant, still sadder hills there lingered, under a cloud bank, a depth of tortoise-shell sky. The heart-rending lights of Waindellville, throbbing in a fold of those dusky hills, were putting on their usual magic, though actually, as Pnin well knew, the place, when you got there, was merely a row of brick houses, a service station, a skating rink, a supermarket. As he walked to the little tavern in Library Lane for a large portion of Virginia ham and a good bottle of beer, Pnin suddenly felt very tired. Not only had the

Zol. Fond tome become even heavier after its unnecessary visit to the library, but something that Pnin had half heard in the course of the day, and had been reluctant to follow up, now bothered and oppressed him, as does, in retrospection, a blunder we have made, a piece of rudeness we have allowed ourselves, or a threat we have chosen to ignore.

VII

Over an unhurried second bottle, Pnin debated with himself his next move or, rather, mediated in a debate between weary-brained Pnin, who had not been sleeping well lately, and an insatiable Pnin, who wished to continue reading at home, as always, till the 2 A.M. freight train moaned its way up the valley. It was decided at last that he would go to bed immediately after attending the program presented by intense Christopher and Louise Starr every second Tuesday at New Hall, rather highbrow music and unusual movie offerings which President Poore, in answer to some absurd criticism last year, had termed "probably the most inspiring and inspired venture in the entire academic community."

ZFL was now asleep in Pnin's lap. To his left sat two Hindu students. At his right there was Professor Hagen's daughter, a hoydenish Drama major. Komarov, thank goodness, was too far behind for his scarcely interesting remarks to carry.

The first part of the program, three ancient movie shorts, bored our friend: that cane, that bowler, that white face, those black, arched eyebrows, those twitchy nostrils meant nothing to him. Whether the incomparable comedian danced in the sun with chapleted nymphs near a waiting cactus, or was a prehistoric man (the supple cane now a supple club), or was glared at by burly Mack Swain at a hectic night club, old-fashioned, humorless Pnin remained indifferent. "Clown," he snorted to himself. "Even Glupishkin and Max Linder used to be more comical."

The second part of the program consisted of an impressive Soviet documentary film, made in the late forties. It was supposed to contain not a jot of propaganda, to be all sheer art, merrymaking, and the euphoria of proud toil. Handsome, unkempt girls marched in an immemorial Spring Festival with banners bearing snatches of old Russian ballads such as *"Ruki proch ot Korei,"* *"Bas les mains devant la Corée,"* *"La paz vencera a la guerra,"* *"Der Friede besiegt den Krief."* A flying ambulance was shown crossing a snowy range in Tajikistan. Kirghiz actors visited a sanatorium for coal miners among palm trees and staged there a spontaneous performance. In a mountain pasture somewhere in legendary Ossetia, a herdsman reported by portable radio to the local Republic's Ministry of Agriculture on the birth of a lamb. The Moscow Metro shimmered, with its columns and statues, and six would-be travelers seated on three marble benches. A factory worker's family spent a quiet evening at home, all dressed up, in a parlor choked with ornamental plants, under a great silk lampshade. Eight thousand soccer fans watched a match between Torpedo and Dynamo. Eight thousand citizens at Moscow's Electrical Equipment Plant unanimously nominated Stalin candidate from the Stalin Election District of Moscow. The latest Zim passenger model started out with the factory worker's family and a few other people for a picnic in the country. And then—

"I must not, I must not, oh it is idiotical," said Pnin to himself as he felt—unaccountably, ridiculously, humiliatingly—his tear glands discharge their hot, infantine, uncontrollable fluid.

In a haze of sunshine—sunshine projecting in vaporous shafts between the white boles of birches, drenching the pendulous foliage, trembling in eyelets upon the bark, dripping onto the long grass, shining and smoking among the ghosts of racemose bird cherries in scumbled bloom—a Russian wildwood enveloped the rambler. It was traversed by an old forest road with two soft furrows and a continuous traffic of mushrooms and daisies. The rambler still followed in mind that road as he trudged back to his anachronistic lodgings; was again the youth who had walked through those woods with a fat book under his arm; the road emerged into the romantic, free, beloved radiance of a great field unmowed by time (the horses galloping away and tossing their silvery manes among the tall flowers), as drowsiness overcame Pnin, who was now fairly snug in bed with two alarm clocks alongside, one set at 7:30, the other at 8, clicking and clucking on his night table.

Komarov, in a sky-blue shirt, bent over the guitar he was tuning. A birthday party was in progress, and calm Stalin cast with a thud his ballot in the election of governmental pallbearers. In fight, in travel . . . waves or Waindell. . . . "Wonderful!" said Dr. Bodo von Falternfels, raising his head from his writing.

Pnin had all but lapsed into velvety oblivion when some frightful accident happened outside; groaning and clutching at its brow, a statue was making an extravagant fuss over a broken bronze wheel—and then Pnin was awake, and a caravan of lights and of shadowy humps progressed across the window shade. A car door slammed, a car drove off, a key unlocked the brittle, transparent house, three vibrant voices spoke; the house, and the chink under Pnin's door, lit up with a shiver. It was a fever, it was an infection. In fear and helplessness, toothless, nightshirted Pnin heard a suitcase one-leggedly but briskly stomping upstairs, and a pair of young feet tripping up steps so familiar to them, and one could already make out the sound of eager breathing. . . . In fact, the automatic revival of happy homecomings from dismal summer camps would have actually had Isabel kick open—Pnin's door, had not her mother's warning yelp stopped her in time.

SHERWOOD ANDERSON

The Egg

My father was, I am sure, intended by nature to be a cheerful, kindly man. Until he was thirty-four years old he worked as a farmhand for a man named Thomas Butterworth whose place lay near the town of Bidwell, Ohio. He had then a horse of his own, and on Saturday evenings drove into town to spend a few hours in social intercourse with other farmhands. In town he drank several glasses of beer and stood about in Ben Head's saloon—crowded on Saturday evenings with visiting farmhands. Songs were sung and glasses thumped on the bar. At ten o'clock father drove home along a lonely country road, made his horse comfortable for the night, and himself went to bed, quite happy in his position in life. He had at that time no notion of trying to rise in the world.

It was in the spring of his thirty-fifth year that father married my mother, then a country school-teacher, and in the following spring I came wriggling and crying into the world. Something happened to the two people. They became ambitious. The American passion for getting up in the world took possession of them.

It may have been that mother was responsible. Being a school-teacher she had no doubt read books and magazines. She had, I presume, read of how Garfield, Lincoln, and other Americans rose from poverty to fame and greatness, and as I lay beside her—in the days of her lying-in—she may have dreamed that I would some day rule men and cities. At any rate she induced father to give up his place as a farmhand, sell his horse, and embark on an independent enterprise of his own. She was a tall silent woman with a long nose and troubled gray eyes. For herself she wanted nothing. For father and myself she was incurably ambitious.

The first venture into which the two people went turned out badly. They rented ten acres of poor stony land on Grigg's Road, eight miles from Bidwell, and launched into chicken-raising. I grew into boyhood on the place and got my first impressions of life there. From the beginning they were impressions of disaster, and if, in my turn, I am a gloomy man inclined to see the darker side of life, I attribute it to the fact that what should have been for me the happy joyous days of childhood were spent on a chicken farm.

One unversed in such matters can have no notion of the many and tragic things that can happen to a chicken. It is born out of an egg, lives for a few weeks as a tiny fluffy thing such as you will see pictured on Easter cards, then becomes hideously naked, eats quantities of corn and meal bought by the sweat of your father's brow, gets diseases called pip, cholera, and other names, stands looking with stupid eyes at the sun, becomes sick and dies. A few hens and now and then a rooster, intended to serve God's mysterious ends, struggle through to maturity. The hens lay eggs out of which come other chickens and the dreadful cycle is thus made complete. It is all unbelievably complex. Most philosophers must have been raised on chicken farms. One hopes for so much from a chicken and is so dreadfully disillusioned. Small chickens, just setting out on the journey of life, look so bright and alert and they are in fact so dreadfully stupid. They are so much like people they mix one up in one's judgments of life. If disease does not kill them, they wait until your expectations are thoroughly aroused and then walk under the wheels of a wagon—to go squashed and dead back to their maker. Vermin infest their youth, and fortunes must be spent for curative powders. In later life I have seen how a literature has been built up on the subject of fortunes to be made out of the raising of chickens. It is intended to be read by the gods who have just eaten of the tree of the knowledge of good and evil. It is a hopeful literature and declares that much may be done by simple ambitious people who own a few hens. Do not be led astray by it. It was not written for you. Go hunt for gold on the frozen hills of Alaska, put your faith in the honesty of a politician, believe if you will that the world is daily growing better and that good will triumph over evil, but do not read and believe the literature that is written concerning the hen. It was not written for you.

I, however, digress. My tale does not primarily concern itself with the hen. If correctly told it will center on the egg. For ten years my father and mother struggled to make our chicken farm pay and then they gave up their struggle and began another. They moved into the town of Bidwell, Ohio, and embarked in the restaurant business. After ten years of worry with incubators that did not hatch, and with tiny—and in their own way lovely—balls of fluff that passed on into semi-naked pullethood and from that into dead henhood, we threw all aside and, packing our belongings on a wagon, drove down Grigg's Road toward Bidwell, a tiny caravan of hope looking for a new place from which to start on our upward journey through life.

We must have been a sad-looking lot, not, I fancy, unlike refugees fleeing from a battlefield. Mother and I walked in the road. The wagon that contained our goods had been borrowed for the day from Mr. Albert Griggs, a neighbor. Out of its sides stuck the legs of cheap chairs, and at the back of the pile of beds, tables, and boxes filled with kitchen utensils was a crate of live chickens, and on top of that the baby carriage in which I had been wheeled about in my infancy. Why we stuck to the baby carriage I don't know. It was unlikely other children would be born and the wheels were broken. People who have few possessions cling tightly to those they have. That is one of the facts that make life so discouraging.

Father rode on top of the wagon. He was then a bald-headed man of forty-five, a little fat, and from long association with mother and the chickens he had become habitually silent and discouraged. All during our ten years on the chicken farm he had worked as a laborer on neighboring farms and most of the money he had earned had been spent for remedies to cure chicken diseases, on Wilmer's White Wonder Cholera Cure or Professor Bidlow's Egg Producer or some other preparations that mother found advertised in the poultry papers. There were two little patches of hair on father's head just above his ears. I remember that as a child I used to sit looking at him when he had gone to sleep in a chair before the stove on Sunday afternoons in the winter. I had at that time already begun to read books and have notions of my own, and the bald path that led over the top of his head was, I fancied, something like a broad road, such a road as Caesar might have made on which to lead his legions out of Rome and into the wonders of an unknown world. The tufts of hair that grew above father's ears were, I thought, like forests. I fell into a half-sleeping, half-waking state and dreamed I was a tiny thing going along the road into a far beautiful place where there were no chicken farms and where life was a happy eggless affair.

One might write a book concerning our flight from the chicken farm into town. Mother and I walked the entire eight miles—she to be sure that nothing fell from the wagon and I to see the wonders of the world. On the seat of the wagon beside father was his greatest treasure. I will tell you of that.

On a chicken farm, where hundreds and even thousands of chickens come out of eggs, surprising things sometimes happen. Grotesques are born out of eggs as out of people. The accident does not often occur—perhaps once in a thousand births. A chicken is, you see, born that has four legs, two pairs of wings, two heads, or what not. The things do not live. They go quickly back to the hand of their maker that has for a moment trembled. The fact that the poor little things could not live was one of the tragedies of life to father. He had some sort of notion that if he could but bring into henhood or roosterhood a five-legged hen or a two-headed rooster his fortune would be made. He dreamed of taking the wonder about the county fairs and of growing rich by exhibiting it to other farmhands.

At any rate, he saved all the little monstrous things that had been born on our chicken farm. They were preserved in alcohol and put each in its own glass bottle. These he had carefully put into a box, and on our journey into town it was carried on the wagon seat beside him. He drove the horses with one hand and with the other clung to the box. When we got to our destination, the box was taken down at once and the bottles removed. All during our days as keepers of a restaurant in the town of Bidwell, Ohio, the grotesques in their little glass bottles sat on a shelf back of the counter. Mother sometimes protested, but father was a rock on the subject of his treasure. The grotesques were, he declared, valuable. People, he said, liked to look at strange and wonderful things.

Did I say that we embarked in the restaurant business in the town of Bidwell, Ohio? I exaggerated a little. The town itself lay at the foot of a low hill and on the shore of a small river. The railroad did not run through the town and the station was a mile away to the north at a place called Pickleville. There had been a cider mill and pickle factory at the station, but before the time of our coming they had both gone out of business. In the morning and in the evening busses came down to the station along a road called Turner's Pike from the hotel on the main street of Bidwell. Our going to the out-of-the-way place to embark in the restaurant business was mother's idea. She talked of it for a year and then one day went off and rented an empty store building opposite the railroad station. It was her idea that the restaurant would be profitable. Traveling men, she said, would be always waiting around to take trains out of town and town people would come to the station to await incoming trains. They would come to the restaurant to buy pieces of pie and drink coffee. Now that I am older I know that she had another motive in going. She was ambitious for me. She wanted me to rise in the world, to get into a town school and become a man of the towns.

At Pickleville father and mother worked hard, as they always had done. At first there was the necessity of putting our place into shape to be a restaurant. That took a month. Father built a shelf on which he put tins of vegetables. He painted a sign on which he put his name in large red letters. Below his name was the sharp command—"EAT HERE"—that was so seldom obeyed. A show-case was bought and filled with cigars and tobacco. Mother scrubbed the floors and the walls of the room. I went to school in the town and was glad to be away from the farm from the pres-ence of the discouraged, sad-looking chickens. Still I was not very joyous. In the evening I walked home from school along Turner's Pike and remembered the children I had seen playing in the town school yard. A troop of little girls had gone hopping about and singing. I tried that. Down along the frozen road I went hopping solemnly on one leg. "Hippity Hop To The Barber Shop," I sang shrilly. Then I stopped and looked doubtfully about. I was afraid of being seen in my gay mood. It must have seemed to me that I was doing a thing that should not be done by one who, like myself, had been raised on a chicken farm where death was a daily visitor.

Mother decided that our restaurant should remain open at night. At ten in the evening a passenger train went north past our door followed by a local freight. The freight crew had switching to do in Pickleville, and when the work was done they came to our restaurant for hot coffee and food. Sometimes one of them ordered a fried egg. In the morning at four they returned north-bound and again visited us. A little trade began to grow up. Mother slept at night and during the day tended the restaurant and fed our board-ers while father slept. He slept in the same bed mother had occu-pied during the night and I went off to the town of Bidwell and to school. During the long nights, while mother and I slept, father cooked meats that were to go into sandwiches for the lunch baskets of our boarders. Then an idea in regard to getting up in the world came into his head. The American spirit took hold of him. He also became ambitious.

In the long nights when there was little to do, father had time to think. That was his undoing. He decided that he had in the past been an unsuccessful man because he had not been cheerful enough and that in the future he would adopt a cheerful outlook on life. In the early morning he came upstairs and got into bed with mother. She woke and the two talked. From my bed in the corner

I listened.

It was father's idea that both he and mother should try to entertain the people who came to eat at our restaurant. I cannot now remember his words, but he gave the impression of one about to become in some obscure way a kind of public entertainer. When people, particularly young people from the town of Bidwell, came into our place, as on very rare occasions they did, bright entertaining conversation was to be made. From father's words I gathered that something of the jolly innkeeper effect was to be sought. Mother must have been doubtful from the first, but she said nothing discouraging. It was father's notion that a passion for the company of himself and mother would spring up in the breasts of the younger people of the town of Bidwell. In the evening bright happy groups would come singing down Turner's Pike. They would troop shouting with joy and laughter into our place. There would be song and festivity. I do not mean to give the impression that father spoke so elaborately of the matter. He was, as I have said, an uncommunicative man. "They want some place to go. I tell you they want some place to go," he said over and over. That was as far as he got. My own imagination has filled in the blanks.

For two or three weeks this notion of father's invaded our house. We did not talk much, but in our daily lives tried earnestly to make smiles take the place of glum looks. Mother smiled at the boarders and I, catching the infection, smiled at our cat. Father became a little feverish in his anxiety to please. There was, no doubt, lurking somewhere in him, a touch of the spirit of the showman. He did not waste much of his ammunition on the railroad men he served at night, but seemed to be waiting for a young man or woman from Bidwell to come in to show what he could do. On the counter in the restaurant there was a wire basket kept always filled with eggs, and it must have been before his eyes when the idea of being entertaining was born in his brain. There was something pre-natal about the way eggs kept themselves connected with the development of his idea. At any rate, an egg ruined his new impulse in life. Late one night I was awakened by a roar of anger coming from father's throat. Both mother and I sat upright in our beds. With trembling hands she lighted a lamp that stood on a table by her head. Downstairs the front door of our restaurant went shut with a bang and in a few minutes father

tramped up the stairs. He held an egg in his hand and his hand
trembled as though he were having a chill. There was a half-insane
light in his eyes. As he stood glaring at us I was sure he intended
throwing the egg at either mother or me. Then he laid it gently
on the table beside the lamp and dropped on his knees beside
mother's bed. He began to cry like a boy, and I, carried away by
his grief, cried with him. The two of us filled the little upstairs
room with our wailing voices. It is ridiculous, but of the picture
we made I can remember only the fact that mother's hand continually stroked the bald path that ran across the top of his head.
I have forgotten what mother said to him and how she induced
him to tell her of what had happened downstairs. His explanation
also has gone out of my mind. I remember only my own grief
and fright and the shiny path over father's head glowing in the
lamplight as he knelt by the bed.

As to what happened downstairs. For some unexplainable reason I know the story as well as though I had been a witness to my
father's discomfiture. One in time gets to know many unexplainable things. On that evening young Joe Kane, son of a merchant
of Bidwell, came to Pickleville to meet his father, who was expected on the ten-o'clock evening train from the South. The train
was three hours late and Joe came into our place to loaf about
and to wait for its arrival. The local freight train came in and the
freight crew were fed. Joe was left alone in the restaurant with
father.

From the moment he came into our place the Bidwell young
man must have been puzzled by my father's actions. It was his
notion that father was angry at him for hanging around. He noticed that the restaurant-keeper was apparently disturbed by his
presence and he thought of going out. However, it began to rain
and he did not fancy the long walk to town and back. He bought
a five-cent cigar and ordered a cup of coffee. He had a newspaper in his pocket and took it out and began to read. "I'm waiting
for the evening train. It's late," he said apologetically.

For a long time father, whom Joe Kane had never seen before,
remained silently gazing at his visitor. He was no doubt suffering from an attack of stage fright. As so often happens in life he
had thought so much and so often of the situation that now confronted him that he was somewhat nervous in its presence.

For one thing, he did not know what to do with his hands. He thrust one of them nervously over the counter and shook hands with Joe Kane. "How-de-do," he said. Joe Kane put his newspaper down and stared at him. Father's eyes lighted on the basket of eggs that sat on the counter and he began to talk. "Well," he began hesitatingly, "well, you have heard of Christopher Columbus, eh?" He seemed to be angry. "That Christopher Columbus was a cheat," he declared emphatically. "He talked of making an egg stand on its end. He talked, he did, and then he went and broke the end of the egg."

My father seemed to his visitor to be beside himself at the duplicity of Christopher Columbus. He muttered and swore. He declared it was wrong to teach children that Christopher Columbus was a great man when, after all, he cheated at the critical moment. He had declared he would make an egg stand on end and then, when his bluff had been called, he had done a trick. Still grumbling at Columbus, father took an egg from the basket on the counter and began to walk up and down. He rolled the egg between the palms of his hands. He smiled genially. He began to mumble words regarding the effect to be produced on an egg by the electricity that comes out of the human body. He declared that, without breaking its shell and by virtue of rolling it back and forth in his hands, he could stand the egg on its end. He explained that the warmth of his hands and the gentle rolling movement he gave the egg created a new center of gravity, and Joe Kane was mildly interested. "I have handled thousands of eggs," father said. "No one knows more about eggs than I do."

He stood the egg on the counter and it fell on its side. He tried the trick again and again, each time rolling the egg between the palms of his hands and saying the words regarding the wonders of electricity and the laws of gravity. When after a half-hour's effort he did succeed in making the egg stand for a moment, he looked up to find that his visitor was no longer watching. By the time he had succeeded in calling Joe Kane's attention to the success of his effort, the egg had again rolled over and lay on its side.

Afire with the showman's passion and at the same time a good deal disconcerted by the failure of his first effort, father now took the bottles containing the poultry monstrosities down from their place on the shelf and began to show them to his visitor. "How would you like to have seven legs and two heads like this fellow?" he asked, exhibiting the most remarkable of his treasures. A cheerful smile played over his face. He reached over the counter and tried to slap Joe Kane on the shoulder as he had seen men do in Ben Head's saloon when he was a young farmhand and drove to town on Saturday evenings. His visitor was made a little ill by the sight of the body of the terribly deformed bird floating in the alcohol in the bottle and got up to go. Coming from behind the counter, father took hold of the young man's arm and led him back to his seat. He grew a little angry and for a moment had to turn his face away and force himself to smile. Then he put the bottles back on the shelf. In an outburst of generosity he fairly compelled Joe Kane to have a fresh cup of coffee and another cigar at his expense. Then he took a pan and filling it with vinegar, taken from a jug that sat beneath the counter, he declared himself about to do a new trick. "I will heat this egg in this pan of vinegar," he said. "Then I will put it through the neck of a bottle without breaking the shell. When the egg is inside the bottle it will resume its normal shape and the shell will become hard again. Then I will give the bottle with the egg in it to you. You can take it about with you wherever you go. People will want to know how you got the egg in the bottle. Don't tell them. Keep them guessing. That is the way to have fun with this trick."

Father grinned and winked at his visitor. Joe Kane decided that the man who confronted him was mildly insane but harmless. He drank the cup of coffee that had been given him and began to read his paper again. When the egg had been heated in vinegar, father carried it on a spoon to the counter and going into a back room got an empty bottle. He was angry because his visitor did not watch him as he began to do his trick, but nevertheless went cheerfully to work. For a long time he struggled, trying to get the egg to go through the neck of the bottle. He put the pan of vinegar back on the stove, intending to reheat the egg, then picked it up and burned his fingers. After a second bath in the hot vinegar, the shell of the egg had been softened a little, but not enough for his purpose. He worked and worked and a spirit of desperate determination took possession of him. When he thought that at last the trick was about to be consummated, the delayed train came in at the station and Joe Kane started to go nonchalantly out at the door. Father made a last desperate effort to conquer the egg and make it do the thing that would establish his reputation as one who knew how to entertain guests who came into his restaurant. He worried the egg. He attempted to be somewhat rough with it. He swore and the sweat stood out on his forehead. The egg broke under his hand. When the contents spurted over his clothes, Joe Kane, who had stopped at the door, turned and laughed.

A roar of anger rose from my father's throat. He danced and shouted a string of inarticulate words. Grabbing another egg from the basket on the counter, he threw it, just missing the head of the young man as he dodged through the door and escaped.

Father came upstairs to mother and me with an egg in his hand. I do not know what he intended to do. I imagine he had some idea of destroying it, of destroying all eggs, and that he intended to let mother and me see him begin. When, however, he got into the presence of mother, something happened to him. He laid the egg gently on the table and dropped on his knees by the bed as I have already explained. He later decided to close the restaurant for the night and to come upstairs and get into bed. When he did so, he blew out the light and after much muttered conversation both he and mother went to sleep. I suppose I went to sleep also, but my sleep was troubled. I awoke at dawn and for a long time looked at the egg that lay on the table. I wondered why eggs had to be and why from the egg came the hen who again laid the egg. The question got into my blood. It has stayed there, I imagine, because I am the son of my father. At any rate, the problem remains unsolved in my mind. And that, I conclude, is but another evidence of the complete and final triumph of the egg—at least as far as my family is concerned.

JAMES JOYCE

Araby

North Richmond Street, being blind, was a quiet street except at the hour when the Christian Brothers School set the boys free. An uninhabited house of two storeys stood at the blind end, detached from its neighbours in a square ground. The other houses of the street, conscious of decent lives within them, gazed at one another with brown imperturbable faces.

The former tenant of our house, a priest, had died in the back drawing-room. Air, musty from having been long enclosed, hung in all the rooms, and the waste room behind the kitchen was littered with old useless papers. Among these I found a few paper-covered books, the pages of which were curled and damp: *The Abbott*, By Walter Scott, *The Devout Communicant* and *The Memoirs of Vidocq*. I liked the last best because it leaves were yellow. The wild garden behind the house contained a central apple-tree and a few straggling bushes under one of which I found the late tenant's rusty bicycle-pump. He had been a very charitable priest; in his will he had left all his money to institutions and the furniture of his house to his sister.

When the short days of winter came dusk fell before we had well eaten our dinners. When we met in the street the houses had grown sombre. The space of sky above us was the colour of ever-changing violet and towards it the lamps of the street lifted their feeble lanterns. The cold air stung us and we played till our bodies glowed. Our shouts echoed in the silent street. The career of our play brought us through the dark muddy lanes behind the houses where we ran the gauntlet of the rough tribes from the cottages, to the back doors of the dark dripping gardens where odours arose from the ashpits, to the dark odorous stables where a coachman smoothed and combed the horse or shook music from the buckled harness. When we returned to the street light from the kitchen windows had filled the areas. If my uncle was seen turning the corner we hid in the shadow until we had seen him safely housed. Or if Mangan's sister came out on the doorstep to call her brother in to his tea we watched her from our shadow peer up and down the street. We waited to see whether she would remain or go in and, if she remained, we left our shadow and walked up to Mangan's steps resignedly. She was waiting for us, her figure defined by the light from the half-opened door. Her brother always teased her before he obeyed and I stood by the railings looking at her. Her dress swung as she moved her body and the soft rope of her hair tossed from side to side.

Every morning I lay on the floor in the front parlour watching her door. The blind was pulled down to within an inch of the sash so that I could not be seen. When she came out on the doorstep my heart leaped. I ran to the hall, seized my books and followed her. I kept her brown figure always in my eye and, when we came near the point at which our ways diverged, I quickened my pace and passed her. This happened morning after morning. I had never spoken to her, except for a few casual words, and yet her name was like a summons to all my foolish blood.

Her image accompanied me even in places the most hostile to romance. On Saturday evenings when my aunt went marketing I had to go to carry some of the parcels. We walked through the flaring streets, jostled by drunken men and bargaining women, amid the curses of labourers, the shrill litanies of shop-boys who stood on guard by the barrels of pigs' cheeks, the nasal chanting of street-singers, who sang a *come-all-you* about O'Donovan Rossa, or a ballad about the troubles in our native land. These noises converged in a single sensation of life for me: I imagined that I bore my chalice safely through a throng of foes. Her name sprang to my lips at moments in strange prayers and praises which I myself did not understand. My eyes were often full of tears (I could not tell why) and at times a flood from my heart seemed to pour itself out into my bosom. I thought little of the future. I did not know whether I would ever speak to her or not or, if I spoke to her, how I could tell her of my confused adoration. But my body was like a harp and her words and gestures were like fingers running upon the wires.

One evening I went into the back drawing-room in which the priest had died. It was a dark rainy evening and there was no sound in the house. Through one of the broken panes I heard the rain impinge upon the earth, the fine incessant needles of water playing in the sodden beds. Some distant lamp or lighted window gleamed below me. I was thankful that I could see so little. All my senses seemed to desire to veil themselves and, feeling that I was about to slip from them, I pressed the palms of my hands together until they trembled, murmuring: "*O love! O love!*" many times.

At last she spoke to me. When she addressed the first words to me I was so confused that I did not know what to answer. She asked me was I going to *Araby*. I forgot whether I answered yes or no. It would be a splendid bazaar, she said she would love to go.

"And why can't you?" I asked.

While she spoke she turned a silver bracelet round and round her wrist. She could not go, she said, because there would be a retreat that week in her convent. Her brother and two other boys were fighting for their caps and I was alone at the railings. She held one of the spikes, bowing her head towards me. The light from the lamp opposite our door caught the white curve of her neck, lit up her hair that rested there and, falling, lit up the hand upon the railing. It fell over one side of her dress and caught the white border of a petticoat, just visible as she stood at ease.

"It's well for you," she said.

"If I go," I said, "I will bring you something."

What innumerable follies laid waste my waking and sleeping thoughts after that evening! I wished to annihilate the tedious intervening days. I chafed against the work of school. At night in my bedroom and by day in the classroom her image came between me and the page I strove to read. The syllables of the word *Araby* were called to me through the silence in which my soul luxuriated and cast an Eastern enchantment over me. I asked for leave to go to the bazaar on Saturday night. My aunt was surprised and hoped it was not some Freemason affair. I answered few questions in class. I watched my master's face pass from amiability to sternness; he hoped I was not beginning to idle. I could not call my wandering thoughts together. I had hardly any patience with the serious work of life which, now that it stood between me and my desire, seemed to me child's play, ugly monotonous child's play.

On Saturday morning I reminded my uncle that I wished to go to the bazaar in the evening. He was fussing at the hallstand, looking for the hat-brush, and answered me curtly:

"Yes, boy, I know."

As he was in the hall I could not go into the front parlour and lie at the window. I left the house in bad humour and walked slowly towards the school. The air was pitilessly raw and already my heart misgave me.

When I came home to dinner my uncle had not yet been home. Still it was early. I sat staring at the clock for some time and, when its ticking began to irritate me, I left the room. I mounted the staircase and gained the upper part of the house. The high cold empty gloomy rooms liberated me and I went from room to room singing. From the front window I saw my companions playing below in the street. Their cries reached me weakened and indistinct and, leaning my forehead against the cool glass, I looked over at the dark house where she lived. I may have stood there for an hour, seeing nothing but the brown-clad figure cast by my imagination, touched discreetly by the lamplight at the curved neck, at the hand upon the railings and at the border below the dress.

When I came downstairs again I found Mrs. Mercer sitting at the fire. She was an old garrulous woman, a pawnbroker's widow, who collected used stamps for some pious purpose. I had to endure the gossip of the tea-table. The meal was prolonged beyond an hour and still my uncle did not come. Mrs. Mercer stood up to go: she was sorry she couldn't wait any longer, but it was after eight o'clock and she did not like to be out late, as the night air was bad for her. When she had gone I began to walk up and down the room, clenching my fists. My aunt said:

"I'm afraid you may put off your bazaar for this night of Our Lord."

At nine o'clock I heard my uncle's latchkey in the halldoor. I heard him talking to himself and heard the hallstand rocking when it had received the weight of his overcoat. I could interpret these signs. When he was midway through his dinner I asked him to give me the money to go to the bazaar. He had forgotten.

"The people are in bed and after their first sleep now," he said.

I did not smile. My aunt said to him energetically:

"Can't you give him the money and let him go? You've kept him late enough as it is."

My uncle said he was very sorry he had forgotten. He said he believed in the old saying: "All work and no play makes Jack a dull boy." He asked me where I was going and, when I had told him a second time he asked me did I know *The Arab's Farewell to his Steed*. When I left the kitchen he was about to recite the opening lines of the piece to my aunt.

I held a florin tightly in my hand as I strode down Buckingham Street towards the station. The sight of the streets thronged with buyers and glaring with gas recalled to me the purpose of my journey. I took my seat in a third-class carriage of a deserted train. After an intolerable delay the train moved out of the station slowly. It crept onward among ruinous houses and over the twinkling river. At Westland Row Station a crowd of people pressed to the carriage doors; but the porters moved them back, saying that it was a special train for the bazaar. I remained alone in the bare carriage. In a few minutes the train drew up beside an improvised wooden platform. I passed out on to the road and saw by the lighted dial of a clock that it was ten minutes to ten. In front of me was a large building which displayed the magical name.

I could not find any sixpenny entrance and, fearing that the bazaar would be closed, I passed in quickly through a turnstile, handing a shilling to a weary-looking man. I found myself in a big hall girdled at half its height by a gallery. Nearly all the stalls were closed and the greater part of the hall was in darkness. I recognised a silence like that which pervades a church after a service. I walked into the centre of the bazaar timidly. A few people were gathered about the stalls which were still open. Before a curtain, over which the words *Café Chantant* were written in coloured lamps, two men were counting money on a salver. I listened to the fall of the coins.

Remembering with difficulty why I had come I went over to one of the stalls and examined porcelain vases and flowered tea-sets. At the door of the stall a young lady was talking and laughing with two young gentlemen. I remarked their English accents and listened vaguely to their conversation.

"O, I never said such a thing!"

"O, but you did!"

"O, but I didn't!"

"Didn't she say that?"

"Yes. I heard her."

"O, there's a . . . fib!"

Observing me the young lady came over and asked me did I wish to buy anything. The tone of her voice was not encouraging; she seemed to have spoken to me out of a sense of duty. I looked humbly at the great jars that stood like eastern guards at either side of the dark entrance to the stall and murmured:

"No, thank you."

The young lady changed the position of one of the vases and went back to the two young men. They began to talk of the same subject. Once or twice the young lady glanced at me over her shoulder.

I lingered before her stall, though I knew my stay was useless, to make my interest in her wares seem the more real. Then I turned away slowly and walked down the middle of the bazaar. I allowed the two pennies to fall against the sixpence in my pocket. I heard a voice call from one end of the gallery that the light was out. The upper part of the hall was now completely dark.

Gazing up into the darkness I saw myself as a creature driven and derided by vanity; and my eyes burned with anguish and anger.

KATHERINE MANSFIELD

Her First Ball

Exactly when the ball began Leila would have found it hard to say. Perhaps her first real partner was the cab. It did not matter that she shared the cab with the Sheridan girls and their brother. She sat back in her own little corner of it, and the bolster on which her hand rested felt like the sleeve of an unknown young man's dress suit; and away they bowled, past waltzing lamp-posts and houses and fences and trees.

"Have you really never been to a ball before, Leila? But, my child, how too weird—" cried the Sheridan girls.

"Our nearest neighbour was fifteen miles," said Leila softly, gently opening and shutting her fan.

Oh, dear, how hard it was to be indifferent like the others! She tried not to smile too much; she tried not to care. But every single thing was so new and exciting . . . Meg's tuberoses, Jose's long loop of amber, Laura's little dark head, pushing above her white fur like a flower through snow. She would remember for ever. It even gave her a pang to see her cousin Laurie throw away the wisps of tissue paper he pulled from the fastenings of his new gloves. She would like to have kept those wisps as a keepsake, as a remembrance. Laurie leaned forward and put his hand on Laura's knee.

"Look here, darling," he said. "The third and the ninth as usual. Twig?"

Oh, how marvellous to have a brother! In her excitement Leila felt that if there had been time, if it hadn't been impossible, she couldn't have helped crying because she was an only child, and no brother had ever said "Twig?" to her; no sister would ever say, as Meg said to Jose that moment, "I've never known your hair go up more successfully than it has to-night!"

But, of course, there was no time. They were at the drill hall already; there were cabs in front of them and cabs behind. The road was bright on either side with moving fan-like lights, and on the pavement gay couples seemed to float through the air; little satin shoes chased each other like birds.

"Hold on to me, Leila; you'll get lost," said Laura.

"Come on, girls, let's make a dash for it," said Laurie.

Leila put two fingers on Laura's pink velvet cloak, and they were somehow lifted past the big golden lantern, carried along the passage, and pushed into the little room marked "Ladies." Here the crowd was so great there was hardly space to take off their things; the noise was deafening. Two benches on either side were stacked high with wraps. Two old women in white aprons ran up and down tossing fresh armfuls. And everybody was pressing forward trying to get at the little dressing-table and mirror at the far end.

A great quivering jet of gas lighted the ladies' room. It couldn't wait; it was dancing already. When the door opened again and there came a burst of tuning from the drill hall, it leaped almost to the ceiling.

Dark girls, fair girls were patting their hair, tying ribbons again, tucking handkerchiefs down the fronts of their bodices, smoothing marble-white gloves. And because they were all laughing it seemed to Leila that they were all lovely.

"Aren't there any invisible hair-pins?" cried a voice. "How most extraordinary! I can't see a single invisible hair-pin."

"Powder my back, there's a darling," cried someone else.

"But I must have a needle and cotton. I've torn simply miles and miles of the frill," wailed a third.

Then "Pass them along, pass them along!" The straw basket of programmes was tossed from arm to arm. Darling little pink-and-silver programmes, with pink pencils and fluffy tassels. Leila's fingers shook as she took one out of the basket. She wanted to ask someone, "Am I meant to have one too?" but she had just time to read: "Waltz 3. *Two, Two, in a Canoe.* Polka 4. *Making the Feathers Fly,*" when Meg cried, "Ready, Leila?" and they pressed their way through the crush in the passage towards the big double doors of the drill hall.

Dancing had not begun yet, but the band had stopped tuning, and the noise was so great it seemed that when it did begin to play it would never be heard. Leila, pressing close to Meg, looking over Meg's shoulder, felt that even the little quivering coloured flags strung across the ceiling were talking. She quite forgot to be shy; she forgot how in the middle of dressing she had sat down on the bed with one shoe off and one shoe on and begged her mother to ring up her cousins and say she couldn't go after all. And the rush of longing she had had to be sitting on the veranda of their forsaken up-country home, listening to the baby owls crying "More pork" in the moonlight, was changed to a rush of joy so sweet that it was hard to bear alone. She clutched her fan, and, gazing at the gleaming, golden floor, the azaleas, the lanterns, the stage at one end with its red carpet and gilt chairs and the band in a corner, she thought breathlessly, "How heavenly; how simply heavenly!"

All the girls stood grouped together at one side of the doors, the men at the other, and the chaperones in dark dresses, smiling rather foolishly, walked with little careful steps over the polished floor towards the stage.

"This is my little country cousin Leila. Be nice to her. Find her partners; she's under my wing," said Meg, going up to one girl after another.

Strange faces smiled at Leila—sweetly, vaguely. Strange voices answered, "Of course, my dear." But Leila felt the girls didn't really see her. They were looking towards the men. Why didn't the men begin? What were they waiting for? There they stood, smoothing their gloves, patting their glossy hair and smiling among themselves. Then, quite suddenly, as if they had only just made up their minds that that was what they had to do, the men came gliding over the parquet. There was a joyful flutter among the girls. A tall, fair man flew up to Meg, seized her programme, scribbled something; Meg passed him on to Leila. "May I have the pleasure?" He ducked and smiled. There came a dark man wearing an eyeglass, then cousin Laurie with a friend, and Laura with a little freckled fellow whose tie was crooked. Then quite an old man—fat, with a big bald patch on his head—took her programme and murmured, "Let me see, let me see!" And he was a long time comparing his programme, which looked black with names, with hers. It seemed to give him so much trouble that Leila was ashamed. "Oh, please don't bother," she said eagerly. But instead of replying the fat man wrote something, glanced at her again. "Do I remember this bright little face?" he said softly. "Is it known to me of yore?" At that moment the band began playing; the fat man disappeared. He was tossed away on a great wave of music that came flying over the gleaming floor, breaking the groups up into couples, scattering them, sending them spinning. . . .

Leila had learned to dance at boarding school. Every Saturday afternoon the boarders were hurried off to a little corrugated iron mission hall where Miss Eccles (of London) held her "select" classes. But the difference between that dusty-smelling hall—with calico texts on the walls, the poor terrified little woman in a brown velvet toque with rabbit's ears thumping the cold piano, Miss Eccles poking the girls' feet with her long white wand—and this was so tremendous that Leila was sure if her partner didn't come and she had to listen to that marvellous music and to watch the others sliding, gliding over the golden floor, she would die at least, or faint, or lift her arms and fly out of one of those dark windows that showed the stars.

"Ours, I think—" Someone bowed, smiled, and offered her his arm; she hadn't to die after all. Someone's hand pressed her waist, and she floated away like a flower that is tossed into a pool.

"Quite a good floor, isn't it?" drawled a faint voice close to her ear.

"I think it's most beautifully slippery," said Leila.

"Pardon!" The faint voice sounded surprised. Leila said it again. And there was a tiny pause before the voice echoed. "Oh, quite!" and she was swung round again.

He steered so beautifully. That was the great difference between dancing with girls and men, Leila decided. Girls banged into each other, and stamped on each other's feet; the girl who was gentleman always clutched you so.

The azaleas were separate flowers no longer; they were pink and white flags streaming by.

"Were you at the Bells' last week?" the voice came again. It sounded tired. Leila wondered whether she ought to ask him if he would like to stop.

"No, this is my first dance," said she.

Her partner gave a little gasping laugh. "Oh, I say," he protested.

"Yes, it is really the first dance I've ever been to." Leila was most fervent. It was such a relief to be able to tell somebody. "You see, I've lived in the country all my life up until now. . . ."

At that moment the music stopped, and they went to sit on two chairs against the wall. Leila tucked her pink satin feet under and fanned herself, while she blissfully watched the other couples passing and disappearing through the swing doors.

"Enjoying yourself, Leila?" asked Jose, nodding her golden head.

Laura passed and gave her the faintest little wink; it made Leila wonder for a moment whether she was quite grown up after all. Certainly her partner did not say very much. He coughed, tucked his handkerchief away, pulled down his waistcoat, took a minute thread off his sleeve. But it didn't matter. Almost immediately the band started, and her second partner seemed to spring from the ceiling.

"Floor's not bad," said the new voice. Did one always begin with the floor? And then, "Were you at the Neaves' on Tuesday?" And again Leila explained. Perhaps it was a little strange that her partners were not more interested. For it was thrilling. Her first ball! She was only at the beginning of everything. It seemed to her that she had never known what the night was like before. Up till now it had been dark, silent, beautiful very often—oh, yes—but mournful somehow. Solemn. And now it would never be like that again —it had opened dazzling bright.

"Care for an ice?" said her partner. And they went through the swing doors, down the passage, to the supper room. Her cheeks burned, she was fearfully thirsty. How sweet the ices looked on little glass plates, and how cold the frosted spoon was, iced too! And when they came back to the hall there was the fat man waiting for her by the door. It gave her quite a shock again to see how old he was; he ought to have been on the stage with the fathers and mothers. And when Leila compared him with her other partners he looked shabby. His waistcoat was creased, there was a button off his glove, his coat looked as if it was dusty with French chalk.

"Come along, little lady," said the fat man. He scarcely troubled to clasp her, and they moved away so gently, it was more like walking than dancing. But he said not a word about the floor. "Your first dance, isn't it?" he murmured.

"How *did* you know?"

"Ah," said the fat man, "that's what it is to be old!" He wheezed faintly as he steered her past an awkward couple. "You see, I've been doing this kind of thing for the last thirty years."

"Thirty years?" cried Leila. Twelve years before she was born!

"It hardly bears thinking about, does it?" said the fat man gloomily. Leila looked at his bald head, and she felt quite sorry for him.

"I think it's marvellous to be still going on," she said kindly.

"Kind little lady," said the fat man, and he pressed her a little closer, and hummed a bar of the waltz. "Of course," he said, "you can't hope to last anything like as long as that. No-o," said the fat man, "long before that you'll be sitting up there on the stage, looking on, in your nice black velvet. And these pretty arms will have turned into little short fat ones, and you'll beat time with such a different kind of fan—a black bony one." The fat man seemed to shudder. "And you'll smile away like the poor old dears up there, and point to your daughter, and tell the elderly lady next to you how some dreadful man tried to kiss her at the club ball. And your heart will ache, ache"—the fat man squeezed her closer still, as if he really was sorry for that poor heart—"because no one wants to kiss you now. And you'll say how unpleasant these polished floors are to walk on, how dangerous they are. Eh, Mademoiselle Twinkletoes?" said the fat man softly.

Leila gave a light little laugh, but she did not feel like laughing. Was it—could it all be true? It sounded terribly true. Was this first ball only the beginning of her last ball after all? At that the music seemed to change; it sounded sad, sad; it rose upon a great sigh. Oh, how quickly things changed! Why didn't happiness last for ever? For ever wasn't a bit too long.

"I want to stop," she said in a breathless voice. The fat man led her to the door.

"No," she said, "I won't go outside. I won't sit down. I'll just stand here, thank you." She leaned against the wall, tapping with her foot, pulling up her gloves and trying to smile. But deep inside her a little girl threw her pinafore over her head and sobbed. Why had he spoiled it all?

"I say, you know," said the fat man, "you mustn't take me seriously, little lady."

"As if I should!" said Leila, tossing her small dark head and sucking her underlip. . . .

Again the couples paraded. The swing doors opened and shut. Now new music was given out by the bandmaster. But Leila didn't want to dance any more. She wanted to be home, or sitting on the veranda listening to those baby owls. When she looked through the dark windows at the stars, they had long beams like wings. . . .

But presently a soft, melting, ravishing tune began, and a young man with curly hair bowed before her. She would have to dance, out of politeness, until she could find Meg. Very stiffly she walked into the middle; very haughtily she put her hand on his sleeve. But in one minute, in one turn, her feet glided, glided. The lights, the azaleas, the dresses, the pink faces, the velvet chairs, all became one beautiful flying wheel. And when her next partner bumped into the fat man and he said, "Par*don*," she smiled at him more radiantly than ever. She didn't even recognize him again.

BERNARD MALAMUD

Take Pity

Davidov, the census-taker, opened the door without knocking, limped into the room and sat wearily down. Out came his notebook and he was on the job. Rosen, the ex-coffee salesman, wasted, eyes despairing, sat motionless, cross-legged, on his cot. The square, clean but cold room, lit by a dim globe, was sparsely furnished: the cot, a folding chair, small table, old unpainted chests—no closets but who needed them?—and a small sink with a rough piece of green, institutional soap on its holder—you could smell it across the room. The worn black shade over the single narrow window was drawn to the ledge, surprising Davidov.

"What's the matter you don't pull the shade up?" he remarked.

Rosen ultimately sighed. "Let it stay."

"Why? Outside is light."

"Who needs light?"

"What then you need?"

"Light I don't need," replied Rosen.

Davidov, sour-faced, flipped through the closely scrawled pages of his notebook until he found a clean one. He attempted to scratch in a word with his fountain pen but it had run dry, so he fished a pencil stub out of his vest pocket and sharpened it with a cracked razor blade. Rosen paid no attention to the feathery shavings falling to the floor. He looked restless, seemed to be listening to or for something, although Davidov was convinced there was absolutely nothing to listen to. It was only when the census-taker somewhat irritably and with increasing loudness repeated a question, that Rosen stirred and identified himself. He was about to furnish an address but caught himself and shrugged.

Davidov did not comment on the salesman's gesture. "So begin," he nodded.

"Who knows where to begin?" Rosen stared at the drawn shade. "Do they know here where to begin?"

"Philosophy we are not interested," said Davidov. "Start in how you met her."

"Who?" pretended Rosen.

"Her," he snapped.

"So if I got to begin, how you know about her already?" Rosen asked triumphantly.

Davidov spoke wearily, "You mentioned before."

Rosen remembered. They had questioned him upon his arrival and he now recalled blurting out her name. It was perhaps something in the air. It did not permit you to retain what you remembered. That was part of the cure, if you wanted a cure.

"Where I met her—?" Rosen murmured. "I met her where she always was—in the back room there in that hole in the wall that it was a waste of time for me I went there. Maybe I sold them a half a bag of coffee a month. This is not business."

"In business we are not interested."

"What then you are interested?" Rosen mimicked Davidov's tone.

Davidov clammed up coldly.

Rosen knew they had him where it hurt, so he went on: "The husband was maybe forty, Axel Kalish, a Polish refugee. He worked like a blind horse when he got to America, and saved maybe two—three thousand dollars that he bought with the money this pisher grocery in a dead neighborhood where he didn't have a chance. He called my company up for credit and they sent me I should see. I recommended okay because I felt sorry. He had a wife, Eva, you know already about her, and two darling girls, one five and one three, little dolls, Fega and Surale, that I didn't want them to suffer. So right away I told him, without tricks, 'Kiddo, this is a mistake. This place is a grave. Here they will bury you if you don't get out quick!' "

Rosen sighed deeply.

"So?" Davidov had thus far written nothing, irking the ex-salesman.

"So?—Nothing. He didn't get out. After a couple months he tried to sell but nobody bought, so he stayed and starved. They never made expenses. Every day they got poorer you couldn't look in their faces. 'Don't be a damn fool,' I told him, 'go in bankruptcy.' But he couldn't stand it to lose all his capital, and he was also afraid it would be hard to find a job. 'My God,' I said, 'do anything. Be a painter, a janitor, a junk man, but get out of here before everybody is a skeleton.'

"This he finally agreed with me, but before he could go in auction he dropped dead."

Davidov made a note. "How did he die?"

"On this I am not an expert," Rosen replied. "You know better than me."

"How did he die?" Davidov spoke impatiently. "Say in one word."

"From what he died?—he died, that's all."

"Answer, please, this question."

"Broke in him something. That's how."

"Broke what?"

"Broke what breaks. He was talking to me how bitter was his life, and he touched me on my sleeve to say something else, but the next minute his face got small and he fell down dead, the wife screaming, the little girls crying that it made in my heart pain. I am myself a sick man and when I saw him laying on the floor, I said to myself, 'Rosen, say goodbye, this guy is finished.' So I said it."

Rosen got up from the cot and strayed despondently around the room, avoiding the window. Davidov was occupying the only chair, so the ex-salesman was finally forced to sit on the edge of the bed again. This irritated him. He badly wanted a cigarette but disliked asking for one.

Davidov permitted him a short interval of silence, then leafed impatiently through his notebook. Rosen, to needle the census-taker, said nothing.

"So what happened?" Davidov finally demanded.

Rosen spoke with ashes in his mouth. "After the funeral—" he paused, tried to wet his lips, then went on, "He belonged to a society that they buried him, and he also left a thousand dollars insurance, but after the funeral I said to her, 'Eva, listen to me. Take the money and your children and run away from here. Let the creditors take the store. What will they get?—Nothing.'

"But she answered me, 'Where will I go, where, with my two orphans that their father left them to starve?'

" 'Go anywhere,' I said. 'Go to your relatives.'

"She laughed like laughs somebody who hasn't got no joy. 'My relatives Hitler took away from me.'

" 'What about Axel—surely an uncle somewheres?'

" 'Nobody,' she said. 'I will stay here like my Axel wanted. With the insurance I will buy new stock and fix up the store. Every week I will decorate the window, and in this way gradually will come in new customers—'

" 'Eva, my darling girl—'

" 'A millionaire I don't expect to be. All I want is I should make a little living and take care on my girls. We will live in the back here like before, and in this way I can work and watch them, too.'

" 'Eva,' I said, 'you are a nice-looking young woman, only thirty-eight years. Don't throw away your life here. Don't flush in the toilet—you should excuse me—the thousand poor dollars from your dead husband. Believe me, I know from such stores. After thirty-five years' experience I know a graveyard when I smell it. Go better some place and find a job. You're young yet. Sometime you will meet somebody and get married.'

" 'No, Rosen, not me,' she said. 'With marriage I am finished. Nobody wants a poor widow with two children.'

" 'This I don't believe it.'

" 'I know,' she said.

"Never in my life I saw so bitter a woman's face.

" 'No,' I said. 'No.'

" 'Yes, Rosen, yes. In my whole life I never had anything. In my whole life I always suffered. I don't expect better. This is my life.'

"I said no and she said yes. What could I do? I am a man with only one kidney, and worse than that, that I won't mention it. When I talked she didn't listen, so I stopped to talk. Who can argue with a widow?"

The ex-salesman glanced up at Davidov but the census-taker did not reply. "What happened then?" he asked.

"What happened?" mocked Rosen. "Happened what happens."

Davidov's face grew red.

"What happened, happened," Rosen said hastily. "She ordered from the wholesalers all kinds goods that she paid for them cash. All week she opened boxes and packed on the shelves cans, jars, packages. Also she cleaned, and she washed, and she mopped with oil the floor. With tissue paper she made new decorations in the window, everything should look nice—but who came in? Nobody except a few poor customers from the tenement around the corner. And when they came? When was closed the supermarkets and they needed some little item that they forgot to buy, like a quart milk, fifteen cents' cheese, a small can sardines for lunch. In a few months was again dusty the cans on the shelves, and her thousand was gone. Credit she couldn't get except from me, and from me she got because I paid out of my pocket the company. This she didn't know. She worked, she dressed clean, she waited that the store should get better. Little by little the shelves got empty, but where was the profit? They ate it up. When I looked on the little girls I knew what she didn't tell me. Their faces were white, they were thin, they were hungry. She kept the little food that was left, on the shelves. One night I brought in a nice piece sirloin, but I could see from her eyes that she didn't like that I did it. So what else could I do? I have a heart and I am human."

Here the ex-salesman wept.

Davidov pretended not to see though once he peeked.

Rosen blew his nose, then went on more calmly, "When the children were sleeping we sat in the dark there, in the back, and not once in four hours opened the door should come in a customer. 'Eva, for Godsakes, *run away*,' I said.

" 'I have no place to go,' she said.

" 'I will give you where you can go, and please don't say to me no. I am a bachelor, this you know. I got whatever I need and more besides. Let me help you and the children. Money don't interest me. Interests me good health, but I can't buy it. I'll tell you what I will do. Let this place go to the creditors and move into a two-family house that I own, which the top floor is now empty. Rent will cost you nothing. In the meantime you can go and find a job. I will also pay the downstairs lady to take care of the girls—God bless them—until you will come home. With your wages you will buy the food, if you need clothes, and also save a little. This you can use when you get married someday. What do you say?'

"She didn't answer me. She only looked on me in such a way, with such burning eyes, like I was small and ugly. For the first time I thought to myself, 'Rosen, this woman don't like you.'

" 'Thank you very kindly, my friend Mr. Rosen,' she answered me, 'but charity we are not needing. I got yet a paying business, and it will get better when times are better. Now is bad times. When comes again good times will get better the business.'

" 'Who charity?' I cried to her. 'What charity? Speaks to you your husband's a friend.'

" 'Mr. Rosen, my husband didn't have no friends.'

" 'Can't you see that I want to help the children?'

" 'The children have their mother.'

" 'Eva, what's the matter with you?' I said. 'Why do you make sound bad something that I mean it should be good?'

"This she didn't answer. I felt sick in my stomach, and was coming also a headache so I left.

"All night I didn't sleep, and then all of a sudden I figured out a reason why she was worried. She was worried I would ask for some kind payment except cash. She got the wrong man. Anyway, this made me think of something that I didn't think about before. I thought now to ask her to marry me. What did she have to lose? I could take care of myself without any trouble to them. Fega and Surale would have a father he could give them for the movies, or sometime to buy a little doll to play with, and when I died, would go to them my investments and insurance policies.

"The next day I spoke to her.

" 'For myself, Eva, I don't want a thing. Absolutely not a thing. For you and your girls—everything. I am not a strong man, Eva. In fact, I am sick. I tell you this you should understand I don't expect to live long. But even for a few years would be nice to have a little family.'

"She was with her back to me and didn't speak.

"When she turned around again her face was white but the mouth was like iron.

" 'No, Mr. Rosen.'

" 'Why not, tell me?'

" 'I had enough with sick men.' She began to cry. 'Please, Mr. Rosen. Go home.'

"I didn't have strength I should argue with her, so I went home. I went home but hurt me my mind. All day long and all night I felt bad. My back pained me where was missing my kidney. Also too much smoking. I tried to understand this woman but I couldn't. Why should somebody that her two children were starving always say no to a man that he wanted to help her? What did I do to her bad? Am I maybe a murderer she should hate me so much? All that I felt in my heart was pity for her and the children, but I couldn't convince her. Then I went back and begged her she should let me help them, and once more she told me no.

" 'Eva,' I said, 'I don't blame you that you don't want a sick man. So come with me to a marriage broker and we will find you a strong, healthy husband that he will support you and your girls. I will give the dowry.'

"She screamed, 'On this I don't need your help, Rosen!'

"I didn't say no more. What more could I say? All day long, from early in the morning till late in the night she worked like an animal. All day she mopped, she washed with soap and a brush the shelves, the few cans she polished, but the store was still rotten. The little girls I was afraid to look at. I could see in their faces their bones. They were tired, they were weak. Little Surale held with her hand all the time the dress of Fega. Once when I saw them in the street I gave them some cakes, but when I tried the next day to give them something else, the mother shouldn't know, Fega answered me, 'We can't take, Momma says today is a fast day.'

"I went inside. I made my voice soft. 'Eva, on my bended knee I am a man with nothing in this world. Allow me that I should have a little pleasure before I die. Allow me that I should help you to stock up once more the store.'

"So what did she do? She cried, it was terrible to see. And after she cried, what did she say? She told me to go away and I shouldn't come back. I felt like to pick up a chair and break her head.

"In my house I was too weak to eat. For two days I took in my mouth nothing except maybe a spoon of chicken noodle soup, or maybe a glass tea without sugar. This wasn't good for me. My health felt bad.

"Then I made up a scheme that I was a friend of Axel's who lived in Jersey. I said I owed Axel seven hundred dollars that he lent me this money fifteen years ago, before he got married. I said I did not have the whole money now, but I would send her every week twenty dollars till it was paid up the debt. I put inside the letter two tens and gave it to a friend of mine, also a salesman, he should mail it in Newark so she would not be suspicious who wrote the letters."

To Rosen's surprise Davidov had stopped writing. The book was full, so he tossed it onto the table, yawned, but listened amiably. His curiosity had died.

Rosen got up and fingered the notebook. He tried to read the small distorted handwriting but could not make out a single word.

"It's not English and it's not Yiddish," he said. "Could it be in Hebrew?"

"No," answered Davidov. "It's an old-fashioned language that they don't use it nowadays."

"Oh?" Rosen returned to the cot. He saw no purpose to going on now that it was not required, but he felt he had to.

"Came back all the letters," he said dully. "The first she opened it, then pasted back again the envelope, but the rest she didn't even open."

" 'Here,' I said to myself, 'is a very strange thing—a person that you can never give her anything.—*But I will give*.'

"I went then to my lawyer and we made out a will that everything I had—all my investments, my two houses that I owned, also furniture, my car, the checking account—every cent would go to her, and when she died, the rest would be left for the two girls. The same with my insurance. They would be my beneficiaries. Then I signed and went home. In the kitchen I turned on the gas and put my head in the stove.

"Let her say now no."

Davidov, scratching his stubbled cheek, nodded. This was the part he already knew. He got up and before Rosen could cry no, idly raised the window shade.

It was twilight in space but a woman stood before the window.

Rosen with a bound was off his cot to see.

It was Eva, staring at him with haunted, beseeching eyes. She raised her arms to him.

Infuriated, the ex-salesman shook his fist.

"Whore, bastard, bitch," he shouted at her. "Go 'way from here. Go home to your children."

Davidov made no move to hinder him as Rosen rammed down the window shade.

RUDYARD KIPLING

The Gardener

Every one in the village knew that Helen Turrell did her duty by all her world, and by none more honourably than by her only brother's unfortunate child. The village knew, too, that George Turrell had tried his family severely since early youth, and were not surprised to be told that, after many fresh starts given and thrown away, he, an Inspector of Indian Police, had entangled himself with the daughter of a retired non-commissioned officer, and had died of a fall from a horse a few weeks before his child was born. Mercifully, George's father and mother were both dead, and though Helen, thirty-five and independent, might well have washed her hands of the whole disgraceful affair, she most nobly took charge, though she was, at the time, under threat of lung trouble which had driven her to the South of France. She arranged for the passage of the child and a nurse from Bombay, met them at Marseilles, nursed the baby through an attack of infantile dysentery due to the carelessness of the nurse, whom she had had to dismiss, and at last, thin and worn but triumphant, brought the boy late in the autumn, wholly restored, to her Hampshire home.

All these details were public property, for Helen was as open as the day, and held that scandals are only increased by hushing them up. She admitted that George had always been rather a black sheep, but things might have been much worse if the mother had insisted on her right to keep the boy. Luckily, it seemed that people of that class would do almost anything for money, and, as George had always turned to her in his scrapes, she felt herself

From: DEBITS AND CREDITS. Copyright 1926 by Rudyard Kipling. Reprinted by permission of Mrs. George Bambridge, Doubleday & Company, Inc. and the Macmillan Company of Canada, Ltd.

justified—her friends agreed with her—in cutting the whole non-commissioned officer connection, and giving the child every advantage. A christening, by the Rector, under the name of Michael, was the first step. So far as she knew herself, she was not, she said, a child-lover, but, for all his faults, she had been very fond of George, and she pointed out that little Michael had his father's mouth to a line; which made something to build upon.

As a matter of fact, it was the Turrell forehead, broad, low, and well-shaped, with the widely-spaced eyes beneath it, that Michael had most faithfully reproduced. His mouth was somewhat better cut than the family type. But Helen, who would concede nothing good to his mother's side, vowed he was a Turrell all over, and, there being no one to contradict, the likeness was established.

In a few years Michael took his place, as accepted as Helen had always been—fearless, philosophical, and fairly good-looking. At six, he wished to know why he could not call her "Mummy," as other boys called their mothers. She explained that she was only his auntie, and that aunties were not quite the same as mummies, but that, if it gave him pleasure, he might call her "Mummy" at bedtime, for a pet-name between themselves.

Michael kept his secret most loyally, but Helen, as usual, explained the fact to her friends; which when Michael heard, he raged.

"Why did you tell? *Why* did you tell?" came at the end of the storm.

"Because it's always best to tell the truth," Helen answered, her arm around him as he shook in his cot.

"All right, but when the troof's ugly I don't think it's nice."

"Don't you, dear?"

"No, I don't, and"—she felt the small body stiffen—"now you've told, I won't call you 'Mummy' any more—not even at bedtimes."

"But isn't that rather unkind?" said Helen, softly.

"I don't care! I don't care! You've hurted me in my insides and I'll hurt you back. I'll hurt you as long as I live!"

"Don't, oh, don't talk like that, dear! You don't know what—"

"I will! And when I'm dead I'll hurt you worse!"

"Thank goodness, I shall be dead long before you, darling."

"Huh! Emma says, ' 'Never know your luck.' " (Michael had

been talking to Helen's elderly, flat-faced maid.) "Lots of little boys die quite soon. So'll I. *Then* you'll see!"

Helen caught her breath and moved towards the door, but the wail of "Mummy! Mummy!" drew her back again, and the two wept together.

At ten years old, after two terms at a prep school, something or somebody gave him the idea that his civil status was not quite regular. He attacked Helen on the subject, breaking down her stammered defences with the family directness.

"Don't believe a word of it," he said, cheerily, at the end. "People wouldn't have talked like they did if my people had been married. But don't you bother, Auntie. I've found out all about my sort in English Hist'ry and the Shakespeare bits. There was William the Conqueror to begin with, and—oh, heaps more, and they all got on first-rate. 'Twon't make any difference to you, my being *that*—will it?"

"As if anything could—" she began.

"All right. We won't talk about it any more if it makes you cry." He never mentioned the thing again of his own will, but when, two years later, he skilfully managed to have measles in the holidays, as his temperature went up to the appointed one hundred and four he muttered of nothing else, till Helen's voice, piercing at last his delirium, reached him with assurance that nothing on earth or beyond could make any difference between them.

The terms at his public school and the wonderful Christmas, Easter, and summer holidays followed each other, variegated and glorious as jewels on a string; and as jewels Helen treasured them. In due time Michael developed his own interests, which ran their courses and gave way to others; but his interest in Helen was constant and increasing throughout. She repaid it with all that she had of affection or could command of counsel and money; and since Michael was no fool, the war took him just before what was like to have been a most promising career.

He was to have gone up to Oxford, with a scholarship, in October. At the end of August he was on the edge of joining the first holocaust of public-school boys who threw themselves into the Line; but the captain of his O.T.C., where he had been sergeant for nearly a year, headed him off and steered him directly to a commission in a battalion so new that half of it still wore the old Army red, and the other half was breeding meningitis through living overcrowdedly in damp tents. Helen had been shocked at the idea of direct enlistment.

"But it's in the family," Michael laughed.

"You don't mean to tell me that you believed that old story all this time?" said Helen. (Emma, her maid, had been dead now several years.) "I gave you my word of honour—and I give it again—that—that it's all right. It is indeed."

"Oh, *that* doesn't worry me. It never did," he replied valiantly. "What I meant was, I should have got into the show earlier if I'd enlisted—like my grandfather."

"Don't talk like that! Are you afraid of its ending so soon, then?"

"No such luck. You know what K. says."

"Yes. But my banker told me last Monday it couldn't *possibly* last beyond Christmas—for financial reasons."

" 'Hope he's right, but our Colonel—and he's a Regular—says it's going to be a long job."

Michael's battalion was fortunate in that, by some chance which meant several "leaves," it was used for coast-defence among shallow trenches on the Norfolk coast; thence sent north to watch the mouth of a Scotch estuary, and, lastly, held for weeks on a baseless rumour of distant service. But, the very day that Michael was to have met Helen for four whole hours at a railway-junction up the line, it was hurled out, to help make good the wastage of Loos, and he had only just time to send her a wire of farewell.

In France luck again helped the battalion. It was put down near the Salient, where it led a meritorious and unexacting life, while the Somme was being manufactured; and enjoyed the peace of the Armentières and Laventie sectors when that battle began. Finding that it had sound views on protecting its own flanks and could dig, a prudent Commander stole it out of its own Division, under pretence of helping to lay telegraphs, and used it round Ypres at large.

A month later, and just after Michael had written Helen that there was nothing special doing and therefore no need to worry, a shell-splinter dropping out of a wet dawn killed him at once. The next shell uprooted and laid down over the body what had been the foundation of a barn wall, so neatly that none but an expert would have guessed that anything unpleasant had happened.

By this time the village was old in experience of war, and, English fashion, had evolved a ritual to meet it. When the postmistress handed her seven-year-old daughter the official telegram to take to Miss Turrell, she observed to the Rector's gardener: "It's Miss Helen's turn now." He replied, thinking of his own son: "Well, he's lasted longer than some." The child herself came to the front-door weeping aloud, because Master Michael had often given her sweets. Helen, presently, found herself pulling down the house-blinds one after one with great care, and saying earnestly to each: "Missing *always* means dead." Then she took her place in the dreary procession that was impelled to go through an inevitable series of unprofitable emotions. The Rector, of course, preached hope and prophesied word, very soon, from a prison camp. Several friends, too, told her perfectly truthful tales, but always about other women, to whom, after months and months of silence, their missing had been miraculously restored. Other people urged her to communicate with infallible Secretaries of organisations who could communicate with benevolent neutrals, who could extract accurate information from the most secretive of Hun prison commandants. Helen did and wrote and signed everything that was suggested or put before her.

Once, on one of Michael's leaves, he had taken her over a munition factory, where she saw the progress of a shell from blank-iron to the all but finished article. It struck her at the time that the wretched thing was never left alone for a single second; and "I'm being manufactured into a bereaved next-of-kin," she told herself, as she prepared her documents.

In due course, when all the organisations had deeply or sincerely regretted their inability to trace, etc., something gave way within her and all sensation—save of thankfulness for the release—came to an end in blessed passivity. Michael had died and her world had stood still and she had been one with the full shock of that arrest. Now she was standing still and the world was going forward, but it did not concern her—in no way or relation did it touch her. She knew this by the ease with which she could slip Michael's name into talk and incline her head to the proper angle, at the proper murmur of sympathy.

In the blessed realisation of that relief, the Armistice with all its bells broke over her and passed unheeded. At the end of another year she had overcome her physical loathing of the living and returned young, so that she could take them by the hand and almost sincerely wish them well. She had no interest in any aftermath, national or personal, of the War, but, moving at an immense distance, she sat on various relief committees and held strong views—she heard herself delivering them—about the site of the proposed village War Memorial.

Then there came to her, as next of kin, an official intimation, backed by a page of a letter to her in indelible pencil, a silver identity-disc, and a watch, to the effect that the body of Lieutenant Michael Turrell had been found, identified, and re-interred in Hagenzeele Third Military Cemetery—the letter of the row and the grave's number in that row duly given.

So Helen found herself moved on to another process of the manufacture—to a world full of exultant or broken relatives, now strong in the certainty that there was an altar upon earth where they might lay their love. These soon told her, and by means of time-tables made clear, how easy it was and how little it interfered with life's affairs to go and see one's grave.

"*So* different," as the Rector's wife said, "if he'd been killed in Mesopotamia, or even Gallipoli."

The agony of being waked up to some sort of second life drove Helen across the Channel, where, in a new world of abbreviated titles, she learnt that Hagenzeele Third could be comfortably reached by an afternoon train which fitted in with the morning boat, and that there was a comfortable little hotel not three kilometres from Hagenzeele itself, where one could spend quite a comfortable night and see one's grave next morning. All this she had from a Central Authority who lived in a board and tarpaper shed on the skirts of a razed city full of whirling lime-dust and blown papers.

"By the way," said he, "you know your grave, of course?"

"Yes, thank you," said Helen, and showed its row and number typed on Michael's own little typewriter. The officer would have checked it, out of one of his many books; but a large Lancashire woman thrust between them and bade him tell her where she might find her son, who had been corporal in the A.S.C. His proper name, she sobbed, was Anderson, but, coming of respectable folk, he had of course enlisted under the name of Smith; and had been killed at Dickiebush, in early 'Fifteen. She had not his number nor did she know which of his two Christian names he might have used with his alias; but her Cook's tourist ticket expired at the end of Easter week, and if by then she could not find her child she should go mad. Whereupon she fell forward on Helen's breast; but the officer's wife came out quickly from a little bedroom behind the office, and the three of them lifted the woman on to the cot.

"They are often like this," said the officer's wife, loosening the tight bonnet-strings. "Yesterday she said he'd been killed at Hooge. Are you sure you know your grave? It makes such a difference."

"Yes, thank you," said Helen, and hurried out before the woman on the bed should begin to lament again.

Tea in a crowded mauve and blue striped wooden structure, with a false front, carried her still further into the nightmare. She paid her bill beside a stolid, plain-featured Englishwoman, who, hearing her inquire about the train to Hagenzeele, volunteered to come with her.

"I'm going to Hagenzeele myself," she explained. "Not to Hagenzeele Third; mine is Sugar Factory, but they call it La Rosière now. It's just south of Hagenzeele Three. Have you got your room at the hotel there?"

"Oh yes, thank you. I've wired."

"That's better. Sometimes the place is quite full, and at others there's hardly a soul. But they've put bathrooms into the old Lion d'Or—that's the hotel on the west side of Sugar Factory—and it draws off a lot of people, luckily."

"It's all new to me. This is the first time I've been over."

"Indeed! This is my ninth time since the Armistice. Not on my own account. *I* haven't lost any one, thank God—but, like every one else, I've a lot of friends at home who have. Coming over as often as I do, I find it helps them to have some one just look at the —the place and tell them about it afterwards. And one can take

photos for them, too. I get quite a list of commissions to execute."
She laughed nervously and tapped her slung Kodak. "There are
two or three to see at Sugar Factory this time, and plenty of others
in the cemeteries all about. My system is to save them up, and
arrange them, you know. And when I've got enough commissions
for one area to make it worth while, I pop over and execute them.
It *does* comfort people."

"I suppose so," Helen answered, shivering as they entered the
little train.

"Of course it does. (Isn't it lucky we've got window-seats?) It
must do or they wouldn't ask one to do it, would they? I've a list
of quite twelve or fifteen commissions here"—she tapped the
Kodak again—"I must sort them out to-night. Oh, I forgot to ask
you. What's yours?"

"My nephew," said Helen. "But I was very fond of him."

"Ah yes! I sometimes wonder whether *they* know after death?
What do you think?"

"Oh, I don't—I haven't dared to think much about that
sort of thing," said Helen, almost lifting her hands to keep her off.

"Perhaps that's better," the woman answered. "The sense of loss
must be enough, I expect. Well, I won't worry you any more."

Helen was grateful, but when they reached the hotel Mrs. Scarsworth (they had exchanged names) insisted on dining at the same
table with her, and after the meal, in the little, hideous salon full of
low-voiced relatives, took Helen through her "commissions" with
biographies of the dead, where she happened to know them, and
sketches of their next of kin. Helen endured till nearly half-past
nine, ere she fled to her room.

Almost at once there was a knock at her door and Mrs. Scarsworth entered; her hands, holding the dreadful list, clasped before
her.

"Yes—yes—*I* know," she began. "You're sick of me, but I want
to tell you something. You—you aren't married are you? Then
perhaps you won't. . . . But it doesn't matter. I've *got* to tell
some one. I can't go on any longer like this."

"But please—" Mrs. Scarsworth had backed against the shut
door, and her mouth worked dryly.

"In a minute," she said. "You—you know about these graves
of mine I was telling you about downstairs, just now? They really

are commissions. At least several of them are." Her eye wandered round the room. "What extraordinary wall-papers they have in Belgium, don't you think? . . . Yes. I swear they are commissions. But there's *one*, d'you see, and—and he was more to me than anything else in the world. Do you understand?"

Helen nodded.

"More than any one else. And, of course, he oughtn't to have been. He ought to have been nothing to me. But he *was*. He *is*. That's why I do the commissions, you see. That's all."

"But why do you tell me?" Helen asked desperately.

"Because I'm *so* tired of lying. Tired of lying—always lying—year in and year out. When I don't tell lies I've got to act 'em and I've got to think 'em always. *You* don't know what that means. He was everything to me that he oughtn't to have been—the one real thing—the only thing that ever happened to me in all my life; and I've had to pretend he wasn't. I've had to watch every word I said, and think out what lie I'd tell next, for years and years!"

"How many years?" Helen asked.

"Six years and four months before, and two and three-quarters after. I've gone to him eight times, since. To-morrow'll make the ninth, and—and I can't—I *can't* go to him again with nobody in the world knowing. I want to be honest with some one before I go. Do you understand? It doesn't matter about *me*. I was never truthful, even as a girl. But it isn't worthy of *him*. So—so I—I had to tell you. I can't keep it up any longer. Oh, I can't!"

She lifted her joined hands almost to the level of her mouth, and brought them down sharply, still joined, to full arms' length below her waist. Helen reached forward, caught them, bowed her head over them, and murmured: "Oh, my dear! My dear!" Mrs. Scarsworth stepped back, her face all mottled.

"My God!" said she. "Is *that* how you take it?"

Helen could not speak, the woman went out; but it was a long while before Helen was able to sleep.

Next morning, Mrs. Scarsworth left early on her round of commissions, and Helen walked alone to Hagenzeele Third. The place was still in the making, and stood some five or six feet above the metalled road, which it flanked for hundreds of yards. Culverts across a deep ditch served for entrances through the unfinished boundary wall. She climbed a few wooden-faced earthen steps and then met the entire crowded level of the thing in one held breath. She did not know that Hagenzeele Third counted twenty-one thousand dead already. All she saw was a merciless sea of black crosses, bearing little strips of stamped tin at all angles across their faces. She could distinguish no order or arrangement in their mass; nothing but a waist-high wilderness as of weeds stricken dead, rushing at her. She went forward, moved to the left and the right hopelessly, wondering by what guidance she should ever come to her own. A great distance away there was a line of whiteness. It proved to be a block of some two or three hundred graves whose headstones had already been set, whose flowers were planted out, and whose new-sown grass showed green. Here she could see clear-cut letters at the ends of the rows, and, referring to her slip, realised that it was not here she must look.

A man knelt behind a line of headstones—evidently a gardener, for he was firming a young plant in the soft earth. She went towards him, her paper in her hand. He rose at her approach and without prelude or salutation asked: "Who are you looking for?"

"Lieutenant Michael Turrell—my nephew," said Helen slowly and word for word, as she had many thousands of times in her life.

The man lifted his eyes and looked at her with infinite compassion before he turned from the fresh-sown grass towards the naked black crosses.

"Come with me," he said, "and I will show you where your son lies."

When Helen left the Cemetery she turned for a last look. In the distance she saw the man bending over his young plants; and she went away, supposing him to be the gardener.

Part Four

INTRODUCTION

This fourth group of stories has a special character of
its own. These are all stories by Southern writers written out of Southern experience. It has often been noticed that a
remarkable number of America's gifted writers of the last fifty
years have come from the South, and this fact indicates that there
is—or was until recently—something about Southern life that is
peculiarly congenial to the creative understanding. It is possible
to see in these stories what that was.

The South has been an agrarian community, dependent for its
economic existence directly on the soil and for its social structure
on an organization compatible with agriculture rather than with
industry. This dependence has required people to live close to
physical nature, not in the romantic or sentimental but in the
practical sense. The grandfather in Robert Penn Warren's *When
the Light Gets Green* has lost nearly everything he loves, and is
loved—if at all—only by his grandson, who finds, at his grandfather's death, that he feels nothing. Mr. Barden has been involuntarily retired from life by his children, and he recognizes
clearly what has happened to him. Yet he cannot separate himself
from the life of nature, from his concern for the proper setting
of the tobacco, from his anxiety about hailstorms when the light
gets green. In the end, the immediate cause of his fatal stroke is a
hailstorm.

Such an agrarian life must be lived in intimate contact with the
physical realities of experience, the human ones as well as the
natural ones. Such a life almost invariably produces a strong sense

of the continuity and stability of experience. Nature may be whimsical and unpredictable over the short run, but over the long run it remains essentially the same. People who live close to it habitually feel that human nature does too. Thus the social and cultural habits most natural to the South have been realistic about the fundamental experience of life—about birth, love, and death —and they have also been conservative, disinclined to assume that the character of human experience can be improved by political or social reforms.

However angry Carothers Edmonds may become at the endless, circuitous cunning by which Lucas Beauchamp in *The Fire and the Hearth* maintains his essential independence and pride, it never occurs to Edmonds to give the whole business up and abandon Lucas to his own devices. We feel confident that Lucas will eventually teach even George Wilkins some of his cunning and that the Negroes will go on producing corn liquor on the Edmonds plantation forever—and that, in his heart, Carothers Edmonds knows it. This whole comic quarrel is conducted within the framework of an institution—the plantation community—whose legal and ethical boundaries seem to Whites and Negroes alike to set permanent and unbreachable limits to action. Neither group would intentionally go beyond these limits; both exercise their skill and cunning in an attempt to triumph within them; and both take an almost aesthetic pleasure in their skill in managing the opportunities available to them within these limits.

In such a stable society, the sense of values and its expression in manners change very slowly; the energy of society goes rather into enriching and refining the customary ways of living than into a restless search for the novelty of change. Like its manners, the South's religious and artistic senses were conservative and ritualized, the characteristic expression of its habitual sense of experience. One of the evident results of these feelings is that the best Southern writers look at life with a clear understanding—an understanding more often than not only unconscious in other regions of the country—that the most meaningful and valuable world we can live in is the longest known and most familiar, that the past must be cherished as part of the present, and that the most important thing to do with the life we actually live from day to day is to love it. Love it adequately and yet without illusion as to its real nature; live it on these terms, and one makes of it, whether he knows it or not, an art, as Alec Maury makes an art of his life of hunting and fishing in *Old Red*. It is accidental but nonetheless significant of the intimate relation between literature and actual experience in the South that Alec Maury is a portrait of Caroline Gordon's father (and Stephen, incidentally, a portrait of her husband, the poet Allen Tate).

Perhaps an even more moving example of the way Southern writers love what is most homely and familiar is Eudora Welty's *The Worn Path*. This Negro grandmother is so old that she can no longer hold an idea in her mind for more than a few minutes; she wanders, with an indestructible, childlike gaiety, from one idea to another as she struggles yet once more along this worn familiar path. When she reaches the dispensary, she has to be told why she has come. Yet somewhere within her, her indomitable love for her grandson keeps driving her—despite her ignorance of where she is going or why—to complete this heroic journey.

The conservative agrarian society of the South was kept from ever becoming merely complacent, was driven insistently back on its deepest ethical self, by the presence of the Negroes. For these Southern writers, the Negroes of the South have been a test of the white man's conscience, and frequently they are seen as a standing rebuke to him. In either case, they force him to confront his own nature directly. Ike McCaslin in Faulkner's *Delta Autumn* is a saintly representative of the old South, a man who refused a fine plantation he had inherited because it was built by slaves; he preferred to live in the village and supported himself as a carpenter. As a young boy he had learned, from an old man who was half Indian and half Negro, the inward significance of man's community with nature in the hunt, and to the end of his days his annual hunting trip—one of them is described in *Delta Autumn*— is like a religious celebration for him. These facts about Uncle Ike are made clear to us in *The Bear*, one of Faulkner's greatest stories; it is much too long for inclusion in a book like this one, but it is only by understanding something of the family history that is made clear in *The Bear* (the Southern imagination is obsessed by genealogy) that we can grasp the full meaning of *Delta Autumn*. To help the reader understand this family history, I have added here a genealogical chart of the McCaslins, black and white.

Unlikely as it may seem, this chart is considerably simplified, and the student who reads Faulkner carefully can easily add detail to it. But what is essential to our understanding of *Delta Autumn* is here.

What this chart of the McCaslins makes clear is that, when the Negro girl with the baby in her arms steps into Uncle Ike's tent, he is being confronted by a repetition of a tragic act deliberately committed by the founder of his family a hundred years earlier. The founder of his family, Lucius Quintus Carothers McCaslin, Uncle Ike's grandfather, had taken as a mistress one of his Negro slaves named Eunice. When the child of that union, Thomasina—called Tomey—was twenty-two, he took her as a mistress. When Eunice discovered that Tomey was with child by Carothers McCaslin, she committed suicide by drowning herself in a creek on Christmas day "six months before her daughter's and her lover's (*Her first lover's*, he thought. *Her first*) child was born. . . ."

Tomey's son, Turl, married a girl named Tennie, and they had a great many children. From the youngest of these children, known as Tennie's Jim, is descended the girl who confronts Uncle Ike in his tent at the end of *Delta Autumn*. The child in her arms is the son of Carothers (Roth) Edmonds, the great-grandson of Carothers McCaslin, as the Negro girl who has been Roth's mistress is the great-granddaughter of Carothers McCaslin. Ike's father and his twin brother, in the previous generation, and Ike, in this one, gave most of their lives to trying to redeem Carothers McCaslin's sin against the Negroes, a sin that consisted ultimately in a refusal to recognize the Negro's humanity. Now, after two devoted generations of sacrifice and struggle, Uncle Ike is confronted with absolute defeat. Carothers Edmonds, the white, male representative of Carothers McCaslin in the present generation, has loved and got with child a Negro girl who is equally Carothers McCaslin's descendant; and now, in anguish and bitterness, Edmonds is denying her because he has learned she is a Negro. It is essentially a repetition of Carothers McCaslin's refusal, after a hundred years have been spent in trying to redeem that refusal.

In his despair, all Uncle Ike can say to the girl who has so rightly called him Uncle Isaac is: "Go North. Marry: a man of your own race." But this is despair; it is, indeed, almost an acceptance of Roth's right to reject the girl, to deny her humanity, as the girl

GENEALOGY OF THE McCASLIN FAMILY

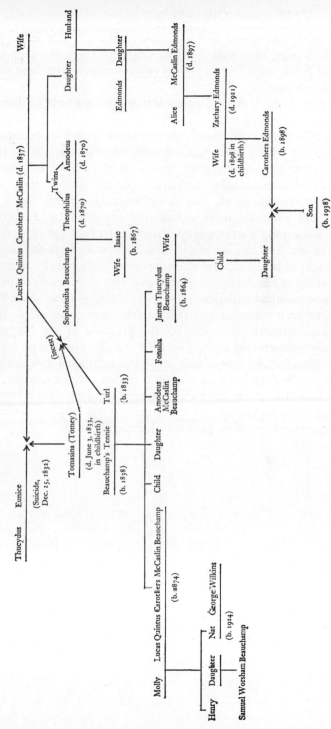

makes quite clear when she looks quietly down at Uncle Ike and says, "Old man, have you lived so long and forgotten so much that you don't remember anything you ever knew or felt or even heard about love?"

One can see in Andrew Lytle's *Mr. McGregor* how brilliantly Southern writers can exploit the fierce dilemma of the Southern White, constantly confronted by the demand that he recognize the Negro as wholly human, filled with reluctance to do so. It is Rhear's humanity, his intimate involvement in the complicated personal relations of the narrator's parents that makes *Mr. McGregor* possible at all. But this dilemma is perhaps most intensely and certainly most extensively exploited by Faulkner, whose work ranges over every aspect and every generation of Southern life. And this is a life in intimate contact wtih the fundamental acts of man's experience, expressing itself socially in manners that are at once simple—in the sense that they are directed to man's few essential experiences—and complex—in the sense that they have been extended and refined for many generations. It is a life kept intensely dramatic by the presence of the Negro—comically exasperating as in *The Fire and the Hearth*, or tragic on the grand scale, where not only the individual but society itself is involved, as in *Delta Autumn*. In one way or another, all the stories in this group have this beautiful and penetrating Southern sense of experience, with its homeliness, its reality, its comic yet tragic awareness of its own very human dilemma.

WILLIAM FAULKNER

The Fire and the Hearth

First, in order to take care of George Wilkins once and
for all, he had to hide his own still. And not only that,
he had to do it singlehanded—dismantle it in the dark and transport it without help to some place far enough away and secret
enough to escape the subsequent uproar and excitement and there
conceal it. It was the prospect of this which had enraged him,
compounding in advance the physical weariness and exhaustion
which would be the night's aftermath. It was not the temporary
interruption of business; the business had been interfered with
once before about five years ago and he had dealt with that crisis
as promptly and efficiently as he was dealing with this present
one—and since which time that other competitor, whose example George Wilkins might quite possibly follow provided Carothers Edmonds were as correctly informed about his intentions
as he professed to be about his bank account, had been plowing
and chopping and picking cotton which was not his on the State
penal farm at Parchman.

And it was not the loss of revenue which the interruption en-
tailed. He was sixty-seven years old; he already had more money
in the bank now than he would ever spend, more than Carothers
Edmonds himself, provided a man believed Carothers Edmonds
when he tried to draw anything extra in the way of cash or supplies from the commissary. It was the fact that he must do it all

himself, singlehanded; had to come up from the field after a long day in the dead middle of planting time and stable and feed Edmonds' mules and eat his own supper and then put his own mare to the single wagon and drive three miles to the still and dismantle it by touch in the dark and carry it another mile to the best place he could think of where it would be reasonably safe after the excitement started, probably getting back home with hardly enough of the night left to make it worth while going to bed before time to return to the field until the time would be ripe to speak the one word to Edmonds;—all this alone and unassisted because the two people from whom he might reasonably and logically have not only expected but demanded help were completely interdict: his wife who was too old and frail for such, even if he could have trusted not her fidelity but her discretion; and as for his daughter, to let her get any inkling of what he was about, he might just as well have asked George Wilkins himself to help him hide the still. It was not that he had anything against George personally, despite the mental exasperation and the physical travail he was having to undergo when he should have been at home in bed asleep. If George had just stuck to farming the land which Edmonds had allotted him he would just as soon Nat married George as anyone else, sooner than most of the nigger bucks he knew. But he was not going to let George Wilkins or anyone else move not only into the section where he had lived for going on seventy years but onto the very place he had been born on and set up competition in a business which he had established and nursed carefully and discreetly for twenty of them, ever since he had fired up for his first fun not a mile from Zack Edmonds' kitchen door;—secretly indeed, for no man needed to tell him what Zack Edmonds or his son, Carothers (or Old Cass Edmonds either, for that matter), would do about it if they ever found it out. He wasn't afraid that George would cut into his established trade, his old regular clientele, with the hog swill which George had begun to turn out two months ago and call whisky. But George Wilkins was a fool innocent of discretion, who sooner or later would be caught, whereupon for the next ten years every bush on the Edmonds place would have a deputy sheriff squatting behind it from sundown to sunup every night. And he not only didn't want a fool for a son-in-law, he didn't intend to have a fool living on the same place he lived on. If George had to go to jail to alleviate that condition, that was between George and Roth Edmonds.

But it was about over now. Another hour or so and he would be back home, getting whatever little of sleep there might be left of the night before time to return to the field to pass the day until the right moment to speak to Edmonds. Probably the outrage would be gone by then, and he would have only the weariness to contend with. But it was his own field, though he neither owned it nor wanted to nor even needed to. He had been cultivating it for forty-five years, since before Carothers Edmonds was born even, plowing and planting and working it when and how he saw fit (or maybe not even doing that, maybe sitting through a whole morning on his front gallery, looking at it and thinking if that's what he felt like doing), with Edmonds riding up on his mare maybe three times a week to look at the field, and maybe once during the season stopping long enough to give him advice about it which he completely ignored, ignoring not only the advice but the very voice which gave it, as though the other had not spoken even, whereupon Edmonds would ride on and he would continue with whatever he had been doing, the incident already forgotten condoned and forgiven, the necessity and the time having been served. So the day would pass at last. Then he would approach Edmonds and speak his word and it would be like dropping the nickel into the slot machine and pulling the lever: all he would have to do then would be just to watch it.

He knew exactly where he intended to go, even in the darkness. He had been born on this land, twenty-five years before the Edmonds who now owned it. He had worked on it ever since he got big enough to hold a plow straight; he had hunted over every foot of it during his childhood and youth and his manhood too, up to the time when he stopped hunting, not because he could no longer walk a day's or a night's hunt, but because he felt that the pursuit of rabbits and 'possums for meat was no longer commensurate with his status as not only the oldest man but the oldest living person on the Edmonds plantation, the oldest McCaslin descendant even though in the world's eye he descended not from McCaslins but from McCaslin slaves, almost as old as old Isaac McCaslin who lived in town, supported by what Roth Edmonds chose to give him, who would own the land and all on it if his just rights were only known, if people just knew how old Cass Edmonds, this one's grandfather, had beat him out of his patrimony; almost as old as old Isaac, almost, as old Isaac was, coeval with old Buck and Buddy McCaslin who had been alive when their father, Carothers McCaslin, got the land from the Indians back in the old time when men black and white were men.

He was in the creek bottom now. Curiously enough, visibility seemed to have increased, as if the rank sunless jungle of cypress and willow and brier, instead of increasing obscurity, had solidified it into the concrete components of trunk and branch, leaving the air, space, free of it and in comparison lighter, penetrable to vision, to the mare's sight anyway, enabling her to see-saw back and forth among the trunks and the impassable thickets. Then he saw the place he sought—a squat, flat-topped, almost symmetrical mound rising without reason from the floor-like flatness of the valley. The white people called it an Indian mound. One day five or six years ago a group of white men, including two women, most of them wearing spectacles and all wearing khaki clothes which had patently lain folded on a store shelf twenty-four hours ago, came with picks and shovels and jars and phials of insect repellent and spent a day digging about it while most of the people, men women and children, came at some time during the day and looked quietly on; later—within the next two or three days, in fact—he was to remember with almost horrified amazement the cold and contemptuous curiosity with which he himself had watched them.

But that would come later. Now he was merely busy. He could not see his watch-face, but he knew it was almost midnight. He stopped the wagon beside the mound and unloaded the still— the copper-lined kettle which had cost him more than he still liked to think about despite his ingrained lifelong scorn of inferior tools—and the worm and his pick and shovel. The spot he sought was a slight overhang on one face of the mound; in a sense one side of his excavation was already dug for him, needing only to be enlarged a little, the earth working easily under the invisible pick, whispering easily and steadily to the invisible shovel until the orifice was deep enough for the worm and kettle to fit into it, when—and it was probably only a sigh but it sounded to him louder than an avalanche, as though the whole mound had stooped roaring down at him—the entire overhang sloughed. It drummed on the hollow kettle, covering it and the worm, and boiled about his feet and, as he leaped backward and tripped and fell, about his body too, hurling clods and dirt at him, striking him a final blow squarely in the face with something larger than a clod—a blow not vicious so much as merely heavy-handed, a sort of final admonitory pat from the spirit of darkness and solitude, the old earth, perhaps the old ancestors themselves. Because, sitting up, getting his breath again at last, gasping and blinking at the apparently unchanged shape of the mound which seemed to loom poised above him in a long roaring wave of silence like a burst of jeering and prolonged laughter, his hand found the object which had struck him and learned it in the blind dark—a fragment of an earthenware vessel which, intact, must have been as big as a churn and which even as he lifted it crumbled again and deposited in his palm, as though it had been handed to him, a single coin.

He could not have said how he knew it was gold. But he didn't even need to strike a match. He dared risk no light at all as, his brain boiling with all the images of buried money he had ever listened to or heard of, for the next five hours he crawled on hands and knees among the loose earth, hunting through the collapsed and now quiet dirt almost grain by grain, pausing from time to time to gauge by the stars how much remained of the rapid and shortening spring night, then probing again in the dry insensate dust which had yawned for an instant and vouchsafed him one blinding glimpse of the absolute and then closed.

When the east began to pale he stopped and straightened up, kneeling, stretching his cramped and painful muscles into something approximating erectness for the first time since midnight. He had found nothing more. He had not even found any other fragments of the churn or crock. That meant that the rest of it might be scattered anywhere beneath the cave-in. He would have to dig for it, coin by coin, with pick and shovel. That meant time, but more than that, solitude. Obviously there must no longer be even the remotest possibility of sheriffs and law men prying about the place hunting whisky stills. So George Wilkins was reprieved without knowing his luck just as he had been in jeopardy without knowing his danger. For an instant, remembering the tremendous power which three hours ago had hurled him onto his back without even actually touching him, he even thought of taking George into partnership on a minor share basis to do the actual digging; indeed, not only to do the actual work but as a sort of justice, balance, libation to Chance and Fortune, since if it had not been for George, he would not have found the single coin. But he dismissed that before it even had time to become an idea. He, Lucas Beauchamp, the oldest living McCaslin descendant still living on the hereditary land, who actually remembered old Buck and Buddy in the living flesh, older than Zack Edmonds even if Zack were still alive, almost as old as old Isaac who in a sense, say what a man would, had turned apostate to his name and lineage by weakly relinquishing the land which was rightfully his to live in town on the charity of his great-nephew;—he, to share one jot, one penny of the money which old Buck and Buddy had buried almost a hundred years ago, with an interloper without forbears and sprung from nowhere and whose very name was unknown in the country twenty-five years ago—a jimber-jawed clown who could not even learn how to make whisky, who had not only attempted to interfere with and jeopardise his business and disrupt his family, but had given him a week of alternating raging anxiety and exasperated outrage culminating in tonight—or last night now—and not even finished yet, since he still had the worm and kettle to conceal. Never. Let George take for his recompense the fact that he would not have to go to the penitentiary to which Roth Edmonds would probably have sent him even if the Law did not.

The light had increased; he could see now. The slide had covered the still. All necessary would be a few branches piled against it so that the recent earth would not be too apparent to a chance passer. He rose to his feet. But he still could not straighten up completely. With one hand pressed to his back and still bent over a little he began to walk stiffly and painfully toward a clump of sapling cottonwoods about fifty feet away, when something crashed into flight within or beyond it and rushed on, the sound fading and already beginning to curve away toward the edge of the jungle while he stood for perhaps ten seconds, slackjawed with amazed and incredulous comprehension, his head turning to pace the invisible running. Then he whirled and leaped, not toward the sound but running parallel with it, leaping with incredible agility and speed among the trees and undergrowth, breaking out of the jungle in time to see, in the wan light of the accelerating dawn, the quarry fleeing like a deer across a field and into the still night-bound woods beyond.

He knew who it was, even before he returned to the thicket where it had flushed, to stand looking down at the print of his daughter's naked feet where she had squatted in the mud, knowing that print as he would have known those of his mare or his dog, standing over it for a while and looking down at it but no longer seeing it at all. So that was that. In a way, it even simplified things. Even if there had been time (another hour and every field along the creek would have a negro and a mule in it), even if he could hope to obliterate all trace and sign of disturbed earth about the mound, it would do no good to move his still to another hiding-place. Because when they came to the mound to dig they must not only find something, they must find it quick and at once and something the discovery and exhumation of which would cause them to desist and go away—say, only partly buried, and with just enough brush in front of it that they couldn't help but find it even before they got the brush dragged off. Because it was a matter open to, admitting, no controversy, not even discussion. George Wilkins must go. He must be on his way before another night had passed.

II

He shoved his chair back from the supper table and stood up. He gave his daughter's lowered, secret face a single look, not grim but cold. But he addressed neither her nor his wife directly. He might have been speaking to either of them or both or to neither: "Going down the road."

"Where you going this time of night?" his wife said. "Messing around up yonder in the bottom all last night! Getting back home just in time to hitch up and get to the field a good hour after sunup! You needs to be in bed if you going to get that creek piece broke like Mister Roth—"

Then he was out of the house and didn't need to hear her any longer. It was night again. The dirt lane ran pale and dim beneath the moonless sky of corn-planting time. Presently it ran along beside the very field which he was getting ready to plant his cotton in when the whippoorwills began. If it had not been for George Wilkins, he would have had it all broken and bedded and ready now. But that was about over now. Another ten minutes and it would be like dropping the nickel into the slot machine, not ringing down a golden shower about him, he didn't ask that, need that; he would attend to the jackpot himself, but giving him peace and solitude in which to do so. That, the labor even at night and without help, even if he had to move half the mound, did not bother him. He was only sixty-seven, a better man still than some men half his age; ten years younger and he could still have done both, the night-work and the day. But now he wouldn't try it. In a way, he was a little sorry to give up farming. He had liked it; he approved of his fields and liked to work them, taking a solid pride in having good tools to use and using them well, scorning both inferior equipment and shoddy work just as he had bought the best kettle he could find when he set up his still—that copper-lined kettle the cost of which he liked less than ever to remember now that he was not only about to lose it but was himself deliberately giving it away. He had even planned the very phrases, dialogue, in which, after the first matter was attended to, he would inform Edmonds that he had decided to quit farming, was old enough to retire, and for Edmonds to allot his land to someone else to finish the crop. "All right," Edmonds would say. "But you cant expect me to furnish a house and wood and water to a family that aint working any land." And he would say, if it really came to that—and it probably would, since he, Lucas, would affirm to his death that Zack Edmonds had been as much better a man than his son as old Cass Edmonds had been than both of them together: "All right. I'll rent the house from you. Name your price and I will pay you every Saturday night as long as I decide to stay here."

But that would take care of itself. The other matter was first and prime. At first, on his return home this morning, his plan had been to notify the sheriff himself, so that there would be absolutely no slip-up, lest Edmonds should be content with merely destroying George's still and cache and just running George off the place. In that case, George would continue to hang around the place, merely keeping out of Edmonds' sight; whereupon, without even any farm work, let alone the still, to keep him occupied, he would be idle all day and therefore up and out all night long and would constitute more of a menace than ever. The report would have to come from Edmonds, the white man, because to the sheriff Lucas was just another nigger and both the sheriff and Lucas knew it, although only one of them knew that to Lucas the sheriff was a redneck without any reason for pride in his forbears nor hope for it in his descendants. And if Edmonds should decide to handle the matter privately, without recourse to the law, there would be someone in Jefferson whom Lucas could inform that not only he and George Wilkins knew of a still on Carothers Edmonds' place, but Carothers Edmonds knew it too.

He entered the wide carriage gate from which the drive curved mounting to the oak and cedar knoll where he could already see, brighter than any kerosene, the gleam of electricity in the house where the better men than this one had been content with lamps or even candles. There was a tractor under the mule-shed which Zack Edmonds would not have allowed on the place too, and an automobile in a house built especially for it which old Cass would not even have put his foot in. But they were the old days, the old time, and better men than these; Lucas himself made one, himself and old Cass coevals in more than spirit even, the analogy only the closer for its paradox:—old Cass a McCaslin only on his mother's side and so bearing his father's name though he possessed the land and its benefits and responsibilities; Lucas a McCaslin on his father's side though bearing his mother's name and possessing the use and benefit of the land with none of the responsibilities. Better men:—old Cass, a McCaslin only by the distaff yet having enough of old Carothers McCaslin in his veins to take the land from the true heir simply because he wanted it and knew he could use it better and was strong enough, ruthless enough, old Carothers McCaslin enough; even Zack, who was not the man his father had been but whom Lucas, the man McCaslin, had accepted as his peer to the extent of intending to kill him, right up to the point when, his affairs all set in order like those of a man preparing for death, he stood over the sleeping white man that morning forty-three years ago with the naked razor in his hand.

He approached the house—the two log wings which Carothers McCaslin had built and which had sufficed old Buck and Buddy, connected by the open hallway which, as his pride's monument and epitaph, old Cass Edmonds had enclosed and superposed with a second storey of white clapboards and faced with a portico. He didn't go around to the back, the kitchen door. He had done that only one time since the present Edmonds was born; he would never do it again as long as he lived. Neither did he mount the steps. Instead he stopped in the darkness beside the gallery and rapped with his knuckles on the edge of it until the white man came up the hall and peered out the front door. "Well?" Edmonds said. "What is it?"

"It's me," Lucas said.

"Well, come in," the other said. "What are you standing out there for?"

"You come out here," Lucas said. "For all you or me either know, George may be laying out yonder right now, listening."

"George?" Edmonds said. "George Wilkins?" He came out onto the gallery—a young man still, a bachelor, forty-three years old last March. Lucas did not need to remember that. He would never forget it—that night of early spring following ten days of such rain that even the old people remembered nothing to compare it with, and the white man's wife's time upon her and the creek out of banks until the whole valley rose, bled a river choked with down timber and drowned livestock until not even a horse could have crossed it in the darkness to reach a telephone and fetch the doctor back. And Molly, a young woman then and nursing their own first child, wakened at midnight by the white man himself and they followed then the white man through the streaming darkness to his house and Lucas waited in the kitchen, keeping the fire going in the stove, and Molly delivered the white child with none to help but Edmonds and then they knew that the doctor had to be fetched. So even before daylight he was in the water and crossed it, how he never knew, and was back by dark with the doctor, emerging from that death (At one time he had believed himself gone, done for, both himself and the mule soon to be two more white-eyed and slack-jawed pieces of flotsam, to be located by the circling of buzzards, swollen and no longer identifiable, a month hence when the water went down.) which he had entered not for his own sake but for that of old Carothers McCaslin who had sired him and Zack Edmonds both, to find the white man's wife dead and his own wife already established in the white man's house. It was as though on that louring and driving day he had crossed and then recrossed a kind of Lethe, emerging, being permitted to escape, buying as the price of life a world outwardly the same yet subtly and irrevocably altered.

It was as though the white woman had not only never quitted the house, she had never existed—the object which they buried in the orchard two days later (they still could not cross the valley to reach the churchyard) a thing of no moment, unsanctified, nothing; his own wife, the black woman, now living alone in the house which old Cass had built for them when they married, keeping alive on the hearth the fire he had lit there on their wedding day and which had burned ever since though there was little enough cooking done on it now;—thus, until almost half a year had passed and one day he went to Zack Edmonds and said, "I wants my wife. I needs her at home." Then—and he hadn't intended to say this. But there had been that half-year almost and himself alone keeping alive the fire which was to burn on the hearth until neither he nor Molly were left to feed it, himself sitting before it night after night through that spring and summer until one night he caught himself standing over it, furious, bursting, blind, the cedar water bucket already poised until he caught himself and set the bucket back on the shelf, still shaking, unable to remember taking the bucket up even—then he said: "I reckon you thought I wouldn't take her back, didn't you?"

The white man was sitting down. In age he and Lucas could have been brothers, almost twins too. He leaned slowly back in the chair, looking at Lucas. "Well, by God," he said quietly. "So that's what you think. What kind of a man do you think I am? What kind of a man do you call yourself?"

"I'm a nigger," Lucas said. "But I'm a man too. I'm more than just a man. The same thing made my pappy that made your grandmaw. I'm going to take her back."

"By God," Edmonds said, "I never thought to ever pass my oath to a nigger. But I will swear—" Lucas had turned, already walking away. He whirled. The other was standing now. They faced one another, though for the instant Lucas couldn't even see him.

"Not to me!" Lucas said. "I wants her in my house tonight. You understand?" He went back to the field, to the plow standing in midfurrow where he had left it when he discovered suddenly that he was going now, this moment, to the commissary or the house or wherever the white man would be, into his bedroom if necessary, and confront him. He had tied the mule under a tree, the gear still on it. He put the mule back to the plow and plowed again. When he turned at the end of each furrow he could have seen his house. But he never looked toward it, not even when he knew that she was in it again, home again, not even when fresh woodsmoke began to rise from the chimney as it had not risen in the middle of the morning in almost half a year; not even when at noon she came along the fence, carrying a pail and a covered pan and stood looking at him for a moment before she set the pail and pan down and went back. Then the plantation bell rang for noon, the flat, musical, deliberate clangs. He took the mule out and watered and fed it and only then went to the fence-corner and there it was—the pan of still-warm biscuit, the lard pail half full of milk, the tin worn and polished with scouring and long use until it had a patina like old silver—just as it had used to be.

Then the afternoon was done too. He stabled and fed Edmonds' mule and hung the gear on its appointed peg against tomorrow. Then in the lane, in the green middledusk of summer while the fireflies winked and drifted and the whippoorwills choired back and forth and the frogs thumped and grunted along the creek, he looked at his house for the first time, at the thin plume of supper smoke windless above the chimney, his breathing harder and harder and deeper and deeper until his faded shirt strained at the buttons on his chest. Maybe when he got old he would become resigned to it. But he knew he would never, not even if he got to be a hundred and forgot her face and name and the white man's and his too. *I will have to kill him*, he thought, *or I will have to take her and go away*. For an instant he thought of going to the white man and telling him they were leaving, now, tonight, at once. *Only if I were to see him again right now, I might kill him*, he thought. *I think I have decided which I am going to do, but if I was to see him, meet him now, my mind might change.—And that's a man!* he thought. *He keeps her in the house with him six months and I dont do nothing: he sends her back to me and I kills him. It would be like I had done said aloud to the whole world that he never sent her back because I told him to but he give her back to me because he was tired of her.*

He entered the gate in the paling fence which he had built himself when old Cass gave them the house, as he had hauled and laid the field stone path across the grassless yard which his wife used to sweep every morning with a broom of bound willow twigs, sweeping the clean dust into curving intricate patterns among the flower-beds outlined with broken brick and bottles and shards of china and colored glass. She had returned from time to time during the spring to work the flower-beds so that they bloomed as usual—the hardy, blatant blooms loved of her and his race: prince's feather and sunflower, canna and hollyhock—but until today the paths among them had not been swept since last year. *Yes*, he thought. *I got to kill him or I got to leave here.*

He entered the hall, then the room where he had lit the fire two years ago which was to have outlasted both of them. He could not always remember afterward what he had said but he never forgot the amazed and incredulous rage with which he thought, *Why she aint even knowed unto right now that I ever even suspected*. She was sitting before the hearth where the supper was cooking, holding the child, shielding its face from the light and heat with her hand—a small woman even then, years before her flesh, her very bones apparently, had begun to wither and shrink inward upon themselves, and he standing over her, looking down not at his own child but at the face of the white one nuzzling into the dark swell of her breast—not Edmonds' wife but his own who had been lost; not his son but the white man's who had been restored to him, his voice loud, his clawed hand darting toward the child as her hand sprang and caught his wrist.

"Whar's ourn?" he cried. "Whar's mine?"

"Right yonder on the bed, sleeping!" she said. "Go and look at him!" He didn't move, standing over her, locked hand and wrist with her. "I couldn't leave him! You know I couldn't! I had to bring him!"

"Dont lie to me!" he said. "Dont tell me Zack Edmonds know where he is."

"He does know! I told him!" He broke his wrist free, flinging her hand and arm back; he heard the faint click of her teeth when the back of her hand struck her chin and he watched her start to raise her hand to her mouth, then let it fall again.

"That's right," he said. "It ain't none of your blood that's trying to break out and run!"

"You fool!" she cried. "Oh God," she said. "Oh God. All right. I'll take him back. I aimed to anyway. Aunt Thisbe can fix him a sugar-tit—"

"Not you," he said. "And not me even. Do you think Zack Edmonds is going to stay in that house yonder when he gets back and finds out he is gone? No!" he said. "I went to Zack Edmonds' house and asked him for my wife. Let him come to my house and ask me for his son!"

He waited on the gallery. He could see, across the valley, the gleam of light in the other house. *He just ain't got home yet*, he thought. He breathed slow and steady. *It ain't no hurry. He will do something and then I will do something and it will be all over. It will be all right.* Then the light disappeared. He began to say quietly, aloud: "Now. Now. He will have to have time to walk over here." He continued to say it long after he knew the other had had time to walk back and forth between the two houses ten times over. It seemed to him then that he had known all the time the other was not coming, as if he were in the house where the white man waited, watching his, Lucas', house in his turn. Then he knew that the other was not even waiting, and it was as if he stood already in the bedroom itself, above the slow respirations of sleep, the undefended and oblivious throat, the naked razor already in his hand.

He re-entered the house, the room where his wife and the two children were asleep on the bed. The supper which had been cooking on the hearth when he entered at dusk had not even been taken up, what was left of it long since charred and simmered away and probably almost cool now among the fading embers. He set the skillet and coffee pot aside and with a stick of wood he raked the ashes from one corner of the fireplace, exposing the bricks, and touched one of them with his wet finger. It was hot, not scorching, searing, but possessing a slow, deep solidity of heat, a condensation of the two years during which the fire had burned constantly above it, a condensation not of fire but of time, as though not the fire's dying and not even water would cool it but only time would. He prised the brick up with his knife blade and scraped away the warm dirt under it and lifted out a small metal dispatch box which his white grandfather, Carothers McCaslin himself, had owned almost a hundred years ago, and took from it the knotted rag tight and solid with the coins, some of which dated back almost to Carothers McCaslin's time, which he had begun to save before he was ten years old. His wife had removed only her shoes (he recognised them too. They had belonged to the white woman who had not died, who had not even ever existed.) before lying down. He put the knotted rag into one of them and went to the walnut bureau which Isaac McCaslin had given him for a wedding present and took his razor from the drawer.

He was waiting for daylight. He could not have said why. He squatted against a tree halfway between the carriage gate and the white man's house, motionless as the windless obscurity itself while the constellations wheeled and the whippoorwills choired faster and faster and ceased and the first cocks crowed and the false dawn came and faded and the birds began and the night was over. In the first of light he mounted the white man's front steps and entered the unlocked front door and traversed the silent hall and entered the bedroom which it seemed to him he had already entered and that only an instant before, standing with the open razor above the breathing, the undefended and defenseless throat, facing again the act which it seemed to him he had already performed. Then he found the eyes of the face on the pillow looking quietly up at him and he knew then why he had had to wait until daylight. "Because you are a McCaslin too," he said. "Even if you was woman-made to it. Maybe that's the reason. Maybe that's why you done it: because what you and your pa got from old Carothers had to come to you through a woman—a critter not responsible like men are responsible, not to be held like men are held. So maybe I have even already forgive you, except I cant forgive you because you can forgive only them that injure you; even the Book itself dont ask a man to forgive them he is fixing to harm because even Jesus found out at last that was too much to ask a man."

"Put the razor down and I will talk to you," Edmonds said.

"You knowed I wasn't afraid, because you knowed I was a McCaslin too and a man-made one. And you never thought that, because I am a McCaslin too, I wouldn't. You never even thought

that, because I am a nigger too, I wouldn't dare. No. You thought
that because I am a nigger I wouldn't even mind. I never figured
on the razor neither. But I gave you your chance. Maybe I didn't
know what I might have done when you walked in my door, but
I knowed what I wanted to do, what I believed I was going to do,
what Carothers McCaslin would have wanted me to do. But you
didn't come. You never even gave me the chance to do what old
Carothers would have told me to do. You tried to beat me. And
you wont never, not even when I am hanging dead from the limb
this time tomorrow with the coal oil still burning, you wont
never."

"Put down the razor, Lucas," Edmonds said.

"What razor?" Lucas said. He raised his hand and looked at
the razor as if he did not know he had it, had never seen it before,
and in the same motion flung it toward the open window, the
naked blade whirling almost blood-colored into the first copper
ray of the sun before it vanished. "I don't need no razor. My nekkid
hands will do. Now get the pistol under your pillow."

Still the other didn't move, not even to draw his hands from
under the sheet. "It's not under the pillow. It's in that drawer
yonder where it always is and you know it. Go and look. I'm not
going to run. I couldn't."

"I know you aint," Lucas said. "And you know you aint. Because you know that's all I needs, all I wants, is for you to try to
run, to turn your back on me and run. I know you aint going to.
Because all you got to beat is me. I got to beat old Carothers.
Get your pistol."

"No," the other said. "Go home. Get out of here. Tonight I will
come to your house—"

"After this?" Lucas said. "Me and you, in the same country,
breathing the same air even? No matter what you could say, what
you could even prove so I would have to believe it, after this? Get
the pistol."

The other drew his hands out from under the sheet and placed
them on top of it. "All right," he said. "Stand over there against
the wall until I get it."

"Hah," Lucas said. "Hah."

The other put his hands back under the sheet. "Then go and
get your razor," he said.

Lucas began to pant, to indraw short breaths without expiration between. The white man could see his foreshortened chest, the worn faded shirt straining across it. "When you just watched me throw it away?" Lucas said. "When you know that if I left this room now, I wouldn't come back?" He went to the wall and stood with his back against it, still facing the bed. "Because I done already beat you," he said. "It's old Carothers. Get your pistol, white man." He stood panting in the rapid inhalations until it seemed that his lungs could not possibly hold more of it. He watched the other rise from the bed and grasp the foot of it and swing it out from the wall until it could be approached from either side; he watched the white man cross to the bureau and take the pistol from the drawer. Still Lucas didn't move. He stood pressed against the wall and watched the white man cross to the door and close it and turn the key and return to the bed and toss the pistol onto it and only then look toward him. Lucas began to tremble. "No," he said.

"You on one side, me on the other," the white man said. "We'll kneel down and grip hands. We wont need to count."

"No!" Lucas said in a strangling voice. "For the last time. Take your pistol. I'm coming."

"Come on then. Do you think I'm any less a McCaslin just because I was what you call woman-made to it? Or maybe you aint even a woman-made McCaslin but just a nigger that's got out of hand?"

Then Lucas was beside the bed. He didn't remember moving at all. He was kneeling, their hands gripped, facing across the bed and the pistol the man whom he had known from infancy, with whom he had lived until they were both grown almost as brothers lived. They had fished and hunted together, they had learned to swim in the same water, they had eaten at the same table in the white boy's kitchen and in the cabin of the negro's mother; they had slept under the same blanket before a fire in the woods.

"For the last time," Lucas said. "I tell you—" Then he cried, and not to the white man and the white man knew it; he saw the whites of the negro's eyes rush suddenly with red like the eyes of a bayed animal—a bear, a fox: "I tell you! Dont ask too much of me!" *I was wrong,* the white man thought. *I have gone too far.* But it was too late. Even as he tried to snatch his hand free Lucas' hand closed on it. He darted his left hand toward the pistol but Lucas caught that wrist too. Then they did not move save their forearms, their gripped hands turning gradually until the white man's hand was pressed back-downward on the pistol. Motionless, locked, incapable of moving, the white man stared at the spent and frantic face opposite his. "I give you your chance," Lucas said. "Then you laid here asleep with your door unlocked and give me mine. Then I throwed the razor away and give it back. And then you throwed it back at me. That's right, aint it?"

"Yes," the white man said.

"Hah!" Lucas said. He flung the white man's left hand and arm away, striking the other backward from the bed as his own right hand wrenched free; he had the pistol in the same motion, springing up and back as the white man rose too, the bed between them. He broke the pistol's breech and glanced quickly at the cylinder and turned it until the empty chamber under the hammer was at the bottom, so that a live cartridge would come beneath the hammer regardless of which direction the cylinder rotated. "Because I'll need two of them," he said. He snapped the breech shut and faced the white man. Again the white man saw his eyes rush until there was neither cornea nor iris. *This is it*, the white man thought, with that rapid and even unamazed clarity, gathering himself as much as he dared. Lucas didn't seem to notice. *He cant even see me right now*, the white man thought. But that was too late too. Lucas was looking at him now. "You thought I wouldn't, didn't you?" Lucas said. "You knowed I could beat you, so you thought to beat me with old Carothers, like Cass Edmonds done Isaac: used old Carothers to make Isaac give up the land that was his because Cass Edmonds was the woman-made McCaslin, the woman-branch, the sister, and old Carothers would have told Isaac to give in to the woman-kin that couldn't fend for herself. And you thought I'd do that too, didn't you? You thought I'd do it quick, quicker than Isaac since it aint any land I would give up. I aint got any fine big McCaslin farm to give up. All I got to give up is McCaslin blood that rightfully aint even mine or at least aint worth much since old Carothers never seemed to miss much what he give to Tomey that night that made my father. And if this is what that McCaslin blood has brought me, I dont want it neither. And if the running of it into my black blood never hurt him any more than the running of it out is going to hurt me, it wont even be old Carothers that had the most pleasure.—Or no," he cried. *He cant see me again*, the white man thought. *Now.* "No!" Lucas cried; "say I dont even use this first bullet at all, say I just uses the last one and beat you and old Carothers both, leave you something to think about now and then when you aint too busy to try to think up what to tell old Carothers when you get where he's done already gone, tomorrow and the one after that and the one after that as long as tomorrow—" The white man sprang, hurling himself across the bed, grasping at the pistol and the hand which held it. Lucas sprang too; they met over the center of the bed where Lucas clasped the other with his left arm almost like an embrace and jammed the pistol against the white man's side and pulled the trigger and flung the white man from him all in one motion, hearing as he did so the light, dry, incredibly loud click of the miss-fire.

That had been a good year, though late in beginning after the rains and flood: the year of the long summer. He would make more this year than he had made in a long time, even though and in August some of his corn had not had its last plowing. He was doing that now, following the single mule between the rows of strong, waist-high stalks and the rich, dark, flashing blades, pausing at the end of each row to back the plow out and swing it and the yawing mule around into the next one, until at last the dinner smoke stood weightless in the bright air above his chimney and then at the old time she came along the fence with the covered pan and the pail. He did not look at her. He plowed on until the plantation bell rang for noon. He watered and fed the mule and himself ate—the milk, the still-warm biscuit—and rested in the shade until the bell rang again. Then, not rising yet, he took the cartridge from his pocket and looked at it again, musing—the live cartridge, not even stained, not corroded, the mark of the firing-pin dented sharp and deep into the unexploded cap—the dull little brass cylinder less long than a match, not much larger than a pencil, not much heavier, yet large enough to contain two lives. Have contained, that is. *Because I wouldn't have used the second one*, he thought. *I would have paid. I would have waited for the rope, even the coal oil. I would have paid. So I reckon I aint got old Carothers' blood for nothing, after all. Old Carothers*, he thought. *I needed him and he come and spoke for me.* He plowed again. Presently she came back along the fence and got the pan and pail herself instead of letting him bring them home when he came. But she would be busy today; and it seemed to him still early in the afternoon when he saw the supper smoke—the supper which she would leave on the hearth for him when she went back to the big house with the children. When he reached home in the dusk, she was just departing. But she didn't wear the white woman's shoes now and her dress was the same shapeless faded calico she had worn in the morning. "Your supper's ready," she said. "I aint had time to milk yet. You'll have to."

"If I can wait on that milk, I reckon the cow can too," he said. "Can you tote them both all right?"

"I reckon I can. I been taking care of both of them a good while now without no man-help." She didn't look back. "I'll come back out when I gets them to sleep."

"I reckon you better put your time on them," he said gruffly. "Since that's what you started out to do." She went on, neither answering nor looking back, impervious, tranquil, somehow serene. Nor was he any longer watching her. He breathed slow and quiet. *Women,* he thought. *Women. I wont never know. I dont want to. I ruther never to know than to find out later I have been fooled.* He turned toward the room where the fire was, where his supper waited. This time he spoke aloud: "How to God," he said, "can a black man ask a white man to please not lay down with his black wife? And even if he could ask it, how to God can the white man promise he wont?"

III

"George Wilkins?" Edmonds said. He came to the edge of the gallery—a young man still, yet possessing already something of that almost choleric shortness of temper which Lucas remembered in old Cass Edmonds but which had skipped Zack. In age he could have been Lucas' son, but actually was the lesser man for more reason than that, since it was not Lucas who paid taxes insurance and interest or owned anything which had to be kept ditched drained fenced and fertilised or gambled anything save his sweat, and that only as he saw fit, against God for his yearly sustenance. "What in hell has George Wilkins—"

Without changing the inflection of his voice and apparently

without effort or even design Lucas became not negro but nigger, not secret so much as impenetrable, not servile and not effacing, but enveloping himself in an aura of timeless and stupid impassivity almost like a smell. "He's running a kettle in that gully behind the Old West field. If you want the whisky too, look under his kitchen floor."

"A still?" Edmonds said. "On my land?" He began to roar. "Haven't I told and told every man woman and child on this place what I would do the first drop of white mule whisky I found on my land?"

"You didn't need to tell me," Lucas said. "I've lived on this place since I was born, since before your pa was. And you or him or old Cass either aint never heard of me having truck with any kind of whisky except that bottle of town whisky you and him give Molly Christmas."

"I know it," Edmonds said. "And I would have thought George Wilkins—" He ceased. He said, "Hah. Have I or haven't I heard something about George wanting to marry that girl of yours?"

For just an instant Lucas didn't answer. Then he said, "That's right."

"Hah," Edmonds said again. "And so you thought that by telling me on George before he got caught himself, I would be satisfied to make him chop up his kettle and pour out his whisky and then forget about it."

"I didn't know," Lucas said.

"Well, you know now," Edmonds said. "And George will too when the sheriff—" he went back into the house. Lucas listened to the hard, rapid, angry clapping of his heels on the floor, then to the prolonged violent grinding of the telephone crank. Then he stopped listening, standing motionless in the half-darkness, blinking a little. He thought, *All that worrying. I never even thought of that.* Edmonds returned. "All right," he said. "You can go on home now. Go to bed. I know it wont do a damn bit of good to mention it, but I would like to see your south creek piece planted by tomorrow night. You doped around in it today like you hadn't been to bed for a week. I dont know what you do at night, but you are too old to be tomcatting around the country whether you think so or not."

He went back home. Now that it was all over, done, he realised how tired he actually was. It was as if the alternating waves of alarm and outrage and anger and fear of the past ten days, culminating in last night's frantic activity and the past thirty-six hours during which he had not even taken off his clothes, had narcotised him, deadened the very weariness itself. But it was all right now. If a little physical exhaustion, even another ten days or two weeks of it, was all required of him in return for that moment last night, he would not complain. Then he remembered that he had not told Edmonds of his decision to quit farming, for Edmonds to arrange to rent the land he had been working to someone else to finish his crop. But perhaps that was just as well too; perhaps even a single night would suffice to find the rest of the money which a churn that size must have contained, and he would keep the land, the crop, from old habit, for something to occupy him.—*Provided I don't need to keep it for a better reason still,* he thought grimly. *Since I probably aint even made a scratch yet on the kind of luck that can wait unto I am sixty-seven years old, almost too old to even want it, to make me rich.*

The house was dark except for a faint glow from the hearth in his and his wife's room. The room across the hallway where his daughter slept was dark too. It would be empty too. He had expected that. *I reckon George Wilkins is entitled to one more night of female company,* he thought. *From what I have heard, he wont find none of it where he's going tomorrow.*

When he got into bed his wife said without waking, "Whar you been? Walking the roads all last night. Walking the roads all tonight, with the ground crying to get planted. You just wait unto Mister Roth—" and then stopped talking without waking either. Sometime later, he waked. It was after midnight. He lay beneath the quilt on the shuck mattress. It would be happening about now. He knew how they did it—the white sheriff and revenue officers and deputies creeping and crawling among the bushes with drawn pistols, surrounding the kettle, sniffing and whiffing like hunting dogs at every stump and disfiguration of earth until every jug and keg was found and carried back to where the car waited; maybe they would even take a sup or two to ward off the night's chill before returning to the still to squat until George walked innocently in. He was neither triumphant nor vindictive. He even felt something personal toward George now. *He is young yet,* he thought. *They wont keep him down there forever.* In fact, as far as he, Lucas, was concerned, two weeks would be enough. *He can afford to give a year or two at it. And maybe when they lets him out it will be a lesson to him about whose daughter to fool with next time.*

Then his wife was leaning over the bed, shaking him and screaming. It was just after dawn. In his shirt and drawers he ran behind her, out onto the back gallery. Sitting on the ground before it was George Wilkins' patched and battered still; on the gallery itself was an assortment of fruit jars and stoneware jugs and a keg or so and one rusted five-gallon oilcan which, to Lucas' horrified and sleep-dulled eyes, appeared capable of holding enough liquid to fill a ten-foot horse trough. He could even see it in the glass jars —a pale, colorless fluid in which still floated the shreds of corn-husks which George's tenth-hand still had not removed. "Whar was Nat last night?" he cried. He grasped his wife by the shoulder, shaking her. "Whar was Nat, old woman?"

"She left right behind you!" his wife cried. "She followed you again, like night before last! Didn't you know it?"

"I knows it now," Lucas said. "Get the axe!" he said. "Bust it! We aint got time to get it away." But there was not time for that either. Neither of them had yet moved when the sheriff of the county, followed by a deputy, came around the corner of the house—a tremendous man, fat, who obviously had been up all night and obviously still did not like it.

"Damn it, Lucas," he said. "I thought you had better sense than this."

"This aint none of mine," Lucas said. "You know it aint. Even if it was, would I have had it here? George Wilkins—"

"Never you mind about George Wilkins," the sheriff said. "I've got him too. He's out there in the car, with that girl of yours. Go get your pants on. We're going to town."

Two hours later he was in the commissioner's office in the federal courthouse in Jefferson. He was still inscrutable of face, blinking a little, listening to George Wilkins breathing hard beside him and to the voices of the white men.

"Confound it, Carothers," the commissioner said, "what the hell kind of Senegambian Montague and Capulet is this anyhow?"

"Ask them!" Edmonds said violently. "Ask them! Wilkins and

that girl of Lucas' want to get married. Lucas wouldn't hear of it for some reason—I just seem to be finding out now why. So last night Lucas came to my house and told me George was running a still on my land because—" without even a pause to draw a fresh breath Edmonds began to roar again "—he knew damn well what I would do because I have been telling every nigger on my place for years just what I would do if I ever found one drop of that damn wildcat—"

"Yes, yes," the commissioner said; "all right, all right. So you telephoned the sheriff—"

"And we got the message—" it was one of the deputies, a plump man though nowhere as big as the sheriff, voluble, muddy about the lower legs and a little strained and weary in the face too "—and we went out there and Mr Roth told us where to look. But there aint no kettle in the gully where he said, so we set down and thought about just where would we hide a still if we was one of Mr Roth's niggers and we went and looked there and sho enough there it was, neat and careful as you please, all took to pieces and about half buried and covered with brush against a kind of mound in the creek bottom. Only it was getting toward daybreak then, so we decided to come on back to George's house and look under the kitchen floor like Mr Roth said, and then have a little talk with George. So we come on back to George's house, only there aint any George or nobody else in it and nothing under the kitchen floor neither and so we are coming on back toward Mr Roth's house to ask him if maybe he aint got the wrong house in mind maybe; it's just about full daylight now and we are about a hundred yards from Lucas's house when what do we see but George and the gal legging it up the hill toward Lucas's cabin with a gallon jug in each hand, only George busted the jugs on a root before we could get to them. And about that time Lucas's wife starts to yelling in the house and we run around to the back and there is another still setting in Lucas's back yard and about forty gallons of whisky setting on his back gallery like he was fixing to hold a auction sale and Lucas standing there in his drawers and shirt-tail, hollering, 'Git the axe and bust it! Git the axe and bust it!' "

"Yes," the commissioner said. "But who do you charge? You went out there to catch George, but all your evidence is against Lucas."

"There was two stills," the deputy said. "And George and that gal both swear Lucas has been making and selling whisky right there in Edmonds' back yard for twenty years." For an instant Lucas looked up and met Edmonds' glare, not of reproach and no longer even of surprise, but of grim and furious outrage. Then he looked away, blinking, listening to George Wilkins breathing hard beside him like a man in the profoundest depths of sleep, and to the voices.

"But you cant make his own daughter testify against him," the commissioner said.

"George can, though," the deputy said. "George aint any kin to him. Not to mention being in a fix where George has got to think up something good to say and think of it quick."

"Let the court settle all that, Tom," the sheriff said. "I was up all last night and I haven't even had my breakfast yet. I've brought you a prisoner and thirty or forty gallons of evidence and two witnesses. Let's get done with this."

"I think you've brought two prisoners," the commissioner said. He began to write on the paper before him. Lucas watched the moving hand, blinking. "I'm going to commit them both. George can testify against Lucas, and that girl can testify against George. She aint any kin to George either."

He could have posted his and George's appearance bonds without altering the first figure of his bank balance. When Edmonds had drawn his own check to cover them, they returned to Edmonds' car. This time George drove it, with Nat in front with him. It was seventeen miles back home. For those seventeen miles he sat beside the grim and seething white man in the back seat, with nothing to look at but those two heads—that of his daughter where she shrank as far as possible from George, into her corner, never once looking back; that of George, the ruined panama hat raked above his right ear, who still seemed to swagger even sitting down. *Leastways his face aint all full of teeth now like it used to be whenever it found anybody looking at it,* he thought viciously. But never mind that either, right now. So he sat in the car when it stopped at the carriage gate and watched Nat spring out and run like a frightened deer up the lane toward his house, still without looking back, never once looking at him. Then they drove on to the mule lot, the stable, and he and George got out and again he could hear George breathing behind him while Edmonds, behind the wheel now, leaned his elbow in the window and glared at them both.

"Get your mules!" Edmonds said. "What in hell are you waiting for?"

"I thought you were fixing to say something," Lucas said. "So a man's kinfolks cant tell on him in court."

"Never you mind about that!" Edmonds said. "George can tell plenty, and he aint any kin to you. And if he should begin to forget, Nat aint any kin to George and she can tell plenty. I know what you are thinking about. But you have waited too late. If George and Nat tried to buy a wedding license now, they would probably hang you and George both. Besides, damn that. I'm going to take you both to the penitentiary myself as soon as you are laid-by. Now you get on down to your south creek piece. By God, this is one time you will take advice from me. And here it is: dont come out until you have finished it. If dark catches you, dont let it worry you. I'll send somebody down there with a lantern."

He was done with the south creek piece before dark; he had intended to finish it today anyhow. He was back at the stable, his mules watered and rubbed down and stalled and fed while George was still unharnessing. Then he entered the lane and in the beginning of twilight walked toward his house above whose chimney the windless supper smoke stood. He didn't walk fast, neither did he look back when he spoke. "George Wilkins," he said.

"Sir," George said behind him. They walked on in single file and almost step for step, about five feet apart.

"Just what was your idea?"

"I dont rightly know, sir," George said. "It uz mostly Nat's. We never aimed to get you into no trouble. She say maybe ifn we took and fotch that kettle from whar you and Mister Roth told them shurfs it was and you would find it settin on yo back porch, maybe when we offered to help you git shet of it fo they got here, yo mind might change about loandin us the money to—I mean to leffen us get married."

"Hah," Lucas said. They walked on. Now he could smell the cooking meat. He reached the gate and turned. George stopped too, lean, wasp-waisted, foppish even in faded overalls below the swaggering rake of the hat. "There's more folks than just me in that trouble."

"Yes sir," George said. "Hit look like it is. I hope it gonter be a lesson to me."

"I hope so too," Lucas said. "When they get done sending you to Parchman you'll have plenty of time between working cotton and corn you aint going to get no third and fourth of even, to study it." They looked at one another.

"Yes sir," George said. "Especially wid you there to help me worry hit out."

"Hah," Lucas said. He didn't move; he hardly raised his voice even: "Nat." He didn't even look toward the house then as the girl came down the path, barefoot, in a clean, faded calico dress and a bright headrag. Her face was swollen from crying, but her voice was defiant, not hysterical.

"It wasn't me that told Mister Roth to telefoam them shurfs!" she cried. He looked at her for the first time. He looked at her until even the defiance began to fade, to be replaced by something alert and speculative. He saw her glance flick past his shoulder to where George stood and return.

"My mind done changed," he said. "I'm going to let you and George get married." She stared at him. Again he watched her glance flick to George and return.

"It changed quick," she said. She stared at him. Her hand, the long, limber, narrow, light-palmed hand of her race, rose and touched for an instant the bright cotton which bound her head. Her inflection, the very tone and pitch of her voice had changed. "Me, marry George Wilkins and go to live in a house whar the whole back porch is done already fell off and whar I got to walk a half a mile and back from the spring to fetch water? He aint even got no stove!"

"My chimbley cooks good," George said. "And I can prop up the porch."

"And I can get used to walking a mile for two lard buckets full of water," she said. "I dont wants no propped-up porch. I wants a new porch on George's house and a cook-stove and a well. And how you gonter get um? What you gonter pay for no stove with, and a new porch, and somebody to help you dig a well?" Yet it was still Lucas she stared at, ceasing with no dying fall of her high, clear soprano voice, watching her father's face as if they were engaged with foils. His face was not grim and neither cold nor angry. It was absolutely expressionless, impenetrable. He might have been asleep standing, as a horse sleeps. When he spoke, he might have been speaking to himself.

"A cook-stove," he said. "The back porch fixed. A well."

"A new back porch," she said. He might not have even heard her. She might not have spoken even.

"The back porch fixed," he said. Then she was not looking at him. Again the hand rose, slender and delicate and markless of any labor, and touched the back of her headkerchief. Lucas moved. "George Wilkins," he said.

"Sir," George said.

"Come into the house," Lucas said.

And so, in its own good time, the other day came at last. In their Sunday clothes he and Nat and George stood beside the carriage gate while the car came up and stopped. "Morning, Nat," Edmonds said. "When did you get home?"

"I got home yistiddy, Mister Roth."

"You stayed in Vicksburg a good while. I didn't know you were going until Aunt Molly told me you were already gone."

"Yassuh," she said. "I lef the next day after them shurfs was here.—I didn't know it neither," she said. "I never much wanted to go. It was pappy's idea for me to go and see my aunt—"

"Hush, and get in the car," Lucas said. "If I'm going to finish my crop in this county or finish somebody's else's crop in Parchman county, I would like to know it soon as I can."

"Yes," Edmonds said. He spoke to Nat again. "You and George go on a minute. I want to talk to Lucas." Nat and George went on. Lucas stood beside the car while Edmonds looked at him. It was the first time Edmonds had spoken to him since that morning three weeks ago, as though it had required those three weeks for his rage to consume itself, or die down at least. Now the white man leaned in the window, looking at the impenetrable face with its definite strain of white blood, the same blood which ran in his own veins, which had not only come to the negro through male descent while it had come to him from a woman, but had reached the negro a generation sooner—a face composed, inscrutable, even a little haughty, shaped even in expression in the pattern of his great-grandfather McCaslin's face. "I reckon you know what's going to happen to you," he said. "When that federal lawyer gets through with Nat, and Nat gets through with George, and George gets through with you and Judge Gowan gets through with all of you. You have been on this place all your life, almost twice as long as I have. You knew all the McCaslins and Edmonds both that ever lived here, except old Carothers. Was that still and that whisky in your back yard yours?"

"You know it wasn't," Lucas said.

"All right," Edmonds said. "Was that still they found in the creek bottom yours?"

They looked at each other. "I aint being tried for that one," Lucas said.

"Was that still yours, Lucas?" Edmonds said. They looked at one another. Yet still the face which Edmonds saw was absolutely blank, impenetrable. Even the eyes appeared to have nothing behind them. He thought, and not for the first time: *I am not only looking at a face older than mine and which has seen and winnowed more, but at a man most of whose blood was pure ten thousand years when my own anonymous beginnings became mixed enough to produce me.*

"Do you want me to answer that?" Lucas said.

"No!" Edmonds said violently. "Get in the car!"

When they reached town, the streets leading into it and the Square itself were crowded with cars and wagons; the flag rippled and flew in the bright May weather above the federal courthouse. Following Edmonds, he and Nat and George crossed the thronged pavement, walking in a narrow lane of faces they knew—other people from their place, people from other places along the creek and in the neighborhood, come the seventeen miles also with no hope of getting into the courtroom itself but just to wait on the street and see them pass—the faces they only knew by hearsay: the rich white lawyers and judges and marshals talking to one another around their proud cigars, the haughty and powerful of the earth. They entered the marble foyer, crowded too and sonorous with voices, where George began to walk gingerly on the hard heels of his Sunday shoes. Then Lucas took from his coat the thick, soiled, folded document which had lain hidden under the loose brick in his fireplace for three weeks now and touched Edmonds' arm with it—the paper thick enough and soiled enough yet which of its own accord apparently fell open at a touch, stiffly but easily too along the old hand-smudged folds, exposing, presenting among the meaningless and unread lettering between salutation and seal the three phrases in the cramped script of whatever nameless clerk which alone of the whole mass of it Lucas at least had bothered to read: *George Wilkins* and *Nathalie Beauchamp* and a date in October of last year.

"Do you mean," Edmonds said, "that you have had this all the time? All these three weeks?" But still the face he glared at was impenetrable, almost sleepy looking.

"You hand it to Judge Gowan," Lucas said.

He and Nat and George sat quietly on a hard wooden bench in a small office, where an oldish white man—Lucas knew him though not particularly that he was a deputy marshal—chewed a toothpick and read a Memphis newspaper. Then a young, brisk, slightly harried white man in glasses opened the door and glinted his glasses an instant and vanished; then, following the old white man they crossed the foyer again, the marble cavern murmurously resonant with the constant slow feet and the voices, the faces watching them again as they mounted the stairs. They crossed the empty courtroom without pausing and entered another office but larger, finer, quieter. There was an angry-looking man whom Lucas did not know—the United States Attorney, who had moved to Jefferson only after the administration changed eight years ago, after Lucas had stopped coming to town very often anymore. But Edmonds was there, and behind the table sat a man whom Lucas did know, who had used to come out in old Cass' time forty and fifty years ago and stay for weeks during the quail season, shooting with Zack, with Lucas to hold the horses while they got down to shoot when the dogs pointed. It took hardly any time at all.

"Lucas Beauchamp?" the judge said. "With thirty gallons of whisky and a still sitting on his back porch in broad daylight? Nonsense."

"Then there you are," the angry man said, flinging out his hands. "I didn't know anything about this either until Edmonds—" But the judge was not even listening to him. He was looking at Nat.

"Come here, girl," he said. Nat moved forward and stopped.

Lucas could see her trembling. She looked small, thin as a lath, young; she was their youngest and last—seventeen, born into his wife's old age and, it sometimes seemed to him, into his too. She was too young to be married and face all the troubles which married people had to get through in order to become old and find out for themselves the taste and savor of peace. Just a stove and a new back porch and a well were not enough. "You're Lucas's girl?" the judge said.

"Yassuh," Nat said in her high, sweet, chanting soprano. "I'm name Nat. Nat Wilkins, Gawge Wilkins' wife. There the paper fer hit in yo hand."

"I see it is," the judge said. "It's dated last October."

"Yes sir, Judge," George said. "We been had it since I sold my cotton last fall. We uz married then, only she wont come to live in my house unto Mister Lu—I mean I gots a stove and the porch fixed and a well dug."

"Have you got that now?"

"Yes sir, Judge," George said. "I got the money for hit now and I'm just fo gittin the rest of it, soon as I gits around to the hammerin and the diggin."

"I see," the judge said. "Henry," he said to the other old man, the one with the toothpick, "have you got that whisky where you can pour it out?"

"Yes, Judge," the other said.

"And both those stills where you can chop them to pieces, destroy them good?"

"Yes, Judge."

"Then clear my office. Get them out of here. Get that jimber-jawed clown out of here at least."

"He's talking about you, George Wilkins," Lucas murmered.

"Yes sir," George said. "Sound like he is."

IV

At first he thought that two or three days at the outside would suffice—or nights, that is, since George would have to be in his crop during the day, let alone getting himself and Nat settled for marriage in their house. But a week passed, and though Nat would come back home at least once during the day, usually to borrow something, he had not seen George at all. He comprehended the root of his impatience—the mound and its secret which someone, anyone else, might stumble upon by chance as he had, the rapid and daily shortening of the allotted span in which he had not only to find the treasure but to get any benefit and pleasure from it, all in abeyance until he could complete the petty business which had intervened, and nothing with which to pass the period of waiting—the good year, the good early season, and cotton and corn springing up almost in the planter's wheel-print, so that there was now nothing to do but lean on the fence and watch it grow;—on the one hand, that which he wanted to do and could not; on the other, that which he could have done and no need for. But at last, in the second week, when he knew that in one more day his patience would be completely gone, he stood just inside his kitchen door and watched George enter and cross the lot in the dusk and enter the stable and emerge with his mare and put her to the wagon and drive away. So the next morning he went no further than his first patch and leaned on the fence in the bright dew looking at his cotton until his wife began to shout at him from the house.

When he entered, Nat was sitting in his chair beside the hearth, bent forward, her long narrow hands dangling limp between her knees, her face swollen and puffed again with crying. "Yawl and your George Wilkins!" Molly said. "Go on and tell him."

"He aint started on the well or nothing," Nat said. "He aint even propped up the back porch. With all that money you give him, he aint even started. And I axed him and he just say he aint got around to it yet, and I waited and I axed him again and he still just say he aint got around to it yet. Unto I told him at last that ifn he didn't get started like he promised, my mind gonter change about whatall I seed that night them shurfs come out here and so last night he say he gwine up the road a piece and do I wants to come back home and stay because he mought not get back unto late and I say I can bar the door because I thought he was going to fix to start on the well. And when I seed him catch up pappy's mare and wagon, I knowed that was it. And it aint unto almost daylight when he got back, and he aint got nothing. Not nothing to dig with and no boards to fix the porch, and he had done spent the money pappy give him. And I told him what I was gonter do and I was waiting at the house soon as Mister Roth got up and I told Mister Roth my mind done changed about what I seed that night and Mister Roth started in to cussing and say I done waited too late because I'm Gawge's wife now and the Law wont listen to me and for me to come and tell you and Gawge both to be offen his place by sundown."

"There now!" Molly cried. "There's your George Wilkins!" Lucas was already moving toward the door. "Whar you gwine?" she said. "Whar we gonter move to?"

"You wait to start worrying about where we will move to when Roth Edmonds starts to worrying about why we aint gone," Lucas said.

The sun was well up now. It was going to be hot today; it was going to make cotton and corn both before the sun went down. When he reached George's house, George stood quietly out from behind the corner of it. Lucas crossed the grassless and sun-glared yard, the light dust swept into the intricate and curving patterns which Molly had taught Nat. "Where is it?" Lucas said.

"I hid hit in that gully where mine used to be," George said. "Since them shurfs never found nothing there the yuther time, they'll think hit aint no use to look there no more."

"You fool," Lucas said. "Dont you know a week aint going to pass from now to the next election without one of them looking in that gully just because Roth Edmonds told them there was a still in it once? And when they catch you this time, you aint going to have any witness you have already been married to since last fall."

"They aint going to catch me this time," George said. "I done had my lesson. I'm gonter run this one the way you tells me to."

"You better had," Lucas said. "As soon as dark falls you take that wagon and get that thing out of that gully. I'll show you where to put it. Hah," he said. "And I reckon this one looks enough like the one that was in that gully before not to even been moved at all."

"No sir," George said. "This is a good one. The worm in hit is almost brand-new. That's how come I couldn't git him down on the price he axed. That porch and well money liked two dollars of being enough, but I just made them up, without needing to bother you. But it aint worrying about gittin caught that troubles my mind. What I cant keep from studying about is what we gonter tell Nat about that back porch and that well."

"What *we* is?" Lucas said.

"What I is, then," George said. Lucas looked at him for a moment.

"George Wilkins," he said.

"Sir," George said.

"I dont give no man advice about his wife," Lucas said.

WILLIAM FAULKNER

Delta Autumn

Soon now they would enter the Delta. The sensation was familiar to him. It had been renewed like this each last week in November for more than fifty years—the last hill, at the foot of which the rich unbroken alluvial flatness began as the sea began at the base of its cliffs, dissolving away beneath the unhurried November rain as the sea itself would dissolve away.

At first they had come in wagons: the guns, the bedding, the dogs, the food, the whisky, the keen heart-lifting anticipation of hunting; the young men who could drive all night and all the following day in the cold rain and pitch a camp in the rain and sleep in the wet blankets and rise at daylight the next morning and hunt. There had been bear then. A man shot a doe or a fawn as quickly as he did a buck, and in the afternoons they shot wild turkey with pistols to test their stalking skill and marksmanship, feeding all but the breast to the dogs. But that time was gone now. Now they went in cars, driving faster and faster each year because the roads were better and they had farther and farther to drive, the territory in which game still existed drawing yearly inward as his life was drawing inward, until now he was the last of those who had once made the journey in wagons without feeling it and now those who accompanied him were the sons and even grand-sons of the men who had ridden for twenty-four hours in the rain or sleet behind the steaming mules. They called him "Uncle Ike" now, and he no longer told anyone how near eighty he actually was because he knew as well as they did that he no longer had any business making such expeditions, even by car.

In fact, each time now, on that first night in camp, lying aching and sleepless in the harsh blankets, his blood only faintly warmed by the single thin whisky-and-water which he allowed himself, he would tell himself that this would be his last. But he would stand that trip—he still shot almost as well as he ever had, still killed almost as much of the game he saw as he ever killed; he no longer even knew how many deer had fallen before his gun—and the fierce long heat of the next summer would renew him. Then November would come again, and again in the car with two of the sons of his old companions, whom he had taught not only how to distinguish between the prints left by a buck or a doe but between the sound they made in moving, he would look ahead past the jerking arc of the windshield wiper and see the land flatten sud-denly and swoop, dissolving away beneath the rain as the sea itself would dissolve, and he would say, "Well, boys, there it is again."

This time though, he didn't have time to speak. The driver of the car stopped it, slamming it to a skidding halt on the greasy pavement without warning, actually flinging the two passengers forward until they caught themselves with their braced hands against the dash. "What the hell, Roth!" the man in the middle said. "Cant you whistle first when you do that? Hurt you, Uncle Ike?"

"No," the old man said. "What's the matter?" The driver didn't answer. Still leaning forward, the old man looked sharply past the face of the man between them, at the face of his kinsman. It was the youngest face of them all, aquiline, saturnine, a little ruthless, the face of his ancestor too, tempered a little, altered a little, staring sombrely through the streaming windshield across which the twin wipers flicked and flicked.

"I didn't intend to come back in here this time," he said suddenly and harshly.

"You said that back in Jefferson last week," the old man said.

"Then you changed your mind. Have you changed it again? This aint a very good time to—"

"Oh, Roth's coming," the man in the middle said. His name was Legate. He seemed to be speaking to no one, as he was looking at neither of them. "If it was just a buck he was coming all this distance for, now. But he's got a doe in here. Of course a old man like Uncle Ike cant be interested in no doe, not one that walks on two legs—when she's standing up, that is. Pretty light-colored, too. The one he was after them nights last fall when he said he was coon-hunting, Uncle Ike. The one I figured maybe he was still running when he was gone all that month last January. But of course a old man like Uncle Ike aint got no interest in nothing like that." He chortled, still looking at no one, not completely jeering.

"What?" the old man said. "What's that?" But he had not even so much as glanced at Legate. He was still watching his kinsman's face. The eyes behind the spectacles were the blurred eyes of an old man, but they were quite sharp too; eyes which could still see a gun-barrel and what ran beyond it as well as any of them could. He was remembering himself now: how last year, during the final stage by motor boat in to where they camped, a box of food had been lost overboard and how on the next day his kinsman had gone back to the nearest town for supplies and had been gone overnight. And when he did return, something had happened to him. He would go into the woods with his rifle each dawn when the others went, but the old man, watching him, knew that he was not hunting. "All right," he said. "Take me and Will on to shelter where we can wait for the truck, and you can go on back."

"I'm going in," the other said harshly. "Dont worry. Because this will be the last of it."

"The last of deer hunting or of doe hunting?" Legate said. This time the old man paid no attention to him even by speech. He still watched the young man's savage and brooding face.

"Why?" he said.

"After Hitler gets through with it? Or Smith or Jones or Roosevelt or Willkie or whatever he will call himself in this country?"

"We'll stop him in this country," Legate said. "Even if he calls himself George Washington."

"How?" Edmonds said. "By singing God bless America in bars

at midnight and wearing dime-store flags in our lapels?"

"So that's what's worrying you," the old man said. "I aint noticed this country being short of defenders yet, when it needed them. You did some of it yourself twenty-odd years ago, before you were a grown man even. This country is a little mite stronger than any one man or group of men, outside of it or even inside of it either. I reckon, when the time comes and some of you have done got tired of hollering we are whipped if we dont go to war and some more are hollering we are whipped if we do, it will cope with one Austrian paper-hanger, no matter what he will be calling himself. My pappy and some other better men than any of them you named tried once to tear it in two with a war, and they failed."

"And what have you got left?" the other said. "Half the people without jobs and half the factories closed by strikes. Half the people on public dole that wont work and half that couldn't work even if they would. Too much cotton and corn and hogs, and not enough for people to eat and wear. The country full of people to tell a man how he cant raise his own cotton whether he will or wont, and Sally Rand with a sergeant's stripes and not even the fan couldn't fill the army rolls. Too much not-butter and not even the guns—"

"We got a deer camp—if we ever get to it," Legate said. "Not to mention does."

"It's a good time to mention does," the old man said. "Does and fawns both. The only fighting anywhere that ever had anything of God's blessing on it has been when men fought to protect does and fawns. If it's going to come to fighting, that's a good thing to mention and remember too."

"Haven't you discovered in—how many years more than seventy is it?—that women and children are one thing there's never any scarcity of?" Edmonds said.

"Maybe that's why all I'm worrying about right now is that ten miles of river we still have got to run before we can make camp," the old man said. "So let's get on."

They went on. Soon they were going fast again, as Edmonds always drove, consulting neither of them about the speed just as he had given neither of them any warning when he slammed the car to stop. The old man relaxed again. He watched, as he did each recurrent November while more than sixty of them passed, the land which he had seen change. At first there had been only the old towns along the River and the old towns along the hills, from each of which the planters with their gangs of slaves and then of hired laborers had wrested from the impenetrable jungle of water-standing cane and cypress, gum and holly and oak and ash, cotton patches which as the years passed became fields and then plantations. The paths made by deer and bear became roads and then highways, with towns in turn springing up along them and along the rivers Tallahatchie and Sunflower which joined and became the Yazoo, the River of the Dead of the Choctaws—the thick, slow, black, unsunned streams almost without current, which once each year ceased to flow at all and then reversed, spreading, drowning the rich land and subsiding again, leaving it still richer.

Most of that was gone now. Now a man drove two hundred miles from Jefferson before he found wilderness to hunt in. Now the land lay open from the cradling hills on the East to the rampart of levee on the West, standing horseman-tall with cotton for the world's looms—the rich black land, imponderable and vast, fecund up to the very doorsteps of the negroes who worked it and of the white men who owned it; which exhausted the hunting life of a dog in one year, the working life of a mule in five and of a man in twenty—the land in which neon flashed past them from the little countless towns and countless shining this-year's automobiles sped past them on the broad plumb-ruled highways, yet in which the only permanent mark of man's occupation seemed to be the tremendous gins, constructed in sections of sheet iron and in a week's time though they were, since no man, millionaire though he be, would build more than a roof and walls to shelter the camping equipment he had lived from when he knew that once each ten years or so his house would be flooded to the second storey and all within it ruined;—the land across which there came now no scream of panther but instead the long hooting of locomotives: trains of incredible length and drawn by a single engine, since there was no gradient anywhere and no elevation save those raised by forgotten aboriginal hands as refuges from the yearly water and used by their Indian successors to sepulchre their fathers' bones, and all that remained of that old time were the Indian names on the little towns and usually pertaining to water—Aluschaskuna, Tillatoba, Homochitto, Yazoo.

By early afternoon, they were on water. At the last little Indian-named town at the end of the pavement they waited until the other car and the two trucks—the one carrying the bedding and tents and food, the other the horses—overtook them. They left the concrete and, after another mile or so, the gravel too. In caravan they ground on through the ceaselessly dissolving afternoon, with skid-chains on the wheels now, lurching and splashing and sliding among the ruts, until presently it seemed to him that the retrograde of his remembering had gained an inverse velocity from their own slow progress, that the land had retreated not in minutes from the last spread of gravel but in years, decades, back toward what it had been when he first knew it: the road they now followed once more the ancient pathway of bear and deer, the diminishing fields they now passed once more scooped punily and terrifically by axe and saw and mule-drawn plow from the wilderness' flank, out of the brooding and immemorial tangle, in place of ruthless mile-wide parallelograms wrought by ditching the dyking machinery.

They reached the river landing and unloaded, the horses to go overland down stream to a point opposite the camp and swim the river, themselves and the bedding and food and dogs and guns in the motor launch. It was himself, though no horseman, no farmer, not even a countryman save by his distant birth and boyhood, who coaxed and soothed the two horses, drawing them by his own single frail hand until, backing, filling, trembling a little, they surged, halted, then sprang scrambling down from the truck, possessing no affinity for them as creatures, beasts, but being merely insulated by his years and time from the corruption of steel and oiled moving parts which tainted the others.

Then, his old hammer double gun which was only twelve years younger than he standing between his knees, he watched even the last puny marks of man—cabin, clearing, the small and irregular fields which a year ago were jungle and in which the skeleton stalks of this year's cotton stood almost as tall and rank as the old cane had stood, as if man had had to marry his planting to the wilderness in order to conquer it—fall away and vanish. The twin banks marched with wilderness as he remembered it—the tangle of brier and cane impenetrable even to sight twenty feet away, the tall tremendous soaring of oak and gum and ash and hickory which had rung to no axe save the hunter's, had echoed to no machinery save the beat of old-time steam boats traversing it or to the snarling of launches like their own of people going into it to dwell for a week or two weeks because it was still wilderness. There was some of it left, although now it was two hundred miles from Jefferson when once it had been thirty. He had watched it, not being conquered, destroyed, so much as retreating since its purpose was served now and its time an outmoded time, retreating southward through this inverted-apex, this ▽ -shaped section of earth between hills and River until what was left of it seemed now to be gathered and for the time arrested in one tremendous density of brooding and inscrutable impenetrability at the ultimate funnelling tip.

They reached the site of their last-year's camp with still two hours left of light. "You go on over under that driest tree and set down," Legate told him. "—if you can find it. Me and these other young boys will do this." He did neither. He was not tired yet. That would come later. *Maybe it wont come at all this time*, he thought, as he had thought at this point each November for the last five or six of them. *Maybe I will go out on stand in the morning too;* knowing that he would not, not even if he took the advice and sat down under the driest shelter and did nothing until camp was made and supper cooked. Because it would not be the fatigue. It would be because he would not sleep tonight but would lie instead wakeful and peaceful on the cot amid the tent-filling snoring and the rain's whisper as he always did on the first night in camp; peaceful, without regret or fretting, telling himself that was all right too, who didn't have so many of them left as to waste one sleeping.

In his slicker he directed the unloading of the boat—the tents, the stove, the bedding, the food for themselves and the dogs until there should be meat in camp. He sent two of the negroes to cut firewood; he had the cook-tent raised and the stove up and a fire going and supper cooking while the big tent was still being staked down. Then in the beginning of dusk he crossed in the boat to where the horses waited, backing and snorting at the water. He took the lead-ropes and with no more weight than that and his voice, he drew them down into the water and held them beside the boat with only their heads above the surface, as though they actually were suspended from his frail and strengthless old man's hands, while the boat recrossed and each horse in turn lay prone in the shallows, panting and trembling, its eyes rolling in the dusk, until the same weightless hand and unraised voice gathered it surging upward, splashing and thrashing up the bank.

Then the meal was ready. The last of light was gone now save the thin stain of it snared somewhere between the river's surface and the rain. He had the single glass of thin whisky-and-water, then, standing in the churned mud beneath the stretched tarpaulin, he said grace over the fried slabs of pork, the hot soft shapeless bread, the canned beans and molasses and coffee in iron plates and cups,—the town food, brought along with them—then covered himself again, the others following. "Eat," he said. "Eat it all up. I dont want a piece of town meat in camp after breakfast tomorrow. Then you boys will hunt. You'll have to. When I first started hunting in this bottom sixty years ago with old General Compson and Major de Spain and Roth's grandfather and Will Legate's too, Major de Spain wouldn't allow but two pieces of foreign grub in his camp. That was one side of pork and one ham of beef. And not to eat for the first supper and breakfast neither. It was to save until along toward the end of camp when everybody was so sick of bear meat and coon and venison that we couldn't even look at it."

"I thought Uncle Ike was going to say the pork and beef was for the dogs," Legate said, chewing. "But that's right; I remember. You just shot the dogs a mess of wild turkey every evening when they got tired of deer guts."

"Times are different now," another said. "There was game here then."

"Yes," the old man said quietly. "There was game here then."

"Besides, they shot does then too," Legate said. "As it is now, we aint got but one doe-hunter in—"

"And better men hunted it," Edmonds said. He stood at the end of the rough plank table, eating rapidly and steadily as the others ate. But again the old man looked sharply across at the sullen, handsome, brooding face which appeared now darker and more sullen still in the light of the smoky lantern. "Go on. Say it."

"I didn't say that," the old man said. "There are good men everywhere, at all times. Most men are. Some are just unlucky, because most men are a little better than their circumstances give them a chance to be. And I've known some that even the circumstances couldn't stop."

592 · WILLIAM FAULKNER

"Well, I wouldn't say—" Legate said.

"So you've lived almost eighty years," Edmonds said. "And that's what you finally learned about the other animals you lived among. I suppose the question to ask you is, where have you been all the time you were dead?"

There was a silence; for the instant even Legate's jaw stopped chewing while he gaped at Edmonds. "Well, by God, Roth—" the third speaker said. But it was the old man who spoke, his voice still peaceful and untroubled and merely grave:

"Maybe so," he said. "But if being what you call alive would have learned me any different, I reckon I'm satisfied, wherever it was I've been."

"Well, I wouldn't say that Roth—" Legate said.

The third speaker was still leaning forward a little over the table, looking at Edmonds. "Meaning that it's only because folks happen to be watching him that a man behaves at all," he said. "Is that it?"

"Yes," Edmonds said. "A man in a blue coat, with a badge on it watching him. Maybe just the badge."

"I deny that," the old man said. "I dont—"

The other two paid no attention to him. Even Legate was listening to them for the moment, his mouth still full of food and still open a little, his knife with another lump of something balanced on the tip of the blade arrested halfway to his mouth. "I'm glad I dont have your opinion of folks," the third speaker said. "I take it you include yourself."

"I see," Edmonds said. "You prefer Uncle Ike's opinion of circumstances. All right. Who makes the circumstances?"

"Luck," the third said. "Chance. Happen-so. I see what you are getting at. But that's just what Uncle Ike said: that now and then, maybe most of the time, man is a little better than the net result of his and his neighbors' doings, when he gets the chance to be."

This time Legate swallowed first. He was not to be stopped this time. "Well, I wouldn't say that Roth Edmonds can hunt one doe every day and night for two weeks and was a poor hunter or a unlucky one neither. A man that still have the same doe left to hunt on again next year—"

"Have some meat," the man next to him said.

"—aint no unlucky— What?" Legate said.

"Have some meat." The other offered the dish.

"I got some," Legate said.

"Have some more," the third speaker said. "You and Roth Edmonds both. Have a heap of it. Clapping your jaws together that way with nothing to break the shock." Someone chortled. Then they all laughed, with relief, the tension broken. But the old man was speaking, even into the laughter, in that peaceful and still untroubled voice:

"I still believe. I see proof everywhere. I grant that man made a heap of his circumstances, him and his living neighbors between them. He even inherited some of them already made, already almost ruined even. A while ago Henry Wyatt there said how there used to be more game here. There was. So much that we even killed does. I seem to remember Will Legate mentioning that too—" Someone laughed, a single guffaw, stillborn. It ceased and they all listened, gravely, looking down at their plates. Edmonds was drinking his coffee, sullen, brooding, inattentive.

"Some folks still kill does," Wyatt said. "There wont be just one buck hanging in this bottom tomorrow night without any head to fit it."

"I didn't say all men," the old man said. "I said most men. And not just because there is a man with a badge to watch us. We probably wont even see him unless maybe he will stop here about noon tomorrow and eat dinner with us and check our licenses—"

"We dont kill does because if we did kill does in a few years there wouldn't even be any bucks left to kill, Uncle Ike," Wyatt said.

"According to Roth yonder, that's one thing we wont never have to worry about," the old man said. "He said on the way here this morning that does and fawns—I believe he said women and children—are two things this world aint ever lacked. But that aint all of it," he said. "That's just the mind's reason a man has to give himself because the heart dont always have time to bother with thinking up words that fit together. God created man and He created the world for him to live in and I reckon He created the kind of world He would have wanted to live in if He had been a man—the ground to walk on, the big woods, the trees and the water, and the game to live in it. And maybe He didn't put the desire to hunt and kill game in man but I reckon He knew it was going to be there, that man was going to teach it to himself, since he wasn't quite God himself yet "

"When will he be?" Wyatt said.

"I think that every man and woman, at the instant when it dont even matter whether they marry or not, I think that whether they marry then or afterward or dont never, at that instant the two of them together were God."

"Then there are some Gods in this world I wouldn't want to touch, and with a damn long stick," Edmonds said. He set his coffee cup down and looked at Wyatt. "And that includes myself, if that's what you want to know. I'm going to bed." He was gone. There was a general movement among the others. But it ceased and they stood again about the table, not looking at the old man, apparently held there yet by his quiet and peaceful voice as the heads of the swimming horses had been held above the water by his weightless hand. The three negroes—the cook and his helper and old Isham—were sitting quietly in the entrance of the kitchen tent, listening too, the three faces dark and motionless and musing.

"He put them both here: man, and the game he would follow and kill, foreknowing it. I believe He said, 'So be it.' I reckon He even foreknew the end. But He said, 'I will give him his chance. I will give him warning and foreknowledge too, along with the desire to follow and the power to slay. The woods and fields he ravages and the game he devastates will be the consequence and signature of his crime and guilt, and his punishment.'—Bed time," he said. His voice and inflection did not change at all. "Breakfast at four oclock, Isham. We want meat on the ground by sunup time."

There was a good fire in the sheet-iron heater; the tent was warm and was beginning to dry out, except for the mud underfoot. Edmonds was already rolled into his blankets, motionless, his face to the wall. Isham had made up his bed too—the strong, battered iron cot, the stained mattress which was not quite soft enough, the worn, often-washed blankets which as the years passed were less and less warm enough. But the tent was warm; presently, when the kitchen was cleaned up and readied for breakfast, the young negro would come in to lie down before the heater, where he could be roused to put fresh wood into it from time to time. And then, he knew now he would not sleep tonight anyway; he no longer needed to tell himself that perhaps he would. But it was all right now. The day was ended now and night faced him, but alarmless, empty of fret. *Maybe I came for this,* he thought: *Not to hunt, but for this. I would come anyway, even if only to go back home tomorrow.* Wearing only his bagging woolen underwear, his spectacles folded away in the worn case beneath the pillow where he could reach them readily and his lean body fitted easily into the old worn groove of mattress and blankets, he lay on his back, his hands crossed on his breast and his eyes closed while the others undressed and went to bed and the last of the sporadic talking died into snoring. Then he opened his eyes and lay peaceful and quiet as a child, looking up at the motionless belly of rain-murmured canvas upon which the glow of the heater was dying slowly away and would fade still further until the young negro, lying on two planks before it, would sit up and stoke it and lie back down again.

They had a house once. That was sixty years ago, when the Big Bottom was only thirty miles from Jefferson and old Major de Spain, who had been his father's cavalry commander in '61 and '2 and '3 and '4, and his cousin (his older brother; his father too) had taken him into the woods for the first time. Old Sam Fathers was alive then, born in slavery, son of a negro slave and a Chickasaw chief, who had taught him how to shoot, not only when to shoot but when not to; such a November dawn as tomorrow would be and the old man led him straight to the great cypress and he had known the buck would pass exactly there because there was something running in Sam Fathers' veins which ran in the veins of the buck too, and they stood there against the tremendous trunk, the old man of seventy and the boy of twelve, and there was nothing save the dawn until suddenly the buck was there, smoke-colored out of nothing, magnificent with speed: and Sam Fathers said, 'Now. Shoot quick and shoot slow:' and the gun levelled rapidly without haste and crashed and he walked to the buck lying still intact and still in the shape of that magnificent speed and bled it with Sam's knife and Sam dipped his hands into the hot blood and marked his face forever while he stood trying not to tremble, humbly and with pride too though the boy of twelve had been unable to phrase it then: *I slew you; my hearing must not shame your quitting life. My conduct forever onward must become your death;* marking him for that and for more than that: that day and himself and McCaslin juxtaposed not against the wilderness but against the tamed land, the old wrong and shame itself, in repudia-

tion and denial at least of the land and the wrong and shame even
if he couldn't cure the wrong and eradicate the shame, who at
fourteen when he learned of it had believed he could do both
when he became competent and when at twenty-one he became
competent he knew that he could do neither but at least he could
repudiate the wrong and shame, at least in principle, and at least
the land itself in fact, for his son at least: and did, thought he had:
then (married then) in a rented cubicle in a back-street stock-
traders' boarding-house, the first and last time he ever saw her
naked body, himself and his wife juxtaposed in their turn against
that same land, that same wrong and shame from whose regret and
grief he would at least save and free his son and, saving and freeing
his son, lost him. They had the house then. That roof, the two
weeks of each November which they spent under it, had become
his home. Although since that time they had lived during the two
fall weeks in tents and not always in the same place two years in
succession and now his companions were the sons and even the
grandsons of them with whom he had lived in the house and for
almost fifty years now the house itself had not even existed, the
conviction, the sense and feeling of home, had been merely transferred into the canvas. He owned a house in Jefferson, a good
house though small, where he had had a wife and lived with her
and lost her, ay, lost her even though he had lost her in the rented
cubicle before he and his old clever dipsomaniac partner had finished the house for them to move into it: but lost her, because she
loved him. But women hope for so much. They never live too long
to still believe that anything within the scope of their passionate
wanting is likewise within the range of their passionate hope: and
it was still kept for him by his dead wife's widowed niece and her
children and he was comfortable in it, his wants and needs and
even the small trying harmless crochets of an old man looked after
by blood at least related to the blood which he had elected out
of all the earth to cherish. But he spent the time within those walls
waiting for November, because even this tent with its muddy floor
and the bed which was not wide enough nor soft enough nor even
warm enough, was his home and these men, some of whom he only
saw during these two November weeks and not one of whom
even bore any name he used to know—De Spain and Compson
and Ewell and Hogganbeck—were more his kin than any. Because
this was his land—

The shadow of the youngest negro loomed. It soared, blotting the heater's dying glow from the ceiling, the wood billets thumping into the iron maw until the glow, the flame, leaped high and bright across the canvas. But the negro's shadow still remained, by its length and breadth, standing, since it covered most of the ceiling, until after a moment he raised himself on one elbow to look. It was not the negro, it was his kinsman; when he spoke the other turned sharp against the red firelight the sullen and ruthless profile.

"Nothing," Edmonds said. "Go on back to sleep."

"Since Will Legate mentioned it," McCaslin said, "I remember you had some trouble sleeping in here last fall too. Only you called it coon-hunting then. Or was it Will Legate called it that?" The other didn't answer. Then he turned and went back to his bed. McCaslin, still propped on his elbow, watched until the other's shadow sank down the wall and vanished, became one with the mass of sleeping shadows. "That's right," he said. "Try to get some sleep. We must have meat in camp tomorrow. You can do all the setting up you want to after that." He lay down again, his hands crossed again on his breast, watching the glow of the heater on the canvas ceiling. It was steady again now, the fresh wood accepted, being assimilated; soon it would begin to fade again, taking with it the last echo of that sudden upflare of a young man's passion and unrest. Let him lie awake for a little while, he thought; He will lie still some day for a long time without even dissatisfaction to disturb him. And lying awake here, in these surroundings, would soothe him if anything could, if anything could soothe a man just forty years old. Yes, he thought; Forty years old or thirty, or even the trembling and sleepless ardor of a boy; already the tent, the rain-murmured canvas globe, was once more filled with it. He lay on his back, his eyes closed, his breathing quiet and peaceful as a child's, listening to it—that silence which was never silence but was myriad. He could almost see it, tremendous, primeval, looming, musing downward upon this puny evanescent clutter of human sojourn which after a single brief week would vanish and in another week would be completely healed, traceless in the unmarked solitude. Because it was his land, although he had never owned a foot of it. He had never wanted to, not even after he saw plain its ultimate doom, watching it retreat year by year before the onslaught of axe and saw and log-lines and then dynamite and tractor plows, because it belonged to no man. It belonged to all; they had only to use it well, humbly and with pride. Then suddenly he knew why he had never wanted to own any of it, arrest at least that much of what people call progress, measure his longevity at least against that much of its ultimate fate. It was because there was just exactly enough of it. He seemed to see the two of them—himself and the wilderness—as coevals, his own span as a hunter, a woodsman, not contemporary with his first breath but transmitted to him, assumed by him gladly, humbly, with joy and pride, from that old Major de Spain and that old Sam Fathers who had taught him to hunt, the two spans running out together, not toward oblivion, nothingness, but into a dimension free of both time and space where once more the untreed land warped and wrung to mathematical squares of rank cotton for the frantic old-world people to turn into shells to shoot at one another, would find ample room for both—the names, the faces of the old men he had known and loved and for a little while outlived, moving again among the shades of tall unaxed trees and sightless brakes where the wild strong immortal game ran forever before the tireless belling immortal hounds, falling and rising phoenix-like to the soundless guns.

He had been asleep. The lantern was lighted now. Outside in the darkness the oldest negro, Isham, was beating a spoon against the bottom of a tin pan and crying, "Raise up and get yo foa clock coffy. Raise up and get yo foa clock coffy," and the tent was full of low talk and of men dressing, and Legate's voice, repeating: "Get out of here now and let Uncle Ike sleep. If you wake him up, he'll go out with us. And he ain't got any business in the woods this morning."

So he didn't move. He lay with his eyes closed, his breathing gentle and peaceful, and heard them one by one leave the tent. He listened to the breakfast sounds from the table beneath the tarpaulin and heard them depart—the horses, the dogs, the last voice until it died away and there was only the sounds of the negroes clearing breakfast away. After a while he might possibly even hear the first faint clear cry of the first hound ring through the wet woods from where the buck had bedded, then he would go back to sleep again— The tent flap swung in and fell. Something jarred sharply against the end of the cot and a hand grasped his knee through the blanket before he could open his eyes. It was Edmonds, carrying a shotgun in place of his rifle. He spoke in a harsh, rapid voice:

"Sorry to wake you. There will be a—"

"I was awake," McCaslin said. "Are you going to shoot that shotgun today?"

"You just told me last night you want meat," Edmonds said. "There will be a—"

"Since when did you start having trouble getting meat with your rifle?"

"All right," the other said, with that harsh, restrained, furious impatience. Then McCaslin saw in his hand a thick oblong: an envelope. "There will be a message here some time this morning, looking for me. Maybe it wont come. If it does, give the messenger this and tell h— say I said No."

"A what?" McCaslin said. "Tell who?" He half rose onto his elbow as Edmonds jerked the envelope onto the blanket, already turning toward the entrance, the envelope striking solid and heavy and without noise and already sliding from the bed until McCaslin caught it, divining by feel through the paper as instantaneously and conclusively as if he had opened the envelope and looked, the thick sheaf of banknotes. "Wait," he said. "Wait:"—more than the blood kinsman, more even than the senior in years, so that the other paused, the canvas lifted, looking back, and McCaslin saw that outside it was already day. "Tell her No," he said. "Tell her." They stared at one another—the old face, wan, sleep-raddled above the tumbled bed, the dark and sullen younger one at once furious and cold. "Will Legate was right. This is what you called coon-hunting. And now this." He didn't raise the envelope. He made no motion, no gesture to indicate it. "What did you promise her that you haven't the courage to face her and retract?"

"Nothing!" the other said. "Nothing! This is all of it. Tell her I said No." He was gone. The tent flap lifted on an in-waft of faint light and the constant murmur of rain, and fell again, leaving the old man still half-raised onto one elbow, the envelope clutched in the other shaking hand. Afterward it seemed to him that he had begun to hear the approaching boat almost immediately, before the other could have got out of sight even. It seemed to him that there had been no interval whatever: the tent flap falling on the same out-waft of faint and rain-filled light like the suspiration and ex-piration of the same breath and then in the next second lifted again—the mounting snarl of the outboard engine, increasing, nearer and nearer and louder and louder then cut short off, ceasing with the absolute instantaneity of a blown-out candle, into the lap and plop of water under the bows as the skiff slid in to the bank, the youngest negro, the youth, raising the tent flap beyond which for that instant he saw the boat—a small skiff with a negro man sitting in the stern beside the up-slanted motor—then the woman entering, in a man's hat and a man's slicker and rubber boots, carrying the blanket-swaddled bundle on one arm and holding the edge of the unbuttoned raincoat over it with the other hand: and bringing something else, something intangible, an effluvium which he knew he would recognise in a moment because Isham had already told him, warned him, by sending the young negro to the tent to announce the visitor instead of coming himself, the flap falling at last on the young negro and they were alone—the face indistinct and as yet only young and with dark eyes, queerly color-less but not ill and not that of a country woman despite the gar-ments she wore, looking down at him where he sat upright on the cot now, clutching the envelope, the soiled undergarment bagging about him and the twisted blankets huddled about his hips.

"Is that his?" he cried. "Dont lie to me!"

"Yes," she said. "He's gone."

"Yes. He's gone. You wont jump him here. Not this time. I dont reckon even you expected that. He left you this. Here." He fumbled at the envelope. It was not to pick it up, because it was still in his hand; he had never put it down. It was as if he had to fumble somehow to co-ordinate physically his heretofore obedi-ent hand with what his brain was commanding of it, as if he had never performed such an action before, extending the envelope at last, saying again, "Here. Take it. Take it:" until he became aware of her eyes, or not the eyes so much as the look, the regard fixed now on his face with that immersed contemplation, that bottomless and intent candor, of a child. If she had ever seen either the envelope or his movement to extend it, she did not show it.

"You're Uncle Isaac," she said.

"Yes," he said. "But never mind that. Here. Take it. He said to tell you No." She looked at the envelope, then she took it. It was sealed and bore no superscription. Nevertheless, even after she glanced at the front of it, he watched her hold it in the one free hand and tear the corner off with her teeth and manage to rip it open and tilt the neat sheaf of bound notes onto the blanket without even glancing at them and look into the empty envelope and take the edge between her teeth and tear it completely open before she crumpled and dropped it.

"That's just money," she said.

"What did you expect? What else did you expect? You have known him long enough or at least often enough to have got that child, and you dont know him any better than that?"

"Not very often. Not very long. Just that week here last fall, and in January he sent for me and we went West, to New Mexico. We were there six weeks, where I could at least sleep in the same apartment where I cooked for him and looked after his clothes—"

"But not marriage," he said. "Not marriage. He didn't promise you that. Dont lie to me. He didn't have to."

"No. He didn't have to. I didn't ask him to. I knew what I was doing. I knew that to begin with, long before honor I imagine he called it told him the time had come to tell me in so many words what his code I suppose he would call it would forbid him forever to do. And we agreed. Then we agreed again before he left New Mexico, to make sure. That that would be all of it. I believed him. No, I dont mean that; I mean I believed myself. I wasn't even listening to him anymore by then because by that time it had been a long time since he had had anything else to tell me for me to have to hear. By then I wasn't even listening enough to ask him to please stop talking. I was listening to myself. And I believed it. I must have believed it. I dont see how I could have helped but believe it, because he was gone then as we had agreed and he didn't write as we had agreed, just the money came to the bank in Vicksburg in my name but coming from nobody as we had agreed. So I must have believed it. I even wrote him last month to make sure again and the letter came back unopened and I was sure. So I left the hospital and rented myself a room to live in until the deer season opened so I could make sure myself and I was waiting beside the road yesterday when your car passed and he saw me and so I was sure."

"Then what do you want?" he said. "What do you want? What do you expect?"

"Yes," she said. And while he glared at her, his white hair awry from the pillow and his eyes, lacking the spectacles to focus them, blurred and irisless and apparently pupilless, he saw again that grave, intent, speculative and detached fixity like a child watching him. "His great great— Wait a minute—great great *great* grand-father was your grandfather. McCaslin. Only it got to be Edmonds. Only it got to be more than that. Your cousin McCaslin was there that day when your father and Uncle Buddy won Tennie from Mr Beauchamp for the one that had no name but Terrel so you called him Tomey's Terrel, to marry. But after that it got to be Edmonds." She regarded him, almost peacefully, with that un-winking and heatless fixity—the dark wide bottomless eyes in the face's dead and toneless pallor which to the old man looked any-thing but dead, but young and incredibly and even ineradicably alive—as though she were not only not looking at anything, she was not even speaking to anyone but herself. "I would have made a man of him. He's not a man yet. You spoiled him. You, and Uncle Lucas and Aunt Mollie. But mostly you."

"Me?" he said. "Me?"

"Yes. When you gave to his grandfather that land which didn't belong to him, not even half of it by will or even law."

"And never mind that too," he said. "Never mind that too. You," he said. "You sound like you have been to college even. You sound almost like a Northerner even, not like the draggle-tailed women of these Delta peckerwoods. Yet you meet a man on the street one afternoon just because a box of groceries happened to fall out of a boat. And a month later you go off with him and live with him until he got a child on you: and then, by your own state-ment, you sat there while he took his hat and said goodbye and walked out. Even a Delta peckerwood would look after even a draggle-tail better than that. Haven't you got any folks at all?"

"Yes," she said. "I was living with one of them. My aunt, in Vicksburg. I came to live with her two years ago when my fa-ther died; we lived in Indianapolis then. But I got a job, teaching school here in Aluschaskuna, because my aunt was a widow, with a big family, taking in washing to sup—"

"Took in what?" he said. "Took in washing?" He sprang, still seated even, flinging himself backward onto one arm, awry-haired, glaring. Now he understood what it was she had brought into the tent with her, what old Isham had already told him by sending the youth to bring her in to him—the pale lips, the skin pallid and dead-looking yet not ill, the dark and tragic and foreknowing eyes. *Maybe in a thousand or two thousand years in America,* he thought. *But not now! Not now!* He cried, not loud, in a voice of amazement, pity, and outrage: "You're a nigger!"

"Yes," she said. "James Beauchamp—you called him Tennie's Jim though he had a name—was my grandfather. I said you were Uncle Isaac."

"And he knows?"

"No," she said. "What good would that have done?"

"But you did," he cried. "But you did. Then what do you expect here?"

"Nothing."

"Then why did you come here? You said you were waiting in Aluschaskuna yesterday and he saw you. Why did you come this morning?"

"I'm going back North. Back home. My cousin brought me up the day before yesterday in his boat. He's going to take me on to Leland to get the train."

"Then go," he said. Then he cried again in that thin not loud and grieving voice: "Get out of here! I can do nothing for you! Cant nobody do nothing for you!" She moved; she was not looking at him again, toward the entrance. "Wait," he said. She paused again, obediently still, turning. He took up the sheaf of banknotes and laid it on the blanket at the foot of the cot and drew his hand back beneath the blanket. "There," he said.

Now she looked at the money, for the first time, one brief blank glance, then away again. "I don't need it. He gave me money last winter. Besides the money he sent to Vicksburg. Provided. Honor and code too. That was all arranged."

"Take it," he said. His voice began to rise again, but he stopped it. "Take it out of my tent." She came back to the cot and took up the money; whereupon once more he said, "Wait:" although she had not turned, still stooping, and he put out his hand. But, sitting, he could not complete the reach until she moved her hand, the single hand which held the money, until she touched it. He didn't grasp it, he merely touched it—the gnarled, bloodless, bone-light bone-dry old man's fingers touching for a second the smooth young flesh where the strong old blood ran after its long lost journey back to home. "Tennie's Jim," he said. "Tennie's Jim." He drew the hand back beneath the blanket again: he said harshly now: "It's a boy, I reckon. They usually are, except that one that was its own mother too."

"Yes," she said. "It's a boy." She stood for a moment longer, looking at him. Just for an instant her free hand moved as though she were about to lift the edge of the raincoat away from the child's face. But she did not. She turned again when once more he said Wait and moved beneath the blanket.

"Turn your back," he said. "I am going to get up. I aint got my pants on." Then he could not get up. He sat in the huddled blanket, shaking, while again she turned and looked down at him in dark interrogation. "There," he said harshly, in the thin and shaking old man's voice. "On the nail there. The tent-pole."

"What?" she said.

"The horn!" he said harshly. "The horn." She went and got it, thrust the money into the slicker's side pocket as if it were a rag, a soiled handkerchief, and lifted down the horn, the one which General Compson had left him in his will, covered with the un-broken skin from a buck's shank and bound with silver.

"What?" she said.

"It's his. Take it."

"Oh," she said. "Yes. Thank you."

"Yes," he said, harshly, rapidly, but not so harsh now and soon not harsh at all but just rapid, urgent, until he knew that his voice was running away with him and he had neither intended it nor could stop it: "That's right. Go back North. Marry: a man in your own race. That's the only salvation for you—for a while yet, maybe a long while yet. We will have to wait. Marry a black man. You are young, handsome, almost white; you could find a black man who would see in you what it was you saw in him, who would ask nothing of you and expect less and get even still less than that, if it's revenge you want. Then you will forget all this, forget it ever happened, that he ever existed—" until he could stop it at last and did, sitting there in his huddle of blankets during the instant when, without moving at all, she blazed silently down at him. Then that was gone too. She stood in the gleaming and still dripping slicker, looking quietly down at him from under the sodden hat.

"Old man," she said, "have you lived so long and forgotten so much that you dont remember anything you ever knew or felt or even heard about love?"

Then she was gone too. The waft of light and the murmur of the constant rain flowed into the tent and then out again as the flap fell. Lying back once more, trembling, panting, the blanket huddled to his chin and his hands crossed on his breast, he listened to the pop and snarl, the mounting then fading whine of the motor until it died away and once again the tent held only silence and the sound of rain. And cold too: he lay shaking faintly and steadily in it, rigid save for the shaking. This Delta, he thought: This Delta. *This land which man has deswamped and denuded and derivered in two generations so that white men can own plantations and commute every night to Memphis and black men own plantations and ride in jim crow cars to Chicago to live in millionaires' mansions on Lakeshore Drive, where white men rent farms and live like niggers and niggers crop on shares and live like animals, where cotton is planted and grows man-tall in the very cracks of the sidewalks, and usury and mortgage and bankruptcy and measureless wealth, Chinese and African and Aryan and Jew, all breed and spawn together until no man has time to say which one is which nor cares. . . .* No wonder the ruined woods I used to know dont cry for retribution! he thought: The people who have destroyed it will accomplish its revenge.

The tent flap jerked rapidly in and fell. He did not move save to turn his head and open his eyes. It was Legate. He went quickly to Edmonds' bed and stooped, rummaging hurriedly among the still-tumbled blankets.

"What is it?" he said.

"Looking for Roth's knife," Legate said. "I come back to get a horse. We got a deer on the ground." He rose, the knife in his hand, and hurried toward the entrance.

"Who killed it?" McCaslin said. "Was it Roth?"

"Yes," Legate said, raising the flap.

"Wait," McCaslin said. He moved, suddenly, onto his elbow. "What was it?" Legate paused for an instant beneath the lifted flap. He did not look back.

"Just a deer, Uncle Ike," he said impatiently. "Nothing extra." He was gone; again the flap fell behind him, wafting out of the tent again the faint light and the constant and grieving rain. McCaslin lay back down, the blanket once more drawn to his chin, his crossed hands once more weightless on his breast in the empty tent.

"It was a doe," he said.

WILLIAM FAULKNER

Raid

Granny wrote the note with pokeberry juice. "Take it straight to Mrs. Compson and come straight back," she said. "Don't you-all stop anywhere."

"You mean we got to walk?" Ringo said. "You gonter make us walk all them four miles to Jefferson and back, with them two horses standing in the lot doing nothing?"

"They are borrowed horses," Granny said. "I'm going to take care of them until I can return them."

"I reckon you calls starting out to be gone you don't know where and you don't know how long taking care of—" Ringo said.

"Do you want me to whup you?" Louvinia said.

"Nome," Ringo said.

We walked to Jefferson and gave Mrs. Compson the note, and got the bat and the parasol and the hand mirror, and walked back home. That afternoon we greased the wagon, and that night after supper Granny got the pokeberry juice again and wrote on a scrap of paper, "Colonel Nathaniel G. Dick, —th Ohio Cavalry," and folded it and pinned it inside her dress. "Now I won't forget it," she said.

"If you was to, I reckon these hellion boys can remind you," Louvinia said. "I reckon they ain't forgot him. Walking in that door just in time to keep them others from snatching them out from under your dress and nailing them to the barn door like two coon hides."

"Yes," Granny said. "Now we'll go to bed."

We lived in Joby's cabin then, with a red quilt nailed by one edge to a rafter and hanging down to make two rooms. Joby was waiting with the wagon when Granny came out with Mrs. Compson's hat on, and got into the wagon and told Ringo to open the parasol and took up the reins. Then we all stopped and watched Joby stick something into the wagon beneath the quilts; it was the barrel and the iron parts of the musket that Ringo and I found in the ashes of the house.

"What's that?" Granny said. Joby didn't look at her.

"Maybe if they just seed the end of hit they mought think hit was the whole gun," he said.

"Then what?" Granny said. Joby didn't look at anybody now.

"I was just doing what I could to help git the silver and the mules back," he said.

Louvinia didn't say anything either. She and Granny just looked at Joby. After a while he took the musket barrel out of the wagon. Granny gathered up the reins.

"Take him with you," Louvinia said. "Leastways he can tend the horses."

"No," Granny said. "Don't you see I have got about all I can look after now?"

"Then you stay here and lemme go," Louvinia said. "I'll git um back."

"No," Granny said. "I'll be all right. I shall inquire until I find Colonel Dick, and then we will load the chest in the wagon and Loosh can lead the mules and we will come back home."

Then Louvinia began to act just like Uncle Buck McCaslin did the morning we started to Memphis. She stood there holding to the wagon wheel and looked at Granny from under Father's old hat, and began to holler. "Don't you waste no time on colonels or nothing!" she hollered. "You tell them niggers to send Loosh to you, and you tell him to get that chest and them mules, and then you whup him!" The wagon was moving now; she had turned loose the wheel, and she walked along beside it, hollering at Granny: "Take that pairsawl and wear hit out on him!"

"All right," Granny said. The wagon went on; we passed the ash pile and the chimneys standing up out of it; Ringo and I found the insides of the big clock too. The sun was just coming up, shining back on the chimneys; I could still see Louvinia between them,

standing in front of the cabin, shading her eyes with her hand to
watch us. Joby was still standing behind her, holding the musket
barrel. They had broken the gates clean off; and then we were in
the road.

"Don't you want me to drive?" I said.

"I'll drive," Granny said. "These are borrowed horses."

"Case even Yankee could look at um and tell they couldn't keep
up with even a walking army," Ringo said. "And I like to know
how anybody can hurt this team lessen he ain't got strength enough
to keep um from laying down in the road and getting run over
with they own wagon."

We drove until dark, and camped. By sunup we were on the
road again. "You better let me drive a while," I said.

"I'll drive," Granny said. "I was the one who borrowed them."

"You can tote this pairsawl a while, if you want something to
do," Ringo said. "And give my arm a rest." I took the parasol and
he laid down in the wagon and put his hat over his eyes. "Call me
when we gitting nigh to Hawkhurst," he said, "so I can commence
to look out for that railroad you tells about."

That was how he travelled for the next six days—lying on his
back in the wagon bed with his hat over his eyes, sleeping, or taking
his turn holding the parasol over Granny and keeping me awake
by talking of the railroad which he had never seen though I had
seen it that Christmas we spent at Hawkhurst. That's how Ringo
and I were. We were almost the same age, and Father always said
that Ringo was a little smarter than I was, but that didn't count
with us, anymore than the difference in the color of our skins
counted. What counted was, what one of us had done or seen that
the other had not, and ever since that Christmas I had been ahead
of Ringo because I had seen a railroad, a locomotive. Only I know
now it was more than that with Ringo, though neither of us were
to see the proof of my belief for some time yet and we were not
to recognise it as such even then. It was as if Ringo felt it too and
that the railroad, the rushing locomotive which he hoped to see
symbolised it—the motion, the impulse to move which had already
seethed to a head among his people, darker than themselves, reason-
less, following and seeking a delusion, a dream, a bright shape
which they could not know since there was nothing in their
heritage, nothing in the memory even of the old men to tell the

others. 'This is what we will find'; he nor they could not have known what it was yet it was there—one of those impulses inexplicable yet invincible which appear among races of people at intervals and drive them to pick up and leave all security and familiarity of earth and home and start out, they don't know where, emptyhanded, blind to everything but a hope and a doom.

We went on; we didn't go fast. Or maybe it seemed slow because we had got into a country where nobody seemed to live at all; all that day we didn't even see a house. I didn't ask and Granny didn't say; she just sat there under the parasol with Mrs. Compson's hat on and the horses walking and even our own dust moving ahead of us; after a while even Ringo sat up and looked around.

"We on the wrong road," he said. "Ain't even nobody live here, let alone pass here."

But after a while the hills stopped, the road ran out flat and straight; and all of a sudden Ringo hollered, "Look out! Here they come again to git these uns!" We saw it, too, then—a cloud of dust away to the west, moving slow—too slow for men riding —and then the road we were on ran square into a big broad one running straight on into the east, as the railroad at Hawkhurst did when Granny and I were there that Christmas before the war; all of a sudden I remembered it.

"This is the road to Hawkhurst," I said. But Ringo was not listening; he was looking at the dust, and the wagon stopped now with the horses' heads hanging and our dust overtaking us again and the big dust cloud coming slow up in the west.

"Can't you see um coming?" Ringo hollered. "Git on away from here!"

"They ain't Yankees," Granny said. "The Yankees have already been here." Then we saw it, too—a burned house like ours, three chimneys standing above a mound of ashes, and then we saw a white woman and a child looking at us from a cabin behind them. Granny looked at the dust cloud, then she looked at the empty broad road going on into the east. "This is the way," she said.

We went on. It seemed like we went slower than ever now, with the dust cloud behind us and the burned houses and gins and thrown-down fences on either side, and the white women and children—we never saw a nigger at all—watching us from the nigger cabins where they lived now like we lived at home; we didn't stop. "Poor folks," Granny said. "I wish we had enough to share with them."

At sunset we drew off the road and camped; Ringo was looking back. "Whatever hit is, we done went off and left hit," he said. "I don't see no dust." We slept in the wagon this time, all three of us. I don't know what time it was, only that all of a sudden I was awake. Granny was already sitting up in the wagon. I could see her head against the branches and the stars. All of a sudden all three of us were sitting up in the wagon, listening. They were coming up the road. It sounded like about fifty of them; we could hear the feet hurrying, and a kind of panting murmur. It was not singing exactly; it was not that loud. It was just a sound, a breathing, a kind of gasping, murmuring chant and the feet whispering fast in the deep dust. I could hear women, too, and then all of a sudden I began to smell them.

"Niggers," I whispered. "Sh-h-h-h," I whispered.

We couldn't see them and they did not see us; maybe they didn't even look, just walking fast in the dark with that panting, hurrying murmuring, going on. And then the sun rose and we went on, too, along that big broad empty road between the burned houses and gins and fences. Before, it had been like passing through a country where nobody had ever lived; now it was like passing through one where everybody had died at the same moment. That night we waked up three times and sat up in the wagon in the dark and heard niggers pass in the road. The last time it was after dawn and we had already fed the horses. It was a big crowd of them this time, and they sounded like they were running, like they had to run to keep ahead of daylight. Then they were gone. Ringo and I had taken up the harness again when Granny said, "Wait. Hush." It was just one, we could hear her panting and sobbing, and then we heard another sound. Granny began to get down from the wagon. "She fell," she said. "You-all hitch up and come on."

When we turned into the road, the woman was kind of crouched beside it, holding something in her arms, and Granny standing beside her. It was a baby, a few months old; she held it like she thought maybe Granny was going to take it away from her. "I been sick and I couldn't keep up," she said. "They went off and left me."

"Is your husband with them?" Granny said.

"Yessum," the woman said. "They's all there."

"Who do you belong to?" Granny said. Then she didn't answer. She squatted there in the dust, crouched over the baby. "If I give you something to eat, will you turn around and go back home?" Granny said. Still she didn't answer. She just squatted there. "You see you can't keep up with them and they ain't going to wait for you," Granny said. "Do you want to die here in the road for buzzards to eat?" But she didn't even look at Granny; she just squatted there.

"Hit's Jordan we coming to," she said. "Jesus gonter see me that far."

"Get in the wagon," Granny said. She got in; she squatted again just like she had in the road, holding the baby and not looking at anything—just hunkered down and swaying on her hams as the wagon rocked and jolted. The sun was up; we went down a long hill and began to cross a creek bottom.

"I'll get out here," she said. Granny stopped the wagon and she got out. There was nothing at all but the thick gum and cypress and thick underbrush still full of shadow.

"You go back home, girl," Granny said. She just stood there. "Hand me the basket," Granny said. I handed it to her and she opened it and gave the woman a piece of bread and meat. We went on; we began to mount the hill. When I looked back she was still standing there, holding the baby and the bread and meat Granny had given her. She was not looking at us. "Were the others there in that bottom?" Granny asked Ringo.

"Yessum," Ringo said. "She done found um. Reckon she gonter lose um again tonight though."

We went on; we mounted the hill and crossed the crest of it. When I looked back this time the road was empty. That was the morning of the sixth day.

II

Late that afternoon we were descending again; we came around a curve in the late level shadows and our own quiet dust and I saw the graveyard on the knoll and the marble shaft at Uncle Dennison's grave; there was a dove somewhere in the cedars. Ringo was asleep again under his hat in the wagon bed but he waked as soon as I spoke, even though I didn't speak loud and didn't speak to him,

"There's Hawkhurst," I said.

"Hawkhurst?" he said, sitting up. "Where's that railroad?" on his knees now and looking for something which he would have to find in order to catch up with me and which he would have to recognise only through hearsay when he saw it: "Where is it? Where?"

"You'll have to wait for it," I said.

"Seem like I been waiting on hit all my life," he said. "I reckon you'll tell me next the Yankees done moved hit too."

The sun was going down. Because suddenly I saw it shining level across the place where the house should have been and there was no house there. And I was not surprised; I remember that; I was just feeling sorry for Ringo, since (I was just fourteen then) if the house was gone, they would have taken the railroad too, since anybody would rather have a railroad than a house. We didn't stop; we just looked quietly at the same mound of ashes, the same four chimneys standing gaunt and blackened in the sun like the chimneys at home. When we reached the gate Cousin Denny was running down the drive toward us. He was ten; he ran up to the wagon with his eyes round and his mouth already open for hollering.

"Denny," Granny said, "do you know us?"

"Yessum," Cousin Denny said. He looked at me, hollering, "Come see—"

"Where's your mother?" Granny said.

"In Jingus' cabin," Cousin Denny said; he didn't even look at Granny. "They burnt the house!" he hollered. "Come see what they done to the railroad!"

We ran, all three of us. Granny hollered something and I turned and put the parasol back into the wagon and hollered "Yessum!" back at her, and ran on and caught up with Cousin Denny and Ringo in the road, and we ran on over the hill, and then it came in sight. When Granny and I were here before, Cousin Denny showed me the railroad, but he was so little then that Jingus had to carry him. It was the straightest thing I ever saw, running straight and empty and quiet through a long empty gash cut through the trees, and the ground, too, and full of sunlight like water in a river, only straighter than any river, with the crossties cut off even and smooth and neat, and the light shining on the rails like on two spider threads, running straight on to where you couldn't even see that far. It looked clean and neat, like the yard behind Louvinia's cabin after she had swept it on Saturday morning, with those two little threads that didn't look strong enough for anything to run on running straight and fast and light, like they were getting up speed to jump clean off the world.

Jingus knew when the train would come; he held my hand and carried Cousin Denny, and we stood between the rails and he showed us where it would come from, and then he showed us where the shadow of a dead pine would come to a stob he had driven in the ground, and then you would hear the whistle. And we got back and watched the shadow, and then we heard it; it whistled and then it got louder and louder fast, and Jingus went to the track and took his hat off and held it out with his face turned back toward us and his mouth hollering, "Watch now! Watch!" even after we couldn't hear him for the train; and then it passed. It came roaring up and went past; the river they had cut through the trees was all full of smoke and noise and sparks and jumping brass, and then empty again, and just Jingus' old hat bouncing and jumping along the empty track behind it like the hat was alive.

But this time what I saw was something that looked like piles of black straws heaped up every few yards, and we ran into the cut and we could see where they had dug the ties up and piled them and set them on fire. But Cousin Denny was still hollering, "Come see what they done to the rails!" he said.

They were back in the trees; it looked like four or five men had taken each rail and tied it around a tree like you knot a green cornstalk around a wagon stake, and Ringo was hollering, too, now.

"What's them?" he hollered. "What's them?"

"That's what it runs on!" Cousin Denny hollered.

"You mean hit have to come in here and run up and down around these here trees like a squirrel?" Ringo hollered. Then we all heard the horse at once; we just had time to look when Bobolink came up the road out of the trees and went across the railroad and into the trees again like a bird, with Cousin Drusilla riding astride like a man and sitting straight and light as a willow branch in the wind. They said she was the best woman rider in the country.

"There's Dru!" Cousin Denny hollered. "Come on! She's been

up to the river to see them niggers! Come on!" He and Ringo ran again. When I passed the chimneys, they were just running into the stable. Cousin Drusilla had already unsaddled Bobolink, and she was rubbing him down with a crokersack when I came in. Cousin Denny was still hollering, "What did you see? What are they doing?"

"I'll tell about it at the house," Cousin Drusilla said. Then she saw me. She was not tall; it was the way she stood and walked. She had on pants, like a man. She was the best woman rider in the country. When Granny and I were here that Christmas before the war and Gavin Breckbridge had just given Bobolink to her, they looked fine together; it didn't need Jingus to say that they were the finest-looking couple in Alabama or Mississippi either. But Gavin was killed at Shiloh and so they didn't marry. She came and put her hand on my shoulder.

"Hello," she said. "Hello, John Sartoris." She looked at Ringo. "Is this Ringo?" she said.

"That's what they tells me," Ringo said. "What about that rail-road?"

"How are you?" Cousin Drusilla said.

"I manages to stand hit," Ringo said. "What about that rail-road?"

"I'll tell you about that tonight too," Drusilla said.

"I'll finish Bobolink for you," I said.

"Will you?" she said. She went to Bobolink's head. "Will you stand for Cousin Bayard, lad?" she said. "I'll see you-all at the house, then," she said. She went out.

"Yawl sho must 'a' had this horse hid good when the Yankees come," Ringo said.

"This horse?" Cousin Denny said. "Ain't no damn Yankee going to fool with Dru's horse no more." He didn't holler now, but pretty soon he began again: "When they come to burn the house, Dru grabbed the pistol and run out here—she had on her Sunday dress—and them right behind her. She run in here and she jumped on Bobolink bareback, without even waiting for the bridle, and one of them right there in the door hollering, 'Stop,' and Dru said, 'Get away, or I'll ride you down,' and him hollering, 'Stop! Stop!' with his pistol out too"—Cousin Denny was hollering good now—"and Dru leaned down to Bobolink's ear and said, 'Kill him, Bob,' and the Yankee jumped back just in time. The lot was full of them, too, and Dru stopped Bobolink and jumped down in her Sunday dress and put the pistol to Bobolink's ear and said, 'I can't shoot you all, because I haven't enough bullets, and it wouldn't do any good anyway; but I won't need but one shot for the horse, and which shall it be?' So they burned the house and went away!" He was hollering good now, with Ringo staring at him so you could have raked Ringo's eyes off his face with a stick. "Come on!" Cousin Denny hollered. "Le's go hear about them niggers at the river!"

"I been having to hear about niggers all my life," Ringo said. "I got to hear about that railroad."

When we reached the house Cousin Drusilla was already talking, telling Granny mostly, though it was not about the railroad. Her hair was cut short; it looked like Father's would when he would tell Granny about him and the men cutting each other's hair with a bayonet. She was sunburned and her hands were hard and scratched like a man's that works. She was telling Granny mostly: "They began to pass in the road yonder while the house was still burning. We couldn't count them; men and women carrying children who couldn't walk and carrying old men and women who should have been at home waiting to die. They were singing, walking along the road singing, not even looking to either side. The dust didn't even settle for two days, because all that night they still passed; we sat up listening to them, and the next morning every few yards along the road would be the old ones who couldn't keep up any more, sitting or lying down and even crawling along, calling to the others to help them; and the others—the young strong ones—not stopping, not even looking at them. I don't think they even heard or saw them. 'Going to Jordan,' they told me. 'Going to cross Jordan.' "

"That was what Loosh said," Granny said. "That General Sherman was leading them all to Jordan."

"Yes," Cousin Drusilla said. "The river. They have stopped there; it's like a river itself, dammed up. The Yankees have thrown out a brigade of cavalry to hold them back while they build the bridge to cross the infantry and artillery; they are all right until they get up there and see or smell the water. That's when they go mad. Not fighting; it's like they can't even see the horses shoving them back and the scabbards beating them; it's like they can't even see anything but the water and the other bank. They aren't angry, aren't fighting; just men, women and children singing and chanting and trying to get to that unfinished bridge or even down into the water itself, and the cavalry beating them back with sword scabbards. I don't know when they have eaten; nobody knows just how far some of them have come. They just pass here without food or anything, exactly as they rose up from whatever they were doing when the spirit or the voice or whatever it was told them to go. They stop during the day and rest in the woods; then, at night, they move again. We will hear them later—I'll wake you —marching on up the road until the cavalry stops them. There was an officer, a major, who finally took time to see I wasn't one of his men; he said, 'Can't you do anything with them? Promise them anything to go back home?' But it was like they couldn't see me or hear me speaking; it was only that water and that bank on the other side. But you will see for yourself tomorrow, when we go back."

"Drusilla," Aunt Louise said, "you're not going back tomorrow or any other time."

"They are going to mine the bridge and blow it up when the army has crossed," Cousin Drusilla said. "Nobody knows what they will do then."

"But we cannot be responsible," Aunt Louise said. "The Yankees brought it on themselves; let them pay the price."

"Those Negroes are not Yankees, Mother," Cousin Drusilla said. "At least there will be one person there who is not a Yankee either." She looked at Granny. "Four, counting Bayard and Ringo."

Aunt Louise looked at Granny. "Rosa, you shan't go. I forbid it. Brother John will thank me to do so."

"I reckon I will," Granny said. "I've got to get the silver anyway."

"And the mules," Ringo said; "don't forget them. And don't yawl worry about Granny. She 'cide what she want and then she kneel down about ten seconds and tell God what she aim to do, and then she git up and do hit. And them that don't like hit can git outen the way or git trompled. But that railroad—"

"And now I reckon we better go to bed," Granny said. But we

didn't go to bed then. I had to hear about the railroad too; possibly it was more the need to keep even with Ringo (or even ahead of him, since I had seen the railroad when it was a railroad, which he had not) than a boy's affinity for smoke and fury and thunder and speed. We sat there in that slave cabin partitioned, like Louvinia's cabin at home, into two rooms by that suspended quilt beyond which Aunt Louise and Granny were already in bed and where Cousin Denny should have been too except for the evening's dispensation he had received, listening too who did not need to hear it again since he had been there to see it when it happened;—we sat there, Ringo and I, listening to Cousin Drusilla and staring at each other with the same amazed and incredulous question: *Where could we have been at that moment? What could we have been doing, even a hundred miles away, not to have sensed, felt this, paused to look at one another, aghast and uplifted, while it was happening?* Because this, to us, was it. Ringo and I had seen Yankees; we had shot at one; we had crouched like two rats and heard Granny, unarmed and not even rising from her chair, rout a whole regiment of them from the library. And we had heard about battles and fighting and seen those who had taken part in them, not only in the person of Father when once or twice each year and without warning he would appear on the strong gaunt horse, arrived from beyond that cloudbank region which Ringo believed was Tennessee, but in the persons of other men who returned home with actual arms and legs missing. But that was it: men had lost arms and legs in sawmills; old men had been telling young men and boys about wars and fighting before they discovered how to write it down: and what petty precision to quibble about locations in space or in chronology, who to care or insist *Now come, old man, tell the truth: did you see this? were you really there?* Because wars are wars: the same exploding powder when there was powder, the same thrust and parry of iron when there was not—one tale, one telling, the same as the next or the one before. So we knew a war existed; we had to believe that, just as we had to believe that the name for the sort of life we had led for the last three years was hardship and suffering. Yet we had no proof of it. In fact, we had even less than no proof; we had had thrust into our faces the very shabby and unavoidable obverse of proof, who had seen Father (and the other men too) return home, afoot like tramps or on crowbait horses, in faded and patched (and at times obviously stolen) clothing, preceded by no flags nor drums and followed not even by two men to keep step with one another, in coats bearing no glitter of golden braid and with scabbards in which no sword reposed, actually almost sneaking home to spend two or three or seven days performing actions not only without glory (plowing land, repairing fences, killing meat for the smoke house) and in which they had no skill but the very necessity for which was the fruit of the absent occupations from which, returning, they bore no proof—actions in the very clumsy performance of which Father's whole presence seemed (to us, Ringo and me) to emanate a kind of humility and apology, as if he were saying, "Believe me, boys; take my word for it: there's more to it than this, no matter what it looks like. I can't prove it, so you'll just have to believe me." And then to have it happen, where we could have been there to see it, and were not: and this no poste and riposte of sweat-reeking cavalry which all war-telling is full of, no galloping thunder of guns to wheel up and unlimber and crash and crash into the lurid grime-glare of their own demon-served inferno which even children would recognise, no ragged lines of gaunt and shrill-yelling infantry beneath a tattered flag which is a very part of that child's make-believe. Because this was it: an interval, a space, in which the toad-squatting guns, the panting men and the trembling horses paused, amphitheatric about the embattled land, beneath the fading fury of the smoke and the puny yelling, and permitted the sorry business which had dragged on for three years now to be congealed into an irrevocable instant and put to an irrevocable gambit, not by two regiments or two batteries or even two generals, but by two locomotives.

Cousin Drusilla told it while we sat there in the cabin which smelled of new whitewash and even (still faintly) of Negroes. She probably told us the reason for it (she must have known)—what point of strategy, what desperate gamble not for preservation, since hope of that was gone, but at least for prolongation, which it served. But that meant nothing to us. We didn't hear, we didn't even listen; we sat there in that cabin and waited and watched that railroad which no longer existed, which was now a few piles of charred ties among which green grass was already growing, a few

threads of steel knotted and twisted about the trunks of trees and
already annealing into the living bark, becoming one and indistinguishable with the jungle growth which had now accepted it,
but which for us ran still pristine and intact and straight and narrow as the path to glory itself, as it ran for all of them who were
there and saw when Ringo and I were not. Drusilla told about
that too; 'Atlanta' and 'Chattanooga' were in it—the names, the
beginning and the end—but they meant no more to us than they
did to the other watchers—the black and the white, the old men,
the children, the women who would not know for months yet
if they were widows or childless or not—gathered, warned by
grapevine, to see the momentary flash and glare of indomitable
spirit starved by three years free of the impeding flesh. She told
it (and now Ringo and I began to see it; we were there too)—
the roundhouse in Atlanta where the engine waited; we were
there, we were of them who (they must have) would slip into
the roundhouse in the dark, to caress the wheels and pistons and
iron flanks, to whisper to it in the darkness like lover to mistress
or rider to horse, cajoling ruthlessly of her or it one supreme effort
in return for making which she or it would receive annihilation
(and who would not pay the price), cajoling, whispering, caressing
her or it toward the one moment; we were of them—the old men,
the children, the women—gathered to watch, drawn and warned
by that grapevine of the oppressed, deprived of everything now
save the will and the ability to deceive, turning inscrutable and
impassive secret faces to the blue enemies who lived among them.
Because they knew it was going to happen; Drusilla told that too:
how they seemed to know somehow the very moment when the
engine left Atlanta; it was as if the gray generals themselves had
sent the word, had told them, "You have suffered for three years;
now we will give to you and your children a glimpse of that for
which you have suffered and been denied." Because that's all it
was. I know that now. Even the successful passage of a hundred
engines with trains of cars could not have changed the situation
or its outcome; certainly not two free engines shrieking along a
hundred yards apart up that drowsing solitude of track which had
seen no smoke and heard no bell in more than a year. I don't think
it was intended to do that. It was like a meeting between two iron
knights of the old time, not for material gain but for principle

—honor denied with honor, courage denied with courage—the deed done not for the end but for the sake of the doing—put to the ultimate test and proving nothing save the finality of death and the vanity of all endeavor. We saw it, we were there, as if Drusilla's voice had transported us to the wandering light-ray in space in which was still held the furious shadow—the brief section of track which existed inside the scope of a single pair of eyes and nowhere else, coming from nowhere and having, needing, no destination, the engine not coming into view but arrested in human sight in thunderous yet dreamy fury, lonely, inviolate and forlorn, wailing through its whistle precious steam which could have meant seconds at the instant of passing and miles at the end of its journey (and cheap at ten times this price)—the flaring and streaming smoke stack, the tossing bell, the starred Saint Andrew's cross nailed to the cab roof, the wheels and the flashing driving rods on which the brass fittings glinted like the golden spurs themselves—then gone, vanished. Only not gone or vanished either, so long as there should be defeated or the descendants of defeated to tell it or listen to the telling.

"The other one, the Yankee one, was right behind it," Drusilla said. "But they never caught it. Then the next day they came and tore the track up. They tore the track up so we couldn't do it again; they could tear the track up but they couldn't take back the fact that we had done it. They couldn't take that from us."

We—Ringo and I—knew what she meant; we stood together just outside the door before Ringo went on to Miss Lena's cabin, where he was to sleep. "I know what you thinking," Ringo said. Father was right; he was smarter than me. "But I heard good as you did. I heard every word you heard."

"Only I saw the track before they tore it up. I saw where it was going to happen."

"But you didn't know hit was fixing to happen when you seed the track. So nemmine that. I heard. And I reckon they ain't gonter git that away from me, neither."

He went on, then I went back into the house and behind the quilt where Denny was already asleep on the pallet. Drusilla was not there only I didn't have time to wonder where she was because I was thinking how I probably wouldn't be able to go to sleep at all now though it was late. Then it was later still and Denny was shaking me and I remember how I thought then that he did not seem to need sleep either, that just by having been exposed for three or four seconds to war he had even at just ten acquired that quality which Father and the other men brought back from the front—the power to do without sleep and food both, needing only the opportunity to endure. "Dru says to come on out doors if you want to hear them passing," he whispered.

She was outside the cabin; she hadn't undressed even. I could see her in the starlight—her short jagged hair and the man's shirt and pants. "Hear them?" she said. We could hear it again, like we had in the wagon—the hurrying feet, the sound like they were singing in panting whispers, hurrying on past the gate and dying away up the road. "That's the third tonight," Cousin Drusilla said. "Two passed while I was down at the gate. You were tired, and so I didn't wake you before."

"I thought it was late," I said. "You haven't been to bed even. Have you?"

"No," she said. "I've quit sleeping."

"Quit sleeping?" I said. "Why?"

She looked at me. I was as tall as she was; we couldn't see each other's faces; it was just her head with the short jagged hair like she had cut it herself without bothering about a mirror, and her neck that had got thin and hard like her hands since Granny and I were here before. "I'm keeping a dog quiet," she said.

"A dog?" I said. "I haven't seen any dog."

"No. It's quiet now," she said. "It doesn't bother anybody any more now. I just have to show it the stick now and then." She was looking at me. "Why not stay awake now? Who wants to sleep now, with so much happening, so much to see? Living used to be dull, you see. Stupid. You lived in the same house your father was born in, and your father's sons and daughters had the sons and daughters of the same Negro slaves to nurse and coddle; and then you grew up and you fell in love with your acceptable young man, and in time you would marry him, in your mother's wedding gown, perhaps, and with the same silver for presents she had received; and then you settled down forevermore while you got children to feed and bathe and dress until they grew up, too; and then you and your husband died quietly and were buried together maybe on a summer afternoon just before suppertime. Stupid, you see. But now you can see for yourself how it is; it's fine now; you don't have to worry now about the house and the silver, because they get burned up and carried away; and you don't have to worry about the Negroes, because they tramp the roads all night waiting for a chance to drown in homemade Jordan; and you don't have to worry about getting children to bathe and feed and change, because the young men can ride away and get killed in the fine battles; and you don't even have to sleep alone, you don't even have to sleep at all; and so, all you have to do is show the stick to the dog now and then and say, 'Thank God for nothing.' You see? There. They've gone now. And you'd better get back to bed, so we can get an early start in the morning. It will take a long time to get through them."

"You're not coming in now?" I said.

"Not yet," she said. But we didn't move. And then she put her hand on my shoulder. "Listen," she said. "When you go back home and see Uncle John, ask him to let me come there and ride with his troop. Tell him I can ride, and maybe I can learn to shoot. Will you?"

"Yes," I said. "I'll tell him you are not afraid too."

"Aren't I?" she said; "I hadn't thought about it. It doesn't matter anyway. Just tell him I can ride and that I don't get tired." Her hand was on my shoulder; it felt thin and hard. "Will you do that for me? Ask him to let me come, Bayard."

"All right," I said. Then I said, "I hope he will let you."

"So do I," she said. "Now you go back to bed. Good night."

I went back to the pallet and then to sleep; again it was Denny shaking me awake; by sunup we were on the road again, Drusilla on Bobolink riding beside the wagon. But not for long.

We began to see the dust almost at once and I even believed that I could already smell them though the distance between us did not appreciably decrease, since they were travelling almost as fast as we were. We never did overtake them, just as you do not overtake a tide. You just keep moving, then suddenly you know that the set is about you, beneath you, overtaking you, as if the slow and ruthless power, become aware of your presence at last, had dropped back a tentacle, a feeler, to gather you in and sweep you remorselessly on. Singly, in couples, in groups and families they began to appear from the woods, ahead of us, alongside of us and behind; they covered and hid from sight the road exactly as an infiltration of flood water would have, hiding the road from sight and then the very wheels of the wagon in which we rode, our two horses as well as Bobolink breasting slowly on, enclosed by a mass of heads and shoulders—men and women carrying babies and dragging older children by the hand, old men and women on improvised sticks and crutches, and very old ones sitting beside the road and even calling to us when we passed; there was one old woman who even walked along beside the wagon, holding to the bed and begging Granny to at least let her see the river before she died.

But mostly they did not look at us. We might not have even been there. We did not even ask them to let us through because we could look at their faces and know they couldn't have heard us. They were not singing yet, they were just hurrying, while our horses pushed slow through them, among the blank eyes not looking at anything out of faces caked with dust and sweat, breasting slowly and terrifically through them as if we were driving in midstream up a creek full of floating logs and the dust and the smell of them everywhere and Granny in Mrs. Compson's hat sitting bolt upright under the parasol which Ringo held and looking sicker and sicker, and it already afternoon though we didn't know it anymore than we knew how many miles we had come. Then all of a sudden we reached the river, where the cavalry was holding them back from the bridge. It was just a sound at first, like wind, like it might be in the dust itself. We didn't even know what it was until we saw Drusilla holding Bobolink reined back, her face turned toward us wan and small above the dust and her mouth open and crying thinly: "Look out, Aunt Rosa! Oh, look out!"

It was like we all heard it at the same time—we in the wagon and on the horse, they all around us in the sweat-caking dust. They made a kind of long wailing sound, and then I felt the whole wagon lift clear of the ground and begin to rush forward. I saw our old rib-gaunted horses standing on their hind feet one minute and then turned sideways in the traces the next, and Drusilla leaning forward a little and taut as a pistol hammer holding Bobolink, and I saw men and women and children going down under the horses and we could feel the wagon going over them and we could hear them screaming. And we couldn't stop anymore than if the earth had tilted up and was sliding us all down toward the river.

It went fast, like that, like it did every time anybody named Sartoris or Millard came within sight, hearing or smell of Yankees, as if Yankees were not a people nor a belief nor even a form of behavior, but instead were a kind of gully, precipice, into which Granny and Ringo and I were sucked pell-mell every time we got close to them. It was sunset; now there was a high bright rosy glow quiet beyond the trees and shining on the river, and now we could see it plain—the tide of niggers dammed back from the entrance to the bridge by a detachment of cavalry, the river like a sheet of rosy glass beneath the delicate arch of the bridge which the tail of the Yankee column was just crossing. They were in silhouette, running tiny and high above the placid water; I remember the horses' and mules' heads all mixed up among the bayonets, and the barrels of cannon tilted up and kind of rushing slow across the high peaceful rosy air like splitcane clothespins being jerked along a clothesline, and the singing everywhere up and down the river bank, with the voices of the women coming out of it thin and high: "Glory! Glory! Hallelujah!"

They were fighting now, the horses rearing and shoving against them, the troopers beating at them with their scabbards, holding them clear of the bridge while the last of the infantry began to cross; all of a sudden there was an officer beside the wagon, holding his scabbarded sword by the little end like a stick and hanging onto the wagon and screaming at us. I don't know where he came from, how he ever got to us, but there he was with his little white face with a stubble of beard and a long streak of blood on it, bareheaded and with his mouth open. "Get back!" he shrieked. "Get back! We're going to blow the bridge!" screaming right into Granny's face while she shouted back at him with Mrs. Compson's hat knocked to one side of her head and hers and the Yankee's faces not a yard apart:

"I want my silver! I'm John Sartoris' mother-in-law! Send Colonel Dick to me!" Then the Yankee officer was gone, right in the middle of shouting and beating at the nigger heads with his sabre, with his little bloody shrieking face and all. I don't know where he went anymore than I know where he came from: he just vanished still holding onto the wagon and flailing about him with the sabre, and then Cousin Drusilla was there on Bobolink; she had our nigh horse by the head-stall and was trying to turn the wagon sideways. I started to jump down to help. "Stay in the wagon," she said. She didn't shout; she just said it. "Take the lines and turn them." When we got the wagon turned sideways we stopped. And then for a minute I thought we were going backward, until I saw it was the niggers. Then I saw that the cavalry had broken; I saw the whole mob of it—horses and men and sabres and niggers—rolling on toward the end of the bridge like when a dam breaks, for about ten clear seconds behind the last of the infantry. And then the bridge vanished. I was looking right at it; I could see the clear gap between the infantry and the wave of niggers and cavalry, with a little empty thread of bridge joining them together in the air above the water, and then there was a bright glare and I felt my insides suck and a clap of wind hit me on the back of the head. I didn't hear anything at all. I just sat there in the wagon with a funny buzzing in my ears and a funny taste in my mouth, and watched little toy men and horses and pieces of plank floating along in the air above the water. But I didn't hear anything at all; I couldn't even hear Cousin Drusilla. She was right beside the wagon now, leaning toward us, her mouth urgent and wide and no sound coming out of it at all.

"What?" I said.

"Stay in the wagon!"

"I can't hear you!" I said. That's what I said, that's what I was thinking; I didn't realise even then that the wagon was moving again. But then I did; it was like the whole long bank of the river had turned and risen under us and was rushing us down toward the water, we sitting in the wagon and rushing down toward the water on another river of faces that couldn't see or hear either. Cousin Drusilla had the nigh horse by the bridle again, and I dragged at them, too, and Granny was standing up in the wagon and beating at the faces with Mrs. Compson's parasol, and then the whole rotten bridle came off in Cousin Drusilla's hand.

"Get away!" I said. "The wagon will float!"

"Yes," she said, "it will float. Just stay in it. Watch Aunt Rosa and Ringo."

"Yes," I said. Then she was gone. We passed her; turned, and holding Bobolink like a rock again and leaning down talking to him and patting his cheek, she was gone. Then maybe the bank did cave. I don't know. I didn't even know we were in the river. It was just like the earth had fallen out from under the wagon and the faces and all, and we all rushed down slow, with the faces looking up and their eyes blind and their mouths open and their arms held up. High up in the air across the river I saw a cliff and a big fire on it running fast sideways; and then all of a sudden the wagon was moving fast sideways, and then a dead horse came shining up from out of the yelling faces and went down slow again, exactly like a fish feeding, with, hanging over his rump by one stirrup, a man in a black uniform, and then I realised that the uniform was blue, only it was wet. They were screaming then, and now I could feel the wagon bed tilt and slide as they caught at it. Granny was kneeling beside me now, hitting at the screaming faces with Mrs. Compson's parasol. Behind us they were still marching down the bank and into the river, singing.

III

A Yankee patrol helped Ringo and me cut the drowned horses out of the harness and drag the wagon ashore. We sprinkled water on Granny until she came to, and they rigged harness with ropes and hitched up two of their horses. There was a road on top of the bluff, and then we could see the fires along the bank. They were still singing on the other side of the river, but it was quieter now. But there were patrols still riding up and down the cliff on this side, and squads of infantry down at the water where the fires were. Then we began to pass between rows of tents, with Granny lying against me, and I could see her face then; it was white and still, and her eyes were shut. She looked old and tired; I hadn't realised how old and little she was. Then we began to pass big fires, with niggers in wet clothes crouching around them and soldiers going among them passing out food; then we came to a broad street, and stopped before a tent with a sentry at the door and a light inside. The soldiers looked at Granny.

"We better take her to the hospital," one of them said.

Granny opened her eyes; she tried to sit up. "No," she said. "Just take me to Colonel Dick. I will be all right then."

They carried her into the tent and put her in a chair. She hadn't moved; she was sitting there with her eyes closed and a strand of wet hair sticking to her face when Colonel Dick came in. I had never seen him before—only heard his voice while Ringo and I were squatting under Granny's skirt and holding our breath—but I knew him at once, with his bright beard and his hard bright eyes, stooping over Granny and saying, "Damn this war. Damn it. Damn it."

"They took the silver and the darkies and the mules," Granny said. "I have come to get them."

"Have them you shall," he said, "if they are anywhere in this corps. I'll see the general myself." He was looking at Ringo and me now. "Ha!" he said. "I believe we have met before also." Then he was gone again.

It was hot in the tent, and quiet, with three bugs swirling around the lantern, and outside the sound of the army like wind far away. Ringo was already asleep, sitting on the ground with his head on his knees, and I wasn't much better, because all of a sudden Colonel Dick was back and there was an orderly writing at the table, and Granny sitting again with her eyes closed in her white face.

"Maybe you can describe them," Colonel Dick said to me.

"I will do it," Granny said. She didn't open her eyes. "The chest of silver tied with hemp rope. The rope was new. Two darkies, Loosh and Philadelphy. The mules, Old Hundred and Tinney."

Colonel Dick turned and watched the orderly writing. "Have you got that?" he said.

The orderly looked at what he had written. "I guess the general will be glad to give them twice the silver and mules just for taking that many niggers," he said.

"Now I'll go see the general," Colonel Dick said.

Then we were moving again. I don't know how long it had been, because they had to wake me and Ringo both; we were in the wagon again, with two Army horses pulling it on down the long broad street, and there was another officer with us and Colonel Dick was gone. We came to a pile of chests and bones that looked higher than a mountain. There was a rope pen behind it full of mules and then, standing to one side and waiting there, was what looked like a thousand niggers, men, women and children, with their wet clothes dried on them. And now it began to go fast again; there was Granny in the wagon with her eyes wide open now and the lieutenant reading from the paper and the soldiers jerking chests and trunks out of the pile. "Ten chests tied with hemp rope," the lieutenant read. "Get them? . . . A hundred and ten mules. It says from Philadelphia—that's in Mississippi. Get these Mississippi mules. They are to have rope and halters."

"We ain't got a hundred and ten Mississippi mules," the sergeant said.

"Get what we have got. Hurry." He turned to Granny. "And there are your niggers, madam."

Granny was looking at him with her eyes wide as Ringo's. She was drawn back a little, with her hand at her chest. "But they're not—they ain't—" she said.

"They ain't all yours?" the lieutenant said. "I know it. The general said to give you another hundred with his compliments."

"But that ain't— We didn't—" Granny said.

"She wants the house back, too," the sergeant said. "We ain't got any houses, grandma," he said. "You'll just have to make out with trunks and niggers and mules. You wouldn't have room for it on the wagon, anyway."

We sat there while they loaded the ten trunks into the wagon. It just did hold them all. They got another set of trees and harness, and hitched four mules to it. "One of you darkies that can handle two span come here," the lieutenant said. One of the niggers came and got on the seat with Granny; none of us had ever seen him before. Behind us they were leading the mules out of the pen.

"You want to let some of the women ride?" the lieutenant said.

"Yes," Granny whispered.

"Come on," the lieutenant said. "Just one to a mule, now." Then he handed me the paper. "Here you are. There's a ford about twenty miles up the river; you can cross there. You better get on away from here before any more of these niggers decide to go with you."

We rode until daylight, with the ten chests in the wagon and the mules and our army of niggers behind. Granny had not moved, sitting there beside the strange nigger with Mrs. Compson's hat on and the parasol in her hand. But she was not asleep, because when it got light enough to see, she said, "Stop the wagon." The wagon stopped. She turned and looked at me. "Let me see that paper," she said.

We opened the paper and looked at it, at the neat writing:

> *Field Headquarters,*
> *—th Army Corps,*
> *Department of Tennessee,*
> *August 14, 1863.*
>
> *To all Brigade, Regimental and Other Commanders: You will see that bearer is repossessed in full of the following property, to wit: Ten (10) chests tied with hemp rope and containing silver. One hundred ten (110) mules captured loose near Philadelphia in Mississippi. One hundred ten (110) Negroes of both sexes belonging to and having strayed from the same locality.*
>
> *You will further see that bearer is supplied with necessary food and forage to expedite his passage to his destination.*
>
> *By order of the General Commanding.*

We looked at one another in the gray light. "I reckon you gonter take um back now," Ringo said.

Granny looked at me. "We can get food and fodder too," I said.

"Yes," Granny said. "I tried to tell them better. You and Ringo heard me. It's the hand of God."

We stopped and slept until noon. That afternoon we came to the ford. We had already started down the bluff when we saw the troop of cavalry camped there. It was too late to stop.

"They done found hit out and headed us off," Ringo said. It was too late; already an officer and two men were riding toward us.

"I will tell them the truth," Granny said. "We have done nothing." She sat there, drawn back a little again, with her hand already raised and holding the paper out in the other when they rode up. The officer was a heavy-built man with a red face; he looked at us and took the paper and read it and began to swear. He sat there on his horse swearing while we watched him.

"How many do you lack?" he said.

"How many do I what?" Granny said.

"Mules!" the officer shouted. "Mules! Mules! Do I look like I had any chests of silver or niggers tied with hemp rope?"

"Do we—" Granny said, with her hand to her chest, looking at him; I reckon it was Ringo that knew first what he meant.

"We like fifty," Ringo said.

"Fifty, hey?" the officer said. He cursed again; he turned to one of the men behind him and cursed him now. "Count 'em!" he said. "Do you think I'm going to take their word for it?"

The man counted the mules; we didn't move; I don't think we even breathed hardly. "Sixty-three," the man said.

The officer looked at us. "Sixty-three from a hundred and ten leaves forty-seven," he said. He cursed. "Get forty-seven mules! Hurry!" He looked at us again. "Think you can beat me out of three mules, hey?"

"Forty-seven will do," Ringo said. "Only I reckon maybe we better eat something, like the paper mention."

We crossed the ford. We didn't stop; we went on as soon as they brought up the other mules, and some more of the women got on them. We went on. It was after sundown then, but we didn't stop.

"Hah!" Ringo said. "Whose hand was that?"

We went on until midnight before we stopped. This time it was Ringo that Granny was looking at. "Ringo," she said.

"I never said nothing the paper never said," Ringo said. "Hit was the one that said it; hit wasn't me. All I done was to told him how much the hundred and ten liked; I never said we liked that many. 'Sides, hit ain't no use in praying about hit now; ain't no telling what we gonter run into 'fore we gits home. The main thing now is, whut we gonter do with all these niggers."

"Yes," Granny said. We cooked and ate the food the cavalry officer gave us; then Granny told all the niggers that lived in Alabama to come forward. It was about half of them. "I suppose you all want to cross some more rivers and run after the Yankee Army, don't you?" Granny said. They stood there, moving their feet in the dust. "What? Don't any of you want to?" They just stood there. "Then who are you going to mind from now on?"

After a while, one of them said, "You, missy."

"All right," Granny said. "Now listen to me. Go home. And if I ever hear of any of you straggling off like this again, I'll see to it. Now line up and come up here one at a time while we divide the food."

It took a long time until the last one was gone; when we started again, we had almost enough mules for everybody to ride, but not quite, and Ringo drove now. He didn't ask; he just got in and took the reins, with Granny on the seat by him; it was just once that she told him not to go so fast. So I rode in the back then, on one of the chests, and that afternoon I was asleep; it was the wagon stopping that woke me. We had just come down a hill onto a flat, and then I saw them beyond a field, about a dozen of them, cavalry in blue coats. They hadn't seen us yet, trotting along, while Granny and Ringo watched them.

"They ain't hardly worth fooling with," Ringo said. "Still, they's horses."

"We've already got a hundred and ten," Granny said. "That's all the paper calls for."

"All right," Ringo said. "You wanter go on?" Granny didn't answer, sitting there drawn back a little, with her hand at her breast again. "Well, what you wanter do?" Ringo said. "You got to 'cide quick, or they be gone." He looked at her; she didn't move. Ringo leaned out of the wagon. "Hey!" he hollered. They looked back quick and saw us and whirled about. "Granny say come here!" Ringo hollered.

"You, Ringo," Granny whispered.

"All right," Ringo said. "You want me to tell um to never mind?" She didn't answer; she was looking past Ringo at the two Yankees who were riding toward us across the field, with that kind of drawnback look on her face and her hand holding the front of her dress. It was a lieutenant and a sergeant; the lieutenant didn't look much older than Ringo and me. He saw Granny and took off his hat. And then all of a sudden she took her hand away from her chest; it had the paper in it; she held it out to the lieutenant without saying a word. The lieutenant opened it, the sergeant looking over his shoulder. Then the sergeant looked at us.

"This says mules, not horses," he said.

"Just the first hundred was mules," Ringo said. "The extra twelve is horses."

"Damn it!" the lieutenant said. He sounded like a girl swearing. "I told Captain Bowen not to mount us with captured stock!"

"You mean you're going to give them the horses?" the sergeant said.

"What else can I do?" the lieutenant said. He looked like he was fixing to cry. "It's the general's own signature!"

So then we had enough stock for all of them to ride except about fifteen or twenty. We went on. The soldiers stood under a tree by the road, with their saddles and bridles on the ground beside them—all but the lieutenant. When we started again, he ran along by the wagon; he looked like he was going to cry, trotting along by the wagon with his hat in his hand, looking at Granny.

"You'll meet some troops somewhere," he said. "I know you will. Will you tell them where we are and to send us something—mounts or wagons—anything we can ride in? You won't forget?"

"They's some of yawl about twenty or thirty miles back that claim to have three extry mules," Ringo said. "But when we sees any more of um, we'll tell um about yawl."

We went on. We came in sight of a town, but we went around it; Ringo didn't even want to stop and send the lieutenant's message in, but Granny made him stop and we sent the message in by one of the niggers.

"That's one more mouth to feed we got shed of," Ringo said.

We went on. We went fast now, changing the mules every few miles; a woman told us we were in Mississippi again, and then, in the afternoon, we came over the hill, and there our chimneys were, standing up into the sunlight, and the cabin behind them and Louvinia bending over a washtub and the clothes on the line, flapping bright and peaceful.

"Stop the wagon," Granny said.

We stopped—the wagon, the hundred and twenty-two mules and horses, and the niggers we never had had time to count.

Granny got out slow and turned to Ringo. "Get out," she said; then she looked at me. "You too," she said. "Because you said nothing at all." We got out of the wagon. She looked at us. "We have lied," she said.

"Hit was the paper that lied; hit wasn't us," Ringo said.

"The paper said a hundred and ten. We have a hundred and twenty-two," Granny said. "Kneel down."

"But they stole them 'fore we did," Ringo said.

"But we lied," Granny said. "Kneel down." She knelt first. Then we all three knelt by the road while she prayed. The washing

blew soft and peaceful and bright on the clothesline. And then
Louvinia saw us; she was already running across the pasture while
Granny was praying.

ROBERT PENN WARREN

When the Light Gets Green

My grandfather had a long white beard and sat under
the cedar tree. The beard, as a matter of fact, was not
very long and not white, only gray, but when I was a child and
was away from him at school during the winter, I would think
of him, not seeing him in my mind's eye, and say: He has a long
white beard. Therefore, it was a shock to me, on the first morning
back home, to watch him lean over the dresser toward the wavy
green mirror, which in his always shadowy room reflected things
like deep water riffled by a little wind, and clip his gray beard to a
point. It is gray and pointed, I would say then, remembering what
I had thought before.

He turned his face to the green wavy glass, first one side and
then the other in quarter profile, and lifted the long shears which
trembled a little, to cut the beard. His face being turned like that,
with his good nose and pointed gray beard, he looked like General
Robert E. Lee, without any white horse to ride. My grandfather
had been a soldier, too, but now he wore blue-jean pants and when
he leaned over like that toward the mirror, I couldn't help but
notice how small his hips and backsides were. Only they weren't
just small, they were shrunken. I noticed how the blue jeans hung
loose from his suspenders and loose off his legs and down around
his shoes. And in the morning when I noticed all this about his legs
and backsides, I felt a tight feeling in my stomach like when you
walk behind a woman and see the high heel of her shoe is worn

and twisted and jerks her ankle every time she takes a step.

Always before my grandfather had finished clipping his beard, my Uncle Kirby came to the door and beat on it for breakfast. "I'll be down in just a minute, thank you, sir," my grandfather said. My uncle called him Mr. Barden. "Mr. Barden, breakfast is ready." It was because my Uncle Kirby was not my real uncle, having married my Aunt Lucy, who lived with my grandfather. Then my grandfather put on a black vest and put his gold watch and chain in the vest and picked up his cob pipe from the dresser top, and he and I went down to breakfast, after Uncle Kirby was already downstairs.

When he came into the dining room, Aunt Lucy was sitting at the foot of the table with the iron coffee pot on a plate beside her. She said, "Good morning, Papa."

"Good morning, Lucy," he said, and sat down at the head of the table, taking one more big puff off his pipe before laying it beside his plate.

"You've brought that old pipe down to breakfast again," my aunt said, while she poured the bright-looking coffee into the cups.

"Don't it stink," he always said.

My uncle never talked at breakfast, but when my grandfather said that, my uncle always opened his lips to grin like a dog panting, and showed his hooked teeth. His teeth were yellow because he chewed tobacco, which my grandfather didn't do, although his beard was yellow around the mouth from smoking. Aunt Lucy didn't like my uncle to chew, that was the whole trouble. So she rode my grandfather for bringing his pipe down, all in fun at first before she got serious about it. But he always brought it down just the same, and said to her, "Don't it stink."

After we ate, my uncle got up and said, "I got to get going," and went out through the kitchen where the cook was knocking and sloshing around. If it had rained right and was a good tobacco-setting season, my grandfather went off with me down to the stable to get his mare, for he had to see the setting. We saddled up the mare and went across the lot, where limestone bunched out of the ground and cedar trees and blue grass grew out of the split rock. A branch of cold water with minnows in it went through the lot between rocks and under the cedar trees; it was where I used to play before I got big enough to go to the river with the niggers to swim.

My grandfather rode across the lot and over the rise back of the house. He sat up pretty straight for an old man, holding the bridle in his left hand, and in his right hand a long hickory tobacco stick whittled down to make a walking cane. I walked behind him and watched the big straw hat he wore waggle a little above his narrow neck, or how he held the stick in the middle, firm and straight up like something carried in a parade, or how smooth and slow the muscles in the mare's flanks worked as she put each hoof down in the ground, going up hill. Sassafras bushes and blackberry bushes grew thick along the lane over the rise. In summer, tufts of hay would catch and hang on the dry bushes and showed that the hay wagons had been that way; but when we went that way in setting time, just after breakfast, the blackberry blooms were hardly gone, only a few rusty patches of white left, and the sassafras leaves showed still wet with dew or maybe the rain.

From the rise we could look back on the house. The shingles were black with damp, and the whitewash grayish, except in spots where the sun already struck it and it was drying. The tops of the cedar trees, too, were below us, very dark green and quiet. When we crossed the rise, there were the fields going down toward the river, all checked off and ready for setting, very even, only for the gullies where brush was piled to stop the washing. The fields were reddish from the wet, not yet steaming. Across them, the green woods and the sycamores showing white far off told where the river was.

The hands were standing at the edge of the field under the trees when we got there. The little niggers were filling their baskets with the wet plants to drop, and I got me a basket and filled it. My Uncle Kirby gave me fifty cents for dropping plants, but he didn't give the little niggers that much, I remember. The hands and women stood around waiting a minute, watching Uncle Kirby, who always fumed around, waving his dibble, his blue shirt already sticking to his arms with sweat. "Get the lead out," he said. The little niggers filled faster, grinning with their teeth at him. "God-dam, get the lead out!" My grandfather sat on his mare under the trees, still holding the walking cane, and said, "Why don't you start 'em, sir?"

Then, all of a sudden, they all moved out into the field, scattering out down the rows, the droppers first, and after a minute the setters, who lurched along, never straightening up, down the rows toward the river. I walked down my row, separating out the plants and dropping them at the hills, while it got hotter and the ground steamed. The sun broke out now and then, making my shadow on the ground, then the cloud would come again, and I could see its shadow drifting at me on the red field.

My grandfather rode very slow along the edge of the field to watch the setting, or stayed still under the trees. After a while, maybe about ten o'clock, he would leave and go home. I could see him riding the mare up the rise and then go over the rise; or if I was working the other way toward the river, when I turned round at the end, the lane would be empty and nothing on top of the rise, with the cloudy, blue-gray sky low behind it.

The tobacco was all he cared about, now we didn't have any horses that were any real good. He had some silver cups, only one real silver one though, that his horses won at fairs, but all that was before I was born. The real silver one, the one he kept on his dresser and kept string and old minnie balls and pins and things in, had *1859* on it because his horse won it then before the War, when he was a young man. Uncle Kirby said horses were foolishness, and Grandfather said, yes, he reckoned horses were foolishness, all right. So what he cared about now was the tobacco. One time he was a tobacco-buyer for three years, but after he bought a lot of tobacco and had it in his sheds, the sheds burned up on him. He didn't have enough insurance to do any good and he was a ruined man. After that all his children, he had all girls and his money was gone, said about him, "Papa's just visionary, he tried to be a tobacco-buyer but he's too visionary and not practical." But he always said, "All tobacco-buyers are sons-of-bitches, and three years is enough of a man's life for him to be a son-of-a-bitch, I reckon." Now he was old, the corn could get the rust or the hay get rained on for all he cared, it was Uncle Kirby's worry, but all summer, off and on, he had to go down to the tobacco field to watch them sucker or plow or worm, and sometimes he pulled a few suckers himself. And when a cloud would blow up black in summer, he got nervous as a cat, not knowing whether it was the rain they needed or maybe a hail storm coming that would cut the tobacco up bad.

Mornings he didn't go down to the field, he went out under the cedar tree where his chair was. Most of the time he took a book with him along with his pipe, for he was an inveterate reader. His being an inveterate reader was one of the things made his children say he was visionary. He read a lot until his eyes went bad the summer before he had his stroke, then after that, I read to him some, but not as much as I ought. He used to read out loud some from Macaulay's *History of England* or Gibbon's *Decline and Fall*, about Flodden Field or about how the Janizaries took Constantinople amid great slaughter and how the Turk surveyed the carnage and quoted from the Persian poet about the lizard keeping the courts of the mighty. My grandfather knew some poetry, too, and he said it to himself when he didn't have anything else to do. I lay on my back on the ground, feeling the grass cool and tickly on the back of my neck, and looked upside down into the cedar tree where the limbs were tangled and black-green like big hairy fern fronds with the sky blue all around, while he said some poetry. Like the "Isles of Greece, the Isles of Greece, where burning Sappho loved and sung." Or like "Roll on, thou deep and dark blue ocean, roll."

But he never read poetry, he just said what he already knew. He only read history and *Napoleon and His Marshals,* having been a soldier and fought in the War himself. He rode off and joined the cavalry, but he never told me whether he took the horse that won the real silver cup or not. He was with Forrest before Forrest was a general. He said Forrest was a great general, and if they had done what Forrest wanted and cleaned the country ahead of the Yankees, like the Russians beat Napoleon, they'd whipped the Yankees sure. He told me about Fort Donelson, how they fought in the winter woods, and how they got away with Forrest at night, splashing through the cold water. And how the dead men looked in the river bottoms in winter, and I lay on my back on the grass, looking up in the thick cedar limbs, and thought how it was to be dead.

After Shiloh was fought and they pushed the Yankees down in the river, my grandfather was a captain, for he raised a cavalry company of his own out of West Tennessee. He was a captain, but he never got promoted after the War; when I was a little boy everybody still called him Captain Barden, though they called lots of other people in our section Colonel and Major. One time I said to him: "Grandpa, did you ever kill any Yankees?" He said: "God-a-Mighty, how do I know?" So, being little, I thought he was just a captain because he never killed anybody, and I was ashamed. He talked about how they took Fort Pillow, and the drunk niggers under the bluff. And one time he said niggers couldn't stand a charge or stand the cold steel, so I thought maybe he killed some of them. But then I thought, Niggers don't count, maybe.

He only talked much in the morning. Almost every afternoon right after dinner, he went to sleep in his chair, with his hands curled up in his lap, one of them holding the pipe that still sent up a little smoke in the shadow, and his head propped back on the tree trunk. His mouth hung open, and under the hairs of his mustache, all yellow with nicotine, you could see his black teeth and his lips that were wet and pink like a baby's. Usually I remember him that way, asleep.

I remember him that way, or else trampling up and down the front porch, nervous as a cat, while a cloud blew up and the trees began to rustle. He tapped his walking cane on the boards and whistled through his teeth with his breath and kept looking off at the sky where the cloud and sometimes the lightning was. Then of a sudden it came, and if it was rain he used to go up to his room and lie down; but if it came hail on the tobacco, he stayed on the front porch, not trampling any more, and watched the hail rattle off the roof and bounce soft on the grass. "God-a-Mighty," he always said, "bigger'n minnie balls," even when it wasn't so big.

In 1914, just before the war began, it was a hot summer with the tobacco mighty good but needing rain. And when the dry spell broke and a cloud blew up, my grandfather came out on the front porch, watching it like that. It was mighty still, with lightning way off, so far you couldn't hardly hear the thunder. Then the leaves began to ruffle like they do when the light gets green, and my grandfather said to me, "Son, it's gonna hail." And he stood still. Down in the pasture, that far off, you could see the cattle bunching up and the white horse charging across the pasture, looking bright, for the sun was shining bright before the cloud struck it all at once. "It's gonna hail," my grandfather said. It was dark, with jagged lightning and the thunder high and steady. And there the hail was.

He just turned around and went in the house. I watched the hail bouncing, then I heard a noise and my aunt yelled. I ran back in the dining room where the noise was, and my grandfather was lying on the floor with the old silver pitcher he dropped and a broken glass. We tried to drag him, but he was too heavy; then my Uncle Kirby came up wet from the stable and we carried my grandfather upstairs and put him on his bed. My aunt tried to call the doctor even if the lightning might hit the telephone. I stayed back in the dining room and picked up the broken glass and the pitcher and wiped up the floor with a rag. After a while Dr. Blake came from town; then he went away.

When Dr. Blake was gone, I went upstairs to see my grandfather. I shut the door and went in his room, which was almost dark, like always, and quiet because the hail didn't beat on the roof any more. He was lying on his back in the featherbed, with a sheet pulled up over him, lying there in the dark. He had his hands curled loose on his stomach, like when he went to sleep in his chair holding the pipe. I sat on a split-bottom chair by the bed and looked at him: he had his eyes shut and his mouth hung loose, but you couldn't hear his breathing. Then I quit looking at him and looked round the room, my eyes getting used to the shadow. I could see his pants on the floor, and the silver cup on the dresser by the mirror, which was green and wavy like water.

When he said something, I almost jumped out of my skin, hearing his voice like that. He said, "Son, I'm gonna die." I tried to say something, but I couldn't. And he waited, then he said, "I'm on borrowed time, it's time to die." I said, "No!" so sudden and loud I jumped. He waited a long time and said, "It's time to die. Nobody loves me." I tried to say, "Grandpa, I love you." And then I did say it all right, feeling like it hadn't been me said it, and knowing all of a sudden it was a lie, because I didn't feel anything. He just lay there; and I went downstairs.

It was sunshiny in the yard, the clouds gone, but the grass was wet. I walked down toward the gate, rubbing my bare feet over the slick cold grass. A hen was in the yard and she kept trying to peck up a piece of hail, like a fool chicken will do after it hails; but every time she pecked, it bounced away from her over the green grass. I leaned against the gate, noticing the ground on one side the posts, close up, was still dry and dusty. I wondered if the tobacco was cut up bad, because Uncle Kirby had gone to see. And while I looked through the gate down across the pasture where everything in the sun was green and shiny with wet and the cattle grazed, I thought about my grandfather, not feeling anything. But I said out loud anyway, "Grandpa, I love you."

My grandfather lived four more years. The year after his stroke they sold the farm and moved away, so I didn't stay with them any more. My grandfather died in 1918, just before the news came that my Uncle Kirby was killed in France, and my aunt had to go to work in a store. I got the letter about my grandfather, who died of flu, but I thought about four years back, and it didn't matter much.

CAROLINE GORDON

Old Red

When the door had closed behind his daughter, Mister Maury went to the window and stood a few moments looking out. The roses that had grown in a riot all along that side of the fence had died or been cleared away, but the sun lay across the garden in the same level lances of light that he remembered. He turned back into the room. The shadows had gathered until it was nearly all in gloom. The top of his minnow bucket just emerging from the duffel bag glinted in the last rays of the sun. He stood looking down at his traps all gathered neatly in a heap at the foot of the bed. He would leave them like that. Even if they came in here sweeping and cleaning up—it was only in hotels that a man was master of his own room—even if they came in here cleaning up, he would tell them to leave all his things exactly as

they were. It was reassuring to see them all there together, ready
to be taken up in the hand, to be carried down and put into a car,
to be driven off to some railroad station at a moment's notice.

As he moved toward the door, he spoke aloud, a habit that
was growing on him:

"Anyhow, I won't stay but a week. . . . I ain't going to stay
but a week, no matter what they say. . . ."

Downstairs in the dining room they were already gathered at
the supper table, his white-haired, shrunken mother-in-law, his
tall sister-in-law who had the proud carriage of the head, the aquiline nose, but not the spirit of his dead wife, his lean, blond new
son-in-law, his black-eyed daughter who, but that she was thin,
looked so much like him, all of them gathered there waiting for
him, Alexander Maury. It occurred to him that this was the first
time he had sat down in the bosom of the family for some years.
They were always writing saying that he must make a visit this
summer or certainly next fall. ". . . all had a happy Christmas together but missed you. . . ." They had even made the pretext
that he ought to come up to inspect his new son-in-law. As if he
hadn't always known exactly the kind of young man Sarah would
marry! What was the boy's name? Stephen, yes, Stephen. He
must be sure and remember that.

He sat down, and shaking out his napkin spread it over his capa-
cious paunch and tucked it well up under his chin in the way his
wife had never allowed him to do. He let his eyes rove over the
table and released a long sigh.

"Hot batter bread," he said, "and ham. Merry Point ham. I
sure am glad to taste them one more time before I die."

The old lady was sending the little Negro girl scurrying back
to the kitchen for a hot plate of batter bread. He pushed aside the
cold plate and waited. She had bridled when he spoke of the batter
bread and a faint flush had dawned on her withered cheeks. Vain
she had always been as a peacock, of her housekeeping, her children, the animals on her place, anything that belonged to her. And
she went on, even at her advanced age, making her batter bread,
smoking her hams according to that old recipe she was so proud
of; but who came here now to this old house to eat or to praise?

He helped himself to a generous slice of batter bread, buttered
it, took the first mouthful and chewed it slowly. He shook his head.

"There ain't anything like it," he said. "There ain't anything else like it in this world."

His dark eyes roving the table fell on his son-in-law. "You like batter bread?" he inquired.

Stephen nodded, smiling. Mister Maury, still masticating slowly, regarded his face, measured the space between the eyes—his favorite test for man, horse, or dog. Yes, there was room enough for sense between the eyes. But how young the boy looked! And infected already with the fatal germ, the *cacoëthes scribendi*.[1] Well, their children would probably escape. It was like certain diseases of the eye, skipped every other generation. His own father had had it badly all his life. He could see him now sitting at the head of the table spouting his own poetry—or Shakespeare's—while the children watched the preserve dish to see if it was going around. He, Aleck Maury, had been lucky to be born in the generation he had. He had escaped that at least. A few translations from Heine in his courting days, a few fragments from the Greek, but no, he had kept clear of that on the whole. . . .

The eyes of his sister-in-law were fixed on him. She was smiling faintly. "You don't look much like dying, Aleck. Florida must agree with you."

The old lady spoke from the head of the table. "I can't see what you do with yourself all winter long. Doesn't time hang heavy on your hands?"

Time, he thought, time! They were always mouthing the word and what did they know about it? Nothing in God's world! He saw time suddenly, a dull, leaden-colored fabric depending from the old lady's hands, from the hands of all of them, a blanket that they pulled about, now this way, now that, trying to cover up their nakedness. Or they would cast it on the ground and creep in among the folds, finding one day a little more tightly rolled than another, but all of it everywhere the same dull gray substance. But time was a banner that whipped before him always in the wind. He stood on tiptoe to catch at the bright folds, to strain them to his bosom. They were bright and glittering. But they whipped by so fast and were whipping always ever faster. The tears came into his eyes. Where, for instance, had this year gone? He could swear he had not wasted a minute of it, for no man living, he

[1] *Cacoëthes scribendi.* Itch for writing.

thought, knew better how to make each day a pleasure to him. Not a minute wasted and yet here it was already May! If he lived to the Biblical three score and ten, which was all he ever allowed himself in his calculations, he had before him only nine more Mays. Only nine more Mays out of all eternity, and they wanted him to waste one of them sitting on the front porch at Merry Point!

The butter plate which had seemed to swim in a glittering mist was coming solidly to rest upon the white tablecloth. He winked his eyes rapidly and laying down his knife and fork squared himself about in his chair to address his mother-in-law:

"Well, ma'am, you know I'm a man that always likes to be learning something. Now this year I learned how to smell out fish." He glanced around the table, holding his head high and allowing his well-cut nostrils to flutter slightly with his indrawn breaths. "Yes, sir," he said, "I'm probably the only white man in this country knows how to smell out feesh."

There was a discreet smile on the faces of the others. Sarah was laughing outright. "Did you have to learn how or did it just come to you?" she asked.

"I learned it from an old nigger woman," her father said. He shook his head reminiscently. "It's wonderful how much you can learn from niggers. But you have to know how to handle them. I was half the winter wooing that old Fanny. . . ."

He waited until their laughter had died down. "We used to start off every morning from the same little cove and we'd drift in there together at night. I noticed how she always brought in a good string, so I says to her, 'Fanny, you just lemme go 'long with you.' But she wouldn't have nothing to do with me. I saw she was going to be a hard nut to crack, but I kept right on. Finally I began giving her presents. . . ."

Laura was regarding him fixedly, a queer look on her face.

"What sort of presents did you give her, Aleck?"

He made his tones hearty in answer. "I gave her a fine string of fish one day and I gave her fifty cents. And finally I made her a present of a Barlow knife. That was when she broke down. She took me with her that morning. . . ."

"Could she really smell fish?" the old lady asked curiously.

"You ought to 'a' seen her," Mister Maury said. "She'd sail over that lake like a hound on the scent. She'd row right along and then all of a sudden she'd stop rowing." He bent over, wrinkling his nose and peering into the depths of imaginary water. " 'Thar they are, White Folks, thar they are. Cain't you smell 'em?' "

Stephen was leaning forward, eyeing his father-in-law intently. "Could you?" he asked.

"I got so I could smell feesh," Mister Maury told him. "I could smell out the feesh, but I couldn't tell which kind they were. Now Fanny could row over a bed and tell just by the smell whether it was bass or bream. But she'd been at it all her life." He paused, sighing. "You can't just pick these things up. You have to give yourself to them. Who was it said 'Genius is an infinite capacity for taking pains'?"

Sarah was rising briskly. Her eyes sought her husband's across the table. She was still laughing. "Sir Izaak Walton," she said, "we'd better go in the other room. Mandy wants to clear the table."

The two older ladies remained in the dining room. Mister Maury walked across the hall to the sitting room, accompanied by Steve and Sarah. He lowered himself cautiously into the most solid-looking of the rocking chairs that were drawn up around the fire. Steve was standing on the hearthrug, back to the fire, gazing abstractedly off across the room.

Mister Maury glanced up at him curiously. "What are you thinking about, feller?" he asked.

Steve looked down. He smiled, but his gaze was still contemplative. "I was thinking about the sonnet," he said, "in the form in which it first came to England."

Mister Maury shook his head, "Wyatt and Surrey," he said. "Hey, nonny, nonny. . . . You'll have hardening of the liver long before you're my age." He looked past Steve's shoulder at the picture that hung over the mantel shelf: Cupid and Psyche holding between them a fluttering veil and running along a rocky path toward the beholder. "Old Merry Point," he said; "it don't change much, does it?"

He settled himself more solidly in his chair. His mind veered from the old house to his own wanderings in brighter places. He regarded his daughter and son-in-law affably.

"Yes, sir," he said, "this winter in Florida was valuable to me just for the acquaintances I made. Take my friend, Jim Barbee. Just to live in the same hotel with that man is an education." He paused, smiling reminiscently into the fire. "I'll never forget the first time I saw him. He came up to me there in the lobby of the hotel. 'Professor Maury!' he says, 'You been hearin' about me for twenty years and I been hearin' about you for twenty years. And now we've done met!' "

Sarah had sat down in the little rocking chair by the fire. She leaned toward him now, laughing. "They ought to have put down a cloth of gold for the meeting," she said.

Mister Maury shook his head. "Nature does that in Florida," he said. "I knew right off the reel it was him. There were half a dozen men standing around. I made 'em witness. 'Jim Barbee,' I says, 'Jim Barbee of Maysville or I'll eat my hat!' "

"Why is he so famous?" Sarah asked.

Mister Maury took out his knife and cut a slice from a plug of tobacco. When he had offered a slice to his son-in-law and it had been refused, he put the plug back in his pocket. "He's a man of imagination," he said slowly. "There ain't many in this world."

He took a small tin box out of his pocket and set it on the little table that held the lamp. Removing the top he tilted the box so that they could see its contents: an artificial lure, a bug with a dark body and a red, bulbous head, a hook protruding from what might be considered its vitals.

"Look at her," he said, "ain't she a killer?"

Sarah leaned forward to look and Steve, still standing on the hearthrug, bent above them. The three heads ringed the light.

Mister Maury disregarded Sarah and addressed himself to Steve. "She takes nine strips of rind," he said, "nine strips just thick enough." He marked off the width of the strips with his two fingers on the table, then picking up the lure and cupping it in his palm he moved it back and forth quickly so that the painted eyes caught the light.

"Look at her," he said, "look at the wicked way she sets forward."

Sarah was poking at the lure with the tip of her finger.

"Wanton," she said, "simply wanton. What does he call her?"

"This is his Devil Bug," Mister Maury said. "He's the only man in this country makes it. I myself had the idea thirty years ago and let it slip by me the way I do with so many of my ideas." He sighed, then elevating his tremendous bulk slightly above the table level and continuing to hold Stephen with his gaze he produced from his coat pocket the oilskin book that held his flies. He spread it open on the table and began to turn the pages. His eyes sought his son-in-law's as his hand paused before a gray, rather draggled-looking lure.

"Old Speck," he said. "I've had that fly for twenty years. I reckon she's taken five hundred pounds of fish in her day. . . ."

The fire burned lower. A fiery coal rolled from the grate and fell onto the hearthrug. Sarah scooped it up with a shovel and threw it among the ashes. In the circle of the lamplight the two men still bent over the table looking at the flies. Steve was absorbed in them but he spoke seldom. It was her father's voice that rising and falling filled the room. He talked a great deal, but he had a beautiful speaking voice. He was telling Steve now about Little West Fork, the first stream ever he put a fly in. "My first love," he kept calling it. It sounded rather pretty, she thought, in his mellow voice. "My first love . . ."

II

When Mister Maury came downstairs the next morning the dining room was empty except for his daughter, Sarah, who sat dawdling over a cup of coffee and a cigarette. Mister Maury sat down opposite her. To the little Negro girl who presented herself at his elbow he outlined his wants briefly. "A cup of coffee and some hot batter bread just like we had last night." He turned to his daughter. "Where's Steve?"

"He's working," she said, "he was up at eight and he's been working ever since."

Mister Maury accepted the cup of coffee from the little girl, poured half of it into his saucer, set it aside to cool. "Ain't it wonderful," he said, "the way a man can sit down and work day after day? When I think of all the work I've done in my time. . . . Can he work *every* morning?"

"He sits down at his desk every morning," she said, "but of course he gets more done some mornings than others."

Mister Maury picked up the saucer, found the coffee cool enough for his taste. He sipped it slowly, looking out of the window. His mind was already busy with his day's program. No water

—no running water—nearer than West Fork three miles away. He couldn't drive a car and Steve was going to be busy writing all morning. There was nothing for it but a pond. The Willow Sink. It was not much but it was better than nothing. He pushed his chair back and rose.

"Well," he said, "I'd better be starting."

When he came downstairs with his rod a few minutes later the hall was still full of the sound of measured typing. Sarah sat in the dining room in the same position in which he had left her, smoking. Mister Maury paused in the doorway while he slung his canvas bag over his shoulders. "How you ever going to get anything done if you don't take advantage of the morning hours?" he asked. He glanced at the door opposite as if it had been the entrance to a sick chamber.

"What's he writing about?" he inquired in a whisper.

"It's an essay on John Skelton."

Mister Maury looked out at the new green leaves framed in the doorway. "John Skelton," he said. "God Almighty!"

He went through the hall and stepped down off the porch onto the ground that was still moist with spring rains. As he crossed the lower yard he looked up into the branches of the maples. Yes, the leaves were full grown already even on the late trees. The year, how swiftly, how steadily it advanced! He had come to the far corner of the yard. Grown up it was in pokeberry shoots and honeysuckle, but there was a place to get through. The top strand of wire had been pulled down and fastened to the others with a ragged piece of rope. He rested his weight on his good leg and swung himself over onto the game one. It gave him a good, sharp twinge when he came down on it. It was getting worse all the time, that leg, but on the other hand he was learning better all the time how to handle it. His mind flew back to a dark, startled moment, that day when the cramp first came on him. He had been sitting still in the boat all day long and that evening when he had stood up to get out his leg had failed him utterly. He had pitched forward among the reeds, had lain there a second, face downwards, before it came to him what had happened. With the realization came a sharp picture of his faraway youth: Uncle Quent lowering himself ponderously out of the saddle after a hard day's hunting had fallen forward in exactly the same way, into a knot of yowling little Negroes. He had got up and cursed them all out of the lot. It had scared the old boy to death, coming down like that. The black dog he had had on his shoulder all that fall. But he himself had never lost one day's fishing on account of his leg. He had known from the start how to handle it. It meant simply that he was slowed down that much. It hadn't really made much difference in fishing. He didn't do as much wading but he got around just about as well on the whole. Hunting, of course, had had to go. You couldn't walk all day shooting birds, dragging a game leg. He had just given it up right off the reel, though it was a shame when a man was as good a shot as he was. That day he was out with Tom Kensington last November, the only day he got out during the season. Nine shots he'd had and he'd bagged nine birds. Yes, it was a shame. But a man couldn't do everything. He had to limit himself. . . .

He was up over the little rise now. The field slanted straight down before him to where the pond lay, silver in the morning sun. A Negro cabin was perched halfway up the opposite slope. A woman was hanging out washing on a line stretched between two trees. From the open doorway little Negroes spilled down the path toward the pond. Mister Maury surveyed the scene, spoke aloud:

"Ain't it funny now? Niggers always live in the good places."

He stopped under a wild cherry tree to light his pipe. It had been hot crossing the field, but the sunlight here was agreeably tempered by the branches. And that pond down there was fringed with willows. His eyes sought the bright disk of the water, then rose to where the smoke from the cabin chimney lay in a soft plume along the crest of the hill.

When he stooped to pick up his rod again it was with a feeling of sudden, keen elation. An image had risen in his memory, an image that was familiar but came to him infrequently of late and that only in moments of elation: the wide field in front of his uncle's old house in Albemarle, on one side the dark line of undergrowth that marked the Rivanna River, on the other the blue of Peters' Mountain. They would be waiting there in that broad plain when they had the first sight of the fox. On that little rise by the river, loping steadily, not yet alarmed. The sun would glint on his bright coat, on his quick-turning head as he dove into the dark of the woods. There would be hullabaloo after that and shouting and riding. Sometimes there was the tailing of the fox —that time old Whisky was brought home on a mattress! All of that to come afterward, but none of it ever like that first sight of the fox there on the broad plain between the river and the mountain.

There was one fox, they grew to know him in time, to call him affectionately by name. Old Red it was who showed himself always like that there on the crest of the hill. "There he goes, the damn' impudent scoundrel!" . . . Uncle Quent would shout and slap his thigh and yell himself hoarse at Whisky and Mag and the pups, but they would have already settled to their work. They knew his course, every turn of it by heart. Through the woods and then down across the fields again to the river. Their hope was always to cut him off before he could circle back to the mountain. If he got in there among those old field pines it was all up. But he always made it. Lost 'em every time and then dodged through to his hole in Pinnacle Rock. . . . A smart fox, Old Red. . . .

He descended the slope and paused in the shade of a clump of willows. The little Negroes who squatted, dabbling in the water, watched him out of round eyes as he unslung his canvas bag and laid it on a stump. He looked down at them gravely.

"D'you ever see a white man that could conjure?" he asked.

The oldest boy laid the brick he was fashioning out of mud down on a plank. He ran the tip of his tongue over his lower lip to moisten it before he spoke. "Naw suh."

"I'm the man," Mister Maury told him. "You chillun better quit that playin' and dig me some worms."

He drew his rod out of the case, jointed it up and laid it down on a stump. Taking out his book of flies he turned the pages, considering. "Silver Spinner," he said aloud. "They ought to take that . . . in May. Naw, I'll just give Old Speck a chance. It's a long time now since we had her out."

The little Negroes had risen and were stepping quietly off along the path toward the cabin, the two little boys hand in hand, the little girl following, the baby astride her hip. They were pausing now before a dilapidated building that might long ago have been a hen-house. Mister Maury shouted at them. "Look under them old boards. That's the place for worms." The biggest boy was turning around. His treble "Yassuh" quavered over the water. Then their voices died away. There was no sound except the light turning of the willow boughs in the wind.

Mister Maury walked along the bank, rod in hand, humming: "Bangum's gone to the wild boar's den . . . *Bangum's* gone to the wild boar's den . . ." He stopped where a white, peeled log protruded six or seven feet into the water. The pond made a little turn here. Two lines of willows curving in framed the whole surface of the water. He stepped out squarely upon the log, still humming. The line rose smoothly, soared against the blue and curved sweetly back upon the still water. His quick ear caught the little whish that the fly made when it clove the surface, his eye followed the tiny ripples of its flight. He cast again, leaning a little backward as he did sometimes when the mood was on him. Again and again his line soared out over the water. His eye rested now and then on his wrist. He noted with detachment the expert play of the muscles, admired each time the accuracy of his aim. It occurred to him that it was four days now since he had wet a line. Four days. One whole day packing up, parts of two days on the train and yesterday wasted sitting there on that front porch with the family. But the abstinence had done him good. He had never cast better than he was casting this morning.

There was a rustling along the bank, a glimpse of blue through the trees. Mister Maury leaned forward and peered around the clump of willows. A hundred yards away Steve, hatless, in an old blue shirt and khaki pants, stood jointing up a rod.

Mister Maury backed off his log and advanced along the path. He called out cheerfully, "Well, feller, do any good?"

Steve looked up. His face had lightened for a moment, but the abstracted expression stole over it again when he spoke. "Oh, I fiddled with it," he said, "all morning, but I didn't do much good."

Mister Maury nodded sympathetically. "*Minerva invita erat,*" [2] he said; "you can do nothing unless Minerva perches on the rooftree. Why, I been castin' here all morning and not a strike. But there's a boat tied up over on the other side. What say we get in it and just drift around?" He paused, looked at the rod Steve had finished jointing up. "I brought another rod along," he said.

_____
[2] *Minerva invita erat.* Minerva was unwilling.

"You want to use it?"

Steve shook his head. "I'm used to this one."

An expression of relief came over Mister Maury's face. "That's right," he said, "a man always does better with his own rod."

The boat was only a quarter full of water. They heaved her over and dumped it out, then dragged her down to the bank. The little Negroes had come up, bringing a can of worms. Mister Maury threw them each a nickel and set the can in the bottom of the boat. "I always like to have a few worms handy," he told Steve, "ever since I was a boy." He lowered himself ponderously into the bow and Steve pushed off and dropped down behind him.

The little Negroes still stood on the bank staring. When the boat was a little distance out on the water the boldest of them spoke: "Yo reckon 'at ole jawnboat going to hold you up, Cap'm?"

Mister Maury turned his head to call over his shoulder. "Go 'way, boy, ain't I done tole you I's a conjure?"

The boat dipped ominously. Steve changed his position a little and she settled to the water. Sitting well forward Mister Maury made graceful casts, now to this side, now to that. Steve, in the stern, made occasional casts, but he laid his rod down every now and then to paddle, though there was really no use in it. The boat drifted well enough with the wind. At the end of half an hour seven sizable bass lay on the bottom of the boat. Mister Maury had caught five of them. He reflected that perhaps he really ought to change places with Steve. The man in the bow certainly had the best chance at the fish. "But no," he thought, "it don't make any difference. He don't hardly know where he is now."

He stole a glance over his shoulder at the young man's serious, abstracted face. It was like that of a person submerged. Steve seemed to float up to the surface every now and then, his expression would lighten, he would make some observation that showed he knew where he was, then he would sink again. If you asked him a question he answered punctiliously, two minutes later. Poor boy, dead to the world and would probably be that way the rest of his life! A pang of pity shot through Mister Maury, and on the heels of it a gust of that black fear that occasionally shook him. It was he, not Steve, that was the queer one! The world was full of people like this boy, all of them walking around with their heads so full of this and that they hardly knew where they were going.

There was hardly anybody—there was *nobody* really in the whole world like him. . . .

Steve, coming out of his abstraction, spoke politely. He had heard that Mister Maury was a fine shot. Did he like to fish better than hunt?

Mister Maury reflected. "Well," he said, "they's something about a covey of birds rising up in front of you . . . they's something. And a good dog. Now they ain't anything in this world that I like better than a good bird dog." He stopped and sighed. "A man has got to come to himself early in life if he's going to amount to anything. Now I was smart, even as a boy. I could look around me and see all the men of my family, Uncle Jeems, Uncle Quent, my father, every one of 'em weighed two hundred by the time he was fifty. You get as heavy on your feet as all that and you can't do any good shooting. But a man can fish as long as he lives. . . . Why, one place I stayed last summer there was an old man ninety years old had himself carried down to the river every morning. . . . Yes, sir, a man can fish as long as he can get down to the water's edge. . . ."

There was a little plop to the right. He turned just in time to see the fish flash out of the water. He watched Steve take it off the hook and drop it on top of the pile in the bottom of the boat. Eight bass that made and two bream. The old lady would be pleased. "Aleck always catches me fish," she'd say.

The boat glided on over the still water. There was no wind at all now. The willows that fringed the bank might have been cut out of paper. The plume of smoke hung perfectly horizontal over the roof of the Negro cabin. Mister Maury watched it stream out in little eddies and disappear into the bright blue.

He spoke softly: "Ain't it wonderful . . . ain't it wonderful now that a man of my gifts can content himself a whole morning on this here little old pond?"

III

Mister Maury woke with a start. He realized that he had been sleeping on his left side again. A bad idea. It always gave him palpitations of the heart. It must be that that had waked him up. He had gone to sleep almost immediately after his head hit the pillow. He rolled over, cautiously, as he always did since that bed in Leesburg had given down with him, and lying flat on his back stared at the opposite wall.

The moon rose late. It must be at its height now. That patch of light was so brilliant he could almost discern the pattern of the wall paper. It hung there, wavering, bitten by the shadows into a semblance of a human figure, a man striding with bent head and swinging arms. All the shadows in the room seemed to be moving toward him. The protruding corner of the washstand was an arrow aimed at his heart, the clumsy old-fashioned dresser was a giant towering above him.

They had put him to sleep in this same room the night after his wife died. In the summer it had been, too, in June, and there must have been a full moon, for the same giant shadows had struggled there with the same towering monsters. It would be like that here on this wall every full moon, for the pieces of furniture would never change their position, had never been changed, probably, since the house was built.

He turned back on his side. The wall before him was dark, but he knew every flower in the pattern of the wall paper, interlacing pink roses with thrusting up between every third cluster the enormous, spreading fronds of ferns. The wall paper in the room across the hall was like that too. The old lady slept there, and in the room next to his own, Laura, his sister-in-law, and in the east bedroom downstairs the young couple. He and Mary had slept there when they were first married, when they were the young couple in the house.

He tried to remember Mary as she must have looked the day he first saw her, the day he arrived from Virginia to open his school in the old office that used to stand there in the corner of the yard. He could see Mister Allard plainly, sitting there under the sugar tree with his chair tilted back, could discern the old lady—young she had been then!—hospitably poised in the doorway, could hear her voice: "Well, here are two of your pupils to start with. . . ." He remembered Laura, a shy child of nine hiding her face in her mother's skirts, but Mary was only a shadow in the dark hall. He could not even remember how her voice had sounded. "Professor Maury," she would have said and her mother would have corrected her with "Cousin Aleck. . . ."

That day a year later when she was getting off her horse at

654 · CAROLINE GORDON

the stile blocks. . . . She had turned as she walked across the lawn to look back at him. Her white sunbonnet had fallen back on her shoulders, her eyes meeting his had been wide and startled. He had gone on and had hitched both the horses before he leaped over the stile to join her. But he had known in that moment that she was the woman he was going to have. He could not remember all the rest of it, only that moment stood out. He had won her. She had become his wife, but the woman he had won was not the woman he had sought. It was as if he had had her only in that moment there on the lawn. As if she had paused there only for that one moment, and was ever after retreating before him down a devious, a dark way that he would never have chosen.

The death of the first baby had been the start of it, of course. It had been a relief when she took so definitely to religion. Before that there had been those sudden, unaccountable forays out of some dark lurking place that she had. Guerrilla warfare and trying to the nerves, but that had been only at the first. For many years they had been two enemies contending in the open. . . . Toward the last she had taken mightily to prayer. He would wake often to find her kneeling by the side of the bed in the dark. It had gone on for years. She had never given up hope. . . .

Ah, a stout-hearted one, Mary! She had never given up hope of changing him, of making him over into the man she thought he ought to be. Time and again she almost had him. And there were long periods, of course, during which he had been worn down by the conflict, one spring when he himself said, when she had told all the neighbors that he was too old now to go fishing any more. . . . But he had made a comeback. She had had to resort to stratagem. His lips curved in a smile, remembering the trick.

It had come over him suddenly, a general lassitude, an odd faintness in the mornings, the time when his spirits ordinarily were always at their highest. He had sat there looking out of the window at the woods glistening with spring rain; he had not even taken his gun down to shoot a squirrel.

Remembering Uncle Quent's last days, he had been alarmed, had decided finally that he must tell her so that they might begin preparations for the future—he had shuddered at the thought of eventual confinement, perhaps in some institution. She had looked up from her sewing, unable to repress a smile.

"You think it's your mind, Aleck. . . . It's coffee. . . . I've been giving you a coffee substitute every morning. . . ."

They had laughed together over her cleverness. He had not gone back to coffee, but the lassitude had worn off. She had gone back to the attack with redoubled vigor. In the afternoons she would stand on the porch calling after him as he slipped down to the creek, "Now, don't stay long enough to get that cramp. You remember how you suffered last time. . . ." He would have forgotten all about the cramp until that moment, but it would hang over him then through the whole afternoon's sport, and it would descend upon him inevitably when he left the river and started for the house.

Yes, he thought with pride. She was wearing him down—he didn't believe there was a man living who could withstand her a lifetime!—she was wearing him down and would have had him in another few months, another year certainly. But she had been struck down just as victory was in her grasp. The paralysis had come on her in the night. It was as if a curtain had descended, dividing their life sharply into two parts. In the bewildered year and a half that followed he had found himself forlornly trying to reconstruct the Mary he had known. The pressure she had so constantly exerted upon him had become for him a part of her personality. This new, calm Mary was not the woman he had loved all these years. She had lain there—heroically they all said—waiting for death. And lying there, waiting, all her faculties engaged now in defensive warfare, she had raised as it were her lifelong siege; she had lost interest in his comings and goings, had once even encouraged him to go out for an afternoon's sport. He felt a rush of warm pity. Poor Mary! She must have realized toward the last that she had wasted herself in conflict; she had spent her arms and her strength against an inglorious foe when all the time the real, the invincible adversary waited. . . .

He turned over on his back again. The moonlight was waning, the contending shadows paler now and retreating toward the door. From across the hall came the sound of long, sibilant breaths, ending each one on a little upward groan. The old lady . . . she would maintain till her dying day that she did not snore. He fancied that he could hear from the next room Laura's light, regular breathing, and downstairs were the young couple asleep in each other's arms. . . .

All of them quiet and relaxed now, but they had been lively enough at dinner time! It had started with the talk about Aunt Sally Crenfew's funeral Tuesday. Living as he had for some years away from women of his family he had forgotten the need to be cautious. He had spoken up before he thought:

"But that's the day Steve and I were going to Barker's Mill. . . ."

Sarah had cried out at the idea. "Barker's Mill!" she had said, "right on the Crenfew land . . . well, if not on the very farm in the very next field." It would be a scandal if he, Professor Maury, known by everybody to be in the neighborhood, could not spare one afternoon, one insignificant summer afternoon from his fishing long enough to attend the funeral of his cousin, the cousin of all of them, the oldest lady in the whole family connection. . . .

She had got him rattled; he had fallen back upon technicalities:

"I'm not a Crenfew. I'm a Maury. Aunt Sally Crenfew is no more kin to me than a catfish. . . ."

An unlucky crack, that about the catfish. Glancing around the table he had caught the same look in every eye. He had felt a gust of the same fright that had shaken him there on the pond. That look! Sooner or later you met it in every human eye. The thing was to be up and ready, ready to run for your life at a moment's notice. Yes, it had always been like that. It always would be. His fear of them was shot through suddenly with contempt. It was as if Mary was there laughing at them with him. *She* knew that none of them could have survived what he had survived, could have paid the price for freedom that he had paid. . . .

Sarah had come to a full stop. He had to say something. He shook his head:

"You think we just go fishing to have a good time. The boy and I hold high converse on that pond. . . . I'm starved for intellectual companionship, I tell you. In Florida I never see anybody but niggers. . . ."

They had all laughed out at that. "As if you didn't *prefer* the society of niggers," Sarah said scornfully.

The old lady had been moved to anecdote:

"I remember when Aleck first came out here from Virginia,

Cousin Sophy said: 'Professor Maury is so well educated. Now Cousin Cave Maynor is dead, who is there in this neighborhood for him to associate with?' 'Well,' I said, 'I don't know about that. He seems perfectly satisfied now with Ben Hooser. They're off to the creek together every evening soon as school is out.' "

Ben Hooser. . . . He could see now the wrinkled face, over-laid with that ashy pallor of the aged Negro, the shrewd, smiling eyes, the pendulous lower lip that dropping away showed always some of the rotten teeth. A fine nigger, Ben, and on to a lot of tricks, the only man really that he'd ever cared to take fishing with him. . . .

But the first real friend of his bosom had been old Uncle Teague, back in Virginia. Once a week, or more likely every ten days, he fed the hounds on the carcass of a calf that had had time to get pretty high. They would drive the spring wagon out into the lot, he, a boy of ten, beside Uncle Teague on the driver's seat. The hounds would come in a great rush and rear their slobbering jowls against the wagon wheels. Uncle Teague would wield his whip, chuckling while he threw the first hunk of meat to Old Mag, his favorite.

"Dey goin' run on dis," he'd say, "dey goin' run like a shadow. . . ."

He shifted his position again, cautiously. People, he thought . . . people . . . so bone ignorant, all of them. Not one person in a thousand realized that a fox hound remains at heart a wild beast and must kill and gorge, and then when he is ravenous kill and gorge again. . . . Or that the channel cat is a night feeder. . . . Or . . . his daughter had told him once that he ought to set all his knowledges down in a book. "Why?" he had asked. "So everybody else can know as much as I do?"

If he allowed his mind to get active, really active, he would never get any sleep. He was fighting an inclination now to get up and find a cigarette. He relaxed again upon his pillows, de-liberately summoned pictures up before his mind's eye. Landscapes and streams. He observed their outlines, watched one flow into another. The Black River into West Fork, that in turn into Spring Creek and Spring Creek into the Withlicoochee. Then they were all flowing together, merging into one broad plain. He watched it take form slowly: the wide field in front of Hawkwood, the

Rivanna River on one side, on the other Peters' Mountain. They
would be waiting there till the fox showed himself on that little
rise by the river. The young men would hold back till Uncle
Quent had wheeled Old Filly, then they would all be off pell-
mell across the plain. He himself would be mounted on Jones-
boro. Blind as a bat, but she would take anything you put her at.
That first thicket on the edge of the woods. They would break
there, one half of them going around, the other half streaking it
through the woods. He was always of those going around to try
to cut the fox off on the other side. No, he was down off his horse.
He was coursing with the fox. He could hear the sharp, pointed
feet padding on the dead leaves, see the quick head turned now
and then over the shoulder.

The trees kept flashing by, one black trunk after another. And
now it was a ragged mountain field and the sage grass running before them in waves to where a narrow stream curved in between
the ridges. The fox's feet were light in the water. He ran steadily,
head down. The hounds' baying was louder now. Old Mag knew
the trick. She had stopped to give tongue by the big rock, and now
they had all leaped the gulch and were scrambling up through
the pines. But the fox's feet were already hard on the mountain
path. He ran slowly now, past the big boulder, past the blasted
pine to where the shadow of the Pinnacle Rock was black across
the path. He ran on and the shadow rose and swayed to meet him.
Its cool touch was on his hot tongue, his heaving flanks. He had
slipped in under it. He was sinking down, panting, in black dark,
on moist earth while the hounds' baying filled the bowl of the
valley and reverberated from the mountainside.

EUDORA WELTY

A Worn Path

It was December—a bright frozen day in the early
morning. Far out in the country there was an old
Negro woman with her head tied in a red rag, coming along a
path through the pinewoods. Her name was Phoenix Jackson. She
was very old and small and she walked slowly in the dark pine
shadows, moving a little from side to side in her steps, with the
balanced heaviness and lightness of a pendulum in a grandfather
clock. She carried a thin, small cane made from an umbrella, and
with this she kept tapping the frozen earth in front of her. This
made a grave and persistent noise in the still air, that seemed
meditative, like the chirping of a solitary little bird.

She wore a dark striped dress reaching down to her shoetops,
and an equally long apron of bleached sugar sacks, with a full
pocket; all neat and tidy, but every time she took a step she might
have fallen over her shoe-laces, which dragged from her unlaced
shoes. She looked straight ahead. Her eyes were blue with age.
Her skin had a pattern all its own of numberless branching wrinkles and as though a whole little tree stood in the middle of her
forehead, but a golden color ran underneath, and the two knobs
of her cheeks were illuminated by a yellow burning under the
dark. Under the red rag her hair came down on her neck in the
frailest of ringlets, still black, and with an odor like copper.

Now and then there was a quivering in the thicket. Old Phoenix
said, "Out of my way, all you foxes, owls, beetles, jack rabbits,
coons, and wild animals! . . . Keep out from under these feet, little bobwhites. . . . Keep the big wild hogs out of my path. Don't

let none of those come running my direction. I got a long way."
Under her small black-freckled hand her cane, limber as a buggy
whip, would switch at the brush as if to rouse up any hiding things.

On she went. The woods were deep and still. The sun made
the pine needles almost too bright to look at, up where the wind
rocked. The cones dropped as light as feathers. Down in the hollow was the mourning dove—it was not too late for him.

The path ran up a hill. "Seem like there is chains about my
feet, time I get this far," she said, in the voice of argument old
people keep to use with themselves. "Something always take a hold
on this hill—pleads I should stay."

After she got to the top she turned and gave a full, severe look
behind her where she had come. "Up through pines," she said at
length. "Now down through oaks."

Her eyes opened their widest and she started down gently. But
before she got to the bottom of the hill a bush caught her dress.

Her fingers were busy and intent, but her skirts were full and
long, so that before she could pull them free in one place they were
caught in another. It was not possible to allow the dress to tear.
"I in the thorny bush," she said. "Thorns, you doing your appointed work. Never want to let folks past—no sir. Old eyes
thought you was a pretty little *green* bush."

Finally, trembling all over, she stood free, and after a moment
dared to stoop for her cane.

"Sun so high!" she cried, leaning back and looking, while the
thick tears went over her eyes. "The time getting all gone here."

At the foot of this hill was a place where a log was laid across
the creek.

"Now comes the trial," said Phoenix.

Putting her right foot out, she mounted the log and shut her
eyes. Lifting her skirt, leveling her cane fiercely before her, like
a festival figure in some parade, she began to march across. Then
she opened her eyes and she was safe on the other side.

"I wasn't as old as I thought," she said.

But she sat down to rest. She spread her skirts on the bank
around her and folded her hands over her knees. Up above her
was a tree in a pearly cloud of mistletoe. She did not dare to close
her eyes, and when a little boy brought her a little plate with a
slice of marble-cake on it she spoke to him. "That would be ac-

ceptable," she said. But when she went to take it there was just her own hand in the air.

So she left that tree, and had to go through a barbed-wire fence. There she had to creep and crawl, spreading her knees and stretching her fingers like a baby trying to climb the steps. But she talked loudly to herself: she could not let her dress be torn now, so late in the day, and she could not pay for having her arm or her leg sawed off if she got caught fast where she was.

At last she was safe through the fence and risen up out in the clearing. Big dead trees, like black men with one arm, were standing in the purple stalks of the withered cotton field. There sat a buzzard.

"Who you watching?"

In the furrow she made her way along.

"Glad this not the season for bulls," she said, looking sideways, "and the good Lord made his snakes to curl up and sleep in the winter. A pleasure I don't see no two-headed snake coming around that tree, where it come once. It took a while to get by him, back in the summer."

She passed through the old cotton and went into a field of dead corn. It whispered and shook, and was taller than her head. "Through the maze now," she said, for there was no path.

Then there was something tall, black, and skinny there, moving before her.

At first she took it for a man. It could have been a man dancing in the field. But she stood still and listened, and it did not make a sound. It was as silent as a ghost.

"Ghost," she said sharply, "who be you the ghost of? For I have heard of nary death close by."

But there was no answer, only the ragged dancing in the wind.

She shut her eyes, reached out her hand, and touched a sleeve. She found a coat and inside that an emptiness, cold as ice.

"You scarecrow," she said. Her face lighted. "I ought to be shut up for good," she said with laughter. "My senses is gone. I too old. I the oldest people I ever know. Dance, old scarecrow," she said, "while I dancing with you."

She kicked her foot over the furrow, and with mouth drawn down shook her head once or twice in a little strutting way. Some husks blew down and whirled in streamers about her skirts.

Then she went on, parting her way from side to side with the cane, through the whispering field. At last she came to the end, to a wagon track, where the silver grass blew between the red ruts. The quail were walking around like pullets, seeming all dainty and unseen.

"Walk pretty," she said. "This the easy place. This the easy going."

She followed the track, swaying through the quiet bare fields, through the little strings of trees silver in their dead leaves, past cabins silver from weather, with the doors and windows boarded shut, all like old women under a spell sitting there. "I walking in their sleep," she said, nodding her head vigorously.

In a ravine she went where a spring was silently flowing through a hollow log. Old Phoenix bent and drank. "Sweetgum makes the water sweet," she said, and drank more. "Nobody knows who made this well, for it was here when I was born."

The track crossed a swampy part where the moss hung as white as lace from every limb. "Sleep on, alligators, and blow your bubbles." Then the track went into the road.

Deep, deep the road went down between the high green-colored banks. Overhead the live-oaks met, and it was as dark as a cave.

A black dog with a lolling tongue came up out of the weeds by the ditch. She was meditating, and not ready, and when he came at her she only hit him a little with her cane. Over she went in the ditch, like a little puff of milk-weed.

Down there, her senses drifted away. A dream visited her, and she reached her hand up, but nothing reached down and gave her a pull. So she lay there and presently went to talking. "Old woman," she said to herself, "that black dog come up out of the weeds to stall you off, and now there he sitting on his fine tail, smiling at you."

A white man finally came along and found her—a hunter, a young man, with his dog on a chain.

"Well, Granny!" he laughed. "What are you doing there?"

"Lying on my back like a June-bug waiting to be turned over, mister," she said, reaching up her hand.

He lifted her up, gave her a swing in the air, and set her down, "Anything broken, Granny?"

"No sir, them old dead weeds is springy enough," said Phoenix, when she had got her breath. "I thank you for your trouble."

"Where do you live, Granny?" he asked, while the two dogs were growling at each other.

"Away back yonder, sir, behind the ridge. You can't even see it from here."

"On your way home?"

"No, sir, I going to town."

"Why, that's too far! That's as far as I walk when I come out myself, and I get something for my trouble." He patted the stuffed bag he carried, and there hung down a little closed claw. It was one of the bobwhites, with its beak hooked bitterly to show it was dead. "Now you go on home, Granny!"

"I bound to go to town, mister," said Phoenix. "The time come around."

He gave another laugh, filling the whole landscape. "I know you colored people! Wouldn't miss going to town to see Santa Claus!"

But something held Old Phoenix very still. The deep lines in her face went into a fierce and different radiation. Without warning she had seen with her own eyes a flashing nickel fall out of the man's pocket on to the ground.

"How old are you, Granny?" he was saying.

"There is no telling, mister," she said, "no telling."

Then she gave a little cry and clapped her hands, and said, "Git on away from here, dog! Look! Look at that dog!" She laughed as if in admiration. "He ain't scared of nobody. He a big black dog." She whispered, "Sick him!"

"Watch me get rid of that cur," said the man. "Sick him, Pete! Sick him!"

Phoenix heard the dogs fighting and heard the man running and throwing sticks. She even heard a gunshot. But she was slowly bending forward by that time, further and further forward, the lids stretched down over her eyes, as if she were doing this in her sleep. Her chin was lowered almost to her knees. The yellow palm of her hand came out from the fold of her apron. Her fingers slid down and along the ground under the piece of money with the grace and care they would have in lifting an egg from under a sitting hen. Then she slowly straightened up, she stood erect, and the nickel was in her apron pocket. A bird flew by. Her lips moved. "God watching me the whole time. I come to stealing."

The man came back, and his own dog panted about them. "Well, I scared him off that time," he said, and then he laughed and lifted his gun and pointed it at Phoenix.

She stood straight and faced him.

"Doesn't the gun scare you?" he said, still pointing it.

"No, sir, I seen plenty go off closer by, in my day, and for less than what I done," she said, holding utterly still.

He smiled, and shouldered the gun. "Well, Granny," he said, "you must be a hundred years old, and scared of nothing. I'd give you a dime if I had any money with me. But you take my advice and stay home, and nothing will happen to you."

"I bound to go on my way, mister," said Phoenix. She inclined her head in the red rag. Then they went in different directions, but she could hear the gun shooting again and again over the hill.

She walked on. The shadows hung from the oak trees to the road like curtains. Then she smelled wood-smoke, and smelled the river, and she saw a steeple and the cabins on their steep steps. Dozens of little black children whirled around her. There ahead was Natchez shining. Bells were ringing. She walked on.

In the paved city it was Christmas time. There were red and green electric lights strung and crisscrossed everywhere, and all turned on in the daytime. Old Phoenix would have been lost if she had not distrusted her eyesight and depended on her feet to know where to take her.

She paused quietly on the sidewalk, where people were passing by. A lady came along in the crowd, carrying an armful of red-, green-, and silver-wrapped presents; she gave off perfume like the red roses in hot summer, and Phoenix stopped her.

"Please, missy, will you lace up my shoe?" She held up her foot.

"What do you want, Grandma?"

"See my shoe," said Phoenix. "Do all right for out in the country, but wouldn't look right to go in a big building."

"Stand still then, Grandma," said the lady. She put her packages down carefully on the sidewalk beside her and laced and tied both shoes tightly.

"Can't lace 'em with a cane," said Phoenix. "Thank you, missy. I doesn't mind asking a nice lady to tie up my shoe when I gets out on the street."

Moving slowly and from side to side, she went into the stone building and into a tower of steps, where she walked up and around and around until her feet knew to stop.

She entered a door, and there she saw nailed up on the wall the document that had been stamped with the gold seal and framed in the gold frame which matched the dream that was hung up in her head.

"Here I be," she said. There was a fixed and ceremonial stiffness over her body.

"A charity case, I suppose," said an attendant who sat at the desk before her.

But Phoenix only looked above her head. There was sweat on her face; the wrinkles shone like a bright net.

"Speak up, Grandma," the woman said. "What's your name? We must have your history, you know. Have you been here before? What seems to be the trouble with you?"

Old Phoenix only gave a twitch to her face as if a fly were bothering her.

"Are you deaf?" cried the attendant.

But then the nurse came in.

"Oh, that's just old Aunt Phoenix," she said. "She doesn't come for herself—she has a little grandson. She makes these trips just as regular as clockwork. She lives away back off the Old Natchez Trace." She bent down. "Well, Aunt Phoenix, why don't you just take a seat? We won't keep you standing after your long trip." She pointed.

The old woman sat down, bolt upright in the chair.

"Now, how is the boy?" asked the nurse.

Old Phoenix did not speak.

"I said, how is the boy?"

But Phoenix only waited and stared straight ahead, her face very solemn and withdrawn into rigidity.

"Is his throat any better?" asked the nurse. "Aunt Phoenix, don't you hear me? Is your grandson's throat any better since the last time you came for the medicine?"

With her hand on her knees, the old woman waited, silent, erect and motionless, just as if she were in armor.

"You mustn't take up our time this way, Aunt Phoenix," the nurse said. "Tell us quickly about your grandson, and get it over.

He isn't dead, is he?"

At last there came a flicker and then a flame of comprehension across her face, and she spoke.

"My grandson. It was my memory had left me. There I sat and forgot why I made my long trip."

"Forgot?" The nurse frowned. "After you came so far?"

Then Phoenix was like an old woman begging a dignified forgiveness for waking up frightened in the night. "I never did go to school—I was too old at the Surrender," she said in a soft voice. "I'm an old woman without an education. It was my memory fail me. My little grandson, he is just the same, and I forgot it in the coming."

"Throat never heals, does it?" said the nurse, speaking in a loud, sure voice to Old Phoenix. By now she had a card with something written on it, a little list. "Yes. Swallowed lye. When was it—January—two—three years ago—"

Phoenix spoke unasked now. "No, missy, he not dead, he just the same. Every little while his throat begin to close up again, and he not able to swallow. He not get his breath. He not able to help himself. So the time come around, and I go on another trip for the soothing medicine."

"All right. The doctor said as long as you came to get it you could have it," said the nurse. "But it's an obstinate case."

"My little grandson, he sit up there in the house all wrapped up, waiting by himself," Phoenix went on. "We is the only two left in the world. He suffer and it don't seem to put him back at all. He got a sweet look. He going to last. He wear a little patch quilt and peep out, holding his mouth open like a little bird. I remembers so plain now. I not going to forget him again, no, the whole enduring time. I could tell him from all the others in creation."

"All right." The nurse was trying to hush her now. She brought her a bottle of medicine. "Charity," she said, making a check mark in a book.

Old Phoenix held the bottle close to her eyes and then carefully put it into her pocket.

"I thank you," she said.

"It's Christmas time, Grandma," said the attendant. "Could I give you a few pennies out of my purse?"

"Five pennies is a nickel," said Phoenix stiffly.

"Here's a nickel," said the attendant.

Phoenix rose carefully and held out her hand. She received the nickel and then fished the other nickel out of her pocket and laid it beside the new one. She stared at her palm closely, with her head on one side.

Then she gave a tap with her cane on the floor.

"This is what come to me to do," she said. "I going to the store and buy my child a little windmill they sells, made out of paper. He going to find it hard to believe there such a thing in the world. I'll march myself back where he waiting, holding it straight up in this hand."

She lifted her free hand, gave a little nod, turned round, and walked out of the doctor's office. Then her slow step began on the stairs, going down.

ANDREW LYTLE

Mister McGregor

"I wants to speak to Mister McGregor."

Yes, sir, that's what he said. Not marster, but MISTER McGREGOR. If I live to be a hundred, and I don't think I will, account of my kidneys, I'll never forget the feelen that come over the room when he said them two words: Mister McGregor. The air shivered into a cold jelly; and all of us, me, ma, and pa, sort of froze in it. I remember thinken how much we favored one of them waxwork figures Sis Lou had learnt to make at Doctor Price's Female Academy. There I was, a little shaver of eight, standen by

Reprinted from A NOVEL, A NOVELLA AND FOUR STORIES by Andrew Lytle, by permission of Ivan Obolensky, Inc.

the window a-blowen my breath on it so's I could draw my name, like chillun'll do when they're kept to the house with a cold. The knock come sudden and sharp, I remember, as I was crossen a T. My heart flopped down in my belly and commenced to flutter around in my breakfast; then popped up to my ears and drawed all the blood out'n my nose except a little sack that got left in the point to swell and tingle. It's a singular thing, but the first time that nigger's fist hit the door I knowed it was the knock of death. I can smell death. It's a gift, I reckon, one of them no-count gifts like good conversation that don't do you no good no more. Once Cousin John Mebane come to see us, and as he leaned over to pat me on the head—he was polite and hog-friendly to everybody, chillun and poverty-wropped kin especial—I said, Cousin John, what makes you smell so funny? Ma all but took the hide off'n me; but four days later they was dressen him in his shroud. Then I didn't know what it was I'd smelled, but by this time I'd got better acquainted with the meanen.

Ma was rollen tapers for the mantel. She stiffened a spell like she was listenen for the North wind to rise; rolled out a taper and laid it down. She went to the door and put her hand square on the knob; hesitated like she knew what was comen; then opened it. There stood Rhears. He was the coachman. Him and his wife Della was ma's pets. They both of'm was give to ma by her pa at the marryen; and in a way that folks don't understand no more, they somehow become a part of her. Ma liked horses that wanted to run away all the time, and Rhears was the only nigger on the place that could manage'm. He was a powerful, dangerous feller. He'd killed the blacksmith and two free niggers in the other county before ma brought him to Long Gourd. His shoulders jest but stretched across the openen, as he stood there in a respectful-arrogant sort of way with a basket-knife in his hand.

"What do you want, Rhears?" his mistress asked.

"I want to speak to Mister McGregor," he said.

Pa had been scratchen away at his secretary. At "Mister" the scratchen stopped. That last scratch made more noise in my ears than the guns at Shiloh. Without a word, without even looken behind him, pa stood up and reached for his gun. The secretary was close to the fireplace and had a mirror over it. He didn't waste no time, but he didn't hurry none either. He just got up, took off his specs, and laid them as careful on the secretary, just like he meant to set'm in one special place and no other place would do. He reached for the gun and turned.

Rhear warn't no common field hand. He was proud, black like the satin in the widow-women's shirt-waists, and spoiled. And his feelens was bad hurt. The day before, pa had whupped Della, and Rhears had had all night to fret and sull over it and think about what was be-en said in the quarters and how glad the field hands was she'd been whupped. He didn't mean to run away from his home like any blue-gum nigger. He jest come a-marchen straight to the house to settle with pa before them hot night thoughts had had time to git cooled down by the frost.

Pa turned and walked towards him. He still moved as steady and solemn. I watched the even distance each boot-heel made and calculated that two more steps would put him up to the threshold. Just to look at him you might have thought he was a-goen towards the courthouse to pay his taxes or walken down the aisle to his pew. All of a sudden he come to a stop. Ma's brown silk skirt had spread out before him. I looked up. There she was, one hand tight around the gun stock, the othern around the barrel. Her left little finger, plunged like a hornet's needle when the skin drew tight over pa's knuckles, made the blood drop on the bristly hairs along his hand; hang there; then spring to the floor. She held there the time it took three drops to bounce down and splatter. That blood put a spell on me.

A gold shiver along ma's dress made me look quick at their faces. Her hair was a shade darker than the dress she was wearen and slicked down around her ears. There wasn't no direct sun on it, but a light sorghum color slipped up and down as if it were playen on grease. The light might have come from her eyes, for they was afire. She was always fine to look at, although her face wasn't soft enough to rightly claim her beautiful. But she would have taken the breeches away from any ordinary man, I tell you. She'd rather manage folks than eat. Pa ought to have let her do a sight more of it than he did. She was happier than I ever seen her the time he went to the legislature. But he didn't take to politics somehow. He said the government rooms smelled too strong of tobacco. He was a mighty clean man, the cleanest I ever come across. Took a washen once a day reg'lar. When I come to think about ma, I see her a-studyen about somethen, with a wrinkle in her eyes. She didn't have to tell the servants not to bother her then. They stayed out of her way or went tippen around if their work took'm near her.

Well, pa saw he couldn't get his gun out of her grip without acting ungentlemanly. He gave her a curious look and a low bow; then turned it loose. Taken off his coat and folden it, he laid it across a chair. Ma was marbly-pale when she stepped out of the way, but she moved easy and steady.

For a long time I never could make out the meanen of them looks, nor why ma done what she done. And she never set us right about it. She wasn't the explainen kind, and you can bet nobody ever asked. I'd just as soon have asked the devil to pop his tail. It's bothered me a heap in my time, more'n it's had any right to. I reckon it's because I always think about it when I'm taperen off. That's a time when a man gits melancholy and thinks about how he come not to be president and sich-like concerns. Well, sir, when I'd run through all my mistakes and seen where if I'd a-done this instead of that how much better off I'd be today, and cuss myself for drinken up my kidneys, I'd always end up by asken myself why that woman acted like that. I've knowed a sight of women in my day, knowed'm as the Bible saints knowed'm, as well as in a social and business way; and I'm here to say, sir, they are stuffed with dynamite, the puniest of'm.

It was a question of authority, and a time when whuppen was out of the argyment. All you had to do was look at Rhears and that basket-knife sharpened thin like a dagger, a-hangen as innocent agen his pant leg, to see he didn't mean to take no whuppen. He must have felt in his Afrykin way that pa had betrayed him. Folks just didn't whup their house servants, and Rhears was a-meanen to teach pa his manners. Niggers can think straight up to a certain point, and beyond that the steadiest of'm let their senses fly like buckshot, high to scatter. It never struck him that Della needed her whuppen. No, sir, he was just a-standen in the door tellen pa he warn't his marster.

Now ma might have thought that pa ought, with his proper

strength, to show him who his marster was. There ain't no doubt but what he had to show it in some way, or he might as well have sold all his niggers for any work he could a got out'n them. Still it was a powerful big risk to run. And it was plain she was a-meanen for him to run it.

Anyway, that was the construction the kin put on it, and it was natural they would. But it never satisfied me. I got it in my head that Rhears warn't the only person on Long Gourd who didn't claim pa his marster. Before I tell you what I mean, give me a little taste of that shuck juice—half a glass'll do, jest enough to settle the dust in my belly. I'm about to choke to death with the drought.

Aah . . . that's sweet to the taste. Now, sir. You'll excuse me if I lean over and whisper this. *That other body was ma.* I know it ain't a-goen to sound right, for she and pa had the name of be-en a mighty loven couple. But a man and woman can fight and still love. Most of'm enjoy fighten. I ain't never seen one get wore out with it. They can go on with a fight for years. Can get fat on it. When they win out, they put the man down amongst the chillun and give him a whuppen when he forgits his manners or sasses back. But if he's stout enough to put her and keep her in her place, she don't hold it agin him. She's proud to think she picked such a game one. That's how come I never married. I'm peaceful by nature. Ain't but one thing ever gits me fighten mad: that's putten salt in my whisky. That riles me. I'll fight a elyphant then.

Well, sir, that morning Della was late. Ma had had to send for her twice, and she come in looken like the hornets stung her. She fluffed down to her sewen and went to work in a sullen way, her lip stuck out so far it looked swole. And they ain't nothing meaner-looken than a blue-black, shiney lip of a sullen nigger woman. It looks like a devil's pillow.

Directly ma said, "Della, take out that seam and do it over again."

"Take it out yourself, if it don't suit," she flounced back.

In a second pa was on his feet: "Woman, lay down that sewen and come with me."

Them was his words; and if a nigger can git pale, Della done it. She seen right away what a mistake she'd made. She fell on the floor and commenced to grab at ma's skirts. "Don't let him whup me, Mistiss. Don't let him." For a while ma didn't say a word.

"Get up off that floor and come with me," said pa again.

"Mister McGregor, what are you going to do with this girl?"

Pa never made her no answer. He walked over and lifted Della up by the arm.

"Don't you tech me: you don't dare tech me. I belongs to Mistiss."

Pa shuck her till her teeth rattled; then she stopped her jumpen and goen on and stood there a-tremblen like a scared horse.

"Mister McGregor," come ma's even tones, "you're not going to punish that girl. She's mine."

And with that pa turned and said in a hard, polite way he never used before to ma: "And so are you mine, my dear." Then he nodded to Della to go before him, and she went.

When he came back, ma was standen in the middle of the floor just where he had left her. She hadn't moved a peg. She just stood there, stiff as a poker, her head thrown up and her eyes as wide as a hawk's.

"I have whipped Della and sent her to the fields for six months. If at the end of that time she has learned not to forget her manners, she may take up again her duties here. In the meantime, so you will not want, I've sent for P'niny. If you find her too old or in any way unsuitable, you may take your choice of the young girls."

He waited a breath for her answer and when it didn't come, got on his horse and went runnen over the back road down to the fields. No other words passed between them that day. At supper the meal went off in quick order. There wasn't no good old-fashioned table talk. Everybody was as polite to one another as if they was visiten. Ma sat at the foot, froze to her chair. Pa at the head like a judge expecten shooten in the court. We knew some-then was bound to blow up and bust; and I do believe if somebody had tromped on a hog bladder, we chillun'd a jumped under the table.

Next mornen it come. That bow of pa's, as he let go of the gun, was his answer to the challenge. For you might almost say pa had whupped ma by proxy. And here was Rhears, agen by proxy, to make him answer for it . . . a nigger and a slave, his mistress's gallant, a-callen her husband and his marster to account for her.

I don't reckon they'd been any such mixed-up arrangement as that before that time; and I know they ain't since.

I scrouched back in the corner and watched, so scared my eyes turned loose in their sockets. If Jesus Christ had a touched me on the shoulder and said, "Come on, little boy, and git your harp," I'd a no more looked at him than if he'd a been my dog come to lick me. For pa and Rhears was a-eyen one another. This fight was to be accorden to no rules. I saw straight off it would start fist and skull and work into stomp and gouge. If pa didn't manage to git that knife away from the nigger, it would be cut and grunt as well.

Pa was the slimberer of the two, but he wouldn't a looked it away from Rhears. From necked heel up he was six feet—no, six feet four—and his boots raised him an ench higher. Right away he took a quick easy step forward, and both of'm tied their muscles together. Rhears tightened his fingers around the knife. I looked at pa's breeches. They fit him tight; and the meat rolled up, snapped, then quivered under the cloth. His butt give in at the sides and squeezed away its sitten-down softness. His waist drawed in and pumped the wind into his chest, a-pushen out his shoulders just as easy and slow. I don't believe you could have found a man in the whole cotton country hung together any purtier.

Pa, quick-like, sunk his hand in and around the black flesh of Rhears' neck. The knife swung backwards, but pa grabbed it with his left hand before it could do its damage. A breath, and Rhears was a-spinnen round the room. The basket-knife lay in the door as still as any of the pine floor boards. This rattled the nigger some. He had figured on gitten Mister McGregor in the door, where he could a used the knife to advantage. Fighten in his mistress's room, a place he didn't feel at home in, rattled him some more. So before he could come to himself good, pa lambed a blow into his black jaw. It was a blow fit to down a mule, but Rhears shook his head and run in to close; changed quick; dropped low and butted. Four quick butts jambed pa agen the wall, where he saved his guts by grabben Rhears' shoulders—to hold. That kinky hunk of iron slowed down. Both men shook under the strain. The noise of destruction held up. All you could hear was a heavy-pumpen blowen, like to wind-broke horses drawen a killen load . . . then a rippen cry from Rhears' coat—and it was good broadcloth—as it split both ways from the small of his back. Both men drawed in their breaths for a long second.

Sudden-like pa's head and chest went down and forward. His feet pressed agen the wall. Slow as candy pullen he broke the nigger's holt on the front muscles of his thighs. But that nigger's grip never give. No, sir. What give was two drippen hunks of leg meat. Just the second that holt was broke pa shifted neat and shoved hard. Rhears smashed a sewen table top into kindlen wood before he hit the wall. That table saved his neck, or I'm as good a man as I used to be. Before he could get his bearens, pa was a-pounden his head into the hard pine floor. I looked for the brains to go a-splatteren any time, and I begun to wonder how far they would slide on the floor's smooth polish. But God never made but one thing tougher'n a nigger's head—and that's ironwood. Slowly Rhears raised up and, with a beautiful strain of muscles, got to his feet. Then him and pa went round the room. It looked like that bangen had set the nigger crazy. A stranger comen into the room would a thought he was set on breaken up every stick of furniture, a-usen pa for his mallet. Once the two of'm come close to ma, so close the wind they made blowed her skirts; but never a peg did she move. She held as rigid as a conjure woman.

Directly the nigger began to wear some. All that crazy spurt of energy hadn't done him no good. Gradually pa's feet touched the floor more and more; then they didn't leave it. The panten got heavier, more like bellows. A chair got in their way. They went over it. They did a sight of rollen—up to the door crowded with house servants, all a-looken like they had fell in the ash-hopper. You could follow how far they'd rolled by the sweat on the floor. It looked like a wet mop had been run by a triflen hand. Then, sir, my hairs straightened up and drawed in to hide under the scalp. Rhears had ended up on top and was a-shiften to gouge. Pa looked all wore down. I tried to holler to ma to shoot, but my throat was as parched as it is right this minute. . . . Thank you, sir. You are very generous.

Have you ever seen a long dead limb stretched between sky and droppen sun? Well, that's how still ma held onto that gun of pa's. I couldn't stand to seen them black thumbs go down. As I turned my head, I heard the nigger holler. Pa had jerked up his knee and hit him in a tender spot. He fell back and grabbed himself. It must have been an accident, for pa made no move to take advantage of the break. He just lay there and let Rhears take hold of himself and git at pa's throat. I never seen such guts in nobody, nigger or white man. Bump went pa's head on the floor. Bump and agen. Ever time he lifted pa, he squeezed tighter. Ever time he come down he pushed him forward.

It had been one of them frosty December mornens, and a fire had been burnen in the chimney since first light. The front stick had been burned in two and left between it and the back stick a heap of red and blue hickory coals. They don't make no hotter fire than that. I saw right away what Rhears had in mind. Every time he bumped my father's head against the floor, he was that much nearer the hearth. Pa wriggled and jerked, but his wind was cut and the black blood ran into his eyes. Those heavy black hands growed deep in the red, greasy flesh of pa's neck.

They moved slower towards the fire, for pa had at last clamped his legs in a way to slow'm down. Then I saw him reach for his pocket. Rhears didn't see this move. His eyes were bucked on what they had in mind to do, and the heat from the hickory logs made'm swell with a dark, dry look of battle luck. After some fumblen pa finally brought out his knife. He opened it in a feeble way over the nigger's back, and let it rip and tear through his ribs. The blood first oozed; then spouted. It fell back from the knife like dirt from a turnen plow. Then pa made a jab back of the kidneys. That done for him. He grunted, turned loose and rolled over like a hunk of meat.

Staggering to his feet, pa went over and leaned agen the mantel. Directly Rhears spoke up, so low you could hardly hear him:

"Marster, if you hadn't got me, I'd a got you."

Then he shook with a chill, straightened out, and rolled back his eyes. Mister McGregor looked at him a minute before he turned to his wife. And then no words passed his mouth. He reached out his hand and she walked over and handed him the gun. He reached over the mantel, and, his arms a-tremblen, set the gun back in its rack.

"Bring me a pan of warm water, the turpentine, and the things out of my medicine chest." That was ma speaken, sharp and peremptory, to the servants in the doorway. "And take this body out of here," she added in a tone she used when the girl Sally failed to dust behind the furniture.

"Sit down in that chair, Mister McGregor, so I can dress your wounds."

Pa done what she told him. She worked away at him with deft, quick fingers. Directly I hears her in a off-hand way, her head benden over and her hands busy wrappen:

"Colonel Winston will be through here on the way South. I think it would be best to sell him Della."

"I think that, my dear," said pa, "would be the most sensible thing to do."

PETER TAYLOR

What You Hear From 'Em?

Whenever someone misunderstood Aunt Munsie's question, she didn't bother to clarify it. She might repeat it two or three times, in order to drown out some fool answer she was getting from some fool white woman, or man, either. "What you hear from 'em?" she'd ask. "What you hear from 'em? *What you hear from 'em?*" She was so deaf that anyone whom she thoroughly drowned out only laughed and said Aunt Munsie had got so deaf she couldn't hear it thunder. It was, of course, only the most utterly fool answers that ever received the drowning-out treatment. For a number of years, Aunt Munsie was willing to listen to those who mistook her " 'em" to mean any and all of the Dr. Tolliver children. And for more years than that she would listen to those who thought she wanted just *any* news of her two favorites among the Tolliver children—Thad and Will. But later on she stopped putting the question to all insensitive and frivolous souls who didn't understand that what she was interested in hearing—and *all* she was interested in hearing—was when Mr. Thad and Mr. Will Tolliver were going to pack up their families and come back to Thornton for good.

They had always promised her to come back—to come back sure enough, that is. On separate occasions, both Thad and Will had promised her. For ten years, she hadn't seen them together, but each of them had made visits to Thornton now and then with his own family. She would see a big car stopping in front of her house on a Sunday afternoon and see either Will or Thad with his wife and children piling out into the dusty street—it was nearly always summer when they came—and then see them filing across the street, jumping the ditch, and unlatching the gate to her yard. She always met them in that pen of a yard, but long before they had jumped the ditch she was clapping her hands and calling out, "Hai-ee! Hai-ee, now! Look-a-here! Whee! Whee! Look-a-here!" She had got so blind that she was never sure whether it was Mr. Thad or Mr. Will until she had her arms about his waist. They had always looked a good deal alike, and their city clothes made them look even more alike nowadays. Aunt Munsie's eyes were so bad, besides being so full of moisture on those occasions, that she really recognized them by their girth. Will had grown a regular washpot of a stomach and Thad was still thin as a rail. They would sit on her porch for twenty or thirty minutes—whichever one it was and his family—and then they would be gone again.

Aunt Munsie wouldn't try to detain them—not seriously. Those short little old visits didn't mean a thing to her. He—Thad or Will —would lean against the banister rail and tell her how well his children were doing in school or college, and she would make each child in turn come and sit beside her on the swing for a minute and receive a hug about the waist or shoulders. They were timid with her, not seeing her any more than they did, but she could tell from their big Tolliver smiles that they liked her to hug them and make over them. Usually, she would lead them all out to her back yard and show them her pigs and dogs and chickens. (She always had at least one frizzly chicken to show the children.) They would traipse through her house to the back yard and then traipse through again to the front porch. It would be time for them to go when they came back, and Aunt Munsie would look up at *him*—Mr. Thad or Mr. Will (she had begun calling them "Mr." the day they married)— and say, "Now, look here. When you comin' back?"

Both Thad and Will knew what she meant, of course, and which-ever it was would tell her he was making definite plans to wind up his business and that he was going to buy a certain piece of prop-erty, "a mile north of town" or "on the old River Road," and build a jim-dandy house there. He would say, too, how good Aunt Munsie's own house was looking, and his wife would say how grand the zinnias and cannas looked in the yard. (The yard was all flowers—not a blade of grass.) The visit was almost over then. There remained only the exchange of presents. One of the children would hand Aunt Munsie a paper bag containing a pint of whiskey or a carton of cigarettes. Aunt Munsie would go to her back porch or to the pit in the yard and get a fern or a wandering Jew, potted in a rusty lard bucket, and make Mrs. Thad or Mrs. Will take it along. Then the visit was over, and they would leave. From the porch, Aunt Munsie would wave goodbye with one hand and lay the other hand, trembling slightly, on the banister rail. (The banis-ters had come off a porch of the house where Thad and Will had grown up. Dr. Tolliver had been one of the first to widen his porches and remove the gingerbread from his house.) The children and their mother would wave to Aunt Munsie from the street. Their father would close the gate, resting his hand a moment on its familiar wrought-iron frame, and wave to her before he jumped the ditch. (The iron fence, with its iron gate, had been around the yard at Dr. Tolliver's till he took it down and set out a hedge, just a few weeks before he died.)

Such paltry little visits meant nothing to Aunt Munsie. No more did the letters that came with "her things" at Christmas. She was supposed to get her daughter, Lucrecie, who lived next door, to read the letters, but in late years she had taken to putting them away unopened, and some of the presents, too. All she wanted to hear from *them* was when they were coming back for good, and she had learned that the Christmas letters never told her that. On her daily route with her slop wagon through the Square, up Jack-son Street, and down Jefferson, there were only four or five houses

left where she asked her question. These were houses where the
amount of pig slop was not worth stopping for, houses where
one old maid, or maybe two, lived, or a widow with one old
bachelor son who had never amounted to anything and ate no
more than a woman. And so—in the summertime, anyway—she
took to calling out at the top of her lungs, when she approached
the house of one of the elect, "What you hear from 'em?" Sometimes a Miss Patty or a Miss Lucille or a Mr. Ralph would get up
out of a porch chair and come down the brick walk to converse
with Aunt Munsie. Or sometimes one of them would just lean out
over the shrubbery planted around the porch and call, "Not a
thing, Munsie. Not a thing lately."

She would shake her head and call back, "Naw. Naw. Not a
thing. Nobody don't hear from 'em. Too busy, they be!"

Aunt Munsie's skin was the color of a faded tow sack. She was
hardly four feet tall. She was generally believed to be totally bald,
and on her head she always wore a white dust cap with an elastic
band. She wore an apron, too, while making her rounds with her
slop wagon. Even when the weather got bad and she tied a wool
scarf about her head and wore an overcoat, she put on an apron
over the coat. Her hands and feet were delicately small, which
made the old-timers sure she was of Guinea stock that had come
to Tennessee out of South Carolina. What most touched the hearts
of old ladies on Jackson and Jefferson Streets was her little feet.
The sight of her feet "took them back to the old days," they said,
because Aunt Munsie still wore flat-heeled, high-button shoes.
Where ever did Munsie find such shoes any more?

She walked down the street, the very center of the street, with a
spry step and was continually turning her head from side to side,
as though looking at the old houses and trees for the first time. If
her sight was as bad as she sometimes let on it was, she probably
recognized the houses only by their roof lines against the Thornton
sky. Since this was nearly thirty years ago, most of the big Vic-
torian and ante-bellum houses were still standing, though with
their yard fences already gone and their lovely gingerbread work
beginning to go. (It went first from houses where there was some
one, like Dr. Tolliver, with a special eye for style and for keeping
up with the times.) The streets hadn't yet been broadened—or
only Nashville Street had—and the maples and elms met above the

streets. In the autumn, their leaves covered the high banks and filled the deep ditches on either side. The dark macadam surfacing itself was barely wide enough for two automobiles to pass. Aunt Munsie, pulling her slop wagon, which was a long, low, four-wheeled vehicle about the size and shape of a coffin, paraded down the center of the street without any regard for, if with any awareness of, the traffic problems she sometimes made. Grasping the wagon's decidedly sawed-off-looking tongue, she pulled it after her with a series of impatient jerks, as though that tongue were the arm of some very stubborn, overgrown white child she had to nurse in her old age. Strangers in town or trifling high-school boys would blow their horns at her, but she was never known to so much as glance over her shoulder at the sound of a horn. Now and then, a pedestrian on the sidewalk would call out to the driver of an automobile, "She's so deaf she can't hear it thunder."

It wouldn't have occurred to anyone in Thornton—not in those days—that something ought to be done about Aunt Munsie and her wagon for the sake of the public good. In those days, everyone had equal rights on the streets of Thornton. A vehicle was a vehicle, and a person was a person, each with the right to move as slowly as he pleased and to stop where and as often as he pleased. In the Thornton mind, there was no imaginary line down the middle of the street, and, indeed, no one there at that time had heard of drawing a real line on *any* street. It was merely out of politeness that you made room for others to pass. Nobody would have blown a horn at an old colored woman with her slop wagon—nobody but some Yankee stranger or a trifling high-school boy or maybe old Mr. Ralph Hadley in a special fit of temper. When citizens of Thornton were in a real hurry and got caught behind Aunt Munsie, they leaned out their car windows and shouted, "Aunt Munsie, can you make a little room?" And Aunt Munsie didn't fail to hear *them*. She would holler "Hai-ee, now! Whee! Look-a-here!" and jerk her wagon to one side. As they passed her, she would wave her little hand and grin a toothless, pink-gummed grin.

Yet, without any concern for the public good, Aunt Munsie's friends among the white women began to worry more and more about the danger of her being run down by an automobile. They talked among themselves and they talked to her about it. They wanted her to give up collecting slop, now she had got so blind and deaf. "Pshaw," said Aunt Munsie, closing her eyes contemptuously. "Not me." She meant by that that no one would dare run into her or her wagon. Sometimes when she crossed the Square on a busy Saturday morning or on a first Monday, she would hold up one hand with the palm turned outward and stop all traffic until she was safely across and in the alley beside the hotel.

Thornton wasn't even then what it had been before the Great World War. In every other house, there was a stranger or a mill hand who had moved up from Factory Town. Some of the biggest old places stood empty, the way Dr. Tolliver's had until it burned. They stood empty not because nobody wanted to rent them or buy them but because the heirs who had gone off somewhere making money could never be got to part with "the home place." The story was that Thad Tolliver nearly went crazy when he heard their old house had burned, and wanted to sue the town, and even said he was going to help get the Republicans into office. Yet Thad had hardly put foot in the house since the day his daddy died. It was said the Tolliver house had caught fire from the Major Pettigru house, which had burned two nights before, and no doubt it had. Sparks could have smoldered in that roof of rotten shingles for a long time before bursting into flame. Some even said the Pettigru house might have caught from the Johnston house, which had burned earlier that same fall. But Thad knew and Will knew and everybody knew the town wasn't to blame, and knew there was no firebug. Why, those old houses stood there empty year after year, and in the fall the leaves fell from the trees and settled around the porches and stoops, and who was there to rake the leaves? Maybe it was a good thing those houses burned, and maybe it would have been as well if some of the houses that still had people in them burned, too. There were houses in Thornton the heirs had never left that looked far worse than the Tolliver or the Pettigru or the Johnston house ever had. The people who lived in them were the ones who gave Aunt Munsie the biggest fool answers to her question, the people whom she soon quit asking her question of or even passing the time of day with, except when she couldn't help it, out of politeness. For, truly, to Aunt Munsie there were things under the sun worse than going off and getting rich in Nashville and Memphis and even in Washington, D.C. This was the subject she and her daughter Lucrecie mouthed at each other about across their back fence sometimes. Lucrecie was shiftless, and she liked shiftless white people like the ones who didn't have the ambition to leave Thornton. She thought their shiftlessness showed they were *quality*. "Quality?" Aunt Munsie would echo, her voice full of sarcasm. "Whee! Hai-ee! You talk like *you* was *my* mammy, Crecie. Well, if there be quality, there be quality *and* quality. There's quality and there's *has-been* quality, Crecie." There was no end to that argument Aunt Munsie had with Crecie, and it wasn't at all important to Aunt Munsie. The people who still lived in these houses—the ones she called has-been quality— meant little more to her than the mill hands, and the strangers from up North who ran the Piggly Wiggly, the five-and-ten-cent store, and the roller-skating rink.

There was this to be said, though, for the has-been quality: They knew *who* Aunt Munsie was, and in a limited, literal way they understood what she said. But those *others*—why, they thought Aunt Munsie a beggar, and she knew they did. They spoke of her as Old What You Have for Mom, because that's what they thought she was saying when she called out, "What you hear from 'em?" Their ears were not attuned to that soft "r" she put in "from" or the elision that made "from 'em" sound to them like "for Mom." Many's the time Aunt Munsie had seen, or sensed the presence of, one of those *other* people, watching from next door, when Miss Leonora Lovell, say, came down her front walk and handed her a little parcel of scraps across the ditch. Aunt Munsie knew what they thought of her—how they laughed at her and felt sorry for her and despised her all at once. But, like the has-been quality, they didn't matter, never had, never would.

Oh, they mattered in a way to Lucrecie. Lucrecie thought about them and talked about them a lot. She called them "white trash" and even "radical Republicans." It made Aunt Munsie grin to hear Crecie go on, because she knew Crecie got all her notions from her own has-been-quality people. And so it didn't matter, except that Aunt Munsie knew Crecie truly had all sorts of good sense and had only been carried away and spoiled by such folks as she had worked for, such folks as had really raised Crecie from the time she was big enough to run errands for them, fifty years back. In her heart, Aunt Munsie knew that even Lucrecie didn't

matter to her the way a daughter might. It was because while Aunt
Munsie had been raising a family of white children, a different sort
of white people from hers had been raising her own child, Crecie.
Sometimes, if Aunt Munsie was in her chicken yard or out in her
little patch of cotton when Mr. Thad or Mr. Will arrived, Crecie
would come out to the fence and say, "Mama, some of your
chillun's out front."

Miss Leonora Lovell and Miss Patty Bean, and especially Miss
Lucille Satterfield, were all the time after Aunt Munsie to give up
collecting slop. "You're going to get run over by one of those
crazy drivers, Munsie," they said. Miss Lucille was the widow of
old Judge Satterfield. "If the Judge were alive, Munsie," she said,
"I'd make him find a way to stop you. But the men down at the
courthouse don't listen to the women in this town any more. And I
think they'd be 'most too scared of you to do what I want them to
do." Aunt Munsie wouldn't listen to any of that. She knew that if
Miss Lucille had come out there to her gate, she must have *something* she was going to say about Mr. Thad or Mr. Will. Miss
Lucille had two brothers and a son of her own who were lawyers
in Memphis, and who lived in style down there and kept Miss
Lucille in style here in Thornton. Memphis was where Thad Tolliver had his Ford-and-Lincoln agency, and so Miss Lucille always
had news about Thad, and, indirectly, about Will, too.

"Is they doin' any good? What you hear from 'em?" Aunt
Munsie asked Miss Lucille one afternoon in early spring. She had
come along just when Miss Lucille was out picking some of the
jonquils that grew in profusion on the steep bank between the
sidewalk and the ditch in front of her house.

"Mr. Thad and his folks will be up one day in April, Munsie,"
Miss Lucille said in her pleasantly hoarse voice. "I understand Mr.
Will and his crowd may come for Easter Sunday."

"One day, and gone again!" said Aunt Munsie.

"We always try to get them to stay at least one night, but
they're busy folks, Munsie."

"When they comin' back sure enough, Miss Lucille?"

"Goodness knows, Munsie. Goodness knows. Goodness knows
when any of them are coming back to stay." Miss Lucille took
three quick little steps down the bank and hopped lightly across

the ditch. "They're prospering so, Munsie," she said, throwing her chin up and smiling proudly. This fragile lady, this daughter, wife, sister, mother of lawyers (and, of course, the darling of all their hearts), stood there in the street with her pretty little feet and shapely ankles close together, and holding a handful of jonquils before her as if it were her bridal bouquet. "They're *all* prospering so, Munsie. Mine *and* yours. You ought to go down to Memphis to see them now and then, the way I do. Or go up to Nashville to see Mr. Will. I understand he's got an even finer establishment than Thad. They've done well, Munsie—yours *and* mine—and we can be proud of them. You owe it to yourself to go and see how well they're fixed. They're rich men by our standards in Thornton, and they're going farther—*all* of them."

Aunt Munsie dropped the tongue of her wagon noisily on the pavement. "What I want go see 'em for?" she said angrily and with a lowering brow. Then she stooped and, picking up the wagon tongue again, she wheeled her vehicle toward the center of the street, to get by Miss Lucille, and started off toward the Square. As she turned out into the street, the brakes of a car, as so often, screeched behind her. Presently everyone in the neighborhood could hear Mr. Ralph Hadley tooting the insignificant little horn on his mama's coupé and shouting at Aunt Munsie in his own tooty voice, above the sound of the horn. Aunt Munsie pulled over, making just enough room to let poor old Mr. Ralph get by but without once looking back at him. Suddenly, before Mr. Ralph could get his car started again, Miss Lucille was running along beside Aunt Munsie, saying, "Munsie, you be careful! You're going to meet your death on the streets of Thornton, Tennessee!"

"Let 'em," said Aunt Munsie. Miss Lucille didn't know whether Munsie meant "Let 'em run over me; I don't care" or meant "Let 'em just dare!" Miss Lucille soon turned back, without Aunt Munsie's ever looking at her. And when Mr. Ralph Hadley did get his motor started, and sailed past in his mama's coupé, Aunt Munsie didn't give him a look, either. Nor did Mr. Ralph turn his face to look at Aunt Munsie. He was on his way to the drugstore, to pick up his mama's prescriptions, and he was too entirely put out, peeved, and upset to endure even the briefest exchange with that ugly, uppity old Munsie of the Tollivers'.

Aunt Munsie continued pulling her slop wagon toward the

Square. There was a more animated expression on her face than usual, and every so often her lips would move rapidly and emphatically over a phrase or sentence. Why should she go to Memphis and Nashville and see how rich they were? No matter how rich they were, what difference did it make, if they didn't own any land, or none in Cameron County. She had heard the old Doctor tell them—tell both his boys and his girls, and the old lady, too, in her day—that nobody was rich who didn't own land, and nobody stayed rich who didn't see after his land first-hand. But, of course, Aunt Munsie had herself mocked the old Doctor to his face for going on about land so much. She used to tell him she hadn't ever seen *him* behind a plow. And was anybody ever more scared of a mule than Dr. Tolliver was? Mules or horses, either? Aunt Munsie had heard him say that the happiest day of his life was the day he first learned that the horseless carriage was a reality.

No, it wasn't really to own land that Thad and Will ought to come back to Thornton. It was more that if they were going to be rich, they ought to come home, where their money counted for something. How could Will or Thad ever be rich anywhere else? They could just have a lot of money in the bank, that was all—like that mill manager from Chi. The mill manager could have a yard full of big cars and a stucco house as big as you like, but who would ever take him for rich? Aunt Munsie would sometimes say all these things to Crecie, or something as nearly like them as she could find words for. Crecie might nod her head in agreement or she might be in a mood to say being rich wasn't any good for anybody and didn't matter, and that you could live on just being quality better than on being rich in Thornton. "Quality's better than land or better than money in the bank here," Crecie would say.

Aunt Munsie would sneer at her and say, "It never were."

Lucrecie could talk all she wanted about the old times! Aunt Munsie knew too much about what they were like, for both the richest white folks and the blackest field hands. Nothing about the old times was as good as these days, and there were going to be better times yet when Mr. Thad and Mr. Will came back. Everybody lived easier now than they used to, and were better off. She could never be got to reminisce about her childhood in slavery, or her life with her husband, or even about those halcyon days after the old Mizziz had died and Aunt Munsie's word had become law in the Tolliver household. Without being able to book-read or even to make numbers, she had finished raising the whole pack of tow-headed Tollivers just as the Mizziz would have wanted it done. The Doctor told her she *had* to—he didn't ever once think about getting another wife, or taking in some cousin, not after his "Molly darling"—and Aunt Munsie *did*. But, as Crecie said, when a time was past in her mama's life, it seemed to be gone and done with in her head, too.

Lucrecie would say frankly she thought her mama was "hard about people and things in the world." She talked about her mama not only to the Blalocks, for whom she had worked all her life, but to anybody else who gave her an opening. It wasn't just about her mama, though, that she would talk to anybody. She liked to talk, and she talked about Aunt Munsie not in any ugly, resentful way but as she would about the rainy season or where the fire was last night. (Crecie was twice the size of her mama, and black the way her old daddy had been, and loud and good-natured the way he was—or at least the way Aunt Munsie wasn't. You wouldn't have known they were mother and daughter, and not many of the young people in town did realize it. Only by accident did they live next door to each other; Mr. Thad and Mr. Will had bought Munsie her house, and Crecie had heired hers from her second husband.) *That* was how she talked about her mama—as she would have about any lonely, eccentric, harmless neighbor. "I may be dead wrong, but I think Mama's kind of hardhearted," she would say. "She's a good old soul, I reckon, but when something's past, it's gone and done with for Mama. She don't think about day before yestiddy—or yestiddy, either. I don't know, maybe that's the way to be. Maybe that's why the old soul's gona outlive us all." Then, obviously thinking about what a picture of health she herself was at sixty, Crecie would throw back her head and laugh so loud you might hear her out at the fairgrounds.

Crecie, however, knew her mama wasn't honest-to-God mean and hadn't ever been mean to the Tolliver children, the way the Blalocks liked to make out she had. All the Tolliver children but Mr. Thad and Mr. Will had quarrelled with her for good by the

time they were grown, but they had quarrelled with the old Doctor, too (and as if they were the only ones who shook off their
old folks this day and time). When Crecie talked about her mama,
she didn't spare her anything, but she was fair to her, too. And
it was in no hateful or disloyal spirit that she took part in the
conspiracy that finally got Aunt Munsie and her slop wagon off
the streets of Thornton. Crecie would have done the same for
any neighbor. She had small part enough, actually, in that conspiracy. Her part was merely to break the news to Aunt Muncie
that there was now a law against keeping pigs within the city
limits. It was a small part but one that no one else quite dared to
take.

"They ain't no such law!" Aunt Munsie roared back at Crecie.
She was slopping her pigs when Crecie came to the fence and
told her about the law. It had seemed the most appropriate time
to Lucrecie. "They ain't never been such a law, Crecie," Aunt
Munsie said. "Every house on Jackson and Jefferson used to keep
pigs."

"It's a brand-new law, Mama."

Aunt Munsie finished bailing out the last of the slop from her
wagon. It was just before twilight. The last, weak rays of the sun
colored the clouds behind the mock-orange tree in Crecie's yard.
When Aunt Munsie turned around from the sty, she pretended
that that little bit of light in the clouds hurt her eyes, and turned
away her head. And when Lucrecie said that everybody had until the first of the year to get rid of their pigs, Aunt Munsie was
in a spell of deafness. She headed out toward the crib to get
some corn for the chickens. She was trying to think whether anybody else inside the town still kept pigs. Herb Mallory did—two
doors beyond Crecie. Then Aunt Munsie remembered Herb didn't
pay city taxes. The town line ran between him and Shad Willis.

That was sometime in June, and before July came, Aunt Munsie
knew all there was worth knowing about the conspiracy. Mr.
Thad and Mr. Will had each been in town for a day during the
spring. They and their families had been to her house and sat on
the porch; the children had gone back to look at her half-grown
collie dog and the two hounds, at the old sow and her farrow
of new pigs, and at the frizzliest frizzly chicken Aunt Munsie had

ever had. And on those visits to Thornton, Mr. Thad and Mr. Will had also made their usual round among their distant kin and close friends. Everywhere they went, they had heard of the near-accidents Aunt Munsie was causing with her slop wagon and the real danger there was of her being run over. Miss Lucille Satterfield and Miss Patty Bean had both been to the Mayor's office and also to see Judge Lawrence to try to get Aunt Munsie "ruled" off the streets, but the men in the courthouse and in the Mayor's office didn't listen to the women in Thornton any more. And so either Mr. Thad or Mr. Will—how would which one of them it was matter to Munsie?—had been prevailed upon to stop by Mayor Lunt's office, and in a few seconds' time had set the wheels of conspiracy in motion. Soon a general inquiry had been made in the town as to how many citizens still kept pigs. Only two property owners besides Aunt Munsie had been found to have pigs on their premises, and they, being men, had been docile and reasonable enough to sell what they had on hand to Mr. Will or Mr. Thad Tolliver. Immediately afterward—within a matter of weeks, that is—a city ordinance had been passed forbidding the possession of swine within the corporate limits of Thornton. Aunt Munsie had got the story bit by bit from Miss Leonora and Miss Patty and Miss Lucille and others, including the constable himself, whom she didn't hesitate to stop right in the middle of the Square on a Saturday noon. Whether it was Mr. Thad or Mr. Will who had been prevailed upon by the ladies she never ferreted out, but that was only because she did not wish to do so.

The constable's word was the last word for her. The constable said yes, it was the law, and he admitted yes, he had sold his own pigs—for the constable was one of those two reasonable souls—to Mr. Thad or Mr. Will. He didn't say which of them it was, or if he did, Aunt Munsie couldn't remember it. After her interview with the constable, Aunt Munsie never again exchanged words with any human being about the ordinance against pigs. That afternoon, she took a fishing pole from under her house and drove the old sow and the nine shoats down to Herb Mallory's, on the outside of town. They were his, she said, if he wanted them, and he could pay her at killing time.

It was literally true that Aunt Munsie never again exchanged words with anyone about the ordinance against pigs or about the conspiracy she had discovered against herself. But her daughter Lucrecie had a tale to tell about what Aunt Munsie did that afternoon after she had seen the constable and before she drove the pigs over to Herb Mallory's. It was mostly a tale of what Aunt Munsie said to her pigs and to her dogs and her chickens.

Crecie was in her own back yard washing her hair when her mama came down the rickety porch steps and into the yard next door. Crecie had her head in the pot of suds, and so she couldn't look up, but she knew by the way Mama flew down the steps that there was trouble. "She came down them steps like she was wasp-nest bit, or like some youngon who's got hisself wasp-nest bit—and her all of eighty, I reckon!" Then, as Crecie told it, her mama scurried around in the yard for a minute or so like she thought Judgment was about to catch up with her, and pretty soon she commenced slamming at something. Crecie wrapped a towel about her soapy head, squatted low, and edged over to the plank fence. She peered between the planks and saw what her mama was up to. Since there never had been a gate to the fence around the pigsty, Mama had taken the wood axe and was knocking a hole in it. But directly, just after Crecie had taken her place by the plank fence, her mama had left off her slamming at the sty and turned about so quickly and so exactly toward Crecie that Crecie thought the poor, blind old soul had managed to spy her squatting here. Right away, though, Crecie realized it was not *her* that Mama was staring at. She saw that all Aunt Munsie's chickens and those three dogs of hers had come up behind her, and were clucking and whining to know why she didn't stop that infernal racket and put out some feed for them.

Crecie's mama set one hand on her hip and rested the axe on the ground. "Just look at yuh!" she said, and then she let the chickens and the dogs—and the pigs, too—have it. She told them what a miscrable bunch of creatures they were, and asked them what right they had to always be looking for handouts from her. She sounded like the boss-man who's caught all his pickers laying off before sundown, and she sounded, too, like the preacher giving his sinners Hail Columbia at camp meeting. Finally, shouting explosively, "Now, g'wine! G'wine! G'wine! G'wine widja!," and swinging the axe wide and broad above their heads, she sent the dogs howling under the house and the chickens scattering in every direction. Only the collie pup, of the three dogs, didn't scamper to the farthest corner underneath the house. He stopped under the steps, and not two seconds later he was poking his long head out again and showing the whites of his doleful brown eyes. Crecie's mama took a step toward him and then she halted. "You want to know what's the commotion about? I reckoned you would," she said with profound contempt, as though the collie were a more reasonable soul than the other animals, and as though there were nothing she held in such thorough disrespect as reason. "I tell you what the commotion's about," she said. "They *ain't* comin' back. They ain't never comin' back. They ain't never had no notion of comin' back." She turned her head to one side, and the only explanation Crecie could find for her mama's next words was that that collie pup did look so much like Miss Lucille Satterfield.

"Why don't I go down to Memphis or up to Nashville and see 'em sometime, like *you* does?" Aunt Munsie asked the collie. "I tell you why. Becaze I ain't nothin' to 'em in Memphis, and they ain't nothin' to me in Nashville. *You* can go!" she said, advancing and shaking the big axe at the dog. "A collie dog's a collie dog anywhar. But Aunt Munsie, she's just their Aunt Munsie here in Thornton. I got sense enough to see *that*." The collie slowly pulled his head back under the steps, and Aunt Munsie watched for a minute to see if he would show himself again. When he didn't, she went and jerked the fishing pole out from under the house and headed toward the pigsty. Crecie remained squatting beside the fence until her mama and the pigs were out in the street and on their way to Herb Mallory's.

That was the end of Aunt Munsie's keeping pigs and the end of her daily rounds with her slop wagon, but it wasn't the end of Aunt Munsie. She lived on for nearly twenty years after that, till long after Lucrecie had been put away, in fine style, by the Blalocks. Ever afterward, though, Aunt Munsie seemed different to people. They said she softened, and everybody said it was a change for the better. She would take paper money from under her carpet, or out of the chinks in her walls, and buy things for up at the church, or buy her own whiskey when she got sick, instead of making somebody bring her a nip. On the Square, she would laugh and holler with the white folks the way Crecie and all the other old-timers did, and she even took to tying a bandanna about her head—took to talking old-nigger foolishness, too, about the Bell Witch, and claiming she remembered the day General N. B. Forrest rode into town and saved all the cotton from the Yankees at the depot. When Mr. Will and Mr. Thad came to see her with their families, she got so she would reminisce with them about their daddy and tease them about all the silly little things they had done when they were growing up. "Mr. Thad —him still in kilts, too—he say, 'Aunt Munsie, reach down in yo' stockin' and get me a copper cent. I want some store candy.'" She told them about how Miss Yola Ewing, the sewing woman, heard her threatening to bust Will's back wide open when he broke the lamp chimney, and how Miss Yola went to the Doctor and told him he ought to run Aunt Munsie off. Aunt Munsie and the Doctor had had a big laugh about it in the kitchen, and Miss Yola must have eavesdropped on them, because she left without finishing the girls' Easter dresses.

The visits from Mr. Thad and Mr. Will continued as long as Aunt Munsie lived, but she never asked them any more about when they were sure enough coming back. And the children, though she hugged them more than ever—and, toward the last, there were the children's children to be hugged—never set foot in her back yard again. Aunt Munsie lived on for nearly twenty years, and when they finally buried her, they put on her tombstone that she was aged one hundred years, though nobody knew how old she was. There was no record of when she was born. All anyone knew was that in her last years she had said she was a girl helping about the big house when freedom came. That would have made her probably about twelve years old in 1865, according to her statements and depictions. But all agreed that in her old age Aunt Munsie, like other old darkies, was not very reliable about such things. Her spirit softened, and she became not very reliable about facts.

REYNOLDS PRICE

Uncle Grant

Supposing he could know I have thought of him all this week. Supposing I was not three thousand miles from northeast North Carolina and supposing he had not been dead six years and I could find him and say, "I have thought of you all this week"—then he would be happy. Supposing though he was alive and I was still here in England—in Oxford whose light and color and trees and even grass would be strange to him as the moon (as they are to me)—and supposing he heard I had thought of him. It would go more or less like this. He would be in my aunt's kitchen in a straight black chair near the stove, having finished his breakfast. My aunt would have finished before he started and by then would be spreading beds or sweeping the porch, in her nightdress still. So he would be alone—his natural way, the way he had spent, say, sixty per cent of his life, counting sleep. His back would be straight as the chair, but his body would lean to the left, resting. The way he rested was to feel out the table beside him with his left elbow (an apple-green table with red oilcloth for a cover) and finding a spot, press down and then lay his head, his *face*, in his hand. His long right arm would lie on his hollow flank, the fingers hinged on the knee, and his legs would be clasped, uncrossed not to wrinkle the starched khaki trousers and ending in high-top shoes that, winter or summer, would be slashed into airy patterns, clean as the day they were bought, just ventilated with a razor blade. His white suspenders would rise from his waist to his shoulders, crossing the starched gray shirt (never with a tie but always buttoned at the neck and when he was dressed, pinned with a dull gold bar), but his face would be covered, his eyes. Only the shape of his skull would be clear—narrow and long, pointed at the chin, domed at the top—and the color of the skin that covered it, unbroken by a single hair except sparse brows, the color of a penny polished down by years of thumbs till Lincoln's face is a featureless shadow but with red life running beneath. That way he would be resting—not waiting, just resting as if he had worked when all he had done was wake at six and reach to his radio and lie on till seven, hearing music and thinking, then shaving and dressing and spreading his bed and stepping through the yard to the kitchen to eat what my aunt cooked (after she fired the stove if it was winter)—and he would rest till half-past eight when the cook would come and say towards him "Mr. Grant" (they were not good friends) and towards my aunt down the hall, "Miss Ida, here's you a letter," having stopped at the post office on her way. My aunt would come and stand by the stove and read with lips moving silent and then say, "Look, Uncle Grant. Here's a letter from Reynolds." He would look up squinting while she read out something like, " 'Tell Uncle Grant I am thinking about him this week,' " but before she could read any more, he would slap his flank and spring to his feet, rocking in his lacework shoes, opening and shutting his five-foot-ten like a bellows, and flicking at his ears—"Great God A-mighty! Where *is* Reynolds?" When she said "England" he would say, "Over yonder with them Hitalians and he been thinking about Grant? Great God A-mighty!" and then trail off into laughing and then for a long time to come into smiling. He would be happy that whole day and it is a fact—there is no one alive or dead I could have made happier with eight or ten words.

But he is dead and the reason I have thought of him these few days is strange—not because I remembered some joke on him and certainly not from seeing his likeness in the blue-black Negroes of the Oxford streets but because I went in a store to buy postcards and saw a card from the Berlin Museum—on a black background an Egyptian head, the tall narrow skull rocked back on the stalky neck, the chin offered out like a flickering tongue, the waving lips set in above (separate as if they were carved by a better man), the ears with their heavy lobes pinned close to the skull, and the black-rimmed sockets holding no eyes at all. I looked on, not knowing why, and turned the card over. The head was Amenhotep IV, pharaoh of Egypt in the eighteenth dynasty who canceled the worship of bestial gods and changed his name to Akhnaton, "it pleases Aton," the one true god, the streaming disc, the sun. I bought the card and left the shop and walked ten yards and said to myself in the street what I suddenly knew, "It's the one picture left of Uncle Grant."

His full name as far as we knew was Grant Terry, and he said he was born near Chatham, Virginia which is some hundred miles to the left of Richmond. (There are still white Terrys near there from whom his family would have taken its name.) He never knew his age but in 1940 when he heard of Old Age Assistance and wanted it (you had to show proof you were sixty-five), my father took him to our doctor who said, "I'll certify him— sure—but if those Welfare Workers took a look at his eyes, they wouldn't need *my* guarantee. He's well past seventy." So assuming he was seventy-five in 1940, that would make him born around 1865—maybe born into freedom and named for a general his parents heard of who set them free—but we didn't know about his youth, what he did to live when he was growing in the years after the war. There was nothing much he could have done but farm for somebody—chopping or picking cotton or ginning cotton or sawing pine timber or at best tending somebody's yard. We did know he had a wife named Ruth who gave him a son named Felix. It is the one thing I recall him telling me from his past (and he told me more than once, never with tears and some- times with laughing at the end as if it was just his best true story)—"When I left my home in Virginia to come down here, I said to Ruth and my boy, 'I'll see you in Heaven if I don't come back.'" And he never went back.

He came south eighty miles to North Carolina. He told my fa- ther he came in a road gang hired by a white contractor to pave the Raleigh streets, but he never said when he came—not to me anyhow, not to anybody still alive. He never said why he came to Macon either. (The streets of Macon are still not paved.) Maybe he had done his Raleigh work and meant to head back to Ruth and Felix but never got farther than sixty miles, stopping in Macon, population two hundred, in Warren County which touches the Virginia line. Or maybe he came to Macon with a railroad gang. (That seems a fair guess. He always called Macon a "seaport town." It was more than a hundred miles from the sea. What he meant was Seaboard Railway—the Norfolk-to-Raleigh tracks split Macon.) Anyhow, he was there by the time I was born in 1933 though he wasn't attached to us, and his work by then—whatever it had been before—was growing things. He planted people's flowers and hoed them, raked dead leaves and burned them, and tended lawns—what lawns there were in Macon where oak tree shade and white sand soil discouraged grass —and then he began tending me.

Not that I needed much tending. My mother was always there and my aunt down the road, and a Negro girl named Millie Mae looked after me in the morning. But sometimes in the evening my parents went visiting or to a picture show (not often, it being the deep Depression), and then Uncle Grant would sit by me while I slept. I don't know why they selected him, *trusted* him, when my aunt could have kept me or Millie Mae. Maybe they thought he could make me grow. (When he first came to Macon and asked for work and somebody said, "What can you do?" he said, "I can make things grow" so they gave him a chance, and he proved it the rest of his life—till my father could say, "Uncle Grant could stick a Coca-Cola bottle in the ground and raise you an ice-cold drink by sunup tomorrow." And God knew I needed growing—I had mysterious convulsions till I was four, sudden blue twitching rigors that rushed me unconscious into sight of death every three or four months.) The best reason though would be that, having no friends of his own, he had taken to me, and there is a joke which seems to show that. One evening when I was nearly two, my parents left me with him, saying they would be back late and that he could sleep in an army cot in my room. But they came back sooner than they expected, and when they drove up under the trees, instead of the house being dark and quiet, there was light streaming from my bedroom and mouth-harp music and laughing enough for a party. In surprise they crept to the porch and peeped in. My high-railed iron bed was by the window, and I was in it in outing pajamas but not lying down—facing Uncle Grant who was standing on the floor playing harp music while I danced in time and laughed. Then he knocked out the spit and

passed the harp to me, and I blew what I could while he clapped
hands. And then they stopped it—not being angry but saying I
had better calm down and maybe Uncle Grant shouldn't pass the
harp to me in case of germs (I had already caught gingivitis from
chewing a brass doorknob)—and that was our first joke on him.

It went on like that another year—him working the yard off
and on and staying with me odd evenings—and then my father
changed jobs (*got* a job after six years of failing to sell insurance
to wiped-out farmers) and we left Macon, going west a hundred
miles to Asheboro, still in North Carolina, where we lived in a
small apartment. Uncle Grant of course stayed on in Macon—he
still wasn't ours and we had no lawn of our own, no room for
him—but before long my father sent bus fare to my aunt and
asked her to put Uncle Grant on the bus (Uncle Grant couldn't
read), and soon he arrived for his first visit. He spent the nights
in a Negro boardinghouse and the days and evenings in our
kitchen. There was nothing he could do to help except wash
dishes (he couldn't cook), but help wasn't what my father
wanted. He wanted just to talk and every evening after supper,
he stayed in the kitchen and talked to Uncle Grant till almost
time to sleep. I was too young then to listen—or if I listened, to
remember the things they said. They laughed a good deal
though—I remember that—and the rest of the time they talked
about the past. My mother says they did but *she* didn't listen, and
now they are dead and nobody knows why they sat there night
after night at a hard kitchen table under a bare light bulb, talking
on and on, and laughing. Unless they loved each other—meaning
there would come times when they needed to meet, and they
never explained the need to themselves. My father would just
send bus fare through my aunt or there would be a letter from
her saying Uncle Grant was ready for a visit and had asked her to
say he was coming, and we would go meet the bus, my father and
I—five or six times in the two years we lived in three small
rooms.

Then we bought two acres of land in the country near Asheboro and built a house. Or began to. The land needed clearing
first—of loblolly pines and blackjack oaks and redbugs and
snakes—so Uncle Grant came and spent the weekdays supervis-
ing that. He spent the nights at the same boardinghouse and as far

as we knew went nowhere and had no Negro friends, but he spent his Sundays with us. We would pick him up in the car after church—my father and I—and drive out to look at our land. He would tell us what trees had gone that week and beg our pardon for, say, sacrificing a dogwood that had stood in the carpenters' path. But what I remember about those mornings—I was five—are two things he did which changed my mind. One Sunday when the clearing had just begun, the three of us were walking around the land—I in shorts and what I called Jesus-sandals—and as we came to a pile of limbs and weeds, six feet of black snake streamed out. It was May and black snakes go crazy in May so he headed for me and reared on his tail to fight. My father and I were locked stiff in surprise, but before the snake could lash at me, Uncle Grant took one step sideways like lightning and grabbed the snake's tail and cracked him on the air like a leather whip. Then we all breathed deep and looked and laughed at two yards of limp dead snake in Uncle Grant's hand. The way that changed my mind was to make me see Uncle Grant, not as the nurse who sat with me nights or talked on and on to my father, but as a fearless hero to imitate, and I never saw him in the old tame way again, not for eight or nine years. Then another Sunday morning we were walking—the land was clear by this time and building had started, but there wasn't a blade of grass, only mud and thousands of rocks that looked identical to me— and Uncle Grant leaned down quick as he had for the snake and came up with a little rock and handed it to me. It was a perfect Indian arrowhead, and in my joy I said, "How in the world did you see it?" and he said, "I'm three parts Indian myself" which deepened the feeling I had had for him since the snake and also made our two rocky acres something grand—a hunting ground of the Occoneechees or a campsite or even, I hoped, a battlefield (though we never found a second head to prove it).

When the house was finished and we moved in, he came with us. There was one small room off the kitchen where the furnace was, and his bed was there and a little low table to carry the things he owned—in the daytime his shaving equipment and his extra shirt, and at night his precious belongings—an Ingersoll watch and a pocket knife. In the daytime he worked to grow us a lawn, and gradually, single-handed, he grew us a beauty. And once it was strong, he began to cut it—with a small hand sickle and his pocket knife. We had a lawn mower and he tried to use it but stopped, saying rocks were too plentiful still—the real reason being he could cut grass better, cut it *right*, by hand and if that meant bending to the ground all day at age about seventy-five and trimming two acres with a three-inch blade, then that was all right. It was what he could do, in spring and summer. In the fall he raked leaves, not waiting till the trees were bare and taking them all at once but raking all day every day. It was one of our jokes on him (a true joke—they were all true) that we once saw him run a few yards and catch a dead leaf as it fell, in the air, and grind it to dust in his hand. In the evening after us he ate at the kitchen counter and washed all our dishes and then went into his room and sat on his bed and looked at picture magazines. Sometimes my father would sit with him and I would fly in and out, but most of the time he sat in silence, thinking whatever his private thoughts were, till we gave him a radio.

That was Christmas 1939 and there wasn't much to hear except black war news, but nothing we gave him ever pleased him more. Not that he had seemed unhappy before—I don't think he thought about happiness—but now he would sit there on into the night. I would sit beside him long as my mother allowed in the dark (the only light was the radio dial), hearing our favorite things which were short-wave programs in German and Spanish with Morse Code bursting in like machine gun fire to make us laugh. We didn't understand a word and my father who thought we were fools would step to the door and shake his head at us in the dark, but Uncle Grant would slap his thigh and say, *"Listen to them Hitalians, Mr. Will!" Hitalians* was what he called all foreigners, and "Great God A-mighty" was his favorite excited expression, the one he used every time some Spaniard would speed up the news or "The Star-Spangled Banner" would play so before long of course I was saying it too—age six. At first I just said it with him when he laughed, but once I slipped and said it in front of my mother, and she asked him not to curse around me and made me stay out of his room for a while. With me being punished my father filled the gap by spending more time in the furnace room, and it was then the jokes piled up. Despite all the war news, he would have a new joke every evening—my father,

that is, on Uncle Grant. One night for instance after they had sat
an hour listening, they switched off the radio to let it cool and to
talk. They talked quite awhile till my father said, "Let's switch it
on. It's time for the midnight news" so they did, and there was
the news, waiting for them. When it had finished and music had
begun, Uncle Grant said, "When does they sleep, Mr. Will?" My
father said "Who?" and he said—pointing through the dark to
the radio—"Them little peoples in yonder." My father whose
work was electrical supplies explained about waves in the air
without wires and Uncle Grant nodded. But some time later
when they had sat up extra-late, Uncle Grant asked if it wasn't
bedtime. My father took the hint but was slow about leaving—
standing in the door, hearing the end of some program—so Uncle
Grant stood and unbuttoned his collar, then thought and
switched off the radio. My father said, "How come you did
that?" and he said, "I can't undress with them little peoples
watching, Mr. Will." So my father never tried explaining again.

Then after three years we lost the house and all that grass and
had to move to another apartment in Asheboro. By then I had a
year-old brother named Bill so again there was no room for Uncle Grant and nothing for him to do if there had been, and my
father explained it a month in advance—that much as we wanted
him around, we couldn't keep paying him three dollars a week
just to wash dishes and that if he stayed on in Asheboro he
would have to find someplace to sleep and hire-out to other people to pay his rent. He told my father he would think it over, and
he thought that whole last month, asking no advice, sitting by
himself most evenings as I was in school and busy and my father
was ashamed in his presence, and giving no sign of his plans till
the day we moved. He helped that day by packing china and
watching how the movers treated our furniture, and when everything had gone except his few belongings, my father said,
"Where are you going, Uncle Grant?" He said, "I'm sleeping in
that boardinghouse till I get you all's windows washed. Then I'm
going to Macon on the bus. I ain't hiring-out in this town."
(Asheboro was a stocking-mill town.) My father said, "You
might break your radio on the bus. Wait till Sunday and I'll
carry you." Uncle Grant said, "I been studying that—where am I
going to plug in a radio in Macon? You keep it here and if I

wants it I'll let you know." My father said, "Maybe when I get a little money I can trade it in on a battery set," and he said "Maybe you can" and two days later went to Macon by bus, saying he would stay with a Nego named Rommie Watson till he found a house. But somewhere in the hundred miles, for some reason, he changed his mind and when the bus set him down, he walked to my aunt's back door and asked could he sleep in her old smokehouse till he found a place of his own? She knew of course why we turned him loose so she told him Yes, and he swept it out and slept on an army cot, coming to her kitchen for meals but not eating well, not looking for a house of his own, not saying a word about work. My aunt finally asked him was he all right, and he said, "I will be soon as I get my bearings." In about two weeks he came in to breakfast with the cot rolled under his arm and his bag of belongings. When he had eaten he said he had found a house at the far end of Macon—a one-room house under oak trees in the yard of a Negro church. Then he left and was gone all day, all night, but my aunt looked out in the morning and there he was, trimming her bushes, having got some sort of bearings, enough to last two years.

We had turned him loose in 1942. He lived on thirteen years and he never let us take hold again. We stayed in Asheboro three years after he left—two years in that apartment and a year in a good-sized house—but he didn't come to visit in all that time. I don't know whether we asked him and if we did, what reason he gave for refusing. He just didn't come and he might have said he was too old. But he worked for my aunt every day, strong as ever, still trimming what he grew with a pocket knife, and the only way he showed age was by not taking supper in my aunt's kitchen. In summer he would stop about six, in winter about five—before dark—and put up his tools and come to the back door, and my aunt would give him cold biscuits and sometimes a little jar of syrup or preserves, and he would walk home a mile and a half and spend his evenings by a kerosene lamp, alone. But that was no change for him, being by himself.

What *was* a change was that after he had been back in Macon two years, he fell in some sort of love with a girl named Katie. She was not from Macon but had come there as cook to a cousin of ours who returned so she had no Negro friends either, and though she was no more than twenty, she began to sit with him some evenings. My aunt didn't know if they got beyond sitting, but she didn't worry much, not at first. Uncle Grant was pushing eighty and it seemed at first that Katie was good to him in ways that made him happy. My aunt *did* say to him once, "Uncle Grant, don't let that girl take your money away," and he said, "No'm. Every penny I lends her, she pay me back." But then it turned bad. After six months or so Katie began taking him to Warrenton on Saturdays (the county seat, five miles away), and they would drink fifty-cent wine called "Sneaky Pete," and every week he would have the few hairs shaved off his head (to hide them from Katie as they were white). For a while he managed to keep his drinking to Saturdays and to be cold-sober when he turned up for Sunday breakfast so my aunt didn't complain but finally he slipped. One Sunday he came in late—about nine—walking straight and of course dressed clean but old around the eyes and with his hat still on. He said "Good morning" and sat by the green kitchen table. My aunt said the same and, not really noticing, gave him a dish of corn flakes. He ate a few spoonfuls in silence. Then he sprang to the floor and slapped his flank and said, "What is the meaning of *this?*"—so loud she could smell the wine and pointing at his bowl. My aunt went over and there was a needle in his food. Thinking fast, she laughed and said, "Excuse me, Uncle Grant. I was sewing in here this week and somebody came to the door, and I stuck the needle in the cereal box, and it must have worked through." That was the truth and, sober, he would have known it, but he stood there rocking a little and then said, "Somebody trying to kill me is all I know." My aunt said, "If you are that big a fool, you can leave my house" so he stood another minute and then he left.

That was in late October—he had just started raking leaves. His shame kept him home the following day—and for two months to come. My aunt reckoned he would come back when he got hungry but he didn't. What food he got he bought from his neighbors or maybe Katie sneaked him things from our cousin's kitchen but he didn't show up at my aunt's, and every leaf fell and thousands of acorns, and she finally hired boys to clear them. He still hadn't showed up by Christmas when we arrived for three days. That was the first we knew of his shame. My fa ther said, "To be sure, he'll show up to see me," but my aunt said, "You are the *last* one he wants to see, feeling like he does," and my father saw she was right. We had brought him a box of Brown Mule chewing tobacco. He surely knew that—we gave him that every Christmas—and we waited but he didn't come. When we left on the 27th my father gave my aunt the Brown Mule and told her to save it till Uncle Grant showed up. She said in that case it would be bone-dry by the time he got it.

But for once she was wrong. About two weeks later in a hard cold spell his house burned down in the night from an overheated stove. My aunt heard that from her cook in the morning and heard that he got out unharmed with the clothes on his back so she packed a lard bucket with food and set our tobacco on top and sent it by the cook to where he was, which was at some neighbor's. The cook came back and said he thanked her and that afternoon he came. My aunt was nodding but the cook waked her and said, "Mr. Grant's out yonder on the porch, Miss Ida." She went and told him she was sorry to hear of his trouble and what was he going to do now? He said, "I don't hardly know but could I just sleep in the smokehouse till I get my bearings?" She thought and said, "Yes, if you'll stay there without having company." He knew who she meant and nodded and spent the rest of the day cleaning the smokehouse and getting the woodstove fit to use.

He stayed there without having company, working on the yard by day and on the smokehouse by night. It was just one room, twice as tall as wide, with pine walls and floor. He scrubbed every board—cold as it was—and when they were dry, tacked newspapers around the walls high as he could reach to keep out wind. And as winter passed he kept finding things to do to that one room till it looked as if he took it to be his home. So when spring came my aunt hired a carpenter, and he put plasterboard on the walls and linoleum underfoot and a lock on the door. Then she took back the army cot and bought an old iron bed and a good felt mattress and gave Uncle Grant a key to the door, saying, "This is your key. I'll keep the spare one in case you lose it." But he never lost it and he lived on there, having got the bearings, somehow or other, that lasted the rest of his life.

We moved back to Warren County in 1945. My father got a

job that let him live in Warrenton (or travel from there, selling freezers to farmers), and we lived in a hotel apartment, still with no yard of our own. But Sunday afternoons we would drive the five miles to Macon for supper with my aunt. When we got there we would sit an hour and talk, and then my father would rise and say he was stepping out back to see Uncle Grant and who wanted to come? That was a signal for me to say "Me," and for a year or so I said it and followed him to the smokehouse. Uncle Grant would have been waiting all afternoon and talk would begin by him asking me about school and what I was doing. I was twelve and wasn't doing much but keeping a diary so my answers wouldn't take long, and he would turn to my father, and they would begin where they left off the week before in the circles of remembering and laughing. Old as I was, I still didn't listen, but soon as they got underway, I would stand and walk round the room, reading the papers on the walls till I knew them by heart. (What I *did* hear was, week after week, my father offering to take Uncle Grant on one of his Virginia business trips and detour to Chatham so he could look up Felix his son and Ruth his wife if she was alive. Uncle Grant would say, "That's a good idea. Let me know when you fixing to go." But he never went. He rode with my father a number of times—down into South Carolina and as far west as Charlotte—but whenever they set the date for a trip to Virginia and the date drew near, Uncle Grant would find yard work that couldn't wait or get sick a day or two with rheumatism.) But a year of such Sundays passed, and I slowed down on the smokehouse visits. My father would rise as before and ask who was going with him to Uncle Grant's, and more and more my brother volunteered, not me. He was going on six, the age I had been when Uncle Grant cracked the snake and found me the arrowhead and we listened to Hitalian news together, so he stepped into whatever place Uncle Grant kept for me and gradually filled more and more of it. But not all, never all, because every time my father came back from a visit he would say, "Uncle Grant asked after you. Step out yonder and speak to him, son." I would look up from what I was doing—seventh grade arithmetic or a Hardy Boys mystery—and say, "Soon as I finish this," and of course before I finished, it would be dark and supper would be ready. But I always saw him after supper when he came in to eat and to wash our dishes—little fidgety meetings with nothing to talk about but how he was feeling and with gaps of silence getting longer and longer till I would say "Goodbye" and he would say "All right" and I would hurry out. (Occasionally though, he would move some way that detained me—by dropping the dishrag, say, and old as he was, stooping for it in a flash that recalled him reaching bare-handed for the snake to save me—and I would find things to say or look on awhile at his slow body, seeing how grand he had been and knowing how happy I could make him, just waiting around.)

It went on like that till the summer of 1947. Then we moved again—sixty miles, to Raleigh, into a house with two good yards and a steam-heated basement room—and as my father arranged, Uncle Grant followed in a day or so. He had not volunteered to follow, even when my father described the basement room and the grass and privet hedge that, since it was August, were nearly out of hand, so my father asked him—"Would you come up and help us get straight?" and he said, "I'll ask Miss Ida can I take off a week." She gave him the week and we gave him the fare and he came. He started next morning at the ankle-high grass, and by sundown he had cut a patch about twenty feet square and sat in the kitchen, bolt-upright but too tired to eat. My father saw the trouble and saw a way out—he said, "I am driving to Clinton tomorrow. Come on and keep me company in this heat." Uncle Grant accepted, not mentioning grass. And none of us mentioned it again. When they got back from Clinton two evenings later, he spent one night, and the next day he went to Macon for good. Busy as my father was, he took Uncle Grant by car and spent a night at my aunt's. Then he came back to Raleigh and at supper that evening said, "He is older than I counted on him being. He won't last long. So I bought him a battery radio to keep him company."

He was maybe eighty-two when he tackled our new lawn and lost. My father was forty-seven. Uncle Grant lasted eight years, working on my aunt's yard till eight months before he died (no slower than ever and with nothing but a boy to rake up behind him), spending his evenings with nothing but his battery radio (Katie having drunk herself jobless and vanished), complaining of nothing but sometimes numb feet, asking for nothing but

Brown Mule tobacco (and getting that whenever we visited, especially at Christmas). My father lasted six.

He died in February, 1954—my father. Cancer of the lung with tumors the size of bird eggs clustered in his throat which nobody noticed till he thought he had bronchitis and called on a doctor. It went very quickly—twenty-one days—and my aunt didn't tell Uncle Grant till she had to. Hoping for the best, she had seen no reason to upset him in advance, but when we phoned her that Sunday night, she put on her coat and went to the smokehouse and knocked. Uncle Grant cracked the door and seeing it was her (she had never called on him after dark before), said, "What's wrong, Miss Ida?" She stood on the doorstep—half of a granite millstone—and said, "Will Price is dead." The heat of his room rushed past her into the dark, and directly he said, "Sit down, Miss Ida," pointing behind him to his single chair. She was my *mother's* sister but she stepped in and sat on his chair, and he sat on the edge of his mattress. Some radio music played on between them, and according to her, he never asked a question but waited. So when she got breath enough, she said the funeral was Tuesday and that he could ride down with her and her son if he wanted to. He thought and said, "Thank you, no'm. I better set here," and she went home to bed. In the morning after his breakfast, he stepped to her bedroom door and called her out and handed her three dollar bills to go towards flowers and she took them. He didn't work all that day or come in again for food so she sent his supper by the cook who reported he wasn't sick, but before she left Tuesday morning for Raleigh, he was stripping ivy off the lightninged oak, too busy to do more than wave goodbye as the car rolled down to the road.

He just never mentioned my father, that was all—for his own reasons, never spoke my father's name in anybody's hearing again. My aunt came back from the funeral and gave him a full description, and he said, "It sounds mighty nice," and ever after that if she brought up the subject—remembering some joke of my father's for instance—he would listen and laugh a little if that was expected but at the first break, get up and leave the room. He went on speaking of others who were someway gone—Ruth his wife and Felix his son and once or twice even Katie—but never my father, not even the last time I saw him.

That was Christmas of 1954 and by then he was flat on his back in a Welfare Home near Warrenton, had been there nearly four months. Six months after my father's death, his feet and legs went back on him totally. He couldn't stand for more than ten minutes without going numb from his waist down, and one night he fell, going to the smokehouse from supper—on his soft grass—so he took his bed, and when he didn't come to breakfast, my aunt went out and hearing of the fall, asked her doctor to come. He came and privately told her nothing was broken—it was poor circulation which would never improve, and didn't she want him to find Uncle Grant a place with nurses? There was nothing she could do but agree, being old herself, and the doctor found space in the house of a woman named Sarah Cawthon who tended old Negroes for the Welfare Department. Then my aunt asked Uncle Grant if going there wasn't the wise thing for him—where he could rest with attention and regular meals and plenty of company and his radio and where she could visit him Saturdays, headed for Warrenton? He thought and said "Yes'm, it is," and she bought him two suits of pajamas and a flannel robe (he had always slept in long underwear), and they committed him early in September—her and her son—as the end of summer slammed down.

We didn't visit Macon in a body that Christmas. My mother wasn't up to it so we spent the day in Raleigh, but early on the 26th I drove to Macon to deliver our gifts and collect what was waiting for us. I stayed with my aunt most of the day, and her children and grandchildren came in for dinner, but after the eating, things got quiet and people took pains not to speak of the past, and at four o'clock I loaded up and said goodbye. My aunt followed me to the car and kissed me and said, "Aren't you going to stop by Sarah Cawthon's and see Uncle Grant?" I looked at the sky to show it was late, and she said, "It won't take long and nobody God made will appreciate it more." So I stopped by and knocked at the holly-wreathed door and Sarah Cawthon came. I said I would like to see Grant Terry, and she said, "Yes sir. Who is calling?" I smiled at that and said "Reynolds Price."—"Mr. Will Price's boy?"— "His oldest boy." She smiled too and said he was waiting for me and headed for a back bedroom. I paused at the door and she went ahead, flicking on the light, saying, "Mr. Grant, here's you a surprise." Then she walked out and I walked in, and the first thing I noticed was his neck. He was sitting up in bed in his clean pajamas. They were buttoned to the top, but they had no collar and his neck was bare. That was the surprise. I had just never seen it before, not down to his shoulders, and the sight of it now—so lean and long but the skin drawn tight—surprised me. *He* was not suprised. He had known *some* Price would turn up at Christmas, and seeing it was me, he laughed, "Great God A-mighty, Reynolds, you bigger than me." (I was twenty-one. I had reached my full growth some time before, but he still didn't say "*Mr.* Reynolds.") Then he pointed to a corner of the room where a two-foot plastic Christmas tree stood on a table, hung with a paper chain but no lights. There were two things under the tree on tissue paper—some bedroom shoes from my aunt and the box of Brown Mule my mother had mailed without telling me—and he said, "I thank you for my present," meaning the tobacco which he had not opened. I noticed when he laughed that his teeth were gone and remembered my aunt commenting on the strangeness of that—how his teeth had vanished since he took his bed, just dissolved with nobody's help. So the Brown Mule was useless, like the shoes. He never stood up any more, he said. But that was the nearest he came to speaking of his health, and I didn't ask questions except to say did he have a radio? He said "Two" and pointed to his own battery set on the far side of him and across the room to one by an empty bed. I asked whose that was and he said, "Freddy's. The Nigger that sleeps yonder." I asked where was Freddy now and he said, "Spending some time with his family, thank God. All that ails him is his water." But before he explained Freddy's symptoms, Sarah Cawthon returned with orange juice for both of us and a slice of fruitcake for me. Then she smoothed the sheets around Uncle Grant and said to him, "Tell Mr. Reynolds your New Year's resolution." He said, "What you driving at?" So she told me—"Mr. Grant's getting baptized for New Year. He's been about to run me crazy to get him baptized—ain't you, Mr. Grant?" He didn't answer, didn't look at her or me but down at his hands on the sheet, and she went on—"Yes sir, he been running me crazy to get him baptized, old as he is, so I have arranged it for New Year's Day with my preacher. I got a big old trough in the back yard, and we are bringing that in the kitchen and spreading a clean sheet in it and filling it up with nice warm water, and *under* he's going—ain't you, Mr. Grant?" Still looking down, he said he would think it over. She said, "Well, of course you are and we wish Mr. Reynolds could be here to see it, don't we?" Then she took our glasses and left. When her steps had faded completely, he looked up at me and said, "I ain't going to be baptized in no hog trough." I said I was sure it wasn't a hog trough, but if he didn't want to be dipped, I saw no reason why he should. He said, "It ain't *me* that wants it. It's that woman. She come in here—last week, I believe—and asked me was I baptized and I said, 'No, not to my knowledge' so she said, 'Don't you know you can't get to Heaven and see your folks till you baptized?'" He waited a moment and asked me, "Is that the truth?" And straight off I said, "No. You'll see everybody you want to see, I'm sure. Give them best wishes from me!" He laughed, "I'll do that thing," then was quiet a moment, and not looking at me, said, "There is two or three I hope to meet, but I ain't studying the rest." Then he looked and said, "You're sure about that?—what you just now told me?" and again not waiting I said I was sure so he smiled, and I reckoned I could leave. I stepped to his window and looked out at what was almost night—"Uncle Grant, I better be heading home." He said "Thank you, sir" (not saying what for), and I stopped at the foot of his bed and asked what I had to ask, what my father would have asked—"Is there any little thing I can do for you?" He said "Not a thing." I said, "You are not still worried about being baptized, are you?" and he said, "No, you have eased my mind. I can tell that woman *my* mind is easy, and if she want to worry, that's *her* red wagon." I laid my hand on the ridge of sheet that was his right foot—"If you need anything, tell Aunt Ida, and she'll either get it or let us know." He said, "I won't need nothing." Then I stepped to the door and told him "Goodbye," and he said "Thank you" again (still not saying what for) and—grinning—he would see me in Heaven if not any sooner. I grinned too and walked easy down Sarah Cawthon's hall and made it to the door without being heard and got in the car and started the sixty miles to Raleigh in full night alone, wondering part of the way (maybe fifteen minutes), "Have I sent him to Hell with my theology?" but knowing that was just a joke and smiling to myself and driving on, thinking gradually of my own business, not thinking of him at all, not working back to what he had been in previous days, feeling I had no reasons.

And went on till late last week—nearly seven years—not thinking of him more than, say fifteen seconds at a stretch, not even when he died just before his afternoon nap, the May after I saw him in December. Freddy his roommate told my aunt, "I was making another police dog and he died"—Freddy made dogs to sell, out of socks and knitting wool—and she and her son handled the funeral. We didn't go, my part of the family (my mother had a job by then and I was deep in college exams and my brother was too young to drive), but my mother sent flowers and they buried him at Mount Zion Church which he never attended, a mile from my aunt's, not in a Welfare coffin but in one she paid for, in a grave I have never seen.

Yet because of an accident—stopping to buy postcards—I have spent a week, three thousand miles from home, thinking of nothing but him, working back to what he may have been, to what we knew anyhow, finding I knew a good deal, finding *reasons*, and thinking how happy he would be if he could know, how long he would laugh, rocking in his lacework shoes, if he heard what reminded me of him (a Hitalian face on a card—Amenhotep IV, pharaoh of Egypt in the eighteenth dynasty who fathered six daughters but no son on Nefertiti his queen and canceled the worship of hawks and bulls and changed his name to Akhnaton, "it pleases Aton," the single god, the sun that causes growth)— and him the son of Negro slaves, named Grant maybe for the Union general (a name he could not recognize or write), who grew up near Chatham, Virginia, and made his one son Felix on a woman named Ruth and left them both to go south to work and somehow settled in Macon near us, finally with us (claiming he could make things grow, which he could), and tended me nights when I was a baby and our yard when we had one and for his own reasons loved my father and was loved by him and maybe loved me, *trusted* me enough to put his salvation in my hands that last day I saw him (him about ninety and me twenty-one) and believed what I said—that in Heaven he would meet the few folks he missed—and claimed he would see me there. And this is the point, this is what I know after this last week—that final joke, if it *was* a joke (him saying he would see me in Heaven), whoever it was on, it was not on him.

Biographical Sketches
of the Authors

JOSEPH CONRAD (1857–1924) was born Jozef Teodor Konrad Nalecz Korzeniowski near Mohilow, Poland, the son of the Polish translator of Shakespeare and a patriot who was exiled for a large part of Conrad's childhood. At seventeen Conrad left Poland to become a sailor, and by 1887 had worked himself up to a command in the British Merchant Marine. In 1893 John Galsworthy, who was traveling on Conrad's ship, the *Torrens*, encouraged him in the writing he had begun, and in 1894 Conrad settled in England, determined to become a novelist. Despite the greatness of the work he did during the first two decades of his career as a writer, during which he produced *The Nigger of the Narcissus* (1897), *Lord Jim* (1900), *Nostromo* (1904), *The Secret Agent* (1907) and *Under Western Eyes* (1911), it was not until 1913, with *Chance*, that he had a popular success. In 1889–1890 he travelled in the Congo and saw the world that is described in *Heart of Darkness*.

F. SCOTT FITZGERALD (1896–1940) was born in St. Paul, Minnesota. His father came of a gentle Maryland family; his mother, he once said, was "straight 1850 potato-famine Irish." He was educated at St. Paul Academy, Newman, and Princeton, where he was a friend of Edmund Wilson and of John Peale Bishop. His first book, *This Side of Paradise* (1920), created a sensation and for a few years he and his wife Zelda were spectacular figures around New York. In 1924 they moved to the Riviera, where he finished his best-known novel, *The Great Gatsby* (1925). In 1930 Zelda went insane and Fitzgerald settled in Baltimore, near her hospital, to try to save her from permanent insanity and himself from alcoholism. In 1934 he published his last com

711

plete novel, *Tender Is the Night,* and shortly thereafter moved to Hollywood, where he died, leaving behind him about half of another novel, *The Last Tycoon* (1941). During his brief career he wrote over one hundred and fifty short stories.

MARY MCCARTHY (1912–   ) was born in Seattle. Both her parents died when she was a child and she grew up in mixed circumstances that she has described in *Memories of a Catholic Girlhood* (1957). She was graduated from Vassar in 1933 and began her career as a writer doing reviews and theatrical criticism for *The Nation, The New Republic,* and *Partisan Review.* She has been married to Edmund Wilson and Bowden Broadwater and is now the wife of James Raymond West. In addition to literary and social criticism and her books on Venice and Florence, she has written half a dozen volumes of fiction, *The Company She Keeps* (1942), *The Oasis* (1949), *Cast a Cold Eye* (1950), *The Groves of Academe* (1952), *A Charmed Life* (1955), and the sensationally popular *The Group* (1963). She is a sharply satirical comic writer whose fiction is always very close to her actual experience.

DYLAN THOMAS (1914–1953) was born in Carmarthenshire, Wales, and educated at Swansea Grammar School, where his father was a teacher. After finishing school, he worked as a newspaperman and did some amateur acting, but he was a born poet, perhaps the most successful of his generation: a romantic of almost hypnotic rhetorical skill who could read his own verse magnificently. He made three highly successful, alcoholically spectacular reading tours in the United States, and died in New York during the course of the third. He wrote little poetry at the end of his life, when he was busy with readings and radio work. Apart from his poetry he wrote two books of prose fiction, *Portrait of the Artist as a Young Dog* (1940) and *Adventures in the Skin Trade* (1955).

FRANK O'CONNOR (1903–1966) was born Michael John O'Donovan, the only child of poor parents, in Cork. As a young man he was a member of the Irish Republican Army and was imprisoned during the troubles, about which he wrote some of his best stories. He worked for some time as a librarian in Cork and Dublin; during this time he did an immense amount of reading. During the 1930's he was a director of the Abbey Theatre. Toward the end of his life he lived a good deal in the United States. For him Chekhov was the greatest of all short-story writers; "I like," he once said, "the feeling I get when a story I've been trying to bring up in the right way gets up and tells me to go to hell." Like so many Irish writers of his generation, he was independent, unfashionable, and very gifted. He published thirty-two books—mostly collections of short stories—and five plays during his lifetime.

KATHERINE ANNE PORTER (1894–   ) was born at Indian Creek, Texas, into a large family that has provided her with the material for some of her best stories. She grew up in Texas and Louisiana and was educated at convent schools. She was in Paris during the 1920's and in Baton Rouge during the great days of the old *Southern Review;* she was then married to its business manager, Albert Erskine. More than most, she is a natural and independent storyteller and has always gone pretty much her own way as a writer. Since the publication of *Flowering Judas* (1930), her first collection of stories, she has been generally recognized as one of the most gifted writers of her generation. Her first and only novel, *Ship of Fools,* published in 1961, was a huge success.

JOHN UPDIKE (1932–   ) was born in Shillington, Pennsylvania, in what he calls "the western periphery of the O'Hara country," where his father was a high-school teacher. He was graduated from Harvard in 1954, and after a year at the Ruskin School of Drawing and Fine Art in London, he joined the staff of *The New Yorker,* for which he worked for two years. Since then he has lived in Ipswich, Massachusetts, writing. He has published three novels, *The Poor House Fair* (1959), *Rabbit, Run* (1960), and *The Centaur* (1963), and two volumes of short stories, *The Same Door* (1959) and *Pigeon Feathers* (1962), as well as several volumes of poems. He is a writer of great verbal skill who appears torn between a desire to write about the homely domestic life of America and a desire to make myths.

DORIS LESSING (1919–   ) was born in Persia, where her British father worked for the Imperial Bank of Persia. In 1925 the family moved to a large farm in Southern Rhodesia and there Doris Lessing grew up, attending a convent school in Salisbury. At eighteen she went to live and work in Salisbury, married, and had two children. Sometime around 1942 she became interested in communism, an interest which has continued to the present, and she is prohibited from returning to Rhodesia because of her political opinions. Her first marriage ended in divorce, and in 1949 she moved to London with her second husband, from whom she is now also divorced. Her books are close to her personal experience; she is much concerned with what she considers the basic conflict of conscience for socialists, the conflict between what is due to the needs of the collective and what to the needs of the individual. She has written over a dozen books, four of which are volumes of short stories, *This Was the Old Chief's Country* (1951), *Five* (1953), *African Stories* (1964, largely a reprint of the previous two collections), *The Habit of Loving* (1957), and *A Man and Two Women* (1963).

FLANNERY O'CONNOR (1925–1964) was born in Savannah and grew up in Milledgeville, Georgia. She was educated at Georgia State College

for Women and at the University of Iowa. In 1950 she began to suffer
from disseminated lupus, the disease that eventually killed her. She
lived most of her short life at home as an impatient invalid. She was a
devout and tough-minded Catholic ("If it were only a symbol," she
once said of the Eucharistic Symbol, "I'd say to hell with it"). In her
brief life she produced four books, *Wise Blood* (1952), *A Good Man
Is Hard To Find* (1955), *The Violent Bear It Away* (1960) and *Everything That Rises Must Converge* (1965). Her work combines her perfectly natural, intensely felt Catholicism with the sense of the grotesque that is common among Southern writers.

HENRY JAMES (1843–1916) was born in New York, the son of a
wealthy transcendentalist theologian. The senior James had distinctive
ideas about how to raise and educate children that had brilliant if odd
results in the cases of Henry and his brother William, the philosopher,
and less happy ones with the other three children of the family. At the
age of thirty-three Henry settled permanently in England, where he
managed to live the life of the upper classes and be a writer too. For
forty years he steadily produced novels and stories of a solidity, a
subtlety, and a technical finish unequalled in his time. He once observed that, up to his time, the history of the English novel had been
"a paradise of the loose end." Without impoverishment of content,
James made it a work of art. His early work—*Roderick Hudson*
(1875), *The American* (1877), *The Portrait of a Lady* (1881)—is
mainly concerned with the "International Theme," the conflict between American and European cultures. During his middle years he
wrote mostly about English life, in novels like *The Princess Casi-
massima* (1886), *The Spoils of Poynton* (1897), and *The Awkward
Age* (1899). The great novels of his final period are *The Wings of the
Dove* (1902), *The Ambassadors* (1903), and *The Golden Bowl*
(1904). Indignant at the failure of the United States to enter the First
World War at the start, he became a British subject six months before his death.

EDITH WHARTON (1862–1937) was born in New York into an
upper-class world. She found herself torn between her commitment to
this world and her intellectual scorn for what she called its "blind
dread of innovation, [its] instinctive shrinking from responsibility."
At twenty-three she married a wealthy Bostonian named Edward
Wharton, who later became a "neurasthenic"; they were divorced in
1913. Brought up in a world that thought serious writing unladylike,
she did not publish a novel until she was forty. Her finest work was
produced during the first two decades of her career, in novels like
The House of Mirth (1905), *The Custom of the Country* (1913), and
The Age of Innocence (1920), though until her death she continued
to write intelligent and often moving fiction. Henry James once said

that in her work "the masculine conclusion" outweighed "the feminine observation." She certainly had a tough mind; yet the ultimate motive of her best work was as certainly an entirely feminine response to experience.

ERNEST HEMINGWAY (1899–1961) was born in Oak Park, Illinois, and had his only formal education in high school there. He worked for a short time as a reporter for the Kansas City *Star* and then went to Italy, where he served as an ambulance driver and in the Italian infantry during the First World War. He was severely wounded there, as is the hero of *A Farewell to Arms* (1929), which draws on this experience. During the 1920's he lived in Paris, writing his early short stories and *The Sun Also Rises* (1926). In the early 1930's he wrote *To Have and Have Not* (1937). Later in the decade he became deeply concerned with the Spanish Civil War; during it he was a reporter in Spain and wrote a play and his novel, *For Whom the Bell Tolls* (1940), about it. He also served as a correspondent during the Second World War, about which he wrote an ill-received novel, *Across the River and into the Trees* (1950). *The Old Man and the Sea* (1952) is a product of his last years, when he lived in Cuba. It earned him the Nobel Prize in 1954. He died by his own hand in Ketchum, Idaho.

JAMES THURBER (1894–1961) was born in Columbus, Ohio, into a family he has described, with perhaps imperfect accuracy, in *My Life and Hard Times* (1933). He was educated at Ohio State University and began his career as a newspaperman with the Columbus *Dispatch;* he later worked for the Paris edition of the Chicago *Tribune*. In 1926 he joined *The New Yorker* and, with E. B. White, gave the magazine its character. He was twice married and spent the last years of his life with his second wife in West Cornwall, Connecticut. "His thoughts," E. B. White said, "have always been a tangle of baseball scores, Civil War tactical problems, Henry James, personal maladjustment, terrier puppies, literary tide rips, ancient myths, and modern apprehensions." He was, like Ring Lardner before him, one of those rare writers whose very real sense of horror at the ordinary dilemmas of American life struck him as comic.

PHILIP ROTH (1933–   ) was born in Newark, New Jersey, and educated at Bucknell. He did a year of graduate work at Chicago, which he later made use of in *Letting Go* (1962). He has taught at Iowa, Harvard, and Princeton. His first book was a remarkable volume of short stories, *Goodbye, Columbus* (1959); it combines an interest in the Jewish community in which he grew up with the typical attitudes of all Americans of Roth's generation. *Letting Go*, the novel which followed, is a big book that seeks to cover the typical experiences of men like him—college, graduate school, marriage, the life of the young intellectual and writer. He has the excessive preoccupation with identity typical of his generation, a preoccupation that may be intensified in his case by his experience of a minority culture; in *Letting Go* the middle-class representatives of that culture are subjected to a satiric attack that is qualified by curious touches of sympathy.

J. F. POWERS (1917–   ) was born in Jacksonville, Illinois, and attended parochial school there. He studied at Chicago and Northwestern but was prevented by the depression from taking a degree. After college he worked for a time in bookstores in Chicago. When his first book, *The Prince of Darkness and Other Stories* (1947), appeared he received a number of awards, including a Guggenheim Fellowship. Since then he has done some teaching (at Marquette), and he continues to live in the Middle West. His remarkable novel, *Morte D'Urban*, won the National Book Award for 1962. He is, however, best known for his short stories, a second collection of which, *Power of Grace*, appeared in 1956. His short stories are mostly about the ecclesiastical life of the Catholic Church and the human dilemmas of priests, about which he writes with wit, understanding, and deep sympathy.

DAN JACOBSON (1929–   ) was born in Johannesburg, South Africa, and educated at the University of Witwatersrand. After graduation he did public relations work for the South African Jewish Board of Deputies in Johannesburg and worked for a firm in Kimberley. In 1956–1957 he held a fellowship in creative writing at Stanford, an experience about which he wrote in *No Further West: California Visited* (1959). Since then he has lived in London. He has written five novels—*The Trap* (1955), *A Dance in the Sun* (1956), *The Price of Diamonds* (1957), *Evidence of Love* (1960), and *The Beginners* (1966)—and two volumes of short stories—*The Zulu and the Zeide* (1956) and *Beggar My Neighbour* (1964). Better perhaps than any other writer of his generation in England, he has combined a concern for social problems that is perhaps unavoidable for a sensitive South African with an undogmatic sympathy for people with views different from his.

JAMES AGEE (1909–1955) was born in Knoxville, Tennessee, and educated at Exeter and Harvard. His first book, a volume of poems called *Permit Me Voyage*, was the selection for the Yale Series of Younger Poets in 1934. After graduation he worked for *Fortune*, which gave him the assignment to write about sharecroppers that led to his eloquently indignant book *Let Us Now Praise Famous Men* (1941). He reviewed movies for *Time* from 1939 to 1943 and for *The Nation* from 1943 to 1948. After 1948 he worked directly in the movies, writing the narration for "The Quiet One" and the scripts for "The African Queen," "Night of the Hunter," and "The Bride Comes to Yellow Sky." In 1951 he published a short poetic novel, *The Morning Watch*, and after his death the "virtually complete" manuscript of *A Death in the Family* (1957) was published. Shortly before that "The Waiting" (chapters eight to ten of the novel) was published as a short story in *The New Yorker*. In this last work, Agee's always powerful feelings are brought under the control of a sharply observed, painstakingly objective narrative.

D. H. LAWRENCE (1885–1930) was born in Eastwood, near Nottingham, the son of a hearty miner and a middle-class mother. He deals more or less autobiographically with his growing up in *Sons and Lovers* (1913). He acquired a teacher's certificate in Nottingham and for a short time taught school in Croydon, where he was discovered by Ford Madox Ford and published in *The English Review*. From the beginning his work was governed by a romantic, even mystical feeling for the inner, hidden self and its secret links with the natural world. Shortly after the publication of *Sons and Lovers* he married Frieda von Richthofen, the beautiful, divorced wife of a Nottingham professor. Lawrence's career was a struggle. He and Frieda were harassed by the authorities during the First World War; his work was constantly under attack for indecency; and he was made unhappy by his own demands on life. In 1919 he left England, living first in Italy and later in Mexico and the American Southwest. He died of tuberculosis, after a long illness, in Vence. His best-known, though not his best novel is *Lady Chatterley's Lover* (1928). He did his finest work in novels like *The Rainbow* (1915) and *Women in Love* (1920), in magnificent travel books like *The Sea and Sardinia* (1921), and in the best of his short stories.

VLADIMIR NABOKOV (1899–   ) was born in St. Petersburg; his father, a prominent liberal, was a member of the first Duma. He was educated in St. Petersburg and at Cambridge University. During the 1920's and 1930's he lived in Germany and France and wrote novels in Russian. In 1940 he moved to the United States, where, until 1959, he taught at Wellesley and Cornell and spent his summers hunting butterflies in the West (he is a professional lepidopterist). He now lives in Europe. When he came to America in 1940 be began writing in English with dazzling skill. His early books in English—*The Real Life of Sebastian Knight* (1941), *Bend Sinister* (1947) and *Conclusive Evidence* (1951)—were great critical successes, but it was with *Lolita* (1955) that he became world famous. He has since written *Pnin* (1957) and *Pale Fire* (1962), and done a learned edition of Pushkin's *Eugene Onegin* (1964). He has published two volumes of short stories, *Nine Stories* (1947) and *Nabokov's Dozen* (1958).

SHERWOOD ANDERSON (1876–1941) came of an impoverished Ohio family and had little formal education. After serving in the Spanish-American War, he settled down as the manager of a paint factory in

Elyria, Ohio. Later he worked in advertising in Chicago, where he made the acquaintance of the gifted group of writers who lived there in his time, and became a writer himself. In 1924 he settled in the small town of Marion, Virginia, where he edited both the local newspapers, one Democratic, the other Republican. He was married four times. He did his best work in his short stories. These characteristically present a fragment of homely experience in which Anderson discovers a moment of self-revelation—and usually of defeat—for an ordinary American of the kind he had grown up with. His work belongs to the slightly self-conscious self-discovery of the Middle West as a region, and is in that respect—if in few others—like Sinclair Lewis's. He was at once a primitive and the first American writer to deal with the fine shades of the inner life of feelings that have so preoccupied modern literature.

JAMES JOYCE (1882–1941) was born in Dublin, the son of a talented and feckless father on whom he drew extensively in his work. He was educated by the Jesuits at Belvedere College and at University College, Dublin. In 1904 he and Nora Barnacle left Dublin for the Continent and, except for brief visits, Joyce never returned to Ireland except in his imagination. He spent the prewar years as a language teacher in Trieste and was in Zürich for most of the First World War. Despite much help from patrons, he managed to keep himself poor most of his life. In 1920 he moved to Paris, where he gradually became the uncrowned king of the expatriate writers there, a position he richly deserved. His volume of short stories, *Dubliners,* was published in 1914, though written a good deal earlier. It was followed in 1916 by *A Portrait of the Artist as a Young Man* and in 1922 by his most famous book, *Ulysses.* He spent the next seventeen years of his life—seriously handicapped by failing eyesight—on his last book, *Finnegans Wake* (1939). Joyce's short stories have a realistic surface so exact and impersonal that it is easy to miss the romantic depth of feeling in them.

KATHERINE MANSFIELD (1888–1923), born Kathleen Beauchamp, was the daughter of a banker in Wellington, New Zealand. She was educated in London and in 1909 married—but never lived with—George Bowden. In 1912 she joined forces with the critic, Middleton Murry; they were finally married in 1918. By that time she was seriously ill, and she spent the rest of her life traveling in search of health, in Italy, Switzerland, and France. Her last resort was the institute near Fontainebleau run by Gurdjieff; there she died of a hemorrhage. Her reputation rests on her four volumes of short stories, *Bliss* (1920), *The Garden Party* (1922), *The Doves' Nest* (1923), and *Something Childish* (1924). In these stories she succeeded in adopting the Chekhovian story to the life of the newly emergent feminine sensibility of the twentieth century, and became the most influential woman writer of her time.

BERNARD MALAMUD (1914–   ) was born and raised in Brooklyn and educated at the City College of New York and Columbia University. From 1949 to 1961 he taught at Oregon State College, which provided the background for *A New Life* (1961). He is now on the faculty of Bennington College. In 1956 he spent a year in Italy, where he found the material for a number of the short stories in *The Magic Barrel* (1958). He is the author of a second volume of stories, *Idiots First* (1963) and of two earlier novels, *The Natural* (1952) and *The Assistant* (1957). Malamud is appealed to by people who are passionately determined to live their own lives, the more recalcitrant the better, and delights in the stubborn oddities of the Jewish world of his childhood in Brooklyn.

RUDYARD KIPLING (1865–1936) came of Yorkshire stock, though he was born in Bombay. He was educated at the United Services College, Westward Ho! which provided the raw material for *Stalky and Co.*, (1899). In 1882 he returned to India to work as a reporter and write short stories and verse. By 1890 he had achieved great fame. In 1892 he married an American girl, Caroline Balestier, and, after a world tour— Kipling was a lifelong traveler—they settled for four years near Brattleboro, Vermont. To this period of his life belong such books as *Many Inventions* (1893), the two *Jungle Books* (1894, 1895), and *Captains Courageous* (1897). In 1896 he moved back to England and in the next decade he produced *Kim* (1901), the *Just So Stories* (1902), and *Puck of Pook's Hill* (1906). He was awarded the Nobel Prize in 1907. Kipling's early experience in India gave him a strong idealistic admiration for British imperialism that was very offensive to professional liberals—one of them called him a "vindictive maniac." Continuous illness and the death of his son at the front in 1915 saddened his last years, during which he wrote the powerful, cryptic, and often bitter stories which make up "the Kipling whom nobody reads" and that everyone ought to.

WILLIAM FAULKNER (1897–1962) was born into an upper-middle-class family near Oxford, Mississippi—the Jefferson of his fiction—where he lived most of his life. He had little formal education, though he did attend the University of Mississippi sporadically for a number of years both before and after the First World War. During the war he served in the Canadian R.A.F. After the war he wandered in New York, New Orleans, and Europe, until he settled down in his home town and went to work on the long series of connected novels and short stories about Yoknapatawpha County that Malcolm Cowley has called his "parable or legend of the Deep South." This legend is made up of the histories of a few families and their friends who live in northern Mississippi, and Faulkner tells their stories from pioneering days to the present. All Faulkner's families have, in addition to their official white members, unofficial colored ones, joined to the families by birth or by self-election. Faulkner's reputation has always been high among critics, but it was not until Malcolm Cowley published his *Viking Portable Faulkner* in 1945 and a movie was made of *Intruder in the Dust* in 1949 that Faulkner achieved wide fame. He was awarded the Nobel Prize in 1950. During his last years he lived a good deal at the University of Virginia, but he was back home in Oxford when he died.

ROBERT PENN WARREN (1905–) was born and grew up in Todd County, Kentucky. He was educated at Vanderbilt, where he met John Crowe Ransom, Donald Davidson, and Allen Tate and became one of the Fugitive Group. After further study at California and Yale he became a Rhodes Scholar. From Oxford he returned to Louisiana State University to teach and to edit, with Cleanth Brooks, *The Southern Review.* He and Brooks also wrote together the most influential textbook of their generation, *Understanding Poetry.* From Louisiana Warren moved to the University of Minnesota in 1942, and in 1950, he went to Yale. He was married to Emma Brescia in 1930; they were divorced in 1951 and he is now married to the writer, Eleanor Clark. Mr. Warren is a poet of great distinction, the author of *Promises* (1957) and *You, Emperors* (1960). His novels include *Night Rider* (1938), *All the King's Men* (1946), and *Flood* (1964). He has also written on social subjects in *Segregation* (1956) and *Who Speaks for the Negro?* (1965). He was the first gifted writer in America to recognize and profit from the greatness of Faulkner's work.

CAROLINE GORDON (1895–) was born in Todd County, Kentucky, and grew up in Clarksville, Tennessee, where her father was a schoolmaster. In 1924 Miss Gordon married the poet, Allen Tate. Since 1928, when she wrote her first novel, *Penhally* (published in 1931), she has been steadily writing skillful fiction to which a doctrinaire but subtle commitment to certain general ideas—the Southern view of the Civil War (*None Shall Look Back*, 1937), the Catholic view of contemporary life (*The Malefactors*, 1956)—gives an almost violent intellectual power. In books like *Aleck Maury, Sportsman* (1934) and the short stories that recall other aspects of her childhood, this severity is moderated by a considerable warmth and affection. She has taught the writing of fiction widely and successfully; she edited, with Allen Tate, a successful anthology of stories, *The House of Fiction* (1950), and has written a critical study of the novel, *How to Read a Novel* (1957).

EUDORA WELTY (1909–   ) was born in Jackson, Mississippi, where her father was the president of an insurance company. She was educated at the Mississippi State College for Women and at Wisconsin, and studied advertising for a year at Columbia. After working briefly in advertising in New York, she returned to Jackson and began to write. She was encouraged by Katherine Anne Porter, who introduced her first book of stories, *A Curtain of Green* (1941). She has since written several other volumes of stories and some longer pieces of fiction. These are *The Robber Bridegroom* (1942), *Delta Wedding* (1946), and *The Ponder Heart* (1954). In spite of her very considerable success she continues to live with quiet naturalness the life of her home town. "I haven't a literary life at all," she once said. "Not much of a confession, maybe. . . . I would not understand a literary life."

ANDREW LYTLE (1902–   ) was born in Murfreesboro, Tennessee. He was educated at Vanderbilt, where he was a member of the Fugitive Group and contributed to the group's two books, *I'll Take My Stand* (1931) and *Who Owns America?* (1936). After graduation he spent some time in France and later studied drama at Yale under George Pierce Baker. For a time he was an actor on Broadway, but eventually became a teacher. He has taught at Southwestern, at the University of Iowa, and the University of Florida, and is at present at the University of the South, where he edits *The Sewanee Review*, as he did briefly once before, during the Second World War. He is the author of four unduly neglected novels, *The Long Night* (1936), *At the Moon's Inn* (1941), *A Name for Evil* (1947), and *The Velvet Horn* (1957). His work is kept vividly alive by his fierce devotion to the old South and is marked by an unusual attack on the problem of reconciling surface and symbol in the contemporary novel.

PETER TAYLOR (1917–   ) is a Tennessean. He grew up in Nashville and was educated at Vanderbilt and at Kenyon College. After serving in the Second World War he became a teacher, first at the Women's College of North Carolina and later at Kenyon. His first volume of stories, *A Long Fourth*, appeared in 1948. It was followed, in 1950, by his first novel, *A Woman of Means*, and later by other volumes of stories, *The Widows of Thornton* (1954), *Happy Families Are All Alike* (1959), and *Miss Leonora, When Last Seen* (1963). Mr. Taylor is a quiet writer with a vivid sense of the surface reality of experience that gives remarkable authority to the feelings in his stories.

REYNOLDS PRICE (1933–   ) was born and grew up in Warren County, North Carolina. He was educated there and at Duke University. After graduation he spent three years as a Rhodes Scholar at Merton College, Oxford, and then returned to North Carolina, where he wrote his first novel, *A Long and Happy Life* (1962). His second novel, *A Generous Man*, was published in 1966. A collection of short stories, *The Names and Faces of Heroes*, came out in 1963. Though Price has said he does not want to make another Yoknapatawpha County (Faulkner's mythical land) out of his native Warren County, the finely observed details of the life he has known there are already taking on a fabulous character.

Questions on the Stories

JOSEPH CONRAD

Heart of Darkness

1. Marlow begins by saying that "this [London and the Thames] also has been one of the dark places of the earth." What was dark about it? Who penetrated that darkness? What did it take in the way of strength for him to do so? What did he have to fight?

2. What is Marlow's opinion of conquest such as the Romans carried out?

3. What does Marlow think justifies conquest?

4. What does Marlow think of savages, of the cannibals and others he meets during his trip up the Congo?

5. Why does he think contact with such savages and with the jungle is such a test of civilized men? How does it test him?

6. What does Marlow think of the Company? Of its office in Brussels? Of its organization in Africa? Of the manifestations of the spirit of commercial exploitation he sees on his trip down the coast of Africa?

7. What is Marlow's first impression of Kurtz?

8. What impression of Kurtz comes to us from Marlow's report of what the young Russian tells him about Kurtz?

9. What does Marlow learn directly from Kurtz that first night when he has to follow Kurtz and bring him back to the boat?

10. What does he learn from Kurtz on the trip down the river before Kurtz dies?

11. Why does Kurtz write at the end of his pamphlet, "Exterminate the brutes"? Why does he say, "The horror! The horror!"

12. Why does the native say "Mistah Kurtz—he dead" "in a tone of scathing contempt"?

13. Why does Marlow lie to Kurtz's intended when they finally meet?

F. SCOTT FITZGERALD
Babylon Revisited

1. What kind of person is Lorraine Quarrles? What can we discover about the kind of life she lives from Charlie's recollections of her during his previous time in Paris and from the note she writes him? From the way she behaves when Charlie runs into her and Dunc at the restaurant? When she and Dunc come to the Peters' house?

2. What kind of a person is Marion Peters? What do we learn about her life from Charlie's visits to the Peters' house? From what Lincoln Peters says about her?

3. What sort of life had Charlie and Helen lived in Paris before Helen's death and Charlie's collapse? How, specifically, had Charlie come to lock Helen out in the snow that night? What had that episode done to their personal relationship? What had Helen died of? How had Charlie collapsed?

4. What parallel is there between Charlie's present relation to Lorraine Quarrles and his present relation to Marion Peters?

5. Why does the story begin with Charlie talking to the bartender in the Ritz Bar and then taking a taxi ride through Paris? Why does Charlie pay a visit to Montmartre?

6. What is Charlie's life like now? Why is Honoria so necessary to its fulfillment?

7. Why does Charlie, at the end of the story, think Helen would certainly not have wanted him to be so alone?

MARY MC CARTHY
Artists in Uniform

1. When Miss McCarthy gets into the discussion in the club car, where the anti-Semitic Colonel is holding forth, she discovers that the occupants of the car have quickly identified her as an artist. How have they done so? Why is she dismayed that they have?

2. In what sense are both she and the Colonel "artists in uniform"?

3. By what process of reasoning does the Colonel persuade himself that, as an anti-Semite, he is a perfectly reasonable and normal man?

4. How does Miss McCarthy set about proving to the Colonel that he is wrong to think so? Why does she fail? What weakness in her own attitude contributes to this failure?

5. How does the Colonel set about explaining to himself why Miss Mc-

Carthy opposes his views? How has Miss McCarthy laid herself open to this kind of explanation?

6. When the Colonel discovers that Miss McCarthy is married to a man named Broadwater and concludes that Mr. Broadwater must be a Jew and that that explains Miss McCarthy's objections to anti-Semitism, how much is he justified in reasoning this way, even though he has the facts wrong? Why does Miss McCarthy not tell him he is wrong in thinking Mr. Broadwater a Jew?

7. What is the story's final implication about how Miss McCarthy ought to have dealt with the Colonel? What mistake does it suggest she made? What does it suggest were the causes for her making that mistake?

DYLAN THOMAS

A Story

1. What age was the narrator and what kind of person was he when he participated in the events he is describing in the story?

2. Why does he describe his uncle as like a buffalo and his aunt as like a mouse? How does his doing so make us feel about them?

3. What is the effect on us of the other images the boy uses? In describing his life with his aunt and uncle?

4. What is the effect of the images he uses in describing the scene at the Mountain Sheep?

5. What effect is created by his treatment of the various characters who appear for the outing and are described during its course? By his account of Will Sentry and Mr. Franklyn when the outing is being prepared for?

6. How are we expected to feel about the men when they go splashing drunkenly in the river? How are we made to take this attitude toward them?

7. Why does Will Sentry cry to the duck and the moon, "Who goes there"?

FRANK O'CONNOR

My Oedipus Complex

1. What do we learn about Larry from his comments on his father's wartime visits at home? From his comparison of his father to Santa Claus? From his offhand remark that it was uncomfortable having his father in the big bed?

2. Why does Larry think his mother is not getting a baby because of the cost? Why is he impatient with her arguing this way?

3. Why does Larry rush in to join his mother in the big bed every morning as soon as he wakes up? What does this habit of theirs show about Larry's mother?

4. Why is Larry so disappointed by his father when they go on a walk together?

5. What tactics does Larry devise for winning his mother's attention away from his father? How does he decide on these particular maneuvers? Why do they not work?

6. What does Larry feel when he first hears that there is going to be a baby?

7. What means does Larry use to keep Sonny in what Larry thinks is Sonny's place? What does his doing so make us feel about Larry?

8. What leads Larry to think there is a possibility of an alliance between him and his father? How does he set about suggesting such an alliance to his father? How does the establishment of the alliance finally come about? How satisfactory is it to Larry?

KATHERINE ANNE PORTER

The Grave

1. Why is Miranda excited by the sight of the dead rabbit and her young? Why does she tremble at the sight of them?

2. Why does Miss Porter introduce the simile about the baby into her description of the young rabbits?

3. In what way does the sight of the dead rabbit and her young connect with the "secret, formless intuitions" of Miranda's mind and body?

4. How likely is it that Paul and Miranda might have found a gold ring and a silver dove in the empty graves? With what are these two objects associated? What kind of ring is the gold ring? What religious significance has the dove?

5. Why does Miranda prefer the ring to the dove, swap with Paul, and wear the ring on her thumb?

6. Why does the ring suggest to Miranda a dislike of her overalls and a longing to dress up in her best dress?

7. Why does the scene in the Indian market awaken the memory of this scene? What have the "piles of raw flesh and wilting flowers" to do with evoking the memory?

8. What is the "dreadful vision" that comes into Miranda's mind when she first remembers her childhood experience?

9. Why is it driven out by the vision of Paul smiling and turning the

dove over in his hand? What has the dove to do with this? What has Paul's age and liking for the dove to do with it?

JOHN UPDIKE
A Sense of Shelter

1. What does the first paragraph show us is the difference for William Young between life inside the high school and life outside it?

2. How does Mr. Updike lead us to think of William's feelings about his life in the high school as like a child playing king of the castle?

3. What are we supposed to think of Mary Landis? What does William think of her?

4. What is the function of the scene in Luke's Luncheonette?

5. Why is William reluctant to leave the school at the end of the day?

6. How is William surprised into telling Mary Landis he loves her?

7. What state of mind does Mary Landis reveal in her conversation with William? What has led her to feel this way?

8. What is Mary Landis' opinion of William? What does she think of his belief that he loves her?

9. Why is William discontented when he first goes back into the school after Mary Landis has left him?

10. What relieves this feeling and makes him once more happy in the sheltered world of the high school?

DORIS LESSING
The Day Stalin Died

1. The object of questions about this story should be to make students see the common source for the grotesque ways these apparently quite different characters behave. Start with Comrade Jean. What is Comrade Jean's social background? How does this affect her idea of how to attain "a correct working-class viewpoint"? How does it reveal the real source of her passionate commitment to the Party? Why does it help to explain her grotesque idea that the Trotskyite Trials of the thirties clearly prove the purity of Soviet justice?

2. Now turn to cousin Jessie. Why will cousin Jessie not have her mother with her in the dress shop? Why does she so hate being photographed? Why is she so self-conscious at the photographers? Why does she apologize when they leave?

3. What are the homosexual photographers trying to do by being so

debonair with their visitors? Why do they not succeed in putting their visitors at ease? How do they take their failure?

4. What is Aunt Emma's obsession? Why is the taxi-driver amused by her? What makes this taxi-driver similar to the newspaper man who comments on Stalin's death?

5. What is the point of introducing into the story the old couple on the bus who quarrel about fish?

FLANNERY O'CONNOR

The Artificial Nigger

1. Start with the end of the story and Miss O'Connor's statement of its lesson, what Mr. Head learned from his experience.

2. Go back to the start and ask questions about the adventure. Why does Mr. Head want to take Nelson on this trip to the city? What does he think it will do for Nelson? Why is Nelson so belligerent about it?

3. What are the feelings of the two on the train? Why does Mr. Head talk to everyone? Why does he take Nelson on a tour of the train? What is his attitude toward the large Negro they see?

4. Why does Miss O'Connor constantly bring in descriptions of the scene outside the train, and of the sunrise that neither Mr. Head nor Nelson notices?

5. What is the point of the episode when Nelson questions the Negro woman about where they are?

6. What is Nelson frightened of when he wakes up and finds himself alone?

7. Why does Mr. Head say Nelson is no boy of his after the accident?

8. What happens to Mr. Head that he admits he is lost? Lost in what sense?

9. What is the effect of the artificial Negro on them?

HENRY JAMES

The Tone of Time

1. Why does the narrator think Mary Tredick a better person to paint the picture for Mrs. Bridgenorth than he is? What does what he tells us about their differences as painters tell us about him?

2. What does the narrator think are Mrs. Bridgenorth's reasons for wanting the painting?

3. Why does Mary Tredick take such an interest in this commission?

4. What feelings does Mary Tredick think her portrait reveals about its subject? What feelings does it really reveal?

5. What does the narrator discover about Mrs. Bridgenorth when she sees the portrait?

6. What leads Mary Tredick to guess Mrs. Bridgenorth's connection with the subject of her portrait?

7. How precisely does she guess what that connection has been?

8. What does Mary Tredick's discovery about Mrs. Bridgenorth reveal to her about herself?

9. What does Mary Tredick's discovery about herself show us about Mary Tredick's gift for giving the tone of time to her portraits?

HENRY JAMES

The Jolly Corner

1. It is probably necessary to deal with the use of ghosts in the story first; this means making students see clearly James's use of the central intelligence. Does *James* say Spencer Brydon saw a ghost?

2. If what James says is that Spencer Brydon believed he saw a ghost, what does this ghost represent?

3. What qualities has Spencer Brydon discovered in himself, on his return to New York, that might make him think he had seen such a ghost?

4. What does his renewed friendship with Alice Staverton mean to Spencer Brydon?

5. What is Alice Staverton's attitude to the ghost?

6. What is Spencer Brydon's attitude to the ghost (a) when he first starts going to the house; (b) when he thinks the ghost is following him; (c) when he actually meets the ghost?

7. What is James's point in having Alice Staverton rescue Spencer Brydon and accept him as a husband?

HENRY JAMES

The Lesson of the Master

1. What kind of a woman does Mrs. St. George appear to be when Paul Overt first meets her?

2. What kind of person does Marion Fancourt appear to be?

3. What do we deduce from Henry St. George's apparent interest in Marion Fancourt during the weekend at Lady Watermouth's?

4. What does St. George reveal about the way he lives and the way his wife manages his life in the smoking-room conversation with Paul? What does he reveal about his own books?

5. In the long conversation between Henry St. George and Paul Overt in St. George's study after the dinner party, what do we learn about (a) St. George's method of work; (b) the kind of books he produces by this method; (c) the reasons he writes such books by this method; (d) his judgment of the general life he lives; (e) his judgment of what marriage to Marion Fancourt will do to Paul Overt as a novelist; (f) his hopes for Overt as a novelist?

6. What does Paul Overt do as a result of this conversation?

7. Why is Paul upset to discover, when he returns to London after two years, that St. George and Marion Fancourt are engaged?

8. What is Paul's impression of Marion at their last meeting?

9. Was Paul right or wrong to think St. George had not played quite fair with him?

EDITH WHARTON
Roman Fever

1. What impression of Mrs. Slade and Mrs. Ansley do we get from the remarks of their daughters and their comments on these remarks? How true is this impression?

2. What impression of each lady do we gain from the thoughts of the other?

3. What is it that Mrs. Slade has always feared in Mrs. Ansley and that makes her hate Mrs. Ansley now?

4. What hints are we given about Mrs. Ansley's real feelings about the view of the Forum?

5. What actually happened that evening twenty-five years ago when Mrs. Ansley received the letter from Delphin Slade that Mrs. Slade had forged?

6. Why does Mrs. Slade now reveal that she had forged this letter?

7. Why does that information upset Mrs. Ansley?

8. Why does Mrs. Ansley's revelation that she had actually met Delphin Slade in the Forum upset Mrs. Slade so much?

9. Why does Mrs. Ansley's revelation that Barbara is Delphin Slade's daughter disturb Mrs. Slade even more?

ERNEST HEMINGWAY

The Gambler, The Nun, and The Radio

1. Where was the Russian wounded, how dangerous was his wound? Where was he when he was hit? Why does the story mention the way he screamed all night when he was brought into the hospital?

2. Does the story use this ironic indirectness to make its points elsewhere?

3. What moral for the story is contained in Mr. Frazer's meditation about "the opium of the people"?

4. What further meaning does Hemingway intend us to see in the story? How does he communicate this further meaning?

5. Define the character of Cayetano and point out the things in the story that reveal it to us.

6. What makes Cayetano a "poor idealist"?

7. Why does Cayetano go on living a disciplined and hopeful life despite his continuous defeats?

8. What kind of a person is Sister Cecilia? What makes her go on living with interest and enthusiasm despite her disappointment at not becoming a saint?

9. Why is the Mexican who is "very strong against religion" in the story?

10. What does Mr. Frazer depend on to keep him going and save him from despair? How well does it work? If not very well, why does he not do something else?

11. If the purpose of *The Gambler, the Nun, and the Radio* is to compare three apparently unlike characters who have in common the problem of the belief they live by, show how the story is constructed to bring these three characters into parallel.

JAMES THURBER

A Couple of Hamburgers

1. Why does the husband insist on using expressions like "dog-wagon," "stay our stomachs," and "stick to your ribs"?

2. What offends the wife about these expressions?

3. What lies behind the wife's queer ideas that diners with nicknames are all run by Greeks and are therefore bad and that diners set at an angle are always poor? Why do these ideas so annoy her husband?

4. Why is the husband so scornful of his wife's suspicion that she has heard a "funny noise" in the car?

5. Why does the husband enjoy singing old popular songs?

6. The wife finally relaxes, content to wait—for her husband to stop singing, for her supper, for the car to break down. Why?

PHILIP ROTH

Defender of the Faith

1. How good a soldier is Sergeant Marx and what things in the story provide the answer to this question?

2. What are Grossbart's reasons for taking the attitude he does in his relations to Sergeant Marx? How sincere would you say he is in doing so?

3. What does Sergeant Marx think of Grossbart's maneuvers?

4. How does Sergeant Marx react to Grossbart's appeals to him?

5. Is Grossbart ashamed of writing the letter for his father to send his congressman about the army food? Why not?

6. Why does Sergeant Marx give the three soldiers weekend passes for St. Louis?

7. Why does Grossbart reveal to Sergeant Marx how he has fooled him into giving the passes to them?

8. Why is Sergeant Marx shocked when he hears that his unit is being sent to the Pacific?

9. Why does Sergeant Marx use his influence to get Grossbart back in the orders for the Pacific?

10. What is Grossbart's judgment of why Marx did this?

11. Why does Sergeant Marx have to make an effort not to beg Grossbart's pardon for having done it?

J. F. POWERS

A Losing Game

1. Why in fact does the pastor give Father Fabre the chair at the end of the story?

2. What happens at the beginning of the story when Father Fabre asks for the table?

3. Why does he think this happens?

4. What does he do about it?

5. What does Father Fabre think of the pastor's preparations for going into the basement?

6. What are we meant to think of them?

7. Why does the pastor not respond to the table as Father Fabre does but accepts Father Fabre's praise of the chair?

8. Compare Father Fabre's reaction to his wound and the pastor's; which is more reasonable?

9. What does the scene at the hospital show us?

10. What final conclusion about the pastor does the story lead us to draw?

DAN JACOBSON

Beggar My Neighbour

1. How does Michael feel about the two African children when he first meets them? Does he think of them as like him?

2. Why is Michael shocked when the two African children wait, long after dark, to thank him the second time he gives them bread?

3. Why is Michael upset when the two African children gently ask him to give them his pen-and-pencil set?

4. Why, after Michael refuses to give them the pen-and-pencil set, do the African children disappear before Dora can bring them bread?

5. Why does Michael begin to hate and even to dread these two children?

6. Why does Michael, when he has a fever, first dream of being lewdly cruel to the girl and brutally violent to the boy and then dream of taking them by the hands and kissing them?

7. Why is this story called *Beggar My Neighbour?*

8. Why does the author make Michael an only child who daydreams a great deal?

JAMES AGEE

The Waiting

1. What do we learn from the telephone call to Mary?

2. What do we learn from the way Mary reacts to that call about her thoughts—from her immediate thought of how Andrew will get to Powell Station, from her rushing to make the bed in the downstairs bedroom, from the thoughts that go through her conscious mind as she does so?

3. Why is it that, during the process, she has a moment of not being "sure where she was or why she was doing this"?

4. What is Mary thinking when she says to Aunt Hannah, "Is he living or *dead*"?

5. What happens when Mary starts to think about the improved relations between her and her husband?

6. What does Aunt Hannah deduce from Mary's saying, "whatever is, is"?

7. What is the point of Mary's having to go to the bathroom?

8. Where does it tell us that it is Mary who says her husband is dead when Andrew comes into the house?

D. H. LAWRENCE
The Odor of Chrysanthemums

1. What means does Lawrence use at the beginning of the story to make the life in the miner's house vivid and familiar to us?

2. Why does Elizabeth touch the dead body of her husband and then kiss it?

3. Is she successful in what she is trying to do?

4. What does this experience reveal to her about their relations when he was alive?

5. What light does this throw on the thoughts she had had when she had been waiting for him to come home, thinking that he was in the local pub drinking?

6. What does she now think of the way she had treated her husband?

D. H. LAWRENCE
The Shadow in the Rose Garden

1. What impression do we get of the husband as we watch him moving about before his wife wakes up?

2. What impression of the wife do we have when we first see her with her husband?

3. What evidence of class differences emerge in these two scenes?

4. What is the wife feeling as she goes back to visit the garden where she had been courted by her former lover?

5. How does Lawrence use exaggerated descriptions of flowers and similes drawn from nature to make us understand her feelings?

6. Why does she focus so hard on the man's hands while they are in the garden together?

7. Why does the wife not want to see the husband when she gets back to their room and feel irritated when he comes in?

8. Why does the husband deliberately give a gross description of the former relationship the wife has just revealed to him?

9. Why is the grossness offensive to the wife in a way he has not fore-seen?

10. What is the result of the wife's revealing the fact that her former lover is now a lunatic?

D. H. LAWRENCE

The White Stocking

1. How does Lawrence suggest to us at the beginning of the story that Elsie is a lively, energetic, gay young woman? How does this momentarily mislead us as to her reason for rushing to the door when the postman knocks? Why does she rush to the door so eagerly?

2. What is it about Elsie that Teddy is most acutely aware of? What is Elsie most acutely aware of about Teddy?

3. What makes Sam Adams' presents and treats so interesting to Elsie?

4. What does Teddy feel about Adams' giving these presents to Elsie when he learns about them?

5. Why is Elsie so upset by Teddy's attitude?

6. Is Teddy right about the meaning of these presents, or is Elsie?

7. What happens between Elsie and Sam Adams at the dance?

8. How does Elsie feel about what happens at the dance? How does Sam Adams feel?

9. Why does Elsie say to Teddy after the dance, "Be good to me. Don't be cruel to me"?

10. When Elsie and Teddy quarrel the evening of Valentine's Day, what does Elsie do to irritate Teddy? Why does she do it? How does she feel while she is doing it?

11. Why does Teddy strike Elsie? How does he feel as he is doing it? How does he feel afterwards?

12. How are Elsie and Teddy reconciled?

13. Define as clearly as you can the kind of human feelings Lawrence has been dealing with in this story.

VLADIMIR NABOKOV

Pnin

1. What life does Pnin dream he is living as he walks back from the film-showing to his room in Waindelville?

2. How does Pnin conduct himself during his daily life in Waindel-

ville? What conception of himself leads him to conduct himself this way?

3. What failures in the conduct of his daily life make Pnin look absurd? Is he aware of these failures?

4. Why does Pnin scorn the Komarovs? Is his attitude toward them justified?

5. Why does Pnin cry at the film? Why does he think his doing so unaccountable, ridiculous, humiliating?

6. Why is Pnin constantly remembering episodes from his past? Does he understand why he does so?

7. Explain how we know that the day of the story is Pnin's birthday.

8. Explain the reasons for the things Pnin dreams of that night.

9. How does the narrator make us understand things about Pnin's life that Pnin does not understand?

10. Why is Pnin fascinated by the pencil-sharpener? Why does the narrator think it significant?

11. What does the narrator wish us to understand from Pnin's discussion of Pushkin's poem?

12. Why does the story end with Pnin's being awakened by the return of Isobel Clements?

SHERWOOD ANDERSON

The Egg

1. What had been the motives of the boy's father and mother in starting a chicken farm?

2. Why had they stuck to it so long?

3. How did the boy's father plan to make a big success of the restaurant?

4. Why is this plan so unlikely to succeed?

5. Why do we feel sorry for the father rather than outraged by his commercialism?

6. Why does the father not realize that Joe Kane is not interested in his trick of standing the egg on end?

7. Why does he not realize that Joe Kane will be sickened by his monstrous chicks in alcohol?

8. Why does he burst into a rage when Joe Kane walks out on his final trick?

9. Why does he fall on his knees beside his wife's bed and weep?

JAMES JOYCE
Araby

1. What impression does the story give us of what the street the boy lived on was really like?

2. What does it look like to the boy?

3. How well does the boy know Mangan's sister? What, then, is it that makes her so fascinating to him?

4. What connects Mangan's sister and the bazaar, Araby, for the boy?

5. What affect does his actual visit to the bazaar have on him? What is it that makes him feel as he does there?

6. Why does his experience at the bazaar make him feel he has been "driven and derided by vanity"?

KATHERINE MANSFIELD
Her First Ball

1. How does Leila feel when she gets into the cab to go to the ball? How does Katherine Mansfield convey that feeling to us?

2. Why does Katherine Mansfield say that the cab seemed to go past "waltzing" lamp-posts?

3. Why is Leila moved by the brother-sister relation between Laurie and Laura?

4. Why does Leila think the lamp jet in the ladies' room is leaping and quivering?

5. What state of feeling is conveyed by Katherine Mansfield's saying Leila "floated away like a flower that is tossed into a pool" when she began to dance?

6. What effect does the conversation of the elderly dancer have on Leila? How long does it last? What puts an end to it? Why?

BERNARD MALAMUD
Take Pity

1. What conception of himself is revealed by Rosen's manner of advising the Kalishes that their store is doomed?

2. Why does Eva so decisively reject Rosen's first scheme to get her out of the store where she can meet somebody and marry again? Why is she sure she is right that the scheme will not work?

3. Why is Eva even more offended by Rosen's second scheme, to set her and the girls up comfortably at his expense?

4. What offends Eva so greatly in Rosen's reply to her assertion that they do not need charity?

5. What offends her about the way Rosen proposes?

6. Rosen's final scheme for giving money to Eva and the girls looks insane; is it rationally explicable?

7. Why is Eva standing outside the window stretching her arms toward Rosen at the end of the story?

RUDYARD KIPLING

The Gardener

1. Start with the ending of the story and ask students what the real relation between Helen and Michael is.

2. What is the truth behind each of the lies Helen tells the village at the beginning of the story? Why does she tell these lies?

3. What is the point of the details about Michael's growing up—the scheme for having him call Helen "Mummy," his suspicion of his illegitimacy, his assertion that it is nothing, his exposed anxiety about it when he is delirious?

4. Why is Helen so unalive after Michael's death?

5. Why is Mrs. Scarsworth introduced into the story?

6. How do we know who the gardener really is?

WILLIAM FAULKNER

The Fire and the Hearth

1. What is Lucas Beauchamp's relation to Carothers McCaslin, the founder of the family?

2. What is Roth Edmonds relation to Carothers McCaslin?

3. What signs are there in Lucas' character that he is descended from Carothers McCaslin?

4. How strong is Lucas' attachment to the McCaslin place? How well does he know it?

5. Why does Lucas want to get rid of George Wilkins and his still?

6. What is Lucas' plan for getting rid of George?

7. Why is Lucas angry that he must carry out alone the physical labor his scheme against George demands?

8. What is the effect on Lucas of finding the gold coin in the Indian mound?

9. Why does Lucas want his still as well as George's found when he

revises his plan after discovering that his daughter Nat has been spying on him? .

10. What did Lucas resent about Molly's living in Zack Edmond's house after Zack's wife died?

11. Why did Lucas want to kill Zack Edmonds?

12. How did he fail to kill him?

13. What unexpected consequences follow from Lucas' reporting George's still to Roth Edmonds?

14. What bargain does Nat strike with Lucas before she agrees not to give evidence against him?

15. Why does Lucas let her talk him out of money?

16. What arrangements do George and Lucas make about the new still?

17. What advice does Lucas give George about explaining the situation to Nat?

WILLIAM FAULKNER
Delta Autumn

1. Explain by reference to the genealogical chart on p. 549 of *Modern Short Stories* the relation between Roth Edmonds and the Negro girl and her son.

2. Why does Roth Edmonds react so harshly when he sees something by the road, brakes abruptly, and then is teased by Legate about having a doe in this country?

3. Why is Roth so bitter about patriotism?

4. Why, that night around the campfire, is he so egregiously rude to Uncle Ike about "the other animals you lived with"?

5. Why does Roth Edmonds react so violently when Uncle Ike speaks of that moment "when it dont even matter whether [a man and woman] marry or not"?

6. Why does the girl who comes to the tent with Roth Edmonds' child call Isaac McCaslin "Uncle Ike"?

7. If the girl knew all along that Roth Edmonds would never marry her and went into the affair with her eyes open, what is she doing in Uncle Ike's tent now?

8. What does Uncle Ike mean when he says, "It's a boy, I reckon. They usually are, except that one that was its own mother too"?

9. Why does Uncle Ike give the girl the hunting horn?

10. Why is Uncle Ike so sure the deer Roth has killed that morning is a doe?

WILLIAM FAULKNER
Raid

1. What is Granny Millard's plan for the recovery of the silver, the mules, and the Negroes?

2. Why does she send the boys to Jefferson to borrow Mrs. Compson's hat and parasol? Why does she write the note to Mrs. Compson in pokeberry juice?

3. Why does Ringo think it foolish not to drive the horses to Jefferson? Why will Granny not allow it?

4. What are Bayard and Ringo most interested in about the ruined plantation house at Sartoris? What interests them most about Hawkshurst?

5. Why are the Negroes walking in great masses toward the river? What is Granny's attitude toward these Negroes? What is Aunt Louisa's? What is Drusilla's?

6. What is Drusilla's attitude toward life in general? What has made her take it?

7. What happens when they get to the river in the wagon? How does Granny meet the disaster?

8. What is Colonel Dick's attitude toward Granny and her request?

9. What is Colonel Dick's attitude toward Bayard and Ringo?

10. What causes the mistake that leads the union troops to give Granny so many chests of silver, mules, and Negroes?

11. Why does Granny keep them? What does she think of herself for doing so?

12. How does Ringo use the order signed by the union general? Why?

13. Why does Faulkner emphasize the peacefulness of home when they finally get there and follow immediately with Granny making them get down and pray?

ROBERT PENN WARREN
When the Light Gets Green

1. Why does Mr. Warren select a narrator who is remembering an experience from his boyhood? Why does Mr. Warren limit what the narrator tells us to what he had understood at the time, when he was a boy? (Be sure to keep this narrator in mind when you come to An-

drew Lytle's *Mister McGregor*, which has a similar narrator but uses him differently.)

2. How much do we understand from the boy's account of his grandfather that the boy himself did not understand?

3. How does the narrator make us see these things without saying anything that the boy himself did not understand?

4. How does the boy see his grandfather most of the time? What does his grandfather look like in fact?

5. What kind of a man had Mr. Barden been when he was young? What things did he love? How did he love them? How good had he been at doing the things he loved?

6. What does our understanding of Mr. Barden as a young man tell us about the ante-bellum and Civil War South?

7. What kind of life has Mr. Barden lived since the war? Why?

8. What kind of people are Mr. and Mrs. Kirby?

9. How had Mr. Barden dealt with the difficulties of living with Mr. and Mrs. Kirby? How does his way of doing so fit with his character?

10. Why does Mr. Barden say to his son, after his stroke, that it is time for him to die?

11. How does Mr. Barden's outburst affect his grandson? How does his death?

12. Why does Mr. Warren include the information that Mr. Kirby was killed in the war and that Mrs. Kirby works in a store?

CAROLINE GORDON

Old Red

1. Why does Mr. Maury devote his life to fishing? What is the similarity between his life and his son-in-law Stephen's?

2. What is the point of Mr. Maury's account of how he learned to smell fish?

3. Why is Mr. Maury impatient of family obligations and family visits? Why would he rather stay in a hotel than in the family house?

4. What is Mr. Maury's attitude toward his game leg?

5. Why does he remember in such detail the coursing of Old Red back in Albemarle County?

6. Why had Mr. Maury given up hunting early in life?

7. What had Mr. Maury's wife, Mary, tried to make of his life?

8. Why does he remember her with respect and affection and even

think of her as the only person who could really appreciate what his life had been?

9. Why does the dream of coursing Old Red become a nightmare of exhaustion for Mr. Maury?

EUDORA WELTY
A Worn Path

1. Why is Phoenix taking this long trip to town?

2. Trace the various obstacles old Phoenix comes up against between the valley where we first pick her up and the wagon track, and describe how she deals with each.

3. What does old Phoenix do when she is knocked down by the dog?

4. How does she describe her situation to the white man who helps her up?

5. How does she feel about stealing the nickel he drops?

6. How does she explain where she is going to him?

7. How does Phoenix know she is in the doctor's office?

8. What happens when old Phoenix is first spoken to by the receptionist and the nurse?

9. How do we know how much old Phoenix loves her grandson?

10. What does old Phoenix plan to do with the money she has got during the day? Why?

ANDREW LYTLE
Mister McGregor

1. What do we know about the narrator of this story?

2. How is his telling of the story affected by the fact that he is a mature man remembering an experience he had had when he was eight? (Be sure to remind students of the narrator of Robert Penn Warren's *When the Light Gets Green*, pp. 633-40, and ask them to compare Mr. Warren's use of his narrator with Mr. Lytle's use of his.)

3. What were Rhears's motives in coming to the house with a knife and asking for Mister McGregor?

4. What kind of woman is Mrs. McGregor? Why does she like spirited horses? Why is she so good at running the place when Mr. McGregor is away?

5. Why is Rhears's request to speak to Mister McGregor so shocking?

6. How does Mr. McGregor react to Rhears's request?

7. Why does Mrs. McGregor force Mr. McGregor to give up the gun? Why does Mr. McGregor agree to do so?

8. What can we deduce from the fact that, even when Rhears is practically killing Mr. McGregor, Mrs. McGregor never makes a move to shoot him?

9. Why, when the fight is over, does Mrs. McGregor walk across the room and hand Mr. McGregor the gun and volunteer to sell Della?

PETER TAYLOR

What Do You Hear from 'Em?

1. What is Munsie's attitude toward mill hands? Toward "has-been quality"?

2. Why does she disagree with Crecie about Crecie's idea that quality, not money, is what counts?

3. Why will she not go to Memphis or Nashville to see Mr. Thad or Mr. Will?

4. Why is Munsie so insistent on continuing to move about the streets of Thornton with her slop wagon? Why is she so sure she will come to no harm in spite of the traffic?

5. Why does Munsie act one way when high-school boys blow their horns at her and when someone she knows says, "Aunt Munsie, can you make a little room"?

6. What is Munsie's attitude when Mr. Thad and Mr. Will come to Thornton for brief visits?

7. What finally persuades Munsie that Mr. Thad and Mr. Will are never going to return to Thornton? How does it do so?

8. What change occurs in Aunt Munsie when she does admit this? Why does that change occur?

REYNOLDS PRICE

Uncle Grant

1. How does Uncle Grant take care of the yard, cutting the grass and raking the leaves? Why does he work this way?

2. How does he take care of the places he lives in and his own person?

3. What is Uncle Grant's idea of entertainment?

4. How deeply does Uncle Grant love Mr. Will and Reynolds? How demanding is he in his love?

5. How did Uncle Grant decide what he was going to do next—

whether to stay with the Prices, go to the aunt's in Macon or, perhaps, settle in his own house and take up with Katie?

6. How does he decide that he is too old to work any more? How much would this realization disturb him? What does he do about it?

7. How much would he be disturbed by going into the welfare home? What complaints does he make about doing so?

8. What is his attitude when Reynolds comes to see him for the last time?